BLOSSOM OF GOLD

NecroSeam Chronicles Book V

NECROSEAM CHRONICLES

Available in eBook, Paperback, Hardcover, and Audiobook (for select titles)

Prequel 1: Princess of Shadow and Dream
Prequel 2: Princess of Grim

Book I: Willow of Ashes
Book II: Orbs of Azure
Book III: Pearl of Emerald
Book IV: Phoenix of Scarlet
Book V: Blossom of Gold

OTHER WORKS BY ELLIE RAINE

Adult
Nightingale: A Paranormal Noir

Children's Illustration
Ballad of the Ice Fairy

BLOSSOM OF GOLD

NecroSeam Chronicles Book V

ELLIE RAINE

Blossom of Gold
NecroSeam Chronicles | Book Five

Copyright © 2020 by Ellie Raine

Cover Design by Ellie Raine
Interior Formatting by Tamara Cribley
Author Photograph by Melissa Giles Photography
Map © 2021 Chris Seckinger

Printed in the United States of America

ISBNs: 978-1-7323238-7-2 (Hardcover),
978-1-7323238-6-5 (Paperback), 978-1-7323238-5-8 (Ebook)

Library of Congress Control Number: 2020902150
First Printing, Edition I: 2020

Published by
ScyntheFy Press, LLC
Peachtree Corners, Georgia
www.ScyntheFy.com

For information about special discounts available for bulk purchases, sales promotions, fund-raising and educational needs, contact ScyntheFy Press at: www.ScyntheFy.com/contact

For special bonus features and up-to-date news, visit the official NecroSeam web site: www.NecroSeam.com

AUTHOR'S NOTE

Dear Adventurer,

Well, here we are: The finale. Thirteen years in the making.

I heed you take caution before you dive back into the Reapers' adventures. This is the last save-point before we reach the End and face the final boss. Stock up on tonics and equip your best gear, because we're in for one Void of a fight… and one terrifying ride of emotional turbulence.

This past decade has been quite a journey for me. It's been thirteen years full of fun adventures, vigorous study, challenging obstacles, leveling wordcraft, and personal growth in my life *and* these characters. In the time I've spent composing this series, I've gone to college (hopped around 3, to be exact), took on several smaller jobs in journalism and editing, joined a rock band with my honorary family (love you guys!), married the love of my life, and had a beautiful daughter (our little dragon princess). After everything I've been through while writing this story, I've learned two vital lessons:

1.   There is no right answer.
2.   Listen to *your* heart, not someone else's.

This series, as I'm sure you've noticed, has been one enormous experiment in the study of this pliable medley of addictive chaos we call "creative writing". At times, this craft can seem like an exercise in futility. We're insane enough to wrangle an ever-shifting ruleset of a wild language and, like the hopeless romantics we are, believe we can bend it to our will like a pilfering ferret determined to fit a whole raw steak in his tiny belly.

I'm sorry to report that, in fact, we cannot.

I've spent years learning *how to write*, attended classes and workshops in creative writing and editing—and perhaps the most frustrating thing about this subject is realizing that, no matter how much you study and analyze its mechanics and techniques, everything you've learned could be considered obsolete the next year (what even *is* the latest number of spaces one should put after a period? Are we still at one, or have we tossed that out alongside the previous two?) Sentence structures, verbification, personification, "show-ing" versus "telling", using sensory words with *punch* to them in favor of more passive words… it's easy to get caught up in the technicalities of this craft and completely miss the bigger picture:

Are you *enjoying* what you write?

I've used this question to guide me through every story I've tackled. If I started yawning, I ditched the original plan and started again in a new direction—one that got my blood pumping and my fingers blurring over the keyboard with giddy cackles. And now that this series is finally coming to a close, I can say without a doubt that I am immensely proud of myself. Proud that I did right by my heart, and proud that I've had the honor of creating—and completing—something that means so much to me. There were times I thought I'd never make it to the end of this adventure, yet here I am. All the doubts, depression, grim desires to let it all end just to stop the terrifying noise from the outside world when agoraphobia flared during its worst times… the only thing that got me through those moments was the overpowering fear of never finishing *this* project. Luckily, strangely, ending this series seems to have given more meaning to life as a whole. I guess that's what I'd been search-ing for all this time. I just couldn't find it until I chipped away the debris and uncovered the sculpture underneath. Funny how our characters can teach *us* the most valuable lessons life has to offer. And those are lessons I'll carry with me as I continue my journey with new stories to come, some in the world of Nirus and some elsewhere.

Whatever comes next, I'll always be sure to have fun along the way—and I hope you will, too. Without further ado, I am proud to present *Blossom of Gold*, the grand finale of *the NecroSeam Chronicles*.

Happy Reading!
~Ellie Raine

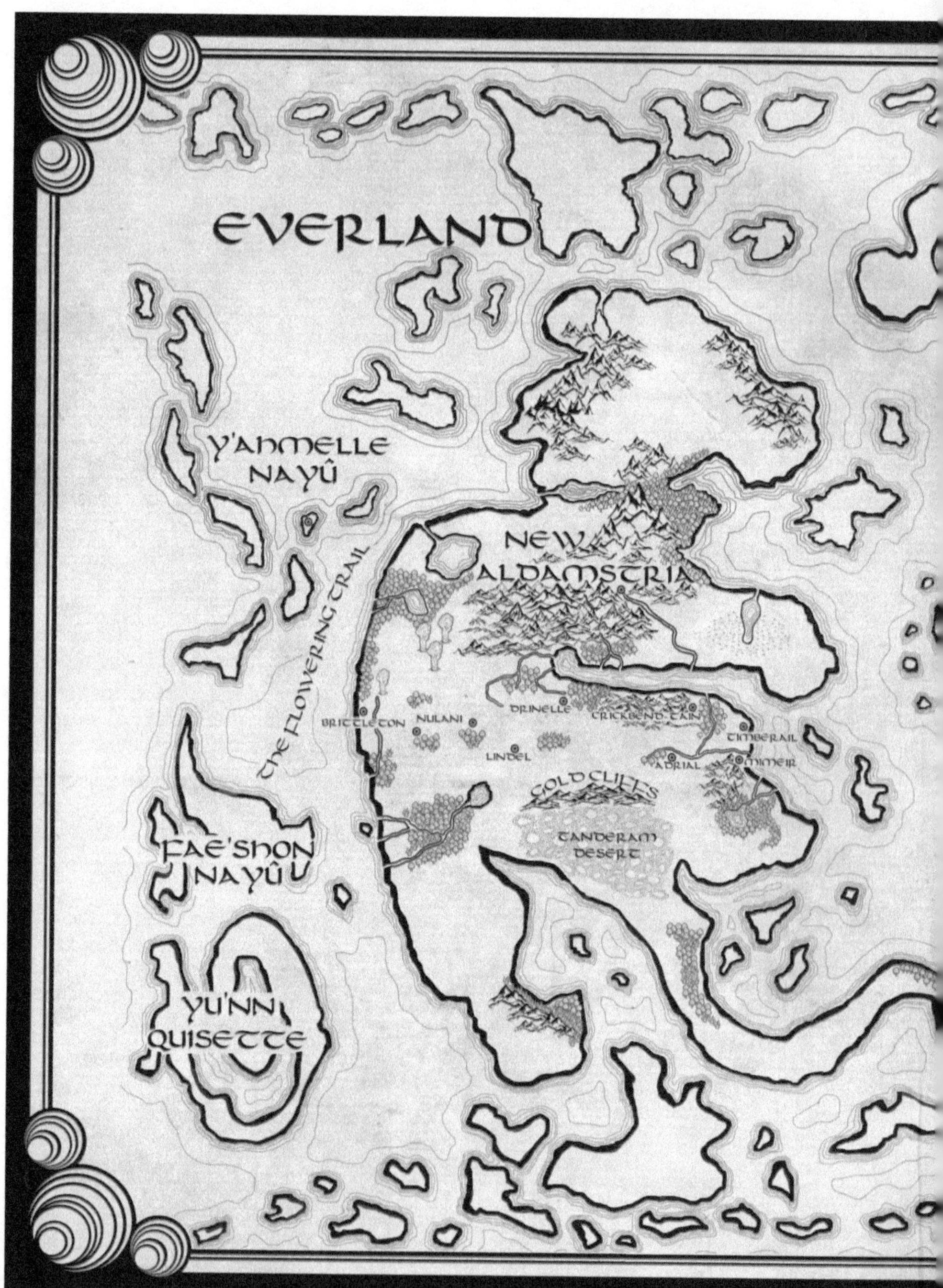

EVERLAND
Y'AHMELLE NAYÛ
NEW ALDAMSTRIA
THE FLOWERING TRAIL
BRITTLETON
NULANI
DRINELLE
CRICKBEND CAIN
TIMBERAIL
LINDEL
ADRIAL
MIMEIR
COLD CLIFFS
TANDERAM DESERT
FAE'SHON NAYÛ
YU'NNI QUISETTE

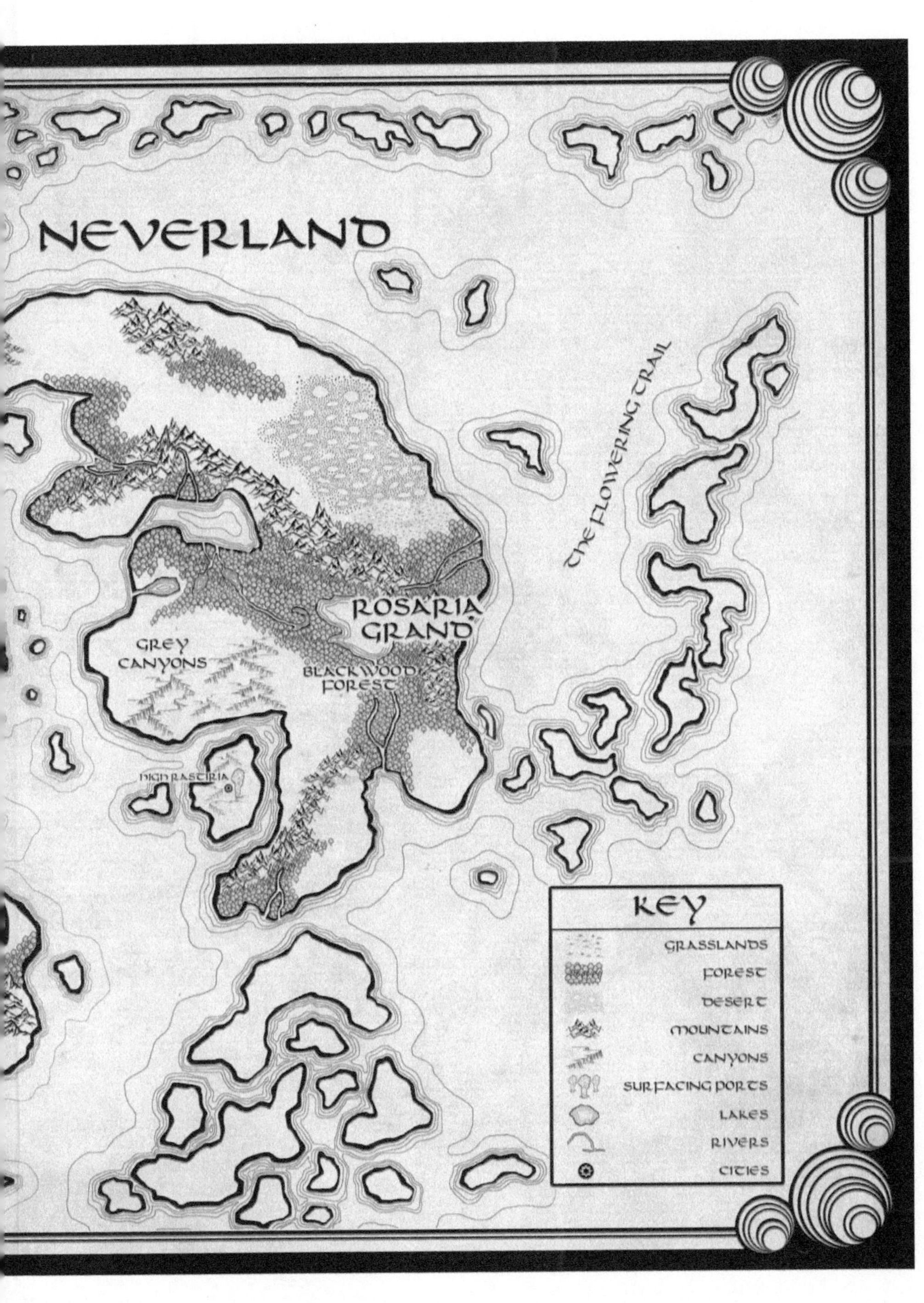
NEVERLAND
THE FLOWERING TRAIL
ROSARIA GRAND
GREY CANYONS
BLACKWOOD FOREST
HIGH RASTIRIA
KEY
GRASSLANDS
FOREST
DESERT
MOUNTAINS
CANYONS
SURFACING PORTS
LAKES
RIVERS
CITIES

TABLE OF CONTENTS

Prologue: Ominous Visions 1
1. What Must Be Done 4
2. Appointed Regent 16
3. A New Voyage 24
4. A Day To Remember 34
5. Captive 38
6. Paranoia 45
7. Parenthood 53
8. Visitation 67
9. Something She Can Use 72
10. The Enemy of My Enemy 79
11. The Blossom of Gold 84
12. Dreams of a Demon 103
13. A New Leaf 113
14. A Royal Wedding 126
15. Like Minds 133
16. For the Children 144
17. Frozen Depths 151
18. Dark Days 159
19. Monstrous Waters 165
20. The Fourth Bearer 172
21. Theories 188
22. Dispensable 196
23. Preparations 199
24. Defectors 209
25. The Queen of Death 212
26. Challenge Accepted 221
27. Death's Duel 228
28. Warning 235
29. Dealings with Demons 240
30. Testimony 250
31. A New Dawn 261

32. The Willow of Ashes 269

33. Usurper 281

34. Answers 290

35. Lost 301

36. Competing Players 309

37. Casualties of War 315

38. Where You Belong 318

39. Mourning 328

40. Acceptance 332

41. The Corpse of a King 340

42. Awakening 344

43. Search Party 351

44. The Crystal Caverns 356

45. World Tour 366

46. Eve of Calamity 377

47. Suit Up 388

48. Honoring Vows 395

49. Crystal Cage 404

50. Rescue Mission 413

51. The Lord of Souls 420

52. On the Cusp 431

53. Reunited 440

54. Brother of the Past 445

55. Final Confrontation 453

56. The End of Existence 458

57. Stranded 461

58. A World in Chaos 467

59. Defenders of Harmony 469

60. Regrets 475

61. Save the Gods 478

62 Last Resort 480

63. A Life Worth Living 483

Epilogue: A New Era 488

Nirussian Travel Guide 495

Nirussian World Notes 501

Dear Readers 505

Acknowledgements 507

About the Author 509

"NO, MY SON... THE FAULT IS NOT WITH YOU.
IT WILL FOREVER BE WITH US."

OMINOUS VISIONS

ASTER

In the hollow depths of the endless Void, wedged between the fragile dreams of helpless shifters, the Seamstress of Souls rattled the abyss with her grueling screams.

The other Gods circled her protectively, their iridescent skin radiating with colors of gold, scarlet, emerald, and azure—and their freshly spilt blood dripped with a luminosity of their own.

Shel, the golden-haired Gardener of Life, dug his gleaming sword into the emptiness as though the blackness were as solid as granite, then leaned against the hilt and puffed for breath.

Ushar, the puckish Archer of Thrill, was hardly his energetic self as he wilted in pain, his scarlet dragon wings scraped bloody and drooping in misery while he limped against his vibrant archer's bow for support.

Rin, the proudest of the Gods known by the mortals as the Artist of Grace, suffered from a cut along his scaled brow, one emerald eye pooling with shimmering blood as his trident nearly slipped from his weak grip.

The child Shepherd of Dreams, Iri, was mounted on his floating shepherd's crook with shaking limbs, looking toward the ashen-haired Seamstress he'd come to call his mother in their small, sundry family.

The Seamstress of Souls, Nira, was crouched over her fallen scythe in the center of them all, curling inwardly in hopes of escaping the searing pain that splintered from the enormous gash split down her middle. The wound shined as bright as a supernova across her torso and thigh.

The Gardener knelt to his injured wife, dragging a golden-glowing finger over her wound to seal it closed. He helped Nira to her wobbling feet and hushed with a voice like grinding stones that rippled through her mind. THAT WAS NEARLY THE END FOR YOU, MY LOVE… YOU WERE ALMOST SPLIT IN TWO, ALONG WITH YOUR LANDS.

It was true. Nira could feel the lone continent within her caverns split apart and drift away. Her people were screaming in terror, their voices crying in her grown wolf ears and quaking her essence.

Rin stabbed his trident down into their barrier's invisible floor, causing an azure shimmer to radiate from the point of impact.

THIS IS RIDICULOUS! *Rin protested, his voice trickling like a flowing river in all of their minds.* IT MATTERS NOT THAT OUR CHILDREN ARE STIFLING THE CHAOS OUT THERE! IT DOES NOTHING TO AID US IN HERE!

Ushar flapped his leathery wings in agreement, his thunderous voice booming. WE CANNOT ALLOW THIS TO CONTINUE. IF WE ALL SUSTAIN THE SAME INJURIES AS MOTHER, THERE WILL BE NOTHING LEFT OF OUR LANDS.

Iri shivered over his shepherd's crook, the azure-glowing child turning to Nira as his crisp voice trilled like a bell. MOTHER…? THERE IS ONE OPTION LEFT FOR US. BUT IT IS A SLIM CHANCE…

Nira panted heavily, ignoring the radiant blood draining onto her tongue as her teeth sharpened, and she growled. WE MUST TAKE IT!

The vision ripped apart.

My perspective was thrown back to the present time so fast, I jolted upright, my shriveled throat burning with a gasp. The sudden intake of air stung so bad, a surge of black blood rushed up my stomach—and spewed onto the prison cell's dank floor under my hands.

The mongrel Necrofera surrounding me hissed and snarled, letting me know they were annoyed with all the noise. Then they went back to sleep in the shadows of the abandoned cell.

I groaned, the pool of black vomit on the floor starting to bubble. It peeled off the stones, crept over my skeletal fingers and slithered up my arms like an army of maggots. They slurped up to my chin, then marched up my lips and slid down my throat, dropping into my stomach where they belonged.

When it finally ended, I flopped to the floor, curling into myself as my starved belly rumbled in agony.

Another day, I thought miserably, *Another unexplained vision…*

I was convinced I would never remember why I was in here—and what I was supposed to do with all these visions when I got out.

If I *ever* got out.

With nothing else to do, I went back to sleep, clutching my empty stomach with a grueling, hungry whimper.

1

WHAT MUST BE DONE

KURN

Idevoured the deli turkey my feathered soldier, Clover, helped me steal. The crow and I feasted on our bounty from atop the fountain's lion-statue in the royal gardens of Everland's palace.

It was a fine day, I had to admit. The week had begun hectically when we first descended from Culatia to fight in the war for Everland's throne. The battle was hard won—many were lost in the battle—but now the weather seemed to have calmed as well as the fights. The sun was glittering down and warming my fur, the birds were twittering their delightful tunes, the flowers and vines were a most brilliant vibrancy that ever graced my sight...

And this palace's food was the most scrumptious delicacy I had the honor of stealing.

This planet certainly had a wide range of spices, far more than my old planet. In fact, we didn't have *any* spices back home. Such was a new concept when I was first stranded here—banished by my own subjects after their ridiculous rebellion.

I ripped off another piece of turkey. *Look who's laughing now, cretins!* I was rather sore about being driven away from my home at first, but now I was glad for it. They were all stuck on that boring, spice-less rock while *I* could enjoy the wonders of Nirussian Cuisine. Emperor Kurn: one. Furry rebels: *zip*.

"KURN'S NOURISHMENT RESERVES FULLY RESTORED," chimed a woman's monotone voice in my thoughts. It was the mouthpiece of the nanites in my blood. She often piped up to report energy levels, or to warn me of danger. *"MEAL EFFICIENTLY DEVOURED."*

I chuckled and rolled to my back, rubbing my newly rotund belly in a satisfied sigh. "Ahhh… A meal fit for kings, indeed!" I patted a paw against Clover's wing. "You've served your emperor well, young knight! Job well done and all… that…"

I paused, noticing the young crow's gaze had drifted off. His neck feathers were fluffed nervously.

"Clover?" I inquired, rolling on all fours again. "Is something the matter?"

I knew Clover couldn't comprehend my words, since the nano-tech translator in my brain only allowed *me* to understand other languages, but Clover must have guessed what I'd asked by my body language.

He grumbled a low caw, "Oliver needs me. Something's wrong."

"Wrong?" I asked, one of my round ears perking. "You mean your Bond with your Reaper is pulling at you again?"

The crow's neck-feathers flared. His gaze snapped to the winged owl-boy, Oliver, beneath us. Clover rumbled, "Where is he going with the sheep girl…?"

I glanced over to find that, indeed, the boy was running off with the copper-haired girl in hand. None of the adult bipeds seemed to notice them leave. I grumbled and chuffed determinedly.

Well! If no one else is going after them, I suppose the responsibility falls to me.

"Right, then," I said and climbed on Clover's back. "I suppose I have enough battery charge left for now… Let's keep an eye on the younglings, shall we?"

Clover gave a caw and spread his wings, flying us off the lion statue to follow the younglings overhead.

The two children dashed out of the gardens beneath us, Oliver leading the way and dragging the sheep-horned girl, Milann, behind him by her wrist. They hurried through the sunlit pathways and pushed through tall hedges, jabbering in panicked tones as they raced onward.

Then, at last, they stopped at the palace's royal pools.

Lounging in the water was a web-eared boy with long, emerald hair that waved down his back like watery fins. This was the little Ocean Prince: Fuérr. The young prince's scaled legs had shifted into a curling Seadragon tail while immersed in the water, and his slender body leaned against the tiled lip of the pool while idly singing a Marincian ballad, his tail waving back and forth in the water along with the tune.

Oliver and Milann charged up to the opposite side of the pool, shouting at the prince and flailing their arms wildly. Fuérr stopped his singing, one of his webbed ears flicking up in question.

"Oleev-a?" Fuérr said in a thick Marincian accent, propping his scaled elbows back against the pool's lip. "What eez proh-bleem?"

"Fuérr, get outta there!" Oliver hollered, spreading his wings and flapping across the pool while Milann ran around its perimeter on foot.

The prince's emerald brow scrunched. "Why eez yuu zo een hurray—"

A scaled man suddenly blinked into existence by the pool's lip, right above the prince, as if having appeared from the air itself.

"Galaxies starve me!" I gasped above them and pulled on Clover's neck feathers, causing the crow to flutter to a stop and flap in small circles. Where had he come from?! Was a cloaking device involved, or had he teleported here? And since when did this primitive planet have such advanced technology?

Or IS it technology? I supposed it could have been part of this world's intriguing magic. But then, the only shifter I'd witnessed doing such things was Dream…

Eureka! That's what was going on! This was the man who'd killed Dream…! He must have taken the man's powers to traverse in and out of the Dream realm.

The intruder wrapped his arms around the prince's head, clasping a smothering hand over the boy's mouth. Fuérr wriggled under the cobra shifter's hold, his tail splashing and thrashing about. Then the cobra's hands glittered with an azure light that wafted into the prince's mouth like blue vapor. The prince's lids grew heavy and he fell into a deep sleep in the intruder's hold. The villain's scaled lips pulled into a grin, displaying his long fangs.

—then he vanished with the prince, leaving naught but ripples in the pool.

"A kidnapping!" I cried, pushing my front paws on Clover's head.

The other two children were still down there, but not for long. Oliver took hold of the sheep-girl and spread his wings, launching into the air and flying out of the palace grounds.

I thrust a paw forward and yelled, "After them, Clover! Your oracle Reaper must have Seen where they're going with his Third Eye! We can't leave the children unattended…!"

Clover screeched and we took off, soaring after the owl boy and the sheep girl.

XAVIER

The gardens of Queen Anabelle's new palace were deceptively mesmerizing.

Sunlight glittered over the vibrant roses and cascading bluebells. Latticed vines draped from the many stone columns laden with gorgeous blossoms speckled with plump berries as red as rubies. Morning dew glistened like jewels over every curling leaf and silken petal, casting the gardens in a shimmering radiance as the droplets glinted all around us. Songbirds twittered and bathed in the trickling fountain at the center of the gardens, our party's ravens and crows fluttering in the lapping pond as the water reflected onto the stone lion statue above them and refracted with soft rainbows…

Except for *my* raven.

Chai stood on the stone wall of the fountain, his black neck-feathers flaring as he hunched over and glared at me with beady eyes. One of those eyes was slashed with a scar that matched the cut running down my right eye. Chai's throat vibrated with a low rumble, our Bond surging with the shared emotion of bubbling rage.

My raven flapped off the fountain wall and alighted onto my shoulder. I welcomed his weight. The closer he was to me, the less our Bond was stretched and strained. Chai turned to the winged woman I glared at—Marian—and croaked at her threateningly.

Beside me, I saw Alexander's raven, Mal, alight on his shoulder also, mimicking Chai's sentiment at Marian.

She was one of the teenaged Enlighteners who'd been chronicling our journey across the realms. Her partner, Herrin, coughed into a fist and sidled back nervously. It seemed he wasn't expecting Marian to make such an outburst, as she'd done moments earlier. Truth be told, I hadn't expected it either. Marian was usually a quiet young woman, focused on her notes and buried in her daily tasks.

Yet here she was, confronting Alexander and me. Her fingers gripped a fist-sized crystal ball that flashed with images so faint, they looked more like smoke.

The ball showed the future. The *last* future the world had left. Marian claimed it would only come if Alex and I continued to gain the rest of our Blessings… as was prophesized.

I glanced at my birthmark under my left knuckles. It was a Crest of three black diamonds. Alexander stared at his similar Crest on his right hand. This was the mark of the Shadowblood… The mark that Macarius shared with us, apparently.

This entire journey, we were told Macarius would bring the End of Existence. And now, we learned that *either of us* may bring the End. Dream had lied to us. And now, Dream was dead, leaving us with no hope of finding any more answers.

The Seers of our party stood quietly around us, all holding crystal balls of different sizes, the globes glinting in the sunlight over their fingers. One of those Seers, the goat-horned Linus who specialized in *present* visions, stood under a vine-wrapped pagoda and hung his head solemnly, his dreadlocked hair falling over his shoulder and clattering with many beads. Another Seer, the Footrunner officer Ringëd who specialized in *past* visions, stood under the breezeway that connected the gardens to the palace, smoke rising from a cigarette between his lips. A third Seer who specialized in *future* visions, little Oliver, was perched atop the fountain's lion-statue, his wings tucked nervously behind him. Princess Rilla, Cayden's younger sister, held a larger, skull-sized crystal ball.

My wife, Willow, didn't have a crystal ball of her own, but she stood by the fountain with her little Songcrow, Jewel, perched on her shoulder beneath her drapery of long, ashen hair. Her marriage-vines glittered in the sunlight, their silver chains shining like glass from atop her hair—and from beneath her crown. Her azure eyes swam with uncertainty as she looked from me to Queen Anabelle, biting her lip.

Waiting on either side of Willow was her azure-haired mother, Myra, and her rust-haired grandmother, Crysalette. They both carried crystal balls the size of their fists, smoke swirling within the clear orbs.

Clinging to Willow's black skirts was a little sheep-horned girl with curling, copper hair and dark bronze skin. This was my soon-to-be adopted daughter, Milann. Willow cupped the girl's face soothingly, as if to assure Milann that the tension in the gardens wouldn't last much longer. Her gaze, however, didn't illustrate much confidence with that.

My newborn son, Lucas, lay sleeping in his hovering basinet beside Willow. The baby's ashen wolf ears twitched and flicked while he dreamt pleasantly in his swaddle, oblivious of the gloom that squeezed the gardens.

Marian didn't break her gaze from us, but stepped back, falling in place beside Herrin once more.

The golden-haired Queen Anabelle stepped forward to face us instead, waiting beside her burly warrior, Kurrick, with her hands cupped patiently at her skirts.

"Please," Ana pleaded. "Sail to the Blossom of Gold with me. We cannot let Macarius gain his Blessings while you both fall behind… It is as Marian said: there will be no one left to match him. There will be no one left to keep him from killing us all." Her golden gaze drifted to my wife and children. "From killing your family."

My wolf ears grew, teeth sharpening.

Alexander and I exchanged a hard glance… then we sighed.

"All right," I said grudgingly. "We'll… go to the Blossom of Gold…"

Alex growled, "But *only* to keep Macarius from killing us. After he's dead, we're done with this nonsense."

Ana nodded, her golden eyes as bright as coins. "I've already gathered a fleet in the Sky Port. I shall contact my generals to prepare for our departure. I advise you to rest while you can." She bowed shallowly, then took her leave and strode back inside.

Baby Lucas began fussing from the nearby basinet. Willow left Milann by the fountain and came to pick up the pup, bouncing him gently over her shoulder as she flicked me an uncertain glance. "Are you sure we should be leaving so soon?"

My face pulled into a brooding glower. "It may be short notice, but I'd personally prefer to get it over with."

"Seconded," Alex snorted. "Especially if it means beating Macarius to the Blossom. If he gets to it first—"

"Oliver?" The voice of Lilli—Willow's bat-winged Hand—interrupted from the breezeway behind us. The black-haired woman entered the gardens with concerned, chartreuse eyes darting from face to face among our group. Her new husband, the bespectacled Reaper knight, Jaq, strode by her side as Lilli continued to call for the boy. "Oliver!"

While she searched the gardens, Jaq came to meet us, adjusting his eyeglasses over his scaled nose. "Hey mates, have ya seen Oliver?" he asked. "We can't find 'im anywhere. He was s'posed to come meet us after he packed his bags, but he never showed."

I glanced over my shoulder at the fountain's statue where I'd last seen the owl boy, murmuring, "Oh, he's been here for some time. He's just up..." I paused, seeing that the boy was, in fact, *not* atop the statue anymore. And when I flicked my gaze down to the fountain's stone base, I noticed that my new daughter, Milann, was no longer sitting there either.

"Erm... Willow?" I began skeptically, my brow furrowing at my wife. "Where have the children gone—*arrrrrgh!*"

Pain split my temples. A whining ring sang through my ears and my vision suddenly blurred. I doubled over, straining to quiet the ringing, but nothing would mute it. Alex had already crumpled beside me, grunting in pain as he, too, clutched his head desperately.

"Xavier?!" Willow's voice was shrill as she hovered over Alex and me, bobbing our wailing baby in her arms. "Alex?! What's happening?"

Through the cloud of agony, I noticed something strange. Willow's image seemed to double, as if a second layer of film coated the original image underneath. A disorienting, small delay streaked her movements.

I waved a hand in front of my face. Yes, there *was* a delay. A second layer...

—the ringing crashed through my ears louder than before, rendering me all but deaf.

Having a discussion in the gardens, are we? A familiar voice purred in my thoughts, crunching like glass. *How lovely... I wonder if the little Ocean Prince is enjoying some leisurely solitude...?*

The voice's chuckles died alongside the ringing, and my vision re-solidified into one image.

I shook over the ground, inching my gaze to Alex who panted beside me on all fours. "That voice," I said, breathless. "That couldn't have been..."

Alex's wolf ears were already grown, and his teeth sharpened. "It was."

The baby still whimpered in Willow's arms as she demanded, "Will you both tell the rest of us what happened?"

"It's Macarius," I said. "We heard his voice—in our thoughts. It's as if... it's as if he were *looking* through us."

All the Seers around us now held grave expressions. I glanced from Linus to Rilla, from Ringëd to Marian... only Marian offered some form of comment, yet all she could muster was, "Oh, dear."

"What does it mean?" I asked Marian.

Her faded brown-and-red wings gave a shudder. "It's difficult to explain... you're familiar with how Seers perceive their visions, correct?"

Alex cocked an eyebrow beside me. "Through another shifter's eyes. Of course we know, we're growing acquainted with our own visions ever since we were given these Hallows."

I licked my lips. "I suppose now that Macarius has prophetic Hallows, he's able to scry on us..."

"But the shifters *I've* scryed were never aware I was doing it," Alex protested. He pushed to his feet. "Between Xavier and me, *I'm* the one who can see visions of the present. Scrying is my territory. None of the shifters I've scryed upon have ever realized I was doing it."

Marian brushed a pensive thumb over her lips. "How many of those shifters were Seers themselves?"

Alex paused. "Er... well, none. Except Dream, on occasion."

Marian's wings lowered in speculation. "And he wouldn't feel the need to tell you when he experienced it, I suppose... Normally, you're correct that shifters aren't aware a Seer is scrying on them. However, when you scry on other *Seers,* they can See you looking through their eyes. There is a delay, an overlap, if you will. We call this 'vision feedback'."

Linus crossed his arms and added, "It occurs when a Seer is having a vision of *you* while *you're* having a vision of them."

Beside me, Willow suddenly gasped. "Like the shared visions…! Only instead of one Seeing the future while the other Sees the past, *both* are Seeing the present at the same time!"

That earned Willow several confused stares by the rest of us.

Then Ringëd broke the silence when he scratched his head and mumbled, "*I've* never had any 'feedback' before."

Linus hummed, "I suspect that's because your emphasis is in visions of the past. I've had many an instance of feedback, but my emphasis is on visions of the present. Logically, since Alexander is the half with *present* visions, you'd think it would only affect him… but Xavier was also affected somehow."

Alex twisted his mouth. "I think I heard the ringing a few seconds before Xavier. He didn't react until after it was already happening to me, so perhaps he was having a *past* vision of me having the feedback. We seem to have a strange connection that way."

Marian gave a considering shrug. "You *are* one soul split into two."

Alex and I declined to comment on that.

Rilla stamped a foot. "Well, what did Macarius *say*? Spit it out already!"

I sighed and shut my eyes, massaging my temple as I recalled back. "He said… something about us being in the gardens…"

"And he made mention of the little Ocean Prince," Alex added. Then he paused. "Wait. Where *is* Fuérr?"

I rubbed my bearded chin. "I don't know. But the other children seem to have disappeared as well."

Willow shushed our fussing newborn and looked about the gardens in concern. "They were here a moment ago, weren't they?"

Linus took the liberty of stalking over to the fountain. The goat-horned Seer touched his fingers over the stone statue, and his eyes glazed with a vision. His expression cracked with dread.

"Oh, no." He jerked back to reality. "The children have flown off—and they're heading to Marincia's capital."

"*What?*" Lilli cried, breaking apart from the rest of us as her bat wings fluttered frantically. "Why would they do such a thing?!"

By the rosebushes, Ringëd threw down his cigarette and stamped it under his boot, trotting to the fountain beside Linus and touching the statue beside the goat's hoof-textured fingers. The officer's eyes staled just like Linus's had, his own vision seeming to hit, and he cursed. "*Oscha!* Prince Fuérr was kidnapped by Macarius in the pools!"

The gardens split with panic.

Alex slammed a fist into a stone column. "That's what the feedback was about! That's why he was scrying on us—Gods damn it, he wanted to be sure Fuérr was alone…!"

Ringëd ripped his hand off the fountain's statue, stumbling as though thrown off balance when he snapped out of his vision, and he stared at his hand while his voice shook. "Bloods… He's going to use the Ocean Prince as bait…"

Willow hefted the baby and started out of the gardens at a furious pace. "We have to retrieve him immediately…!"

"You can't." Ringëd's breath was hollow. His hand balled. "He's… already long gone now. *Inside* Aspirre. Where we can't enter physically without the Orbs of Azure…" He slumped against a nearby pillar. "And I have *past* visions, remember? If Linus's vision of the *present* showed the kids were only now on their way to Marincia…" He rocked his head back against the pillar, staring blankly at the sky. "They're already gone, too…"

Willow's fox ears grew and curled tight to her head. "Then… then we missed them…? Just like that?"

Ringëd drew a long breath. "Just like that."

Willow's eyes began to well. She clutched baby Lucas tight, anger so thick in her snarl, it practically leaked from her pores. "That… Gods damned… snake…" To my fright, it *did* leak from her pores—her hands to be exact. Her palms began wavering with small, orange flames, which singed the cotton swaddle wrapped around our baby, smoke curling from the fabric.

"Willow!" I clipped, grabbing her arm in a panic. "Don't burn the blasted baby!"

My icy fingers snapped her out of her fury long enough to glare at me. "What do you mean don't—*Ahh!*" She noticed the burning swaddle and gasped, quickly extinguishing her fire and patting the fabric to snuff the lingering embers. When the fire was out, she exhaled a long, traumatized breath. "Bloods be good, I do *not* need this added stress…!" She glowered at me angrily. "And I wouldn't have burned the *baby*, Xavier, he's a Pyrovoker just as I am! Fire doesn't harm us! The most it would have done is turn his swaddle to ash and leave him naked, so don't startle me like that over something so trivial!"

I gawked at her, horrified. "Trivial—?!"

Lucas began wailing harder, making both of us stop cold.

We sighed, and Willow's grasp eased around him tenderly. "I'm sorry… I suppose I need to learn how to better quell my temper now, don't I…?"

I loosened a breath through my nose, calming, and slid an arm around her waist. "We both do… We'll discuss this later. There's too much happening right now that needs our attention."

She nodded, turning to Ringëd again and asked, "What can we do to retrieve the children?"

Ringëd loosened his shirt collar with an awkward finger, looking uncomfortable. "Well, uh," Ringëd began. "Past visions are great for investigating what already happened, but… it's not so helpful for figuring out *current* situations… or future ones." He rubbed his arm. If he had any ears to grow, I imagine they would have sprouted by now. "But," he said with a more hopeful tone, "Oliver and Milann went to *save* Fuérr. They weren't captured, they went on their own. So that's something, I guess." He paused as another vision came to him. Then he added, "And, apparently, Kurn went with them to babysit. Another positive—"

"A ferret is not a babysitter!" Willow roared, breaking out of my hold and startling the baby into another frightened cry. "Oh, for the love of… Xavier, will you please take him until I calm down?"

Willow abruptly handed me the screaming baby, and I fumbled to bob Lucas over my shoulder, trying to soothe him with quiet hushes. I completely failed at quieting him, but Willow didn't seem to care so long as I kept hold of him for a turn. *All right, then… I suppose this is the best way I can help.* Not knowing what else to do, I kept to my bobbing and swaying, watching as Willow stamped her foot in front of Ringëd.

"The children can't run off by themselves!" she insisted. "They're going after a psychotic murderer!"

Jaq, who'd been quiet all this time, threw a scaled thumb over his shoulder. "Sorry, but guess ya forgot to tell *them* that. They're already gone."

Willow gave an explosive scream at the sky, her hands bursting with orange fire before turning on her heels and starting to storm out the gardens.

I still held the baby, who was finally settling down, as I hurried after her. "Willow, wait! This isn't over yet. There must be something we can do. I say we go after them and—"

"Wait!" Marian held up a hand as she seemed to have a vision herself. "Hang on. If the Shadowblood goes to Marincia now… the only future we have left will be gone."

That stopped Willow just before she ducked into the palace, and I nearly stumbled into her with Lucas.

Alex came to stand beside me, both of us staring at the cardinal woman and questioning in unison, "How?"

Marian shook her head gravely. "I don't know, exactly… but my visions show me that, if you leave the children be, Nirus still has that future."

Willow's face was absolutely livid now. She opened her mouth, likely about to scream at Marian, but I stopped my wife with a halting hand.

"Marian," I said sternly, pinching my nose as I sucked in a hard breath. "Now I *can't* fault Willow for being angry over this nonsense. Do you hear yourself? You mean to tell me that in order to give our new daughter a future to live, we have to let her run to her *death*?" I kept hold of Lucas with one arm while smearing a hand over my face. "That's sure to win us the Parents-of-the-Year prize."

"—My mother and I will retrieve the children," Willow's mother, Myra, announced from beside the fountain. She stalked toward us. "In the future *I* See with my own Third Eye, their future still lingers if my mother and I rescue them from Marincia." She gestured to the rust-haired Crysalette, who held baby Eryn, Aspirre's new king-in-waiting, and stepped beside Myra. My mother-in-law nodded at us solemnly. "You all keep to your course and go to the Blossom. We will find the children."

"I'm going with you!" Lilli insisted with a flap of her wings.

Jaq crossed his scaled arms beside her. "If she's goin', so am I. We didn't just get hitched only to get separated right after." He cast Alexander and me an apologetic grimace. "Sorry, mates... But *I* don't have any new Hallows to get."

"Nor a coronation waiting for us when we return to Grim," Lilli added with an expectant glance at Willow and me.

Willow's shoulders slumped, seeming to share my daunted sting. Her father had died in the last battle with the demons. The Death King was gone. And now, she and I were the unofficial monarchs of Grim... But even more terrifying was the reminder that, after we went to the Blossom of Gold, we were supposed to return home to Grim so Willow could claim the throne officially. But with this new dilemma...

I sighed. "We'll have to delay our return home, it seems... We'll come to Marincia straight after we see the Blossom and meet with you all again—"

"No," Herrin interrupted, tucking his wings nervously behind Marian. The scholar lifted an anxious finger. "After the Blossom, you *have* to hurry to the Willow of Ashes for your last set of Hallows." He waved a hand at everyone. "I say both parties should descend to Grim immediately after you're all done with your missions. We can all meet again in the Death Palace afterward, all while heading Macarius off in the process."

Alexander rubbed his chin with a hum. "That does sound like the most logical move..." He flicked his heterochromic eyes at me. "What say you? It's your daughter who's in danger."

I rubbed my eyes. "I know... but I have to remind myself that Milann had a life before meeting us. She'd even spent months on her own, despite her age. I should hope, with Oliver there to tell her the future... and Jaq and Lilli going after them for protection…" I sighed. "If Marian's *and* Myra's Third Eyes tell them the children will be safe, then I've no choice but to trust them." I nodded to Jaq. "Keep Milann away from that cobra for me, will you?"

Jaq saluted with a fist to his chest. "You got it, mate." He paused and amended, "Sire."

I shuddered, and saw Willow do the same beside me.

"Yes, well…" I cleared my throat awkwardly. "We'll see you in Grim…"

With a final nod, he and Lilli dashed out of the gardens. Crysalette followed after them. Myra began to leave as well, but the azure-haired woman paused when she passed Willow.

"Darling," Myra said to her daughter, hesitating. "I don't suppose… could I… carry your father with me…?"

Willow's stare grew morose, and she fetched the Storagecoffin that was strapped to the chain around her waist. It was a translucent teal box the size of her hand, made of a gummy gem that shrank non-living objects within its confines. Inside this particular box was the wrapped corpse of the previous Death King—Willow's father.

"Of course, Mother," Willow whispered as she passed the coffin to Myra.

Myra gripped the coffin delicately. Then a large Songcrow—the late Death King's messenger, Locke—flew down from the sky and alighted on Myra's wrist, rubbing his beak on the coffin with a wounded coo.

Myra's eyes spilled with tears, nuzzling Locke and hugging the small coffin to her chest, a small sob escaping her lips. She pulled her daughter in for a loving embrace, kissing her crown. "Please be safe, Willow… We'll meet again at home."

Willow held her mother fast, her own eyes welling. "Home can't come soon enough… Take care, Mother. Tell Milann I'll have her chambers ready for her return."

Myra allowed herself a chuckle, dabbing at her eyes before kissing Willow's head once more, then took her leave after the others.

Willow drew in a calming breath and took our wolf-eared son from me, giving me an exhausted gaze. "Come… I suppose there is much to be done now…"

2

APPOINTED REGENT

ANABELLE

"The fleet is prepped and on schedule, your grace," the brown-scaled viper woman informed me from my communicator's screen of light, the device's gears and springs whirring in my hand. *"I shall tell the captains to prepare for our departure."*

I nodded to the viper while striding down the corridor of New Aldamstria's palace beside Kurrick. "Thank you, Genevieve. We'll be there posthaste."

When I ended the call, Kurrick grunted his disapproval, his armor clattering as he folded his arms over his chest.

I gave him a narrow glance. "Still have your reservations with Genevieve?"

He retorted, "I believe I was commanded to hold my tongue on the matter."

"I'm willing to revoke that command if it means you'll cease being a mute gargoyle every waking moment," I muttered, stopping to turn on him. "You've barely spoken a word to me since the battle. I know you've much on your mind, so for the love of Shel, speak it."

He faltered. "I… er… haven't much to say, your grace. Most topics I've tried to speak of, you've either forbidden me from speaking them, or I have no interest in broaching them."

My huffed. "Nonsense. The only topic I've forbidden is that of your grievance with Genevieve."

He opened a gesturing hand at me. "Precisely, my lady."

"Oh, will you stop with the formalities? I've told you before that I wish for you to call me by name."

He grumbled and rolled his head back. "Yet another decree that your majesty has demanded of me to still my tongue."

"That wasn't a…" My lion ears flicked in annoyance. "Kurrick, *you* are not required to follow my orders. You can do so if you wish, but you've no obligation."

"Of course, I've an obligation," he contradicted. "You are my queen. *I* am your guard. To disobey you would be crossing a dangerous line—"

"That we've spent the last five-hundred years crossing already!" I threw up my hands. "Five centuries, Kurrick! What is two years compared to five *hundred*?" I grabbed his arm, startling him. "Kurrick, please. I'm tired of this game. I may have reclaimed my lands, but that changes nothing." My stomach tangled sickly. "Do you even care for me anymore…?"

His scared face tightened. "I…" He exhaled hollowly, grasping my hand. "I am no *king*, Ana." He tore his arm from my grasp and stepped back, keeping his cold distance while still lingering at my side.

"<… sure you're going to be okay, Zyl?>" King Roji's voice bounced through the tall corridor.

The scarlet-winged man approached from up ahead, carrying a bundle of luggage full of many Storagespheres and Storageboxes. Alongside him was his emerald-haired wife, Dalminia, whose webbed ears flicked while their youngest daughter tugged at Dalminia's fin-like hair from her straining arms. The toddler, Prylan, giggled with delight, the scarlet feathers of her tiny wings fluttering hectically… making it *more* difficult for Dalminia to keep her afloat.

Their second daughter, the 3-year-old Mavis, was much better behaved. The girl happily held hands with her aunt—Roji's younger sister, Zylveia.

Zylveia wasn't really alive, merely resurrected for the time being. She had been killed weeks ago… tricked by Macarius. The cobra had slit her throat to gain all of Sky's Hallows before he fled into the veiling storm. Zyl's death had been tragic for all of us, but her ghost had formed a Bloodpact with Howless Lilliana Tessinger, who granted her this temporary revival now.

Zyl's new affiliation with an important Reaper such as Lilliana meant she would forever travel with their party… Which, to her obvious delight, included her cat-jay friend, El.

El walked alongside the resurrected princess with perked cat ears, her pale-blue wings flicking behind her. Beside El was, of course, Octavius. The black-haired cat shifter chatted with El fervently, his laughter flighty and his bronze cheeks painted with a subtle blush. It seemed their courtship was still going well, from what I could glean… although, I noticed El's attention would periodically be called back to Zyl when the princess grabbed El's fingers and pulled her away to ogle at a new part of the castle she found particularly marvelous.

Her elder brother, King Roji, continued with his concerns in their language, <A lot happened these last few weeks… I mean, I had to watch you… you know…>" His voice dimmed, unwilling to finish.

Zyl snorted and wafted a hand at her brother, answering him in a thick Culatian accent. "I being the fine one, Roji! I get to be traveling with El now! Ees happy thing!"

El giggled with a vigorous nod, her accent far lighter. "Definitely a happy thing, Zyl. Don't worry, your Majesty… I'll keep an eye on her." A flash of pain flitted through her yellow eyes, but it vanished just as soon as it came, and she exhaled a hard breath. "I won't let anything happen to her soul."

Roji's grin was tight. "Thanks, El… I'm glad she'll be surrounded by the best Reapers Grim has to offer." He paused, noticing Kurrick and I were here. His grin grew more sincere as he approached me with a wave. "How's it going, Land? Are you liking the queen life after that hectic battle?"

I replied politely, "I'm certainly enjoying this moment of peace, if that is what you mean, Sky. I see your family is ready to return to Culatia?"

He hefted the string of Storageboxes he held and tossed his chin up in a gesture. "Yep. All ready to go. Thanks for giving us a place to crash, Ana."

I nodded. "It is I who should be thanking you, Roji. Your Stormchasers were a great help in our success." I smiled at his wife next. "And you as well, Dalminia. Without both of your assistance, I dare say I may not have my lands now."

Dalminia balanced her youngest daughter over her hip and tossed a scaled hand. "Oh, you would have done just fine on your own, I've no doubt." Her expression drained then, as if remembering something depressing, and she murmured, "Although… I'm sorry to hear about… well, about Dream… I know you mentioned he was your foster father."

My mood soured, and I saw Kurrick lower his eyes beside me. I sighed. "Yes… I only hope he achieved all he worked for before he…" I shut my eyes, my chest squeezing tight. I now understood Roji's reluctance to acknowledge Zylveia's death. Speaking it aloud seemed to make it… *real*. If left silent, perhaps I could pretend it never happened? That he was still here to guide us…?

Roji patted my shoulder. "Knowing him, I'm sure he did. Well…" He cleared his throat and gave a wan grin. "I guess we'll see you around?"

My returning smile was thin. "Yes… We will be sure to visit when next your islands drift our way—"

"Tavius!" A familiar voice shouted behind us.

I whirled, seeing Ringëd had appeared and was running through the corridor, a rather urgent look painting his face. He skidded to a stop in front of

Octavius and panted over his knees. "Tavius, have… have you seen Mika? We have to leave *now*."

Octavius blinked at him from beside El, his legs staggering back. "Uh, I think she and my dad are still packing up for the trip to Grim…"

"We're not going to Grim anymore," Ringëd puffed. "There's been a change of plans."

"Ah—yes," I agreed with a clap of my hands, realizing I'd forgotten to mention this. "I've asked the twins and your company to join me at the Gyle Islands before you all descend—"

"Not those plans," Ringëd interrupted. "*New* change of plans. At least, for some of us." The Seer tossed his head at Roji and Dalminia. "Macarius just kidnapped your nephew, Prince Fuérr."

We all stiffened.

Ringëd didn't wait for any of us to reply, continuing with a rush of breath, "He's taking the kid to Marincia to use him as bait for his father. Oliver and Milann flew off on their own after them, and Kurn left with them, too. Some of us are splitting from the group to follow them while Ana and the twins head to the Gyle Islands. We're all going to meet at Grim's Grand Capital. Roji, Mini, you can go with whoever you want, but I need to find my wife so we can get going already."

Dalminia's webbed ears folded down, and she hauled her younger daughter, Prylan, over her shoulder as she stammered, "Y-yes! We'll come with you to save Fuérr!"

"Great, follow me!" Ringëd ran ahead and called back. "I'm going to check the kitchens for Mika!"

Roji, Mini and their two daughters hurried behind him, disappearing around the corner and leaving Kurrick and I with Octavius, El, and Zyl.

Octavius glanced at me warily. "U-um… who should *I* go with?"

My mind was still struggling to keep pace with the urgent news. This was all happening so fast.

"I suppose…" I began absently, "You should go with whomever you wish…"

Octavius thought on it, then looked at El. "I guess wherever El wants to go?"

One of El's white cat ears dropped, and she turned to Zylveia. "And I'll go wherever *Zyl* goes."

I sighed and massaged my brow. Those were quite the *non*-answers, weren't they?

"Very well…" I said, my brain still sluggish as I tried to formulate an immediate plan of action. "Zylveia, you seem to be the deciding factor. I suggest you choose quickly, given how hurried Ringëd had been."

Zylveia blinked and glanced from face to face, troubled. "*Ye, ye, ye…*" Zylveia scratched her scarlet-feathered head. "I think I need go with *Da'torr* Lilli, now that I ees being the dead one…" She puffed up her lips thoughtfully. "But since *Da'torr* Lilli ees being the mother of Oliver, I be thinking she will be choosing to go for him." She shrugged. "I can only be guessing we go to Marincia?"

I nodded. She had phrased it like an uncertainty, but Shel bless her, it was an answer at last. "Very well. Then I suggest you return to your *Da'torr* posthaste to prepare."

She nodded, and the three left promptly… leaving Kurrick and I alone in the corridor again.

Anger roiled my blood, my teeth sharpening. I flicked my gaze at the now tense Kurrick. "How had Macarius breached our defenses?"

Kurrick shook his head. "I do not know, your grace… With the Orbs of Azure now in his possession, I'm afraid there is only so much we can do. The realm of Dreams is compromised. The only knights capable of securing defenses are our small supply of Dreamcatchers."

"Then I shall ask some of those Catchers to join *our* party to the islands," I decided. "I'll request Yulia and Jimmy to accompany us immediately."

Kurrick grunted. "I doubt it will stop Macarius from breaking through, regardless. Dream had said Macar was his only equal with Somniovoking. Even Myra could never reach the level of her father."

I bit my sharpened thumbnail. "Then… If he's going to Marincia with Fuérr, let us hope he'll be too distracted over *there* to care about interrupting us on the islands."

Kurrick nodded. "Best we do not dally, then?"

"Indeed," I growled, storming toward the throne room. "But first, I have some things to settle here."

Kurrick followed me to the throne room.

Inside, we found Prince Cayden—well, *former* prince—speaking with Linus and the young, ex-princess Rilla.

It seemed the Seers were explaining the situation to Cayden now. Cayden's lion ears were folded down in horror as he listened to what had happened with the children.

"Well, what are we still doing here, then?" Cayden demanded, his lion tail swishing at his legs. "We have to go after them—!"

"Sky and his wife are already preparing to do so," I interrupted, my voice echoing in the domed chamber.

They all snapped to attention as I crossed the marble floor, and they quickly bowed to me in respect.

I stopped in front of Cayden, humming, "I have a different task for you three, if you wouldn't mind taking on the responsibility."

One of Cayden's lion ears perked in confusion. "What task, my lady?"

Linus froze as the Dream mark on his shoulder gleamed azure, and his eyes slid into a distant stare as if having a vision. "Ah," he said, turning to Cayden. "Her Majesty wishes to make you her regent here in Everland's palace."

Cayden blinked, pointing a dumbstruck finger at his own chest. "M... me, your grace?"

"This was your home to begin with," I explained, "and you've been trained to be this land's ruler your entire life, as your late father's heir. Not to mention your experience with leading the rebel army and *success* in rallying the country together for me." I gestured to Linus and Rilla kindly. "And, of course, every regent would benefit from having two Seers as his advisors, if they wished."

Rilla's olive eyes brightened excitedly. "An official advisor? Me? No more having to hide my Hallows—no more beatings if I See nothing?"

My expression dampened at the young teen. *Beatings? Gardener's Spade, that poor girl...* It was unacceptable for anyone her age to endure something so heinous from her own father. If I had any regrets left for Galden's death, they were thoroughly vanquished now.

I stroked Rilla's honey-blonde head softly. "No more beatings... ever again. And neither of *you* need hide yourselves, either," I added, shifting my gaze up at Cayden and Linus. "I find it quite ridiculous to be threatened with public execution over love of any sort."

The two blanched ghostly pale.

Rilla scrunched her brow at her elder brother. "What does she mean, Cayden?"

"Er..." Cayden coughed into a fist, ignoring Rilla and turning to me. "That is... I, er... *Khm-hmm!* While we're ever thankful for the sentiment, your grace, I... *Khm!* Don't think it would be wise to, er, expose *that* quite yet... if ever." He grimaced. "If I'm to be a public figure in your kingdom, we'd be a target for those who still, er... wouldn't *approve*..."

I frowned. "Oh. I suppose you've a point... It's still the same for Somniovokers in all realms, isn't it?" I sighed, my lion ears folding down. "Well, regardless of what you choose, I at least hope it'll bring you some relief to know it won't *lawfully* cost you your head?"

Cayden smiled thinly. "It does, your grace... Thank you."

"Cayden!" A woman's bubbly voice chimed suddenly from the east entryway. It was Lady Revinna, the lioness who was forced into marriage with Cayden when King Galden was still alive.

The woman was quite cheery as she practically skipped to Cayden's side, kissing his cheek in a chuckle. "There you are! I've barely seen much of you in days. Have you been celebrating our freedom without me?"

Cayden lifted an absent finger. Then he bit his knuckle, looking as though he'd completely forgotten about Revinna. "Right…" He glanced at me to find his confidence. I merely shrugged, conveying that it was his choice regarding what to share. He sucked in a breath. "Revinna… Now that my father is dead, you realize that makes our marriage void… don't you?"

Her smile faded with confusion. "What do you…?" His meaning dawned on her sagging face. "Oh… oh, I… see…" She sounded hollow. "You don't wish to keep our marriage, do you?"

Cayden pursed his lips in a wince. Then with a deflating sigh, he hung his head. "I'm sorry, Revinna. I was already… *with* someone. Before all of this." He hesitated for only a moment, then clutched Linus's hand, lacing their fingers together as he cleared his throat. "Now that he's back… I can't in good conscience keep up the charade. Please accept my sincerest apologies…"

Both she and Rilla stared at them; at their intertwined hands.

"What!" Rilla cried, clapping her hands on her gaping face.

"You…!" Revinna stabbed a shocked finger at Cayden, gasping. "*That's* why you never seemed interested in laying with me!"

Cayden's lion ears curled in a furious blush, mortified. "I beg your pardon—!"

Linus broke into sharp laughter, snickering, "Straight to the point, isn't she! I like this one."

"I thought you simply didn't find me attractive!" She said, sounding relieved. "I thought there was something wrong with me!"

"Why would there be something wrong with…!" Cayden cursed and ducked his head, stealing a habitual glance over his shoulder. "As I said, I was *with* someone already and…"

Rilla let out a piercing shriek, hopping next to her brother with a sudden rush of energy. "*THAT'S* why Linus visited so much when I was little—!"

"Will you *keep it down*?" Cayden hissed and clasped a hand over his sister's mouth. "I'm only saying this around *you* because I'm comfortable around my sister. Don't go spouting other people's business to the whole Bloody kingdom!"

I chuckled and tucked my arms behind me. "Speaking of business, I'll leave you all to yours…" I nodded to Cayden. "I'll return to discuss the details of your new role before I leave for the Gyle Islands, Regent Cayden… In the meantime, could you see that Tanderam Prison is made aware of the change in power? I believe we still have prisoners of war locked away that we weren't able to free in our last raid."

Cayden flushed, bowing hurriedly and seeming more than happy for the change in subject. "Y-yes, your majesty! I'll see to it immediately!"

I turned and left them in the throne room, Kurrick striding at my side in a grimace.

"I will never understand why Cayden would choose a *man* over his queen," he muttered.

I hummed blithely. "I'd have thought you'd be relieved, Kurrick." I smirked over my shoulder. "Now my list of qualified suitors is, once again, reduced to one—"

Crack!

Kurrick slammed his fist so hard on a nearby pillar, a small fissure split where he struck. I drew back in surprise, my lion ears folding down to see his frightful, curdled glare.

"You *do not* understand." His voice scraped like a knife over flint. "Without Cayden, that list is reduced to *zero*. Now I must find someone else who actually has some sense…!"

When my shock ebbed, I ground my sharpened teeth. "Enough, Kurrick! I don't know why you insist in being so difficult, but I'm tired of this irritating game of yours—"

"*This isn't a game!*" He roared, his lion ears growing and curling back, his voice dripping with venom as he rumbled so low and deep, I could barely hear him, "I… cannot marry someone I do not care for… *Ana.*"

My blood ran cold.

He let out a smooth stream of breath through his nose… then stormed off.

My view of his back blurred behind hollow, angry tears.

3

A NEW VOYAGE

WILLOW

The sea breeze swept my long hair back, and I stared out at the watery horizon from the deck of our ship. It was a relieving change of pace to finally travel by sea rather than thousands of feet in the Bloody air.

The sky was awash with vibrant shades of pink and orange as the setting sun lowered behind the shimmering waves, the sight unnervingly exquisite despite the dark path that lay ahead. Two messengers flew alongside our ship in that sky. They were Barrach and Ethil: the messengers of Mother Alice and Father Lucas. With their Reapers gone, they followed us now. Having them here was a small solace… it was said that the messengers were pieces of our very souls. In this way, I supposed, my Spirit Parents were still with us…

We'd set sail hours ago, along with thirty seaward ships and ten Airships, as part of both Anabelle's and my fleet. We were headed toward the Gyle Islands nestled between the two continents of Land. Most of our party had gone to Yu'nn Quisette, Marincia's capital city, while the few of us still left went in the opposite direction.

Xavier was watching over our son somewhere inside the ship's cabin. Hired crew members, floating ghosts, and resurrected vassals bustled across the deck where I overlooked the sea by myself. I found my two resurrected vassals, Rossette and Nikolai, patrolling the ship's perimeter with vigilant gazes. The twins had also resurrected their ghostly vassals for this voyage, and they were clustered together and carrying out similar tasks.

The rabbit-eared Vendy had her Crystal sword sheathed at her hip and looked Deathly ready to use it if the need arose. Her braid wafted gently in the breeze that rolled over the ship, her expression hardened. Striding alongside her was her fellow vassal, Hugh, who had been given a pair of glowing scythe-spheres to wear around his neck, giving the boy a means to defend himself and everyone else. Hugh was Xavier's apprentice Reaper as well as his vassal… it was a strange combination, but it's what the boy requested, so Xavier went along with it.

Our party's Blacksmith, Henry, was polishing the iron hook he'd attached to his stubbed hand after he'd lost it in the Battle of New Aldamstria weeks before this. He had apparently been hit with an Infection-arrow on that hand and had quickly cut it off to prevent the disease from spreading.

The rest of the twins' vassals—Dalen, Aiden, and Apson—stalked the upper deck by the helm, where Nathaniel steered the pegged wheel, acting as our ship's captain.

I found Alexander leaning over the railing to my left. He was stealing a glance at our rabbit-eared Alchemist… Bianca. The Mistress Chemist was too busy taking notes on a ledger to notice him, surrounded by a crowd of her Alchemy guild members as they spouted off their current assignments for brews to craft during their travels. Alex resigned himself to staring off at the horizon, letting loose a brooding grumble.

You've stalled long enough, Willow, I chided myself.

With a deep breath, I pulled out my silver communicator. There was a brief moment of hesitation, but I forced myself to dial the number of King Ninumel's correspondent. Once entered, the gears and springs whirled to life as a screen of light projected from the green vision-gem imbedded in the center of the device.

The web-eared correspondent's face appeared on the screen.

He opened his mouth to speak, but I cut him off, speaking in their native tongue of Marincian, "<I am Willow Ashleya Ember, Princess of…>" I stopped short, my chest tightening along with my throat. "<*Queen* of Death… I must speak with King Ninumel immediately. It's of dire importance.>"

The correspondent glanced about, flabbergasted, but redirected my call right away and connected me to Ninumel's personal line. After a short wait, the Seadragon appeared on the screen with a shocked look painting his features.

"<*QUEEN?*>" Ninumel questioned in Marincian with wide, emerald eyes. "<*What's happened with Serdin? Has he…?*>"

"<My father is dead,>" I croaked, swallowing before continuing, "<I suppose you haven't heard from your sister Dalminia quite yet. Then I'll be the first to tell you what's happened. Yes, my father was killed. As was the Sky Princess… as well as Dream.>"

Ninumel fell Deathly silent. Then he breathed in horror, "*<Even Dream…? But I… who could have possibly killed the two-thousand-year-old oracle?>*"

"<Macarius Lysandre.>" I closed my eyes as another breeze rolled past my face, tugging my hair with it. "<I'm sure by now you've heard your wife speak of the Shadowblood and the Lightcaster?>"

He nodded gravely, rubbing his scaled fingers over his long moustache. "*<I've heard, yes… She says your fiancé and his brother are the Shadow.>*"

"<Husband,>" I corrected, realizing it had been some time since I last saw Ninumel myself. Roji and Dalminia were the last to speak with Ninumel on com last month. He wouldn't have known that Xavier and I wedded after we left his palace in Yu'nn Quisette. "<Yes, the twins are the Shadowblood. Macarius is their opposite, the Lightcaster. Has your wife spoken of what the Lightcaster intends to do with us Relicbloods?>"

He gave a low rumble. "<He seeks to kill us. And take our Hallows…>" He paused, then asked, "<If three Relicbloods have fallen, does this mean he has their Blessings…?>"

"<Two of them. Sky and Dream. My father fell in battle here on the surface, killed by a… a Sentient Necrofera…>" I hadn't been present for that battle, but I'd heard the horrifying description of my father's death. It was enough to send a crisp chill through my soul. Xavier had said my father's heart was ripped straight out of his chest by La'Lunaî… I could only imagine the agony he must have endured before being devoured and…

I forced my thoughts to halt. It was just so… so painful… I willed back tears and exhaled a heavy breath, continuing in a shivering voice, "Macarius does not have the Death Hallows. He cannot gain his powers unless the Relicbloods are killed under the witness of their Relics… Which brings me to the reason I've called you.>" I cleared my throat, my voice darkening. "<I wished to warn you, Ninumel. It is about your son.>"

Terror creased his scaled face. "*<Do not DARE tell me Fuérr was also—!>*"

"<Your son is alive,>" I assured. "<For now. But he's been kidnapped by the Lightcaster himself. Macarius intends to wager Fuérr's life for the location of the Pearl of Emerald…>" I sighed, shame twisting my stomach. "<I'm sorry, Ninumel… he was taken under our watch. I take full responsibility…>"

Ninumel was clearly livid, though he said nothing. He simply breathed deeply for several moments, his teeth sharpening until he finally spoke again. "<So… he is coming here with my son?>"

I nodded. "<Last our oracles Saw, he escaped by way of Airship. I suggest you have your Skyports searched thoroughly across your islands. But be warned, he is in possession of the Orbs of Azure. He is no longer bound to the physical

realms, and will likely use this to his advantage. Your sister is on her way with Roji and his fleet as we speak, along with half of our company. I will also contact my Reapers stationed on your islands to assist in the search immediately.>"

His webbed ears folded downward. "<Thank you… and… I suppose if this Lightcaster was conniving enough to best the Great Oracle, I… cannot blame any of you for what's happened…>" His ears flicked back angrily. "<But by the Artist, when that snake sets foot on my glacier, he will find my trident in his ribs before his next step…!>"

"<For the sake of my father and grandfather, I pray that you do. Be prepared, Ninumel. And be safe.>"

The call ended.

Then a man's rumbling voice suddenly commented beside me, "I suppose you've many a task ahead, haven't you, Death Queen?"

Hecrûshou had suddenly appeared beside me, the shark shifter leaned against the ship's railing. He must have approached while I was distracted with the call. The Demon King's indigo, fin-textured hair waved from the sides of his smooth shoulders, which were bare under his opened vest, revealing his sharp elbows and defined muscles along his triceps and torso. His pupils, which I knew were naturally white and glowing, were disguised with an illusion to make them look black, to hide what he was from the unsuspecting members of our hired crew. And wrapped in a covering cloth was his Spiritcrystal trident that he'd leaned beside him on the rail.

I sighed and put away my com. "You look strange with normal eyes, Hecrûshou. I never would have thought I'd find them more unsettling than their natural radiance."

He hummed. "Yes, well… if you keep to your promise, I suppose there oughtn't be a need to hide them, will there?" His gaze narrowed at me. "Now that you're queen, I do hope you intend to *honor* that promise? Not only for me, but for all of us?" He swept his attention to the several Sentients occupying our ship.

The old jackal woman, Miranda, clipped across the deck behind us with her cane; the dragon shifter, Thörd, was taking advantage of his disguised eyes and flirting with some of the female Reapers on board; lastly, the web-eared pacifist demon, Khol, sat at a bench and knitted away at his latest, vibrant creation, whistling a jolly tune.

"Of course, I intend to honor our agreement," I assured. "But keep in mind, swaying the people of Grim to grant you all citizenship will be enormously difficult, let alone convincing the council not to call me a traitor and vote to take away my throne in the process."

He crossed his arms. "What will you need from us to change their minds?"

"Your collective testimonies?" I offered, waving a hand in the air. "Perhaps if you tell each of your stories in turn, the people will find sympathy for you all."

He grumbled, "Assuming we're given the chance to tell our stories in the first place. Should any of your Reapers break your command and come after us—"

"I will ensure that won't happen," I promised, pausing as an afterthought hit me. "Although… have we learned what's become of Cilia?"

Hecrûshou shook his head. "Thörd flew around the mountains and neighboring cities in the valleys, but there was no sign of her. Nor of her husband. Since they fell from Culatia mere hours before we descended on our Airships, there is no other place they could have landed."

I bit my lip in thought. Considering they'd fallen from thousands of feet, I could only assume Kael was dead. Even if Cilia had broken his fall, the impact would have surely killed him regardless. No, I thought it more likely she'd let his soul rot, like hers, and fled with him somewhere to keep him safe. At least, that's what *I* would have done, were I in her situation and such a thing had happened to Xavier…

What sort of Death Queen are you?

I rubbed my temples. Seamstress prick me, even *I* was shocked by my own blasphemous thoughts. To let anyone's soul rot was amongst the foulest of sins, the strictest Law of Death that all citizens of Nirus were expected to follow, else they face severe consequences. All this talk of reforming Grim's sacred laws was pulling my moral conscience in all sorts of uncomfortable directions. How will granting citizenship for Sentient demons change our world? How will it affect our long-set culture? And that was only assuming I could convince my people to change their way of life at all.

"We need Cilia," I said in a long sigh. "Her testimony will be vital, along with Kael's."

Hecrûshou tilted his head to the side. "I'd say it's likely we'll find them at our destination."

I cocked an eyebrow. "At the Gyle Islands? What makes you say that?"

"That is her home," he explained with a shrug. "Where she first awoke, just like Miranda. If she fled from La'Lunaî's horde to protect Kael, going there seems the most sensible."

"I see… Then, I'll leave her to you all. In the meantime, are there any more of you who may be of help for this trial?"

"Oh, there are thousands of Sentients. Though, I have a feeling that most of them have been rounded up by La'Lunaî, from the Land *and* Sea. And having Thörd search for any in the skies would take far too long in the short amount of time we have before we descend to Grim."

"Then what of the Sentients in Grim?" I asked. "Or better yet, do you know of any Ancients like yourselves down in the caverns?"

His lips pulled into a brooding frown. "There are two sisters down there, last I knew… Ashya and Charra. Vipers, both rivaling even La'Lunaî's power. Though, it's been ages since I visited their domain. I haven't a clue if they'd be willing to testify for us."

My breath iced. "Vipers? Oh, Seamstress…"

He gave me a furrowed look. "What's wrong?"

"My father once told me the story of how he became king," I muttered, pounding a frustrated knuckle over my brow. "He said he and my mother fought a very powerful Sentient woman. She and her horde killed my grandfather, then my parents killed the demon herself…" I exhaled sharply. "They said she was a viper."

His expression tightened. "Ah. Yes, that was likely one of the sisters…"

"Then the only one left down there who *could* testify probably hates the stones I walk on, thanks to my parents." I threw up my hands. "Wonderful. And if La'lunaî is working with Macarius, I have a feeling she'll soon descend to Grim and recruit that other sister and storm the palace eventually. What a lovely disaster I've inherited as the new queen."

Hecrûshou gave an agreeing hum. "Indeed. Well, rest assured, the rest of *us* will be recruiting any Sentients we find along our travels in the meantime. Should your fears of a demon invasion come to pass, you'll have a counter defense on your side."

"Thank you… and that only means I have to make damn sure you're all granted citizenship for your help."

He chuckled. "I suppose you're right. I look forward to seeing how our coexistence will benefit one another." He nodded respectfully before stalking away, going to Miranda and filling her in on the plan.

I folded my arms over the railing and gazed at the watery horizon. Jewel twittered from the sky and alighted on my shoulder, the little crow rubbing her beak lovingly against my jaw. I patted her head.

"It really could be a mutual benefit, couldn't it, Jewel?" I asked my messenger, propping my chin up with a dreary hand. "I only hope I can prove it to the people of Grim."

And that won't be the only thing I'll need to convince them of, I thought. There was also the matter of my vow to Land's Tailors. To Sirra-Lynn, to Rochelle, to the other Healers who had spent decades protecting living vessels whose

NecroSeams were cut before their deaths… protecting them from my family. It was against the fifth Law of Death to keep a living vessel alive without its soul. But, as Xavier had proven, it was possible to weave a temporary NecroSeam for those vessels, despite the fact they were still alive. The temporary Seams only lasted for a few weeks at a time, but the fact it was possible at all was nothing short of astounding. Because of this new discovery, I'd say it was worth discussing a revision to the law with the council. The only difficulty would be proving more than a handful of Necrovokers could pull it off. Even *I* still hadn't found success at it and…

I deflated. If the Bloody *queen* couldn't do it, how would I convince them anyone else could?

Perhaps I needed a new tutor, of sorts. Someone other than Xavier, who could use terms I actually understood…

Decision made, I twisted round, looking for the one person Xavier had successfully taught the skill to:

Matthiel Inion.

I spotted Matthiel's silken black locks peeking just above the railing of the upper deck. His voice wafted from up there as he conversed with what sounded like Neal Treble—Octavius's cocky brother who had joined us on our voyage. The two were members of Xavier's and my royal guard, so they were often paired together while on patrol.

Gritting my teeth, I climbed the steps to the upper deck. Past the helm where Nathaniel steered the ship, I found Matthiel and Neal leaning over the far railing with their backs facing me, staring off at the horizon and laughing cheerily. Their silver plate clattered as they traded wide gestures, as if sharing old stories to pass the time.

My footfalls vibrated the floorboards as I walked up behind Matthiel and cleared my throat. "Pardon, Matthiel…"

Matthiel flinched and spun around. When he saw my face, he didn't hesitate to bow, his armor crinkling noisily. "Y-Your Highness!" He paused and amended. "I mean… your *majesty*…"

I ignored the sickening pang that came with the new honorific and stood taller—though, I was still far shorter than the sienna-eyed Howllord. "Matthiel, I have a request."

He blinked at me. "Y-yes, of course. Anything you wish."

"I understand you're teaching miss Lëtta how to thread a NecroSeam for living vessels?"

He frowned, puzzled. "Yes… I am. She's making great progress, but she still has some practice to do before—"

"I hoped you could include me in your lessons," I said quickly, before the embarrassment had a chance to take root. "It is… shameful if the Death Queen cannot do such a task… I wish to amend that."

Matthiel's grey cheeks bled scarlet, then flushed paler than a ghost in the mist. "Y… yes, of—of course, your grace…! But…" He coughed into a fist, as if panicking. "Wouldn't your husband be a more… *convenient* tutor?"

"Xavier's tried to teach me," I admitted, the humiliation hitting at last. I cupped my face miserably. "But I suppose his method of teaching isn't suitable for the way *I* learn… Apparently, having a severe advantage over other Necrovokers leaves him at a loss for training those of us who *aren't* extraordinary at our Hallows…"

"Ah…" Matthiel rubbed his neck. "I see… Then, shall… shall I come find you when it's time for Miss Lëtta's lessons?"

I nodded. "That would be wonderful. Thank you."

He smiled warmly, bending into a low bow. "Of course, Your Majesty."

The title made me bristle again. But I kept my steps dignified as I retreated down the steps, crossing the lower deck toward the door to the ship's inner cabins. Once safely inside, I staggered down the hall and let out a long, exhausted breath, rubbing my pounding temples.

Waaaahhh!

My steps dwindled, hearing a baby's muffled cries up ahead.

Wahhh! Waaaaahhh!

It was coming from Xavier's and my door.

That must be Lucas, I thought, steeling myself as I gripped the door's handle. *And thus ends my short break from motherhood…*

I pushed open the door.

"—WAAAAAAAAHHHHHHH!!!"

The baby's piercing wail blasted my eardrums at full volume now, the sound so grating, it made my blood shiver.

"WAAAAAAAAAHHHHHH!!

Xavier was struggling to keep hold of our thrashing, wolf-eared son. The newborn wriggled as he screamed bloody murder over Xavier's shoulder, my poor husband desperately bobbing the pup and trying to shush him calmly. It was all for naught. Lucas only screamed louder, and Xavier's grown wolf ears twitched from under his tousled grey hair. His messenger raven, Chai, ducked his head under his wings as if trying to muffle the sound from the dresser in the corner. I noticed Xavier's heterochromic eyes were heavy and sagging with dark rings, neither of us having slept in days.

When I shut the door behind me, Xavier whirled and exhaled in relief. "Oh, thank *Death!* Willow, could you—*huah!*—" Lucas wriggled violently and nearly fell off of Xavier's shoulder. Xavier quickly secured his hold, shouting over the noise, "I-I don't know what's wrong! I've changed him, I've swaddled him, I tried to give him a bottle, but he—!"

I took Lucas and cradled the babe in my arms. Only when I pulled away the loose bodice of my gown and let the baby suckle did the shrieking stop at last.

Xavier dripped facedown onto the nearby bed with a groan. "Thank you... Bloody Death, thank you..."

I chuckled and kept Lucas balanced while sitting on the mattress beside him, kissing Xavier's cheek. "Thank you for watching him, love. I had a few things to attend to."

"Mmn... good. I'm..." He yawned. "... glad you enjoyed your break..." He fell asleep almost immediately, snoring softly over the comforter as if it was the most comfortable bed he'd ever had in his life.

I sighed and smiled at the nursing newborn. Lucas had Xavier's face, that much was certain. His sturdy nose, his broad chin, his distinct brow... much of him resembled my husband so astoundingly, one could have thought he was a belated triplet of Xavier's and Alexander's. Lucas's wisps of ashen hair, though, were inherited from me. The sharp shape of his eyes were also mine, but his white irises, which stared up at me like frozen pools in a grey winter, only reminded me of my father.

Tears stung so suddenly, they flooded over without warning, dripping over Lucas's cheek. I hurried to wipe them dry, sniffing and holding my breath to compose myself. But my lungs only held for a moment, trembling as a sob escaped.

Xavier stirred from his groggy sleep at the sound. He pushed up beside me in concern. "Willow...? What's wrong?"

"I..." Another sob choked as I kept a secure hold of our child. It seemed absolutely absurd, but every instinct I had screamed at me to keep Lucas close... that if his warmth wasn't heating my chest, I would scatter to pieces over the floorboards. My voice was tight as I whispered, "I can't do this, Xavier... I can't be queen—I've barely had time to be a mother, and now my father is gone, my grandfather is gone, my new *daughter* is gone, and I..."

He wrapped his arms around my waist and squeezed.

"I... I know..." he hushed, his grip strengthening as his icy soul soothed the fire in mine. Even still, his arms trembled around me, and he buried his face in the crook of my neck. "It feels like everyone is leaving, all at once... Even my parents are..." He couldn't finish, and I felt cold tears hitting my neck as he hugged me tighter. "But… we have each other. You're still here… and I'm still here." He turned my chin toward him and stole my lips, pushing hard. When he pulled away, he re-secured his grip around me and whispered, "I'll always be here."

I leaned into him, watching our wolf-eared son close his eyes as he nursed peacefully in my arms.

Oblivious to the painful circumstance he'd been born into.

4

A DAY TO REMEMBER

CILIA

500 YEARS PRIOR

The corpse's dismembered arm was shoved down my throat, the raw flesh dripping with blood over my tongue and trickling over my chin.

"All of it," Master Hector—the Sentient Necrofera who'd Marked me when I'd first Changed and woken—ordered testily, shoving the arm farther down until the limp fingers tickled my esophagus. "Can't have you getting weak on me, newborn."

I gagged and sputtered, pained tears streaking down my face, my protesting screams choking on the feast. As mind-numbingly delicious as it was, I'd been stuffed with 'meals' for weeks nonstop, I feared I would burst. When I couldn't take it anymore, I clamped my sharpened teeth shut—and the remainder of the arm ripped off and dropped at my feet. I blinked as I swallowed what was still in my throat, surprised and disturbed by how easily my teeth had severed through flesh and bone in a single, effortless bite. As always, it tasted hauntingly glorious… but the scene soured that delight.

I coughed and wheezed over the ground, a gush of blood pouring down my chin and pooling at my shaking, stained hands.

"Please…" I croaked, hacking my throat raw as those fingers I'd swallowed whole rubbed against my stomach. "Please, Master… no more—"

He struck my cheek so sharply, my skull *cracked* out of line, my neck snapping. I fell on my back in a puff of dirt, gasping for breath as I waited for my neck to heal itself with black, sticky tar.

I tried to prop myself up with my elbows, but Master shoved my head to the dirt and mounted me, his nasty glare shining bright with white pupils.

"What have I told you about giving me orders, *newborn*?" He growled, ripping my gown until I was naked under him. He pinned my legs open, as he always did when I displeased him. "You know the price for…"

The ground quaked under us.

Master paused, confused as the tremors grew stronger, nearly throwing him off as he released me to keep his balance—

There's my chance!

Thanking Shel for the distraction, I shoved my clawed hand through Master's bare chest—and *ripped* out his heart. Master barely squeezed out a pained gasp before I crushed my fingers over the juicy muscle like a plum— and cut his rotten NecroSeam with my claws.

Master's flesh deteriorated to ash above me. His blackened soul evaporated. Then his bones clattered over my nude belly and legs. Shivering, I crawled on all fours, keeping low to the dirt as the ground still shook and trembled from the unexpected quake.

At last…! I gasped and heaved for breath. *At last, I'd been given an opportunity…!*

I'd planned to kill that bastard for years. My every attempt before this had been met with horrible, painful failure… his Ancient Weight was always too strong for me to overpower. All I'd needed was a chance to catch him off-guard—a chance that the Gods had deemed me worthy at long, long last.

But the ground was still shaking. This was no normal quake, either. I heard the trees in the forest nearby splinter and crash to the ground, I heard the echoing *crick, crick, crick* of stones and boulders split apart.

An incredible *crack* came from deep within the ground. Under my hands, a hairline fracture appeared in the dirt. The fracture spread on both sides and crept over the ground. It crumbled and grew, splitting deeper, gaping wider…

Until, at last, the land broke apart.

I gasped as rock and stone drifted away right under my fingers. The ocean waters that waited miles from here along the coast suddenly came rushing forth to fill the new, ever-stretching trench. I stumbled back and shied away from the new ledge that had formed, staring in both horror and wonder as the gap grew and grew and grew, the bones of my former master left behind on the other retreating ledge…

PRESENT DAY

"The land *split*?" Kael questioned after I'd finished my tale. "Is that how the Neverland continent came to be?"

We trudged through the humid jungles of the Gyle Islands, stepping over tall roots, ducking under enormous leaves, and evading gossamer webs frosted in morning dew. Kael and I had swum here on the backs of two lesser Fera, the salty seawater still clinging to our skin and brittle, dried hair. Kael's newly white pupils were an odd sight, but I supposed I would grow accustomed to them in time. I was sure he, too, found much unfamiliarity in me, now that he's seen what I'd become over the centuries. But whatever he thought of it, at least he seemed to accept this was who I was now. A monster. A murderer…

Then again, he was now a demon himself. And as he'd assured me time and time again, his conscience was not any cleaner.

"Yes," I said after batting away a dangling vine. "It was said to be remarkably similar to when Grim's continents split at the end of the Time of Discord. And just as similarly, no one truly knows what caused either realms to split. At the time, there were many theories. The most popular among them was that Shel was angry with the people of Everland for their civil war that had broken out and set his wrath upon them."

Kael swatted a squealing mosquito on his neck. "Civil war?"

I hummed. "After the last King of Land was killed…" I stopped. "Oh. That's right. That was *your* doing, wasn't it?"

Kael's expression fell. "I… can't remember…" He clutched his head, squeezing his eyes shut. "All I can think about is how… how Macar butchered you…" His claw grew and pierced his scalp, black blood squirming from the wounds. "And how desperately I want to shred him to pieces…!"

I cupped his bristly face. "You'll still have your chance, darling. And now that you're a Necrofera, it will be easier than you think." An afterthought struck me, and I amended. "That is, if we can find a way past La'Lunaî and her horde."

Kael calmed at my touch, nodding. "Yes… Right. Those are the other Ancients you mentioned? Remind me which ones are on our side again?"

"Only a handful." I counted on my fingers. "There is Hecrûshou of the Western Seas, Khol of the Northern Seas, Thörd of the Storming Skies, Miranda of the Neverland continent…" I snapped my fingers, remembering something. "Ah, that's right. Do you happen to remember Miranda? She was a nurse under your employ in Land's Palace when we were alive."

Kael rubbed his head as if in mild pain. "I… don't remember much of the palace, still. Most of the memories I've regained have all been of you." He smiled at me suddenly, his yellow eyes bright and warm. "I thought… I'd never see you again, Cilia. Nira has truly blessed me if she granted me that precious gift after everything I've done."

"Everything you've done was caused by Macarius in the first place," I reminded.

His gaze darkened again. "I suppose…" He sighed and looked about as I continued forward, Kael following at my heels. "Is this really where our home is now?"

"Just ahead, yes. The entirety of Aldamstria was split from *both* continents during the Great Divide. The palace ruins are here as well, though they're riddled with vines and wildlife now. It's quite a mess."

He grunted curiously as I led us through the jungle. When we approached the overgrown ruins of the ancient city, we stopped at the only domicile that wasn't latticed with tangled greenery. The only plants that decorated the humble cabin were the daisies I usually set at the windowsills. They were shriveled now, having passed nearly three winters since I left for Everland with Macar, but they still made the cabin look like the coziest home in the wild city.

When I opened the door and walked inside, Kael lingered under the frame, running a reminiscent hand over the wood. He whispered wistfully, "Our home… It's still here?"

"After I killed my demon master," I began as I grabbed a nearby rag from the adjoining kitchen and began cleaning the dust that had collected in my absence, "I came back here, to the place where I first Awoke. I'd hoped it would bring back my memories… but none ever returned." I growled low. "I suppose that was because Macar had already trapped them in that damned mirror-sphere of his… I'm lucky he missed some of *you*, at least."

My cleaning slowed to a dismal stop. *That's right*… Macar still had my memories. I'd broken his leash before I could get them back. I'd completely forgotten…

Kael strode through our old home in wonder, slowing at every insignificant piece of furniture he passed by. "It's all the same…" he whispered, as if only now recalling the memories. "Exactly how it was…"

He stopped cold when he glanced at his feet and found the ancient blood stains that had long soaked into the hardwood for the rest of eternity. His cat ears grew, and he knelt to touch his fingers over the stain. "This was where I found you…"

I left the rag on the countertop and crouched beside him. "And this was where I Awoke. Alone… with no memories save for a voice calling my name." I kissed his cheek. "Your voice, Kael."

His eyes began to well, and he suddenly reeled me in to cradle my head. "He will die for this…" he hissed. "I'll see that he faces the same horrors he put you through. Every last one…"

I held him close, welcoming his warmth. "It will be a day to remember, my love."

5

CAPTIVE

KURN

TRANSLATED FROM FERRET

I scurried through the ship's creaking corridor and hobbled behind splintered barrels to hide from the stalking, bi-pedal crew members.

I sniffed the air, trying to discern the familiar scent of the young fish-prince, Fuérr, from the rest of the salty seawater. He was here, I was sure of it. His signature scent was a unique blend of ice water and salt, and a bit of a flowery potpourri. When I'd checked the other ships along the docks of Brittleton's harbor, I hadn't caught so much as a whiff of him. Here, though, it was present. Faint, but present. That was enough to tell me this was indeed the ship we sought.

I'd left Clover with the children outside, since they were all too large to sneak about this vessel unnoticed. I, on the other hand, was well practiced in the art of espionage, thanks to Ringëd's career of investigative work over the years.

My nose led me down the stairwell—far, *far* down the stairwell, all the way to the bottom of the ship. This must have been the brig. Several barred cells were lined flush along the walls. A single, dim lamp hung from the ceiling, swinging lazily along with the waves that rocked the ship.

A single prisoner waited in the farthest cell.

"KURN'S MEMORY ARCHIVES ACCESSED," chimed a woman's voice in my thoughts—the mouthpiece of my nanites' core processing unit. *"FACIAL IDENTITIFICATION CONFIRMED: SEADRAGON SHIFTER. AGE EIGHT. NAME: FUÉRR ASCHÎT'AQUA. CROWNED PRINCE OF MARINCIA."*

I sighed in relief. "Eureka… just who I was looking for."

The boy's arms were chained above his head against the wall, dampening-gloves strapped to his hands and feet. His emerald, fin-textured hair was loose and fell down the middle of his bare, scaled back. His eyes were closed but he was breathing softly, likely asleep. Stale tears coated his cheeks, the poor lad looking exhausted with dark rings sagging his lids.

Since my furry body was thin enough to slip through the bars of Fuérr's cell, I hobbled inside and scampered beside him, laying my front paws on one of his scaled legs.

"Youngling!" I huffed in my breathy language, bouncing my paws over his scales. "Youngling, wake up!"

His green eyes cracked open groggily. When he saw me, he jolted.

"Kurnna!" He exclaimed in his Marincian accent. He continued in that language and the nanite-translator in my brain helped me understand him. "Are you really here, little furry one?"

"I am indeed," I said, though I knew he couldn't comprehend my snickering language. My speech was limited to a few mere *dook, dook, dooks.*

His webbed ears flicked as he asked. "Is Oliver here? Or Auntie Mini?"

I threw my head upward in a gesture, knowing that explaining in detail was beyond my control at this point. Perhaps it would be best to retrieve Oliver and Milann—the ones who were actually large enough to get him out of here.

I patted Fuérr's leg and huffed encouragingly, "I'll be right back, young one."

When I scurried back the way I'd come, I heard Fuérr calling out for me in a panic. *Poor youngling,* I thought with a sinking heart. *Don't you worry. We'll get you out of here in a moment.*

I hobbled up the stairwell, through the corridors, out to the decks and down the ramp onto the loading docks.

Oliver and Milann were right where I'd left them: behind the stack of fish crates. Clover the crow hid within the veil of Oliver's shaggy, feathered hair from his shoulder.

When they spotted me, Oliver's wings fluttered hopefully. "Was he there?!"

I nodded, gesturing to the ship urgently.

Milann exhaled, "Finally! Let's go get him."

They snuck to a cart of barrels that waited beside the ship. These were some of the food supplies that workers were now bringing onboard. The children found separate barrels and dumped the contents into the water, then hid within the barrels.

A part of me grieved for all that delicious food being wasted, seeing an apple bobbing in the water… but, as I reminded myself, I supposed desperate times called for desperate measures. I climbed into Milann's barrel, since Oliver's was already cramped with Clover, and I peeked out the knothole.

Two web-eared workers strode toward us. When they fell out of sight from my spying hole, our barrels suddenly vibrated, making us tense as we lurched upward. The workers chatted above us as they hauled our barrels onto the ship.

Clunk! Clunk!

Milann and I stifled pained winces when we were tossed down haphazardly… then the barrel remained still. The sound of the worker's chatter faded away.

After five whole minutes of silence, I popped up the lid and peered around.

Ah, I recognized this room! We were in the pantry, second floor. I had passed these shelves of potatoes and cabbages during my first inspection of the ship.

We were alone for now, so we all crawled out of the barrels quietly. I scampered ahead to lead the way to the imprisoned prince, remembering the route from here.

We reached the brig at last. Fuérr was still chained where I'd left him. But now, he was straining against his shackles, pulling them with noisy rattles.

"Fuérr!" Oliver hissed and ran over to the barred cell door.

The prince ceased his clattery tugging, and his eyes spilled over with tears when he saw the boy. *"Olee-va!"*

Milann shuffled beside Oliver and scrutinized the thick lock on the door. Her nose scrunched. "How do we get this thing open—?"

A foghorn sounded, and the crew up top began shouting commands. Then the ship began to dip and bob more drastically in the water.

I cursed, "Blast, they've set sail!"

Footsteps creaked from the stairwell, and the two children and I scattered behind a wide support beam. I sidled beside Milann's boot, keeping low to the floorboards as I peeked round the beam with a thundering pulse.

A lone figure entered the brig. She was a brown-scaled woman dressed in fine silks and lace sleeves. Her long, brown hair was pulled into a tight bun, and she held a communicator in one manicured hand. The screen of light displayed an oddly familiar face of a viper woman in gilded armor and no helm.

I craned my neck farther around the beam, my ears perking as I squinted to get a better view of the woman on screen. If I didn't know any better, I'd say she was…

Genevieve?

I *did* recognize her! That was one of the golden queen's guards, wasn't it?

"*They've split toward separate destinations,*" Genevieve reported from the screen, glancing over her shoulder like a weasel in the midst of thieving eggs from a nest, "*The Ocean King's sister has gone with the Sky King to retrieve the prince. They're bringing a fleet of Stormchasers with them. The rest of us are sailing to the Gyle Islands to find the Blossom of Gold.*"

Above me, I saw Milann's copper brow furrow, and she hissed to Oliver, "Wasn't that lady at the Land Palace with us?"

Oliver grumbled low, "That's Genevieve… I guess the scary sword guy was right about her."

Anger simmered in my nanite-riddled blood, glaring at the viper on screen with curled ears. "A traitor, is she?" My teeth barred as a quiet growl slipped through my throat. "Perhaps she'll learn just what an emperor does to traitors when next I see her…"

The snake woman holding the com hummed in delight. "Brilliant news. And you know what to do once you're there with the queen?"

Genevieve gave a dismal, but resolute sigh from the screen. "*Yes… Father and I discussed the plan some time ago. Do not worry, mother. I'll make sure to see it through.*"

"That's a good girl. You honor us with your dedication, dear… Be sure you aren't discovered before then."

She nodded. "*Yes, mother. I shall contact you after my task is done.*" She took a breath before adding, "*Also, you should be aware that two children have left on their own to find the prince. They left earlier than the others, so you may run into them soon.*"

The woman's eyebrow cocked. "Oh? Well, then. We'll have to keep a few cells open for them, won't we?"

Muffled voices sounded from off screen, and Genevieve's face tightened with panic. "*They're coming—I have to go, Mother.*"

The call ended, and the viper woman pocketed the com with a sigh.

Creeeeeeaaaaaak…

The door creaked open from atop the stairs.

A man's voice called down in a whimsical purr, "How is my dearest step-daughter faring with the Shadowblood…?"

The voice was so pleasant, it ruffled my fur in a chill. I curled against Milann's boot in a shiver.

The stairs creaked and squeaked as the man strode down to the brig to meet the woman. He was a tan-scaled snake with oddly colored, azure-and-scarlet splotched hair, with strange eyes to match.

"FACIAL IDENTIFICATION CONFIRMED," chimed the nanite woman's voice in my thoughts as it accessed my memory archives again. *"COBRA SHIFTER. AGE UNKNOWN. NAME: MACARIUS LYSANDRE."*

I huffed, "Yes, I know. He's the man trying to kill us."

"ENEMY CONFIRMED," she announced. *"ARCHIVING MACARIUS LYSANDRE AS IMMIDIATE THREAT. TERMINATION PROCESSING…"* she paused. *"TERMINATION DELAYED. EMPEROR KURN HAS INSUFFICIENT POWER LEVELS."*

I rolled my eyes. "Have I *ever* had sufficient power levels for termination?" I couldn't remember the last time I had to use that command. I recalled coming close to it a few times when I fled my planet during the rebellion, but I didn't have sufficient power levels even then. Useless, outdated little bots…

I turned my attention back to Macarius—the man who kidnapped the prince.

The scaled woman slid an arm over his and smiled. "All according to plan, darling. Though she warns that Sky is coming for us with his fleet, along with the Ocean King's sister."

"And we're sure our last Airship has been thoroughly burnt to ashes?" Macarius questioned as the two stalked toward the prince's cell. "The last thing we need is for any of their Seers to use its planks as a medium."

The woman purred. "Not a single splinter is left, I checked it myself."

"Splendid." The man smiled, his fangs on display as he gazed at Fuérr behind his half-moon spectacles. "They'll be inspecting Airships in Yu'nn Quisette's ports. Going by way of sea ought to give us the freedom we need to dock there and…" He drew a sudden breath, his eyes growing distant. An azure light radiated from his chest beneath his tunic, and I guessed that was where his Dream mark was now gleaming. He had the look that Ringëd often wore when he was having a vision.

Then his head snapped directly at the support beam where we hid.

"Why, hello there, children," he said with a fang-filled smile, walking toward us—and twisted around the beam, startling Milann and Oliver. "I wasn't aware we had stowaways with us…"

"Run!" I yelled and scampered away, diving into a large knothole in one of the floorboards and peeking an eye through. Clover screeched and fluttered up the stairwell out of sight.

Milann and Oliver moved to flee—

but Macarius snagged their wrists. The fiend's hands glittered with azure light that seeped into the children's skin, and the two fell limp in Macarius's hold.

They were sound asleep. Macarius had used his dream Hallows to make them slumber.

His splotched gaze flicked toward the Ocean Prince in his cell. "Friends of yours, I presume?"

Fuérr chewed on a string of Marincian curses, spitting at the ground.

"It was an endearing attempt," Macarius commended in a chuckle. His wife opened two separate cells beside Fuérr's and he tossed each child into one, locking the barred doors. "But not an effective one, I'm afraid. Though, perhaps there is some use for you both. If the prince has an attachment to his friends, he'll be less likely to leave you both here, should he find a way to escape. I thank you for that." He tipped his head to the prince and left up the steps with his wicked wife, murmuring blithely, "Now, I believe I spied a messenger escaping upstairs. I suspect it belongs to one of the new children. Tell the crew to find it and kill it immediately. We don't want it finding help and leading any Reapers to our vessel."

"A wise plan, dear," she said, the two of them disappearing upstairs.

When I heard the metal door up there creak closed, I sniffed the air through my spying knothole. I didn't smell any additional shifters, but there was a familiar scent still present by the stairwell. I crawled out and hobbled to the source, craning my head up to look at the underside of the steps.

"They're gone, Clover!" I called up to the young crow shivering from a metal support bar under the well. "You can come down now!"

The crow sheepishly peeked his head out from his wings, dropping them in relief when he saw me. He hopped off the bar and soared down, flying to the cell where Oliver was sleeping. The crow squeezed through the bars and nudged his beak against the boy's cheek. Oliver didn't stir.

I crawled into Milann's cell and patted her nose with my paw, but she didn't wake either. I sighed and scurried two cells over to Fuérr's cage, crawling up his torso and stretching over his arm to take a look at his shackles. The locks were too small for even *my* little paws to toy around in there. In a huff, I hopped off the prince and crawled back through Oliver's cell to meet with Clover, shaking my head.

"There's nothing we can do to get them out of this, I'm afraid," I said dejectedly. I knew Clover couldn't understand me, but I went on regardless, wanting to talk myself through a plan of action. "We'll have to wait until we dock again to escape… For now, we need to warn the others about Genevieve. It sounds as if they're sailing right into a trap."

Clover cocked his head, not comprehending.

I tapped a paw to my nose in thought. "Although, *how* are we going to warn them? Even if the ship's crew doesn't see you flying out of here and kill you, you wouldn't get to the twins for weeks. They'll probably already be there by that time."

I hummed broodingly, rubbing my ear. "No… the children's safety takes priority. Wherever they go, we follow…" I sighed. "However long that will take…"

6

PARANOIA

KURRICK

300 YEARS PRIOR

The gilded engagement-vines shined under the sunbeams that filtered through the forest's canopy. The amethyst centerpiece sat in its proper place in the long box, glinting in colorful flashes as I leaned against a moss-dressed boulder to scrutinize the jewelry.

"Yes… these will do nicely." I grinned at the vines and snapped the box closed.

I'd purchased these earlier today in the markets, outside the forest. I was fortunate Ana hadn't been here to see me leave. I only hoped the surprise wasn't spoiled.

We'd spent the last few months in the physical plane—outside of Aspirre—to sharpen our physical training. It was impossible to gain any physical strength in the realm of Dreams. If Ana and I were to prepare ourselves for the End of Existence, we would need all the strength we could garner.

And today was our last day outside. For what could be years.

I wished to make this a *memorable* day.

I fiddled with the Shelish coin dangling from my neck with a chuckle. She'd gifted me this coin some weeks ago. I'd expected some sort of present—it wasn't often either of us ventured out to the physical realms, so the occasions were always precious to us—but this particular gift had been different. It was far more expensive than previous gifts… and Shel, but the smile it brought her when she presented it…

My grin widened, and I gripped the box of vines with determination. I'd be damned if I let her best me this time. By nightfall, I'd see Ana as my wife and return to Aspirre a married man. I'd like to see her compete against *that…*

I let out a nervous breath. Was there a chance she wouldn't accept? What if I waited too long? To say I'd dragged my feet for two-hundred years would be an understatement, yet…

I shut my eyes stubbornly. *She'll accept. She's been with me for two lifetimes already, it'd be ludicrous to think she wouldn't stay with me for another few—*

"Kurrick."

I yelped and spun about, nearly dropping the box.

Dream had suddenly appeared beside me. The young, azure-haired king stared at the nearby river with his usual, blank expression.

I breathed out my panic in a hard exhale. "By the Gardener, Dream, you *must* stop doing that—"

He snatched the box out of my hand and opened it, examining the vines with a placid gaze.

"E-Excuse me!" I tried to swipe them back, but he wheeled about to avoid me. I stamped a foot. "Return those at once, Dream! She'll be here any moment, and…!"

"They're the same," he murmured, his lids narrowing. "Precisely the same…"

I staggered. "The same as what?"

"The ones Ana wore in my vision," Dream said, finally facing me and returning the box to me. "This does not bode well."

My lungs tightened at that grave tone. "Wh… what doesn't bode well…? What was the vision?"

His lips drew into a thin line. Then his azure eyes drifted to the flowing river, electing to remain silent and allow the screeching cicadas to fill the emptiness.

"Dream," I chewed, seizing his shoulder. *"What was the vision?"*

He cast his gaze down at his bare feet. Then reluctantly reached for the velvet sack tied to his waist.

He produced one of the Orbs of Azure.

Upon lifting the Orb to my face, it gleamed with sparkling light, bleeding with smoky images inside.

The face it showed was Ana's. Her hair shined in its golden brilliance in the warm sun. The vines and its amethyst jewels glittered from her head and brow. Her metallic eyes stared at the sky as someone held her in his arms.

And her neck was flooded with blood from the gash slit across her neck.

I reeled back, knocking the Orb out of Dream's hand and causing it to *thmp* along the moss at his feet.

"H-h… how?" I hushed, panic thrumming at full alert now. "How do we stop it?!"

Dream bent to retrieve the Orb. "I don't know. I'm not sure how it comes to pass, either. All I know is that one day, when you face death yourself, she will come to protect you." His tone deadened. "And she will die."

I gripped the box of vines, my fists shaking. "But *how do I stop it?!*"

"I don't know," he repeated. "I only came to be sure it wasn't a *current* vision. Whenever it will happen, it seems it will be after you wed." His expression grew stern. "Perhaps the best course of action would be to stay alert, for now. Watch your back. If you're fortunate, simply knowing it will happen may change its course." He grumbled under his breath. "I will let Crysa and Myra know. Perhaps we can all guard her as a whole."

—He vanished in a blinding light, leaving me in the forest.

I glared at the vines I still held.

Then hurled them into the river with a furious scream. The currents swallowed the sparkling jewelry as they sank beneath its lapping surface.

My teeth sharpened. "It will *never* come to pass."

PRESENT DAY

I stomped through the ship's corridors on patrol, keeping a strict hand on the hilt of the sword at my hip.

Scrich-scrich-scrich-scrich…

I flinched and drew my blade, jabbing it toward the source of the danger…!

My grip faltered. There was naught but a feral mouse under my blade, nibbling at a piece of celery it likely pilfered from the galley.

My lion ears grew and twitched in annoyance, my tail swishing at my legs as I jammed my blade back in its sheath and continued my patrol.

Bloods have mercy… if a damned rodent had me this terrified, this was certainly a terrible voyage indeed. I was on edge more than any journey we'd undertaken thus far.

This was the sacred time we had awaited for so many centuries—the time when Ana would take the Shadowblood to the Blossom of Gold to fulfill their destiny. But smothering the excitement of it all was the looming fear that Macarius would pop into existence from Aspirre at any moment.

Dream was now dead. Macarius had the Orbs of Azure. What could protect us now?

The question had my fingers twitching over my hilt. *Shel, please, let Macarius be too distracted with the Ocean King to come for us.* The only consolation I had was knowing that it was damn near impossible to pinpoint the coordinates of a moving ship from Aspirre. Logically, him suddenly appearing on this vessel was nothing to worry about, but damn it, my paranoia didn't care for logic.

I passed by an unoccupied room and threw open the door, inspecting the cabin to be sure it was empty. Then I marched to the next one and did the same. Then the next one. Then the next.

Without Cayden or Linus, the only other honor guards who could protect Ana were me and that leery-eyed viper, Genevieve. Last I saw of her, she was patrolling the deck outside for any strange activity. Of course, *I* knew that she was the only suspicious passenger on this damned ship. Why did Ana trust her so? Is it to spite me? To irritate me? Oh, Ana would certainly go to great lengths to pull at my nerves, as she always had…

But what reason do I have to distrust Genevieve? I wondered in silence. *I do not fear Cayden nor Linus the same way… Although, I suppose I once did, before I grew more familiar with them.*

I frowned. Blast, that meant Ana may be right to dismiss my concerns… It could be that I'll come to trust Genevieve later, as I did with those two. But how will I do that if the viper woman never *speaks*? For Land's sake, she's as reserved and guarded about her past as… as…

As I am. My eye twitched in annoyance. *Damn it.* If I had my reasons to keep my own life a secret for five hundred years, then of course Genevieve did as well. What right did I have to suspect her for that?

But Dream's vision could still come to pass.

My grip tightened on my sword, and I resumed my fervent inspection of the ship.

Yet I slowed when passing the door to Ana's private cabin. She'd hardly emerged during these three weeks of voyage. She only took her meals in her room, delivered personally by Claude or Sirra-Lynn. She hadn't once asked to see me.

I was worried I'd gone too far when last we spoke. I wasn't sure if she believed my excuse or if she was pouting until I retracted. Either way, it had clearly struck a chord. But I had to admit, locking herself in her cabin was probably the best way to keep her safe at this point. Well, as safe as I could control. With only two of her guards present, it would have been difficult to keep at her side at all times.

I rounded to the stairwell and descended into the galley. Many crew members were here enjoying their meals, and a few of them—the Shadowblood twins included—turned their heads to nod at me. Of the two, Xavier especially looked exhausted. His wife sat beside him, nursing their son as she spoke with Herrin across the long table.

I crossed the galley and headed straight for the kitchens, leaning my head through the open wall over the chef's counter. There, I found the black-haired, yellow-eyed man I sought.

"Claude," I called gruffly, "A word?"

Claude glanced at me curiously and set down his skillet, wiping his hands on his apron before coming toward the counter across from me. "What's up?" He questioned.

"I wished to ask after her majesty," I said, licking my lips hesitantly. "She hasn't left her cabin in weeks, and I know you and your wife deliver her meals, so…"

Claude propped his chin up with a fist. "You can't go in there and ask yourself?"

"I'm… preoccupied," I said flatly. "The rest of our usual guard was left in Everland. As such, I've spent night and day inspecting the ship for any unwanted passengers—passengers who could very easily pop into existence at will, mind you."

Claude grimaced, minding full well. "Oh… right. Forgot about that bit…" He shuddered. "It was bad enough being watched by Macarius 24/7, but with him having a VIP ticket to whatever damn locked room he wants, I can see why you're asking… Bloods, Now *I'm* not going to sleep. Thanks a lot."

I raised my brow expectantly, waiting for him to remember my original question.

"Right, right." He snapped his fingers and knocked on his skull. "You want an update on your queen. I saw her last night and she was fine, but if you want a more recent report, might want to ask Genevieve. She came here a few minutes ago to pick up her majesty's lunch. She might be in there by now, but give her a few minutes and I bet she'll be done."

I scowled, but nodded in thanks and stormed back up the stairwell.

GENEVIEVE

As her majesty ate her meal, I stood guard by the window of her private cabin. I pretended to stare at the watery horizon, but stole a sidelong glance at the golden-haired queen in secret.

She was eerily silent. The only sounds in the cabin were her delicately clinking silverware. I'd asked Claude if I could deliver her meal myself this time to find out why she'd been so reclusive during the voyage, but thus far, she hadn't uttered a peep and I'd learned nothing. There was something unnervingly morose about her doll-like expression. Her arms absently maneuvered her silverware as if by habit rather than command. Her bright eyes stared at the woodgrain of the wall before her, looking yet not seeing, as if she were gazing past the planks and watching the waves behind them instead. I couldn't tell if she was depressed or wracking her brain over a formidable riddle.

What is it that burdens your mind, my lady? I thought, worry twisting my stomach.

Why did I care? She was the enemy. She would help bring the End of Existence to us all, alongside the Shadowblood. For the sake of our world, I've risked exposure for an entire year and served at her side, knowing that I would have to carry out my assigned task—*eager* to play my part in our deliverance once we arrived at the Blossom of Gold…

But Shel, how can I do it now? I gripped my scaled arms to stifle the tremors, venom leaking from my fangs. *Her majesty is just so…*

So enchantingly perfect.

My heart squeezed. She was, without a doubt, the most kindhearted, powerful, and clever queen I have ever had the honor to meet. She made short work of both the continents' rulers, as if they were trifling children and she their disciplining mother. She rallied the realm together and joined them with incredible grace and ease, her smile able to calm anyone's rage into a relaxing, trickling stream…

But now, her smile was gone. Her bronze face was blank. Whatever captured her mind must have been ground-shattering indeed—

"Genevieve," she whispered suddenly.

I jolted at attention and saluted. "Y-yes, my queen?"

She hummed absently, "How can you tell if someone is hiding something from you?"

My scales crawled. Was that a trick question? Did she suspect me…?

I swallowed, positioning my feet toward the door in case I was forced to run. "W… what do you mean, your grace?"

She set down her silverware, still staring at the wall. "Kurrick is acting stranger than usual."

I resisted the urge to gasp in relief. "I… I see…" I cleared my throat. "Strange how?"

"He claims he doesn't care for me," she said. Her head cocked to one side, her golden curls tumbling over one shoulder. "Yet he is taking even more pains than usual to protect me. I've heard him stalking outside my door like a paranoid bloodhound night and day, I've heard the utter fear in his voice when he speaks to anyone in the hall regarding potential threats…" She flicked her metallic gaze to me. "If he truly felt nothing for me, why go to such lengths to keep me alive?"

I blinked at her. "I suppose… actions speak louder than words, my lady…"

One of her lion-ears flicked back. "Yes, they do… which tells me he lied. But then it begs the question: *why?*"

"Perhaps he doesn't wish to be king?" I offered. *Though,* I thought to myself, *imagining that pain-in-the-tail as king is infuriating enough.* Her majesty may be the epitome of royalty and grace, but her brutish lover had the refinement of a three-legged platypus—a platypus that tried to unveil my plans and get me killed at every turn for an entire year.

Her Majesty shook her head. "He claims that is the reason, but it holds no ground. Being the husband of a Relicblood comes with little to no obligation of *any* responsibility, if he chose. The burden would completely fall to me, and he knows this."

"Then commitment frightens him?" I suggested.

She snorted. "He has no qualms committing to stay with me for five centuries, yet the concept of marriage scares him in name? No. That logic is just as contradicting." She sighed dismally. "*I* think he knows something will happen if we wed. Dream was my foster father, it's likely he Saw something in a vision and told Kurrick of it." Her tone dripped into a growl. "I think I'm going to die soon."

I went cold, frozen where I stood. "Your Majesty…?"

"It's only a theory," she said, folding her arms over her desk. "But it's the only explanation that fits his unusual behavior."

A shiver prickled my spine. *It will be me,* I realized, my eyes starting to sting, *it will be my doing. I… will be the one to kill her.*

As much as I hated it… I knew it had to be done. For all of us. For our world… For existence itself.

I whispered, "Neither of us will let that happen." The lie was as sour as the venom leaking over my tongue. "I guarantee you that."

She gave me a gentle, beautiful smile. "Well… let us hope it stays as a theory. Thank you for the meal, Genevieve… you're dismissed."

I bowed, keeping my gaze on the floorboards. "Yes, my queen…"

When I left her in her cabin, I shut the door behind me, trying to calm my thundering pulse. *I must do it,* I reminded, clutching my chest as a knot thrashed and tangled. *I MUST…*

"Genevieve," a biting growl blurted.

My head snapped up, and I found myself staring at the ugly, scarred glare of Kurrick.

I steeled myself and stormed forward, shouldered past him in the usual sneer we often shared, and replied dully, "Kurrick."

He seized my shoulder. "Wait."

I glowered at him. "What?"

"How…" He hesitated, inhaling in a brace. "How is she?"

My gaze narrowed at him. Her majesty had been right. He *was* obviously worried. "She is… troubled," I answered. "She is attempting to unravel a mystery that plagues her mind."

His face tightened. He must have presumed that *he* was the mystery.

"I see…" He said. "Then, I… hope the burden leaves her soon…"

"We shall see," I huffed and continued forward.

"One more thing, Genevieve," he called.

I pivoted back with a groan. "Yes?"

"I've realized recently that…" He coughed behind a fist, clearly reluctant to continue, but he did so regardless. "I haven't given you much chance to gain my trust… I'd hope that, perhaps, I could amend that… Whomever you keep calling in private, I've decided to give you the benefit of the doubt." He added in a rueful grumble, "But you'd better not make me regret it."

I stared at him, shocked. This brute was backing off? *Now?* Of all the times for him to show some damned sympathy, it had to be hours before I would fulfill my task and…

I bit my lip. *No. This may be to my advantage.* If I could get him to finally drop his guard, it would be just in time.

Kurrick let out a sharp breath through his nose, likely presuming I'd opted for silence, and continued down the hall.

"It's my mother," I said, making him pause and twist back to me. I was sure to give my best, depressed sigh. "My mother is still in Neverland, in our home… with my father. He beats her. She only calls me when he isn't around to hear, and I've been trying to convince her to run, but she's afraid she won't have anywhere to go. I just… I just want her to be safe, but I'm so far away, I…"

He crossed his arms in an understanding grunt. "Have you told our queen of this? I suspect she'll be more than willing to call upon her knights in the area and assist."

"I… hadn't thought of that," I lied. "That would be… wise, I think. Thank you." I nodded appreciatively and hurried down the hall in the opposite direction, hoping he would think my welling eyes were due to a different sort of hurt.

It was hurt for existence itself.

7

PARENTHOOD

XAVIER

"*Augh…!*" I flopped over the railing of the upper deck in a deflated groan, smearing a hand over my heavy lids so hard, I half expected them to peel off like Jaq's snakeskin in summer. "*Please* tell me we'll be off this blasted ship soon…?"

Alexander chuckled and bobbed my son in his arms playfully. "Nathaniel believes so."

His raven, Mal, was perched on his shoulder while rubbing his beak over the boy's ashen wisps of hair teasingly. Lucas giggled and reached for Mal's feathers—*yanking* them so hard, the bird screeched in pain. Mal flew off Alexander's shoulder and grumpily alighted on the railing beside me instead, joining our parents' messengers, Barrach and Ethil, who croaked and twittered playful jeers at Mal as he bit at his crumpled feathers.

My own raven, Chai, wasn't here. Again. My messenger had been absent for the last few weeks. I knew he was still around the ship, I could feel our Bond was safely close and out of danger, yet… where *was* he? And what in Bloods was he doing?

"I'm told we should arrive in a few moments, in fact," Alex hummed cheerfully. He wagged a finger in front of his nephew's nose. The boy went cross-eyed as his ashen wolf ears swiveled and flicked at the curious finger. Alex chuckled. "Why? In need of some proper sleep?"

"I'll take *improper* sleep at this point!" I pushed upright and clapped my hands furiously. "Any sleep! Any! That's all I ask! Every time we finally get Lucas to sleep—*every Bloody time*—someone storms by in the hall and shouts orders, or drunkenly stumbles into our door, or laughs too loud or, or…*ARGH!*" I scratched my tangled, tied-up hair like a madman, my scalp screaming in protest. "The sooner we get our own private chambers the better! I see why so few parents travel with their children this early. This fathering business is *exhausting…*" I dripped over the railing again with my arms dangling over the side of the ship like a sopping coat.

From the rail beside my head, the tiny Ethil hopped onto my grown wolf ear, her thin talons gripping my fur softly. She twittered what sounded like a scolding tune and beat her red-striped wings like an irritating moth and caused my ear to flick in a reflex, shooing her off. She alighted on the rail to my left and nudged her beak against my cheek instead. The larger raven, Barrach, likewise nudged his beak against my *other* cheek.

I sighed, letting my parents' messengers do as they pleased with their attempted consoling. It didn't help, but… their hearts were in the right places. I was far too tired to stop them, anyway.

Alex's face wrenched with a sympathetic grimace, but he tried to stifle it into a grin. "Well, er… just be thankful you didn't have twins, eh? I'm sure *our* father and mother had more trouble with the both of us and…" He trailed off, letting it die there.

Along with the stinging reminder that our parents were gone.

I sighed again, heavier this time, and scratched Ethil's and Barrach's heads before pushing up. I pressed a solemn hand against my vest's hidden pocket. The Storagecoffin that held our father's wrapped body was there. I saw Alexander lay a hand on his own vest's pocket, probably where he kept our *mother's* Storagecoffin, while hefting Lucas to his other arm.

We'd watched our parents fall in the Battle of New Aldamstria; watched their souls deteriorate from the poison they were struck with… All we had left of them were their messengers. Ethil and Barrach were small fragments of their souls, lost and adrift without their Reapers. I was glad they were still here with us, at the very least.

Alex cleared his throat and shifted topic, bouncing a smiling Lucas in his arms. "So, then, er… *Kmm!* Where is Willow?"

"Ah… She's taking lessons with Matthiel." I folded my arms over the rail, pushing down the squall of emotions twisting my chest. It was times like this I wished Chai would come out of hiding, wherever he was… I could use some comforting from *my* messenger, instead of ones I didn't share a Bond with. I loosened a solemn breath. "He's… teaching Willow and Lëtta how to tie souls to living vessels."

Alex cocked an eyebrow at me. "Weren't *you* teaching her that?"

"I tried, but…" I rubbed my knuckles, *really* wishing Chai was here now. The constant reminder of his absence was pulling at my nerves again. "Apparently,

I'm a terrible Hallows instructor… She said I made her feel incompetent and ashamed and…" I massaged my eyes. "Have you had trouble explaining how *you* resurrected enormous skeletons of Stonedragons?"

He grunted. "I have, actually. I tried teaching it to Matthiel once. He did eventually manage to resurrect a smaller dragon, but he did so on his own… apparently 'push really hard' wasn't explicit enough for him."

"Exactly!"

"How would I even begin to explain how I did it if *I* barely understood it?"

"Yes—precisely!" I threw up my hands. "When I try to teach Willow any of that, it turns into an argument." I exhaled a hard breath, smearing a hand over my beard…

"—Today should be the day, Bazil," a familiar woman's voice perked up my ears.

Across the deck, I spotted the rabbit-eared woman over by the cabin walls. It was Bianca, our party's chief Alchemist—and one of Alexander's and my oldest friends.

Bianca wore her usual overalls riddled with pockets and vials of tonics she always kept on hand, her pale-orange hair pulled into a loose bun between her long ears and topped with a pair of smudged goggles. At her heels was her pet Barkdragon, Bazil. The skinny, tree-like creature creaked like branches as it strode at her side with twig-thin limbs, various plants and sprouts growing like moss from its barky skin.

I watched skeptically as Bianca inspected a knothole in the cabin wall's wooden planks, muttering to her dragon while scribbling notes in a leather bound journal. "They've been incubating it for eighteen days now," she said to Bazil, who gave a creaking noise in excitement. "And it's been wiggling all day, so it could be any minute now…"

I flicked a sidelong glance at Alex beside me. He was also watching Bianca. But his face sagged as he looked at her with pained longing, and he pried his gaze away to stare at the watery horizon instead, bobbing Lucas in his arms as if to distract himself.

I cleared my throat. "I suppose… you haven't had any luck with Bianca?"

His face dripped into a grimace, and he stared at my son as Mal played a game of peek-a-boo with the boy by covering his face with a wing. "No," Alex grumbled. "She won't speak to me. She won't even look at me."

"Has she at least told you the reason?"

"She hasn't a need to." He said. "When she slapped me, I Saw a vision through her eyes. Heard what she was thinking."

"Which was?" I prodded.

"That I only saw her as a spare option," he rumbled miserably. "A backup plan… She's convinced I don't care about her, and I only came crawling back after Lilli left me for Jaq, and I… I don't think I can fix that."

I rubbed my thick beard in thought, looking back at Bianca as she continued studying whatever had her fixated in that knothole. "I should think talking to her would be a good start," I suggested.

"I've tried," Alex groaned. "But she keeps running off before I can explain anything. I messed up, Xavier. I don't know how to get through to her—I can't navigate women anywhere *near* as well as you…" He handed back Lucas to me and sighed. "I don't know how you always seem to miraculously know what to say when Willow is cross with you… What am I doing wrong?"

I kept a firm hold of Lucas as he wiggled in my arms, the boy flopping over my shoulder and reaching for the three messengers perched on the railing. His wolf ears flicked against my neck softly, making me chuckle… but I stifled it when I saw Alex's morose face had worsened. He exhaled and buried his head in his hands.

"Alex…" I began, "I—*huah!*"

Lucas nearly dropped out of my arms. I hurried to catch him by his armpits, pulling him back up as my nerves were now stinging at full alert.

The boy was thrashing more than usual suddenly, fussing as he tried to escape my hold, reaching toward where Bianca was studying that knot in the cabin wall. I kept Lucas tight over my shoulder, determined to give Alex the attention I haven't been able to provide since I become a father.

"I'm… not a couple's therapist…" I grunted, struggling against Lucas's unwavering efforts to leap from my arms. "I'm truthfully no better at relationships… outside of Willow. I only know what to say—*Lucas, don't you even!*—to my wife because we've had our share of—*Oh, no you don't!*—arguments beforehand… I had to learn what vexes her, what pleases her, and—*Lucas, what is the matter with…!*"

Lucas shoved his hands over my face, his fingers finding their way into my mouth as the boy cried desperately. I secured my grip on the writhing child, but his fussing wouldn't cease.

Alex groaned and thunked his head on the rail. "I already *know* what vexes and pleases Bianca. And I know why she's upset. The problem is that I don't know what to *do* about it."

I raised my voice to be heard over Lucas's cries. "Do something that will… get her attention…! Maybe bring her flowers—*ouch!*" Lucas grabbed my beard and yanked the hairs at my chin painfully.

Alex laughed hollowly. "Bianca doesn't care about flowers. Not unless she can use them for her tonics."

"Well, there you… have it…! Get her something she can use in her tonics!" He grumbled. "I suppose…"

"—There's the little pup!" a woman's wispy voice chimed from the steps.

Yulia had climbed to the upper deck. The Dreamcatcher's white hair had grown a bit over the years, her snowy locks tumbling just over her shoulders in lovely waves. As always, Yulia wore modest attire, consisting of flattering grey trousers and an indigo blouse that was buttoned all the way up to her neck in a tall collar. She wore a wide-brimmed hat to hide her delicate skin from the sunlight, and a sheer veil fell over her sharp eyes from the headwear. Somehow, our honorary sister had once again found a way to look sporty without compromising her elegant poise.

Climbing the steps behind her was our other Dreamcatcher, Jimmy. The antlered man wore a simple shirt and tan shorts, his casual look contrasting Yulia's wardrobe.

When Yulia spotted me struggling with Lucas, she gave a delighted giggle and hurried to take the whining pup from me, bouncing him gently and wagging a playful finger before his nose.

"Who's a precious boy?" She said brightly, smiling up at me. At last, the boy calmed, distracted by Yulia's efforts. "Oh, Xavier, he really does look just like you when you were his age."

I panted from exhaustion, my throat still scratchy from lack of sleep. "So you keep saying… but he isn't even a month old. You didn't join our family until Alex and I were a year old."

She lifted her chin. "Oh, it's all the same."

Jimmy cocked an eyebrow at me and tipped his antlered head to the side, grinning a laugh. "Have you been sleeping all right, Howllord? Can't say I've counted too many times I've seen your soul in Aspirre day *or* night. Might want to catch up, there."

I cast the Dreamcatcher a glare so grueling, he cringed and sidled behind Yulia for protection, flinching when I growled, "Unless you have advice on *how* exactly I can do that, Jimmy, I suggest shoving your comments up your—"

CLANG! CLANG! CLANG!

The ship's bell gonged thrice, and Aiden called down from the crow's nest, "Land! We have land!"

We all peered at the horizon. Lucas hefted his head over Yulia's shoulder to look, but he couldn't hold it for long. He settled with nuzzling his face into the crook of her neck, and she laughed as his wolf ears tickled her throat.

In the distance were the speckled masses of what I could only assume were the Gyle Islands. They consisted of a ring of smaller islands that encircled a larger piece of land. According to Herrin, the center island was our destination.

From the helm, Nathaniel shouted for the crew to prepare for our arrival on the shores, and the decks were suddenly bustling with shifters at every turn.

Two of those faces were our Enlighteners, Herrin and Marian. They both carried sack-fulls of papers and scrolls and books slung over their backs. When the two bird shifters came out of the cabin, they found Alexander and me on the upper deck and climbed the steps toward us.

"We're all set to go," Herrin announced as he pulled the straps of his rucksack tight around his arms. "We just talked to Hecrûshou. He and the other Ancients went ahead by sea and sky to look for Cilia and Kael, in case they're already there… Ready to get your fourth set of Hallows?"

Alex and I shared a wary scowl.

My brother pushed off the rail. "We're ready to get it over with, if that's what you mean. But I've some… *research* to conduct before we leave." He coughed into a fist, and I thought I saw the hint of a blush paint his cheeks, and he stalked into the ship's cabin to disappear.

I grinned, betting that his 'research' had something to do with Bianca.

I took Lucas back from Yulia, the pup hugging my neck while I sighed. "Well, better get *this* one ready for the journey—"

A scratchy croak blurted above me, suddenly.

I glanced up.

And spotted Chai soaring down to me.

"Chai!" I lifted my arm toward my raven, hefting the wriggling Lucas over my shoulder. "There you are! Bloods, where have you been? You've been gone for weeks—"

Chai flew straight past my face, ignoring me completely.

"Ch… Chai…?" I blinked after him, watching my raven soar across the deck.

And flap to where Bianca was standing with her Barkdragon. Chai stuck his beak in the knothole she was studying—and swirled it around its loosened nail, opening up a hidden cubby hole. Chai climbed inside and swirled the plank closed again, hiding him safely within the wall.

"What in the five realms…?" My gaze narrowed, and I hefted Lucas over my shoulder as I stalked over to Bianca suspiciously.

The Alchemist didn't notice me come up behind her, still scribbling away at her notes while peeking into the knothole where Chai vanished. I hummed, "Bianca, what is—?"

She jolted and whirled in a start. When she saw it was only me, she relaxed, her rabbit ears draping over her shoulders. "Bloods, Xavier, don't sneak up on me like that."

"Er, sorry…" Lucas started wiggling again, and I tightened my grip on him. "What is Chai doing in there, exactly?"

Bianca gave me a blank expression. "You don't know?"

"Know what?" I demanded. "I haven't seen him in weeks. Is this where he's been hiding?"

"I don't know if I'd call it 'hiding'," she said, scratching her nose with her fountain quill—and getting an ink stain on her dark skin. She tossed her head in a gesture toward the loose plank. "Well, just take a look. You'll see."

I frowned. Then stuck my finger in the knothole and swirled the plank open. When the contents inside were revealed…

I fell still, whispering, "Bloods be good."

WILLOW

"Yes—very good, your grace," Matthiel praised from over my shoulder as I evoked my violet Hallows, forming a glowing thread inside my assigned ghost's translucent chest. "Now thicken it. Living souls are far tougher to thread than expired ones."

I hesitated, keeping my thin Seam of light hovering before my face. "How do I thicken it, exactly?"

"By adding more layers," he explained, rubbing his black goatee in thought. "Or, I suppose *twist on* more layers. Create multiple Seams and wind them together."

"Oh. That actually makes sense." I twiddled my fingers and created three more Seams, wrapping each one over the first Seam until they were a singular, gleaming mass of violet light inside the ghost's wispy chest. "Now what?"

"Try to stitch the ghost into his living body," Matthiel said and gestured to the sleeping vessel that shared the same face as my assigned soul.

I took a deep breath and dragged the soul over to his vessel by his new NecroSeam, gently lowering the specter into the skin—

The ghost slipped out like soap on tile, and I yelped while quickly pulling him back inside, straining to keep the Bloody man still—

He slipped out again, and my Hallows dissolved as I lost control and the violet NecroSeam disappeared from the soul's hollow chest.

I groaned. "Why does this keep happening?"

"Don't be discouraged, your grace," Matthiel said with a reassuring smile. "You're making great progress, just like Lëtta." He nodded to the black-haired teenager, who'd at least managed to make *one* stitch in her assigned vessel before she'd lost control. "It's like a muscle—you must train to make it stronger before mastering control. Do you remember how long it took all of us to get to our current level of fitness during our early Reaper training in the palace?"

I sighed. "You make it sound as if we *stopped* training since then."

"Precisely," he chuckled. "If one wishes to keep their strength, one must continue to nurture that strength... 'use it or lose it', as they say."

I hummed. "I suppose you're right... Well, if nothing else, you're a far better instructor than Xavier when it comes to Hallows, Matthiel. I actually *understand* you."

He beamed at that, properly chuffed. "Really? Why, thank you, your grace. That's very..." He seemed distracted by something behind me, and his brow furrowed. "Alexander? What are you doing over there?"

I twisted back to look. Alexander had slipped into this Healing cabin without a sound, and he was now surreptitiously peeking at an open page of an Alchemist textbook that had been left on a cluttered desk filled with glass vials, jars and dirty beakers. The book's owner, Bianca, had been there when I'd first started the lesson with Matthiel, but it seemed she had left since then—and Alexander had snuck in to peruse the pages she had been studying, leafing through them with a determined scowl on his face.

When Matthiel called him, Alex's fingers snapped away from the page corner and he quickly tucked his hand behind his back.

"Hmm? What?" Alex cleared his throat and leaned against the wall casually. "I was... er..." He coughed behind a fist. "Scouting. I should, er, be going, and..." He awkwardly took his leave and slipped out.

Matthiel and I exchanged perplexed glances.

—Slam!

The door was shoved open with a loud clatter, rattling the glass beakers over the countertops.

Under the doorframe was my husband. His long hair was tangled over his shoulders, apparently having fallen out of its tail from earlier this morning and veiling the left half of his face, leaving his scared right side exposed. He was holding our wriggling son with a vice-grip while panting for breath as if he'd sprinted all the way here.

"Willow!" Xavier puffed, seeming rattled. "You... You have to... to come... outside and...!"

"What's wrong?" I asked, my tone hardening as panic simmered. "Is it Macarius? Or one of the demons—?"

"No, no, no!" Xavier assured, shaking his head as he regained more of his breath. "It's nothing like that! It's about…! Well, it's—*ouch!*" Lucas tugged on his beard, making him wince and give up in a groan. "Oh, just come and see!"

Xavier hurriedly led the way out to the corridor, and I fumbled after him, stumbling outside to the sunlit deck. He turned the corner around the cabin walls—and screeched to a halt in front of Bianca and her woody Barkdragon.

"Xavier," I huffed impatiently, plucking our son from his tired arms and let him wheeze over his knees to catch his breath. Lucas wriggled and fussed in my hold, but I wasn't as exhausted as Xavier and kept my grip firm on the boy. "Will someone tell me—*ouch!*" Lucas tugged my long hair and made my scalp sting. One of the ashen strands snapped off and flaked to ashes before it reattached where it belonged. I groaned. "What exactly is going on?"

Bianca chuckled, sticking her fountain quill into the knothole of a loose plank along the wall and swirled it upward—revealing a hidden cubby hole within the wall.

A twitter chirped from inside.

"That sounds like Jewel…" I murmured, peering inside with a furrowed brow. She'd been absent for weeks, hearing her voice sent a rush of relief. "Is this where you've been hiding…?"

My breath died.

The cubby hole was furnished with spare pieces of fabric and cottony nesting material. And at its center, snuggled between my tiny Jewel *and* Xavier's larger Chai…

Was an egg.

"Death's Head!" I gasped, holding Lucas to my chest as I gawked at the egg between the messengers, amazed. "Jewel! Is *this* what you've been up to? *Motherhood?*"

Jewel chirped and rubbed her head against her small egg lovingly. Chai gave a warm coo and wrapped Jewel and the egg with a long wing.

Bianca tapped her quill against her journal and hummed. "I've been documenting them when they started nesting a few weeks ago. I actually thought you guys knew." She rubbed her neck with a laugh. "Sorry. Guess I should have mentioned something so you guys wouldn't worry."

"But… But how could they have…" I struggled to decide which question to ask first, turning to Bianca desperately. "They're two different *species!*"

Bianca only shrugged, flipping through her journal to address her notes. "Ravens and crows have been known to interbreed and produce offspring, on rare occasions. The rareness is out of *preference*, not capability. I guess the same goes for Songcrows, too." She scanned through her annotations curiously and continued, "I've heard that messenger breeding patterns are different from normal black birds, since they both share the same mates for life, but messengers only breed a few times *in* that life since they live longer than regular birds—but I've never had the chance to see it for myself. I thought this was the perfect time to document it. Top that with the fact these messengers belong to two *married* Reapers, and that adds another layer of intrigue not commonly seen." She was giggling with thrill now, flipping through her notes in a flurry. "I just couldn't resist the chance to study them!"

Xavier and I marveled at the raven and Songcrow who nuzzled their egg like a loving family.

Beside me, Xavier frowned and rubbed his beard as if puzzled. "But Chai is so…" he began skeptically. He used his hands to measure Chai's tall stature against Jewel's tiny size with a perplexed expression, sputtering, "And Jewel is so… just so… I mean…" He scratched his head, giving up. "How did you *fit*, Chai?"

Bianca snickered. "That's not how it works with ravens—"

Crrrk!

The egg cracked with a small fissure, quivering between our messengers. Bianca squealed excitedly. "Oooooh, it's hatching, it's hatching…!"

We all held our breaths, and I hugged Lucas tight to my chest.

Crrrrk… Crrk-crrk-crrk…

Crack!

A tiny beak pipped through the shell, and a small, bald head peeked out with the sweetest little chirp.

Jewel burst into a flurry of jovial twitters and clucked as the hatchling pipped its way through the rest of the shell, cuddling the bare thing in her wings as Chai encircled them both with his larger wings.

The three of us gave heartwarming sighs as we watched the new family—

Lucas suddenly gave a shrill, deafening shriek from my arms, making my ears ring. The baby squirmed wildly, thrashing and writhing like mad and nearly falling out of my hold as he *lunged* forward, reaching for the nest and…

And touched a gentle hand over the hatchling's head. The hatchling chirped, pushing his little beak against Lucas's palm happily. Lucas gave another thrilled squeal with the brightest smile to ever split the pup's face.

Xavier, Bianca and I blinked at Lucas and the hatchling.

I breathed, "Is… is this…?"

"Lucas's messenger?" Xavier finished for me.

I re-secured my grip on Lucas, but didn't dare tear him away from the hatchling. "Seamstress prick me! I nearly forgot we should have been expecting one to come for Lucas!" I stared wide-eyed at the pair. "But I… I never expected *Jewel* to birth that messenger herself…"

Bianca was now jumping in circles. "You've *got* to be kidding me! A baby's messenger born from his *parents'* messenger?! This is *so* unheard of!" She began scribbling as if in a trance, her toothy smile stretched so wide, I was surprised her face didn't crack with sores.

Xavier was still staring, dumbfounded. He lifted a limp finger. "But… I don't understand. He's not even a month old. How could his messenger already be here?"

"He *is* a Relicblood of Death, Xavier," I explained, rubbing a finger over the tiny chick's featherless head. "All those of the Royal Bloodline are found by their messengers at an early age. Typically, they come shortly after the time of their births, as Jewel did for me."

Lucas squealed again and giggled as his little messenger nuzzled his palm cheerfully.

"Well, then," Xavier laughed and circled his arms around me and Lucas from behind, the ice in his soul cooling our Pyrovoker's heat as he murmured, "How about that, Lucas? Your very own messenger… Congratulations."

"Congratulations indeed," I echoed, kissing Lucas's crown. "And to you as well, Jewel and Chai. Nira bless your little hatchling."

The birds chirped and croaked happily, snuggling each other with fluffed feathers.

Hours after the new chick was hatched, we finally arrived at the shores of Gyle Island and dropped anchor.

Lucas clung to my neck while I looked over the railing to admire the sandy beach. Behind it was a thick jungle, with deep green foliage and twisting vines and vibrant blossoms the likes of which I'd never seen. The exotic flowers were enormous! Their stamens spilled out like thin tongues and their pollen-coated anthers were as long as Ringëd's pet ferret. The sunlight barely split inside the greenery through the canopy, but outside of the jungle, the beach shimmered against the foaming tide. In truth, it resembled a postcard one would see of a romantic, tropical holiday resort… if only we hadn't come for a much less cheerful reason.

Anabelle's fleet of seaward ships and Airships were landing around us. Soon, the sandy bank bustled with shifters and soldiers.

Footfalls clomped up the steps behind me, and I turned to find our golden haired hostess had appeared. Anabelle was dressed in violet leather armor. Her petal-like curls had a metallic sheen under the sunlight, practically glowing along with her golden eyes that shined like brilliant coins.

Ana rested a hand over the hilt of a sword at her hip and spoke softly, "Do you have everything you'll need for the trek? It will take some time to reach the palace ruins."

I hefted Lucas over my shoulder, seeing Jewel flutter by my head while Chai soared to the railing next to me. On Chai's back was their little hatchling, nestled in his feathers. I asked Ana, "You already know the way?"

"Of course," Ana hummed, "this was once our home, when we were children."

I frowned. "'We'?"

"Your mother and I," she explained, walking back toward the ship's steps. She added idly, "And Kurrick, of course."

I watched her descend to the lower deck to meet with Genevieve. Oddly, Kurrick wasn't there, as he usually was. I spotted him tromping along the opposite side of the deck and leaning over the rail as if inspecting the ship's walls for assassins. But his head snapped up when Ana and Genevieve strode down the ship's ramp onto the sandy beach, and he hustled after them. He still kept his distance from the women, but stayed within a protective range with his hand firmly clasped around the hilt of his sword.

I glanced at Xavier beside me. "Is Kurrick acting stranger than usual?"

Xavier rubbed his beard. "I was wondering that myself, yes… Perhaps he's anxious to be back in his old home?"

"Maybe…" I shook my head, deciding to save that question for later, and led the way off the ship as we began our trek into the jungle.

MILANN

Kc-coh… Tck!

Kc-coh… Tck!

I tossed a pebble against my cell's mildewy wall, catching it as it bounced back to me.

Kc-coh… Tck!

Kc-coh… Tck!

My breath fogged in the super cold air, and I hugged my knees in a shiver. We'd been locked in this ship for what felt like forever. And each day, it just kept getting colder and colder.

Oliver and Fuérr were in the two cells to my left. Fuérr was still chained up like always, and Oliver sat cross-legged on the gross floor with his hands hovering over his 'crystal ball'. It was really a rubber, glittery water ball, but it worked anyways. The blue glitter inside swirled with pictures as Oliver stared at the ball super hard. The Dream mark on his neck was shining with blue light as he evoked his Hallows to see into the future. Apparently, he wasn't all that good with past and present events. He mostly just saw what was *going* to happen… or, I guess, what *could* happen.

His messenger crow, Clover, sat on Oliver's feathered head and picked at an itch with his beak. That little ferret, Kurn, was curled up asleep on Fuérr's lap.

Kc-coh… Tck!

I leaned back against my cell bars and grumbled, "Tell me again why we had to get caught?"

Oliver didn't break his stare from the glitter ball. "It was the only path that'll get us to the right ending," he said absently, "to save Fuérr."

"But we still have to make the right choices?" I asked, remembering what he was talking about when we first woke up in here.

He nodded. Then the glitter settled at the bottom of the water ball and he rubbed his eyes, his Dream mark dimming. "Yeah… we're on the right street now, but we still got a few more crossroads to get to. Gotta make sure we take the right turns when they come up."

I sighed and thunked my head on the bars. "Great…"

Kc-coh… Tck!

—BrrrRRRRUMMM!

The ship jerked to a sudden stop, throwing me off the cell bars and straight into the wall. Oliver and Fuérr had been thrown, too, and I wasn't the only one to fumble upright.

Fuérr's webbed ears flicked upward in question. "We eez stopping? Where eez?"

Oliver grumbled and picked up his glitter ball again. "I'll try and See with a scrying… I'm not very good at present events, but—"

Squeee!

The brig's door suddenly squealed open from the top of the stairwell.

Footsteps echoed from the metal stairs, and those two snake shifters from before came down.

Clover fluttered off Oliver's head and quickly hid under his feathered hair. Oliver scooped up his glitter ball and hurried to toss it into the Storagebox he still had from when we got on the ship. Fuérr's chains rattled when he strained to look at the snakes, and the ferret on his lap scurried down and hid behind the prince's scaly back.

"We've docked at Yu'nn Quisette's harbor now," the woman said to the com screen she held in front of her scaled face. That other lady, Genevieve, was on the other end again. "Have you all arrived at the Gyle Islands yet?"

"*Yes, Mother,*" Genevieve answered from the screen. "*We've just left the ships and are traversing the jungle... I'm not sure how long it will be before we reach the ruins.*"

"As long as you've arrived at the islands," the woman hummed, "Be wary, Genevieve. We can't have your mission spoiled right at the cusp of victory."

She bowed her head. "*Yes, Mother...*"

The call ended.

8

VISITATION

ASTER

I sat on the grody stone floor of my cell and flopped against the disgusting wall. Tanderam Prison was dark, as usual. The torches on this floor had burned out who-Bloody-knows how many years ago. And I was *so hungry...*

The rotten corpses of my old cellmates munched uselessly on the bars, their blackened souls slithering like worms over their skin and white eyes shining with a wild hunger for clean souls that, unfortunately for all of us, were nowhere in sight.

I didn't really care about eating souls right now. I just needed a cheeseburger—*anything* to stop the constant, shriveling pain in my stomach. I guessed souls would fit the bill at this point, but it wasn't like I needed the power boost. And I wasn't a primal beast like these guys, thanks to my prophetic Hallows. So, I could wait on soul-eating if someone just got me a damn sandwich.

Then again, that demon army I've had visions about looked pretty bad, and I sure as Bloods didn't want to be caught in that mess. That would have been *worse* than this boring, grimy cell. But if I could just get that cheeseburger...

"Aster?"

My head snapped up.

A muscular, scaled man with brown-and-blonde streaked hair was suddenly standing in front of me in the cell full of demons. The mongrels nipped and swiped at him, but their teeth just caught colored air.

I squinted at the guy. "I... I-I know you..." My dried throat stung painfully, parched lips cracking. I focused on this cobra's face. He was so... familiar...

My hazy memory *clapped* back like an icy bolt.

"Accursius…?" I whispered hoarsely. Everything rushed back. Memories flooded like a breaking dam, flying so quickly I was having trouble keeping up with them all.

I remembered my parents… my home in Mimier. My Master Oracle who trained me in the art of fortune telling… Then came my vision of the twins surfacing, my journey toward the capital, my imprisonment after the war started…

And my death, when the guards on our floor abandoned us and left us to starve.

I coughed and dropped to the floor, my twig-like arm shuddering under me. I was too weak to push myself up.

My throat scratched like needles. "Accursius…!"

The cobra shifter rushed to help me up—

But his fingers fizzled through my arms like mist.

"Gardener sow me…" Accursius knelt beside me helplessly. "I am sorry, Aster… I cannot affect anything in our shared visions. Just as you cannot affect *my* surroundings when you visit my time." His gaze wrenched with sadness. "I… cannot help you…"

"It… it isn't that…!" I fell into a hacking fit, managing to pull myself up to face him. "I remember…! I remember everything—with us, with *you*…!" Tears blurred my vision. "You're going to die, Accur."

He paused, looking confused. "Everyone dies, Aster. Look at you, now—"

"But it's Macar who kills you!" I wheezed. "I Saw the vision of your future… of *my* past. Macar uses Kael to kill Adam. And then Macar kills *you*."

His face streaked with shock. "Macar…? But Dream said we were to work together to stop the End?"

I shook my heavy head, my neck too weak to hold it high. "Macar *hates* you. He hates that you've ignored him, always treated him like a spare child all your lives—and he thinks the End can be stopped another way."

"I… I-I…" Accur clutched his temples, his breaths ragged. "It cannot be… I won't allow it…! I can… I can stop him!" Accursius straightened and stopped a foot. "I can fix this! If I talk to Macar—!"

"It's too late." I let my skull hang down in an exhausted pant. "There's nothing you can do… your future is already set. I wouldn't be here, otherwise."

Accursius fell to his knees and hid his face in his hands. "Macar… What have I done…?" He broke into a miserable sob. "When…? When will this happen?"

"When you leave your inspection at Tanderam and go back to the Land Palace… King Adam will already be dead. You'll save a lot of guests and servants when you get there, but… then you'll run into Macar. And he'll kill you."

"What if I survive?" he asked. "What if I stop Macar *before* he kills me?"

"You won't," I grunted. "If there was a way for you to survive, *I* wouldn't be here."

He looked away, troubled. "Why…? Why did the Gods allow this to happen…? Why allow *any* of this to happen? We could have resolved this in *my* time and…"

"Actually… you couldn't have." I sighed. "There were supposed to be *two* pairs of twins… They *all* needed to survive birth together. All four. I don't know why, but that's what had to happen… the other pair didn't survive their births in your time. You two did. When you think about it… Macar and Dream causing the glitch in the loop allowed the other pair's reincarnation to… to have another chance at survival and growth… So, here we are." I waved a skeletal hand in a gesture.

He rubbed his red eyes and looked around in disgust, changing the subject to get his mind off his grim future. "How long have you been in here?" he asked. "During our last shared vision, you were apprenticing under your Master Oracle… For you to be here—and worse, to have Changed into a Necrofera—what have you endured?"

I grimaced. "It's a long story… and I'm not sure how long I've been in here. Feels like years, I think…"

"No one has come to save you?"

I furrowed my brow, thinking back. "Most of us were freed in a raid some years ago… They never reached our floor, though. So that was some luck…"

Accursius's face fell solemn. "I'm sorry…"

I shrugged—then started hacking. "It's fine, I guess… I don't have to worry about dying anymore. Already there. But the country's under new management now, so they're going to free us today anyway… if I'm timing my visions right, at least."

He nodded thoughtfully. "Then you'll be able to do what you must? To warn them?"

"I can do more than…" I stopped cold, my meercat ears perking straight up.

What was that amazing *smell?*

Accursius frowned. "What's wrong?"

I sniffed the air, my ears swiveling all around and listening for sounds above me. I could barely hear shouting and footsteps up there. But that scent was new. Different. It was tingly and tantalizing, so agonizingly mouthwatering that my years-long dried throat was almost choking with saliva. "I smell… *souls…*"

—Sirens blared, then explosions pounded the upper floors.

Pckoww! BRRRRM!

The ceiling fell right on top of Accursius—but since he wasn't actually here, the stones phased through him like mist.

Torchlight stung my eyes as the cell washed with a new brightness... and the scent of souls crashed through my nostrils like a river of fire.

As the mongrel demons scattered into the shadowed corners, I peered up at the hole in the ceiling. Four silhouettes of armored soldiers popped into view. They lifted their visors and stared down at me.

"H... hey...!" I called up to them with a weak voice, still shielding my eyes from the stinging brightness. "Can... can I get a cheeseburger down here...?"

The soldiers scratched their heads in bewilderment.

Their souls smelled so *good*, but... I wanted to save what little sliver of humanity I had left before I succumbed to that temptation. If I had *something* to eat, it would keep that impulse at bay.

I looked down at Accursius and saluted him with two thin, quivering fingers. "S-see you around, Accur... or not."

The cobra grimaced. "Yes... I am... sorry. For having failed in my time..."

"Don't worry about it. We didn't know what would happen back then. We know better now. So we have another chance to fix things."

He gave a scaled smile. "Yes... I suppose you're right."

My chapped lips split into a grin. "You mean *we're* right. And yeah. We are. Now, go off and save some of those palace guests—they're going to need you, no matter *what* your future is."

He sucked in a breath, nodded dutifully... Then his image hissed into vapor.

I flopped against the wall and called up to the soldiers again, "So, about that cheeseburger..."

An armored woman with feathery wings dropped into the cell, landing with her back facing me. In her hands were a pair of dual-scythes, the crooked blades glowing a haunting, ghostly blue.

A Reaper? They must have guessed some of the prisoners would have died and Changed into Necrofera. *Prisoners like me.*

Fear hit me like a river or needles. I pressed my back further against the grimy wall and threw my arms over my head in a shiver. *Bloods!* She came down to kill me, didn't she? She's an exterminator...!

"Get on my back!" she barked suddenly. Her eyes were glued to the mongrel demons in the shadowy corners. She raised her scythes to them as they snarled at her, but they seemed to sense danger and kept their distance.

I blinked at her, croaking, "Wh... what?"

"Get on my back!" she repeated, spreading her wings as an invitation. "Hurry! Or these Fera will tear *both* of us apart and save our souls for dessert!"

She thinks I'm alive, I realized.

Before she could change her mind, I scrambled for her and latched to her back like a terrified squid out of water. She leapt up in a rush of wind and flew us toward the hole in the ceiling—just as the mongrels sprang for her feet. She barely made it out with her toes, but cleared the ceiling and dropped both of us on the floor of the upper level cell where her sword-wielding comrades were waiting.

I flopped on all fours in a heavy pant. "Shel, thank you…! Thank you…!"

The soldiers surrounding me whispered about how skeletal I looked, their tones pitying.

"We have some bread," one of the younger-looking men offered, reaching into his pack that was slung around his shoulder and offered me a loaf. "It isn't much, but—"

I snatched the loaf and shoved it down my throat in one go. The bread sank into my shriveled stomach like lead. I must have gained a whole pound that minute.

The soldiers gave each other skeptical looks before the younger man offered me a waterskin next. "We… we also have water…"

I grabbed that just as quick as the bread and poured the entire thing straight into my mouth. Some of it splashed onto my grody tunic and I desperately sucked on the fabric to get what was damn well mine.

The Reaper woman from before rubbed my back in sympathy. "You poor thing… don't worry. We'll see that you and the other prisoners are…" She paused above me. I felt her fingers drag over my boney spine where the too-long tunic's neckline exposed my skin.

Where my Evocator's mark was.

She sounded confused. "Isn't this… the Shadowblood's Crest…?"

I twisted back to her. "Hey, um, do you have any more bread?"

She finally saw my face—and yelped, stumbling back to get away from me. She was staring at my eyes.

Land! I forgot about my glowing pupils!

Before she could draw out her scythes again, I bolted through the group and ran out to the halls. Now that I'd had *something* to eat, I had just enough strength to get the Land out of here.

"Sorry…!" I called back, my bare feet thumping against the hard stones. "I have someone to find…!"

9

SOMETHING SHE CAN USE

ALEXANDER

I used one of my scythes to cut down a giant leaf as I followed everyone into the jungle.

My brother mimicked me with his own scythes beside his wife, their tunics showing dark splotches of sweat just like mine as the humidity seemed to swallow us the farther we walked. Willow's bundled hair was tangled and greasy as she carried their baby on her back using a twisted sling.

Flying from branch to branch beside them were Jewel and Chai. Chai carried their tiny, featherless hatchling on his back, Jewel fluttering over to them frequently to feed the chick when she found food in the jungle.

Through the incessant whine of insects and chittering birdcalls, I could hear Xavier and Willow chatting fervently about the joyous occasion of their son's messenger, their voices echoing in the expansive foliage ahead of me.

"How do we handle the little thing's naming, exactly?" Xavier speculated curiously. "Lucas can't speak yet himself. Do *we* name it?"

Willow chuckled. "No, Xavier. As a child of the Death family, his first word will be the name of his messenger. It's something we all know, instinctively. Other Reapers do the same if they happen to be chosen at an early age as well, though such a thing rarely happens to those outside our family line. My first word was *Jewel*, for example."

Xavier scratched his sweat-ridden beard. "Hrm… *Jewel* seems rather advanced for a shiftling so young. The books we've read all say most children can't say many syllables until they're at least twelve months or so…"

"Not if that shiftling is a Reaper who has Bonded with their messenger," Willow said matter-of-factly. "Our messenger's name is something we simply…

know. It's so ingrained into our souls that it becomes the only word we obsess over—no matter how difficult the syllables are—until we finally speak it."

Xavier seemed intrigued yet disappointed. "I was hoping his first word would be 'Da Da' or 'Pa Pa'."

Willow wafted a prim hand at him. "That will likely come after his messenger's name. *And* after 'Ma Ma', of course."

Xavier shot her a narrow glance. "Sure of that are you? Well, we'll just have to see who wins that race, won't we?"

They shared delighted laughter, shoving each other's shoulders teasingly.

I sighed, slicing down another giant leaf as Mal flapped above me nearby.

It just isn't Bloody fair… They were such a perfect couple, even their damned *messengers* became mates? I supposed Mother's and Father's messengers acted like mates, but… Barrach and Ethil never laid an egg. Or was that because Ethil wasn't even a crow at all? She was a common, east-Grimish blackbird, so perhaps those couldn't interbreed with Corvids…

I rubbed my eyes, the logic giving me a headache. This was a conundrum Bianca could certainly unravel…

If she were still talking to me.

I growled, my wolf ears growing, and I swatted a vine out of my way. Xavier said he couldn't provide counsel, but maybe if I studied him and Willow enough, I could glean something useful?

I glanced to my right, watching as Bianca stopped to inspect a new plant for the fifth time since we left the ship. She crouched over some patch of herbs I sure as Void couldn't name. She collected their blossoms, leaves, and roots in separate jars which she tucked into her satchel before climbing onto her Barkdragon, Bazil, and continued forward.

She spared a terse glance over her shoulder at me. The glare was so curdled, I was glad as Bloods she was a Healer and not a *dangerous* Evocator.

Get her something she can use, Xavier's advice rolled back to mind.

I grumbled, looking about the jungle to look for anything that might fit the bill. But there were so many damned plants here, how was I supposed to know which would be useful and which would be decoration?

Skrlch!

My boot crunched over something sticky.

I'd stepped on a patch of what looked like clovers. But these had frilled leaves and intriguing, blue berries with turquoise spots. The dozen I'd stepped on had squished onto my boot and stained it with purplish ooze.

I blinked, recognizing the plants. It had been in the Alchemist textbook I'd stolen a look in, back on the ship.

Perhaps Bianca could use these?

I bent over and plucked three handfuls of the odd-looking clovers and their berries, enough to make a nice bouquet, and stuffed them into my Storagebox that was clipped to my belt.

I continued back on the trek with a grin as I sliced at the jungle's thick foliage with my scythe again, Mal flying by my head with a puffed chest and a proud flap.

Hours passed before we reached the end of the thick jungle. The stone ruins of an ancient city began to crop up around us, and although the trees and brush were sparser here than before, it was still overrun with vines and various wildlife. I saw a feral python dozing on the roof of one structure, and several orangutans hustled into a brittle enclosure as Anabelle's soldiers entered the ruins.

Few buildings were still intact, from what I could tell. There were chipped statues of Shel and His son, Land. Most of their features were hidden by thick patches of moss that had accumulated over time.

As our troupe stomped through the ancient city, Anabelle led the way to the abandoned palace that waited in the heart of the ruins.

I stepped under a crumbled archway that led inside the palace. The interior of the palace was just as dusty and overgrown as the rest of the city. When I stepped down the eastern corridor—

I saw Bianca riding her Barkdragon down the northern hallway. I spun on my heels and hurried after her.

"Bianca!" I called, jogging up to her. "Bianca, I…! I was hoping we could spare a moment to—!"

She steered Bazil around a corner without a reply. She went out of her way to make no eye contact.

My teeth sharpened, wolf ears growing. I continued to follow her around the corner. "I-I've brought something…! for *you*, erm…" My palms were sweating so much, they were starting to itch. I scratched them nervously. "Look, I…" The itch grew, and I scratched harder. "I know you think I…" Now they were stinging, and I had to grow my claws to scratch more vigorously. "I know you… I know I haven't… Gods, Bloody—*why are my hands burning?!*"

I hunched over to focus on the incredible stinging, growling in pain.

Bianca lifted one of her rabbit ears. Then she sighed and slid off Bazil, holding out a hand to me as she gave a patronizing drawl. "Let me see."

She grabbed my burning hands and examined the palms. They were now red and covered in small, irritated bumps and blisters which had started to trail up my arms.

Her brow furrowed. "Alex, you have a rash…" She shot me an accusing look. "What did you *touch?*"

"I didn't… touch anything…" I seethed and scratched my hands furiously, the rash spreading up my forearms at an alarming rate. Then I remembered something, and blushed. "W-well… except, er… there *was* that one plant, I suppose…" I scratched more, the burning endless.

"Stop, stop!" She grabbed my wrists and pulled my blistered hands away from each other. Her glare could have melted a hole in my skull. "What was the plant?"

"It's… it's in my Storagebox—"

She snatched my Storagebox and pulled out a handkerchief from her coat pocket, reaching into the box's gummy surface. She plucked out the bouquet of that strange plant from earlier.

Her long ears dropped in shock.

"ALEX!" She shrieked and dropped to her knees to rummage through her satchel. "These are Varish Vanulars!"

I didn't like her panicked tone. "Er, what does that mean?"

"They're *poisonous!*" She quickly stuffed the Varish Vanulars in a spare jar she found in her satchel, making sure not to make direct contact with them by using the handkerchief, and screwed the lid shut. Then she plucked out a different jar with some sort of cream inside and jumped to her feet, spreading the cream over my palms and forearms. It soothed the stinging to an extent, but the burn threatened to creep up again before she clasped her hands over mine and evoked her remedy Hallows. Her hands gleamed with gold light over my palms. The cream's soothing effect amplified, and I sighed in relief when the pain subsided.

She also let out a relieved breath, still evoking her Hallows on my palms. "What were you doing with those? That stuff can spread like wildfire until you're covered from head to foot."

I flushed. "I… er… saw it in your Alchemy book and thought…" I cleared my throat. "I thought you might find them useful for some tonic…"

Her dark cheeks grew pink. Then she scowled and dismissed her Hallows, crossing her arms. "Obviously they're useful for tonics," she muttered, seeming loathe to admit it. "But you shouldn't touch random plants you find in the jungle! You're lucky it wasn't something worse."

I winced. "There's something worse?"

"There's a plant out there that secrets venom so powerful, they say the pain lasts for fifty years."

I grimaced. "Ah…"

"Yeah," she grunted. "So, what have we learned?"

"... Don't touch anymore jungle plants..."

"Good boy." She put the jar of soothing cream into my Storagebox. "Bloody idiot. One day, I'm going to find you keeled over in a ditch and find out you ate a whole handful of nightshade berries, I swear..." She paused, then added, "Just in case, if you see any berries that you think are blueberries, *don't* eat them. In fact, don't eat anything in the wild. Assume everything will kill you."

"R-right..." *Back to square one,* I thought miserably. I could cross 'getting her something useful' off the list of ways to make amends. But that left me with nothing. Brilliant.

Though, I considered cheerfully, *at least she's speaking to me again.*

"Look, Bianca..." I cleared my throat, seizing the opportunity while I had her here. "I know I've been..."

"Stupid?" she offered as she slung her satchel over her shoulder again.

I coughed into a fist. "Er, yes... stupid. *Immeasurably* stupid. I shouldn't have waited so long to call off my arrangement with Lilli—"

—He shouldn't have considered going through with it in the first place—

"—I mean, I shouldn't have considered going through with it in the first place," I corrected swiftly.

"Seriously?" She perked an eyebrow. "Reading my mind with your dumb prophetic Hallows is cheating. That's not an apology. That's plagiarism."

Damn it. "Er, right, sorry... I don't have an excuse, Bianca. I messed up. I know that." Sickness twisted as I flicked my pained look at her. "But I swear on my life... *and* my afterlife... that I will not make that mistake again."

She hesitated for a moment. Then snorted. "I'll believe that when I see it."

"You will," I promised. "Bianca, I couldn't marry someone else even if I tried... and I *did* try."

Her long ears folded back angrily, and her thoughts rang through my head. *The fact that he tried is the problem!*

My shoulders locked in a cringe. "Oh. Death..."

"'Oh Death' is right." She muttered, catching on to my mind-reading again. "Better luck next time, Alex. Can't wait to hear the next horrible attempt."

With that, she climbed onto Bazil and stalked away.

I kicked the wall, a piece of it crumbling off in a puff of dust.

Da'torr Alex? The voice of Hugh suddenly hit my thoughts, my vassal calling for me through our mental connection. *Queen Anabelle has summoned the Shadowblood.*

I smeared a hand over my face... and sighed.

BIANCA

"Stupid, Bloody, idiot…" I muttered, flattening over Bazil's mossy back and plopping my head over the Barkdragon's skull. "He can read minds, but *still* hasn't figured out the problem? How can he be that dense, Bazil?"

Bazil creaked under me pleasantly, strolling us through the palace ruins. The Barkdragon twisted his long snout back and started sniffing my satchel.

"Woah, woah, woah—careful, Bazil!" I pulled the satchel onto my lap so he couldn't nose through it. "I've got Varish Vanulars in there. You don't want to go sniffing those anytime soon. Look what they did to Alex."

I shuddered at the reminder. That rash had gotten really bad by the time I noticed it. What was he thinking, grabbing random plants in the jungle like that? Was he trying to give me a heart attack? If he'd found something worse, he could have dropped dead out there and…

I flapped my rabbit ears over my eyes in a groan. "Note to self: do *not* let Alex explore the wild by himself anymore…"

I sighed and gripped my satchel, biting my lip to stop the dumb smile from breaking through. As much as I hated to admit it, I actually kind of… liked… the gift…

I gave a muted scream into my hands, cupping my face in a furious blush.

Who was I kidding? I *loved* the gift. The fact he took the time to get me something—anything—was enough to send my rebellious pulse into a swooning frenzy.

I pounded my head, angry with myself. Why did his stupid plan have to work? It was reckless! It was dangerous! He could have gotten himself killed…!

But I looked everywhere in that jungle for Varish Vanulars… I was so disappointed when I didn't find any. Then Alex happened to show up with an entire bouquet of them just for me?

I melted onto Bazil in a long exhale. For all his idiocy, the fact he did *some* research into what I was looking for was, well… sweet.

Then again, it was also super rude of him to look through my book without permission. But Gods damn it, why do I *like* the privacy violation—?

"Hey, boss!" a familiar voice piped behind me. "Boss, slow up!"

I eased Bazil to a stop and craned back.

My second-in-command Alchemist, Red, was trotting up to me. His splotched goggles hung from his neck, and he had a satchel of his own slung over a shoulder and clinking with glass jars and vials.

"Did the harvest go well?" I asked, squinting a strict eye at him. "I better not hear about someone *else* getting a rash from touching something they shouldn't have."

Red frowned. "What? Naw, no one's that dumb, boss. We know how to follow protocol."

I snorted a laugh. "Good. You should have seen the blisters on Alex's hands—it was *bad*."

"Ya mean that Howllord 'a yours?" His face bunched up in question. "Oh Land, what'd he get his grubs on?"

"Varish Vanulars." I couldn't help my toothy grin as I pulled out my jar of the bouquet to show Red. "The idiot was picking them like daisies out there."

Red went bug-eyed at the jar. "Varish Vanulars?! That clod found some?! We've been lookin' all over that damn jungle for those!"

I giggled like a giddy six-year-old. "I know!"

"And he just waltzed through a patch and thought he'd make 'imself a nice garnish?" Red shook his head, setting gloved fists at his sides. "I swear, the best luck always goes to blockheads who have no Bloody clue what they're doin'… Could've gotten himself killed if he found somethin' worse."

"That's what I said!" I threw up a frustrated hand. "He's *so* not allowed to go out there unsupervised anymore. Think you and the guys could tail him if you see him wandering off?"

Red gave me a thumbs up. "Sure thing, boss. I'll get Rob and Harri on it, if I'm too busy myself. Can't have your boyfriend keelin' over if he's supposed to save the world, right?"

I snapped out of my glee, remembering I was still mad at Alex, and grimaced. "Save the world? Yes. Boyfriend? No."

Red shrugged and started walking backward in a chuckle. "Whatever ya say, boss."

I crossed my arms bitterly, having Bazil stroll forward again down the hall so Red wouldn't see me blushing.

10

THE ENEMY OF MY ENEMY

WILLOW

I strode into the vine-infested ballroom of the ancient palace. Some of the ceiling had crumbled over time and thin slits of golden sunrays sliced into the room to provide us dim lighting, thick clouds of dust glittering down in the gorgeous rays.

Xavier strode beside me with our son over his shoulder. The pup gave a small sneeze from the dust before nuzzling his father again, his wolf ears flicking under Xavier's chin.

I ran my fingers over a dusty pillar.

—the ballroom flashed with light suddenly. The darkness blinked away, and the dust vanished from the air.

The ballroom looked *new*, somehow. Decorative and golden, its brilliant walls and high ceiling gleamed in the chandelier's light.

But staining its majesty were the droves of corpses littering the floor. Their faces were burnt away and blackened, skulls gleaning through and sockets ravaged with black veins.

Clang!

The clash of metal rang through the ballroom behind me. I spun around—

The battling men misted through me like smoke. Or rather, *I* misted through *them.*

Both men had Grimish hair, but one was an inky black and the other an ashen white. The latter had a skull-crown atop his head, and unlike his sword-wielding opponent, he battled with a long-staved scythe.

A Relicblood of Death, I noted in confusion. *This must be a past vision…*

I knew I was correct when I registered The Death King's dueling adversary: Kael Treble.

Like a crazed madman, Kael thrust his poison-infested blade at the Death King for want of caution or care. His yellow eyes were blistering red. Tears streaked down his face and cleared the soot clinging to his cheeks in sleek trails. Every agonized scream shook the ballroom as he demanded over and over, "Where is my son...?!"

This must have been the night he found Cilia butchered, I realized, my hand quivering as I brought it to my lips. *And he couldn't find his son...*

This was the face of a man who had lost everything. A man who had been robbed of all he held dear. My eyes welled, the cruelty too much even for me. To witness the birth of his insanity... to watch his spirit unravel and warp into a disfigured heap of hatred and wrath...

This was a torture I would *never* wish upon any soul.

As their battle raged on, I noticed several more figures hiding in the shadows. There was a little girl with golden locks weeping over the corpse of what could only be the Land King, given his equally golden hair. Could that have been Anabelle?

I stepped through the ballroom, finding what looked like a young Kurrick, but without the scars creasing his face. The boy was slinking his way toward Anabelle and making sure not to draw Kael's attention.

"Myra...!" A frantic voice hissed to my left. "Myra, darling...! Where are you...?!"

I found my rust-haired grandmother Crysa sidling from pillar to pillar, her face sullied with panic.

Then a soft whimper caught my ears from behind a fallen table. I peered over, and found myself staring at a pair of icy, azure eyes hidden under a tangle of curly blue hair. It was a small child, with tears staining her bronze cheeks and blue fox ears folded tight to her neck in utter fear.

And she was staring directly at me.

"Mother...?" I whispered, starstruck.

The child flinched as if I'd bitten her. *So, she CAN See me,* I thought. *Does this mean I'm sharing this vision with her, instead of Grandfather Dream?*

I stepped toward her—and misted through the table so I could crouch beside her. She yelped in fright and shuffled away from me.

"You...!" She sniffled shakily. "You're a dream-walker copy...?"

"Not exactly, Moth... er, Myra," I said.

The child's azure brow crinkled. "How do you know my name?"

"I'm... a friend," I explained, trying to put it in words a youngling could understand. It sounded ridiculous to hear it aloud, but I did my best. "Or rather, we *will* be friends later. Much later."

I gazed about the room full of carnage and death. It was enough to make me ill. When I looked back at my young mother, I noticed her tiny feet were stained red from the puddles on the marble floor. I could only think of my son… What if Lucas had been in her place? So small and helpless, in the middle of an event as terrifying as this, witnessing such horrors he surely would never forget…?

"This is no place for a child," I hushed to her. "You shouldn't be here. You must leave."

Her fox ears folded back as she peeked over the fallen table, hesitant. "But… but Uncle Kael will see me…" Her eyes began to well, and she shut her lids in a squeal. "Why is he doing this…? H-He… he would never…" She sniffled and rubbed her eyes raw. "Why is he evil now…?"

Her sobs grated against my new mother's instincts. I wanted to hold her, to comfort her, *anything*… but I was only witnessing this event. I wasn't physically here.

And *here* had already happened.

"No," I began softly, "If I've learned anything these last few years, it's that there is no such thing as evil… Wars can be caused through misunderstandings. They can be caused through greed and envy. They can be caused by revenge… these are all the errors of mortals. We all have them inside us. Kael would not have come to this madness on his own. He was manipulated. *Cilia* was manipulated. And Macarius…" I took a deep, hollow breath, the realization striking like a scythe to my spirit. "Macarius was afraid… because Grandfather told him *he* was to save us from the End of Existence…"

One of my mother's fox ears lifted in confusion, not understanding.

Then a yell rang out in the ballroom.

I whirled in time to see that Kael was gleaming with a bright light, his entire body glowing with a strange radiance. A similar light flashed from a man's blinding figure by the balcony—

And then both men vanished in a blink.

The Death King whipped his gaze about in bewilderment, his poisonous foe nowhere in sight. And at the balcony, a blue-haired teen wheezed on all fours over the marble floor, his arms trembling and sobs painfully strained.

I rose, leaving my mother behind her shielding table, and approached the simpering man.

"Grandfather…" I whispered.

Grandfather Dream flicked one of his grown fox ears toward me. He did not look. "Of course…" His voice was coarse as he sucked in a shuddering breath. "Of course, Iri would see it fit to bring you here for this, Granddaughter… to see my greatest *failure…*" His lungs squeezed at the last word, and he wept over the floor, pounding his fist on the marble. "I was such a fool…! I should have listened to you…! And now we will all meet our deaths because of the monster *I* created…!" He cupped his face, whispering, "I've killed us all… I thought I could finally—*finally*—have a friend… have a life…" His tone dripped with loathing. "But it was never meant for me, was it…? I was always meant to choose the *wrong* path…"

My eyes stung, the tears spilling freely now. There was no willing them back. Never in my life had I ever seen Grandfather like this.

I crouched beside him. "Grandfather… do you know what you once told me when I was a young girl? What you *will* say to me when our timelines cross?"

He scoffed bitterly. "Whatever it is, I'm confident it will be awful advice…"

"You told me that the greatest illusions in life are 'right' and 'wrong'. I was too young to understand it at the time, but now, I know what it means." I closed my eyes. "'Right' and 'wrong' are simply… words. They mean nothing. They are myths that we mortals cling to as we ceaselessly attempt to find the fabricated lie of 'morals'. They are manmade. The truth is that we only want what is best for *us* and those we love. None of this is your fault, Grandfather… it is the fault of your love for all of us. And we will never blame you for that."

—the ballroom slammed back to its original dimness again, the corpses vanishing around me.

Along with Grandfather.

"—Er, Willow?" Xavier's voice rasped in concern above me. He still held our son, staring at me like I was a madwoman. "What in Death just happened? You were talking to the dust all over the room… and you're, er… crying…"

I rose to my feet, dabbing my wettened eyes. "I… Saw my mother as a child. And my Grandfather…"

His expression fell grim. "Oh. I see…"

Footfalls echoed from the shadows.

Two figures lingered there, just shy of the beams of light. But in the darkness, I could see their glowing, white pupils.

"Cilia," I greeted quietly.

Xavier held our baby closer as he stared at the second figure beside Cilia, my husband growling, "Kael… I see Hecrûshou and the others found you."

Cilia stepped into the light, her grey hair shining softly in the rays of light as she purred, "He and Thörd found us. They say Miranda and Khol are searching the grounds for signs of La'Lunaî. Though, I doubt she and her army are here. Hiding a Weight that large and numerous would be near impossible."

She glanced at Kael beside her. "We've elected to… reacquaint ourselves with the palace instead. It seems to have helped Kael regain some of his memories."

Kael ran a hand over one of the dusty pillars, his expression distant. I had to wonder if he was remembering the carnage he had caused here five centuries ago. Judging from his sickened expression, I suspected he was indeed.

"What have I done…?" Kael rumbled in shame. "So much death… and I…" He hushed. "I didn't care…"

Cilia cupped his bristled face, and he leaned into her touch as tears stung his glowing eyes.

Xavier and I exchanged a solemn glance. Then I sighed. "While your actions can never be forgotten… we understand your reasons for them."

Xavier lowered his gaze. "You were both victims yourselves… of Macarius's plot."

Cilia shook her head. "It does not excuse what we've done."

"True," I said. "You cannot change your past. But you *can* change what you do now." I offered her my hand, teeth sharpening as I rumbled, "Help us kill Macarius. Help us protect the realms… and as the new Death Queen, I will do everything in my power to grant your kind citizenship. Including the both of you."

Cilia's lips curled with dark delight as she snagged my hand, sealing our agreement. "With pleasure, Your Majesty."

11

THE BLOSSOM OF GOLD

XAVIER

I hefted baby Lucas over my shoulder, walking alongside Willow and our newest, demon allies.

The moment we stepped outside, I noticed my Crest began to gleam with a pulsing light over my left knuckles.

Land's Relic is near…

Thus far, Alexander's and my Crests only glowed like this when we were close to the Lost Relics. When only one of the three diamonds on my hand pulsed with light, I strode in the direction it was pointing, leading the others as they followed me. Our footfalls echoed through the jungle ridden breeze-way, wildlife chittering and chirping all around the ruins. According to Kael, he remembered this was the way to the central gardens. That was where Hugh had told me to meet with Anabelle.

Which meant it was also where the Relic of Land awaited.

Kael walked beside me in silence until he squinted at my face, as if only now remembering who I was. He rumbled, "You are… the boy from the canyons…?"

I cocked an eyebrow. "Recognize my eyes, do you?"

"Yes…" Kael seemed perplexed, his white pupils glowing in the breeze-way's shade. "You've grown since then. No longer a boy… a father, even." He glanced at my son who snoozed in my arms. Remorse sagged Kael's face. "And I nearly stole this future from you… I am… so sorry…"

Hearing an apology had my insides simmer with conflictions I never expected to feel for this man. It was Kael who'd thrown me off that cliff so long ago. It was Kael who tore me away from Willow; ripped me of a normal life, where I was forced to share a body with my twin for six years and suffer endless night terrors reliving that horrific memory over and over until I nearly went mad…

And now he was sorry?

"I will never forget what you've done to me," I said darkly, my voice a low hiss. My teeth sharpened, wolf ears growing and curling back... But after a moment, the anger subsided, and I sighed. "Even so, I... equally will never forget that you tried to protect my family in Culatia..." I hugged my infant son tighter, relishing his Pyrovoker's heat against my neck. Having proof he was still here was enough to calm my nerves, and my voice softened. "If not for your interference, my son may not have survived... Nor would my wife. If I'd lost them, I..." My throat tightened, remembering the chaotic storm in the colosseum, Willow lying along the stone rows in the middle of labor, her skin marred by burn scars as Macarius electrocuted her with his new Hallows, her agonized screams drilling through my eardrums...

Willow suddenly squeezed my shoulder, breaking my trance and throwing me back into the present.

I found my wife casting me a misty gaze. Willow stole my lips, then touched her brow to mine. Steam hissed between our flesh, my Glaciavoker's ice cooling her fiery soul and filling me with a dazed euphoria. She was alive. She was still here with me.

And I would *never* let Macarius take her away.

"—Interference?" Kael suddenly echoed next to us. I'd nearly forgotten he and Cilia were even here. Kael looked delighted as he gripped hands with Cilia, the two seeming warmed by our family's bonding moment... but Kael *also* seemed horribly puzzled.

"I had been in Culatia?" Kael asked, sounding unsure. "What was I doing in Culatia?"

"Ah..." I tapped a knuckle to my chin. "You must not remember that quite yet... My wife tells me you tried to protect her from Macarius while she was in labor with our son."

His brow raised in surprise. "I... did?"

"Yes." I hesitated. "Though, Macarius killed you for it... Part of me wonders if he always planned to dispose of you once you were of no use to him. It seems to be his way."

Kael brooded over this for a moment, looking troubled as we continued through the breezeway, my Crest lighting the way. One of Lucas's wolf ears flicked against my bearded neck while I ducked under a low-hanging vine and stepped out of the breezeway into the gardens themselves—

"Master!" the voice of my apprentice, Hugh, called from under a stone archway wrapped with blooming vines.

The resurrected boy was with the rabbit-eared Vendy and the winged Dalen. The three vassals were armed with their Spiritcrystal weapons in hand. Hugh wielded his very own pair of short handled dual-scythes, Vendy shouldered her glowing broadsword, and Dalen tossed one of his Crystal daggers idly in the air. When Hugh called us, the other two turned, and all three trotted over.

"*Da'torr* Xavier," Vendy greeted and stopped in front of me. She flicked one of her rabbit ears toward Cilia and Kael. Her nose scrunched. "I see you two are back…" She looked at me and threw her head over her shoulder in a questioning gesture. "They still on our side?"

I nodded. "They're starting a new path."

Willow took Lucas from my arms and added, "One where our goals align."

Dalen snorted. "Fine with me, 'long as they don't turn around and eat your souls." He flapped his wings sharply for emphasis and pointed at the demon pair with one of his Crystal daggers. "If I see either of ya *slobberin'* in their direction, I'm gonna sic one of your demon king friends on ya." He tossed his chin toward Khol, who was having an absolute blast befriending a cloud of butterflies.

Cilia chuckled and patted Dalen's cheek. "Your intentions are noted, poppet, but might I suggest your first choice *not* be Khol the Kindhearted? A newborn is more terrifying than our in-house butterfly whisperer."

She strode past Dalen with a light shove of her hip, tugging Kael alongside her and went to introduce Kael to their rotten brethren scattered about the gardens.

Dalen grumbled his annoyance. "Bloody cretin… come on, *Da'torr.* Your brother's over this way."

Willow and I followed Dalen through the expansive ruins of the central gardens. Vendy patrolled behind us while Hugh guarded our left side, where Willow strode with the slumbering baby in her arms.

The ruins were ghosts of a beautiful landscape, echoes of an ancient majesty that had been abandoned and left at the mercy of the wild jungle. Stone and brick fountains were dried up and overgrown with ivy. Statues were crumbled and hidden under thick, leafy vines. Littering the tangle of plants were hordes of reptiles, birds, and colorful butterflies…

And leaning against a tree while *covered* in such butterflies was my irritated brother. Alexander had his arms crossed as he glared at the swarm of butterflies resting all over him. A few sat on his grown wolf ears, and when we approached him, the fairy-like bugs fluttered gently to his shoulders when he flicked an ear toward us.

"There you are," he growled and pushed off the tree. The butterflies fled from his clothes as he stalked over to meet us. Two of them still clung to his hair until he vigorously ruffled them off, then smacked a mosquito on his sweaty neck.

"Bloody pests…" he muttered. "Can we get this over with? The sooner we have these damned Blessings, the sooner we can leave this overgrown, infested *nest* of things that wish to burden me." He smacked another mosquito that landed on his arm, then swatted away another flurry of butterflies that tried to perch on his head.

One of the blue and black butterflies fluttered to my wife and son. It landed on Lucas's nose, waking him. The pup marveled at the creature's colorful wings, going cross-eyed. Willow chuckled and gently scooped a finger under the butterfly's legs, encouraging it to stick to her instead. When it complied, she lifted it with a smile. "It's not so terrible," she said.

Alex muttered curses under his breath as he followed us deeper into the gardens. He and I followed our glowing Crests until all three diamonds pulsed with a steady glow under our knuckles, signaling we were upon the Relic.

There, between two hollow stumps in the middle of the ruins, stood the golden-haired Queen Anabelle. Her two closest guards, Kurrick and Genevieve, were at attention on either side of her, as usual. Herrin and Marian stood anxiously off to the side with parchment and quill at the ready, their wings shivering in anticipation.

I noticed Claude and Sirra-Lynn were by a dried-up fountain. Their armored son, Neal, was leaned against a tree beside a fully-plated Matthiel, their messengers perched on their silver shoulders. As the two Reapers chatted, Neal idly tossed a throwing-scythe in hand. But when his raven gave an alerting croak and drew his attention to his parents by the fountain—he spotted Kael and Cilia there. They were speaking to Claude and Sirra with hushed tones. Neal almost dropped the scythe in his rush over, probably to hear what the demons had to say, and left Matthiel behind to scratch his head in confusion.

The family seemed to be making amends, from what I could tell. Soft words were exchanged, far too quiet for me to hear, but given their posture and gentle expressions, I assumed their Ancient ancestors had been formally welcomed and forgiven.

Yet, when Kael's gaze moved toward the golden queen and her guards—his face tightened. His brow furrowed at Genevieve, as if her face struck his memory.

Strange… I mulled, suspicious. *Could he know her, somehow?*

But that question died the moment my eyes fell on Kurrick.

By Gods, the scarred man was drastically more tense than usual. Kurrick glared over his shoulder at every birdcall and rodent chitter that sounded from the jungle. For the first time since I've known him, the angry man looked… well, *terrified.*

And Kurrick aside, there was also something foreboding about Anabelle's empty stare. Her coin-like eyes were heavy with thought as she stared ahead into the jungle, her mind seeming miles away. But she blinked back to reality when she noticed Alexander and me approach.

"Thank you for coming," Anabelle whispered. One of her lion ears swiveled toward us. "I apologize for calling you so soon after we've arrived. But I'm sure I haven't a need to emphasize our rushed timeline… to dally could mean the End of us all."

Alex chewed under his breath to me, "or the *salvation* of us all."

I ignored him, turning to Ana as I crossed my arms. "Well, then? Shall we begin?"

She nodded. Then she closed her eyes, took a breath… and sang.

Breathe ye child your life begins

Cherish thine hallowed garden again

It was a slow and wavering melody. It was also… familiar. This was the tune for *the Ode of Hope,* the song Linus and the old rebellion would sing in hopes of catching the ears of the true heir; the ears of Anabelle.

But although the melody was the same, Anabelle sang different lyrics. Had this been the original purpose for the song? The Call of Land's Relic?

Spread your roots honor all your kin

And allow all thy branches to bend
Strengthen the stem
Sunlight will mend
And mind all the weeds till the end

My Crest gleamed brighter. One of the black diamonds shifted gold, as did Alexander's beside me.

As Anabelle sang, the two hollow stumps on either side of her began to creak and moan. Their chipped bark began to grow, turning and twisting as its veiny fibers sparkled with golden light.

How the mountains ever extend

They have lived proud and never condemned
Their stones have seen all of time's ill winds
Like them now your journey begins
Stand on the brim
Strong stones defend
But strongest is your soul's ascent

The stumps became sturdy trunks that bowed and twisted together above Anabelle's head, like a golden archway of branches that crisscrossed and looped with interlacing fingers. Flowers of every kind bloomed from golden buds, splitting and spinning in intricate designs along the archway as it continued to rise above our heads like a swelling canopy.

the second diamond of our Crests shifted gold.

Strengthen the stem

Sunlight will mend
And mind all the weeds till the end

The top of the enormous plant peeled open, revealing colossal flower petals that unfurled like a golden rose and fanned over our heads to blot out the sunlight. The blossom's own golden glow replaced that light and washed over us all.

Stand on the brim

Strong stones defend

My attention flicked to the side when I noticed our demon companions were forced back by some invisible barrier. Kael was screaming something, tossing a frantic hand toward Genevieve, but he was too far back to be heard.

But strongest is your soul's ascent

Our last diamond shifted gold—
And the gardens fell to blackness.

My eyes flew open. I was on my back, staring at the sky.

Clsch!

A crack split through a cloud, making me blink. The line grew longer as I watched it branch apart into thousands of fissures, creaking and echoing throughout the world like a mighty oak tree about to split in two.

Then the sky shattered to pieces.

Screams ripped all around me, blasting my grown wolf ears and scrambling my blood in a panic. I shoved my hands over my ears, desperate to block out the shrieks of agony and torture. Fragments of the broken sky rained upon the landscape and sliced my scalp as they became tangled in my hair like deadly snow. I threw my arms over my head, but the shards sliced and cut my skin mercilessly, my stinging arms spitting with blood.

"Here again…!" I clenched my sharpened teeth and pushed to my feet.

It was the same vision as before, at the previous Relics.

It was the End of Existence.

"—Xavier!" Alexander's voice cut through the chaos behind me. My brother came panting to my side, his skin coated in bloody cuts like mine. His heterochromic glare was fixated on the carnage around us. "It's still the same as before… the future hasn't changed." His hands balled as he snarled, "But how does it come? Do we bring this? Or does Macarius?"

"I don't know," I growled, my wolf ears curling. "Keep watch. There must be a clue here if we pay enough attention."

Alex grunted. "If we don't die before we can find it."

I had no reply for that. He was right. Every other vision of the End only stopped when we died—each time more horrific than the last. We had no evidence suggesting this vision would end any differently.

Then we'll have to search quickly, I decided, scanning the terrain with a furious glare.

Through the holes in the sky, only darkness waited. Black sand poured down from the gaps, hissing softly as it glopped onto the ground. The gelatinous clumps bubbled and writhed, the mounds of sand shifting into horrifying creatures. The creatures' shapes were never the same. They lurched and slurped and molded themselves in nauseating patterns, barely taking consistent forms of enormous animals.

Noctis Golems.

The nightmarish sand-beasts slaughtered the crowd of people, tearing them apart in gruesome pieces before devouring them alive. The familiar faces of our party were doing their best to exterminate the Golems. There was Anabelle slicing them with her sword, Roji flying above them with his bow and arrows, Dalminia sweeping a trident of ice through the horde, Willow cutting them with her scythe left and right… But there were too many. The death toll rose like a tidal wave, flesh ripped from bone, bone splintered from joint, entrails slurped from soaking bellies…

I clapped a disgusted hand to my mouth, sick. These visions were worsening… It was always horrifying, but it seemed the longer we stayed on this path, the closer we came to this future coming true.

I staggered back—bumping into Alex.

He didn't seem to notice. He was too busy staring at the blackness waiting behind the fragmented sky above us. I followed his gaze.

My brow knitted.

There were five colorful lights zipping through the empty void. *No, wait… those weren't lights.* I squinted for closer inspection. Those lights were… people. *Glowing* people.

The one sparkling with golden light was a man clad in gilded armor. He was armed with a heavy sword that he swung and thrust at the sand-beasts swarming the dark terrain, splitting them in half as their grains hissed away into vapor with every mighty cut.

Beside him, a scarlet-glowing man soared through the blackness with his brilliant red wings. He shot at the beasts with arrows of light using more speed than any mortal could ever achieve.

Behind him was an emerald-glowing man who obliterated creature after creature with his trident made of green light, his motions so fluid, I thought he was dancing.

Beneath the three men, an azure-gleaming child swept the beasts aside with his radiant-blue shepherd's crook. Lastly, a violet-shining woman with long, ashen hair sliced through the grainy monsters with a long-staved scythe.

My lungs drained cold. "It's… It's the Gods…"

Alex's voice softened with a mix of wonder and confusion. "They're… fighting the Noctis Golems…? But why?"

—a powerful scream split the air suddenly, so agonized that its echoes rippled through time itself.

It had come from above us, where the Gods battled the monsters. The azure child God, Iri, had been pierced through the heart by one of the Golem's sandy claws. He was the one whose cry shook the world, his wound festering with white light that split across his radiant body, crawling all throughout his flesh until—

He exploded in a blinding flash.

The burst of light swept outward from all directions, swallowing everything in its wake. And then, as Alex and I were engulfed in the light…

It devoured existence itself.

The whiteness faded black.

Alex and I now floated in an empty Void.

Before us sat a lion, its fur gleaming a brilliant golden light.

YOU HAVE GROWN SO MUCH, *the lion's rumbling voice growled, crawling through our thoughts like soothing vines,* YOU'VE ONE RELIC LEFT. BUT PERIL AWAITS, AS YOU SAW… AND MY SOUL DAUGHTER HASN'T MUCH TIME.

The lion rose on its paws, its tail flicking urgently.

TAKE MY BLESSINGS, *it rasped,* HEAL MY DAUGHTER…

My vision flashed with golden light—and I woke on the jungle floor beside Alex.

I squeezed in a reviving breath.

My lungs filled with humid air as I felt it tangle in my soul. It wrapped and knotted so tremendously, I fumbled to sit up and panted on all fours, clenching the grass between my fingers. The soil beneath was soft and warm under my nails. It seemed to have a… a pulse. The roots under my fingertips beat and pounded gently like an echo in the ground that pulled at my soul and beckoned me to free it… The pulse blistered through me, so intense it twisted together, wrapping my very being and strangling me until…

The roots sprouted under my hands.

A radiant, golden shimmer lit the grass between my fingers. Dandelions and lilies and clovers sprouted up from the ever-rising blades of grass, climbing higher until they unfurled under my nose. Their delightful perfume made my head feel like cotton, and a laugh escaped me.

I turned to Alex beside me. My brother sat surrounded by an alcove of stones that I didn't remember being there before. They were jagged and crooked, yet tall and sturdy, circling around Alex as if to form a backing for him to rest against as he panted in hoarse wheezes. The rocks seemed to have come from two moss-covered boulders near him. Their bases were still intact, but they had stretched upward unnaturally.

He was looking at his golden-glowing hands… Staring at the crowned Land mark that had replaced the Crest under his right knuckles.

I turned over my left hand to stare at mine. Like his, my Crest was gleaming gold with a crowned Land mark. But it soon faded and returned to my original birthmark of three black diamonds.

The now-familiar feeling of *fullness* welled in my soul. Which meant these new elements of Land Hallows were now imbued within me, as with the first three Relics.

Yet, despite the prickling thrill fighting to burst out of me, I couldn't shake off the feeling of dread.

Heal my daughter… The golden lion had rumbled in that vision. It was no doubt Shel, the Holy Gardener. He'd said to heal his daughter…

I stiffened. Shel's daughter was *Land*.

My head snapped to Anabelle, panic sparking as I prepared for the worst…

But I relaxed. Ana still stood under the enormous, glowing Blossom of Gold beside Kurrick and Genevieve. It seemed little time had passed while we were having that vision. Nothing seemed out of place. Ana cast me an eager smile, her golden hair glistening beneath the ethereal gleam of the Blossom towering over us.

I smiled back. The normalcy of the scene was… calming. I thanked Bloods we were done with this latest vision. Now that it was over with, I was eager to find something to take my mind off the horrors and…

A glint flashed over my vision, distracting me. Where was that coming from? I flicked my gaze to Genevieve. The shine came from something in her scaled hand. Something sharp.

My calm vanished.

"ANABELLE!" I shouted, bursting to my feet and breaking into a sprint.

Ana's metallic eyes peered curiously at me.

—then a dagger sliced over her throat.

A line of red peeled across Anabelle's neck. It was so sudden, she was still standing in a shocked silence.

Kurrick was not.

"ANA!" His scream was like shattered glass, his hard expression shattering. He drew his sword in a wild rage, thrusting it at Genevieve like a lunatic.

Clang!

His blade clashed on impact. In front of Genevieve, now chipped under his blade's edge, was a stone wall that had stretched up from a boulder at Genevieve's feet. And Genevieve's hands were glittering with golden light.

Genevieve's brown eyes were now as bright as gilded coins. Her hair was bleeding the same metallic hue, viper fangs unfolded and dripping with venom.

Kurrick's rage only burned hotter, and he screamed while going around her stone wall to slice horizontally.

Genevieve gave an effortless flick of her wrist—and tossed Kurrick's sword aside with her new Hallows.

Kurrick's claws grew, and he lunged for the viper woman—

Anabelle swayed beside him, her eerie stance faltering at last as her legs crumpled like a ragdoll.

Kurrick dropped everything and quickly caught her before she hit the ground, sinking to his knees. "Ana…!" His voice was a tight whisper. He cradled her head like a delicate, glass sculpture. "No, no, no, no, no…"

Red flowed down Ana's neck. She sputtered up crimson bubbles, raising a weak hand to her wound as she struggled to evoke her remedy Hallows over the cut. Golden light flickered from her palm, but soon blinked out as her arm lost its strength and dropped to her side. She looked up at her scar-faced warrior with a placid gaze. Then her eyes drifted to Genevieve.

She whispered with as much breath as she could muster, "Why…?"

Genevieve said nothing. She hung her head, and for a moment, I could swear I saw tears. Then she ducked away and ran out of the gardens.

From the sidelines, Willow clutched the baby and barked in command, "AFTER HER!"

Our vassals broke into a sprint at the order, Dalen and Rossette taking to the air and Nikolai, Vendy, and Hugh dashing through the jungle on foot. Matthiel had his scythe materialize and sprinted off as well, and Neal fumbled after him in a curse, readying his throwing-scythes as they disappeared into the jungle.

I sprinted after her as well, my hands sparking with lightning as the electricity festered in my soul like static—

The ground shook suddenly, throwing me off balance.

The Blossom of Gold was twisting and curling its colossal petals closed. As the bark-like stem unwound itself from its arching shape, it shrank back into its original form: two hollowed stumps on either side of the bleeding queen and her sobbing warrior.

Once the tremors subsided, I cursed and bounded for Anabelle. Alex hurried to his feet to follow after me. We fumbled beside Anabelle in Kurrick's arms, crouching down in heavy pants.

Ana's eyes rolled back, gagging on blood that poured from her mouth and throat, staining her flesh, her teeth… and Kurrick's armor.

Kurrick held her head to his chest and sobbed. "Ana… I-I tried to stop this—I tried… I… I'm sorry…" He squeezed his eyes shut and rocked her gently, petting her hair. "Don't leave me…" His usually gruff voice tightened into an agonized squeal. "Please… *Don't leave me…*"

It was painful to watch. Painful to listen. In the two years Kurrick had spent with us on our journey, not once had I seen him so… broken.

"Let me see her!" the voice of Bianca broke through the jungle. The rabbit girl came from around a tree she'd apparently been hiding behind. "Let me see her *now!*"

Alex and I split apart to let Bianca kneel between us. She shoved her hands over Ana's wound with panicked mutters, blood seeping between Bianca's dark fingers. The Alchemist's palms gleamed with golden light… but only one layer of skin sealed shut on Ana's throat, and it took several minutes for even that much to work. "Damn it…!" Bianca chewed, pushing more Hallows onto the cut. "I should have brought my tonics…!"

Bianca's face turned red as she pushed out her Hallows as fast and as hard as she could manage—then like a popped bubble, Bianca's Hallows shut itself off, and she swayed. Alex caught her before she hit the ground, and once she'd righted herself, she coughed in a ragged voice. "Bloods… that was all of my Hallows…" Tears stung her eyes as she looked at Kurrick. "I'm sorry… It's just too deep. Not even remedy Hallows can heal it…"

Kurrick roared, "What do you mean you can't heal it—?!"

"Let us try," I blurted. All eyes were on me, now. I looked at Alex urgently. "Shel asked us to Heal His daughter, before we were thrown out of the vision. Maybe there's something *we* can do."

Alex took a breath, hesitant, then nodded. "It's worth a try."

I swallowed, cautiously clasping a hand over Ana's soaking throat. Alex laid his own hand over mine. I didn't know which half of the Healing Hallows either of us had been granted, but if both of us used it at the same time, *something* had to work.

I closed my eyes and drew in a deep breath. A warm buzz came from my soul. The vibration hummed stronger as I focused on the command to *heal*, until it sloshed about like a raging tsunami begging to break through. I trapped it there—and evoked the Hallows down my arms.

Golden lights leaked from my palm and fingertips. They latched onto Ana's open flesh like plant roots, causing her skin to stretch and grow. The wound healed itself from the inside of her sliced voicebox first. But it was incredibly slow. She was losing blood faster than I could heal the cut. At this rate, she would still die if I couldn't force the healing to go faster… But no matter how hard I pushed out the Hallows, it healed no quicker—

Alex's hand suddenly gleamed golden on top of mine. His Hallows seeped into my pores and latched onto my soul—catching a ride on the stream of magic I evoked into Anabelle.

Her wounds healed at lightning speed. The magic streams crossed and zigzagged and laced together in dizzying circles around Anabelle's wound, the tissue and skin sealing closed in a ray of golden light.

When it was over, Alex and I removed our hands. A scar ran across Ana's throat, but it spilled no more blood.

Anabelle spasmed and rolled on her side, coughing out the blood that had pooled in her throat. She gasped and wheezed, her skin shuddering as her eyes flitted back into consciousness and focused on Kurrick's face.

"Ana…!" Kurrick held her closer. "I'm sorry…! I'm so sorry, I…!"

Ana lifted a weak hand to Kurrick's scruffy face. Her lips moved as if trying to speak, but all that came was a soft breath of silence.

Kurrick hushed her, "Save your voice… you need rest, Ana."

She whispered more empty breaths, then closed her eyes as her hand fell limp and she drifted to sleep in his arms.

Kurrick huddled there with her for what felt like hours. I was sure it was only minutes, but time seemed to stretch around them. No one spoke for a long time. It looked like I wasn't the only one who dared not disturb them.

Then, at last, Kurrick whispered, "Shadowblood." He didn't pry his gaze from Ana's face. "Have you… Seen another vision of the future…? When you gained your Hallows?"

I answered hesitantly, "We did…"

His grown lion ears curled against his head. "Was Anabelle there? In your vision?"

I nodded. "She was fighting the Noctis Golems alongside her Soul Brothers and Sisters."

He let out a heavy, croaking sigh. "I… I see… Then, I've no more excuses have I, Ana…?" He stroked her petal-like curls and lifted her as he rose to his feet. Then he bowed his head in a solemn nod to Alex and me. "Thank you… Shadowblood. Both of you… Perhaps you'll be our salvation after all…"

Kurrick carried his queen out of the gardens toward the palace ruins. Alex and I were left alone in the jungle with Willow, Lucas, and Bianca.

Then the crunch of dry pine needles sounded as two figures emerged behind me. It was Cilia and Kael. The demons had been pushed back from the Relic's invisible barrier that warded off their kind, but now that the Blossom had returned to its dormant state, it seemed they were able to approach again.

I rose to my feet, growling at Kael. "You were yelling at Genevieve before you were pushed away. Did you know her?"

Kael's voice was guttural. "She is Macarius's step-daughter. I didn't know exactly what she had planned, but I knew she couldn't be trusted. By the time I remembered where I'd seen her face, I was shoved back by the Relic."

Alex's teeth sharpened. "That Bloody witch…"

I rubbed my eyes. "At least we learned our Healing Hallows in time to save Ana…"

"—I'll say!" Herrin suddenly piped from atop a vined tree branch at the edge of the jungle. His winged assistant, Marian, clung to the branch beside Herrin with a traumatized shiver. The Enlighteners had apparently flapped up there when the trouble began. That was for the best, I decided. The Scholars weren't trained in combat.

Herrin flapped down to us and fluttered his wings, flicking away the stray leaves that had wedged themselves between his feathers. Marian did the same, still seeming rattled as she clutched a ledger to her chest meekly.

"That was amazing!" Herrin exclaimed. He grabbed my left hand and Alexander's right hand, examining our Crests in wonder. "Bloods, it's a good thing Healing is part of the Land Hallows…! I didn't think Ana was going to make it—Bianca couldn't heal a wound *that* fatal!"

Bianca, who had been catching her breath on the jungle floor, groaned and hacked in exhaustion. "Don't remind me…"

Alex hurried to crouch down and sling Bianca's arm over his neck, helping her to her feet. She swayed and clutched her head tenderly. "Ugh…" Her long ears drooped down miserably. "I think I'm gonna hurl…"

Alex worriedly touched his knuckles to her brow. "You're burning up… You shouldn't have used all your Hallows like that."

She glowered at him. "Yeah, well, if I knew your 'chosen one' arse was going to do the job, I wouldn't have—*woah*…!" She tried to push away from him, but almost fell, flopping against him again. Her ears folded over her eyes. "Gods damn it…"

Alex couldn't help his blushing smile. But it faded when he blinked at her, frowning. "I'm not pretending to care—"

"*Stop reading my mind, Alex,*" she snapped, giving a muted scream behind her mortified hands.

He cleared his throat. "S-sorry…"

"I swear to Bloods, do you have any idea what privacy is—*urrgh…!*" She turned green, gagging as she clapped a sickened hand over her mouth, then bent over to vomit on the grass.

Alex winced and reached for her back, but retracted as another slosh of bile spewed from her throat.

While she emptied her stomach, Herrin came up to me with a leger and quill in hand.

"So, um, anyway," Herrin began. "We saw that Xavier can seal wounds, and Alex can amplify the effect and speed up the remedies. What about your Arbor and Terravoking? What's the split there?"

I cringed at the sound of another vomiting fit from Bianca, trying to avert my gaze and give her some space. "I, er, seem to be able to grow plants at will," I told Herrin, waving a glowing hand over the grass at my feet. Flowers and weeds sprouted there in seconds.

Herrin turned to Alex, who still hovered over Bianca helplessly. "Can you grow plants like him?" Herrin asked.

Alex seemed conflicted whether to give his attention to Bianca or Herrin. Since Bianca was still preoccupied, he sighed and humored Herrin. My brother evoked his Hallows and tried to grow something from the ground, as I had done, but the result was a failure. Not a single blade of grass rose higher. However, the small stone by his boot stretched upward in a thin spire. His mouth twisted, muttering, "I grow… rocks?"

Alex and I shared a contemplative glance. Then we waved our hands across the other's arms and tested those same Hallows on the other's grown object.

My magic pulled up his spired stone, and I made it hover in the air before me. Alex's magic plucked one of my flowers from its stem and had it float up to him. Then he seemed to have another idea, and instead made it float down to Bianca's soured face.

She scowled at the flower, hanging her head in a groan. *"Read the Bloody room, Alex—hurh…!"* She wretched again, dry heaving. It seemed she'd emptied her stomach completely. Alex coughed into a fist and dismissed his Hallows immediately, dropping the flower and crushing it under his boot as if to erase his mistake.

Herrin grimaced, trying to stay on topic. "Uh, right… One grows stuff, the other lifts the stuff… Got it."

—Da'torr? The voice of Dalen fuzzed in my thoughts. It must have hit Alex as well, since his heterochromic eyes snapped up the moment Dalen spoke through our mental connection.

My tone hardened. "Have you caught Genevieve?"

Not exactly, Dalen replied, *She sorta… well…*

Hugh's voice mumbled bashfully next. *She caught us in a tangle of vines with her Hallows...*

Vendy's voice chewed irritably. *She made me drop my damn sword! Can you two hurry up and get us down before one of these feral monkeys swipes it? They're pulling on my ears over here!*

"Death," Alex and I cursed. "We're on our way."

I turned to Willow, ruffling Lucas's ashen wisps of hair between his wolf ears as I addressed my wife, "Our vassals lost sight of Genevieve. How are Rossette and Nikolai faring?"

Willow glanced to the side and questioned to the air, "Rossette? Nikolai? What is your status on our quarry?"

There was a pause, then Willow shook her head. "They've lost sight of her."

Kael stepped beside me, the demon's cat ears showing as he growled. "She couldn't have gotten far. You all arrived by sea and Airship, yes?"

I nodded. "Yes. And Anabelle has her fleet standing guard at the coast. Though, speaking of which..." I pulled out my com and called the fleet's general, a tiger woman named Darleen Quintez.

When the round-eared general answered and her face appeared on the screen, she straightened upright in surprise. *"Death King Xavier?"*

My stomach clenched at the name, but I tried to keep if off my face and announced, "General Quintez, I am speaking on behalf of Queen Anabelle while she is in recovery."

The general's ears folded back uneasily. *"Recovery? Has something happened?"*

"We were betrayed," I rumbled, my tone gritty as anger simmered back to life at the reminder. "Captain Genevieve was a spy. She tried to assassinate your queen. She's escaped our pursuit, and we fear she may attempt to flee the island aboard one of your ships."

Her teeth sharpened. *"If that traitor takes one step on any ship, my soldiers will lop off her foot along with her head!"*

"If you must," I grunted callously. "Keep alert, General. She has Land Hallows now. Be sure to warn your captains."

I ended the call, then tossed my head over a shoulder to tell Alex and the others to come with me.

"They've been warned," I muttered. "Now let's go cut down our tangled vassals."

Bianca groaned from the ground. "You do that... I'm going to take a nap..."

EVERLAND

12

DREAMS OF A DEMON

TAYMEN

A feral lizard scurried over my hand.

I lifted him up and stared at his beady eyes with a sigh. "Hey, little guy. You hungry?" I brought up the leftover shifter-finger I didn't finish from our camp's last meal. I hated eating raw flesh… well, actually, I guess I hated how *delicious* it was… There was something intoxicating about it—not just the flesh, but the soul inside was enough to put you in a dazed trance and…

Damn it, stop thinking about it!

I shook my head, trying to knock out the morbid thoughts. *Great… now I'm normalizing eating shifters. I'm officially a monster…*

But despite how much I hated what I was becoming… shifter corpses were the only meals Mistress La'Lunaî allowed us to eat. I guessed I could eat the lizard, but I was stuffed from 'dinner', so I wasn't desperate.

The lizard sniffed at the half-chewed finger I offered him, then chomped it in its gummy mouth and hopped off my hand. I watched it crawl under a stone to hide from the morning sunlight, then I leaned back and looked around the expansive nest.

The other demons were asleep all over the wastelands. Our Sentient numbers had grown by the hundreds over the months; our mongrel numbers by the thousands. The mongrels usually kept within their respective, squirming groups, and us Sentients stayed in our assigned squads.

My squad of twelve snoozed on the dirt around me. Some were men, some were women, some were old and some were young like me, all of us having different Hallows. We were a mismatched bunch, but so were the other squads.

Our captain, Jace, snored like a noisy steam engine as he rolled into an awkward sprawling position. He wore our army's newest uniforms the Mistress had handed out months ago. They were wrinkly, muddy-green tunics and ankle-length pants. Jace's uniform was way too small on his long limbs, so he looked kind of ridiculous with his dark brown hair in a tangled mess, and his yellowed teeth were crooked as he snored with an open mouth. He had a wiry goatee framing his cracked lips, and his bronze skin practically glowed in the sunlight.

Demons slept during the day, most times. Jace said that was usually just the mongrels who needed to do that, but since Mistress La'Lunaî wanted us to move as a unit, we adjusted our schedules to fit theirs.

Jace's lieutenant, Syreen, lay curled up in the dirt beside me. Syreen was a muscular girl, probably around my age from what I could tell. She had cropped, blonde hair and angry scars running all over her face and neck. Demons didn't *get* scars after they Changed, so I knew she got those while she was alive, which meant she must have been in a *lot* of battles in her time.

Rumor among the squad was that Syreen had been a queen in Neverland. None of us ever asked her directly though. She didn't *talk* with anyone. She either glared until you ran away, or drove her claws through your eye sockets if you pissed her off enough. The only person she didn't swipe her claws at was Mistress La'Lunaî… but I had a hunch that was only because of Mistress's Mark she'd injected in all of us. The Mark stopped us from disobeying her. That was the only reason none of us had tried to make a run for it out of the nest. Mistress would know where we were. And she'd hunt us down.

"Hugh…" Syreen whispered in her sleep, her head thrashing. "Brother… I don't… understand…"

She talked in her sleep pretty much every night. She didn't say much, it was usually just a name. *Hugh.* She often paired it with 'little brother', so it was a safe bet Hugh was her brother. Duh. It was weird, though, because she didn't start saying that stuff until after the battle in New Aldamstria with the Reapers. That battle did *not* go well. We lost two-thirds of our previous numbers, so Mistress La'Lunaî had been sending us on recruiting missions in the night.

Since demons didn't technically 'dream', I could only assume Syreen was reliving a memory. One with her brother Hugh, from when she was alive.

Did I have any brothers? I wondered with a twisted mouth. I'd been in this nest for months, but I couldn't remember a damned thing about my life except for my name.

And my Hallows.

I stared at my hands, evoking my dream Hallows as blue light glowed from my palms. *What good is being a dream walker if I can't dream?*

From what I could tell, I was the only Somniovoker in the entire nest… and therefore, the most useless Sentient Mistress complained about. She was probably right. Though, I couldn't help but wonder if I could somehow use my Hallows to find some of my lost memories. I vaguely remembered someone—a teacher?—telling me how all forgotten memories were scattered in Aspirre, floating around in there waiting to be remembered. The memories only disappeared when our souls Descended to Nira. So, by that logic, a *rotten* soul wasn't a Descended soul, and my memories should still be in the Dream realm. If I could just find a way to get *into* Aspirre, maybe I could find my memories?

Okay, Taymen. I took a preparing breath and raised my glowing-blue hand to my head. *You can do this. Dream Hallows means you can FORCE yourself to sleep… and force your soul into Aspirre… right?*

It was a weak theory, and I hadn't had a chance to test it yet, but… I had to try, didn't I? I shut my eyes and heaved my magic into my skull, pouring everything I had out of my soul and…

The world spun suddenly, my skull splitting with pain. "Land…!" I grunted, bearing the throbs as I pushed more Hallows into my head. "Come on…! Just… a little more…!"

My vision spotted, and I broke into a cold sweat, wheezing as my magic drained out of me at full speed…

Until I collapsed to the dirt.

And Everything went black.

I jolted upright, my stomach lurching as I started falling way, way down into a dark, empty abyss.

I screamed and evoked my azure Hallows beneath my feet.

Strings of light spewed from my fingertips, twisting and knotting and swirling together as I conducted them to my will. It was like painting a picture—or, more accurately, weaving a tapestry of light.

The lights wove into brick shapes, attaching to one another and forming a road that gleamed a bright azure. When the glow dimmed, they became solid pieces of real brick—

Which I slammed into stomach-first.

I gave a winded groan, my lungs shuddering in heavy pants as I pushed myself upright and whipped my head around.

There was nothing but blackness everywhere I turned.

I ran a confused hand through my hair, my lion ears growing. Okay, let's see… I'm in an empty abyss of nothingness. And I just created a piece of a road out of thin air.

A laugh bubbled out of me. "I… I did it…!" I jumped to my feet in a thrill. "I'm in Aspirre…! Take that, rotten soul! Your demon deterrent can suck it!"

A glimmer of light caught my eye a few yards away from me. Oh, I remember those! It's a memory!

I twiddled my glowing fingers, evoking more of my dream Hallows. The road expanded with another dozen rows of bricks. I tapped my foot against them to test their stability. Yep, they would hold me… I guessed the little road I wove earlier had come out from habit, so I shouldn't be worried, but still. Without my memories, it didn't hurt to be careful.

More bricks continued to zip into existence with azure wisps of light, and as each row of stones clunked and clicked into place, I walked over them and headed for the floating ball of light: the memory. When I reached it, I crouched over it and eagerly scooped it up—

HSSSSSSSSSHHHHHAAAAAAHHH…

I stopped cold, my blackened blood freezing over. I knew that sound… somewhere in my foggy memories, I knew that sound meant…

Danger.

SHHHHHhhhh…!

Grains of black sand poured onto the road at my feet.

Then I remembered.

"LAND!" my muscles moved on their own, hand whipping above my head in a glowing-blue arch as I wove a see-through bubble above my head and around my side, encasing myself in a small barrier.

CRASH!

A swarm of black sand hit my barrier, the grains scattering all around my bubble and coating it black like Aspirre's void.

Then the sand froze in place and slid back together, forming an ever shifting shape that resembled a terrifying shark, and a creepy skeleton of a demonic shifter.

I trembled, but didn't dare take down my barrier. "R-r-r-right…" I stuttered. "I r-r-remember you guys now…"

Noctis Golems. They were the demons of Aspirre. If I was going to come in here more often to find my memories, I'd have to remember to weave a barrier like this BEFORE exploring the abyss.

I shook myself off, assuring myself that, if my long-term memory was right, these guys couldn't eat my soul so long as I had my barrier up. Swallowing, I turned back to the ball of light I'd trapped with me. I scooped it up and brought it to my brow, letting the light sink into my skull.

The abyss and the Golem vanished.

Now, I stood in a snow-covered field, staring at a litter of corpses. Smoke clung to my lungs and damn near choked me to death, my throat burning as I fell into a coughing fit.

Then I saw a new corpse beside me. One I recognized.

"Da…!" I cried over the almost-headless man in front of me. It was my Da… his empty eyes were staring up at the sky. Lifeless.

—The memory ended, and I shivered on my woven road, that Golem still slamming against my barrier uselessly.

"Da…" Tears hit, rolling down my nose as I heaved in heavy gasps. "That was… my Da…!"

The pain of losing him squeezed my chest so hard, I thought it would pop—but the bliss of remembering something from my life was insanely relieving.

I found my memory. Which meant I could find more…

"—Wake up, idiots!"

I bolted awake and scuttled over the dirt in a hurry.

Jace towered over me with his hands on his hips, looking impatient as he barked to the rest of the squad, "I said wake up! Mistress gave marching orders. We're descending to Grim."

The others groaned awake and pushed to their feet. I followed suit meekly, hoping no one saw my Dream mark glowing from my neck while I was out. Judging by their same-old, placid expressions, it looked like I'd gotten away with it.

Syreen was the last to wake up. She sluggishly rose and followed the others, a sad look sagging her face as I followed behind her timidly.

ASTER

Aw man, this was *torture…!*

Timberail's harbor was full of so many delicious scents, my tears were mixing with the drool on my chin.

Succulent meat simmered from kabobs, steam peeled off grilled carrots along with the mouthwatering smell of onions and spices and garlic and…

And *souls.* So. Many. *Souls…*

The harbor bustled with shifters all around me, each one perfumed with a scent so tantalizing, my vision started to blur, meercat ears perking and teeth sharpening hungrily…

Don't you dare, Aster!

I shoved my hand in my mouth and bit down hard, black blood seeping over my tongue. The taste of my demon blood was disgusting enough to stave off my appetite a little. But not for long.

My shrunken stomach roared painfully, my eyes stinging with tears. Why did Shel have to torture me like this?! All these souls right here in one place, vendors selling all this food I couldn't afford…!

If only those Bloody soldiers didn't have a Reaper with them when they got me out of Tanderam. She would have skewered me on the spot if I'd stayed any longer. But that meant no government-funded refugee relief. Demons weren't considered refugees. They were at *war* with us. So, no money, no aid, and no *food*—

Someone ran into me, knocking me back.

—the faces of the heterochromic twins stared at me in disbelief, neither brother sure what to make of me—

The vision ended as quick as it came.

The mustached guy who ran into me didn't seem to notice and was stalking over to one of the ships at the harbor.

I hurried over and snatched his wrist. "Sir…!" I panted. "Sir, please, can you take me on your ship?"

The guy jolted when he looked at my face, but not because of my white pupils. Those were hidden behind a pair of shades I swiped off a tourist earlier. A vision of the Present showed me he was looking at my horrifically sunken cheeks and skinny fingers.

"Good Gods, boy!" the man grimaced in a sympathetic wince. "You look like a walking skeleton!"

"Technically, we're *all* walking skeletons, Sir," I said with a weak grin. Then started again more seriously, "Please, Sir, let me board your ship?"

His thick brow bunched up. "You have something to do in Neverland, boy?"

Neverland? "Uh, y… yeah," I said. "It's really important that I get there as quick as possible… I… I need to go back home to my parents. I've been in Tanderam Prison for two years, the regent just got us out. I didn't have a way to tell my family where I've been…"

It was only a half lie. I really had been trapped in Tanderam for two years—two years!—but my family lived in Mimier a few towns over from here in Everland. Well… they *used* to live there. I had stopped by my old house before I came to Timberail and found it empty. I used my prophetic Hallows to see what happened to them.

They were killed by the Raiders when the war started. Apparently, they thought my parents were hiding their only son whose birth records showed a

Dream mark—even a *half* Dream mark was considered illegal at the time. My parents were declared traitors, they resisted, and were slaughtered right then and there. Their bloodstains were still on the front porch when I got back… and I found out the same thing happened to my Master Oracle. So… there was no one left to go back home to anymore.

Nowhere to go but up, huh…?

The man's expression softened at me. "You were a prisoner there…?"

I nodded solemnly. "They rounded up anyone with a Dream or Death mark… I'm an apprentice oracle—or, I guess I *was*… they killed my master when he resisted arrest, so, um…" I sighed. "It's… been a long two years. I just want to get home…"

His bearded frown was heartfelt, and he clapped a hand on my boney shoulder. "I understand, boy. Think you can work for your fare?"

My meercat ears perked. "Yeah…! Yeah, I can do that! Anything!"

He chuckled and thumped my back, leading me up the ramp of the ship. "What's your name, boy?"

"Aster," I told him in a relieved breath. "Aster Sorelles."

"Well then, Aster, welcome aboard." He led us onto the deck where a flurry of crewmembers were busy at work. "I'm Captain Bardell. These are your new crewmates. They'll show you the ropes—literally." He laughed at his own joke and slapped a knee. He whistled for one of the men to come meet us, and ordered, "Show our new recruit Aster what his duties will be while we ferry this young lad to Neverland." He frowned while getting another look at me, then added, "But, er, maybe show this gangly skeleton to the galley first?"

The sailor flicked me a confused glance—winced when his eyes landed on my sunken cheeks. He shuddered a little before saluting dutifully. "A… Aye, Captain! Come with me, erm, s-sir…"

THE GYLE ISLANDS

Queen's Treasure

13

A NEW LEAF

ANABELLE

My bleary eyes were slow to open. A fluorescent light spilled into my stinging retinas. I was in what looked to be an infirmary.

My throat was throbbing dully, and I brought a hand to my neck and felt a ridge of scar tissue running across it.

That's right… Genevieve…

Humiliation slammed through me, so powerful I nearly vomited. The stinging mass of fury writhed within me at the cruel reminder of my stupidity, prickling my stomach like a ball of scurrying rats that mourned the loss of a trusted friend—and craved the head of a vile betrayer.

She will face a horrid death for this, I thought bitterly, using the guardrails on the side of the bed to slowly pull myself up. This proved difficult with the tangle of wires and fluid-tubes hanging from my veins, but I managed to brush those aside, finding the hovering stand of fluid-sacks next to the bedside table.

I paused. There was a bouquet of beautiful, vibrant flowers waiting for me on the table. In fact, now that I looked round the room, there were *dozens* of colorful bouquets surrounding me. There was even a lovely, tan scarf with knitted roses, which I assumed must have been courtesy of Khol. I donned the warm scarf, partly to relish its soft fibers and also to hide the scar across my throat. Then I noticed the bouquet on the table had a note attached. I lifted the wrapped flowers curiously and pinched the note to read the inked script:

Soul Sister Land,

Praying for your swift recovery. Xavier grew these with his new Hallows in hopes of bringing you some cheer upon your waking—which Sirra-Lynn and Kael assures us should be this afternoon.

Come find us in the markets once you're well enough. Much has transpired during your rest these last few weeks and I'm sure you wish to be informed.

    P.S: To relieve you of unnecessary stress, Xavier and I took the liberty of coordinating the resurrection of your Grand Capital… with Kurrick's guidance, of course. The locals have taken to calling it "Queen's Treasure". We hope all will be to your liking.

    Resurrections are a Necrovoker's specialty, after all.

Thala ul wuw shefta,
Your Soul Sister Death

My brow furrowed. *It has been weeks?* How many weeks? And what markets did she speak of? I lifted my hand with the fluid-tubes skeptically. *When had this equipment arrived here…?*

Bloods be good, they must have already commenced trade!

I hurriedly set aside the bouquet on the table—

Clack—Shhhink!

A long box fell off the table. Its contents spilled onto the marble floor and glinted in the light. They looked like… wedding-vines?

Confused, I slid off the bed and crouched down, grasping the fluid stand for support as I scooped up the vines. They were made of golden chains embedded with amethyst gemstones, the detached centerpiece glittering with the largest gem. A small sliver of parchment had fallen out of the box as well. I opened it and read five simple words in harsh script:

Yours… if you still wish.

Despite my aching throat, I smiled. Then eagerly clipped the vines in my hair, leaving the centerpiece in the box.

"—Ah," a rumbling voice said from the opened doorway. "It seems our patient is awake, Dr. Treble."

I rose and turned about, still clutching the long box. Three figures stood under the doorframe.

One was our party's morning Dreamcatcher, the enchanting Yulia, who wore her traditional indigo Catcher's cloak with silver buttons lining from her chest to her hips, tied together with thin, glistening chains. Her white fox tail curled around the hem of her cloak and her hair had been pinned up in a braided bun.

Beside her was the cat-eared Sirra-Lynn. When the blonde Healer spotted me standing here, holding the fluid stand to steady myself, she grinned and lifted one of her coned ears.

The black-haired man who'd spoken stood between the women. His yellow eyes glowed with white pupils.

My lion ears curled back, hesitant. *Kael...* Willow's note had mentioned him, but I hadn't considered the gravity of what his presence meant... and the casual acceptance Willow had used when referring to him was certainly bizarre.

Kael looked vastly different from the last time I'd seen him. There was a strange air of peace around him now. His once callous face was now soft and serene. If not for his glowing white pupils, I could almost recognize the man I'd originally known as Uncle Kael in my youth... before Cilia's butchery. And before Kael's deadly insanity.

Somehow, the tension had evaporated with his current smile. Strange, how swiftly we can change our nature if given nurturing support from those around you... strange and disorienting.

Since Kael was suddenly here, I supposed the other demons had retrieved Cilia and him sometime while I was resting. And it seemed he had already assumed his previous role as royal surgeon in that time... How *long* had it been?

Kael didn't seem to notice my skepticism and instead nodded to Yulia appreciatively, giving a cheerful hum, "Thank you for informing us of her waking, Sil... and thank you again for finding another memory of mine in Aspirre. I truly appreciate it."

Yulia gave a humble nod and murmured, "It *is* part of the job, doctor. Jimmy and I are always on the lookout for lost memories as well as nightmares." She smiled to me and offered a delicate curtsey. "Your majesty, welcome back to the physical realm. I hope we made sure your dreams were to your liking while you slept?"

I frowned, trying to recall my dreams. I vaguely remembered Kurrick's face... or had that been *before* I was asleep? I hummed in reply, my throat dry and coarse, "I must assume so, for I don't remember what they were... and I feel quite refreshed."

Yulia seemed pleased by this. "I'm glad to hear it, your majesty. Be well."

She curtseyed again, and took her leave.

Sirra-Lynn stalked over to take down my fluid bag. "Well, your majesty," Sirra began as she removed the tubes from my hand and checked the monitors with strict eyes. "How are you feeling?"

I swallowed the burn in my throat, "Well enough to walk... My legs feel rather stiff."

Kael flashed a penlight in my eyes and checked my pulse as he rumbled, "I am at least glad to see you're on your feet so soon, your majesty. I'd sensed that you might awaken this morning." He rubbed the stubble on his neck with a proud grin. "Dr. Treble was skeptical, but Infeciovoking is rarely wrong about such things."

Sirra huffed. "There was still a chance she wouldn't wake up, Dr. Treble. You *are* an old geezer, your senses could have been fading."

He flicked his white pupiled gaze at her. "Old geezer? Shouldn't such names be reserved for those who *look* the part? I should think Miranda would be better suited—"

"I heard that!" the voice of Miranda clipped as the elderly demon woman herself stomped inside with a tray of tonics and medicine. She gave a wrinkly scowl at Kael. "The number should count just as well as the face, I say." She placed the tray on the bed beside me, then flashed me a warm smile. "Good morning, my dear!" She cheerily cupped my face with her shriveled fingers and gave a gruff chuckle. "I'm so glad you've recovered enough to stand! But my goodness, you must be famished. Come, let's take your medicine and find you a meal."

Once I took the prescribed medication, two more figures strode into the room.

It was the scale-skinned Rochelle and the black-haired teenager, Lëtta. The young nurse changed the bedsheets while Rochelle handed me a white smock with a lavender floral print to wear instead of the open-backed clinic gown. I went behind a curtain in the corner to change into it. After I was in the new dress, I glanced at my reflection in the wall-mirror. The scar on my throat was ghastly and puckered… the redness was dulled, but it was not a flattering sight. In a sigh, I rewrapped Khol's gifted scarf around my neck to hide my shame.

I should have listened to Kurrick, I thought broodingly as I clutched the vine-box to my chest and stared at the jewelry glittering with purple gem-stones on either side of my hair. *He was wise to suspect her all this time…* my claws grew, pricking the leather case of the box. *And I was an idealistic fool…*

Sighing, I emerged from behind the curtain. With a painful swallow, and a burning voicebox, I announced, "I would like to dine in the markets. Willow has asked that I find her and Xavier there."

Everyone nodded their understanding. Kael and Miranda offered to take me there themselves, and the three of us stepped out to the halls, leaving the others in the clinic room.

Kael waved a hand in front of my scarf-hidden throat, rumbling, "I'm glad you're able to use your voice so well. The Shadowblood's Healing is quite marvelous, certainly. No shifter would have survived a cut such as that, let alone still have their voice afterward. It is a miracle, no doubt." He lowered his hand in a chuckle. "That scarf Khol gifted you, however, is more of a tragedy."

My throat burned dully as I gave a low whisper, "I rather like it… it was kind of him to knit it for me. My father once gave me a scarf like this when I was a girl, and…" The breath fell from my lips at the memory. And then I remembered that, painfully… my foster father was gone.

Kael's calm expression dripped into sorrow. His black cat ears grew, and his voice fell as we strode through the corridors. "I… am sorry… for what I've done to your father…"

My lion ear flicked in confusion. Then I realized what he'd meant. "Oh…" I whispered. "You speak of my *birth* father. I was quite young when you poisoned him. I'd only just met him."

Kael winced in shame. "It seems I cannot find many a soul I haven't wronged, can I…?"

I hummed dully, "I should think not… but in truth, I spoke of the man that *raised* me like a father. You were not the one behind Dream's death." My whisper dimmed. "That was the work of Macarius."

Kael's cat ears folded down farther. "Yet it was the poison *I* had infused in his blade that sealed Dream's fate… For which I am also… deeply sorry…" He hesitated. "But I've no right to apologize. Especially not to you, Ana. I hadn't known you were Adam's blood-daughter then, but I remember Dream and Crysa would bring you and your sister to visit us, to play with Caleb…" He sighed. "Those days seem so faint, after everything I've done…"

I exhaled a long, slow breath. "If I'm to be honest, I cannot forgive your actions. You are right to be ashamed by them."

He cast down his gaze.

"But you, yourself," I added softly, "I *can* forgive."

One of his cat ears perked up, puzzled. "What do you mean?"

"You weren't yourself after Cilia's death," I explained. "You were no longer Dr. Kael Treble, the royal surgeon of King Adam's court. You were a different being, a shell of a man consumed by grief and rage… such trauma can twist any of our mortal souls, if the wrong influences come to pull our strings for their personal gain. You were Macar's puppet. A hollow doll." Oddly, I found my lips tugging with a small smile. "But it is a warm sight indeed to see the real Kael Treble again."

His returning smile pursed into a flat line. "It is the strangest feeling. Although my memories continue to return, the years spent in anger are hazy. I was barely aware of my surroundings. Barely aware that I was still alive, even. Now that the mist has cleared as I looked around, it's hard to believe I wasn't a ghost—*less* than a ghost." He scratched his stubbled chin, troubled. "It's admittedly rather frightening to think I've spent the last five centuries in such a state… How had I not seen what was happening?"

I re-wrapped my scarf round my neck in a thoughtful hum. "How many times had you strayed from Macar's watch, during then?"

He took a moment to recall, then said, "None. He never left my side while we were trapped in Aspirre."

"And when was the first moment you began to doubt that what you were doing was right?"

"After he sent Claude and I to Tanderam Prison…" He cupped his mouth pensively. "After I met my descendant, Mikani." A smile washed over his features. "She reminded me of Cilia… it brought back many a memory of our earlier years together."

I nodded. "It is interesting how our true selves crack through the mask when the ones who forced it on our faces are absent. I wager Macarius was not pleased to hear you'd met someone who reminded you of joyful times?"

Kael grimaced. "Indeed not… In fact, he became more adamant to remind me of the horrifying times afterward."

I huffed. "I thought as much. I am glad your leave of him has seemed to bring more joyous days to you."

"—as am I," the voice of Cilia purred behind us. She strode beside us and circled an arm around Kael's waist as she took her place at his side, holding a silver platter of teacakes in front of him. "Claude and I are trying something new with our latest shipment of produce from overseas. We're seeking opinions. What do you think?"

Kael delightedly picked one up and took a bite. "Blackberry?" he asked.

She beamed. "Precisely."

"They're delicious, darling." He kissed her cheek.

I blinked as the white-pupiled couple shared cheerful laughter. *I certainly HAVE missed much while recovering,* I thought, *They look so… happy. As they used to be.*

Land's Blade, I even spied a few braids in Cilia's steel-grey locks. She looked like any young maiden with her blissful husband, despite the radiance of her pupils. It was such a drastic change from the last time I'd seen her.

To my other side, Miranda snorted. "Bloody younglings—you could never keep your sappy personal life out of the clinic, could you, Kael?"

Kael laughed. "Oh, now I'm a youngling again? What happened to agreeing that I was an old geezer? Have you remembered that you had wrinkles even when you were one of my nurses?"

I paused, gasping softly, "That's right…! I'd forgotten you both were colleagues here in this very palace back then."

Miranda muttered, "Oh yes. And it was no picnic to work under a young prodigy, I'll tell you what." The old woman slapped Kael's shoulder with a cackle. "But Bloods, I'm lucky I wasn't in the ballroom when *this* lunatic snapped. Bastard didn't leave me many survivors to treat after that. Not to mention, the replacement surgeon after him was a real arse. Gave us nurses Void for years before I died of old age."

Kael rubbed his chin. "Who replaced me?"

Miranda tossed a flippant hand. "Dr. Trasoul, the old hack. He'd been after your job for years, so he didn't hide his thrill when you went nuts."

They spoke more of their history as we stepped out to the open courtyard.

Much had *indeed* changed. The jungle overgrowth had been fully cleared away, I couldn't spot a single out-of-place vine or ivy on any columns or trees or statues or… were those *working* fountains? How had they gotten those up and running again so quickly? I suspected the Shadowblood may have used their Hallows of water to speed up the process. I would have to ask them later.

Along with the new landscaping, the courtyard was bustling with shifters. Some I recognized, but most were new faces I couldn't recall in the slightest.

As we strolled onward, we entered the construction site of what could only be the new markets. There were lumbermills and wooden beams, a plethora of building framework between pitched tents, merchants and cooks already selling their food and wares… I spotted a blacksmith's tent in the distance. My word, was that Henry teaching a group of apprentices how to use the forge? He was waving around his hook-hand in a gesture at his prospective students. And that wasn't the only blacksmith's tent, I noticed.

"Oh, it's Ana!" a boyish voice chimed happily from my left. The web-eared Khol practically danced over before he caught me in a heartfelt embrace, singing, "You're awake! And you found your scarf! Do you like it?"

I chuckled. "I love it. Thank you for the wonderful gift. It was a joy to see upon waking."

He clapped his hands in delight. "Oh, I'm so glad—!"

"What atrocity have you bestowed the queen with now?" Hecrûshou's gritty voice condemned next. The shark-demon stalked up behind his rotted comrade. Hecrûshou's Crystal trident was wrapped in a cloth and strapped to his back. His little Bindragon, Aahn, was curled around his scaled bicep as Hecrûshou folded his arms and cast Khol a disgusted grimace. "Look at that monstrosity. How is that fit for a royal throat?"

Khol pouted, "She said she loves it, thank you very much!"

Hecrûshou snorted and looked at me with white, glowing pupils. "Was your sight injured as well as your voice?"

I gave him a wry smile. "I rather like it. I think it's quite fetching."

Khol preened and flapped his webbed ears.

Hecrûshou rolled his eyes.

Then, as the wind swept through the markets, I saw a braid of long, ashen hair waft gently in the breeze.

Willow.

She stood with her back facing me under a lumbermill tent with her husband, who carried their baby as he assisted her in giving direction to the builders surrounding them. I started toward them, the demons staying behind to chat amongst themselves.

"… will need one structure here," Willow told the builders as she pointed to the blueprints spread over the table before them. "There is a large oak tree in that area, so do be sure to build around it carefully. But we'll need another three buildings in the eastern district as well. Then once that is finished, we'll need…" She quieted when she noticed the builders had stopped paying attention to her. They were looking behind her with open mouths. When she turned and spotted me, she gasped, "Ana! Thank Bloods, Kael was right about your waking today."

She asked the builders to take a short reprieve, and hurried over to me. Xavier followed at her heels, playfully trotting in zigzags as he carried their giggling wolf-eared son by the belly to pretend the pup was flying. There was a tiny, white-necked Songcrow following the boy. Was that his little messenger? The hatchling that hadn't even grown its feathers the last time I saw it?

The royal Death couple was dressed oddly formally, for being in a half constructed kingdom. Willow wore black, fine silks with long-lace sleeves hugging her arms down to her wrists. A sheer chiffon top-skirt ruffled in the breeze along with her pinned up, braided hair. She was dazzling with her many trinkets shimmering in the sunlight: there was her music watch hanging from her neck, her marriage-vines dangling from her brow, a pair of glittering earrings adorning her lobes, and, most magnificent of all, her silver crowns etched with skulls and decorated with precious gems and diamonds.

Xavier wore a similar crown under his tied-up locks. His long bangs were neatly groomed along with his hugging beard, and his marriage-stud gleamed from his left ear while his matching ring glinted from his left ring-finger. Even with the scar running down his clear white eye, he looked nothing short of regal and refined.

Even their son wore his own, tiny skull-crown in the same motif as his parents' headwear.

Those are new Death crowns, I observed. *They are nothing like the crowns of old…*

There must have been a jeweler in the markets, as well as the Blacksmiths. And, as I reached a hand to the engagement-vines clipped to my hair, I suspected Kurrick used the same jewelers for these.

Willow stopped before me and placed a hand on her hip. "Well, Sister Land? What do you think of your Grand Capital-In-Progress?"

I hushed, "It is wonderful… you and Xavier coordinated all this?"

Xavier popped up behind her with a pleased smile. "We did indeed. It was fair practice before we take on our new roles in Grim. Wasn't it, Lucas?" He hefted the baby against his chest so the pup could face me. Lucas's colorless eyes went wide at the sight of my golden curls.

I giggled and patted the boy's head between his wolf ears. "Well, if you've achieved this much progress in such a short time, I think you're ready to be acting rulers…" I paused. "How long *has* it been, exactly?"

Xavier scratched his neck and hummed, "Nearly five weeks."

My eyes bulged open. "*Five weeks?* I've been asleep for nearly a month? But that's… that's almost 50 days!"

Willow pursed her lips. "Kael said you were in a temporary coma. Either way, we couldn't leave your budding city unfortified while our enemies plan to invade sometime in the near future."

My mood dampened at the reminder. "That's right… Is there news of the children?"

Xavier bobbed their son as he murmured darkly, "None, as of yet… we've spoken with Ninumel, however. There's been no sign of Macarius and Fuérr. If Macarius intends to use Fuérr as bait to force Ninumel to lead him to the Pearl of Emerald, it's reasonable to assume Macar hasn't gained any Ocean Hallows yet. And assuming he's at least *near* Marincia's capital, we highly doubt he'll change course to the Blossom of Gold before his goal is met. Kael tells us Macarius is a methodical man—he isn't one to stray from his tightly-knit schedule unless he's given no other option."

Willow added, "In the meantime, Kurrick has called for reinforcement soldiers from your regents."

My brow rose in surprise. "Kurrick called Vanessa and Cayden? By his own volition?"

Willow shrugged. "He's made quite a lot of executive decisions this last month, believe it or not." She grinned. "And it's about Bloody time. He's been willfully abandoning his opinions since you first overtook Neverland, I was beginning to think he'd lost the ability to *have* any at all."

"As had I," Xavier chuckled as the baby reached for his beard and marveled at the thick hairs. "Suddenly he's quite involved in the city's resurrection. He's quite involved in *many* things, at that. Who would have thought?"

I smiled and reached for the dangling vines in my hair, still clutching the box with the centerpiece inside. "It is not as surprising as you think," I said. "It's simply... overdue."

Willow's expression warmed at my vines. But it fell when she glanced down at my attire—which was a simple smock with a lavender floral pattern, paired with Khol's gifted scarf.

"Shouldn't you be in your gown?" she asked.

I frowned. "Gown?"

She and Xavier exchanged a hesitant look. Then she questioned, "Have you not seen Kurrick since you awakened?"

I shook my head. "His note didn't say where to find him."

Xavier rubbed the back of his neck. "Er... I think I last saw him at the tailor's tent in the western district. We can take you there, if you like?"

"I would," I said. "Please, lead the way. I do wish to speak with him, if he has the time to spare."

Willow laughed as we strode westward, "Oh, he'll have the time. Believe you me. He's been leading the preparations for your waking all month."

As I followed them, I spied several familiar faces throughout the city. Our two winged Enlighteners, Herrin and Marian, were outside one of the fully constructed brick buildings speaking with what looked to be a group of scholars. They must have been more Enlighteners, like themselves.

There was also Yulia at a small teashop's outdoor, iron table. She was joined by Jimmy and a few others whom I suspected were the various Dreamcatchers the two had rescued during the war in Everland. Next door was a lively tavern where I saw Neal and Matthiel sharing a pint of ale.

Across the street was the rabbit-eared Bianca and her second-in-command Alchemist, Red, who were browsing an apothecary.

And sitting on the lip of a trickling, stone fountain was Alexander. With grown wolf ears, he watched Bianca from the apothecary's open door, giving an intense scowl as if waiting for some sort of opportunity to arise.

When Bianca lifted to her toes and tried in vain to reach a jar of herbs on the top shelf, Alex's ears perked. He quickly evoked his Land Hallows over the clay jar.

The jar gleamed with golden light, startling Bianca. The jar floated off the shelf and into her hands, causing her face to twist with bewilderment. When she seemed to realize what had happened, her gaze grew angry—and her head snapped to Alex outside by the fountain.

He gave a meek wave, coughing nervously. She grimaced and shoved the jar onto the nearest shelf and stalked out in a huff, Red hurrying after her. As she stormed away, Alex's ears dropped and his scowl returned.

In front of me, Xavier gave a sympathetic wince and stopped to meet his brother by the fountain. "I see you haven't made much progress winning her back?" he asked, bobbing Lucas from his shoulder.

Alexander's ears curled back. "No."

Willow took the baby from her husband and twisted her mouth. "Is it wise to follow her around so much? If Xavier did that, I would be driven mad."

Alex looked dumbfounded at her. "You would? Gods Bloody damn it!" He hit a fist against the fountain's stone lip—causing the stone to shoot upward around his hand when his Hallows activated on instinct. He gave a frustrated breath. "Why am I so terrible at this?"

Xavier used his own Hallows to smooth the stone back to normal and murmured, "You may simply be trying too hard, Alex… Just give her the space she needs. I'm sure she'll come around on her own."

Alex grumbled indignantly, hunching over.

"… still no sign of the witch after this long?" A familiar voice demanded from behind the fountain.

Kurrick…

My lion ears perked, thrill prickling as I left Willow and the twins to circle round the fountain.

Like a dream, Kurrick was there. He was dressed in a fine, silken doublet woven with gold and deep indigo embroidery, the high collar adorned with golden buttons and ranking pins. I staggered back at the sight. I couldn't remember the last time I'd seen Kurrick in such fine garments. It had been some time since I'd seen him in anything other than armor, in fact. What was the occasion? Or has he been dressing this way all month?

"I want her *found*, do you understand?" Kurrick growled testily to the soldier who cowered under him. "It is unacceptable that the traitor has been free this long! Find her and throw her in the dungeons—I intend to question her myself if I must, and…!"

A rust-haired woman with antlers suddenly ran up to him in a furious pant, holding up a large bouquet of orange carnations. "Are…" She puffed for air, as if she'd sprinted all the way here, "Are these acceptable, Sir Kurrick…?"

Kurrick inspected the bouquet with a strict gaze, then shook his head. And—to my great surprise—he softened his tone. "They are lovely, miss Jilla, but she prefers marigolds. They are her favorite. Please inform your Mistress to prepare those instead. I'm terribly sorry for the trouble."

She nodded and hurried off to comply.

Kurrick turned back to the soldier, assuming his harsher tone once again, "Keep searching! The jungles, the palace, the city, the coast, it matters not! I want her behind bars!"

The soldier saluted. "Y-yes, Sir Kurrick!"

"—Sir Kurrick!" a new man's voice piped. It was a thick man with blubbery cheeks who waddled over, looking rather sweaty and upset. "These damnable chimps are still trouncing about the vineyard! I can't find the Bloody Feral Control officer!"

Kurrick clicked his tongue. "He's likely still clearing the stables of feral snakes. You might find him there."

The man thanked Kurrick and waddled off to do just that.

When Kurrick noticed the soldier was still standing in front of him, he barked, "What are you still doing here? I told you to…!"

The soldier dropped to his knees in an incredibly low bow. It was meant for me.

Kurrick was befuddled by the action. In a frown, he turned to look at the fountain—and saw me.

"Ana!" He sprinted over, stumbling over a stray bucket that was left on the cobbled road. He kicked it aside and rushed toward me.

I chuckled. "You seem to be handling things well, Kurr—*ah!*"

He scooped me up and squeezed me to his chest, kissing my head and my cheek and finally catching my lips with a deep, lingering push. When he finally let me up for air, he set me back on my feet, but kept his arms circled around me.

"You're wearing your vines?" he asked with an elated smile.

I was still dizzy from all the attention, blearily reaching for the vines in my hair. "Of… Of course I am… You were worried I wouldn't?"

"Only slightly," he admitted in a blush. "There was a small chance you… wouldn't forgive me…"

"Forgive…?" My brow knitted desperately, trying to remember. "Oh. You mean for trying to fool me?" I shook my head, the vines wavering. "I knew you were only trying to protect me. There's nothing to forgive. Well, except for your *lateness* in giving me these." I touched one of my vines with a smile, then brushed an admiring hand over his silken doublet. "But I'm quite stumped on why you're wearing such a fine garb? What is the occasion?"

His laugh was spritely. "Our wedding."

I paused. My brain was slow to process that. "Our… but I…" I gawked at him. "*Today?*"

"I was waiting for you to wake," he said, rubbing his thick neck anxiously. "Is it too soon?"

"No, no, it's just… It's only…" I narrowed my gaze at him, suspicious. "You're acting so strange. Or… so *un*-strange? It's almost as if you're the *old* Kurrick again. It's baffling… I haven't seen you like this since we trained at the river."

Bloods, that was so long ago. But it was true. Kurrick had been unbearably cryptic and cold ever since the last day at the river. So many lifetimes ago… And now he was suddenly back?

"Kurrick," I hesitated. "What is happening? Where has this part of you been—and why is it suddenly back now? What's changed?"

He took my hand and cupped it to his scarred cheek. "Your *future* has changed, Ana… Now that Dream's vision has already come to pass, and you did *not* die…" He melted into my palm as if in a whimsical daze. "You are as safe as I can make you. Finally… Though, I feel as though I've… wasted the last three centuries. For that, I am sorry." He took my chin and stole my lips. "But I'll be damned if I'm wasting any more time. Now…" He cleared his throat, his tone finally gaining its familiar crunch. "Will you have me or won't you?"

I took hold of his arm and gave a swooning sigh. "I have waited far too long to hear that… Lead the way."

He beamed, and we strode forward arm in arm. I stole a glance over my shoulder, seeing that Willow and Xavier were chuckling after us in delight.

Alexander, however, had his mouth hanging open in disbelief.

"*Really?*" Alex fumed. He hit the stone fountain's lip furiously, the rocks shooting upward around his fist once again. He smeared a hand over his face and groaned in misery, "Seamstress help me… *Kurrick* is better at this than I am…"

Xavier snorted a laugh—and Alex punched his shoulder.

I chuckled, leaning against Kurrick as relief lifted my heavy soul after so, *so* long… and we strode through the city together.

Our city.

14

A ROYAL WEDDING

XAVIER

The royal wedding was the very image of peace and magnificence.

I stood next to Willow, looming behind the stone altar in the royal rose gardens on the palace grounds. Willow and I were officiating the union… or rather, *Willow* was officiating. I was merely here as a showpiece; a public display to show that Grim had both hands of support in the affair. For some ridiculous reason, if the King of Death was not present while the queen officiated the wedding of another Relic Bloodline, the public would assume I disagreed with the union—which I certainly didn't. I thought it was about damned time.

Ana was dressed in a beautiful, golden gown with short, lace sleeves and a satin ribbon tied around her throat to hide the scar. Marigolds and violets decorated the gown at the collar and hip, and her gilded crown had the same type of flowers laced between the curling metal hoops.

Kurrick was still in his fine silken doublet from this morning. I don't think I've seen him smile so wide as he connected Ana's vines with the amethyst centerpiece at her brow. He didn't even flinch when Ana pierced his ear with his marriage-stud, and kissed her fingers after she slipped on his gold ring.

I glanced at my wife. Willow herself glistened with regal beauty. But while Ana was the vision of warmth and sunlight, Willow was the vision of cool mists and cavern lights. Her new silver skull-crown was more effeminate than mine. The diamonds quivered where they hung at the tops of the wiry metal curls, shimmering in the light and casting colorful prisms. Her azure eyes welled as she dubbed the royal couple husband and wife.

As the crowd clapped and cheered—save for Alexander who had already helped himself to the open bar in the back and was stumbling over a stool—the king and queen strode arm-in-arm through the crowd to begin their first dance together. I quietly slipped out the kerchief from my breast-pocket and dabbed Willow's newly wettened cheeks.

She blushed, murmuring, "I'm sorry… I know it's silly, but I… I'm just so…"

"Happy?" I turned her chin to me. Stole her lips. "You're allowed to be. Besides…" My tune saddened. "It is far more cheerful to officiate weddings than reapings."

"Yes…" she agreed. "We've had more reapings than weddings of late, haven't we?"

"Such is the burden of the rulers of Death," I remarked. "It almost doesn't seem fair, does it?"

"No… it doesn't." she agreed. "I'm glad to be given as many opportunities for brighter events. I say we enjoy it while we can… especially since Yulia was kind enough to give us a short break from parenthood. I hope Lucas isn't giving her much trouble."

I grinned and scratched my bearded jaw. "I'm sure she can handle him. It's only *one* child this time—she looked after Alex and me, for Death's sake. Anyone who survives the likes of us can surely survive *half* of me."

She laughed and took my hand. "Let's hope *my* half balances yours out. Now come, let's enjoy the celebration and—"

"*Da'torr*," a thick voice called. I spotted my vassal, Nathaniel, wading through the crowd toward us. Behind him were two other vassals of mine: the winged Aiden and the scale-skinned Apson.

"*Da'torr*," Nathaniel grunted once he and Aiden stepped up to me. He threw a thick thumb over his shoulder. "Yer ship's ready for depart're, when ye be wantin' to leave. The other three vassals ar' packing up yer luggage as we be speakin'."

My heart sank. I'd nearly forgotten Willow and I had promised the Grimish council we'd return to the caverns. For our coronation. They'd given us leniency considering the Land Queen's recovery…

But now it was our duty to be present for *our* country.

Aiden's wings quivered anxiously in the wind. "You'd best leave soon, *Da'torr*… The council is not a patient bunch."

Apson added apologetically, "And I know from *my* experience as an old king's Hand that you do not wish to try the council members' patience…"

I nodded, rubbing Willow's knuckles before releasing her. "Very well…" I said. "We'll gather those who wish to join us. Please have the ship ready to set sail, Nathaniel."

Nathaniel saluted with a thick hand to his chest. "Aye, *Da'torr*."

The three left.

Willow and I gave solemn sighs.

"—*aaahhh…!*"

Alexander cried in pain from the back of the crowd. Heads turned as his screams worsened.

"Alex…?!" Panic split, my wolf ears growing as I started toward my brother with hurried steps, Willow close at my heels.

Alex clutched his head, falling to his knees and pushing his temples as if trying to squeeze his skull into oblivion. "*Rrgh…!* Get… out…! Get *out*…!"

—*Riiiiiiii…!*

A sharp ring whined in my eardrums suddenly, and I doubled over.

"Xavier?!" Willow crouched over me. There was a delayed, overlapping image with her movements.

Enjoying ourselves, are we…? Macarius's voice purred in my thoughts, the ringing intensifying as he chuckled. *What a lovely celebration… I'll be sure to congratulate the couple after our holiday in Marincia…*

His voice died into silence at last, and the ringing finally ebbed along with the pain in my temples.

"Xavier?" Willow asked again. She laid a concerned hand on my back. "What happened?"

"Vision feedback…" I panted. She helped me to my feet, and I saw Alex was being hauled up by a few men from the crowd. Alex found my gaze, and his stare sharpened furiously at me. I turned back to Willow. "Macarius was scrying on us again. To see what we were up to. He… he still plans to come for Land's Hallows… for Ana…" I cupped my face in a hard sigh. "But it sounds as if he still hasn't left Marincia, at the least… there's still time."

Willow's expression hardened, her fox ears growing. Then she let out a hard breath. "We've done all we can to secure the island. Kurrick and Ana have their soldiers here, and more are on their way. All we can do is… remain on course. Perhaps we'd best hurry and give you both your Death Hallows…?"

I nodded grimly.

Bloods, I was not looking forward to this…

GENEVIEVE

I watched from my hidden perch at the harbor as the Death Queen and King sailed off with their party.

At the boardwalk, the newly wedded Land Queen and King waved them off hand in hand.

She lives…

I released a hard breath as relief washed over me.

Thank the Gardener, she LIVES… I stared at my hand. *And yet… I was still granted Land's Blessings…*

Father had told me one could obtain a Relicblood's Hallows even if they weren't Crest Bearers. He told of a time that had been lost to historians for centuries, where the Bloodline of Sky had once been Skydragons, before a swallow had killed the old Relicblood in the eyes of their Relic and claimed his Hallows… But in those tales, Father was certain the challenger had to kill the ruler. Yet, I was given Land's Blessings, despite having failed to kill my queen. Perhaps one doesn't have to kill a Relicblood to acquire the Hallows? Perhaps it's simply a matter of spilling blood?

Still, my breaths shuddered.

Perhaps I, too, can live…?

MARINCIA

Yu'nn Quisette

15

LIKE MINDS

MACARIUS

SEVEN YEARS PRIOR

Slam!

I hit a furious fist on the wooden table, our plates and ale mugs clattering, drawing attention from the other patrons of this tavern in Neverland's capital city, Rosaria Grand.

"How could you lose her?" I demanded of Kael, my anger bursting. We'd regrouped after their infiltration of Grim's palace beneath this continent—but Kael had *not* delivered favorable news. "She was a child!"

Both Kael and Claude ducked their heads and pulled their cowls farther over their faces, hiding from the curious onlookers around us. Bloody idiots, why were they concerned? I'd given them illusions to disguise their matching black hair and yellow eyes. It was an obvious precaution, given how many Wanted sketches had been drawn of them. Though, I supposed I had to offer them some leniency. It had been only five days after their infiltration, yet the five realms seemed to find it a hot topic of discussion already. Still, their failure was not to be excused.

Kael's gritty voice chewed through clenched teeth as he kept his tone quiet. "A child, yes… but you forget, the princess is said to be Death's new incarnation. She had greater skill than I'd anticipated, for one so young. Not to mention, as Dream's granddaughter, she held *his* Hallows as well as Death's." He rubbed a contemplative finger under his nose, hesitating. "Though… something else called to my attention down there. Something I believe you'll find to your liking, Macar."

I leaked into my seat, hissing, "With these current circumstances, I *highly* doubt any news from you will be to my liking, Kael."

"There was a boy with the princess. Her betrothed. He had the most peculiar eyes… one clear and the other blue. It is a condition known as heterochromia, if I remember my studies correctly."

I rubbed my eyes behind my spectacles. "And this is relevant how?"

Kael's stubbled grin was wicked. "He bore the Crest of Nirus on his hand."

I stiffened.

Kael chuckled, entertained that he'd caught my attention. "It was the Shadowblood," he said. "I've no doubt. And you'll be pleased to know that I disposed of *him*, at the least."

I brushed calculating fingers over my lips. "If the Shadowblood was born again… then the cycle must have continued during our absence…" I flicked my gaze at Kael again. "And what of his brother?"

Claude, who'd been silent during this whole conversation, suddenly found his voice. "Uh—he's not a problem!"

I cocked an eyebrow at Kael's middle-aged descendant.

Claude's cat ears grew from under his cowl, and he coughed before amending, "I mean, uh… he doesn't have a brother. So, uh, nothing to worry about, right?"

I folded my arms. "Of course he has a brother. According to Dream, the Shadowblood and the Lightcaster have always been reincarnated as twins, with every cycle. Just as Accur and I had been in our era. The Shadowblood had even been born on the same day as us, but they'd been stillborn."

"Uh… yeah," Claude gave me a twitching smile. "That's what I meant. He, uh, *used* to have a brother. But he died at birth. So…" He lifted his hands in a shrug. "Not a problem."

I tilted my head thoughtfully. "Ah… Dream had said it was rare for any of us to survive our births at all, let alone *together*… I suppose this incarnation was no different."

Claude seemed to relax at that.

"*—has been five days since the attack on the Death Palace in Grim's caverns,*" fuzzed the strangely glowing 'vision-screen' in the corner.

I turned to stare at the device curiously. The shifters of this era seemed to obsess over these things and relied on them for their daily news. On the screen of light displayed the burnt remains of the palace ballroom in Grim. A reporter woman was off-screen and explaining the results of the aftermath. According to her, the assassin—who, amusingly, sat across from me—was still at large. Then the view changed to a different scene. This one showed a bearded man with sapphire eyes and a thick beard. The man clasped a strong hand over a young teen's shoulder, though the teen faced away from the screen.

"The Devouhs are still searching for their son along the surface canyons and—"

Claude suddenly jerked up and sprinted to the screen, punching buttons like a madman until the screen showed nothing but fizzling static.

The patrons around us shouted complaints, and Claude apologized, clearing his throat before returning to our table and dumping a handful of Mel beads between our mugs. A few of those beads clattered to the floor in soft *plink, plink, plinks!*

"Let's go," he ordered. "I'd rather not give anyone a chance to see either of our faces. On screen or in person."

My mouth twisted, suspicious, but Kael and I rose to follow him out to the streets among the flower-filled buildings and latticed archways. The fall-dressed foliage partially shaded us from the sunlight that split through their curling vines in golden rays. Bloods, how I missed the physical realm—how I missed the sun. I'd have to study this beauty more closely from now on, so I can weave its likeness inside Aspirre when I build our Sanctuary.

I grumbled to Claude, "You're being far too paranoid. My illusions are seamless. No one will recognize either of you, rest assured."

Claude only hunched his shoulder further, tugging on his cowl. "I just don't want to take any chances."

I rolled my eyes.

Then stopped short. An arching, iron gate caught my attention right beside me. It wasn't the gate itself that drew my shock, but the gold letters lining the archway:

The Lysandre Academy of Rosaria Grand.

"I don't believe it," I whispered, dumbfounded. I lifted my hood and adjusted my half-moon spectacles to better see the gilded letters. Yes, it *did* say the Lysandre Academy. The school my father founded—where *I* had been Headmaster, for a short time.

Kael was the first to notice I'd stopped. He grabbed Claude's arm to halt him as well.

"Macar?" Kael called. "What is…" He read the letters on the archway. His eyes widened. "Seamstress Cleanse me! Isn't that your school?"

I muttered, "It has my name on it, doesn't it?"

"But it's been five hundred years!" he protested. "How is it still standing?"

I cocked my head. "Why don't we find out?"

I pushed open the gates and… simply strolled inside. No one tried to stop me. No one tried to stop Kael or Claude from following behind me. I didn't recognize a single piece of architecture or landscaping, but my word, it was so serene... so *relaxing*. There were rosebushes in bloom despite the autumn season, there were trees of vibrant purples and crimsons, there were persimmon and pear trees scattered all throughout the grounds in pristine order... it was magnificent.

The schoolground's temple chimed the high-noon hour, the bells echoing across the town itself. Not moments after, various students and teachers bustled along the cobbled pathways, all wearing the same colored uniforms that I vaguely recognized from my time as Headmaster. The garbs were sleeker and more modern than I remembered. The girls wore long navy skirts and vests with gold blouses underneath while the boys wore similar navy vests and trousers, their throats decorated with gold neckties. Everything was so different, but somehow, the school's color scheme had remained the same. How peculiar.

As the crowd of students and professors passed our group, herds of them flicked their gazes at me—and did double-takes. Some professors even bumped into their students to gawk at me in length.

Strange, I thought, twisting toward Kael and Claude. No one paid either cat any attention. I was the sole subject of their shocked stares. *How curious. I wonder...*

I found the largest building across the courtyard and stalked over, the teeming students all making way for me as I entered without complication, Kael and Claude following at my heels.

Yes, I was correct in assuming this was the official building of the school administration. I walked along the hallway, noting the dozens of portraits lining the walls of previous Headmasters... no, Head*mistresses*. These were all women. Only two men were pictured at the very end of the hall.

And those two men were my father... and me.

I laughed. I hadn't aged a day since this portrait was taken. I'd been sealed away in Aspirre shortly after I'd become Headmaster. Time had passed right over me, physically. It was a small wonder I was acquiring so many stares here.

This could be most advantageous. If this school was still here, was it possible the other locations in the other realms were still there as well? I could easily claim to be a... a *descendant* of the original founder, surely, perhaps contest the Headmistress in charge that it was my birthright and inheritance to overtake the Academies...

Or I could kill her.

Yes, I liked that plan better. Less arduous... and I was itching for a rush after so many years of imprisonment.

I turned round to find the portrait of the current Headmistress. The gilded nameplate informed me her name was Vivianna Erestead.

I hummed. An antlered man wearing an administrator's pin on his breast pocket passed me, and I snagged his arm to query, "Where might I find Headmistress Erestead?"

The administrator blinked at me. He looked at the portrait of my face on the wall, then back at my physical face in front of him. He stammered. "Er, uh, I suppose... She is visiting her assistant, Lannyse Fenerral... erm, in Roaress Fenerral's manor?"

"And that is... where?"

He threw a hesitant thumb over his shoulder. "East... east campus..." He stole another glance at my portrait, then added uncertainly, "sir..."

My lips rolled into a smile. "Thank you. Kael, Claude," I called back to my comrades. "Let's go for a stroll."

They looked perplexed, but followed me outside nonetheless. It took less than twenty minutes to find the manor whose gate held the sign with silver letters that read, *House Fenerral*. I was met by a number of armored women holding spears and casting me wary glances.

The captain of the guard stepped in front to block my way, sizing me up. "Do you have an appointment with the Lady Fenerral?" she demanded.

I smiled. "I am here to request one, in fact. I'm sure she will accept."

The captain cocked an eyebrow. Then she reached up to touch her ear—which I noticed was hooked with one of those strange communicator devices this era held. She spoke off to the side, presumably to the receiver of the communicator whom I could neither see nor hear.

"Lady Fenerral," addressed the captain, "There is a man here to see you. He wishes to request an appointment."

Silence followed, the captain listening. Then she turned to me again and asked, "Name?"

I folded my arms behind my back. "Macarius Lysandre."

The captain's brow knitted terribly. She repeated the name through the communicator with uncertainty, then listened for a response. I assumed she'd received one since she cleared her throat and stepped aside.

"You've been permitted entry," she said. "Though, she is currently in meeting with Headmistress Erestead. Lady Fenerral has instructed you to wait for her in the second floor's parlor... the butler will direct you."

I nodded my thanks, stepping forward. Kael and Claude began to follow, but I stopped them with a hand. "Perhaps this would be best handled alone," I told them. "I suggest you both wait in the courtyard for me. I oughtn't be long. I merely wish to speak with this Headmistress for… negotiations." My smile curled with a chuckle.

They didn't protest as I entered the manor alone. The butler met me at the tall, arching doorway, then led me to the second floor's parlor. I sat on the leather chair, pretending to wait for the Lady Fenerral, until the butler took his leave.

Once he was gone, I evoked my Dream Hallows. My hands gleamed with an azure light as my figure split in two, creating a phantom copy of myself who took my place on the chair while he waited for the Lady Fenerral—and *I* slipped out of the parlor, evoking my illusion Hallows to disguise myself as the butler.

I made my way through the halls undetected. Many a servant passed me in the corridors, but none thought anything was amiss. I found the kitchens soon enough and plucked a cleaver from the cutlery block, tucking it into my cloak behind my disguise.

Now that my 'negotiating' tool was acquired, I leisurely strode through the manor, searching each door for the Headmistress.

"… how many times do I need to explain this?" a woman's voice clipped from the latest door I approached. "This is a *school,* Lannyse. This is no place for politics. Think of the children!"

I cracked the door open and peered inside.

Two women stood across a small coffee table, surrounded by many couches and chairs. It looked to be a master bedchamber. One of the women matched the Headmistress Erestead's portrait to the letter. The other woman was a viper shifter from the looks of it, with dark scales and angled eyes as sharp as her fangs—which I noticed dripped with venom as anger flared in her dangerous glare at the Headmistress. Though, she confined her fury to her gaze alone. The rest of her pristine features remained calm and collected… almost calculated.

This must be Lannyse Fenerral, I concluded.

Lady Fenerral kept her voice level. "The children are the very reason politics are imperative for their future. There is a rebellion in our midst, Vivianna. The extremists are touting lies of a lost Relicblood of Land. If they have their way and kill our beloved queen, what do you think will happen to our beautiful country? The other Relicbloods will attempt to dominate us again. They already dictate our queen's rule, they are waiting for their opportunity to control us."

My brow perked in surprise. *A sensible woman… I suppose there is hope for this world after all.*

The Headmistress rubbed her temples and dropped into one of the cushioned chairs, grabbing a glass of wine on the coffee table and taking a large glug. She drained it in one setting before exhaling heavily. "Lannyse… for the last time, you *must* stop this talk of the Relicbloods."

"Why?" she challenged and lowered into the chair across the table. She sat with an air of elegance while taking the second glass of wine, swirling the crimson liquid ponderously. "They gained their kingdoms through years of conquest. We hail them as heroes, the saviors who delivered us from the Time of Discord… yet we ignore the death and destruction they caused to get there. I only wish to teach the children the *true* history that the world choses to ignore—"

"If I hear you spouting your anti-Relicblood rhetoric on this campus again, I'm afraid I will have to ask you to leave our staff entirely." The Headmistress *clacked* her empty wine glass on the table and leaned forward threateningly. "Do *not* speak of your politics again. Do you understand me?"

Lannyse lifted her nose, staring at her wine with a hum. "Very well… as you wish, Headmistress…"

My smile was insatiable as I used my illusion Hallows to render myself invisible and slipped inside. I would have to time the seconds carefully since such a complex guise had a limited life span even for me. I brandished my cleaver and stalked toward the Headmistress.

Poor Lannyse, I lamented in silence, *You are a wise woman indeed, but I'm afraid I need a scapegoat at the moment. You will have the misfortune of taking the blame for the Headmistress's brutal…*

—Thmp!

The Headmistress collapsed. Her mouth began to foam as she shook there, curled on the floor and gagging for breath.

Lannyse gently set down her wineglass and reclined in her seat with a weary sigh. "Or, should I say *former* Headmistress?"

The Headmistress's tremors finally settled, her now lifeless body still curled on the carpet as the foam bubbled from her lips.

"Fool woman," Lannyse intoned dully. She circled a manicured finger over her temple, a yawn displaying her long fangs. "How an idiot like you became Headmistress will forever be a mystery. But not to worry. I will be sure that our impressionable youths are led down the proper path."

I stood over the Headmistress's limp body, my cleaver still raised like a dumbstruck fool. I was so shocked, I'd forgotten to keep my Hallows flowing, and my invisible guise dripped away three seconds too soon.

Lady Fenerral froze in her seat when I suddenly appeared out of thin air. Then she noticed my cleaver, which I'd lowered in my daze, and her shoulders relaxed.

"You're too late, I'm afraid," she said. Her hand primly lifted up her sharp, scaled chin. "If you were looking to steal the title, I'm afraid you'll have to go through me now."

I stared at her. For all my preparation, I found myself speechless.

She cocked her head in a hum. "Nothing to say, Macarius Lysandre? Has your five hundred years in a timeless purgatory rendered you mute?"

My gaze narrowed at her. Still, no response came to mind.

"You must be wondering how I know of your purgatory, mm?" She motioned at the chair behind the corpse. "Please, do make yourself comfortable. I am most intrigued to hear what became of the Lost Lysandre twin."

I hesitated, but found my legs lowering into the chair of their own accord, my gaze still affixed on Lady Fenerral's chillingly calm face. At last, I found my voice. "I suppose my short time as Headmaster was enough to keep my history records?"

Her smile had a strangely dangerous allure. "Indeed. Though, the mystery behind your disappearance after the Land King's assassination is discussed quite fervently among the history professors here. It's an enticing conundrum, you see. There are thousands of theories out there."

I cocked an eyebrow. "And how many have theorized my purgatory in Aspirre, exactly?"

"Only me," she said and reached behind her chair to pull out a different, unopened bottle of wine. She collected two new glasses from the table's undercarriage and poured each of us a glass. I didn't touch mine until she pinched the stem of *her* glass and took a sip, demonstrating that this bottle was *not* poisoned.

When I finally deigned to drink from my glass, Lannyse continued, "I've studied your biography extensively. What intrigues me most is your constant mention of your friendship with the King of Dreams. You had detailed notes of how he was wont to vanish into Aspirre, physically and spiritually, out of thin air, and pop back into our reality at will. My theory was that you somehow convinced the King of Dreams to bring you into Aspirre so you may live a prolonged life… how accurate was I?"

I grimaced. "Partially. There was no convincing Dream of anything. He *trapped* me there for five centuries. I only escaped that timeless prison weeks ago when his sealing Evocation wore off."

Her head cocked. "Curious… why would he trap you?"

"I may have given him quite a fright." I couldn't help my wicked chuckle at the memory. "I was the one to orchestrate the Land King's death, after all… and I had some fun along the way, as I see you're quite familiar with yourself." I kicked the corpse's boot. "Though, my methods were far… messier." I flipped my cleaver casually.

Her lips rolled into a smile. "This was one of my cleaner projects, I admit… Now. Since you were planning to assassinate the Headmistress, and *I* am now Headmistress… do you plan to assassinate me, Macarius Lysandre?"

I set down my wine and tapped a finger over the leather chair's arm, thinking. I frowned at the corpse at my feet.

"I have another idea." I declared, waving my cleaver at the body. "Why don't I dispose of *her*…" I grinned wide, my fangs displaying hungrily as I cast this viciously beautiful woman an admiring leer. "And you become the Lady Lysandre?"

She paused. Then gave a dark chuckle. "Well. I suppose I've already made myself a widow some years ago…" She leaned forward, purposefully exposing her gown's open neckline. "And you seem like a man after my own heart, by the sound of it…"

I smiled, a strange, pleasant flutter meeting my chest that I'd never felt before. "My thoughts precisely."

PRESENT DAY

Genevieve ran her blade over the golden-haired lioness's throat. Tears welled and blurred her vision, a silent scream raging in her heart, mourning her queen yet rejoicing at the safety of the world's future as her soul filled with power she'd never known…

My vision dissolved with a smile.

Lannyse's sharp face came into view in front of me again, our hands still intertwined so I could use her as a medium to check on our daughter's progress on the islands.

"Genevieve has done it," I announced delightedly. My scaled fingers squeezed her hands tenderly. "She has gained Land's Hallows."

Lannyse sighed with relief. "Then she must be in hiding. If our calls aren't getting through, she must be in a precarious situation indeed."

"Then best we complete *our* mission here and rescue her," I hummed, rising from my chair. I strode to the door to leave our private cabin.

Lannyse followed at my side and slid her arm over mine. She wrapped her fur cloak tighter around her shoulders and rubbed her now swollen belly. Our son had grown over the month in there, so much that there was no hiding that my wife was with child.

It was strange and glorious all at once, to think that I would be a blood-father. The child I'd apparently given Cilia so long ago never gave me such a thrill.

And such a fright.

What if I failed to stop the End? What if everything I've worked for was meaningless—what if our fate was inevitable…?

It won't be, I decided, searching through my Third Eye to see the one, single vision that still held a future. *I will force the timeline toward success… by any means.*

Lannyse and I stepped out to the snow-covered deck, the bitter cold stinging the scales on my cheeks. The watery horizon was littered with tumbling snowfall, the glaciers and cityscape lining the distance with beautiful Heliogems full of rich, glowing colors of ruby, amber, violet and jade.

Lannyse's lips pulled into a thin, grimacing line. "It seems we're within docking range… and judging by the number of ships lined up in waiting, I suspect they are searching each vessel for the little prince."

I patted her hand with a chuckle. "Not to worry, my love. We now have a *new* means of transportation… come. Let us collect the children."

We entered the ship's front cabins and opened the metal door leading to the brig. The hinges squealed heavily, and as we descended the spiraling staircase, our footfalls echoed over the metal steps.

Our three prisoners were in their respective cells. They all huddled against the wall when Lannyse and I entered, watching us like feral sheep facing gluttonous wolves.

I reached into my cloak's hidden pocket and pulled out the velvet sack which held the Orbs of Azure. I singled out one specific Orb—the Orb of Present—and gave a fang-filled smile.

"Come along children." I mentally tapped into the Orb's powers, and it began to gleam in my hand. "We're embarking on a trip."

The Orb flashed all around us—and the ship vanished.

KURN

"Where did they go?!" I demanded, my breathy voice echoing a startled squeak in the brig as I hobbled out of the large hole in the floorboards. "They just popped away out of thin air!"

Clover gave a screeching caw as the crow flapped down to me, his neck feathers flaring as he bounced his beak up and down.

"Something feels weird…!" Clover hollered. He ruffled his wings in a shiver. "I don't see Oliver, but… but I *feel* him—through our Bond! I think he's still here…!" He swept his beak back and forth, frantic now. "They're moving fast, we got to hurry!" He lowered his wing to me. "Come on! We got to follow them!"

I hesitated, "I don't rightly understand what you're on about, Clover, but I suppose Ringëd always *did* say to trust a messenger's Bond with their Reaper." I scurried back into the hole in the floorboards and clamped onto the scythe-sphere necklace Milann had entrusted to me moments before those snake shifters came down here. The little owl had told her to give me her weapon. I presumed it had something to do with the future. I've worked with Ringëd and his strange visions long enough to know *not* to question the methods of a Seer.

But I was running low on power for my nanites. I wasn't sure how long I could make myself light enough for Clover to carry my weight without recharging and…

Something caught my eye, and I gasped. There was a communicator on the floorboards, where that viper woman must have dropped it before they popped out of the physical plane!

Gripping Milann's scythe necklace with my teeth, I scurried to the communicator and pressed my paws against its silvery surface. The device thrummed as the nanites in my blood sucked the power from the com and recharged themselves as much as they could manage. It wasn't much, but I suspected it would be enough to get us where we needed to go.

I hurriedly climbed onto Clover's back, activating my nanites to make me levitate slightly and take off some of my weight for the crow.

"Tally ho!" I huffed, and we took flight, speeding out of the open brig and hustling over the glacier's icy lands.

16

FOR THE CHILDREN

MYRA

I walked down the ramp onto the snow-dressed docks of Marincia's capital, *Yu'nn Quisette*.

With my alabaster cowl ruffling in the sharp wind, I took a shivering, fogged breath and patted the Storagecoffin that hid in my cloak's inside pocket.

"Well, Serdin," I whispered, drawing in a breath. My husband's Songcrow, Locke, gave a melancholy whistle from my shoulder. He pushed his beak against my cheek, and I leaned into the crow, stroking his neck feathers lovingly. "We've a granddaughter to retrieve, haven't we?"

Locke shook himself over my shoulder, singing a deep tune and shifting his determined glare ahead.

I did likewise, then stepped onto the snowy dock—

"*Plann!*" A grating voice barked in Marincian. They had ordered me to halt.

I peeked up from under my cowl and saw a scale-skinned, web-eared man clad in jade armor glaring at me while pointing a trident at my face.

"<We are inspecting all ships that enter port!>" he said in Marincian. "<Gather the rest of your crew out here where we can see them!>" He jerked his head over a shoulder, gesturing to the cluster of soldiers armed and ready with tridents and lances of their own.

I sighed. Then lifted my hood to show my azure locks and blue eyes.

The commanding soldier staggered back, along with his squad of Wavecrashers. He stammered in his watery language, "<D… Dream Princess…? I-I mean Death Queen Myra…?>"

"<My daughter is queen now,>" I corrected in his tongue. Locke whistled his impatience at the man. "<If you must search the ship, do so. The man you

seek is a Decepiovoker—finding an illusionist of his caliber can prove to be difficult.>"

Of course, came the unsettling afterthought, *I would be surprised if Macarius didn't simply slip through their watch by bringing the hostages into Aspirre using the Orbs of Azure...*

I sighed, deciding there was nothing to do about it since he may have already done so, but it was best not to add to this soldier's stress. Instead, I politely said, "<You may carry on, Sir... We'll not disrupt your work.>"

"<—but I suggest working quickly,>" Dalminia clipped behind me.

She and her winged husband, Roji, stomped down the ramp beside me. Dalminia folded her scaled arms. "<I have an appointment with my brother and I would rather not be tardy, thank you.>"

The soldier's webbed ears dropped along with his jaw. He quickly jerked his trident away from my face and took a knee, gasping, "<Your Highness...! A-a-a thousand pardons, my lady...!>" He swallowed meekly. "<b-b-but... as Her Highness Dream made clear... we... we're looking for an illusionist...>" He rubbed his neck. "<Is... is there any way you could, er... provide *proof* of your... erm... identity...?>"

Beside her, Roji snorted—then plucked one of his scarlet feathers from his scalp and handed it to the soldier.

The man's face scrunched, baffled. "<What is this supposed to—*ah!*>"

The feather *zapped* apart in a thousand scarlet bolts of lightning, sparking in the man's fingers and causing his fin-like hair to stand on end. The electric bolt then shot back onto Roji's scalp before reforming itself as a scarlet feather once more.

The soldier stood gaping at Roji, his scaled fingers still twitching slightly from being shocked.

Roji grinned. "<Sky reincarnate here. Lightning hair. I'd like to see a Decepiovoker do *that.*>"

The soldier attempted to smooth back his frazzled hair-fins, grumbling, "<Yes... I would only expect the soul of Sky to be so frivolous in such dire times...>" His expression softened at Dalminia. "<My apologies, Your Highness. The king gave word of your imminent arrival, so we have your guards waiting for you by the royal coaches. Please allow them to escort your party to the palace... it is for your protection.>"

Dalminia nodded. "<Thank you, Sir. And I'm loath to inform you, but you have quite a large workload ahead. We've brought many ships for you to inspect.>" She pointed to the flurrying clouds overhead, where Roji's fleet of battle-Airships speckled the sky. "<They are reinforcement troops from Culatia, to help with your search and defenses.>"

The soldier's webbed ears flapped down, as if daunted, but he quickly resumed a dutiful tone. "<Yes, your Highness Ocean...>"

Roji laughed and nudged the soldier in the ribs. "<She's the Sky Queen now, pal. Better get used to calling her 'Majesty Sky', eh?>" He patted the annoyed man's shoulder. "<And don't worry about searching the Airships. My Stormchasers are inspecting those at the station.>" Roji twisted back and whistled. "<Come on, kids! Time to go meet your Uncle Ninumel!>"

Their two scale-skinned, winged daughters barreled onto the boardwalk with thrilled giggles, hopping in the snow and leaving prints as the family headed for the awaiting hover-coach.

I exhaled a shivering breath, drew my cowl over my face again, and stepped after them—

"Oi! Roji!" the voice of Zyl called from the ship's deck. Zyl herself, resurrected by Lilli earlier this week, was dressed in a heavier coat than I wore, her puffy hood hiding her scarlet, feathered hair and gloves warming her hands. She spread her wings and quickly flapped down to the boardwalk to chase after her brother, sharply jabbering to him in the Culatian tongue.

Then Zyl's cat-eared, blue-winged friend, El, came down the ramp beside Octavius, followed by Lilli and Jaq, then Ringëd and Mikani...

They all nodded as they passed me, climbing into their own hover-coaches.

The last to step onto the boardwalk was my rust-haired mother. As she carried my baby brother, Eryn, against her hip, I noticed her fox ears were draped down the sides of her neck solemnly. And like me, she wore all white, blending with the icy terrain around us.

It was the color of mourning.

Anger simmered at the hue, my fox ears growing. I hated having to wear it... hated that it had come to this. I'd chosen a life of mortality—*with* Serdin. We were meant to grow old together, not be separated by a blood-lusting, Gods damned *demon* and...

Tears stung at the reminder. I'd Seen the vision of his death when it happened. That *beast* had murdered him... and eaten his soul. All I had left of Serdin was his empty vessel and... and Locke.

I stroked Locke's wings from my shoulder, the ghostly pain swelling again, and the Songcrow rested his beak on my head to comfort me.

My mother came down the ramp to meet me. Her solemn features didn't seem any brighter than mine, I noticed.

Serdin wasn't the only one to fall in Aldamstria. My father, Dream, was lost as well. I hadn't seen much of my father since I came to live with Serdin in the physical plane, but... it was absurd to imagine a world where the two-thousand-year-old king wasn't waiting in the background to offer his wisdom—that I, the daughter who chose a life of mortality, outlived the man who lived outside of time.

It was just so ludicrous… and hardly fair.

Mother stepped beside me, hefting Eryn as the azure-haired boy played with the fur cowl ruffling against his cheeks. We strode side by side as we made our way toward our designated coach. Atop the buggy, silver flags wafted in the chilled wind. They were embroidered with Marincia's royal emblem: a crowned, emerald Ocean mark. Frostdragons were harnessed to the hovering vehicle, and they shook their furry heads, freeing their coats of the loose snowfall, and chuffed idly as they waited for us.

This wasn't my first time strolling through the enchanting city of Yu'nn Quisette, but this icy realm never ceased to steal my breath. The glaciers lining the horizon shimmered like glass and reflected the wavering green aurora lights that ribboned through the dark sky. The rounded buildings and seashell mosaics were always a sight to behold, ice sculptures standing proud and magnificent while fish-tailed shifters lounged in the hotspring pools and curling streams that split through the city.

I climbed into our awaiting coach, Locke ducking his head from my shoulder to avoid the doorframe.

Mother climbed in behind me with Baby Eryn, the fox eared kit marveling at the snowy sights outside as his azure tail curled around his little waist. Mother was quiet for a time, but when the Frostdragons pulled our coach forward, she cleared her throat.

"Has there been word from Willow?" She asked.

I hummed low, my tone as dry as my spirit. "Yes… She says Ana is awake and well. It seems the Shadowblood's Healing is something to behold…" I paused, a small bubble of cheer melting a hole in the thick layer of grief. "I hear she and Kurrick have finally wedded… I'm glad that my sister, at least, is finding good fortune…"

Mother sighed and stroked baby Eryn's azure curls absently. "Fortune seems to flee from our family as of late… I suppose all we can do is cherish the few moments that catch it."

I nodded, exhaling a long breath and fogging the window. Locke fluffed his feathers and squatted lower over my shoulder, leaning into my head. It brought a small glimmer of cheer.

We arrived at the palace's frosted courtyard at last, and just as we climbed out of the coach—

"Crysalette!" a woman's heavily accented voice called to my mother.

It was Queen Veyazelle. She was hurrying through the courtyard toward us, King Ninumel trotting in the snow at her heels. Veyazelle swept to my mother and wrapped her arms around her, catching baby Eryn in the embrace as well.

"Zank yuu for coming…!" she cried in a thick Marincian accent. She kissed Mother's cheeks, and did the same for baby Eryn in her hold. "And yuu had ze baby…! Artizt zink me, he eez zo big…!" Her cheer fell suddenly, and her webbed ears folded. "Have yuu… heard from my Fuérr…?"

My mother shook her head. "Not yet. But we will find him, Veya."

I stepped beside my mother with Locke, a growl slipping from my throat, "We'll find *all* the children. My granddaughter went after them and I intend to see her safe just as well."

"—Along with my *reckless* son!" Lilli huffed behind me. She and Jaq had stepped out of their own coach and joined us. Lilli's bat wings gave a sharp flap as she grumbled, "That boy is in for a harsh reprimanding when we retrieve him."

Jaq gripped his wife's shoulder, grunting assuredly, "And we *will* retrieve him. Along with the others."

Veyazelle loosened a hollow sigh of hope. "Rin praize yuu all… Pleaze, come inzide where it eez warm. We can dizcuz planz over a fire."

Our party followed her and Ninumel through the courtyard, their boots crunching over the snow and leaving a wide path of prints as they headed for the palace.

I lagged behind them all, casting Locke a dreary gaze. I drew in a tight breath. My hand absently touched the hidden pocket of my cloak, feeling the edges of Serdin's Storagecoffin under my shivering fingers.

"Serdin…" I whispered, letting the swell of pain in my chest boil into angry determination. "Wish me luck, darling…"

I stormed inside after the others.

My azure-glowing hands hovered over the crystal ball Veyazelle had fetched for me.

I sat on the carpeted floor of the royal library, my legs tucked delicately under me. My stance unintentionally mimicked Ringëd's across from me as he waved his hands over his own crystal ball that Veyazelle had given *him*.

My Mother sat behind me on one of the many couches surrounding the royal library's crackling hearth. Roji and Dalminia were here of course, but without their daughters. The girls were being seen to by Princess Zyl, along with baby Eryn.

Joining us were Jaq and Lilli on their own separate couch while Mikani, El and Octavius sat on the floor to watch Ringëd and me work our prophetic Hallows over the crystal balls.

Ninumel and Veya refused to sit. They watched our orbs gleam and flit with images of various scenes—some from the eyes of the children, and some from the eyes of their captors.

Ringëd's visions, however, had a far *lower* vantage than any of mine. His view was limited to ground-level objects and floorboards on a ship, as if he were looking through the eyes of a rodent.

Ninumel's emerald brow knitted skeptically at Ringëd, muttering in Marincian, "<Why is your vision so… little? It's practically on the ground.>"

Ringëd answered in the same language, "<My best medium is through my pet ferret. He's pretty much ground-level.>"

Ninumel's baffled looked only worsened. "<A ferret?>"

Veyazelle murmured with a hand to her lips. "<It looks as if they're still on a ship?>"

Ringëd grimaced. "<No telling at this point. I'm better at *past* visions, so this is the best I can do right now.>"

I hummed, Locke fluttering from my shoulder as I considered, "<They may have already docked, keep in mind… wait." I tensed, an image of scaled hands finally manifesting within *my* orb. "<I've got him…!>"

The terrain was a white landscape.

The crunch of snow could be heard beneath my narrator's feet, and many prints littered the powder as their entourage marched forward. A body of water waited at the tundra's lip with glaciers lining the horizon. But in that water bobbed a vehicle I didn't recognize. It was sleek and bulbous with copper walls and round, double-reinforced windows. A pair of propellers were rigged to the back while electric lamps brightened the front. It looked large enough to fit two handfuls of people.

My narrator knew precisely what it was—he had requested its creation from his students here in Yu'nn Quisette. They assured him it was ready to dive into the depths of the ocean and carry his crew within.

Now that he saw it in person, he was quite pleased with the results. There were no visible gears or springs to be seen, so he assumed those must have been hidden inside the machine itself—

A whining ring split through his eardrums. He doubled over, clutching his throbbing temples and gritting his teeth in pain… Was he seeing double?

He lifted his shaking hands to inspect them. Yes, there was a slight delay with the action. An echo of images. Accur once mentioned a phenomenon like this, hadn't he?

Accur? I thought with a frown as I continued to watch through Macarius's eyes. *What phenomenon does he speak of?*

—I speak of an opposing Seer scrying through your eyes, a foreign thought answered suddenly, making me jump in fright.

Fascinating… he purred in my thoughts through the vision. *Even the Shadowblood hasn't discovered how to scry on me. I wonder who could be strong enough to break through my prophetic defenses?*

I went rigid.

The narrator hummed. *Let's find out, shall we?*

The machine in the icy water disappeared from the crystal's view, puffing away like smoke. In its place, blackness filled the crystal, like ink swirling in water… until new images grew within. Now, inside the ball was a panoramic scene depicting… all of *us*, surrounding the orb. As if the orb itself were looking at us.

Is that little Myra I See? the voice questioned in my thoughts, my heart shocked alive. *And with the other royals, are you?*

An audible chuckle sounded from the orb, and the voice of Macarius rumbled aloud from the crystal, "Do tell Ninumel that his son wishes him well… but we won't be needing the king for this endeavor any longer. I've acquired *other* incentive for our little prince." His laughter curdled. "The other children say 'hello'."

—He cut off his Hallows, and the crystal ball went blank.

I shook to my feet, fox ears growing. Locke screeched and whistled furiously from my shoulder.

"He… he *Saw* me…" I whispered in a shiver, my skin crawling at the thought. I flicked my gaze to Ninumel, my teeth sharpening. "We must leave! He's heading to the Pearl of Emerald as we speak…!"

17

FROZEN DEPTHS

KURN

Kshhh!

Hissing steam sprayed behind me from the ship's intricate pipework on the ceiling, which was my chosen place of hiding.

Poorly chosen, I admitted, but there were few places on this tiny, metal vessel where I could traverse the cabins undetected. I had to be careful. We were inside enemy lines—and these bipedal foes were giants compared to me.

My teeth kept a firm grip on Milann's scythe-sphere necklace. The metal chain tasted salty on my tongue. The girl had slipped it to me when the children's captors weren't looking. She'd tasked me with keeping it safe until the 'right time' came. I hadn't a clue when the 'right time' would be, but she assured me that Oliver would give me some sort of signal… whatever that would be.

But first I had to *find* the children.

I peered over the pipe and observed the handfuls of crew members below. Few words were shared amongst this eerily quiet crew. They would receive orders on occasion from their communicators, but otherwise they were silent, only their footfalls ringing through the ship.

"DANGER DETECTED," blared the female voice from my thoughts, the nanites whirring in my blood as her pleasant voice said, *"CAUTION IS ADVISED."*

My round ears flattened, and I set down Milann's necklace to mutter, "Your software calendar must be out of date. We've been in enemy territory for days."

"KURN WAS NOT IN IMMIDIATE DANGER HIMSELF," she justified. *"HIGHER LEVELS OF ADRENALINE DETECTED TODAY. PRECAUTIONARY WARNING: ONE WRONG MOVE AND TONIGHT'S DINNER WILL BE FERRET STEW WITH A SIDE OF KURN LEGS."*

I grimaced. "Thank you for that lovely imagery…"

Pull yourself together, Kurn, I chided myself and scooped up Milann's necklace with my teeth again. *The children are counting on their emperor. A ruler does not let his people suffer because of his cowardice.*

My round ears folded in a frightened shiver as I nervously scurried onward—

Chuf-chuf-chuf!

The pipes chugged and rumbled under my paws menacingly, and I yelped, scrambling onto a different network of pipes—

Kshhh!

Another spray of vapor hissed in front of my long nose, so close that I could smell the brassy scent of the water within, and I squealed in terror before leaping off the pipe and clung to a third one that wove beneath me along this ship's cramped ceiling.

"DANGER DETECTED," the nanite's voice chimed in my thoughts. *"SUGGESTED ACTION: GET OFF THE DAMNED CEILING."*

"Ah 'unt ha' a'her e'e hoo hi!" I growled with my mouth clamped tight over the necklace. I was trying to say *I don't have anywhere else to hide,* but given my limited timeframe, I decided it wasn't worth the effort to correct. I was glad Clover had stayed outside to find help, at least. If *I* had trouble finding a suitable hiding place in this miniature ship, Clover certainly would have been captured by now.

My claws gripped the pipe tighter, and I carefully followed the network across the main cabin. I peered at the small, circular windows which displayed nothing but blackness and rolling bubbles as our metal vessel chugged farther into the dark depths of the ocean. The walls creaked and groaned hauntingly, and I saw a few Seadragons slither around out there, their whiskers wavering in rhythmic curls.

Keeping my teeth clamped on the necklace, I scampered along the pipes, searching numerous tiny rooms in hopes of finding the children. The pipes dipped and curved around the vessel, twisting this way and that like a confounding maze. I hopped down three series of paths, crawled over the wall leading to the front cabin—and spotted my quarries.

Little Prince Fuérr was chained at the sharp cornered front of the cabin below the bow of the ship. He was facing that cornered wall, which was made of double-reinforced glass from floor to ceiling, displaying the watery depths of the ocean outside as the ship's rotating lamps scanned the terrain.

The helm was in this cabin, looking like a copper hourglass as a scaled crew member piloted the vessel.

Behind him were Oliver and Milann, both in shackles and chained to the back wall.

And guarding them was the scarlet-and-azure haired cobra himself.

Fuérr pointed eastward at the window, croaking hoarsely in Marincian as the pilot steered the ship in that direction. The little prince peered over his shoulder at Oliver and Milann.

The pied cobra patted Oliver's feathered hair—then a spark of electricity zapped from his fingers threateningly, pulling Oliver's feathers straight up from the static.

Fuérr's webbed ears folded in panic and he snapped his head toward the windowed walls again, continuing his directions with a tighter voice.

My teeth ground against Milann's necklace angrily. *Bastard.*

Milann's gaze drifted upward. She spotted me. My ears perked, wondering if this was the time to return her scythe-necklace, but she subtly shook her sheep-horned head.

I grumbled. More waiting, then. I laid on my long belly, consigning myself to simply watching them as Fuérr led their ship deeper into the dark waters.

MILANN

The ship bobbed violently as we finally popped up from the water inside a glacier's icy cave. The two snake shifters had their guards haul Fuérr, Oliver and me out of the ship, following Fuérr's lead into the ice cave.

Wow… it's so pretty… I couldn't help but stare at the sparkly walls. There were glowy gems in all kinds of bright colors that painted the ice with sleek and shiny washes and—

Not the time, Milann!

I wriggled my shackled wrists behind my back, the chains noisy in this echoy tunnel. I gritted my teeth and glared at the guards surrounding Oliver and me. They had pointy spears aimed at us as we followed the snake shifters through the cave. The man with red-and-blue patched hair had one hand clasped on Fuérr's shoulder up ahead.

Fuérr was still crying, but he looked like he was trying not to shake as much. His webbed ears were glued to his jaw, but he held his chin up and walked on anyway, rubbing his eyes with a sniff. He must have been thinking about the plan Oliver told us to follow. It was the only plan we had, so Fuérr could only pin his hopes on that future.

I flicked a sideways look at Oliver next to me. His chestnut wings were shivering from the cold, rattling the chains keeping them closed.

Wait for Kurn. That's what Oliver said to do when we got to the cave. I gave the ferret my scythe-necklace before we left our cell on the old ship. Oliver said it was Kurn's job to bring it to me at the Ocean Relic.

I scrunched up my nose at Oliver and sighed, my breath fogging in the cold. *Either Oliver's right, or we're all dead after this.* My teeth started chattering, but not just from the cold.

We were getting closer to the end of the cave where a wide opening waited with more of those pretty, glowy gems. The closer we got, the faster my heart pounded in my grown sheep ears, and my head sank.

Fuérr led us into the opening. The domed ceiling was huge and filled with spikey icicles aimed down at our heads, a cold fog misting over them and making the colorful light-gems bloom all over the place. There were upside-down icicles on the floor, too, but these ones had holes in them, and they looked hollow.

I stopped short when I saw the giant, humongous clam made of ice right in the center of the cave.

I gasped, "That thing's as big as a *house!*"

Oliver grumbled in a shiver next to me. "Y-y-y-yeah… the R-Relics-s-s tend t-to be big-g-g…" He frowned, his chained-up wings tightening on his back as he added, "W-well, exc-c-cept for the Orbs-s-s of Az-zure…"

Orbs of Azure… Those were the glittery crystal balls—the ones that the weird-haired snake shifter used to bring us into that black void. If those were Relics, why did *he* have them?

The snake man shoved Fuérr in front of the giant ice-clam, making the little prince stumble on all fours.

"Give the Pearl its Call," the snake demanded and raised a scaled hand—which burst into a tangle of zapping lightning, which he aimed at Oliver and me. "And I advise against giving a *fake* Call."

The guards surrounding us brought their spears closer to us, making Oliver and me touch backs nervously. Those metal tips looked *real* sharp.

Fuérr's webbed ears flicked in a panic, and he swallowed hard before pushing to his feet. He raised shaking, green-glowing hands, and…

Started dancing?

I thought it was weird at first, his movements wobbly and hurried yet still fluid and mesmerizing, but after he waved his glowing hands in the air for several minutes, the giant clam suddenly vibrated and *cracked* apart at the seam. Fog spilled out as it groaned all the way open.

Inside the icy clam was a huge, sparkly-green pearl. It floated on a clear pool of water, where the cold fog licked over it like white smoke.

The Pearl of Emerald, I realized in wonder. My old parents used to read me stories about this—I Saw drawings of it in old fairy tale books when I was little.

Fuérr continued his dancing, his glowing hands streaking and waving in circles, which made the pool of water under the Pearl ripple and churn chaotically. Then the water swirled *into* the hole-filled icicles on the floor, making them whistle with pretty, flute-like music. The faster the water spiraled inside, the louder the music got—and the faster the Pearl of Emerald spun over the water in the clam. It started to glow, brighter and brighter, and the whole cave started to rumble under my feet.

Some of the icicles started breaking off the ceiling and hurtled down around us. I yelped in a flinch, but Fuérr quickly used his magic to grab the ice out of the air and made them swirl around in a sparkling snowstorm.

The snake man started laughing. Then he grabbed one of his guard's spears and stalked up behind Fuérr, raising the tip over Fuérr's head. Fuérr didn't notice. He was too busy dancing.

"Fuérr!" Oliver shouted next to me.

But Fuérr didn't hear. Oliver's voice was drowned under the whistling icicles and rumbling cave. It was getting so intense, the guards around us had to put down their spears to keep their balance, ignoring us as they watched the impressive show Fuérr was giving, the Pearl now a steady, blinding gleam.

Oliver tried to spread his wings, but the chains around his feathers clinked tight and stopped them from opening. He wriggled his arms behind his back, but his shackles were too tight to move them at all, like mine.

—Something brushed against my leg, making me flinch.

The ferret!

"Kurn!" I shouted.

The ferret hobbled in a circle excitedly—or panicked?—my scythe necklace clutched in his mouth.

I knelt down as the little weasel climbed onto my back and stuck its paws in the large keyhole of my shackles.

Click!

The shackles opened and fell to the icy floor.

I rubbed my wrists in a wince. The metal had chaffed so much, it left sore red marks.

"Thanks, little guy!" I hollered, taking my necklace back from Kurn's teeth. I plucked off the scythe-sphere from the magnetic holder and tossed the chain aside, touching the sealing rune on the sphere. My long scythe grew in a golden light, pouring into my hands like liquid metal.

Kurn hurried over to Oliver next.

Click!

Click!

The ferret popped open Oliver's shackles from around his wrists and wings—

Oliver stretched his newly freed wings and bolted in the air toward Fuérr, startling the distracted guards around us.

I cursed and ran after Oliver. The guards regripped their spears, and one of them thrust their weapon at my head. I ducked under it, then hopped over another that swung for my legs, *thwacking* a third spear away with my scythe as I sped up.

In front of me, the snake man drove his spear down toward Fuérr's head—

"NO!" I shouted, skidding between them and *ripping* my scythe in an arc over my head.

Clang!

My crooked blade caught the man's spear, and I heaved with all my strength to pry it out of his fingers—sending it flying to the icy floor.

I held my scythe out and glared daggers at the snake. "Get away from him!"

The snake blinked at me. "Who gave the *child* a scythe—?"

"Fuérr!" Oliver shouted overhead. Then he swooped down and grabbed Fuérr by the waist, hauling him in the air and flying him back toward the tunnel we'd come from—

Crrrack—zap!

CRASH!

A blast of lightning shot from the snake's hand and struck the ceiling of the tunnel's entrance. Ice crumbled in heavy chunks and blocked the tunnel before Oliver and Fuérr could make it through.

Zap!

Zap!

Zap!

The snake kept shooting bolts of lightning from his hands, forcing Oliver to dip and dodge and flap in circles to evade them all, ice spraying from the walls where the bolts hit.

"A valiant attempt…" the snake hissed and stalked closer to them with his hands raised and sparking with static. "But children must learn their place—"

I roared and swung my scythe at his back.

He spun on me so fast, I barely had time to stagger. He snatched my staff and *kicked* me in the stomach, making me gag and almost puke, and he ripped my scythe out of my fingers.

"Irritating child," he spat, tossing my scythe away.

I pushed down the sickness in my gut and heaved to my shaking feet, stumbling after him. "Get… back here…"

He shot more lightning from his hands—and formed an electric cage around Oliver and Fuérr in the air, trapping them in the strings of static. He kept one hand raised to make the cage hold while his other hand retrieved his spear from the floor. He lifted it over a shoulder, aiming at Oliver and Fuérr.

Rrrrrrrrr…

The icy rubble blocking the exit vibrated suddenly. Then all at once, the frosted chunks lifted in the air, making way for the crowd of people who rushed inside.

One of them was my blue-haired Nana Myra.

The snake didn't pay them any attention, though, and launched his spear at Oliver and Fuérr. The weapon sailed fast and steady, its aim deadly perfect—

"FUÉRR!" a deep, rumbling voice roared, so fierce it rattled my bones.

A scaled man with emerald hair suddenly leapt into the air, his hands glowing green and spewing a strong stream of ice beneath him, shooting him higher and higher toward the airborne boys. He kept the stream going with one hand while he shot bursts of ice at the flying spear, but his aim was so chaotic that it missed every time. In a furious scream, the man sped up his icy stream and lifted himself higher until he blocked the path of the flying spear and—

The man was struck in the back by the spear, the tip crunching through the other side.

He dropped like a stone onto the ice stream he'd created, blood staining the sleek crystals as he slid to the cavern floor with his neck twisted in an unnatural angle.

Fuérr screamed. "PAPA!"

The Pearl of Emerald suddenly flashed with a bright light.

I held my hand to my eyes, trying to see what was going on, but the flash stung my eyes so bad it made them water. When the light dimmed, I found the snake man towering over the dead man's corpse. The snake's two-toned hair now had a third, green color splotched in his strands, and his eyes bled with a matching, third color, too.

The group who just entered came rushing in all directions—two of them, a blonde viper and a black-haired bat woman, went straight for the multi-colored snake, their scythes drawn and hurled at him as they both gave angry yells.

The snake tilted his head at them, giving a smile as all his guards—and the snake woman—huddled around him.

Then they all vanished.

The viper and bat's scythes sliced nothing but the cold fog.

The Pearl's green light dimmed into nothing, the clam rumbling shut… and the cave was suddenly quiet.

Nana Myra ran over to me and scooped me up. "Milann!" She hugged me tight, out of breath. "Bloods, don't you scare us like that again…!"

I blushed, mumbling. "Sorry, Nana…"

I peeked over her shoulder. Oliver was flapping Fuérr down between the bat woman and viper man. When they touched the ground, Fuérr ran over to the dead man bleeding on the ice.

Fuérr's sobs echoed throughout the cave.

My chest squeezed at the sound, my stomach lurching as I watched Fuérr shake the limp body of his dad with a desperate squeal…

Fuérr… I'm so sorry…

I buried my own tears in Nana's shoulder.

18

DARK DAYS

MYRA

On the third dawn after Ninumel's death, I watched from the front pew of the Rinish Temple as High Howless Lilliana swept her pure Crystal scythe over the fallen Ocean King's NecroSeam.

A gentle *snap* echoed through the temple.

The Seadragon's ghost rose from his vessel, floating up to stare at his corpse with a gloomy expression. He turned to Lilliana, the Hand of the Death Queen, as she informed him of the ill events… and welcomed him to his new Afterlife.

Beside me, my rust-haired mother, Crysalette, kept her head bowed beside Ninumel's wife, Veyazelle. Both their faces hid beneath mourning-white veils that were sewn to their wide brimmed hats. Prince Fuérr wept beside Veyazelle in his own chair, Oliver and my adopted granddaughter, Milann, seated beside him. Most of us in the audience wore soul-seeing masks for the occasion. Only the faces of the Treble family and Lilliana were unobscured.

I was surprised to see Jaq wore no mask either. He was Hallowless and therefore couldn't see ghosts, but when he adjusted his spectacles over his scaled nose, I spotted a rippled engraving etched on the black frames. That was a Sealing-rune. Which meant his eyeglasses had been enchanted with an Evocation that allowed him to see detached souls.

Sky King Roji sat on the other side of the Temple's pews with his two daughters, waiting respectfully as his wife, Ocean Princess Dalminia, accepted her role as Regent of Marincia, in her brother's place. Since Prince Fuérr was far too young to take the throne, the responsibility fell to the eldest Relicblood of Ocean. I saw Roji fidget in his seat as his wife donned her brother's crown. He seemed to fight back a sob, hugging their daughters tight.

How will this affect their kingdoms...? I wondered solemnly. Roji had his own responsibilities in Culatia, once this war with Macarius was over. With the family separated until Fuérr came of age, it would surely mean their daughters would be split for a time as well. *I suppose this is what the old Sky King had warned, before his son took the crown...*

I reached for the Storagecoffin strapped to my waist.

Serdin... I unclipped his Storagecoffin and hugged it to my chest, drawing in a slow breath. *We were indeed fortunate to keep our family together... weren't we?*

I remembered a time Serdin had worried over that. I'd assured him I had no obligation to take the throne after my father—since Father was, by most shifters' standards, something of an immortal—I didn't think I would be needed.

But now even Father is gone...

I glanced at my mother beside me. In her lap sat her fox-eared and tailed toddler... my brother, Eryn.

Eryn looked remarkably similar to our father. He had our family's curling, azure locks and matching eyes, but his cheeks, his nose, his brow and chin... it was like looking at an old portrait of the Little Blue King. And attached to our mother's waist was that very king's Storagecoffin.

Since I had chosen a life of mortality with Serdin, I had given up my title as Father's heiress to Aspirre's throne... but now that Serdin was gone along with Father, Eryn was too young to take up that burden. My daughter had stepped up to her role as Grim's new queen, so...

There was nothing keeping me in the physical plane anymore, was there?

Mother asked me to act as Regent to Aspirre. Mother wasn't a Relicblood, as she explained, and so the Dreamcatchers would likely prefer one of the true Bloodline of Dreams...

And I had accepted.

But first, I reminded in a sigh, *we must ensure the End is evaded.*

I put Serdin's Storagecoffin back on my waist, settling back in my seat. Perched on the bench beside me was Locke, who nudged my shoulder with his beak to console me.

Ninumel's family was called to the front of the temple to greet his ghost. Then, the other Relicbloods were invited up as well. I exhaled and pushed to my feet, my fingers still brushing Serdin's coffin in hopes of steadying my nerves.

—The flames rose high and devastating among the spired rooftops of Grim's blackstone palace. Her sister's two killers flitted through the veil of smoke: the azure-haired princess and her ashen-haired lover, the Prince of Death.

The narrator's fangs unfolded, venom dripping as hatred burned her heart hotter than the flames surrounding the royals, swearing vengeance—

The vision vanished as quickly as it had come. My mother was staring at me, concern creasing her orange brow.

"Myra?" she asked. "What's wrong? Was it a vision?"

I shook my head, dazed. "I… think so… but it was strange. I was looking at myself…" I touched the Storagecoffin at my waist. "Myself and Serdin…"

But whosever vision it was, I thought in a shiver, *is a most worrying question…*

SAILING TOWARD NEVERLAND

19

MONSTROUS WATERS

ASTER

Rain ravaged the ship.

I was sloshed around the deck with the rest of the crew, the ship tilting like crazy as the harsh waves thrashed against the bow and knocked us off our feet.

"Get those sails down!" Captain Bardell shouted from the helm. He fought the wheel for control. "Stop wasting time!"

The crew leapt onto the masts and started climbing up the shrouds to reach the sails. I hustled over to the bottom of the main mast and grabbed the ropes alongside the others—

Then a vision flashed in my Third Eye. A *bad* one.

I dropped the rope and leapt onto the mast in a rush, climbing after the man who was balancing on the yard, trying to tie up the sails.

I reached the top—then *tackled* the guy off the mast, keeping hold of him as we both hurtled down to the deck.

Smash!

I broke his fall on the floorboards, my spine shattering on impact. Thankfully, I was already dead, so my broken pieces just glopped back together in a mess of sticky blackness.

CRRRRAAAAACKK!

A powerful bolt of lightning struck the mast where the guy had been sitting, splitting it in half. The splintered beam came swinging down toward the deck.

I threw the guy off me and rolled to my feet, shoving the other crewmembers out of the way just as the beam *crashed* into the deck.

Then another vision struck. I whipped my head to the helm. "CAPTAIN!" I hollered and sprinted up the stairs to the upper deck. "GET DOWN!"

I shoved his head down before he could protest—

SPLIKCH!

A large fishing hook the size of a head plunged into my skull in a spray of black blood. I yanked it out and glared at the thing. *Bloody hook.* We'd put it out there this morning hoping to catch some larger fish. We weren't expecting this storm to hit, so we forgot to pull it up.

The captain had been too busy scrambling to get back on his feet to see that the hook actually hurt me—my wound had already healed—but he saw me holding it now and his brown skin went ghostly pale.

He looked at me like I was a damned prophet. "How did you know that would…?"

I tapped my forehead. "Third Eye, Captain! I'm a Seer, remember?"

"Aye…" He said gruffly, his brow furrowing. "Aye, that ye are, boy…*ARGH!*"

The gale cut through again, and the captain grabbed the wheel to keep the ship under control. "You did your part helping me, boy!" He yelled. "Now go help *them* get those other sails down!"

I saluted and hurried back down to the main deck to do just that.

When the storm finally settled and morning came around, I sank my teeth into my fifth burger today. Warm juices dribbled down my fingers and filled up my wilted, shriveled stomach so satisfyingly, I was already sobbing with joy.

The ship's bell gonged twice as seagulls cried overhead in the clear blue sky, the breeze licking over my face as the salty air filled my nose from the deck's table where I sat with a mountain of food scattered around me.

The crewmembers were all cheering me on, encouraging me to beat my past record of seven burgers in one setting. I wasn't about to disappoint.

But as great as the food was, I wished I could take off these damn sunglasses and see the sun in all its glory… but I'd been stuck in Tanderam for so long—over two years, apparently—that my eyes still hadn't adjusted to the brightness. If I took off my glasses, my eyes would burn out of their sockets. Aaaand then slurp back *into* their sockets like black worms.

I guessed it was a good thing I couldn't take off the glasses yet. At least this way, the crewmembers couldn't see my white pupils. I'd hitched a ride on this nice merchant ship and they were kind enough to let me onboard as they sailed to Neverland. But if they knew I was a Necrofera, they probably wouldn't take that so well.

According to my visions, I knew the Shadowblood was supposed to be on the Gyle Islands for a while. But I *also* knew they had to go to Neverland before they could descend to Grim. If I could head them off and get to Neverland before them, I could just meet them at the harbor. Either way, my prophetic Hallows showed me that I wouldn't meet them unless I got on this specific ship. I didn't See any visions about *why*, but if it got me the future I wanted, I wasn't going to question it.

"Aster, slow down, boy!" Captain Bardell clapped a thick hand on my shoulder just as I finished the fifth burger and picked up the sixth. "I know you're glad to eat after nearly starving to death in a prison cell, but you'll *eat* yourself to death if you block all your arteries with grease!"

I took a rebellious bite and swallowed. "Sounds like a *much* better way to go than starving, Captain." I went back to my meal.

He sighed, but chuckled, shaking his head. "You youngsters and your reckless diets…"

I finished the sixth burger and gave a loud belch, prompting an uproar of laughter from the crewmembers. "I'm 22, Captain. I'm not that young."

"Young enough," he argued pleasantly. He patted my shoulder and nodded toward the ship's railing. "When you're done, I want to have a few words with you, Aster. Don't puke on me when you do, got it?"

I shrugged, still chewing, "Gof'fit, Ca'ffin."

He chuckled and stalked over to the railing to wait for me. I quickly scarfed down two more burgers, breaking my old record and making the crew go wild over it before I finally got around to trotting over to the captain, wiping my mouth with a sleeve.

When I reached him, the captain cocked an eyebrow at me. "How do you keep all of that down, anyway? You're all skin and bones." He gestured to my scrawny limbs, which were visible through my short-sleeved vest and cargo capris. "You're like a walking skeleton. How do you fit so much food in there without gaining a lick of weight?"

I shrugged. "I don't know, captain. I guess I have a fast metabolism."

The truth was, demons didn't gain or lose weight. Whatever we ate, we converted into energy—using *all* of it without leaving anything to 'expel'. It was a cool perk, but I knew from experience that even if you couldn't die from starvation as a Fera, it still hurt like Land and left you too weak to move. And I particularly didn't want to fall into the temptation of eating souls if I could help it. The *real* food helped stave off the appeal.

The captain scratched his head. "Must be *really* fast, in your case…" He cleared his throat. "Aster, I wanted to thank you for your help with that storm last night. If it wasn't for your predictions, our ship would have drowned… along with us in it."

I turned a finger in my meercat ear to get an itch. "Aw, it was nothing. I was pretty much done with my apprenticeship with my Master Oracle before the war started, so I've had a lot of practice." I glanced at the broken mast sticking out of the deck, wincing. "Uh, sorry I couldn't do anything about the mast, Captain…"

He tossed a dismissive hand and snorted. "A mast isn't worth a damn compared to the crew. I've already called Neverland's coastguard to come and give us a tow the rest of the way, so don't worry over a Bloody piece of wood." He stabbed a thick finger into my ribbed chest. "We *all* would have been dead if it wasn't for you, Aster. For that, I owe you a debt. It isn't much, but… I wanted to give you this as thanks."

He reached into the Storagebox tied to his belt and pulled out a fancy, velvet box with golden cords and tassels.

I took the box skeptically and opened it. Inside was a fist-sized crystal ball sitting on a satin pillow.

"A crystal ball?" I asked, blinking dumbly. "But these are expensive! I can't take this."

"You can and you will." He gave a bearded grin and chuckled. "I got it from a trader down in Adrial. I was planning to sell it for a pretty bead in Neverland to a rich oracle, but… I think it'd be better off in a *talented* oracle's hands."

I hesitated. "Are you sure…?"

"Of course I'm damn well sure, boy. You saved all the lives of these men and women, and you can't put a price on that. This is the *least* I can do to show my gratitude."

I closed the box and held it to my chest in a blush. "Okay… thank you. But I don't have anything to keep it safe in?"

He frowned thoughtfully. Then he unclasped his Storagebox and handed it to me. "Then take this, too. I have several."

I thanked him again and strapped it to my own belt—which was cinched as tight as it could get around my skeletal waist—and put the crystal ball's box inside for safe storage.

"Now," the captain said, "there's one more thing I wanted to talk to you about. You said you're going to Neverland to see your family?"

Oh, I thought in a wince, *I almost forgot that was my excuse.* "Yeah," I told him. "I've been gone for so long, I want them to know I'm all right."

He rubbed his beard in a hum. "Well, when you're done reuniting with them… Have you considered a future with this ship?"

One of my meercat ears flicked up curiously. "What do you mean?"

"Aster, your visions are incredibly powerful." He waved to me. "Stronger than any oracle I've ever seen. I think it's no coincidence that the Shepherd sent you to *my* ship." He crossed his arms. "Not to mention, the boys have taken to you like family. We'd be sad to see you go… what do you say?"

I glanced down at the waves beneath us. "I mean… that really means a lot to me, Captain…" My mouth twisted. "But I made a promise to—"

BRRRRRRRRRR…!

The ship suddenly rumbled, throwing the captain and me off balance.

When the tremor settled, we stood there frozen, sharing a worried glance.

"Uh," I began sheepishly. "Captain? What was that?"

He grimaced. "Er… Turbulence?"

"On a ship?—*woah!*"

Another quake shook the ship, and the water around us hissed and sloshed wildly. The crew members around us began shouting, screaming in fright, but it was muted under the sudden roar of water that splashed onto the deck—

An enormous, fifteen-foot tentacle sluggishly *peeled* out of the water.

The captain and I stood gaping at the suckered limb. "Holy Bloods…!"

CRASH!

The tentacle hurtled down over the ship and *snapped* one of the remaining masts in half. The limb wrapped around the deck and began crushing the sides, the wood cracking and splintering under the pressure.

"*Sea monster!*" The captain cried. "*Those Bloody tales were true!*"

AAAAHHNNNNNNN…? Came an echoing sound from beneath the sea.

The water parted as the creature's enormous head emerged… and it cocked at us curiously. Its large eyes blinked down at us. The webbed fins on the side of its head flapped in question, and the beast gave another cry.

AAAAAAAHHHNNNNNNNNN?

The captain took off his hat in shock. "Bloods be good…! Is… is that a Bindragon?"

I flicked him a bewildered look. "Bindragons are supposed to be tiny! This thing is as big as a house!"

AAAAHHHNNNNN! It cried again, the low tone vibrating my bones. Its head-fins flapped downward, and it suddenly gave a sad look. *AAAAAAHHNNNNN…?*

The captain scratched his head. "Does it want something?"

"Dunno…" I hesitated before inching over to its enormous tentacle—which I realized was really its long, serpentine body. I drew in a breath, then laid a hand between two of its suckers, evoking my prophetic Hallows.

I was met with a vision full of pain and discomfort, as if a sharp knife were cutting into my back.

The vision faded, and my meercat ears perked. "Oh. So that's what's up, huh?" I went to the railing and hopped atop it, twisting back to the baffled captain. "I'll be back in a minute!"

I dove into the water.

Luckily, I didn't have to worry about running out of breath. I didn't have to breathe at all, as a demon. I swam under the ship, following the long body of the colossal Bindragon until I found what I was looking for:

The large, jagged tooth of a Seadragon stuck in his back.

It was bigger than two of my heads. I grabbed the tooth's sides and got a good footing on the Bindragon's body, then grunted as I *yanked* the thing out of its skin—

AAAAHHHNNN… Came the bone-shaking sigh of relief from the dragon.

It uncurled its body from around the ship, releasing it as the vessel bobbed clumsily in the now-still waters.

I started to swim back—but its tail wrapped around my waist and *hauled* me above water so quick, my hood fell off my head and flopped straight to my shoulders.

My sunglasses ripped off my face. I dangled in the air, dripping wet and still caught in the Bindragon's tail. The dragon pulled me over to its head. Then nuzzled its face into my stomach lovingly.

Its fins tickled me into a laughing frenzy, and I pet its head with a grin. "Aw, you're welcome, big guy. It was no problem."

The Bindragon gave a cheerful *AAAAHHNNN* and swung me onto its skull between its head-fins. My Third Eye opened when I was seated there. Sometime in the near future, the faces of the Shadowblood twins were looking up at me in disbelieving shock, beholding the gigantic dragon underneath me.

I hummed and patted the dragon's head. "Well, aren't you a good luck charm?" I looked down at the crewmembers on the ship below me—specifically at the captain. His mouth was wide open, and a vision showed me that he was looking directly at my white, glowing pupils. I'd lost my second set of sunglasses in the water.

I clicked my tongue. "Well, guess the jig is up… Hey captain!" I shouted down at him, waving goodbye. "Thanks for the offer, but I have a job to do! This guy can take me the rest of the way!"

The captain still stared at me in shocked silence.

I waved a boney hand at him and the crew. "See you around!"

The Bindragon sang an excited *AAAAAHHHNNNN* and dove underwater, taking me with him as we swam wherever the Void this guy felt like taking me. I didn't really care about our path.

I already knew we were heading to the right destination.

20

THE FOURTH BEARER

XAVIER

My father's bearded face melted in my arms, his flesh dripping away from his skull as it blackened and rotted off—

Waaaaaaaaahhh!

I bolted awake and stumbled out of bed, hitting the carpeted floor sharply on my side.

Waaaaaaaaahhhh!

I panted over the floor, bleary and disoriented. Where was I? What happened to the battlefield…? To father…?

WAAAAAHHH!!

I heard Willow yawn from atop the bed. "Oh, all right, Lucas…"

My brain still swam, the name echoing in my memory. *Lucas… Father…?*

No, not Father. Wrong Lucas. She spoke of the baby.

I groggily remembered we were on a ship heading to High Neverland. I reached for the nightstand next to the bed and heaved myself up. Then found myself staring at my father's Storagecoffin, which I'd set on the nightstand earlier in the night.

Father…

I tore my eyes away and focused on Willow instead. My wife sat on the edge of the bed as she plucked our wolf-eared son out of his bassinet and opened the top of her sleepgown to nurse him.

When his crying finally settled, she glanced at me warily. "Xavier? Are you well?"

"I…" My throat burned, and I dragged a hand over my face, my heart still pounding. "I'll be fine… but I don't think I'll return to sleep anytime soon. Do you need anything?"

She cradled our son with one arm and rubbed her eyes with her free hand. "Mm… Perhaps some water?"

I nodded, grabbing an empty glass from my nightstand. But I paused when my gaze fell on Father's Storagecoffin again.

Don't think about it.

I squeezed my eyes shut and stomped over to our cabin's private washroom. I flipped on the dim lamp along the wall—

A man's bearded face caught my peripherals to the left, his sapphire eye staring at me.

I quickly turned to him. "Father…?!"

I stopped. It was only a mirror. The bearded face I'd seen was mine. The sapphire eye was my left iris. My clear, white eye was still beside it, my scar dragging down my brow and stretching to my cheek.

Hands shaking, I *clacked* the glass on the countertop, pushing out a hard breath. A straight razor caught my eye beside the sink. I grabbed it, lathering shaving cream over my entire face and rid myself of every last blasted hair. By the time I finished, my slender face was as bare as Khol's bald head.

I patted a towel to my face and filled up the empty glass of water for Willow, then stormed back into the cabin.

I found Willow still nursing the baby. Her music-watch was now on her nightstand, the case flipped open and the innerworkings revolving round as the Requiem's twinkling music played its soft lullaby for Lucas.

The Crest on my left hand gleamed dimly toward the amulet. *That's right… the crystals inside the watch are from the Willow of Ashes.* Our current destination…

And the final Relic where Alexander and I were to gain our last set of Hallows.

When Willow noticed me emerge from the washroom, she flicked her gaze at me. "That certainly took you some time for a simple glass of…" She saw my cleanly shaven face and flinched, covering her open breast. Then she relaxed. "Death, Xavier! I thought you were Alexander."

I grunted. "It's been some time since anyone said *that* to me."

"But… You shaved?" She asked. "Why the sudden change?"

I scratched my chin, one of the small cuts stinging where I nicked myself. "I… reminded myself of my father." Sickness twisted. "It was *too* much of a reminder…"

She pursed her lips. Then offered encouragingly, "Well, it's… quite dashing."

"Thank you… here's your water, darling." I gently clacked down her glass of water on her nightstand.

Then I glanced at my own nightstand, where my father's Storagecoffin waited. I wandered over to it, touching it with tender fingers… and slid back into bed beside Willow.

When Lucas finally fell back asleep, she laid him in his bassinet, closed her music-watch to stop the twinkling music, and settled against me. She cupped my face as steam hissed between our flesh, her warm fingers heating my freezing jaw. She gave a light chuckle.

"It's so cold without it. And *smooth*." She kissed my cheek. "It feels like ages since I've seen *all* of your face."

I hummed and reminded her, "It was bare when we first arrived in Neverland."

"As I said." She took my lips, the touch pleasantly electric, and wrapped an arm around me. "Ages."

I chuckled, then closed my eyes and drifted back to sleep at long, long last…

—PRIRIRIRIRIRIRIRIRII!!!

The blaring ring of my communicator blasted our cabin with sound from my nightstand.

PRIRIRIRIRIRIRIRIIRIRII!!!

I cupped my ears and cringed. "No, no, no, no, no…"

… *Wwwwaaaaahhhh….!* Lucas wailed, now fully awake. Again.

Willow and I groaned. She tended to Lucas while I grabbed my noisy com, answering it in a curse, "What in DEATH could it be at this hour…!"

The screen of light blipped alive, and I stopped cold.

It was Jaq.

"Sorry, mate," Jaq apologized on the screen, scratching his scaled chin awkwardly. *"I mean, uh, SIRE… I forgot about the time difference over there."*

I exhaled, too exhausted to protest his discomforting use of *sire* for now. "It's fine…" I grumbled instead. "Damage done, I suppose… What's the status on the children?"

"That's the good news," Jaq announced with a fang-filled smile. The screen changed view as it streaked downward, and the face of a little sheep-horned girl appeared as she took hold of Jaq's com.

"Hiiii!" My recently adopted daughter, Milann, greeted with a proud grin. Her copper hair and curling horns were shaded by a furry cowl, her breath fogging from her lips.

"Milann!" I cried, adrenaline bursting as I shot to my feet. "Thank Bloods you're all right…!"

Willow hurried beside me with the baby, exasperated. "There you are, young lady! For the love of Bloods, *never* make us worry like that again!"

Milann rubbed her neck in a nervous laugh. *"R-right... sorry... But Oliver said that the good future wasn't going to happen if I didn't help save Fuérr, so... I didn't really have a lot of time to explain all that."*

Willow pinched the rim of her nose. "These Bloody Seers are trying my patience at every turn..." She sighed. "But I'm happy you're safe, Milann. We'll see you at home in Grim. If you leave now, I should think we'll arrive at nearly the same time—and we'll be sure to give you a proper orientation. I hope you'll be pleased with your new living quarters."

I hummed, not having considered that. "A palace is quite an upgrade, Willow. I'd be *very* surprised if she wasn't pleased with your old chambers."

Willow paused. "Ah... that's right. I suppose those *won't* be my chambers anymore, now that I'm queen..." A depressing thought seemed to flash in her eyes, but she dismissed it with a shake of her head, addressing Milann again on the screen. "Milann, could you please give the com to Jaq again?"

Milann nodded, and the screen streaked upward.

Jaq's face appeared again, and Willow asked, "Will you all be descending to Grim now, or will Ninumel need additional assistance in guarding the palace from Macarius?"

Jaq's expression dripped into a wince. *"There's no point in guarding the palace anymore,"* he said, his tone hauntingly dim.

I inquired beside Willow, "What do you mean?"

Jaq took a moment to answer, and when he did, his voice was so, so quiet. *"... Ninumel is dead."*

Willow and I were silent.

"Macarius gained all of Ocean's Hallows," Jaq added. *"And then he just... left. Popped out of existence again. I'm sorry, Sire..."*

The impact was slow to sink in. My breath shook with a building rage, fists clenching as my wolf ears grew.

"I see..." My voice was tight. "At least... the children were spared..."

Jaq's features softened. *"Yeah... Yeah, they were. And they're doing great, now that we've got them back..."* Whatever he saw on my face must have made him uncomfortable, and he cleared his throat. *"We'll, er, see you in Grim, Sire...?"*

I nodded, my throat too cinched to respond verbally, and ended the call.

My fingers wrapped around the com, claws sharpening as my rising fury bubbled hotter.

It festered and shook my hand that held the com, fighting to break free until—

"rrrRRRRRRAAAAAAAAH!" my lungs blistered with a vicious snarl, and I chucked the com against the wall.

—CLACK—Spictch!

The com burst into pieces, gears and springs raining to the floor. There was now a dent in the wall.

Waaaahhhh!! Cried Lucas in Willow's arms. *Waahh…! Waaaahhhh!*

"Xavier!" Willow chided. "You're scaring him…!"

I tried to keep my breaths even, the rage threatening to escape again. "I… I'm sorry…" I clutched my throbbing head, Lucas's wails ringing through my wolf ears and scratching against my amplified hearing. "I… I need some air."

She sighed, but nodded in understanding. I grabbed Father's Storagecoffin, pocketed it, and stormed out to the hall.

After shoving open the door leading out to the deck, I saw the night sky was speckled with stars, the cool light of the full moon washing over the ship and giving it a calming radiance. I loosened my lungs, letting the brisk wind cool my temper as I turned my gaze across the deck.

Then I paused.

Alexander was out here, his arms folded over the rail.

Our messenger ravens, Mal and Chai, were perched beside his arm. Lucas's little Songcrow—who the boy had recently started calling *Virro*—was snuggled against Chai's back and sleeping soundly.

My lips pulled into a tight line, wondering if I should leave Alex be… then decided against it, striding over stubbornly.

Chai gave a low croak when I approached. My raven lowered his head in greeting, but made no attempt to fly to me for fear of disturbing the little crow on his back. I came beside Alex and folded my arms over the rail.

"Ninumel is dead," I chewed bitterly. "Macarius has his Ocean Hallows now."

"I know," Alex said, staring at the dark, ocean waters beneath us. Mal mimicked his distant gaze at the sea, his feathers ruffling in the warm breeze. "I had a vision of your conversation with Jaq," He explained. Then he gave me a sidelong glance—did a double-take. "What happened to the beard?" He questioned. "I thought the point was that we didn't look alike?"

"It was." I gave a half-hearted shrug. "But right now, I'd rather look like my twin… and not our father."

He blinked at me. Offered no comment. Then he slid his gaze back toward the waters with a sigh. He reached into his pocket and pulled out a Storagecoffin. The one that held our mother.

I pulled out Father's Storagecoffin, the two of us standing in silence for a lingering moment.

Then I hushed, "It feels strange without them."

He grunted. "Like missing a leg. Everything just feels so…"

"Off balance?"

"Yes… Exactly."

Silence again. The waves hissed and slapped against the ship in a lulling rhythm.

Then Alex murmured, "Grandfather Edric called, you should know. He's made arrangements with our parents' old vassals to send their vessels to the Death Palace for us to receive. It seems they *all* wish to form a Bloodpact with us."

"That's quite a number of vassals," I remarked. "At least Willow will be taking on *her* father's vassals in the palace. He had just as many—if not more. I couldn't fathom having that many on top of our parents' vassals."

"Bloods, no." He relented to a light chuckle. "I'm exhausted with the six we have."

We shared a laugh—

BRRRRRRR…!!

The ship rumbled suddenly, making us stagger.

"What was that?" we questioned warily.

BRRRRR…!

AAAAAAAAAAHNNNNNN?

The waters sloshed below the ship—

A scream ripped from below the floorboards under our feet. It was coming from the galley below deck.

Alex and I raced inside and dashed down the spiral steps, kicking open the galley's door, our scythes drawn at the ready.

"Guys!" Bianca squeaked in fright when she saw us. She must have been the one who'd screamed earlier. She hurried behind Alexander and me and pointed at the intruder currently stuffing his face with every morsel he could find in the cabinets. "I-I-I was just getting some tea and this guy just *jumped* through the window and started eating everything! He's like a black hole! He's eating all of our rations…!"

Alex cocked an eyebrow at her. "You didn't stop him?"

"How can *I* Bloody stop him?!" She demanded, thrusting a terse hand at the stranger. "He's a Necrofera!"

We gaped at her. Then shouted. "Lead with that!"

Clank, clash, clink-clink-clink!

The intruding Fera emptied the cabinets with an insatiable hunger, pots and pans and bowls and goblets clattering to the floor in his wake.

Footfalls came trotting down the stairs behind us. It seemed we weren't the only ones to hear Bianca's scream. She'd woken up the entire ship. Willow came down with the baby, Neal and Claude ran down behind her, Yulia and Jimmy hurried alongside Nathaniel, Apson and Aiden, our troupe of demons followed behind—

"MY MUFFINS!" Cilia shrieked and pushed her way to the front of the crowd. Her hands burst into flames as she evoked her fire Hallows. "Those took me *HOURS* to make, you gluttonous Clean One…!"

"It's a demon," I growled, keeping my scythes raised.

Cilia blinked at me. Then pointed at the intruder. "*That* is a demon?"

Alex questioned, "Can't you tell that sort of thing? You said every demon has a Weight of some kind?"

"They do," Cilia said, perplexed. "But *that* one doesn't."

Hecrûshou stalked around us alongside the rest of our demons to get a closer look. His Crystal trident was still wrapped in its cloth as he rumbled, "Artist sink me, he's weaker than *Khol*."

"What!" Khol fanned an insulted hand at his scaled chest. "You're comparing me to a newborn?! That isn't fair! How can I best a newborn at being weaker if I don't have Hallows like you all—I didn't know I was eating all those souls when I was still a mongrel! I haven't had a soul *since*, so don't you hold my blank past against me!"

"That was a compliment, Khol," Hecrûshou sighed, rubbing his eyes. "Only *you* would compete for the title of weakest demon, I swear…"

Miranda cocked her head at the intruder. "Strange. This newborn's Weight is so light, it's almost like he isn't there at all. Like he's invisible."

The dragon-winged Thörd scratched his head as if puzzled, mumbling in a thick Culatian accent, "Maybe new demon *just* born recent-recent? No eat souls yet?"

"Like me?" Kael questioned beside Cilia. "Do I hold the same Weight as him?"

Cilia hummed. "Exactly the same… which means Thörd is right. He hasn't eaten any souls yet."

Bianca muttered under her breath, "It looks like he's eating more than enough *food* to make up for it."

Hecrûshou rubbed his chin. "Perhaps that is how he's staved off the soul-thirst thus far, as Kael has been doing…" Hecrûshou unwrapped his Crystal trident and approached the voracious Necrofera in the kitchens. "Little newborn! Cease your gluttony and identify yourself!"

"*Rhfhh—hurrr—mmmffnnrr?*" The intruder intoned with his mouthful of raw salmon, holding up a finger to tell Hecrûshou to wait.

From my spectating vantage, I flicked a wary glance at Alex beside me. "Er… Did he just tell a Demon King to *wait*?"

Alex muttered, "Technically, he didn't say anything."

Hecrûshou bristled, his webbed ears flaring. "Now see here, newborn! You are in the presence of Ancients! I am willing to assume you are ignorant of us, so believe you me when I tell you we can crush you like a worthless bug. Now *cease and desist. Right. Bloody. Now.*"

The young man swallowed the salmon whole, then finally looked at Hecrûshou. Though, not two second passed before his gaze dropped to the little Bindragon who was coiled around the Demon King's trident.

"Oh, hey!" The new demon flashed an adoring smile and rubbed the Bindragon's finned head with a finger. "You have one too! Awww, yours is so little! That's cute. Who's a widdle fella? Who's a cute widdle fella?"

The Bindragon squealed with delighted *aaaaahns* and happily flapped his fins under the man's finger.

The intruder seemed to forget Hecrûshou was there and unceremoniously resumed his task of emptying the cabinets and stuffing his face.

Hecrûshou's throat clicked with annoyance. He *slammed* the butt of his trident on the floor—and the intruder was hit by some invisible force, his back *crashing* into the pantry, wooden plates and bowls raining onto the floor in a tangle of noise. The intruder was stuck to the splintered pantry, struggling with his twig-thin limbs to move. Then his white-pupiled gaze caught a vine of grapes dangling above him. He stuck out his tongue to shamelessly pluck off a grape and swallowed it whole.

Hecrûshou was not amused. "Did you climb aboard this vessel for a *snack?*"

The young demon smiled nervously, which looked freakish with his hollow cheeks and sunken eye sockets.

"Actually…" the demon wheezed under Hecrûshou's invisible Weight that crushed his lungs. He flicked his glowing gaze at Alexander and me. "I came to find *them*…" His bronze cheeks flushed pink. "But then I smelled all the food and… I couldn't help myself…" He gave a girthy belch. Then his stomach rumbled. "Um… do you guys have any more of those amazing muffins—*Hurrhhh…!*"

He was pushed farther into the pantry when Cilia stormed in with a scowl so heated it rivaled the flames engulfing her hands. "You ate them all, you greedy little…!"

"Cilia, be calm." Hecrûshou evoked his water Hallow and clapped a hand over one of Cilia's fiery fists, dousing the flames with a splash of water. He turned back to the newborn. "What exactly do you want with the Shadow twins?"

The new demon opened his mouth to reply—

BRRRRRRR…!

The entire ship trembled suddenly.

CRICK-CRICK-CRICK-CRICK…!

A strange sound like wood on the brink of splintering echoed through the ship's bones, vibrating the structure itself along with us inside it.

Alex and I shuffled back to back nervously. "What was that?"

The intruding demon winced. "Oh, crap! Hey—uh, you got to let me go real quick, or…"

Movement caught my eye from the open, circular window of the kitchens. It looked like… My brow knitted terribly low. "Is that an *eye?*"

AAAAAAAAAAAAHNNNN?

The deep growl shook my bones. Or had that been the ship quivering?

The newborn squirmed under Hecrûshou and Cilia's heavy Weights. "H-hey! Seriously, let me go for a minute! He's just worried about me!"

Hecrûshou stared at him. "He'?"

"I have to calm him down before he crushes your ship!"

Hecrûshou and Cilia exchanged perplexed glances, then reluctantly released the intruder, who dropped to his spindly knees. His meercat ears perked and he pushed through our party, sprinting up the stairs as he called down, "Be right back…!"

Like *Death* I was going to leave an unknown Necrofera unsupervised.

I pushed through everyone to lead the way up the steps, Alex running at my side as the others followed at our heels. When I stalked out to the deck—

I screeched to a halt, Alex slamming into my back.

"What in Death is *that?*" We both demanded.

Wrapped around the ship was an enormous tentacle. Its underside was covered in suckers the size of my head while its smooth top was sleek with wavering fins. The tentacle tightened around the ship, causing one of the railings to *crack* as splinters spat out from under its grip.

The others came outside to see what was happening. Like us, they gawked at the tentacle crushing the ship, all of us rendered speechless.

Except for our captain, the resurrected Nathaniel.

"Seamstress prick me!" Nathaniel shouted in awe, taking off his plumed hat. His black bear ears folded downward. "It's the Beast o' the Dark Waters!"

I flicked him a wary look. "The what?"

"When I were alive," Nathaniel explained, still staring at the frightening sight with wonder, "There were tales o' monsters that ruled the seas. One for each cardinal direction. Legends spoke o' terrifying creatures like *Shëfaux the Gelid,* and *Hecrûshou the Hunter*—"

"For *Oscha's* sake!" Hecrûshou groaned beside him, shouldering his glowing trident—his little Bindragon coiled around the fork—and massaged his temples. "*I'm* Hecrûshou the Hunter!"

Nathaniel paused. "Oh… I thought ye were just named after 'im?"

"No! I'm five hundred years old! *I'm* the Bloody original!" His webbed ears folded down in annoyance. "And the twins already killed Shëfaux in Neverland. How did you not know this?"

Nathaniel rubbed his thick neck. "No one Bloody told *me* 'is name…"

"—I'm sorry," I interjected, clearing my throat as I waved a hand at our current problem. "Could you get back on topic and explain *what in Death this thing is before it crushes our ship in half?*"

Nathaniel coughed. "Right… There were rumors among the sailors about a seabeast called the Kraken. It was a ruthless monster that crushed unfortunate ships and—"

"HEY!" the newborn demon shouted at the tentacle from across the deck. He climbed on top of it and walked along its length, waving his arms in the air like a maniac. "Dude! Chill! I'm right here, everything's cool!"

AAAAAAAAAAHHHHNNN? came the rumbling cry from underwater. I could swear it sounded like a whale's call.

Then the ship rocked wildly, waves thrashing from under the bow. I heard Willow yelp behind me as she stumbled to keep balance, our baby wailing in her arms.

"Death!" I snatched her waist to keep her steady and grabbed a nearby rope—

The water below peeled away, and a gigantic, finned head rose higher and higher over the deck. The towering beast opened its huge, black eyes and stared at the skeletal demon on its back.

AAAAAAAAHHHNNN? it rumbled, shaking my belly to its core.

Hecrûshou's little Bindragon perked its finned head at the colossus. It gave a small, curious squeak. *Aaaaahhnnn?*

The giant beast looked at Aahn. Then replied. *AAAAAAHHHHNNN?*

Aaaahnnn! Aahn uncoiled himself from Hecrûshou's trident and slithered down its staff onto the deck. He slithered onto the railing beside the enormous creature. *Aaaahhnn? Aaaaahhhn? Aaaaaahhhnn?*

AAAAAHHHHHNNNN…

The beast lowered its head and playfully touched snouts with Aahn.

I gave Nathaniel a flat stare. "So. The great Kraken is just a giant Bindragon?"

Nathaniel seemed at a loss for words. "Uh… I s'pose it is…"

"See, dude?" the newborn demon patted the beast's head, its fins flapping cheerfully. "Told you everything was cool—*woah!*" The dragon pushed its head into the demon's stomach and flipped him onto its giant skull, causing the man to laugh.

Willow stepped beside me with the baby, giving me a sidelong glance. "This new demon seems rather... bubbly." She commented. "Do you think we can trust him?"

I murmured, "I think I'll leave that judgement to his own kind... but I suppose he hasn't attacked anyone save for the pantry."

Our baby reached for the Bindragon's enormous, snake-like body that was still wrapped around the ship. The boy giggled when his fingers brushed its smooth skin. I chuckled while ruffling Lucas's ashen wisps of hair, the boy's wolf ears flopping in a laugh—

Crrrreeeeaaaaa...!

The Bindragon's grip tightened ever so slightly on our ship, the wood groaning on both sides, splinters puffing out.

I grimaced. "*That*, however, could pose a problem." I cupped my hands around my mouth and shouted up to the scrawny demon atop the dragon. "Could you tell your dragon to release our ship before it snaps the whole vessel in two? I'd rather not risk my child drowning, thank you!"

"Oh, right!" The demon scratched the dragon's brow. "Hey, dude, you think you could let go?"

AAAAAHHHNNNN...

The dragon's suckers *pop, pop, popped* off row by row. The creature slithered off our ship and splashed into the water, bobbing our ship from the residual waves. The dragon leaned its head down to allow the demon to hop onto the deck. He patted his dragon's head, then turned back to us.

"Sorry about him, Your Majesties." He flashed Willow and me a skeletal smile. "He thinks he's the size of a poodle sometimes."

Willow perked an eyebrow beside me. "I see... You seem to know who *we* are. Do you mind telling us who *you* are?"

"And what in Death you want?" Alex added from my other side, his wolf ears grown and curled.

"Right!" The demon snapped his bony fingers. "I almost forgot. My name is Aster Sorelles. I guess you could say I'm here to help the cause." He winked. "And Bloods, are you going to need me."

I eyed him suspiciously. "Why would we need *you*, exact—"

"*Arrrrrgh...!*" Alex suddenly grunted in pain, doubling over. My brother crumpled over the floorboards and clutched his temples with desperate, clawed hands.

"Alex?!" I crouched over him, panicking as I watched my brother writhe on the deck like a wild animal. "What's wrong?! What's going ..."

—rrrrrrrRRRRRRRRRRRrrrrr—

My own temples burst in agony, a deafening ring scratching my eardrums and making my head throb. The pounding intensified, my vision shivering so violently the ship around me blurred into hazy shapes…

Then the shapes solidified again. But everything was wrong. Willow was farther away from me than she'd been a moment ago, and Alex had flipped to my right side somehow. I knew I was thrashing around from the pain, but my vision didn't *match* my movements. It was almost as if…

The answer struck like a gong.

I wasn't looking through my own eyes. I was looking through *Alexander's*. And his vision was doubled, a second layer of the world sluggishly following after the original view beneath its veil.

"Death…!" I sucked in a pained breath, that incessant ring slicing my eardrums. "Not him again…!"

—Sailing, are we? The familiar, hissing voice of Macarius wafted in our shared thoughts. *I suppose the royal couple must return home to claim their throne…*

"Damn it…" Alex chewed through sharpened teeth.

The throbbing burned my temples like hot coals, the whining ring worsening in my ears. "You…" I growled, shaking my head to try and knock Alex's vision out of my eyes. All it did was make me look like a madman in Alexander's peripherals. My throat clicked. "You can go to Void, bastard…"

His chuckles rolled through our thoughts. *How inconsiderate. And here I only thought to pay a friendly check up to—*

I felt someone's thin fingers suddenly latch onto my head. I Saw through Alexander's vision that *his* head was grasped by another, similar hand.

It was the new demon: Aster. He had come between us and grabbed our skulls.

"Hey, Macar," Aster said in a blithe hum. "Long time no see. How you been?"

Macarius's voice paused from our thoughts. *Who are you?*

"What, you don't remember me?" Aster's tone was mockingly overdramatic. He feigned a wounded look, rolling back Alexander's head as he shifted his weight—and shoved *my* head down like an armrest. "That's pretty rude. You went to all that trouble to kill me and don't recognize your own brother's reincarnation?"

Silence from our thoughts—and from the deck around us.

Then Macarius's voice returned in a whisper. *Accursius…?*

"In the flesh," Aster said. "Well. *New* flesh. You get it." His fingers gripped our scalps tighter, making Alex and me wince. "So, things ended kind of rough for us on our last run. But I've got some plans to make *this* run a winner. But part of that means these two are with me." He wobbled Alex and my heads, shaking Alexander's doubled vision in all of our Third Eyes. "Along with their prophetic Hallows. You understand. That's always been my department. Now…"

My vision of Alexander's sight boiled black, dripping away until my own point of view returned at last. The whining ring dimmed in my ears, the throbbing pain receding from my temples.

Now that my own vision was back, the first thing I saw was Aster's hollow face wrought with deep-seeded rage. The demon dug his fingers into my scalp so hard, my eyes watered.

His throat clicked in a heated rumble. "Mind your own fucking business, Macar."

Aster released us, and Alex and I collapsed to the deck in a winded cough.

"There you go," Aster declared. "I put up interference walls around your Third Eyes. Macar won't be able to spy on you while I'm around." He winked a glowing eye. "You're welcome."

I pushed up and stared at the horrifically thin demon, stammering, "You're… you're Accursius Lysandre?"

Aster shrugged. "I was, in my last life. Macar killed me and now I'm here." He gestured to himself. "New vessel, new bloodline. Guess the Lysandre line died with me in the 15th century."

"Where is your proof?" Willow demanded, her fox ears growing as she came to help me to my feet. She balanced our son with her other arm and glaring at Aster. "You don't expect us to simply take your word for it?"

Aster lifted a thoughtful knuckle to his lips. "Hm… I guess I have *this* as proof?" He turned around and uplifted his soaked tunic. Displayed on the very center of his sharp, skeletal back…

Was a Crest of three black diamonds.

"Macar and I were born with the same Crest as you guys," he said, then produced a fist sized crystal ball from his Storagebox. As his hands gleamed azure and poured into the crystal he held, his Crest shifted into a glowing-blue Dream mark. "Does that count?"

The deck was smothered with silence.

Aster hefted himself onto the now-splintered railing and sat with one leg swinging off the edge, patting the enormous head of his Bindragon, who cooed a low, reverberating *AAAAAAAHHHNNNN* from the sea.

Alex and I flicked each other disbelieving stares.

I opened my mouth to protest. Shut it. Then scratched my head and asked, "What of the rest of your Hallows? If you're the other half of the Lightcaster, won't you have the other half of the Hallows your brother gained?"

Aster turned a finger in his meercat ear and hummed. "That's not how it works. Macar and I aren't like you two. The Shadowblood twins gain all elements that are *split* between them. Macar and I could, in theory, only gain *whole* elements where each set of three would be scattered between us. Back in my past life, he was born with two whole elements from the Dream realm while *I* was born with one whole element from the Dream realm—the one he didn't have. Supposedly that's how our Hallows would have been gained, too."

Alex scowled. "What do you mean 'in theory' and 'supposedly'? Macar gained three sets of Hallows already, so shouldn't you have them as well now?"

"First off." He lifted a skinny finger. "Dream was pretty sure we *both* needed to be present at the Relics to properly gain our Hallows. Macar got them alone, without me. And strictly speaking, he didn't gain his Hallows the way he was supposed to—he *killed* to get those. If he'd gotten them the way Dream intended, he only would have come out with either one or two, and *I* would have gotten the leftovers. But since I wasn't there for all that, he's got nine Hallows and I have… well, just the one I was born with."

I crossed my arms. "So… where have you been? If you were here the whole time, why wait until now to appear?"

Alex grunted, "And as a Necrofera no less?"

Aster rubbed his boney neck, his pleasant expression falling. "Oh. Well, uh… when I first had a vision of you guys surfacing to Everland, I tried to make my way to the capital to meet up with you all. But I was so busy looking ahead at where you *would* be, I… lost track of what was happening *now*. After the war started, a Rockraider saw my Dream mark activate with another vision and they locked me up, then shipped me to Tanderam Prison. Your rescue team shook things up in there, but…" He gave a shallow shrug. "You never made it to my floor. Because of all the guards they lost, they had to reprioritize the soldiers. The ones on my floor all abandoned us, and after a few weeks…" He gestured to his ribbed, freakishly skinny stomach. "I, uh… sort of starved to death. I've been trapped in there for a couple years since."

The night fell quiet as we took in his story, horrified.

As a light breezed rolled through, Willow broke the silence. "I… I'm so sorry…"

Aster rubbed a finger under his nose. "It's all good now, I guess… I knew I'd get out eventually. I had a vision that the new regent of Everland would send another team to overtake the prison, so it was really just a waiting game for me."

"But we…" My fists clenched, sickened with myself at this news. "We were right there… If we'd gone just a little further, we could have found you and…" I hung my head. "You wouldn't have met your death if we'd finished the job. Your life was in *our* hands, and we… we failed you…"

"Actually." Aster lifted an informative, twig-thin finger. "If you *did* get me out back then, it wouldn't have led to the one future we have left." He threw up his hands in a laugh. "Sometimes, you just got to do what needs to be done so the rest of us can keep existing. It sucks being a Seer sometimes, huh?"

Alex and I sighed our agreement there.

Alex scratched his head in a frown. "There's still something I don't understand… Dream claimed we four could only be born *together*. Macarius has been alive for centuries and—"

"And broke the cycle," Aster finished for me with a shrug. "By your own rules, if *I* couldn't have been reborn while Macar was still alive, neither could *you* both. The four of us are supposed to be born together. But since Macar royally screwed up the cycle, the three of *us* were reborn together while Macarius was still alive."

My brow furrowed. "You mean… you were born on…"

"The First of Spiridel, 2082," he said. "Only, *I* was born on the surface in High Everland. I'm from Mimier, common-born this time."

I rubbed my temples desperately. "Nira help me, this doesn't make any sense…"

Alex muttered, "Nothing ever makes sense anymore. By that logic, this makes perfect sense."

Aster coughed into a fist and looked up at his Bindragon. "So, uh… is it cool if I stick around? That's what leads to the good future, so…"

I glanced at Willow in question. "What say you, love?"

Lucas began to fuss in her arms, and she sighed. "I suppose so long as our Ancients agree to keep an eye on you, you may stay with us…"

Alex growled threateningly, "But if you lay one *tooth* on anyone from our ship, we won't hesitate to reap your rotted NecroSeam and send you to the Void. Understood?"

Aster shot up pacifying hands. "Oh, I got it. And like I said, I don't want to eat souls right now."

Willow quirked an eyebrow. "What do you mean 'right now'? Do you plan to eat souls later?"

He circled a hand in the air. "I'm just thinking if that huge army of Fera ever show up, they'll have like, *zero* trouble forcing me to eat souls. So, I can't exactly rule out the possibility. I thought if I didn't eat any souls, they wouldn't feel my tiny existence. But if that didn't work out, I'd have to eat a *ton* to stand up against them, but I haven't had even one soul yet, so they'd overpower me in a heartbeat." He shrugged. "So, never say never."

Hecrûshou rubbed his chin and mumbled, "He has a point… La'Lunaî could easily Mark him if she so pleased."

Miranda sneered, "And considering she's collecting stray demons like rare Evocator cards, she *would* please."

Cilia snorted. "Fine. He can stay. But my kitchen is *off limits.*" She shot Aster a rueful glare. "If you need to stave off your soul-thirst, you come directly to me. I'll give you your fair ration. If I see your slimy tongue exploring my cabinets again, I'll singe you to a crisp and serve your roasted arse to your Bindragon. Am I understood, newborn?"

Aster gave a nervous smile. "Y-yeah…! Got it!"

Willow massaged her eyes, murmuring to me, "Well, I suppose this addition will provide us another perspective for the council, when I propose demon citizenship…" She yawned, hefting the cooing baby over her shoulder.

I laid a hand on her back softly. "Perhaps we should continue this conversation in the morning, love…" I kissed her cheek, and kissed Lucas's brow. "You both should get some rest."

She hummed tiredly. "As should you."

I glanced over my shoulder at Alexander.

His wolf ears were still grown, and he flicked one in my direction as he met my gaze. Then he nodded toward Willow, as if telling me to follow her and let him handle our new party member.

I nodded my thanks, my lids suddenly heavy with exhaustion now that the excitement had waned.

With a yawn, I followed after Willow, heading back to our cabin to sleep.

Well… as much as my dreams would allow, at least…

21

THEORIES

HERRIN

"Okay!" I huffed and scattered my notes over the iron table. "Let's see what we've got…"

The foredeck glowed with sunlight, seagulls squalling overhead in the cheery blue sky as our party's black birds croaked and cawed at them testily. I sucked in an invigorating breath, my lungs feeling as light as the fluffy clouds drifting overhead.

It was a great day to find some answers!

Across from me sat Xavier and Willow. The royal couple had given their son to Yulia this morning, since our meeting here required their full attention. They looked exhausted and groggy, but tried their best to keep poised for this occasion.

Alexander was here too, but he sure as Bloods wasn't happy about it, glaring at the fourth member of our meeting:

Aster Sorelles. The reincarnation of Accursius Lysandre.

I couldn't help my stupid grin, my wings twitching anxiously as I shuffled my notes on the table.

Accursius Lysandre—right here in front of us…! The missing piece of the equation, the variable so overlooked we didn't even think he was *part* of this anymore… and he stumbled right onto our ship!

I was laughing like a maniac now, scrambling to organize my chaotic notes. Some pages fluttered in the breeze, almost flying off, but I quickly snatched them up and tried like Land to pin them all down with as many appendages as I could offer. Fingers, knees, elbows, wings… Bloods, my muscles were screaming…

"Er…" Xavier began across the table, raising a concerned hand, "Do you need some help, Herrin?"

"Nnn… nope…" I strained to keep my papers steady. One slipped out with a new gust of wind, and I snagged it with my teeth in a panic.

"—Really, Herrin," the voice of my assistant, Marian, scolded behind me. "Do you plan to enroll as the circus's new contortionist?"

I craned my head back to her—

Stopped.

Marian was giving me a disapproving look as she walked over, carrying a silver tray of iced tea and lemon cakes. Tucked under an arm was a leather bound ledger, a fountain-quill clipped to the cover.

But what had me staring was her frilly, yellow-and-cream stripped dress. Her *short* dress.

My face burned, and not from the beating sun.

Never once had I *ever* seen Marian's legs—*or* her shoulders, even. I'd gotten so used to her in long sleeves and gloves, I guess I figured it wasn't her thing. Then again, I knew the long sleeves were usually her way of hiding the latticed scars that were slashed all the way down her arms that wrapped to her fingers.

Scars that were now in full view under the bright sunlight, marring her deep-bronze skin with hardened, crisscrossed lines.

It always hurt to look at them. The few times she'd rolled up her sleeves around me, it was a cruel reminder that I screwed up… She'd gone missing when we rounded up the other Enlighteners in Neverland, when the war started. It was *my* job to find her as the Archchancellor of the guild…

It turned out, the old queen of Neverland, Syreen, had captured her and thrown her in the dungeons. Marian told me she'd been tortured into giving our location away with her prophetic Hallows… how the queen had used her Arborvoking to pry thick vines under her skin, twisting them from the inside and…

My feathers shuddered. I didn't blame Marian for wanting to cover up the scars. But now, with them so exposed like that so casually, in the most out-of-character dress I've ever seen her wear… I guess that meant she was ready to put that painful chapter of her life behind her?

Marian plucked the loose paper out of my teeth and set down her tray on the table, the iced tea clinking in their sweating glasses.

"Bloods, look at this mess," Marian sighed, shaking her feathered head at my disorganized notes. She used the glasses to pin down the papers so I didn't have to strain myself anymore. Her auburn wings tucked against her back as she lowered into the seat beside me. "You really ought to take more care with these things, Herrin. Otherwise, we'll be running around like headless chickens trying to piece these chronicles together and…"

She paused, seeing I was still staring at her, and she questioned, "What?"

"Uh…" I scratched my feathered hair, flicking my attention to my notes instead. "N-nothing…"

"—Why, what a lovely dress, Marian," Willow complimented across the table. The Death Queen took up one of the iced teas and sipped it heartily, smiling at Marian. "It suits you quite nicely."

Marian's face turned beet red. She mumbled, "Er, thank you… but it isn't mine, actually. I, er… spilled the first batch of tea on my other dress, so Sirra-Lynn gave me this one for today…"

Willow chuckled. "Well, I think it's quite fetching on you. Perhaps you should consider adding something similar to your daily wardrobe?"

Marian coughed into a fist, mortified. "I, uhm… I supposed I will think on it, Your Majesty… Thank you…" Looking desperate to change the subject, Marian started again in a nervous laugh, "S-so, er… Shall we begin?"

"Yes!" I squeaked, a little too loud, and I cleared my throat, quickly dipping my quill in the inkwell by my *blank* paper. "All right, so… Aster." I glanced up at the white-pupiled demon across the table. He was already stuffing his face with every last lemon cake on the tray Marian had brought. "We have a few questions for you, if you're okay with that?"

Aster shoved the last lemon cake down his throat and gave a satisfied belch. He kicked his feet on the table and folded his arms behind his head, glancing at the sea to watch his enormous Bindragon play in the water with Hecrûshou's tiny Bindragon, Aahn.

"Shoot," Aster encouraged.

"Firstly," I began, "How do you know so much about your past life? No one ever *consciously* remembers anything from their past incarnations, so how did you learn about it?"

Aster rubbed a finger under his nose, one of his meercat ears perking. "Oh, that one's easy. I'm a Seer."

Marian muttered, "As am I, mind you. I certainly don't know my past incarnation."

Aster shrugged. "I'm half the Lightcaster, here. Most oracles tell me they've never experienced the things I have."

Marian didn't sound impressed. "Such as?"

"Well, I've had a ton of shared visions with Accursius, for one thing."

Willow's brow furrowed across from me. "Shared visions…? With your past self?"

Xavier rubbed his newly shaven chin—and I absently noted how *thin* his face was compared to Alexander without the beard—and looked at his wife curiously. "You mean like those visions you've had with your grandfather?"

Hold up. My attention snapped to the Death Queen, and I prodded, "Your grandfather? You mean Dream?"

"Yes." Willow tucked a lock of ashen hair behind her ear, the light breeze catching the strands and sweeping them behind her. "I've had several shared visions with him. They occur when two Seers have simultaneous visions of one another. For me, I would have visions of Grandfather in the past, while he had visions of me in the future."

Marian took the liberty of scribbling that down on her own paper, a look of fascination prying her eyes wide.

"Wow…" I breathed, looking at Aster. "Does that describe what you've had with Accursius?"

"Yep." Aster winked one white-pupiled eye at me. "That's it exactly."

Marian paused her note-taking. "I've heard of shared visions among few talented Seers, but… to share visions of a past self?" Her wings shuddered anxiously. "That's simply unheard of! Even Dream never mentioned such a thing!"

Aster snorted. "No offense to Dream, but his visions were never as strong as mine. Not even when I was Accursius."

Alexander, who'd been silent this whole time, rolled his mismatched eyes and leaned back in a mutter, "A humble one, he is…"

I twisted my mouth in thought. "But that makes sense, considering the Shadowblood's abilities have outmatched *all* the Relic Children's incarnations…" I pointed my quill at Aster. "But instead of exceeding in Death Hallows, the Lightcaster was said to exceed in Dream Hallows, which seems to match up with you and Macar."

Aster perked an eyebrow. "Where was that said?"

"In Dream's journal," I explained, picking up the dusty, thin journal from the table and opening it to the page I quoted, showing it to Aster. "Dream wrote how all the incarnations of the two twins followed the same pattern every time. One pair was born with Death Hallows, split in half between them, with half-colored eyes." I gestured to Xavier and Alexander. The brothers shifted uncomfortably now that they were under the spotlight. Then I waved to Aster. "And the other pair was born with Dream Hallows, split in *whole* elements, where one was a Dual-Evocator with Blessings of dream and illusion, and the other with a single Blessing of prophecy."

Aster crossed his arms over his chest. "Huh… Dream told me about that when I was Accursius, but he didn't mention he had a journal about it."

Marian drummed her scarred fingers over the table. "But that brings up another question that Dream himself couldn't answer in the journal. *Why* are one pair's Hallows split into halves, and the other pair's are not?"

The twins only shrugged alongside Aster, and Willow shook her head.

I pursed my lips, scratching my feathered hair in a grumble. "I guess… that probably means… unlike the Shadowblood, the Lightcaster must *not* be one soul split in two. They must be two *whole* souls on their own."

Aster flicked up one of his meercat ears. "Makes sense, I guess. But why *weren't* Macar and I one soul?"

"I… don't' know." I set down my quill and pinched the brim of my nose, mulling it over.

Okay, Herrin, I thought determinedly. *Think! The Shadowblood and the Lightcaster were both created by the Gods. One of the pair will bring destruction— the other pair will bring salvation… but then…*

"Why would the Gods create Their own destruction in the first place?" I questioned out loud.

It just didn't add up. The Gods wouldn't willingly create someone who would kill them. If they'd meant to, they would have created the *second* pair to counter them. There had to be something I was missing.

Marian hummed beside me. "Is it possible the End will *not* be caused by either pair?"

I stared at her. Everyone else did, too.

"What do you mean?" I asked, rifling through my notes. "The prophecy says…"

"*One will save,*" Marian recited by heart, lifting a finger. "*One will ruin. One will defend, or cometh the True End.*" She lowered her hand and tapped the journal. "The prophecy gives three roles. The Savior, the Ruiner, and the Defender. At first, Herrin and I thought these roles were for Xavier, Alexander, and Macarius…" She waved to Aster. "But with a fourth member now at play, the math doesn't match. Yet, if we consider that Xavier and Alexander are two halves of *one whole* soul…"

"The three roles still fit!" I gasped, her point clicking. "That would mean the prophecy isn't talking about all four of them—but all three *whole* souls! And…!" I ruffled my hair-feathers anxiously. "Holy Bloods…! Marian, what if we've been reading that line completely wrong? *One will save. One will ruin. One will defend, or cometh the True End*—What if it isn't saying the End will come if one doesn't save and defend? What if it means the End will come if all *three* roles aren't filled?"

Marian's feathers quivered with excitement. "Which would mean this isn't about them causing the End, but—!"

"All three of them stopping it *together!*"

"—If you're quite finished!" Willow's impatient voice called from, weirdly, below us. I looked down. *Oh.* Apparently, Marian and I got so excited, we didn't realize we'd flapped in the air a few yards. Below our dangling feet, I saw Willow set an expectant hand on her hip. "Would you mind coming down and walking the rest of us through your sudden breakthrough?"

Marian and I coughed and flew back down to the table. "Uh, right," I said in a blush. "Sorry…"

"In short," Marian said after clearing her throat. "There is a possibility *none* of you will cause the End of Existence. Not even Macarius."

Xavier and Alex perked at that, asking in unison, "You're sure?"

She nodded. "I'm almost positive. There may be an outside source that causes the End that the Gods need you *all* to stop."

The twins' hopeful faces drained away like water on oil.

Xavier mumbled, "So… you mean we'll have to work… *with*… Macarius?"

Alex gave an irritated rumble. "You must be joking?"

Aster, at least, seemed to accept it well enough as he scratched his chin and hummed, "Could be cool. Why not?"

Willow snapped at him, "Why not?! He's trying to kill us!"

Aster shrugged. "Maybe we can convince him to stop?"

"He's already killed my Grandfather Dream!" Willow jabbed a sharp hand all around the ship. "He killed Cilia, he killed *you*—He has slaughtered anyone and everyone whenever it fancies him! He *enjoys* it! He killed Ninumel just last night! And now that blood-lusting madman is on his way to *my* home, intending to kill *my family!*"

Aster sucked on wincing teeth. "Right… so, 'making friends' is out…"

"Oh, Seamstress Cleanse me…" Willow rubbed her face with harsh hands, her white fox ears growing and curling tight to her long hair. She flicked a furious glare straight at me. "Herrin? Tell me this is only a foolish theory and not a definite fact?"

My wings dipped. *Ouch…* It was a shot in the dark, sure, but 'foolish'?

"Um…" I mumbled, rubbing an arm as my confidence fell. "It's only a theory… I guess…"

Slam!

Marian hit her hands on the table, making the drinks clatter. Bloods, Marian was *seething* mad. I'd never seen her this angry. Her glare curdled at Willow as her wing feathers bristled, her talons sharpening from her fingers.

"It may be a theory," Marian rumbled, her tone edged. "But Herrin's logic makes far too much sense to ignore, *Your Majesty*." Marian curtly collected our notes from the table and *clacked* them in order.

Then she snagged my arm and jerked me away from the table with her. "If you don't mind, the Archchancellor and I have some discussing to conduct regarding our *foolish theory*."

I tripped behind Marian, her talons digging into my arm so hard, it hurt like Land. "U-um, Marian?" I said meekly as she dragged me into the ship's inner hallways. "Could you, uh… ease up a bit—?"

"I can't *believe* she said that to you…!" Marian fumed, her wings flapping hard and smacking me in the face. "The audacity! The gall! If she'd been paying *any* attention, she'd see that you were right and…!"

"Marian, it's okay!" I pulled her to a stop, grabbing her arms to calm her down. "Seriously. It's all right. I don't care."

Her anger evaporated. "But… she was so rude to you, and…"

"It's fine. Really." I gripped her arms for assurance. "Thanks for the support but… I really can't blame her for being resistant to a theory like this. Not after what Macarius did to everyone she loved… You've got to keep that in mind, Marian."

Marian ground her teeth, looking away indignantly. Then she blushed, noticing my hands were still clutching her scar-ridden arms.

Embarrassed, I quickly let her go. "S-sorry… I didn't mean to…"

"It's… fine…" She self-consciously hugged herself and gripped her arms, as if trying to hide the scars from sight. But without her usual gloves or long sleeves, it didn't cover a single crease. She sighed, shutting her eyes as she changed the subject. "I'm positive this is the true meaning behind the prophecy… It's the only explanation that fits Aster's sudden appearance."

I nodded. "Agreed. But we'll need to find proof. If the world needs Macarius alive to bring us that single future we have left, it's going to take a *lot* of convincing for the others. They're set on killing him right now." I knuckled my temple, thinking hard. "So, the question is, how do we *find* that proof? We don't even know which of the three souls belong to which roles from the prophecy…"

"All could be he, by choice or by say," Marian recited from the prophecy's second line. It was the line Dream failed to mention until the night before he was murdered. *"And can change if they please, by claiming thy name."*

I bit my knuckle. "Right… they decide which roles they fill…" I paused, a thought hitting me. "Unless it actually means… what they call themselves doesn't matter. And if their self-labels don't matter, they're already predestined as the other roles…" I took a breath, then turned to Marian. "Have you read Faulin's theory of the Soul's Origin?"

Marian put a fist at her hip. "Of course. It's the theory that energy cannot be created or destroyed, only displaced. Similarly, Faulin theorized that Soulenergy is created by various origins, from which Nira borrows to create our souls. Some souls are theorized to originate from the physical planet itself, such as trees and dirt and water—or in *our* case, the animals that inhabited the planet before shifters evolved—and some originate from the collective beliefs and ideologies shared by massive groups of shifters from their various cultures."

I grinned, adding, "And what, would you say, are the three most *massively* shared beliefs that all cultures have in common? So much that we consider them absolute truths?"

"I suppose… that would be…" Her eyes widened with a gasp. "Life, Death, and Rebirth!"

"And the prophecy's three roles are the Savior, the Ruiner, and the Defender." I held up three fingers. "Now if we assign those three collective truths, Life would be the Savior, Death would be the Ruiner, and Rebirth would be the Defender."

She rubbed her temples furiously. "But there's a flaw, there. By that theory, *Death* would be created from Death, *Land* would be created from Life…"

I shook my head. "You're thinking too literally. What other parallels are there for life, death, and rebirth? For Savior, Ruiner, and Defender?"

She took longer to think on that. "I suppose… Preservation, Destruction, and Re-construction? Or…" She frowned. "Wait. What if *Conservation* parallels the Savior? To conserve the life that already exists—or to conserve past lives that once lived… which would mean, if the Ruiner represents Death, that could mean destruction *of* that past life—which represents the concept of *change!*" She threw up her hands—along with the papers she was holding, the notes fluttering around her as she grabbed my shirt and shook me ecstatically. "That's it, Herrin! That's the key! The Savior saves the past, the Ruiner saves the future, and the Defender saves the present!" She let me go in a shrill giggle, her wings fluttering. "When together, they save *existence!*"

"And now that we know what we're looking for, we'll know how to determine which souls belong to which roles!" I fumbled back toward the deck outside. "Come on, Marian! We're not done with our interviewing—!"

"Wait!" She grabbed my wrist to stop me. "Perhaps it would be wiser to draw up a few notes first? To organize our presentation for our…" She grimaced. "*Reluctant* audience?"

My excitement faded at the reminder. "Oh. Right… Good idea, Marian."

She beamed at that, and I found myself blushing. Weirdly enough, with her new dress and that smile… she was actually really cute.

But she would probably slap me if I mentioned that.

I coughed and mumbled, "Um, maybe *you* should do the organizing this time…"

She gave a considering frown. "Agreed."

22

DISPENSABLE

GENEVIEVE

I hid inside the vine-covered brush in the center of the royal gardens, quivering under the cover of leaves.

I was too close to being discovered. The trembling ball of fear tightening my chest threatened to leap out of my throat, but I suppressed the impulse to run.

I had my orders. Father instructed me to meet him and mother at this spot, where the Blossom of Gold awaited.

I peeled back a large leaf to steal a glance at the two hollow, twisted stumps in the open field in front of me. Sunlight spilled over the well-kempt grass and beautiful flowers with such majesty, you could truly feel Shel's presence warming your soul.

And I, the betrayer, felt the mountain of his wrath upon my back.

Just to be sure I was well hidden, I evoked my new plant Hallows onto my hiding brush to grow more leaves, shielding my trembling figure. Oh, when were Father and Mother arriving—?

"Genevieve," the rumbling voice of my step-father hissed above me, making me start. "It is time."

I peeled back the brush with shivering arms, rising into a kneel before him and my pregnant mother, who waited at his side with a proud smile splitting her face. Father now had *three* colors patching his hair and eyes, a mixed painting of scarlet, azure and emerald. He had successfully gained the Ocean Relic's Hallows during his journey.

And now, I was to give him his fourth set of Hallows.

"Yes, Father," I whispered, bowing my head in reverence. "I am ready to help the realms steer toward a thriving future."

I took a deep breath, strode to the twin trunks… and began to sing.

Breathe ye child your life begins…

I mimicked the song my queen had sung, when she gave the Blossom its Call. My voice was hardly as beautiful as hers, yet it seemed to be enough. The trunks twisted and stretched upward, growing larger until the Blossom of Gold towered over us and blocked the sunlight in its glowing majesty.

When I finished the song, I fell into silence and turned to Father and Mother.

"I-I… I am ready, Father…" I said. But I paused. "However… I did not kill the queen to gain these Hallows…" I slid two fingers through my newly golden locks. "It seems that only the spilling of blood is needed to gain the Blessings… so, I offer you my willing blood, Father. This way, I may continue to fight for our future… by your side."

I withdrew a dagger from my belt, handing it to Father. Then I offered him my palm, kneeling.

Father smiled warmly, a sigh spilling from his scaled lips. He cupped my chin and whispered, "That won't be necessary, dearest daughter."

My gaze was confused. "But Father… you need your Hallows, don't you? You are the Lightcaster…"

"Oh, I certainly need my rightful Hallows," Father hummed.

—Pain suddenly speared through my chest, an icy numbness splintering my blood.

I tried to gasp for breath, but none came, my lungs tight with pain. My gaze drifted down in panic.

Father had evoked his ice Hallows—and driven a frozen spire through my heart.

"What I *don't* need, Genevieve…" His scaled smile dripped into a callous glower as a golden, fourth patch of color bled into his hair and eyes. "Is a flight risk daughter who has been bewitched by the golden charm of a *Relicblood queen.*"

I struggled under his icy spire, fear exacerbating the pain, my breaths strained and ragged. My gaze flicked to my mother behind him. I reached for her desperately. "M… mother…" I wheezed. "H-help…"

Mother's once caring smile curdled, and she rubbed her swollen belly with a sigh. "Terribly sorry, dear. You father and I have already made arrangements with a certain Queen of Demons. You understand."

My soul hollowed. "Wh… what…?"

"Honestly," Mother drawled cruelly. "I blame your birth-father for your poor judgement…" She cupped her face with disappointment. "I had hoped you'd evaded his weakness… but it seems I was wrong."

Tears stung, venom building in my glands and leaking over my tongue.

Father chuckled. "Don't despair, Lannyse. She was of use to us, in the end." His face wrenched with hate. "And if my supposed *twin* is to be believed… Ashya the Ravager will find *great* use for a new Relicblood in her army."

The metallic taste of blood flooded over my lips. I collapsed on my back, staring up at the Blossom of Gold… until my vision spotted and turned to blackness.

My mother's voice drifted in my ears in the void. "Fear not, Genevieve… your new brother will surely succeed in your place. He, at least, holds the blood of our Savior…"

23

PREPARATIONS

WILLOW

"Vi, Vi, Vi, Vi, Vi…" Lucas babbled in my arms, the boy patting his white-necked Songcrow's feathers gently. "Virro! Virro… *ro, ro, ro, Virro…*"

"Very good, Lucas," I chuckled, kissing his head as I held him close, rocking him for a heartfelt moment from inside Yulia's private cabin. "You and Virro be good to Auntie Yulia. I don't want to hear about any troublesome behavior."

Yulia laughed behind a polite hand. "Oh, he's far too sweet for such a thing. Not to worry."

I sighed, handing Lucas over to her.

The baby giggled in Yulia's arms, reaching for the Dreamcatcher's beautiful face. Virro buzzed around them now, and Lucas continued babbling his name—the only word he knew, at the moment—as he tried to catch the little bird.

Xavier and Alexander stood on either side of me. Alex leaned against the wall with his arms folded while Xavier scratched the thin beard that had regrown along his jaw over the weeks at sea. He'd kept it groomed and trimmed this time, keeping it only around the frame of his face and not around his lips like he'd done before.

Xavier smiled cheerily, "He's certainly taken a liking to you, Yulia."

Yulia bobbed him with a bright smile and tapped his nose with a finger. "Well, the feeling's mutual, little deary."

I chuckled and reached for the satchel slung around my shoulder, gripping the strap… but I bit my lip. "Are you sure you'll be fine watching him for so long? We've only ever needed him looked after for a few hours at a time… This will be the first time we'll need you to watch him for an entire day, and…"

"Your Majesty," Yulia interrupted in a light laugh, "I understand perfectly. We're descending to Grim tonight. A returning queen and king have much to prepare for. And I'm more than happy to watch over my honorary nephew." She lifted the boy in the air and nuzzled his nose against hers, prompting a giggle from him. "And he is *far* easier to watch than the twins ever were." She eyed Xavier with a grin. "It's quite clear that he didn't gain his docile nature from *you*, Xavier."

Alex snickered from the wall while Xavier gave a nervous smile. "I have to agree with you, there…"

I hummed. "Well, if you're sure you'll be fine…" I slipped off my satchel and flipped it open, pulling out the several Storagespheres and boxes cluttered inside. "*This* one is his milk with a few icepacks, *this* one is extra clothes and bibs, *this* one is his solid foods and spoons, *this* one is full of toys and his blanket and his pacifier—"

"—Do *not* forget his pacifier!" Xavier added hurriedly. "He only ever takes to this particular one. He'll throw anything else away."

I nodded fervently. "Yes, yes, and then his bath time is exactly 6 o'clock—"

"—and he only eats the *chicken* solid foods after that—"

"—and then he'll only take the milk to get him to sleep, and…"

Yulia stopped us with a gentle hand.

"Your Majesties," she began, closing my satchel and slinging it around her shoulder as she hefted Lucas on her hip. "I do remember all this from the last time I watched him during the Land Queen's wedding. My memory hasn't dwindled that swiftly."

I blushed. Xavier cleared his throat. "A-ah… yes. Right… er, good…"

I scratched my head, dragging my boot over the floorboards in thought. "I suppose, if that's everything…" I lingered awkwardly, feeling like I'd forgotten something. I was sure there was *one* more point to make… wasn't there? I rubbed my temple, exhaustion weighing down my mood. "Let's see… you have the bottles, the toys, the clothes…"

Xavier snapped his fingers. "Ah! And the diapers! We included the rash cream in the same sphere, and extra wipes in case—"

"For Death's sake!" Alexander groaned, *thunking* his head against the wall. "Just hand over the coffins and *go!*"

I smacked my brow. "The *coffins!* That was it…!"

Yulia seemed confused. "Coffins?"

Alex pushed off the wall and reached into his coat pocket, producing his mother's Storagecoffin where her shrunken vessel was wrapped in a modest cloth. He handed the coffin to Yulia.

"Xavier and I wondered if…" Alex drew in a long breath, closing his eyes, "if you could watch after our parents' vessels while we prepare for the descent into Grim?"

Yulia blinked at him, then at Xavier when *he* stepped beside his brother and offered her the Storagecoffin that held their father's vessel. Yulia's lips quivered, tentatively accepting the coffins with thin, grey fingers.

"I…" She grew quiet. "You're certain you wish for… *me* to carry them…?"

The twins spoke as one. "Of course we're certain." Xavier added separately, "They may as well have been your parents just as well as ours."

Alex grunted his agreement. "There's no one else we trust more with them."

Yulia's eyes began to mist. Then she smiled in a sniffle. "Of… Of course… I shall take great care of them…"

"—Hey, Yulia, you up?" a new voice sounded from the open doorway. Jimmy appeared under the frame, ducking to avoid hitting his antlers on it. He found Alexander, Xavier and me. Then he saw Yulia with the baby, dabbing at her eyes while clutching the two Storagecoffins.

Jimmy retracted. "Oh… Uh, sorry. I guess I'll, uh… come back later?"

"No, no!" I blurted—quickly pushing the twins toward the door as I flashed him a smile. "No need! We were just… er, leaving. Now. Yes…" I shoved the twins past him into the hall, turning back to blow Lucas a kiss. "Don't give Yulia a difficult time, dear! We love you!"

With that, we left, crossing the hallway as a trio.

Alex muttered back at me. "What in Bloods was that about?"

I jerked my head back toward Yulia's door. "I'm not about to disrupt the couple when they barely have time to see each other as it is."

Alex scowled, perplexed. "What do you mean?"

Xavier hummed. "They've been taking opposite shifts while watching over our dreams. Yulia has the morning shift and Jimmy takes the night shift."

"I *meant* what do you mean 'the couple'?" Alex demanded. "Since when were they courting?"

I tapped a contemplative finger to my lips. "I'm not sure it's official quite yet… They tend to keep to themselves about such things."

Alex's scowl deepened. "Then how do you know… why would that…" He rubbed his eyes. "Oh, never mind. I don't care enough."

Xavier and I chuckled.

"… would have to determine which soul fits which role," a girl's voice mumbled from a cracked door we passed by.

I knew that voice. It was Marian.

The three of us stopped and peeked inside. We found the cardinal girl sitting at a parchment-cluttered table beside Herrin, the two Enlighteners sorting through dozens of notes and texts with determination.

Herrin's wings bowed up and down in thought as he murmured, "We'll have to come up with specific questions for each of them. See which of the twins prefer which philosophy, and ask Aster which one *he…*"

My mood dripped in annoyance, my fox ears growing. They were *still* discussing that ridiculous theory? The one that suggested we had to work with the man who was trying to kill us?

I stormed onward, stomping outside to the deck. Xavier and Alex followed behind me.

Most of our party was out and about, here. The ghosts of Vendy and Hugh chatted across the deck, their arms folded over the railing as Hugh's crow, Lady Lilac, cawed playfully with the little Bindragon—and the *giant* Bindragon that followed our ship. Henry leaned on the rail beside them like a watchful chaperone, wearing a face-mask over his eyes that gave him temporary soul-sight. He crossed his burly arms over his chest and lightly scratched his stubbled chin with his hook-hand.

I found Cilia and Kael sharing a meal with their descendants, Neal and Claude. Neal's messenger raven, Ace, wolfed down his own snack that Neal had set aside for him.

Nathaniel was at the helm as always, muttering to Aiden and Apson about some wager he'd lost this morning.

Matthiel was speaking with Lëtta on the other side of the deck, his hands waving in instructive gestures that mimicked a stitching motion. I presumed they were discussing their soul-tying lessons… which I hadn't been able to attend myself, of late. My list of duties had been piling up.

Near the bow, I spotted Aster sitting round a wooden table eating breakfast. As expected, Aster had several plates surrounding him, each one piled higher than his skeletal head.

I led the way toward the gluttonous demon. Alexander plopped into the seat to Aster's left while Xavier eased into the chair on his right.

I, on the other hand, was too furious to sit, tapping my foot and muttering, "I can't *believe* those Enlighteners are still obsessing over their detestable theory…" I stalked around the table. My long hair drifted and wavered with every turn I made, loose strands picking up in the wind and streaking across my face irritably. I brushed them away in a string of obscenities.

Alexander hunched over the table, swiping one of Aster's many plates for himself. Aster shot him a wounded look, but Alexander's glower was so fierce, the demon raised no verbal protest, and returned his attention to his own meal in a depressed pout.

Alex didn't seem to care. He looked groggier than usual, dark rings puffing under his lids as he stabbed a potato cube with a spare fork lying on the table as if it were the source of all his troubles in the world.

Xavier looked exhausted as well, but I knew that was from Lucas. The baby was teething last night, so he'd broken his usual sleeping pattern and woken every two hours. None of us had slept well.

As Xavier took a plate for himself, his dark grey hair fell freely to his shoulders and drifted behind him in the breeze, his bangs ruffling away from his face to expose the scar running down his right, colorless eye. He yawned and found an extra set of silverware, sluggishly eating his claimed meal with the rest of them.

I ceased my pacing, one of my fox ears twitching as I looked between the three men who'd blatantly ignored me. "Am I the only one who sees how ludicrous their... their *theory* is?"

Alex was the first to answer grittily. "No."

Aster leaned back in his chair and folded his arms behind his head thoughtfully. "I don't know. I mean, it could make sense."

I gawked at the skeletal demon. "How?!"

Aster threw up his hands. "I'm not saying I like it! Just, you know, think about it. Why else would the Gods bother to make Macar's soul in the first place? They wouldn't willingly make a soul they thought would end existence."

"But that...!" I ground my sharpened teeth. "It doesn't...! *ARGH!*" My soul's fire exploded out of my hands in a burst of blue flames.

I paused. *Blue flames?* Bloods, I don't remember the last time I was this livid; if I ever *had* been.

My rage ebbed as I stared at my smoking hands, the fire puffing out. *Odd...* Blue flames usually made me exhausted, even after a short usage. I didn't feel the least bit tired now. *I must have grown stronger these last few years away from the palace...*

Xavier drummed his fingers over the back of his chair. "Is this the proper time to worry over this? We have far more pressing matters to see to tonight—"

"I can't accept them humoring that *lunatic* idea of theirs!" I shouted.

Alex picked at his meal and grunted, "I've already decided to ignore those two. I'm killing the cobra first chance I'm given. We had a plan. I'm not changing it now."

Xavier hesitantly lifted a considering finger. "But what if they're right? What if we do need him alive for all of us to survive? We wouldn't have much of a choice *except* to change the plan, would we?"

"Xavier!" I snapped, my blood rupturing as I whirled on my husband. "Don't you dare encourage their ridiculous theory!"

Xavier cringed. "I'm only suggesting we ensure that, with whatever we decide, it leads to the right future…"

"How in Bloods are we supposed to know if…!"

A baby wailed from inside the cabin.

My fox ears swiveled toward the cry so swiftly, I winced as they pulled the skin on the sides of my head.

Blast this Mother's instinct, I cursed to myself. I was warned about that post-partum chemical change, but I hadn't been prepared for its strength. It didn't matter if it was a baby crying or something else that *sounded* like a baby. Even the slightest whimper from Hecrûshou's tiny Bindragon shocked my blood with adrenaline. More mortifying, though, was when those cries made my milk leak and stain my gown… I'd had to order special binding-straps from the tailor on Anabelle's island to help absorb it all, which I was thankful for *now* as my breasts prickled painfully at the sound of Lucas's wailing.

Moments later, Yulia entered the deck from inside the cabin. The lovely Dreamcatcher's snow-white fox tail swished behind her as she sauntered toward me with the crying pup in her arms. But despite the boy's complaints, Yulia's face was painted with a smile.

"I'm terribly sorry to interrupt," Yulia began. "I normally wouldn't bring him back so soon, but I believe you and Xavier would prefer to hear what Lucas has to say."

I glanced over my shoulder at Xavier, who perked at the mention. I turned back to Yulia and the baby in question, "What he has to 'say'?" I asked. "Other than *Virro?*"

Lucas whimpered in her hold, his ashen wolf ears folded to his shoulders. *"Nnnn…"* Lucas whined. He reached for Xavier behind me. *"Nnnn…"* Lucas struggled with the sound, his face bunching into a knot and turning red. *"Nnnn—DA…!"* He warped his lips as he tongued the syllable. *"Da… Dada…!"*

Xavier sprang to his feet and fumbled beside me. He grabbed my shoulders in excitement. "Did he just…!"

"Dada!" Lucas said again, blowing raspberries playfully as he reached for Xavier with his tiny hands. *"DaDA! Da, Da, Da, Da, Da…!"*

Xavier practically squealed with joy and lifted the boy. "That's right! That's right—*Dada!* Brilliant job, Lucas…!"

Lucas giggled, proud of himself. He continued to babble with the one syllable in sing-song tones, *"Da, Da, Da, Da, Da, Da, Da…"*

I clapped my hands in delight. "Oh, wonderful, dear! Can you say *Mama* next? Hmm? *Mama! MaaaaMaaaa!"*

Lucas swiveled a wolf ear at me. Then said, "*Mmmm… Mmmmm…*"

My smile split twofold. "That's it…!"

"*Mmmmm…*" He sneezed, a small puff of red fire licking from his little palms for but a moment. Then he smiled at me from Xavier's arms and said, "Dada!"

I hung my head in defeat, chuckling. "Well… at least you said *something* other than Virro."

Xavier chortled and lifted the boy high overhead, Virro buzzing in circles around them. "Daddy wins this time, doesn't he? Yes he does! Yes he does!"

Phweeeeee!

A whistle sounded from the upper deck, where Nathaniel was steering the helm.

"A'right, ye lads 'n lassies!" Nathaniel's booming voice announced as the burly bear-shifter stalked to the railing of his deck above us. His wide-brimmed hat shaded his face from the sunlight, its long plume ruffling in the sea breeze. Nathaniel nodded to Xavier and me. "Yer Majesties… We be an hour's time from High Rastiria's eastern harbor. Best pack yer things and prepare for yer Descent into Grim." His bearded face fell solemn, his tone softening. "And make sure prep'rations be set for the pyre when we get there… before yer coronation."

I wasn't the only one to shiver. Beside me, I saw Xavier give a visible swallow, holding Lucas tight to his chest. Xavier sighed, then reluctantly handed Lucas back to Yulia.

"Well, that was short lived…" He lamented, rubbing a thumb over the baby's cheek. "Thank you, Yulia. That was a wonderful surprise…"

Yulia smiled with a nod and took the baby, walking back into the cabin.

Much to prepare, I thought with a heavy heart.

One of those preparations involved the eulogy I was to give during the funeral tonight. I'd written the speech months ago, fighting through tearful bouts at every word. I thought *that* had been the most difficult part… until I began rehearsing it. Writing it down was painful enough, but to say it aloud was agony. Thus far, I'd managed to get through it with mildly welling eyes… but that was only in practice. When the time came to give the real eulogy, I wasn't confident I wouldn't choke under the pressure.

I'll rehearse one last time during our descent, I decided and reached into the Storagesphere at my hip. *For now, I must check on the preparations down in Grim.* I pulled out my communicator, dialing the number of the Death Palace's Master Servant: Morice.

The com's screen brightened in front of me, and after a few moments of the screen swirling within itself, Morice's face appeared.

"Your Majesty Willow," Morice greeted, bowing his head deeply. There was a thickness to his voice that he'd adopted since I first gave him the news of my father's passing. I'd called him frequently these last months to coordinate certain… events that were due on the night of our arrival back home.

Once we docked in High Rastiria—the city in High Neverland located directly above Grim's Grand Capital, *Low* Rastiria—we were scheduled to take the Surfacing Port down to Grim in the geyser canyons. Likewise, my mother was arriving in a short few hours before us with the rest of their group. From what we've discussed, they were bringing Ninumel's ghost with them. Now that the Ocean King was deceased, it was the duty of the Death Queen to arrange a fellow Relicblood's Afterlife… and *I* was that queen.

I steeled my voice. "Morice. We're on time to Descend tonight. Is everything in order down there?"

"Of course, your grace," he said. *"I've spoken with First Fangs Inion to gather the guards for your procession. He informs me all is in order."*

I nodded. Matthiel's father was now acting as First Fangs, after Mother Alice's death.

"And the pyre?" I asked Morice. "The coronation ceremony?"

"All coordinated and ready for your arrival, my queen," he confirmed. *"And Conrad has gathered your father's vassals for the Bloodpact exchange tomorrow afternoon."*

I sighed. "Very well. Thank you, Morice… I suppose I'll see you tonight."

He bowed in respect. *"Yes, my queen… safe travels. Thala ul wuw shefta."*

"Thala ul wuw shefta," I said in return.

I ended the call with a long, morose breath, looking about the deck.

Aster was saying his goodbyes to his colossal Bindragon, which gave a low *AAAAAHHNN* and disappeared into the water. Alexander had left the table and was now speaking to his three vassals' ghosts beside them.

Xavier stood at my side with his arms crossed patiently, his hair wavering in the wind. "Well, darling?" he began. "What's next?"

I took his arm and leaned my head against his refreshingly cold shoulder. "More planning," I sighed. "I don't suppose… we could wait a few moments longer?" I suppressed the throbbing knot in my chest that threatened to tear my nerves apart. "I… would like to be *us* again, if only for a short time…" I melted against him. "Not parents. Not royalty… merely… *us.*"

His mismatched eyes grew weary. After a moment, he nodded, lifting my chin and stealing my lips with a delicate, frosted kiss. "That sounds lovely."

GRIM

The Realm of Death

24

DEFECTORS

TAYMEN

I trotted along the isolated, floating roads in Aspirre's endless void, scanning the abyss.

In the distance, I spotted a gleaming ball of light drifting like a delicate bubble. I evoked my dream Hallows, my hands glowing azure, and wove a new connecting road leading to the light. When I reached it, I scooped it up and pushed it into my forehead.

The abyss disappeared as the memory played around me.

I found myself staring at a slender face with mismatched, blue-and-clear eyes. His right, colorless eye had a scar dragging down to his cheek, his shoulder-length, grey hair pulled back in a thin tail by a silken ribbon.

Whosever eyes I was looking through handed him a glass of oddly-colored wine, then turned away, walking inside a crowded ballroom full of partying guests who bowed to the narrator and greeted her with 'your majesty' and 'my queen'.

She saw a glimpse of a blond-haired boy with lion ears rushing through the crowd, and she cocked her head at the young teen. She wondered what mischief her little brother, Hugh, had gotten himself into now.

The memory ended, and the ballroom dripped away as Aspirre's abyss surrounded me again.

The ball of light was still in my hands. I frowned at it. It wasn't MY memory, but... I had a hunch who it belonged to. A palace, a queen, a little brother named Hugh...

I hurried back to my subconscious parallel—back where my body was sleeping, and evoked my Hallows to wake myself up.

My eyes flew open, and I jolted up from the rock I was sleeping on. The memory-light was still clutched in my palm.

I scanned the area. The rest of the demon army was still asleep under Grim's bright, Floating Lights that drifted in the overhanging mist of the cavern's ceiling. The nest was all gathered on some weird rock formation, surrounded by gigantic straights that I guessed was Grim's 'ocean'.

My squad mates snoozed in our designated huddle, Captain Jace snoring the loudest like always. I spotted the squad mate I was looking for next to Jace: Syreen.

I cupped the ball of light and scooted over to her nervously. I'd never spoken to Syreen—no one had, really. She didn't talk to anyone, but Bloods, did she slice you up if you got on her bad side. The only time she did talk was in her sleep. And the only thing she said was *Hugh*.

Like from this memory…

I bit my lip, steeling myself as I reached down and ever so gently shook her shoulder. "H-hey," I whispered, swallowing. "Syreen—?"

Her white-pupiled eyes snapped open in less than a second, and before I could move out of the way, she grabbed my throat and sank her claws into my neck, black blood spurting painfully like a fountain full of holes.

I wheezed under her grip. "W… wait…! I… have something… for you…!" I held up the ball of light.

She said nothing, scowling from me to the light. Her grown lion-ears lowered in confusion.

I sucked in a breath. *Here goes nothing.* With a quick snap of my arm, I shoved the ball of light into her forehead.

Her lids widened, and she dropped me. I crashed to the rock in a winded cough, hacking as my throat healed itself with tiny tendrils of black sludge.

"Hugh…" she whispered. Then she flicked her gaze down at me. "Where did you…? *How* did you…?"

"I-I'm a Somniovoker," I explained, panting. I peeked over my shoulder to look around the squad of sleeping demons. "Um… Come with me. I can't talk here."

She didn't complain, following me away from the others so we could talk in private. I found a wide boulder that would block us from view, and when I was sure no one was awake and listening in, I cleared my throat.

"S-so," I began, "A while back, I figured out I can force my soul into Aspirre. From there, I've been trying to collect any memories of mine I could find…

then I found one I figured was yours." I gestured to her with a meek shrug. "I mean, you kept saying that name in your sleep every night, so… was it yours?"

"It… was," she confirmed softly. She hesitated. "Can… can you find more?"

I shrugged. "I'll be looking around. If I find any of yours, I'll send them your way." I rubbed my neck. "By the way… that guy with the weird eyes in your memory… wasn't that the Death Prince we went up against in High Everland?"

Syreen hummed in thought. "Yes… though, considering our troops felled the previous king, I suspect he is now the Death *King*…" She tapped a rapid finger to her lips. "The very king Mistress La'Lunaî wishes for us to march upon tonight…"

I hesitated. "You look like you're planning something."

"Yes…" she rumbled, "When last I saw my brother, before my death, he was already… dead." She shook her head, staying focused. "But during the battle on the surface, he was there in front of me, alive and breathing again… well, for a short time."

I was super confused now. "He died twice?"

"So it would seem," she agreed, well aware how bizarre that sounded. "I think his ghost may have formed a vassalship with the Death King. And if that's so…" Her fists clenched, lion ears curling to her head. "I must find him… and warn him of La'Lunaî's attack."

I shivered. "Uh… okay. But how are you going to do *that*?" I gestured to the horde of sleeping demons that waited behind the boulder. "The minute you leave, you'll be caught in a heartbeat."

Her face soured. Then she narrowed her glowing eyes at me. "You say you're a Somniovoker?"

"Uh…" I gulped nervously, not liking her devious tone. "Y-yeah?"

Her lips peeled into a sharp-toothed grin. "Then I know *exactly* how to bring them a warning…"

25

THE QUEEN OF DEATH

WILLOW

After our surfacing pod arrived in the nether caverns of Grim, I watched Xavier button on his alabaster doublet in our private compartment.

He'd tied back his long, grey hair with a white ribbon, the thin tail falling between his shoulder blades while his bangs fluttered above his thinly bearded jaw.

I wore a flowing gown with lace sleeves that poured to my hands with delicate designs, my alabaster cloak made of the same lace that fanned behind me in a long train. Checking my complexion in the mirror along the wall, I pulled my thick, long braid over a shoulder. The bell attached to the loosely-tied, black ribbon jingled with the motion. My ashen locks fell to my ankles, a few strands remaining loose around my cheekbones. My butterfly marriage-vines were pinned to the sides of my head with diamonds and azure gemstones. They resembled frosted dewdrops rolling down a spider's silken web that gathered into a larger teardrop at the center of my forehead.

Atop those vines hugged my silver skull-crown. With jewels shimmering like berries from intricate vines, the grandiose artwork of curling leaves twisted and knotted between glassy carvings of raven skulls, the crest of Grim etched around the main rim with glorious filigree. There was writing in the Grimish script above and beneath it, the same phrase repeated around its circumference like a beautiful frame:

Mu Necros Neschali Yettek.

With Death Comes Rebirth.

It was the last strike of punctuation—the declaration that it was now my turn to bare this heavy mantle. Fitting, how this concept was so perfectly illustrated by the weight of the headpiece gently squeezing my temples with its velvet lining.

I turned to Xavier, seeing he was staring at my crown with a sunken gaze. He went to the table along the wall where his own silver skull-crown awaited. Both of our crowns had been made on Anabelle's new capital island.

He lifted the royal headpiece with hesitant fingers. Then he turned to me.

"Is it appropriate to wear our crowns before the coronation?" He asked.

I strode to Xavier and plucked the crown from his grasp, laying it on his brow for him. "Grim's people are expecting the arrival of their new monarchs," I said. "Especially during the funeral pyre of the previous king…"

Pain twisted at the reminder.

My father was gone. And now, Grim fell to my shivering hands. *Seamstress Cleanse me, I am NOT ready for this.* My eyes welled and burned. Motherhood was one daunting responsibility, but to be a queen on top of it all? Right after losing my father? My Grandfather? Mother Alice, Father Lucas—and so many others?

Xavier must have noticed my trepidation. He cupped my face and brushed his thumb over my cheek. I clutched his cold hand in a sigh.

No, I thought, letting out a sharp exhale. *I am Death. I will honor those whose souls were lost.* I clenched my fists. *I will not bring shame to my family.*

I sucked in a breath and turned to Xavier. "Come, darling… we've a ceremony to conduct."

Xavier offered a thin smile.

I took his arm in mine and we strode out of the compartment together. The others were waiting for us, all dressed in mourning white attire like Xavier and I, save for Neal, Alexander and Matthiel, who had all donned their silver armor under alabaster cloaks, their hoods drawn over their heads and casting their faces in shadow.

Yulia and Jimmy stepped through the party to meet us. Jimmy held my son, who was dressed in his own miniature suit and small skull-tiara. Yulia held the two Storagecoffins the twins had given her this morning. She strode to Alexander and handed him one of the coffins.

"Your mother," she whispered.

Alexander gripped the coffin tenderly. His eyes misted. He tried to reply, but his throat cinched and he instead drew Yulia in for a heartfelt embrace, yielding to a quiet sob as they both wept in silence. I rarely saw Alexander in tears. I rarely saw him embrace *anyone*, but here, he seemed to lean on Yulia like a younger brother to his elder sister, sharing the pain of losing their parents. It was enough to make my own eyes sting, my fox ears folding down my neck.

Yulia released Alex and moved to Xavier next, handing *him* the last Storagecoffin.

"Your father," she hushed.

Xavier's fingers quivered as he accepted the coffin. He, too, embraced Yulia with fresh tears.

Once they collected themselves, I turned to the Surfacing Pod's metal door that led to the station in Grim's capital.

The door that led home.

Nikolai lingered beside the exit, awaiting the order to open the door. I nodded to him, and he turned the latch with an echoing *clank*, then pushed it open with a slow hiss.

Through the doorframe, I spied two lines of Reaper guards standing at attention on either side of our path. Delicate, mourning music lulled through the crowded station from the speakers all around the building. Grimish shifters of every kind stood behind the wall of guards, all dressed in white and holding candle-lilies with burning anthers. Despite the mass, none of their whispering voices reached higher than a light murmur.

They awaited their queen.

I took a deep, shuddering breath, then stepped out to the pod's metal staircase, Xavier at my side.

The tunnel of Reapers beneath us jerked to attention, their armor clattering in unison as their messengers, which were all perched on their shoulders, raised their beaks in respect. One Reaper in particular was clad in more decorative armor that lacked a helmet—whom I recognized as First Fangs Matthew Inion, Matthiel's father.

Fangs Matthew stepped out of line and bellowed with authority, "Announcing the arrival of Her Majesty, Death Queen Willow Ember! And her husband, Death King Xavier Ember! Salute!"

The Reapers slammed fists to their chests with an echoing clatter, the sound rattling my bones.

I flicked my eyes to Xavier beside me. My husband's wolf ears had flattened to his neck in terror. His petrified gaze flew all around the massive crowd that was so long, shifters spilled out of the station and overflowed the streets outside. *Death*, I cursed to myself, seeing Xavier's arms tremble. *He's panicking.*

"Darling," I hissed under my breath, sliding an arm around his. "One step at a time. We walk as one. Are you ready?"

He sucked in a shaking breath, then nodded.

I held my head high…

And we took the first step down the metal stairs together.

The crowd's murmurs hushed when we touched the platform. Yulia followed behind us with Lucas in her arms. Alexander strode beside her carrying his mother's coffin. Neal came after them beside Matthiel, whom I could hear exchanging soft words with his father.

Xavier and I continued forward, the shifters quieting when we neared each section, striding out to the streets where many horses and a royal hover-carriage waited for us. They were to bring us to the palace, where the pyre would be held.

Xavier and I stepped into our carriage. Yulia entered after us with the baby and sat on the bench across from us. Alexander, Matthiel, and Neal climbed onto the three horses surrounding our carriage, and the rest of our entourage found their own steeds to mount. Once we were all accounted for, the coachman whipped the horses into motion, and we glided through the streets of Low Rastiria.

The spired roofs and grey-stone buildings were such a relieving sight. We'd spent years among so many different architectures, it was refreshing to see something familiar again. And the best sight of all was the Floating Lights swirling above us in the cavern's twisting clouds of mist. *Bloods, how I missed home…*

It took half an hour to reach the palace's iron gates. The servants and ghosts crowded around the courtyard as Xavier, Yulia and I stepped out of the carriage—

"There you are!" a young girl's voice blurted to my left. "Over here, over here!"

It was Milann. She was dressed in a silken white gown and fur-lined cloak, a sparkling tiara combed in her copper hair between her sheep horns. Her wide cowl fell to her shoulders as she ran to me and Xavier, latching onto both our waists in a tight embrace.

"Milann," Xavier and I greeted warmly. We knelt to wrap our arms around her.

Xavier smiled. "I'm glad to see you're safe."

I tucked a lock of her curly hair behind her ear, sighing. "Royalty certainly becomes you, dear… What a lovely gown."

Milann's cheeks flushed pink, lifting her skirts and turning round experimentally, then twisted to glance at the woman who stepped behind her. "Nana Myra got it for me."

My gaze lifted. My mother was standing by Milann. Her grey-streaked, azure hair wavered in the cavern winds as she looked down at us with a fatigued smile that creased her cheeks.

"It's so good to see you, Willow," Mother said softly. She squeezed one of Milann's shoulders. "Come, Milann… Your mother and I have… something very important to see to."

Milann nodded and walked toward a cluster of people whom I hadn't noticed were standing there until now. The group consisted of familiar faces. Jaq and Lilli caught my eye first, Oliver waiting between them with sagging wings.

Beside our carriage, Alex dismounted his horse and went to clasp hands with Jaq welcomingly. Ringёd and Mikani were here as well, that feral ferret laying over Ringёd's shoulders around his neck. Octavius waited beside them alongside the cat-eared, winged El, their black-and-white messengers perched on their shoulders with their feathered heads bowed in sorrow. Roji had his scarlet wings lowered as he stood beside his sister's ghost, Zyl, who floated there with a translucent hand rubbing her arm. Roji's two daughters hugged both of his legs. Roji's wife, however, wasn't standing beside him.

I found Dalminia's emerald-haired figure standing beside Queen Veyazelle, Prince Fuérr, and…

And the ghost of Ocean King Ninumel.

Next to him was my rust-haired grandmother Crysa. She wore a warm cloak and a soul-seeing mask over her eyes. When she found my gaze, she nodded to Ninumel's specter and the two approached me, stepping beside my mother.

I bowed my head to Ninumel, guilt festering. "I'm sorry we couldn't help you in time, Ninumel… Please, forgive us…"

Ninumel's ghost shook his head and spoke in his watery language, "<It wasn't your fault that lunatic killed me… I'm just thankful your Hand was there to reap my soul before I rotted.>" He twisted back to look at Lilli, who bowed.

My Hand… I thought belatedly. *No longer my Aide.* I'd nearly forgotten Lilli's role had changed when I became queen. She'd left so soon after the shift, I hadn't had time to consider it.

My grandmother Crysa pulled out a Storagecoffin from her cloak. She handed it to me in a murmur, "Here you are, dear… give your grandfather a proper ceremony for me…"

My mother breathed a slow, sorrowed sigh as she retrieved a coffin of her own and gave that to me as well. "And one for you father," she said tightly, her cheeks wet with tears. Locke, my father's Songcrow, flew down from the sky and perched on her shoulder, singing a low, remorseful whistle.

The coffins were heavy in my suddenly-frail hands. Through my fingers gleaned the shifter-shaped forms that were wrapped in modest draping, hiding the shrunken corpses of my father and grandfather within. The palm-sized coffins weighed so little. It seemed preposterous. The king of Grim and the king of Aspirre now weighed as light as meager coin purses?

My stomach twisted. It felt so wrong… These were the men who'd tossed me in the air so effortlessly when I was a child; who were strong enough to haul me over their shoulders when I threw a tantrum; who pulled me to my feet when I fell during scythe training in my teen years… They were my *family.* And now, it was my turn to carry them, weighing as little as boxes of precious diamonds inside the Storagecoffins' translucent-blue confines.

Tears broke, blurring my sight until they spilled through. I wilted and collapsed into my mother and grandmother. We stayed huddled together for an eternal moment, sharing the hurt.

When at last I broke away, I kept the two coffins clasped to my chest and turned forward. Xavier met my gaze and nodded to me, holding his father's coffin. Alexander joined him soon after, carrying their mother's coffin.

Misery shuddered my bones as I stepped forward, taking the lead toward the royal cemetery. The twins followed behind me… along with the rest of Grim in our wake.

When we reached the cemetery, the palace's Master Servant, Morice, was waiting by the enormous pyre he and the Head Vassal, the spectral Conrad, had arranged.

I stepped before them, prompting a bow from the two. They stepped aside and allowed Xavier, Alexander and me to lay the four coffins on the stone rim of the pyre's platform.

Xavier folded his hands behind his back patiently while Alexander and I evoked our Death Hallows onto the coffins, violet lights streaming from our fingers and delicately grasping the wrapped corpses within. We carefully pulled the bodies out, the hidden figures growing to their original sizes once they touched the crisp air. We laid each one under the pyre's logs in a neat row, keeping them wrapped in their cloths. Their bodies had been too disfigured from the poison to be… presentable for the public.

I took a deep breath, then turned to face the conglomerate of Grimlings and Grimlettes who had come to witness the ceremony. This cued Morice to bring me a small com earpiece, and once he stepped back beside Conrad's ghost, I announced:

"The Seamstress bless you all for coming to this sorrowed ceremony…" My voice was amplified by the earpiece and echoing throughout the speakers, which Morice had had set up around the cemetery. "The souls we honor today are First Fangs Alice Devouh, High Howllord Lucas Devouh… The King of Aspirre, Dream Sandist… and the King of Grim, Serdin Ember…"

My voice had cinched during the announcement, but I pushed through. "Each of these souls had been part of my family. They fought bravely for the lives of this country." I gestured toward Roji and Dalminia; toward Veyazelle, Fuérr, and the ghost of Ninumel. "They fought for the lives of *all* countries. It has been centuries since the five realms felt it imperative to intercede in each others' affairs in the face of war. But we have learned that, without a doubt, a war amongst one of us affects *all* of us… the four souls we honor today recognized this. They fought for the world as a whole, because they believed that only together could we overcome fear… and overcome any threat that may tear our bonds apart. In this time of grief, we must remember the strength that our unity possesses, and commit it to memory. It is far easier to read about our historic alliance than *experience* it in our lifetime. When historians write of battles in the past, they give us numbers of those whose lives were lost. Statistics to us, the readers. But to those who were there, they were friends… families. Every soul is more than a mere number, and each loss is one to grieve."

My breath shuddered as I continued, "Those were my father's words, when I was a child… he understood how precious our lives were, and that none should be forgotten. Neither should my father… nor his Fangs, nor his Eyes… nor my grandfather Dream."

My eyes misted, obscuring my sight. *Not again…* This always happened, no matter how many times I rehearsed this… *But I MUST finish.*

I exhaled in a shiver, raising a hand—which puffed with orange fire as I evoked my Hallows and announced, "Tonight, we honor their sacrifice…! We honor their souls that have returned to Nira too early! May the Seamstress guide your souls through the Great Unknown, and gift you with a new vessel full of life and prosperity…!" Tears rolled down my face, and I gave a final, blazing cry—lighting the pyre with my flames. "*Mu necros, neschali yettek…!*"

"*MU NECROS NESCHALI YETTEK!*" came the echoing replies of the Grimish people, their voices reverberating through the caverns in such unison, I could swear it shook the ground under my boots.

The fire licked and crackled as the wood was scorched, and I returned the com earpiece to Morice before stepping back beside Xavier to watch the flames rise.

His own eyes misted, and he slid an arm around my waist as I leaned into him, watching the smoke pepper the winds.

"—such audacity!" a voice sneered behind us.

Xavier and I wheeled round.

Stalking toward us through the crowd was an ashen-haired, clear-eyed young man. His wolf ears were grown and curled as he glared at me with such biting vehemence, his eyes may as well have grown fangs along with his mouth.

"Death's Head…" Xavier's brow knitted at the young man, who looked barely younger than ourselves. My husband flicked me a perplexed gaze. "Isn't that… your cousin?"

I glowered. "Unfortunately, yes…"

As my cousin made his way over, he pushed several shifters out of his way, causing one woman to stumble to the ground.

My grown fox ears curled. "Felix. To what do I owe the displeasure—?"

"How *dare* you return to Grim after abandoning your people for two Bloody years!" He bellowed, halting before me. He straightened so tall his shadow towered over me. "You disgrace the Seamstress with that crown…! You have no right to wear it!"

I suppressed a groan when the reporters hurriedly pointed their cameras at Felix, his chest puffing up as their bulbs blinked and flashed over him. *He's just posturing,* I reminded myself, struggling to keep a calm façade. I caught sight of my ashen-haired uncle, Yvan Ember, who stood beside his wife, Councilwoman Rovinne. The couple wore smug grins as they watched their son berate me, as if they'd written his script themselves.

I growled, "And you have no right disrupting my family's funeral pyre." I shot a hand toward the burning flames, my fox ear twitching. "Which is *also* your family. Their corpses still burn with fresh ash. Your disrespectful tantrum can wait until after—"

"I've done enough waiting, *vermin*," he snarled, baring his sharpened teeth. "I'll not be spoken to like a child by a grotesque hybrid! You thought I would forget about you if you stayed away long enough? Don't think me such a fool that I would allow you to waltz down here as if nothing were amiss!" He stabbed an accusing finger at me. "You've been running away from me for too long, and your cowardice ends tonight!"

My eyebrow lifted, anger simmering into confusion. "Running away… from you?" I questioned. "Why in Bloods would you think…"

—Memory pricked me like a faint, forgotten spider. It was so small and long ago, I'd nearly forgotten it had happened at all.

That's right. Felix had planned to challenge me to Death's Duel. He wished to fight me for the throne.

I stared at him. A snicker spurted out of me, and I hurriedly clasped a hand over my mouth to control my quivering lungs. After a moment, I finally collected my wits with a slow, steady sigh.

"Is that what you believe, Felix?" I tapped a ponderous knuckle to my chin. "Let me see if I've gathered this… You believe my time battling three separate wars across the realms was a means for me to 'run away'…" I pointed at him, another chuckle breaking through. "from *you*?"

For only a moment, Felix's wolf ears wilted.

"Of… of course it was!" He suddenly didn't sound as sure of that statement as he had so clearly planned—or rather, as his *parents* had so clearly planned. But as the reporters continued to blink their lights over him, the flashes seemed to rekindle Felix's determination, and he lifted his chin higher. "You knew I was about to challenge you to Death's Duel! You were so frightened of me, you fled to the surface to—!"

"Felix, please," I wafted a hand in the air. "You were so far from my mind, I all but forgot you were still down here. If you wish to die that swiftly, I suppose I'll accommodate you and your silly Duel." I looked at Xavier and squeezed his shoulder. "Darling, do you mind if I take care of this small nuisance?"

Xavier hesitated. "Are you sure about this…?"

I scoffed. "I'll take no joy in claiming another life so unnecessarily, but what can I do? He wishes to publicize his execution throughout the country. That is *his* choice."

Felix bristled. "What arrogance…! I'll have you know that I am a well acclaimed athlete in the Evocator Games, and—!"

"And how adorable you are, playing your fun little games," I said flatly, stalking past him and patting his shoulder as I strode toward the palace to find myself an attire more suitable for battle.

I flicked him a curdled glare over my shoulder. "Be warned, cousin. This Duel will be no game." My voice dropped into a low rumble. "It will be yet another war."

26

CHALLENGE ACCEPTED

WILLOW

The tunneled entryway of the colosseum vibrated under the roar of the crowd outside.

I could see the dirt-ridden arena ahead, and I tied the drawstrings of my black, half jerkin tight over my chest. It was hemmed at my midriff, displaying the crowned Dream mark that waited there like a stylized, azure eye.

The jerkin was an unusual length for a duel, true, but this was more than a duel. It was a showcase of one's valor and leadership; a test of one's soul; a demonstration of one's pride in themselves.

And I, as the daughter of two Relic Bloodlines, was determined to show the pride of *both* houses I represented. Which meant that both my Death mark and Dream mark must be exposed.

Xavier paced the tunnel like an anxious wreck, circling the ghosts of Rossette and Nikolai who waited patiently for me to prepare. My vassals would be joining me in this battle, as was customary for Death's Duel. They were tied to me through our Bloodpact, and so they would be an indication of my Necrovoker's strength.

"You're sure about this?" Xavier asked for what must have been the dozenth time.

I gave a patient hum. "Yes."

He turned his wedding ring nervously. "You're *sure* you're sure?"

"Xavier," I sighed, "For the last time, I am sure."

He still didn't sound convinced. "But you're not even wearing armor?"

"Neither will he, if he isn't a fool," I said. "It's never wise to wear metal against a rivaling Pyrovoker. Fire cannot burn us directly, but hot *armor* will cook us underneath it."

He swallowed. "A-ah… but… the winner of Death's Duel must… execute the loser…"

"Xavier." I took his hand. "I'll be fine. If I were two years younger, perhaps Felix would have the advantage. But after everything we've been through, I now have far more experience in battle than he ever did."

"I Bloody know that," he grumbled. "Why do you think I'm worried? This is hardly a fair fight. How will it affect you when it comes time to take his head after you've won?"

I laughed. "Thank you for the vote of confidence, love… But in truth, I was only countering his posturing earlier. I don't intend to take Felix's head." I coiled my braided hair in a large bundle, tying it tight with my bell and ribbon. "I intend to make him yield."

"—I'm afraid eet won't be az zimple az yuu zink," a heavily accented voice said behind me.

I turned. The ghost of Ninumel was floating toward us.

His wife, Queen Veyazelle, strode beside the web-eared ghost while wearing a soul-seeing mask and holding her husband's Storagecoffin in one hand as the other clutched little Fuérr's fingers to her other side.

"Ninumel?" I met them halfway. "If you've come to worry over me as well, I can assure you, I'm fully capable of—"

"Yuu might be capable," Ninumel interrupted, then he switched to his native Marincian tongue. "<*If* this were an even match. But Death's Duel allows for each combatant to fight alongside their vassals, correct?>"

I put a hand on my hip. "<Yes. A competent ruler of Grim must demonstrate their skills of diplomacy and cooperation by displaying the bonds they've created with those closest to them.>"

"<And have you ever watched your cousin play in the Evocator Games?>" he asked.

I frowned. "<Well… admittedly, no. I haven't exactly had the time, have I?>"

"<I have,>" he said. "<I watched the Evocator Games when they came to my islands last year. Prince Felix is his team's designated Necrovoker. Most Necrovokers at these games usually bring a handful of vassals who are trained in combat. But the Death Prince…>" He shook his spectral head, his ghostly moustache wavering hauntingly. "<He keeps twenty-six combative vassals.>"

My eyes bulged. "*Twenty-six?*"

Xavier murmured beside me, "I don't recall your cousin being particularly talented with Necrovoking. How has he managed to coordinate that many vassals at once during a high-stakes battle?"

"<He doesn't,>" Ninumel grunted. "<Not very well, at least. And in the Games, they only allow six vassals on the field at a time. Here, however, he'll be allowed to utilize *all* of them… luckily, he himself isn't much of a threat. But that still leaves you, Death, at a disadvantage. You only have two vassals, yes?>" He gestured to Rosette and Nikolai. "<If it suits your liking, *I* would like to be added, to assist you.>"

I stared at the Ninumel in shock. "<You wish to form a vassalship? To help with Felix?>"

He scoffed, "<Not just Felix. Your *real* war is with the man who kidnapped my son and killed me. I hardly wish to stand aside in some retirement after-home without doing my part to kill the bastard.>" He extended his hand. "<What say you?>"

I hesitated. Then pushed out a breath and slid my scythe-stick out of my coiled, braided hair, having my weapon materialize in a golden gleam. I took the radiant, blue blade and sliced it over my palm to draw blood… then clasped the ghost's offered hand.

"<Welcome to the family, Ninumel,>" I said.

My blood leaked into the specter like branching veins, my soul thrumming tightly as the Pact was sealed.

When it was done, Ninumel lifted his translucent chest. "<Brilliant. Now… resurrect me so we can deal with this boy swiftly. Artist sink me if we allow this child to delay our preparations for the real threat.>"

I nodded and evoked my Hallows, my hands glittering with violet light. "<I couldn't agree more.>"

I waved my glowing hands, the lights streaking with the motion, and had my Hallows flow into the two Storagecoffins strapped to my hip, along with the third coffin in the Ocean Queen's hands. I pulled out their clothed skeletons—in Ninumel's case, his fleshy, scaled corpse—and linked their joints and ligaments together, accelerating the growth of their muscles and veins and skin and hair.

Rosette's green feathers sprouted as her childish form was constructed, and I poured more of my Hallows into her bones, aging her into a late teen to allow her wings the strength to fly, and her muscles the strength to defend herself if needed.

Nikolai's fin-like hair fell to his shoulders, his smooth scales growing prominent along with his webbed ears.

Ninumel's scales and webbed ears grew as well, his emerald, translucent hair wavering like bright seaweed against his sharp cheekbones.

When all three vessels were fully alive and resurrected before me, I curled my arms inward, then *shoved* them forward, my Hallows slamming into their chests and jumpstarting their newly pumping hearts.

With that done, I wove each of their souls temporary NecroSeams, the violet threads gleaming with the ghosts' wispy chests. I used those Seams to stitch the ghosts into their awaiting bodies, making sure to add extra strength to keep their souls attached, should their vessels die during battle.

Seconds passed in silence. Then, my three vassals sucked in reviving breaths, their eyes snapping open. They straightened, proud and resilient, then nodded to me. They were ready to fight.

I stepped past Xavier through the tunnel with the trio at my side.

"Willow?" Xavier called after me.

I paused as he trotted to me and took my hand; the hand I'd sliced with my scythe to form the Bloodpact. Xavier evoked his new, golden Hallows, the shimmering lights sealing the cut on my palm and leaving a faint scar.

He kept hold of my fingers, hesitating. Then said, "Don't trip."

I laughed. "Of course, dear… I'll see you after I've won."

I stole his lips, then walked out to the arena.

HUGH

"Five minutes," the resurrected Aiden huffed with a flap of his wings, placing five silver Yln coins on the table we surrounded. Yln was the Grimish currency. If I understood correctly, the silver coins were the second highest denomination, called Tallohs.

Nathaniel, Lady Vendy and I occupied the other seats, placing our bets inside the royal box-seat of the colosseum.

Everything was grey and white around me, since I was a ghost and *not* resurrected right now. The only shifter here in full color was Lady Vendy across from me, since she also wasn't resurrected and still a ghost.

Lady Vendy scowled at the coins Aiden had set on the table with great contemplation. One of her brown rabbit ears lowered. Then she motioned for Aiden to take out six Tallohs from his pouch—since she couldn't touch them, as a ghost—and after he placed them into the pile, Lady Vendy said, "*Ten* minutes."

Nathaniel was next, beside her. One of his bear ears perked in consideration. He scratched a single, gold coin—the highest denomination, called a Challan—against the thick hairs at his jaw. After a moment, he *clacked* it down and declared, "Twenty minutes."

Aiden's gaze flattened at him. "You have that little faith in Her Majesty's chances of ending this quickly?"

"Aye," Nathaniel guffawed with a toothy grin. "'coz I have nothin' *but* faith she's gon'a try talkin' the sorry sod out o' it. I says that'll take another fifteen minutes, on top o' the five it'll take to wipe the floor with the wee lad. What do *you* say, Hugh?"

They all looked at me next. I bit my lip in thought, then sighed and held up five fingers to Nathaniel, prompting him to place five Tallohs into the pile. "U-um... I think it will take fifteen minutes..."

Aiden cocked his head at me. "Playing the middle-ground, are we?"

I blushed, but I supposed they wouldn't be able to tell since I was a ghost and, in their newly alive eyes, misty white. "I-I'm not very good at gambling... it wasn't seen as something... masculine, in Neverland..."

My heart sank at the reminder of home. The home that I left; that didn't belong to me anymore, regardless. Remembering all the bruises and scratches and beatings Mother would give me alongside my half-brothers... remembering the day my father died from illness... remembering Sy, always being there for me, to protect me...

If I'd been resurrected, tears would have stung. Was it possible that, if I hadn't left the palace to be Master Xavier's apprentice, I wouldn't even *be* a ghost? Would Sy not have gone to war with them in the first place? Would she not have accidentally killed me...?

And would she not have been captured by La'Lunaî and forced to fight in her demon army?

I shivered. Sy's white-pupiled face flashed back to memory. She'd been there during our battle in New Aldamstria. It had definitely been her standing over me, before I died again from too much damage. She'd vanished when *Da'torr* Alexander revived me, along with the rest of La'Lunaî's forces.

Sister... we will free you from La'Lunaî. I promise.

"Ah," Aiden gave a sympathetic sigh, breaking me from my brooding. It took me some time to remember what we'd been talking about. What was it? Ah, right! He'd only heard my mention of gambling not being 'masculine' in Neverland.

"I suppose not much has changed there since I died," Aiden said. Then he reconsidered, his feathers lifting as he amended, "Well, then again, it actually seemed a tad *better* when we picked you up there." He motioned to his trousers and laughed. "They've severely lessened the padding in recent fashions. You should have seen what they made us wear three centuries ago! Bloods, *that* was a mistake."

Nathaniel guffawed and slapped the table, making the coins jingle. "I *did* see what they made ye lads wear back then, and '*mistake*' is the understatement of the millennia! Thank Bloods they don't make ye wear it now!"

They chatted on about their long afterlives, and I saw Lady Vendy chuckle.

I smiled dreamily. *Lady Vendy...* Even as a ghost, she was enchanting. Her misty brown hair was braided over her shoulder, like it had been when she died, or so she'd told me. I'd learned that we ghosts could make ourselves look however we wanted, so long as it stayed within the parameters of what we could look like while alive, but changing clothing was a bit... difficult, unless a soul-seamster like Master Xavier made us new spirit-clothes. It was all very complex and I barely understood any of it, but I supposed it didn't really matter.

At the end of the day, we were still dead.

It was crowded in this expansive box-seat, everyone still whitened to my ghostly eyes. By the window sat the two Dreamcatchers, Sir Jimmy and Sil Yulia, with the baby Death Prince in her arms. The tyke ogled the colosseum outside with amazement, his wolf ears perking straight up. Sir Jaq and Sil Lilliana were in the back with Oliver, Apson and Lilliana's father, Howllord Daniel Tessinger. The Queen of Dreams held her fox-tailed baby while she conversed with her daughter Myra.

Out on the terrace attached to the windowed-wall, the new sheep-horned Death Princess, Milann, overlooked the railing. Sir Octavius also waited there alongside Sil El and the resurrected Sky Princess, Zylveia.

I found *Da'torr* Alexander leaned against the back corner. He was dressed in full armor save for his head and was scowling at the skeletal demon-man, Aster, who pulled his sweater's hood over his head miserably.

"But I'm *starving*...!" Aster whined as his freakishly thin stomach groaned and rumbled. "I can't take it anymore...! There's too many souls out here, I-I-I need *something* to help me ignore how..." He leaned closer to *Da'torr* Alex and gave a long, hungry inhale, his mouth watering and his white-glowing eyes turning wild. "How *good* they smell..."

Alex bristled and shoved him off, grabbing him by the neck. "Death, *all right!* Find your Bloody food! But I'm not about to let you go alone, sniffing every shifter like that..." He opened the door in a string of curses with the demon still in his grasp.

Squeak!

The terrace door pushed open, and Princess Milann peeked her head inside. She watched anxiously as *Da'torr* Alex stormed out of the box-seat.

Then she followed after him.

"Oh, Land," I grimaced timidly, looking over my shoulder to the others at our table. Lady Vendy was the only one who noticed my worried gaze. Aiden and Nathaniel were still deep in reminiscent conversation.

Lady Vendy lifted a rabbit ear. "What's wrong, Hugh?"

I swallowed and pointed at the door. "The, u-um… new Death Princess just went after *Da'torr* Alex… and I don't think he's aware she's following him."

Vendy winced and floated off her seat. "Aw, Land. That won't go over too well with *Da'torr* Xavier. Come on." She grabbed my spectral wrist and pulled me outside with her. "We better keep an eye on her."

We walked round the top row, which was filled with those of our party who didn't wish to stay in the box-seat—our demon companions among them—and spotted the retreating tiara of Princess Milann walking into the inner-ring of the colosseum. She followed after *Da'torr* Alex and the groaning Aster, and we hurried to float up to them.

"*Da'torr* Alex!" Lady Vendy called. "Better watch your six!"

Princess Milann couldn't hear us with her living ears, but *Da'torr* could. He turned to us—then spotted the young Death Princess mid-slink, and flinched.

"Milann!" *Da'torr* barked, his voice echoing in the corridors. "What are you doing out here? You shouldn't be *anywhere* without guards!"

The princess froze, her sheep ears growing. "I-I… I just wanted to see Mom and Dad…"

Da'torr paused, not expecting that. He let out a hard breath through his nose and ran a hand through his hair. He looked at Lady Vendy and me.

"Vendy," he said, "Hugh. Come with us to find Xavier. I want you both to guard her… but I need Xavier to stitch your souls to your vessels…"

I nodded, as did Vendy, and we both followed behind the trio dutifully.

27

DEATH'S DUEL

WILLOW

My vassals and I strode into the open area, my scythe firmly secured in my grasp.

The blinking lights of cameras and reporters flashed all around us as the crowd roared with enthused cheers. A blaring announcer boomed from the speakers at our entrance. *"Announcing her royal majesty, Death Queen Willow Ember! Accompanying her in this Duel are her two…"* he paused, confused. Then he quickly amended, *"No! THREE vassals! It seems the queen has just formed a Bloodpact with the late Ocean King, Ninumel Aschit'aqua!"*

The surprise sent the audience in an uproar.

"And her challenger…!" The announcer blared, and I spied an ashen-haired young man entering the arena from the opposite end of the colosseum. *"Death Prince Felix Ember! Accompanying him are his record breaking twenty-six combative vassals!"*

Felix stepped into the arena. Like me, the teenaged Death Prince wore thin, black garments consisting of ankle-length trousers and a simple half jerkin that was hemmed at his midriff to display the crowned Death mark on the small of his back—which I saw when he spun round to wave proudly at his adoring fans in the audience. In his grasp was his long-staved scythe, the glowing blade arching over his head as if to look more intimidating.

Surrounding Felix was a small army of shifters, all with different colored hair, some with horns and some with wings, some with scales and webbed ears, all wearing similar, black uniforms akin to what Felix and I wore.

And they *all* glared dangerously at my three vassals. They focused the brunt of their ire at my latest, royal comrade, Ninumel.

Ninumel paid them no mind and rumbled to me in Marincian, "<Don't let them intimidate you. Prince Felix only recruits past contestants of the Evocator Games as his vassals. None of these shifters have been forced to fight for their lives.>"

A growl clicked in my throat. "<This would normally put me at ease… but Bloods, this will be more difficult than I expected.>"

Felix and I stopped yards away in the center of the arena, close enough for me to see the loathing scowl he dedicated to me.

"And now…!" The announcer boomed. *"A moment of silence, as the High Priestess Merillin will give the holy prayer!"*

The crowd's cheers dampened respectfully.

A woman with long, leathery bat wings soared down to the arena, landing between our parties. Her clerical robes billowed around her in the cavern winds. In her grasp was a thick volume of the holy Choir, which she held out between Felix and me.

"Your royal highnesses," she said to us, "Please place your hands upon the Choir, and recite the prayer to the Mother Goddess."

Felix and I laid our hands on the embossed cover, neither of us breaking eye contact as we recited in unison, "Mother Nira, Sorrowed Seamstress of Souls, grace this duel with your sacred presence and bear witness. As is your will, the winner of this ritual shall henceforth be recognized as the only soul worthy to rule Grim in this lifetime. The one who falls shall have their soul sent to you in the Great Unknown, and see that their next life is long and prosperous." Felix had recited the last line with a mocking tone. I resisted the urge to roll my eyes as we ended with, *"Mu Necros Neschali Yettek."*

We removed our hands from the cover. The priestess nodded her approval and bowed to us, spreading her bat wings and flying out of the arena.

The announcer's voice came roaring back. *"Duelers, prepare your party!"*

The crowd rippled back to life around us.

"Felix," I began, my fox ears growing as anxiety prickled. I twirled my scythe behind me, the blade cocked at my feet. "This is your last warning. Yield now, and live to fight beside our Brothers and Sisters against the real threat."

His sharpened teeth barred as he sneered, "The *real threat* is allowing a vermin princess to drive our nation into ruin. The danger that comes for us was instigated by your irresponsible jaunt on the surface."

I drew in a slow breath, keeping my calm as the cavern winds blew past my face and ruffled my braided hair, my bell jingling from its ribbon.

"I believe you mean vermin *queen*," I corrected. "And do tell me more of my irresponsible… how did you phrase it?" I set a hand on my hip. "Jaunt on the surface'? Yes, that accurately describes my efforts to help rescue our soldiers from a high-security fortress in a foreign land who declared war on us." I could hear my voice echoing through the Colosseum's many speakers. I presumed they'd had microphones listening in on us nearby.

Perhaps that's for the best.

I went on in mock shame, "It truly paints a brilliant picture of the thousands upon thousands of demons I've slain alongside my fellow Reapers... as well as the commanding Sentients who stalked us across the realms for two grueling years. And let's not forget my leisurely stroll from the Sky realm down to High Everland in the battle where both my father and grandfather had their *souls destroyed*..." Anger bubbled, my spirit's fire igniting as smoke began to lick from my fingers. My teeth sharpened and I snarled at my ignorant cousin, "But *do* tell me of your gallant little games you chose to play down in the safety of the caverns instead of joining us in the battlefield?"

Half the audience members rippled with laughter. Some drew concerned gasps, others shouted derisive jeers. There were still some shifters in the mix chanting Felix's name and holding supportive signs for him. I supposed they were his fans from the Evocator Games.

Felix's wolf ear twitched furiously.

"*Ten...!*" The announcer blurted as the surrounding vision-screens displayed the bright numbers for the countdown. "*Nine...! Eight...! Seven...!*"

He continued his countdown. My vassals slid into offensive stances, readying their Hallows with glowing hands. Felix's vassals did the same. I quickly surveyed the number of different colors gleaming from those hands, counting several gold magic, green magic, red magic, violet magic... there were no azure lights that I could see. *So, Felix detests my Dream blood so much that he refused to take on any vassals with Aspirrian Hallows.*

I gave a sharp-toothed grin. *Then he won't expect me to use it.*

"*Three...!*" The announcer boomed.

I evoked my Dream Hallows, azure lights gleaming around my hands.

"*Two...!*"

Felix's brow furrowed at the sight of my blue Hallows. My grin stretched wider.

"*ONE!*"

A horn blared through the speakers to signal the start of the Duel—

The entirety of Felix's vassals sent a barrage of lightning, fire, ice, and stone straight for me.

I quickly wove my glowing-azure hands and created five phantom copies of myself with my Somniovoking, the new figures breaking apart and spreading out. Felix was just as confused as his vassals. The *real* me rolled away from the volley of attacks, which Ninumel quickly blocked by conjuring an enormous wall of ice.

The audience went ballistic.

"Her Majesty Willow begins the Duel with Somniovoking!" The announcer exclaimed with confused excitement. *"An unexpected choice! Felix's party isn't sure which one is the real queen!"*

<*Brilliant idea,*> Ninumel commended in Marincian through our mental connection, his voice fuzzing in my thoughts. He was too far away to speak directly, since both of us were on the run and dodging Felix's vassals without pause. He panted through our connection, <*I haven't seen you use phantom copies before... Serdin told me you weren't as adept with your Dream Hallows.*>

"<I hadn't been, until recently!>" I threw a puff of fire at a flurry of ice-shards thrown at my head, melting them into water puddles. After finding the Glaciavoker responsible, I bolted toward her. She barely had time to panic before I *sliced* her Temporary NecroSeam with a solid snap. I knew Felix could easily re-attach her soul and revive her, but he'd have to *notice* her first, then get close enough to her body to resurrect her all over again. Which would take him time.

That was my only focus, for the time being. I moved from vassal to vassal, cutting and ripping and wheeling my scythe over their chests one after another, muscle memory taking over from all the chaotic battles of war I'd faced these last few years.

The few times I was able to steal a glance at my own vassals, I saw Ninumel seemed to be holding his ground with his combination of Ocean Hallows all on his own. He evoked his water Hallows and flooded a cluster of Pyrovokers, trapping them in a lapping bubble of water. I presumed he must have increased the water pressure with his Pregravoking, judging from how their bones *cracked* and *snapped* to splinters, their faces and ribs crushed as their mouths bubbled silent screams. Ninumel waited until the last of the bubbles faded from their breaths before dismissing his Hallows. The trapped corpses of Felix's vassals splashed to the dirt, their eyes rolled back and faces painted with a blotchy purple hue.

The audience above that section shrieked with startled excitement.

They cheer for this cruelty? My soul mourned for the ghosts we were forced to torment. *What sort of sacred duel romanticizes death like this?*

I shook my head, staying focused. *These vassals knew what they would face when they made their Bloodpact with Felix. Just as MY vassals had volunteered to assist me. For all my cousin's faults, he would never force an unwilling soul to fight.*

The reminder was all I needed to stay on task.

I searched the misted ceiling and found Rossette's green wings high above me. A team of Felix's winged vassals were sending relentless volleys at her, gusts of wind spiraling from the glowing-red hands of an Aerovoker, lightning sparking from another Astravoker, and fire streams shooting at her wings in an attempt to burn her feathers from a Pyrovoker. Rossette expertly dodged and rolled away from all of them, zapping her lightning and sending one of them straight to the dirt just feet away from where I was standing.

Rossette and Ninumel seem to be holding up well, I noted, looking round the chaos. My phantom copies were still running about and distracting the other vassals. I even spied Felix himself chasing after one of those copies, swiping his scythe into their false chests and screaming furiously when colored mist came from them instead of blood.

But where is Nikolai?

My head snapped to a web-eared corpse lying yards away. *There!* Bloods, they'd already gotten to him. A rocky spike jutted out from Nikolai's ribs, smeared with blood.

I gripped my scythe and sprinted over to him, evoking my Death Hallows with my free hand. Violet lights streamed from my palm and fingers, wrapping around Nikolai's body as I pulled him off the large spike and healed his wound, jumpstarting his heart once again.

Nikolai breathed to life and his eyes snapped open. "I s-s-sorry, *Da'torr…!*" He shivered and shuffled to a new battle stance.

SHHH-POW!

A thick blast of water shot between us, and we both hopped away. Nikolai evoked his green Hallows to freeze the stream and broke it apart, heaving with all his might to throw the heavy, frosted pillar straight at the Aquavoker who'd attacked us. The pillar knocked the Aquavoker to the ground and crushed her skull in a mess of blood.

Nikolai's webbed ears flicked down, looking ill. "I think I no like this Duel, *Da'torr…*"

I grimaced. "In that, we agree, Nikolai… just stay focused. If I can convince Felix to yield—"

A ferocious scream ripped to my left, and I quickly lifted my scythe to block—

CLANG!

Felix's crooked blade clashed against my staff. His colorless glare blazed with hatred.

"There you are, you dishonorable mongrel," he growled, the words oozing like molasses. "You've evaded me with those phantoms long enough! It's time to rid our sacred Bloodline of your *taint!*"

He unhooked his blade and swung for my stomach. I lurched back, sweeping my staff forward.

CLANG!

I blocked that attack.

CLANG! CLANG!

Two more for my head and ribs.

CLANG! CLASH! CLANG!

We stepped to this deadly dance over and over, my feet skidding back each time. Felix managed to cut my shoulder shallowly, and I seethed when he barely caught my side, making me stagger.

"Felix!" I shouted over the clamor, ducking under another swipe for my head. "I don't wish to kill you…! We have far more threatening enemies to be concerned with!"

"All the more reason to have a true Relicblood of Death to lead us!" He lifted his scythe overhead and *slammed* it down, forcing me to block with my staff again in a piercing *clash!*

My fox ears curled back, anger bubbling as my grip tightened on my weapon. "A true Relicblood of Death?" I echoed with sharpened teeth. "Seamstress Cleanse me, Felix—*I AM DEATH!*"

I bent low to avoid another slice, swept my staff under his legs with such strength, he crashed to the dirt in a winded cough. I snagged his scythe with my own blade and *ripped* it from his fingers, hurling it several yards away, prompting the crowd to shout in a start.

I twirled my scythe in a heated snarl and touched the blade to his throat. "I have tolerated your bile our entire lives, *little cousin,*" I rumbled, my throat crackling. I straightened until my shadow fell over his startled face, my short-self looming over the taller boy for the first time in a very long time. "You are too quick to judge a shifter on their size and their blood… Just as you were too quick to judge my humble trio of vassals against your numerous followers."

I jerked a hand around the arena. The field was littered with corpses and frustrated ghosts. Only a handful of Felix's vassals were still standing against my team. I turned back to the downed prince. "It's over, Felix. I've won your silly game. Yield now, and…"

The ground began to quake under my feet.

The dirt split into large sections with golden lights, then began lifting in the air—bringing me along with it.

Death!

I knelt and grasped the edge of my crumbly dirt-island with my free hand, trying to keep balanced while still clutching my scythe. Peering over the shrinking field, I saw that a single leopard-tailed Terravoker was responsible for my new ride. The rock-thrower woman strained against my weight as she lifted me on this piece of ground higher and higher, floating me above the audience.

Damn it…! Panic set in, the battle beneath me spinning nauseatingly. *This could pose a problem…!*

28

WARNING

XAVIER

From our vantage down in the arena's tunnels, Veyazelle, Fuérr and I watched the ground around my wife's feet break apart and lift her high in the air. "Mother of Death," I cursed, my wolf ears growing.

Willow had been on the verge of winning not seconds ago. Now that she was up in the air, her phobia was certainly going to drive her into a panic. But would it be devastating enough to bring her back to where she started?

"What a surprising setback!" The announcer's voice blared to life from the speakers. *"Just when the queen had gained the advantage, she was snagged by one of Felix's still-standing Terravokers!"*

The large vision-screens surrounding the colosseum zoomed on a leopard eared woman with golden-glowing hands, struggling with exertion as she used her rock Hallows to keep Willow stranded on that lone piece of ground high above the arena. The woman's brown skin was sleek with sweat, her leopard tail twitching when her foot slipped an inch over the dirt.

She can't keep Willow up there much longer, I thought as the screens shifted to Willow on the rocky island. My wife's fox ears were fully grown and stuck to the nape of her neck, her azure eyes drastically wide as she overlooked the field beneath her. To the unsuspecting audience, it wouldn't be difficult to assume her scowl was caused by fury for her opponent. But *I* knew it was a look of terror. I cursed to myself, *Blast it, Willow, don't panic now. The Terravoker will run out of Hallows stamina soon.*

Beside me, Fuérr gripped his mother's skirts anxiously and stammered in Marincian, "<Is-is Death going to die now?>"

Veyazelle laid a scaled hand on her son's emerald hair and soothed, "<She'll be fine, darling. She's faced worse when you traveled with her.>"

I grunted my agreement and spoke in their tongue, "<She won't lose, Fuérr. She has your father with her, remember?>"

This seemed to give Fuérr more confidence, and he nodded, returning his watch to the Duel.

From the ground, I spotted Felix pushing to his feet and brushing the dirt from his trousers. His wolf ears were curled, trying to keep a determined expression, but he still seemed rattled.

I grinned. He didn't expect my wife to come that close to severing his head, did he?

Only four of Felix's vassals were still standing. The furious prince began shouting orders at them, rushing over to the others' corpses to resurrect them again. His plan was proving to take longer than he probably liked. Willow had severed most of their souls from their vessels, so he had double the work-load ahead of him. Judging from his exhausted panting, it looked like he was running low on Hallows stamina just as well as his vassals. Even if he did manage to revive them all in time, I doubted they'd have much left in them to continue fighting. Felix could return their physical strength, but he couldn't replenish their *soul's* strength.

"—Is she gonna lose now?"

I jolted at the young girl's voice, whirling round.

Milann was looking up at me from under her curly copper hair, the skull-motif tiara sparkling with diamonds between her sheep horns.

"Milann?" I knelt to her, startled. "What are you doing down here? You're supposed to be with Yulia and your grandmother."

"—Apologies," the voice of my brother rumbled as he approached us next. The ghosts of Vendy and Hugh drifted on either side of him, floating quietly as Alexander's polished armor clattered in the echoing tunnel.

Along with them, the skeletal Aster strode unabashedly in his hooded sweater, the meercat demon carrying two armloads of candied almonds, lamb kabobs, and caramel apples— which he was currently in the middle of chewing happily.

They stopped in front of me, and Alex crossed his arms, jerking his head at Aster. "This gluttonous idiot decided to peruse every damned concession in the whole Colosseum. Our other demons might be well versed in blending in with the living, but I don't trust *this* dolt... So, I chaperoned. But Milann followed us. She wished to see you down here." He rubbed his neck hesitantly. "I, er... hope that isn't a problem?"

I pursed my lips. "Hrmm... I suppose as long as you stay in the tunnel with us, it's safe enough..."

Vendy tossed a spectral hand dismissively. "No worries, *Da'torr*. Hugh and I came along in case you wanted us to watch her."

Hugh smiled helpfully beside her. "Which we're more than glad to… But we thought you'd wish to resurrect us first. And *Da'torr* Alexander cannot do so without you, Master."

I nodded, considering. "Right… Perhaps we should have assigned you to guard Milann beforehand?"

"Probably," Alexander agreed with a shrug. "She *is* a princess now. You and I both know the risk of assassins and swindlers."

That shocked me awake. *Death… Of course.* I mentally kicked myself for not having thought of that. Of course Milann was at risk of such dangers now. I was so distracted with Willow's Duel, it hadn't even crossed my mind.

I rubbed my eyes in a groan. "Bloods, you're right… Vendy, Hugh, *please* watch Milann while she wanders out in public?"

Vendy and Hugh voiced their affirmations.

Alex chuckled and evoked his violet Hallows, pulling out Vendy's and Hugh's vessels from two of the numerous Storagecoffins strapped to his belt. The lights weaved all around the corpses until the two were standing before us, fully alive and waiting for their souls.

I wove them temporary NecroSeams and stitched them to their vessels, allowing them to waken and take their places alongside Milann as requested.

Milann dragged her foot over the dirt bashfully, fingering the glowing scythe-sphere dangling from her necklace. "I don't need guards… I want to help Mom."

I paused. It was strange to hear her calling Willow that. It was drastically informal for a new princess, but… Bloods help me, I couldn't help but smile. I supposed that meant she truly did think of us as her parents now. Adopted or not.

I clasped a hand on her shoulder and chuckled. "That is gallant of you, Milann… but I'm afraid your mother must face this alone. It's part of Grim's ancient traditions."

The sheep girl's face still dripped with concern. "But she's losing…"

"Losing?" I laughed, pointing at the Terravoker who struggled to keep Willow lifted on that floating rock. "Do you see that leopard woman? The Terravoker?"

Milann nodded.

"She's running out of stamina. Swiftly. Give it a moment, and your mother will be free."

"But then she'll *fall* and die," she protested.

I moved my pointing finger to the green-winged Rossette, who was blasting a barrage of lightning bolts around Felix and his vassals—which he desperately continued to revive in an endless loop. The moment they breathed back to life, Willow's three vassals killed them all over again.

"Do you see that parrot-shifter up there?" I murmured to Milann, "She's on our side. She can easily grab your mother and put her safely on her feet again—"

"H-hey," a new, unfamiliar voice interrupted behind me suddenly. "You're the, um… the Death K-K-King, right…?"

I turned, frowning.

Hiding in the shadows and avoiding the dim lamplight was a skittish figure. Whoever he was, he shook like a nervous wreck and peered over his shoulder as if afraid to be discovered by someone who didn't want him here.

"Who are you?" I demanded, rising as Alex and I stepped in front of Milann protectively. Vendy drew her Crystal sword while Hugh brandished his dual-scythes. Veyazelle pushed Fuérr behind her, her webbed ears flicking in suspicion.

Aster was the only one who didn't look a bit worried, still chewing on his snacks as he cast the newcomer a disinterested glance. I noticed Aster's back gleamed with an azure light from beneath his sweater, and he blinked mid-chew. He promptly swallowed.

"What the Void?" Aster complained to the intruder. "Why can't I scry on you?"

The intruder tensed from the shadows.

I turned to Aster with a knitted brow. "What do you mean you can't scry on him?"

Aster shrugged, looking troubled. "Usually, I can get a scrying on someone if we're touching the same ground. I can use the stones as a medium. But I'm not getting anything on this guy."

"O-o-oh," the intruder shivered, finally stepping out into the light. "Th-that's probably because I'm not actually here…"

He was a Landish, lion-eared teenager. His lanky torso was wrapped in an open vest with nothing underneath, his scrawny legs clothed in ankle-length trousers that were tattered and stained with greasy blotches. The boy skittishly peeked his gaze up to face me.

My blood froze. I was staring at two white pupils, glowing like brilliant stars from his irises.

"A demon…!" I ripped my scythe-spheres from my neck-chain, my blades materializing. Alexander did the same and drew out his own blades, ready to strike—

"W-w-wait!" The lion demon squeaked and threw his hands over his head. "I-I'm not here to eat you…! L-like I said, I'm n-not actually here!" He went to the walls of the tunnel and sank his hand into the stone, his skin misting without contact. "S-s-see? I'm a Somniovoker. A-at least, my original is… I'm just a copy."

Alex and I exchanged confused glances.

I demanded, "Then what do you want?"

"W-w-well… Um…" His gaze moved to the rest of our group. His lion ears perked when he spotted Hugh. "H-Hey…! I know you! You're—you're *Hugh*, right?!"

Hugh jolted.

I gave my apprentice a furrowed glance. "Hugh? Do you know him?"

Hugh shook his head. "No, Master… I don't recognize him."

"We've never met," the demon clarified. He looked hard-pressed to find the right words. "Like I said, I'm a Somniovoker, so… A-after I Changed into a Fera, I've been going into Aspirre, looking for my memories—"

"Get to the point," Alexander barked, his teeth sharpening with impatience.

The boy cringed. "I-I found someone *else's* memory there, with H-Hugh in it…! Another demon girl, in my troop…! S… S-Syreen Lowery! Y-y-your s-s-sister…!"

We all fell still.

I growled. "Why *exactly* are you here, demon?"

"T-To warn you…!" He said. "Syreen wanted me to find her brother—and tell you all to get the Void out of here!"

I had a sinking feeling I knew the reason, but questioned anyway. "Why?"

He swallowed. "B… because La'Lunaî is coming." His voice was grave and terrified. "We're already here."

—He vanished into mist.

29

DEALINGS WITH DEMONS

WILLOW

Far above the chaotic arena, I shivered on my floating piece of rock, my fox ears folded down the nape of my neck as my stomach churned at the sight of the tiny duelers far below in the arena.

Damn him! I tried to calm my frazzled blood. Felix must have planned to use my fear of heights as a contingency plan.

"The queen's phantom copies have faded!" the announcer declared. Then the vision-screens around the colosseum zoomed on my face from atop this piece of rock. Luckily, my fox-eared face looked tight with determination instead of panic. *"Her true form has been snagged by Felix's Terravoker...!"*

I suppressed a whimper, thanking Nira when the screens focused on Felix down on the field instead. It looked like Felix was using this chance to resurrect as many of his vassals as he could. Unfortunately for him, *my* vassals killed them all with quick strikes of their magic before they could so much as take a step. Felix couldn't keep up. He was losing energy... and growing more furious.

All right, I thought, forcing out calm breaths. *We still have the advantage. Felix will run out of stamina soon enough, and he'll have nothing left to resurrect ANYONE with anymore... which also means his Terravoker will have nothing left to keep me up here either...*

The realization brought back the panic in full force. *Bloods! I'll die from the fall...!*

"R-Rossette...!" I called shakily, tapping into *all* my vassals' mental connections. "Nikolai, *someone...!* If this Terravoker drops me, this duel will be over...!"

The voice of Ninumel rumbled from my thoughts in Marincian, *<One moment, Death! Your Astravoker is needed down here, to cover more ground! The Glaciavoker and I will assist! Hold fast!>*

I watched as the distant figures of Ninumel and Nikolai broke apart from their routine of killing Felix's ever-reviving vassals. In their stead, Rossette swooped down to keep our opponents preoccupied with her lightning.

My two Marincian vassals ran under my floating piece of ground, evoked their ice Hallows, and sculpted a thick, arching pillar of sleek ice. The pillar rose all the way up to my island and latched on, the rock quaking under me, then steadied itself securely.

<There,> Ninumel said through our mental connection—and I saw him shoot a spear of ice into the Terravoker's chest with a mere flick of his wrist. *<Now you can slide down safely.>*

I skeptically looked down the steep arch. There were no curved edges to keep me from slipping over the sides of it… and it was terribly narrow…

I muttered in Marincian, "*<I can't help but question your idea of safe…>*"

Fwooooosh…!

—A powerful gust of wind burst from behind me, so strong that it *shoved* me halfway over the edge of my floating piece of ground. I shrieked and dug my claws into the dirt ledge to keep hold.

Another burst of air pushed over me, and I strained to hold tight, my claws burning painfully as I left trailing scratch marks over the dirt. The new gale blew my braided hair out of its bundle, my ribbon and bell slipping off and tumbling down to the arena below as my loose braid whipped about wildly.

I managed to swing my legs over the icy arch, my feet slipping for a moment, but it was enough to steady me. My lungs burned with terrified breaths while I searched for the source of the wind—

"Just shove off already!" A woman with pale blue wings roared as she soared toward me, her scarlet-glowing hands pushing a vortex of wind at me again.

I braced and dug my claws deeper into the rock, my braid unraveling in the gust. The Aerovoker swooped down, snatched my loose locks, and *tugged* as hard as she could. She was trying to pull me over the ledge. I thought my scalp would rip at any moment, making my eyes water with pain.

"Damn it…!" My teeth sharpened. I flicked my eyes toward my scythe, which was still on the rock next to me. "I will *not* die… from such… a childish… *trick!*" I grabbed the weapon and twirled it behind me—

The blade *sliced* off my long hair.

I was free!

… But instantly dropped onto the slippery ice my vassals had made. I yelped and fumbled to stay on both feet as I slid down the slope, using my scythe to balance myself. I dug the hooked blade into the ice behind me, kicking up frost as it left a deep trench in my wake, my stomach lurching sickly as I descended at a hazardous speed toward the ground.

My head snapped back for only a moment, but it was enough to see the shocked look on the winged Aerovoker's face. Her fingers still clutched my detached strands… which, to her bewilderment, deteriorated into flakes of ash.

The ash drifted after me as I continued my frightening descent, the soft flakes reattaching to the shortened strands that flared at my neck.

The closer I neared the field again, the clearer my destination became:

I was headed straight for Felix.

The Death Prince didn't seem to notice this, however. He was gasping for breath, his hands glowing a faint violet, which sputtered into nothing. His stamina had weakened. He was drenched in sweat, looking ripe to faint soon. With his Hallows empty, he couldn't resurrect anymore vassals. Nikolai, Ninumel, and Rossette killed the remainder while I slid past the carnage.

And *slammed* my shoulder into Felix's chest, knocking him down. I skidded to a stop and leapt onto the dirt, lowering my scythe to his neck.

"*Yield*," I snarled, the command blazing between my heavy pants. "I will not ask again."

Felix wheezed and shivered under my blade, his sneer indignant. "Y-y-you… disgusting… *vermin*…" His ashen wolf ears curled back angrily. His glare flicked to Ninumel. "It's because you have a… a *true* Relicblood with you… You… tricked him to align with you…"

I muttered. "Then I suppose, considering you believe a 'true Relicblood' beat you, it sounds as if you don't believe *yourself* a true Relicblood."

His face puckered tight under my blade.

"And," I added. "I hardly think you have a right to claim that my victory was not from my own efforts. You barely fought in this duel, hiding behind your superfluous number of vassals so you wouldn't have to lift your due weight. What you fail to understand, Felix, is that a *coward prince* orders his soldiers to fight for him."

I withdrew my weapon from his neck and erected it in the dirt at my side, leaning against it as I crouched down, evoked my dream Hallows, and clasped an azure-glowing hand to his brow. "But a *queen* orders her soldiers to fight *with* her."

The azure lights sank into his skin. Felix's eyes rolled back, and his head flopped onto the dirt, caught in a deep slumber from my Hallows.

The colosseum died into utter silence.

The audience stilled.

"Prince Felix has... fallen..." the announcer blared on the speakers, his voice still full of energy, but it carried a more respectful tone as he declared, *"Queen Willow is the victor of Death's Duel... the prince did not yield. According to tradition, the queen has won the right to send his soul to the Mother Goddess."*

The speakers echoed for several long moments, then was swallowed by the resounding silence.

They were waiting for me to reap Felix's soul... and destroy it with Infeciovoking. This was our sacred tradition; the tradition of Death's Relic Bloodline; the tradition of Grim's ancient culture.

A tradition that has outlived its necessity.

I lowered my scythe, my fox ears curling back. "No."

My voice echoed through the colosseum again. They'd focused the microphones on me again, and a quick glance at the large vision-screens showed me the cameramen had zoomed on my sweat-ridden face.

Good, I thought, lifting my head as I shouted, "I will not end the life of a capable soldier. The war with High Everland may be over, but there is a Necrofera army waiting to march on our fair country. It would be reckless and unnecessary to rid our ranks of even one reaper."

Mutters buzzed from the audience. They were uncertain. Some clapped their agreement while others hollered their disapproval.

"I have won this sacred Duel!" I shouted, my voice still amplified for all to hear. "I have proven that I am worthy to rule Grim, witnessed by the Seamstress of Souls! Despite being outnumbered, my allies and I have shattered the odds and were victorious...! My crown remains uncontested! If there are others who wish to challenge my right to rule, let them face me this very moment and meet the same fate as the prince...!"

The crowd hushed in an instant.

I looked round the colosseum. No soul dared stir from their seats.

I snarled, "I shall take your silence as a sign of acknowledgement... I am your queen. I am *Death.* And after two-thousand years of ruling, the times have proven to change our culture in many ways. Why, then, should I be questioned for sparing the life of one who could help *preserve* our country?" I twirled my scythe upright and *pounded* the staff over the dirt. "Prince Felix will keep his soul. He and his vassals will fight with us when it comes time to battle, if they choose. Now, bring down the Healers and tend to His Highness... I have a coronation to attend."

I stormed off, the audience bursting into a roar of cheers around me...

... but they were drowned by a sudden cacophony of screeching black birds throughout the colosseum.

I halted mid-step. Those were all messengers, from the patrolling Reapers in the aisles. Their shrieks made the hairs on my neck prickle, the noise tangling and knotting into a frazzled mess of noise.

An earsplitting twitter cut through the madness behind me. Jewel, my tiny Songcrow who'd stayed with Xavier during the duel, fluttered to my face in frantic twitters. Our Bond pulsed with warning signals.

My fox ears swiveled straight up. I twisted round to search the colosseum with a furrowed brow. "It can't be...?"

The other messengers croaked and cawed and screeched wildly from the aisles, the other Reaper knights looking round in confusion.

"—Willow!" the voice of my husband barked behind me.

I found Xavier sprinting alongside Alexander and our skeletal Sentient, Aster. They skidded to a stop before me and my vassals, panting.

"Willow," Xavier puffed, his scythes already in hand. "It's La'Lunaî! She's here—!"

Screams ripped through the audience.

Like a towering wave ready to crash into the colosseum, the horrifying forms of dripping beasts poured into view from overhead. They blotted out the ceiling mists, they flew in on crooked wings and scampered on disjointed limbs—

"*To arms!*" I roared, my amplified voice rumbling throughout the arena, my blood sparked into immediate action.

The Reapers between the aisles rushed to slide between the spectators and the monsters... but the demons declined to attack. They merely hissed and growled at the terrified shifters.

"Sorry to crash the party," a drawling voice said to my left, the man's voice picked up by the microphones and reverberating through the arena's speakers. "We got tired of waiting for an invitation."

Shadows appeared in my peripherals. I spun on my heels and held out my scythe, staring down the sudden collection of Sentient demons who'd appeared around us. Their white pupils gleamed hungrily.

The man who'd spoken was a tall shifter with brown hair and spindly limbs that were too long for his leather jerkin and trousers. His grin displayed a row of crooked, yellow teeth. "That was a fun little game you had there," he commended, clapping entertained hands. "We *all* enjoyed the show..."

As he gestured around the colosseum, I noticed various shifters in the audience rose as if commanded. *Other Sentients... They were waiting among the crowd?*

"Now, here's what's going to happen," the demon man said. "You're going to give up the location of the Willow of Ashes..." He flipped his head toward the audience. "… or we're going to eat every soul in this Bloody colosseum. What'll it be, Your Majesty?"

My sharpened teeth gritted—

Crack!

Someone dropped down beside us, the ground forming a small crater around the newcomer.

It was Hecrûshou. His radiant trident was pointed at the leader of the opposing demons. The shark's pupils glowed a brilliant white, his illusion disguise discarded.

"Tell your Mistress to stand down," Hecrûshou growled—and he must have shoved his rotten soul's Weight against the cluster of Sentients, because they all suddenly flew backward, hitting the dirt and squirming as if pinned in place by an invisible force. I noticed the demons in the audience had all done the same, confused squeals of fright spilling from their lips.

"*Bloody… Land…!*" The leading demon sputtered from the ground, wheezing as if his lungs were being crushed. Still, he grinned wide. "La'Lunaî… told us about you, *shark*… She says… she can't wait to tear out your Seam…"

Hecrûshou rumbled, "If I were alone, she just might. But we've gained a few allies along the way."

Crack!

Miranda dropped beside the shark and tapped her cane in a *hmph*. "I find it funny that La'Lunaî spouts her threats through an underling. I wonder, was she too frightened of the Reapers here to show up for her own ambush? What do you think, Thörd?"

The lavender-haired dragon demon flew down beside her, his hands sparking with lightning as he laughed. "Thörd say Little La'Lunaî ees being the scared one! We Ancients not threatened by newborns!"

Crack! Crack! Cilia and Kael dropped down next, fire burning from Cilia's hands and black poison festering from Kael's fingers.

Cilia purred, "What an adorable little daycare La'Lunaî created… Perhaps we should start our own, darling? For you and Aster?"

Kael chuckled. "I'm not sure I like the idea of being stuck in a room with Macar's bottomless pit of a soul-brother."

"Hey!" Aster pouted from behind the safety of Alexander's armored back. "Would you *rather* I eat everyone's souls—?"

"*Oh-ho-ho, dear, no, no, no—aaah…!*" our last demon, Khol, squealed as he ungracefully flopped stomach-first on the ground next, giving a winded cough as he fumbled to his feet and shivered meekly. "Is-is-is… is L-L-La'Lunaî here…?"

"No," Hecrûshou grunted and shouldered his trident. "It seems her fear of Reapers got the best of her, now that we're in the center of Reaper territory… She left this poorly conceived ambush to non-Ancients. Most of them are newborns. Even *you* would overpower this lot, Khol."

"Oh, good!" Khol clapped delighted hands. "I was hoping you'd say that! Thank Bloods for La'Lunaî's fear of—"

"You…"The opposing demon man pushed himself to his elbows, seeming to break out of Hecrûshou's hold slightly as black tendrils writhed from his forehead like disgusting worms. "You stupid… bastards…"The tendrils slithered back into his skin, and he relaxed, heaving upright. "You actually thought Mistress wouldn't Mark the lot of us to keep you from shoving us around?"

Cilia hummed. Then raised a hand.

She snapped her fingers.

Immediately, the mongrel beasts in the stands jerked at her command, turning away from the helpless spectators to now snarl at the Sentient demons scattered throughout.

Cilia murmured, "I suppose she failed to remember that mongrels cannot be Marked, then?"

Thörd and Miranda did the same with their Weight, commanding separate portions of the mongrels to drop into the arena like festering maggots pouring into a bowl of cereal—and they attacked the opposing Sentients.

It was mayhem around us. We living shifters squeezed together, still keeping a protective stance around Felix and his vassals, while we watched the mongrel demons brawl against the unprepared Sentients.

Bloods, I thought frantically, *Most of these Sentients really are newborn… majority of them weren't here for the last two battles. They didn't know what to expect at this showdown, did they.*

Suddenly, Hecrûshou launched his trident at a nearby Sentient man. The fork *cracked* into his ribs in a splatter of black blood. Hecrûshou rushed him and regripped his weapon, jerking it inside his chest.

Snap!

He severed the demon's rotten NecroSeam without hesitation.

The Sentient's skin deteriorated, boiling away from his bones, which clattered to the ground at Hecrûshou's feet.

Hecrûshou kicked the Sentient's discarded skull, rolling it before the cluster of brawling demons. The shark raised a commanding fist in the air.

The mongrel demons ceased their mauling.

The Sentients still alive panted for breath, their wounds healing, standing shakily as they looked at Hecrûshou with pure terror.

Hecrûshou propped his Crystal trident over a shoulder and looked around the cluster of faces from the remaining Sentients. "Anyone else care to be Cleansed?" He offered. "Or would any of you rather have your Mark removed? Other Ancients such as ourselves can dig it out of you, if you wish."

They looked at one another, uneasy.

Hecrûshou clicked his tongue. "No one? Hrm. Very well. You had a chance of being granted citizenship if you chose to renounce your life of soul-eating and join *our* ranks, but…" He sighed. "I suppose you all prefer a second death."

They all shuffled their feet. Finally, one woman questioned, "We… we can be citizens…?"

"—You can protect us from La'Lunaî?" a young man asked next. "You can do that?"

They were all asking questions now, shouting over one another ecstatically—

Then the crowd of Sentients were hit with an invisible force all at once, their foreheads squirming with black sludge as they dropped to their knees. Half of them suddenly broke into a run, fleeing the arena. The other half resisted whatever urge was raging through them, dragging their claws over the dirt and leaving marks as their feet tried like Death to get away.

Cilia cursed. "La'Lunaî is ordering them to retreat! She must be near…!"

Hecrûshou roared, "Free as many as you can!"

Our Ancients dashed after the Sentients who clung to the ground. They snatched the newborns by their necks, pried their fingers into the Sentient's foreheads, and plucked out the black sludge that was La'Lunaî's mark. Our Ancients threw each sludge piece into the dirt, and I watched in disgust as the pieces oozed over the ground like worms, slithering out of the arena and chasing after the retreating demons.

I flinched when a piece slithered over my feet, and I hopped out of its way. It crawled toward Kael, who snatched it with clawed fingers. Kael evoked his Infection Hallows over the sludge, black veins spewing over the thing. It deteriorated, misting between his fingers like rotted vapor, until his hand was clean.

I blinked at him. *The Marks can be destroyed by Infeciovoking…?*

Over time, our Ancients had freed a dozen newborns, who all puffed over the dirt in confusion and relief. Some were sobbing with joy. Others were clinging to our Ancients and begging them for their protection.

The rest, unfortunately, had fled. Along with the mongrels.

I rubbed my eyes, exhaling. "Thank Bloods…"

"—Felix…!" a shrill voice screamed from the east tunnel of the field.

My gaze whipped toward the woman hurrying after us with a squad of guarding Reapers clattering around her. One of the most decorated Reapers, I noticed, was my Uncle Yvan, who ran at the woman's side with a dangerously livid scowl aimed directly at me.

I grimaced, recognizing the slender, beak-nosed woman beside my uncle. *The Head of Council. Aunt Rovinne... Felix's mother.*

Rovinne rushed to their slumbering son, and while Uncle Yvan lifted him from the dirt, Aunt Rovinne turned to her guarding Reapers and stabbed an ordering finger at our Ancient demons with a ripping scream, "Exterminate these demons immediately—!"

"You will do no such thing," I commanded, snapping a stern glare at the now hesitant guards. I stepped between them and the Ancients, sweeping my scythe before them protectively.

Alexander and Xavier ran to my side and guarded the Ancients as well. Then from the east tunnels ran Jaq, Matthiel, Neal, and Octavius—from the skies soared Roji, El, and Lilli—whom all took a defensive stance between Rovinne's guards and the Sentients.

Our formation seemed to confuse her soldiers.

"Lower your weapons," I ordered, gripping my scythe tighter and holding my ground. I drew in a deep breath, my nerves rattling. *Now the REAL challenge arrives.* "These are our allies."

The Councilwoman stared aghast at me. "Allies?! Those beasts are—!"

"—the only force keeping back the Necrofera who retreated for their lives," the voice of my mother interrupted.

The azure-haired woman stalked into the arena from the west tunnel, Grandmother Crysa following at her side. The two women stepped in front of me to face Rovinne, primly cupping their hands at their skirts with deceptively polite smiles.

"And I would refrain from calling them beasts, Councilwoman," Grandmother Crysa suggested, her fox ears flicking. "They have agreed to strengthen our efforts against a common enemy, and thus deserve respect."

Rovinne's grown wolf ears folded down. What little color her grey face held quickly drained white. "*Respect?* They're demons, for Death's sake! What sort of queen conspires with the very demons she's expected to kill?! Guards...! Get rid of these abominations—!"

Crrrack! Zzap!

Bolts of lightning burst from King Roji's hands, exploding at the guards' armored boots in warning.

"I'd think twice before going head-to-head against *four* Relicbloods." Roji gestured with a wing toward my mother, the resurrected Ninumel, and me. He then nodded to the Sentients. "These guys are with us. If you condemn Death for allying with them, you condemn *all* the Bloodlines."

My mother hummed, "Precisely. And the Queen of Land, too, will confirm her alliance. You have but to contact her from the surface." She gave a polite gesture toward Rovinne. "Which we will all be more than delighted to do before the Court of Lords, if it would please you. There is much the realm of Grim must be made aware of, regardless." She cupped her hands on her skirts again. "Please, allow us to tell the nation of our discoveries in length."

Rovinne's claws grew. The glower she gave our Ancients curdled. Her piercing gaze snapped to me, her voice low and gritty. "Very well... *Your Majesty...*" The words oozed ruefully. "You and your *demons* are summoned to the Council..." She turned away with Uncle Yvan and their guard, Felix still slumbering in his arms. As she left, she chewed over her shoulder to me, "We shall unveil whatever devious plot you've concocted under trial... may Nira have mercy on your soul."

She and her guard left, and I exhaled the breath I was holding, rubbing my eyes. "Wonderful."

30

TESTIMONY

WILLOW

Clack! Clack! Clack!

Head Councilwoman Rovinne slammed her gavel from her podium in Grim's courtroom, declaring, "Court is now in session!"

Her vicious glare burned past Xavier and my lecterns to stare at the Sentient demons.

My husband and I wore our royal-black court robes, our crowns glinting from our brows in the court's lamplight. I'd been to court with my father a number of times before, so I was familiar with the proceedings… but this session was *far* different.

The Howllords and Howlesses that occupied the Councilwoman's side of benches had crammed themselves behind her lectern with frightened shivers, animal ears grown, wings fidgeting in horror, and tails firmly tucked between their legs. They flinched at every subtle movement the demons behind me made. I flicked my gaze back to see Cilia's entertained smirk, seeing she was enjoying the show as she deliberately crossed her legs to watch them jump. Adversely, the web-eared Khol was quietly knitting a scarf. Prince Fuérr, Oliver, and Milann sat around the pacifist demon, the children swinging their feet with carefree giggles as they tried their hand at knitting alongside him.

In slightly shorter lecterns on either side of Xavier and I were the other Relicbloods: Roji and Dalminia, my mother and grandmother, and the resurrected Ninumel and Zylveia.

There was a line of Reapers guarding the Council's side of benches, all with their scythes drawn while Cousin Felix led them with a fixed glare.

Alexander and his squad lined *our* side of benches, in case the other knights were ordered to strike at any moment.

Perched atop Xavier and my lectern was a large crystal ball. I knew it was connected by wires and circuits underneath the desk's framework, allowing access to the council's individual vision-screens. Through this, the whole court could view what the crystal ball revealed from the convenience of their personal screens. On the crystal's surface was etched a rippled sealing-rune, which a Seer previously engraved to trap their prophetic Hallows into the globe.

My gaze narrowed at the crystal ball. It was unusual to see it present. They normally brought it out for interrogations, to unveil the truth behind the accused's past. I supposed, then, that *I* was being interrogated.

And this will be televised throughout Grim, I thought as I glanced at the two cameramen on either side of the room. One was focused on Rovinne's side and the other was focused on mine.

"Death Queen Willow Ember," Aunt Rovinne rumbled. "Place your hand on the crystal ball before you."

I didn't protest and clasped the crystal orb without an ounce of hesitation.

Rovinne didn't seem pleased at my lack of trepidation. She went on haughtily, "You stand accused of conspiring with the Necrofera enemy…" She clutched her lectern's edges with grown claws and craned forward menacingly. "… to win your crown against Death Prince Felix Ember in our realm's sacred Duel." Her tone darkened. "How. Do. You. *Plea?*"

I cocked an eyebrow. I expected an accusation of conspiracy, but not over the Duel.

"Not guilty," I intoned dismissively, my hand still on the crystal ball. As I recalled the memory of *my* perspective of the Duel, that same memory replayed on the orb, lighting up on the council members' personal screens—including Rovinne's. I huffed and continued, "On two accounts. As for the Duel, the only souls who fought alongside me during the Duel were my three vassals. The Necrofera did not come forth until *after* I was declared the winner. For your accusation to hold any truth, my vassals would have to be the enemy demons you speak of. Which, as you can clearly see…" I gestured to my three resurrected vassals: Ninumel, Nikolai, and Rossette, who sat on my side of the courtroom among our peers. "… Their souls have *not* rotted. As for your second false point…"

I gestured to the Sentients behind me, and the crystal ball flashed with bits of my memories, each one showing different interactions with the demons throughout our journey. "*These* Necrofera are not our enemy. As I have stated before, those present here are our allies. They are fighting with us against the *real* enemy demons, whom you'd witnessed invading the colosseum not hours ago."

The ball displayed my memories of La'Lunaî and her army. The council members slowly began to peer over one another at the various screens brightening over their abandoned desks.

I blinked when two members broke away from the safety of Rovinne's lectern and returned to their desks. One was Dr. Yshia Lochart, an antlered woman whom I remembered was an Evocational Studies expert. Her face held a mixture of fascination and shock every time one of my memories of Xavier's and Alexander's multiple Hallows flashed over her screen.

The other, interestingly enough, was Dr. Gorron Mallesch, the council's Demonology Specialist. His look of wonder and intrigue made me grin.

Of course these two would find our discoveries interesting. I was glad they were present today. They were perhaps the two most important minds we needed to sway. Their recognized expertise meant that, if they acknowledged our previous information on demons was incomplete—and the Shadowbloods' Hallows was legitimate—our claims would hold credibility.

The Councilwoman didn't seem to notice her two colleagues had strayed away from the pack, and she sneered, "All demons are the enemy! There are no 'good' demons and 'bad' demons—!"

"I beg your pardon?" Hecrûshou piped from the benches, affronted. The little Bindragon wrapped around his bicep lifted its head, flapping his webbed ears with a curious *aaahn* as Hecrûshou growled, "We protected your simpleton son from being slaughtered and recruited into La'Lunaî's rotten army, yet you have the gall to have us stand trial while you push to have him overthrow your rightful queen—even after he was proven unworthy, according to your own customs?" The shark crossed his arms. "If anyone is conspiring, it is unequivocally *you*."

The others of the council began to murmur uncertainly.

Rovinne bristled. "You *dare* to speak in this council, beast?! Your ilk deserves to be exterminated upon sight! And my son has yet to be proven unworthy! Your influence during the Duel stained a holy tradition! Her *Majesty* is hardly in any position to debate this topic in the first place, given she is clearly biased from being emotionally compromised and having a conflict of interest—!"

"Pardon, Councilwoman," Xavier interrupted beside me, lifting a pacifying hand. He kept his tone cordial as he questioned in a hum, "If my wife is emotionally compromised due to her involvement in the Duel, as you say…" He cocked his head. "Does this not mean that *you*, likewise, are emotionally compromised?"

Her curdling glare narrowed at him. "Excuse me?"

"It *is* your son we speak of," Xavier said, opening a hand in her direction. "And, should the crown be given to him, this means that you will have a hand in your son's opinion when it comes time to vote for anything regarding the laws of this country. But if you have a hand in the *royal* vote, your position as Councilwoman will also give you a hand in the *judicial* vote, as you currently have." Xavier laced his fingers on our lectern, offering a polite smile. "And, correct me if I'm wrong, but such power on both sides would make your position a *tyrannical* one, unable to avoid a conflict of interest on all matters… would it not?"

The rest of the court's murmurs grew more fervent. It seemed most of them hadn't realized this.

The Councilwoman was Deathly still. She opened her mouth, but clicked her teeth shut. It seemed she had no retort.

I flashed Xavier an appreciative smile, then used the new silence as an opportunity to begin my prepared debate. I rose from my seat and cleared my throat.

"For centuries," I began, raising my voice to be sure the whole court could hear me, "it has been my family's duty to rid the realms of the Necrofera, and to prevent their creation… But in these two-thousand years, what do we truly know of the Fera?" I turned my attention to the council's Demonology expert, who was casting our Sentients a focused, studying look. "Dr. Mallesch?"

The man nearly leapt out of his seat, as if having forgotten that his queen was here until now. "I—I-I, er… *khm-hmm!* Yes, Your Majesty…?"

"Could you please tell us what data you and your colleagues in the Demonology Studies Society have gathered over the last two centuries?"

Dr. Mallesch shakily retrieved a pair of reading-spectacles from his breast pocket. "A-ah… yes… Well, we know of the varying classes…" I doubted he noticed his fingers were running over his curled moustache as he continued, "We know the most commonly formed ones are the Class 3 demons: the monstrous, mindless Fera… And less common are the Class 2 demons: Monstrous Class 3's that have eaten enough souls to become Sentient and reclaim their shifter forms—"

"Why does *everyone* have to bring that up?" Khol cried from the benches, though he didn't cease his knitting. His webbed ears flapped in a huff. "It's not as if we're aware we're eating any souls when we're like that! If I'd started as a Sentient, I wouldn't have eaten any—"

"*Khol,*" Miranda warned with a sharp look. "Don't interrupt."

Khol resigned himself to his knitting again, his nose to the ceiling. I suppressed a groan as I waved for Dr. Mallesch to go on.

He did so, but meekly, "a-a-and… there is also… erm…" He glanced at the many Sentients in our party. "The Class 1 demons: *Evocators* who have died and had their souls rot... who keep their shifter forms from the very beginning of the Change."

I nodded. "And would you say this is the most information we've gleaned on the demons thus far?"

He retrieved a kerchief from his desk and dabbed the sweat beading his brow. "W-well... yes, that's the most we've gathered..."

"I see," I hummed and rapped my fingers over the lectern. "Then, Doctor, I'm to assume you were unaware that the Class 1 and Class 2 Sentients followed a hierarchical system of power of their own design?"

The council members muttered their confusion to one another, and Dr. Mallesch stared dumbfounded at me. "They... they do...?"

"They do indeed. And while I'm sure you were aware that the older a Sentient becomes, the more power they have over other Sentients, but did you *also* know that they have formed hidden societies and cultures among us? Wishing for order among their own kind just as we have formed order among ours?" I cocked my head, ashen hair drifting over my shoulder. "And, lastly... were you aware that there is *royalty* among the Fera?"

Dr. Mallesch was want for breath. "Royalty...?"

"Among their kind, they are called the Ancients." I swept a hand toward our awaiting Sentients. "And we are in the presence of all but *two* of those royals now."

There was silence. I didn't even hear so much as a rustle of feathers from the winged members of the Council. Dr. Mallesch's face flushed white, his gaze awed at the Sentients filling the benches.

Then, Aunt Rovinne let out a skeptical breath. "Ridiculous!" she spat. "Royal demons? I've never heard of anything so preposterous in all my—!"

"My parents unknowingly fought against an Ancient before I was born," I said. "A viper, as I'm told. The one who killed the previous king at the time." I turned to Hecrûshou and waved him toward me. "Hecrûshou, could you please place your hand on the crystal ball to show them the Ancient I speak of?"

Hecrûshou nodded and came to the lectern beside me. He was tall enough that he only needed to reach his hand up to touch the ball, his fingers brushing over the crystal lightly.

Within the ball, two scaled, grey faces dripped into view. The images were mimicked on the individual screens at the other lecterns. I didn't recognize either woman from personal experience, but one viper's features matched what my parents had always described: long, plaited black hair, her face narrow and sharp, and her white-pupiled eyes glowing with pure hatred.

At the sight of that particular face, Rovinne's words died on her lips. She looked as though she recognized this demon; as if she were looking into her nightmares.

Hecrûshou rumbled, "Which of these two had been the Ancient killed by the old king?"

Rovinne's voice was meek with fear. "The…"

"—the left one," my azure-haired mother answered first. She had risen from her short lectern, her eyes locked on her individual screen with a haunted glare. "Serdin and I… we killed that one. Together…" Her claws grew, scratching the wood of the lectern.

Rovinne glanced down at Uncle Yvan beneath her. He gave a rigid nod in agreement. I'd nearly forgotten they were *all* there for that event.

Hecrûshou cocked his head. "*Charra the Callous,* was it? Which means her sister, *Ashya the Ravager*, is the one who still remains…"

Rovinne found her voice again and protested. "H-Hang on…! Do you mean to tell me that *thing* had a sister? And she… she's still out there, lurking in the caves somewhere…?"

Hecrûshou muttered, "Unless you've encountered a second viper demon these past years, yes. Be warned… The Grim Sisters are as old as the Ancient who pursues us… and just as powerful."

Rovinne hesitated. "When you say powerful…" Her grown wolf ears dropped to her neck, seeming too frightened to finish.

She didn't need to, though. Hecrûshou kept his fingers on the crystal ball and had scenes form within—and Rovinne watched on her screen as the fires of past massacres razed entire cities, viewed through the horrified eyes of Hecrûshou himself.

No one was spared in those slaughters.

Men, women, *children*… centuries of destruction… centuries of pure, helpless terror for the ancient citizens of Grim. And the viper sisters were at the center of it all, their crooked smiles splitting with hunger.

Dr. Mallesch leapt to his feet in a shriek. "It's the Rastiria Massacre of 1763!"

Hecrûshou's sneer was low. "Yes… I'm not surprised it became a historic event for your country. The Grim Sisters tried to overthrow Death's Bloodline and claim Grim for all demons… They wished to free our people from our oppressors. Free them from the endless exterminations, of being executed without trial…" He hung his head, looking ill. "They… killed so many. Some of us here now were nearing two-hundred years into our Afterlives, and they called us down, hoping to sway us into joining their efforts. I will never forget the screams. The sight of shifters being burned alive… nor will I forget the *scent*…" His voice shook, and he took a moment to compose himself. His tone was thick with disgust. "La'Lunaî joined them happily. As did Shëfaux the Gelid. The rest of us refused." He swept his gaze to Cilia, Miranda, Thörd, and Khol. All held sickened expressions.

I was surprised that even Cilia, the fire-thrower responsible for countless slaughters in High Everland in recent years, looked discomforted by the memory. Perhaps her mass-killing spree hadn't started until she'd met Macarius.

Hecrûshou removed his fingers from the crystal ball. "Some of us declined out of self-preservation. Others, like myself, refused out of revulsion…" He sighed. "Eventually, there was a coalition of Reapers and Grimish citizens who came to drive their horde out. The sisters and La'Lunaî nearly met their end by the royal family themselves… but now, La'Lunaî has returned to the caverns. And if history is any indication, I do not doubt she plans to join forces with Ashya the Ravager once again."

Rovinne's shoulders dropped. She sounded out of breath. "Then… what can we do…? If another Rastiria Massacre comes…"

"If another comes," I said, keeping my tone confident to ease her worries. "We will have something our ancestors didn't." I swept my hand toward the Sentients. "We have *allies* that know their kind. These Ancients have power over the weaker Fera, some sort of Soul Weight that pushes them into obedience."

Rovinne flicked an unsure gaze at the demons. "If this is true, what's to stop *these* demons from being overpowered by the *other* demon's 'Weight'?"

"Us." I placed a hand on my hip determinedly. "Yes, the enemy Ancients will certainly attempt to overpower our allying demons… but this power of theirs has no effect on Clean Souls, such as ourselves. These shifters here with us wish to stop the massacre that's coming—"

"But why?" Dr. Mallesch interjected. It wasn't out of fear or suspicion, the man looked inexpressibly curious. "Why would they care what happens if only the *living* shifters are at risk?"

There were agreeing murmurs from the Council members.

My voice was thick. "Because the living shifters are *not* the only ones at risk. Ancients have a peculiar… *trick* over the younger Sentients. They can take a piece of their rotten souls and imbed it within the minds of the weaker Necrofera. With this, Sentients such as the ones on *this* side of the benches…" I gestured to the collection of newly-freed Sentients who had their Marks removed in the arena. "Can be enslaved to do whatever the controlling Ancient wishes of them, against their will. These Sentients here had been enslaved by La'Lunaî until *our* Ancients pried out her Mark from their skulls and freed them in the colosseum. But as you saw, La'Lunaî fled with countless more Sentients still under her control—which tells you that the ones sitting here wished *not* to follow her, once they were free."

Dr. Mallesch breathed in amazement. "Markings, now… This… this is incredible…"

I waved a hand toward the Council. "The demons have as much to lose as we do, should La'Lunaî and Ashya succeed in overrunning the realms. They will face a long and tortuous Afterlife under the control of others… Just as we need their help to stop the coming massacre, they need the help of the Reapers to protect their freedom."

Dr. Mallesch cupped his mouth, still starstruck. "Bloods… For all our research, we never *knew*…"

I nodded heavily. "We've spent so much time killing the Necrofera without hesitation, we never stopped to think they could be civil enough to simply *ask them* all of these facts…" I laid a hand on my chest. "I, too, hadn't known any of this. I hadn't even considered such a thing was possible. It was by mere chance, and much danger, that I discovered there was more to the demons. *Some* crave nothing but souls, yes… but others, I learned, wished for freedom. For love. For acceptance, and knowledge, and equality…" My throat tightened. "And some wished only for death…"

My mind slid to the memory of Janson, tears threatening to build. I pushed down the guilt and took a new breath. "I ask the court: does this sound any different from living shifters? We have murderers and thieves just as they do. But we also have those who believe in honor and loyalty… and so, too, do they. We have painted an inadequate picture of the demons. We thought they were all in agreement with their goals. As if they were some sort of hivemind, working as one sinister organization. We thought there was nothing new to be learned. That mentality was disgustingly narrow, as I have come to find out."

I waved to the Sentients in offering. "I ask that the Council listen to each of their stories, and look into their pasts as they share their tales through their own eyes. Judge for yourselves if they are to be trusted as allies."

I stepped down from the podium alongside Xavier, allowing Hecrûshou to be the first to place his hand on the crystal ball once more, and allow his memories to play on the members' screens.

One by one, the rest of the Council returned to their seats, enraptured by what they witnessed. Each demon took their turn to tell their stories: verbally *and* through their displayed memories. The whole process took hours. There were many moments of frightened screams among the members; moments of laughter; of sympathy; warmed hearts… and moments of tears. Even knowing a small piece of their backgrounds myself, I still found myself unprepared for the level of devastation a Sentient endures. Centuries of misery and fear... it was far more horrific than I'd imagined.

Cilia and Kael were the only two left to share their stories. They approached the lectern together, and laid their joined hands over the crystal ball.

The scene they opened with their wedding day.

There were flowers in Cilia's hair, as we saw through Kael's eyes. Through Cilia's view, Kael's smile was warm and brimming with pure joy. They shared pieces of the next five years together. Kael's work as a surgeon in Everland's royal palace, Cilia's baking experiments that he would sample when he returned home, the birth of their son Caleb and his growth into a giggling toddler.

Then, the bright scenes darkened.

We could hear Cilia gasping for breath, the point of view through her eyes as she glanced down at her own chest. It poured crimson through her gown. A knife was skewered through her ribs. She fumbled to the floor, crawling. Macarius's scaled face flashed over her as he followed Cilia with a fang-filled smile. He picked up a cleaver from the counter.

THUNK!

Cilia's screams ripped in agony as he chopped her into pieces, blood spurting and bones cracking with disgusting sounds that made the Council members cringe and gag sickly. I even saw Dr. Mallesch clasp his lips as if holding back vomit.

The next scene was through Kael's eyes. He stepped into their home to find what remained of Cilia. Her severed head hung from the wall by her hair, which had been nailed to a wooden plank. Beside the dripping horror was a message painted in blood: *Your failure's payment.*

To my surprise, Macarius stepped in next. His clothes were free of blood now, and he acted ignorant of what had transpired not hours before. He convinced Kael it had been the Land King's doing... and when Kael rushed out to the snowy streets, he saw a glimpse of his five-year-old son being kidnapped by a man with glittering golden hair.

It must have been an illusion Macarius conjured, I thought, anger simmering. I'd seen Cilia's memory of that night, but this was the first time I'd witnessed Kael's version.

As I watched him storm the palace in his memory, slaughtering all who stood in his way on his rampage to save his son, I wanted nothing more but to hate him... but after seeing what he'd witnessed, it was no surprise that he'd snapped. If I found Xavier in such a state, and Lucas being carted off... what would *I* have done...?

There was a flash of white light in the memory—then Kael and Macarius found themselves floating in a black abyss. This must have been the moment my grandfather sealed them into Aspirre.

The point of view changed to Cilia's again. She had woken in her blood-soaked home three days after. She was confused and disoriented, stumbling out to the snow. She couldn't remember who she was. She couldn't remember *anything*.

Except a voice, echoing in her mind.

Cilia…

She presumed that must have been her name. She vaguely remembered it. But she didn't know whose voice that had been.

A series of different scenes flashed in a row, months spent wandering the forests and mountains alone, trying to remember that voice. If she could just find who it had been…

Then she met a man with glowing white pupils. He called her a new-born, which puzzled her. He peeled off a piece of his skull, which turned into a writhing black sludge—and jammed it into her brow.

She screamed as it squirmed through her brain. He gave a command, and her limbs obeyed without her control. He shoved her to dirt and ripped her gown to shreds, exposing her naked body, and ordered her not to run.

She couldn't disobey.

Her sobbing screams were ordered to be stifled, and were now terrified whimpers as he ravaged her over and over, days after weeks after months of the same torture—

"That's enough…!" Rovinne begged from her podium. "Please…! Remove your hands…"

Cilia and Kael did so—and Kael drew in his wife for a soothing embrace, the pair sobbing in each other's arms after reliving their nightmarish horrors.

The councilwoman cupped her face, her eyes still wet with her own tears. She sucked in calming breaths—but slammed a fist on her lectern, as if angry to feel even an ounce of sympathy, let alone enough to cause such a reaction from her.

"No more…" Her voice wavered tightly. "Never… in my *life*… have I seen such a horrifying…" She couldn't even find the words to finish, choking into a sob.

Cilia and Kael left my podium, and I reentered, sighing.

"What I wish to propose…" I leaned on the lectern. "Is a vote… A vote to grant citizenship to any Sentient who abides by our laws; to any who refuse our enemy's desire to slaughter and feast on souls. In exchange for aiding us in our struggle to survive the coming massacre, I wish to give them the freedom they have longed for during *countless* lifetimes…" I straightened and declared, "In this, my vote is Yae."

There was resounding silence that squeezed the room. Some members were still sobbing, some were fidgeting with various quills or kerchiefs or rings or robes…

"—Yae," piped Dr. Mallesch, breaking the silence. He sniffed and lifted his chin. "I-I… I vote Yae."

"Yae," another member, Dr. Yshia Lochart, agreed next.

The room flooded with the same response, not even a minute passing until we were left with one, unanswered vote.

Rovinne's.

"Well, Councilwoman?" I said softly, opening a hand to her. "What say you?"

For the first time since I've known my aunt, I saw mind-breaking confliction in her eyes. She bit her lip, her features stained with indignance.

Then she sighed. "I… vote Yae…"

She *clacked* her gavel, and I loosened my breath.

"But," Rovinne chewed with sharpened teeth, "I expect to see *detailed* documents from this. I'll not have every demon flocking to Grim hoping for salvation. Speak with your Ancients. Create your restrictions… I expect *order* to be upheld, at all costs." She rose to her feet. "Inform the Council once you've drafted the appropriate bill… Adjourned."

As she left, I smiled after her, nodding to her respectfully. Then I turned to Hecrûshou.

The shark demon was stalk still, staring distantly into space.

"Well, Hecrûshou," I said, pride buzzing in my chest. "Was I true to my word?"

At first, he said nothing.

Then his eyes suddenly leaked with tears.

"Yes," he whispered. A croaking laugh escaped him, his smile so wide, it stretched his skin with pure elation. "Yes, you were. Thank you…" He quaked, his sobs worsening—then he bent down and wrapped me in an enthused embrace. "*Thank you…*"

I chuckled, returning the embrace with long, relieved sigh. "Congratulations, Hecrûshou… you've certainly earned it."

31

A NEW DAWN

XAVIER

The courtroom was now buzzing with fervent chatter.

Willow was discussing the next course of action with Hecrûshou, telling him that, if he expected to be treated as a regular citizen, then he had to abide by the laws of a regular citizen: which entailed handing over his Spiritcrystal trident, since only Reapers were legally allowed to wield weapons of that mineral. The shark looked forlorn as he picked up his trident from the benches, sighed, and handed it to Willow. He claimed there wasn't a need for it anymore, if he was to be working with the Reapers officially now.

From the corner of my eye, I saw Yulia peek her lovely head inside the courtroom. She'd been waiting outside during the hearing, looking after Lucas until we were finished. She held my infant son in her arms as she crossed the room to meet with Willow. Lucas cried when he saw Willow, reaching for her desperately. My wife chuckled and took him from Yulia, kissing his cheek and calming the baby now that he was with his mother.

I smiled at my family… but my cheer faded when I remembered the last memory with Cilia and Kael, and a sickened knot clenched my chest.

The two demons were near the back of the room, whispering about their trialing lives apart. They were still sobbing.

Macarius destroyed their happiness… I turned back to Willow and Lucas. Milann had hopped over and asked to hold the baby, making silly faces to make him giggle.

My hands balled into angry fists. *I'll be damned if he shatters mine.*

"—Xavier?" Alex blurted behind me, clasping my shoulder with a gauntleted hand. He cocked an eyebrow at me. "You look troubled. Shouldn't you be more… *celebratory,* after a victory like this?"

My grown wolf ears curled, rumbling, "How can I celebrate…? If La'Lunai's army is here, Macarius can't be far behind…" I stole another glance at my family. Willow's cheerful gaze caught mine. She suddenly looked concerned that I didn't return that cheer. I shook my head and turned back to Alex. "I can't let Macarius near my family, Alex. If he exacts a *fraction* of the horrors onto them that he did to Cilia and Kael…"

Alex squeezed my shoulder. "He won't. We'll kill him before he comes anywhere near us."

"—You can't!"

We both jumped at Herrin's interjection. The winged scholar had popped up behind us alongside Marian, the two clutching packets of notes in their arms and struggling to keep them all from falling.

"You can't kill Macarius, remember?" Herrin insisted.

Marian huffed at his side, "We may need him *alive* to stop the End! No killing until after we've proven our theory!"

Alex put a fist on his armored side. "Still on about that, are you? Look, I don't care about your ridiculous theory. I'm killing him, and that's final."

"Not yet!" They cried. Herrin spoke separately, "Kill him *after* we stop the End…! Can you at least do that?"

I twisted my mouth, annoyance simmering. "How close are you both to proving your theory, exactly?"

Herrin beamed. "Super close! We just have to ask you both—oh, and Aster—a few last questions, and we should have what we need."

Alex and I exchanged a glance. Then we twisted back to the benches, where Aster was stuffing his face with that same collection of snacks he'd acquired at the colosseum.

"Aster," I called, getting the skeletal demon's attention, "Herrin and Marian have questions for us."

Aster hurried to his feet, taking a bag of popcorn with him, and hopped over the benches to meet us. "What's up?" He asked, crunching on his popcorn.

Herrin cleared his throat. "I need to know each of your answers to this one question: Which is more important? The past?" He leaned his head to the side. "Or the future?"

My brow knitted. "That's all?"

"That's all," Herrin affirmed.

I laughed. "Well, that's simple. Obviously—"

"—The future—"

"—The past—"

The three of us paused. Aster and I had answered 'the future' together. Alexander had answered 'the past'.

I frowned at Alexander. "The future is more important. Without that, we have nowhere to go."

Aster swallowed another mouthful of popcorn. "What he said."

Alex crossed his arms. "Without the past, there would *be* no future. So, the past is more important."

"But that still means you need to consider what's to come with care," I insisted.

We glared at each other for a long moment. Then a different thought struck me—and seemed to strike Alex at the same time, our expressions softening. Alex and I turned to Herrin.

"The present," we both answered in unison. It was a third option Herrin had neglected to offer.

Marian flicked her gaze at Aster. "And do you still keep to *your* original answer?"

Aster snorted. "Duh. The only place everyone tries to get to is the future."

Herrin exchanged a thrilled grin with Marian. "That proves it!"

I sighed, rubbing my temple. "Proves what, exactly?"

Herrin pointed at Aster. "Aster is the Ruiner. Which means Macarius is the Savior."

Marian nodded to Alex and me. "And you two are the Defender—where Xavier represents the Ruiner, and Alexander represents the Savior."

We all gave them flat stares, our unified tones unamused. "What?"

"Don't you see?" Marian urged, her wings fanning out for emphasis. "The prophecy from Iri stated that One will Save, One will Ruin, and one will Defend. We all assumed Macarius was the Ruiner, which led us to believe that he would bring the End. But he *isn't* the Ruiner! *Aster* is!"

Aster looked hurt. "I'm not a Ruiner…"

Herrin chimed in, "Not literally, Aster. Iri's prophecy is all metaphorical. 'To ruin' can also be interpreted as 'to change'. And if we take that into consideration, this means that what you 'ruin' is the *past*."

Marian gestured to me next. "Xavier's first answer was also 'the future'—which makes you the Ruiner *half* of the Defender." She gestured to Alexander. "And since 'to save' can also be seen as 'to preserve', Macarius and Alexander fit the Savior role, since they believe that protecting the past is the way to ensure the future."

Alex scowled. "Am I supposed to take that comparison as a *complement?* Why am I lumped in with a psychopathic murderer?"

"But you're not," Herrin insisted. "You're the Savior half of the *Defender*. Both you and Xavier might lean toward different answers, but you both decided that, together, the *present* was more important—that both the past and the future are equally important and need balance. That's *your* role."

Marian chuffed, quite proud of herself. "And since Aster is the Ruiner, our entire assumption that the Ruiner would bring the End must be incorrect. Aster has only one of the Blessings he's meant to have—Macarius has majority of them, and therefore has more means to do damage. But Iri wouldn't have called an End Bringer the 'Savior'."

Herrin stabbed an excited finger in the air. "Which means that *none* of you will bring the End! But you're *all* needed to stop it!" He directed his pointing finger at Alexander and me. "So no killing Macarius until *after* he helps save us from the End!"

Alex and I glowered at him.

Then I noticed someone new was standing beside me. I turned to face her, perplexed. It was an antlered woman from the Council. She flinched when I turned to her, flushing pink.

"Oh—uh, um," she stammered, clearing her throat. "I-I don't mean to interrupt, Your M-Majesty, but, erm…" Her gaze alternated between Alexander and me. "You're the Shadowblood, aren't you?"

Herrin swooped in to answer for us, "Yep, that's them!"

The woman squealed with barely-contained excitement. "Oh, my goodness gracious—it's true…! My name is Dr. Yshia Lochart, I represent the Evocational Studies Association! I've read all the NecroSeam Chronicles— Could you *please, please, please* demonstrate your multiple Hallows?!" She stopped herself when Alex and I cringed back, and she gave a nervous laugh, dialing back her enthusiasm. "*Khm-hmm…* For science, of course…"

I felt uneasy at her wide-eyed look at us, and mumbled, "Erm… perhaps some other time…?"

Councilwoman Rovinne suddenly caught my eyes from across the benches. She was stalking toward Willow, pulling her aside as Milann played with baby Lucas, and the two women hissed under their breaths about something that, judging from their grave expressions, must have been serious.

My gaze narrowed at them.

"Excuse me," I said to the still-jabbering Evocations expert, stepping away as she instead bombarded Alexander with her questions.

As I neared my wife and her aunt, I overheard Rovinne whispering, "… thought I recognized that man." She nodded her sharp chin toward Kael, who still stood with Cilia in the back, tucking a lock of her grey hair behind her ear lovingly. Rovinne's tone was harsh. "That *is* the assassin from the Death Palace, isn't it? The Infeciovoker?"

Willow kept her voice hushed. "Yes. His name is Kael Treble. And his wife is the Demon Queen who tried to kill us in High Everland."

Rovinne's face fractured. "How in the five Bloody realms did you tame those two? Neither of them look like bloodthirsty monsters anymore—especially given their gruesome history!"

I cut in from over Willow's shoulder, "They were both being manipulated by the cobra shifter you saw in their memories."

Rovinne whirled on me, befuddled. "The lunatic *butcher* from the 16th century?"

I nodded. "We've had many encounters with him during our time on the surface… he's like my brother and I." I paused, my look turning quizzical at Rovinne. "Have you read Herrin Tesler's books? Regarding the Shadowblood and the Lightcaster?"

Rovinne's stare grew stale at me. "I don't have time to read silly fairytales."

"It's no fairytale, Councilwoman." I raised my hand and evoked my ice Hallows, my palm glowing emerald as ice crystalized above my fingers in the shape of a frosted candle-lily.

I handed the glossy flower to Rovinne, who took it with a gaping mouth. She was staring at the crowned Ocean mark on my left hand. Then the mark changed scarlet, becoming a crowned *Sky* mark as I evoked my lightning Hallows and very delicately had a spark of electricity zap from my fingers.

When the mark dissipated back to its original Crest of three black diamonds, her grey face drained pale.

"Bloods Almighty…" Her voice shook. "The rumors… they're actually true…?"

"I'm afraid so," I said with a grim tone. "But my brother and I aren't the only ones who can receive these Blessings… the cobra shifter you saw is like us. His name is Macarius Lysandre. He's also known as the Lightcaster." I nodded toward Cilia and Kael. "And he used *them* to get those Blessings… they've agreed to stand trial for their crimes after we've taken care of their murderer, but you'll have to trust us when we say those two are no longer a threat to us." I put fists to my sides and turned to Willow. "Willow and I have more reason to hate them than anyone. They've almost killed us on several occasions."

Willow grumbled vindictively, "Not to mention, Cilia smeared my name when she wore *my face* during a demon invasion in High Everland."

I hummed, "I'm quite certain that was Macarius's idea, since he was the Decepiovoker of their morbid troupe. I doubt Cilia would have cared—"

"Hang on," Rovinne interrupted, rubbing her temples in desperate confusion. "Are you trying to tell me that this… Macarius… is still out there? In *this* century?"

"Yes." I cocked my head. "Who do you think is pulling the strings in La'Lunaï's demon army? You heard them ask for the location of the Willow of Ashes. This means they're still working with him…" I hesitated, glancing at Willow as a new spike of anxiety ran over my skin. "… and he's after our last set of Blessings…"

The set that *we* still didn't have, either.

Rovinne's confusion only doubled. "You're not making sense. The Willow of Ashes is a myth?"

Willow sighed and pinched the rim of her nose. "You really ought to read Herrin's books… Rovinne, I am not sure how else to tell you this but…" Willow let out a breath. "The Lost Relics are not myths. And they were never lost to begin with. The Relicbloods of each realm have kept them hidden from the public for over a thousand years."

I crossed my arms. "We discovered that Dream had issued their secrecy in the first place… and he recently lifted that secrecy before his death. He taught us that anyone can become a Relicblood if they draw the blood of a *current* Relicblood at their respective realm's lost Relic. And this is how Macarius is gaining his Hallows."

Willow's voice rumbled, "You can ask any of the Relicbloods here today. This was how Ninumel died. And Sky Princess Zylveia. And, nearly, the resurfaced Land Queen. Though, *she* was fortunate enough to survive. My Grandfather Dream was… not so fortunate…" Her fox ears grew. "I have watched my fellow Relicbloods die at the hands of a ruthless murderer too many times. I will not allow it to continue, especially not with my family." Willow laid a hand on Rovinne's quivering shoulder. "*All* of my family. I warn you now, Rovinne, you must tell Uncle Yvan what's to come. Protect him. And protect Felix. *Every* Relicblood of Death is in danger. Have your guards watch them every waking moment until we capture Macarius. Do you understand?"

The color had completely drained from Rovinne's face, but she nodded vigorously, then hurried back to her armored husband from the other side of the courtroom.

Willow cast me a morose glance. "Perhaps… given that our timeframe has been shortened so drastically…" She bit her lip. Then sighed. "It's time I brought you to the Willow…"

I swallowed, my blood shivering anxiously.

All I could do was nod.

FELIX

My eyes were slow to open, the fluorescent light stinging my retinas.

Was I... in the palace infirmary?

I struggled to sit up on the patient bed, my arms hooked to various fluid-tubes and wires. My shirtless chest and arms were bandaged, dark bruises and puckered scars visible where my skin was exposed around my torso.

How had I gotten here...?

My head throbbed, ruing these damned lights that burned my adjusting eyes. I vaguely remembered being in the colosseum... I was fighting that Bloody vermin queen.

I'd LOST to that Bloody vermin queen, I corrected in a rage, my wolf ears sprouting and curling back as the sting of pure, unrivaled *hatred* boiled over.

... but it was overtaken by shame.

"How... could I have lost...?" My vision blurred with tears, burying my wretched face in my hands, a disgraceful sob breaking my voice. "I was better... I-I was *pure*... And yet, she *bested me*...?"

"—Well," a woman's voice hummed to my left, startling me. "For what it's worth, you would have won, had it been a fair duel."

I squinted against the glaring ceiling lights. There was a scaled, pregnant woman sitting in a visitor chair. She was reading a book and delicately sipping a glass of lemonade.

"Who... who are you?" I demanded weakly. "How long have you been there...?"

She chuckled and set down her glass, closing the book in a warm sigh. "I've been here for a few hours. I was waiting for you to waken, Your Highness. My name is Lannyse Lysandre." She smiled. "I am a school teacher, visiting one of our Academy's locations here in Low Rastiria."

"A school teacher?" I was only more perplexed. "What are you doing here?"

"I'm here to right a wrong I couldn't help but notice," she said. "The queen did not fight fairly in your Duel..." Her tone was suddenly gritty. "She had *demons* fighting for her against you..."

My eyes bulged. "Demons...? But... but how could she...?"

My bandaged hands balled, fury bubbling. I threw off the sheets and roared, "That traitorous *insect*...! I cannot allow such a sin to go unpunished...! Grim *must* be protected!" I glared at the scaled woman in the chair. "*Where is she?*"

I thought I saw a twitching grin roll over her lips. "She is on her way to the Willow of Ashes… You'd best get to her soon. There is no telling what evils she plans to bring to the sacred Relic…"

"That witch…!" I jerked out the fluid-tubes and wires, dashing out to the halls. "I won't let her get away with this…!"

32

THE WILLOW OF ASHES

XAVIER

The eerie silence of the Weeping Woods had me on edge.

Our usual party traversed the misted forest in a protective formation, the Reapers just as alert as the Sentient Necrofera in the darkness.

Well, save for Aster, of course.

The bumbling demon was too busy scarfing down skewered sausages to notice the trickling stream right in front of him—and his feet *plunked* into the water. He slogged his way out of the stream to cross to the other side, still chewing on his sausages while kicking the water from his boots in an annoyed grumble.

Myra and Crysalette were the quietest of our group, taking turns to carry the azure-haired, baby Eryn.

My adopted daughter, Milann, trekked alongside Oliver and Fuérr, the three children mumbling to each other.

"… and it's like, *this big*," Oliver described as he stretched his arms as tall as he could. "And it's white, and all pretty, and…"

Milann scrunched her nose at him. "You're just copying the description in the Choir."

Fuérr nodded his agreement with a flap of his webbed ears, tossing a long lock of his fin-like, emerald hair and huffing in a thick Marincian accent. "Eez truu. Zat eez een Quai-or."

Oliver's feathers flared on his wings, giving a sharp flutter. "I'm not copying! I Saw it in future visions! You'll see…!"

"<… Feels incredibly lighter than I expected,>" Ninumel hummed to Willow in Marincian to my left. The resurrected king hefted a Spiritcrystal trident—the one that had previously belonged to Hecrûshou. He admired the curling fork and frowned at Willow. "<Are you sure I'm allowed to wield this? You just told *that* one he couldn't legally have it if he wasn't a Reaper.>" He pointed the trident at Hecrûshou ahead of us, who twisted back at the mention and snorted indignantly.

Willow bobbed Lucas in her arms as she replied in Ninumel's tongue, "<There are allowances granted to certain individuals, in specific cases. The vassal of a Reaper may wield a Crystal weapon if given permission by that Reaper. Since you and I formed a Bloodpact—and I'm the Bloody Queen of Death—there is nothing illegal about you wielding this. Plus...>" She shrugged, Lucas's wolf ears folding in question as he marveled at the glowing trident. "<As a Relicblood of Ocean, you're more familiar with wielding a trident, correct? I thought it was convenient that Hecrûshou needed to relinquish this in exchange for his new citizenship, while *you* needed to be equipped for demon-slaying while fighting alongside me.>"

Ninumel rubbed his long moustache. "<Are you sure he doesn't mind...?>"

"<I asked if he objected, but he thought it would be idiotic not to arm you appropriately. Though, he says he would like a new trident to replace it, once he acquires a legal permit, so Henry thinks he can forge one within the week and...>"

—smack!

One of Roji's scarlet wings thwacked the back of my head as he and his wife walked by me, nearly toppling my crown. As his feathers brushed over my hair, static sparked from them and I leapt away in a confused yelp.

"Do you mind?" I grumbled, replacing my crown so it hugged my skull properly again. I still wasn't accustomed to its weight. My neck ached to take it off, but there hadn't been time to grab a Storagebox to stuff it in, so the only place I could conveniently carry it was... on my head.

Roji hadn't seemed to notice he'd run into me, and rubbed his neck apologetically. "Oh, sorry, Xavier. Was trying to avoid this stupid creek." He gestured to the stream of water that bowed next to his wife's boots.

I exhaled, calming as I watched their two young daughters run around the misted woods in delighted giggles. When they splashed into the many creeks, their legs shifted into tails, and they fluttered their little wings to spray each other with the cold droplets.

Roji's resurrected sister, Zylveia, walked up ahead with her cat-jay friend, El, jabbering in Culatian with wild gestures. Beside El, Octavius seemed to be struggling with understanding them. His grasp of the language was juvenile, but he tried to keep up regardless.

Beside them, Matthiel and Neal murmured under their breaths about how late it was, wishing the demon army could have given it a rest for another week.

Vendy, Hugh, and Dalen had taken their wide formation around Milann and the other children, watching them carefully as I'd requested. Aiden, Nathaniel, and Apson had been asked to stay behind in the palace to keep an eye out for any intruders. They could report straight to me, should any calamity arise there.

"—Hey mate," Jaq suddenly piped beside me cheerily. The viper had slowed his pace to walk beside me, his armored steps clattering. "Er, I mean… *Sire*," he amended awkwardly. "Sorry. Still ain't used to it."

I groaned and rubbed my lids. "Jaq, do me a favor and *never* get used to it. I haven't seen you in months. And quite frankly, I'm due for some normalcy back in my schedule before I forget I'd ever been *just Xavier*."

Jaq gave a sympathetic grin and tapped my crown with a knuckle, the knocks vibrating over the metal and rumbling softly over my scalp. "Not diggin' the royal life, eh?"

I sighed. "It isn't that, it's just… Oh, I don't know. Willow was raised to be a queen all her life—I was raised to be a knight, or… or an ambassador, like my father—or even a general, like my mother. But a king?" I gave a hollow laugh. "I knew marrying Willow would eventually lead to this, but… I suppose I'd hoped I would have a bit more… *preparation* before actually getting here."

Jaq shrugged. "Looked like you were gettin' the hang of it pretty quick, in the courtroom."

I cocked an eyebrow at him. "Really? I felt like I was grasping at mist in there. My palms were certainly cold enough with sweat." I balled my hands in demonstration, chuckling. "I was waiting for someone to scream at me for having the audacity to sit next to Willow."

Jaq chortled and thumped my back. "Well, can't blame ya there, mate! After that epic ass-beating your wife gave her cousin, anyone would be scared to sit next to her!"

I laughed. "No argument there. So, did you simply wish to chat, or did something need my attention?"

He flicked a thumb over his nose with a sniff. "Nah, Alex asked me to stick close to ya, for protection. He asked Lilli to do the same for the queen."

I glanced over at Willow, seeing an armored Lilli had indeed joined her, the two conversing and playing with baby Lucas in Willow's arms.

"Ah." I cast Jaq a curious smile. "How are you and Lilli enjoying married life, by the way? You hadn't been wedded a whole day before we sailed off to different countries. I'm still not sure how that happened in the first place?"

He scratched his scaled chin, puzzled. "Alex didn't tell ya all that?"

"He's been a bit… preoccupied." I nodded up ahead where Alex had stopped before a large stream.

My brother was about to hop onto the stones between the water, but paused when Bianca came up to the stream next. Alex flushed and quickly evoked his stone Hallows over the rocks, his hands glittering gold as the stones stretched and connected together, forming a bridge over the stream at Bianca's feet.

Bianca lowered a rabbit ear at him. He smiled hopefully. She rolled her eyes and walked across, relenting, and muttered, "Thanks…"

Alex beamed like a dumbstruck fool, following behind her with more confidence—

Schhrr—THUNK!

He slipped over the wet, stony bridge and fell on his back in a yelp, scraping his flailing hand on the rough rock. He sat up in a seethe, cursing under his breath.

Bianca saw him and gave a hopeless sigh, going back to crouch beside him. She took his scraped hand and used her remedy Hallows to heal the wound, then rose without a word and blushingly stormed across the bridge to the other side of the stream.

Alex sat there for what seemed like a full minute before stumbling to his feet and practically floated after her in an airy daze.

"Oh," Jaq grunted next to me. "She's still mad, huh?"

I grinned. "She seems to be warming up. She is quite stubborn, though."

"—It isn't stubbornness that drives her," Lilli clipped suddenly beside us.

She and Willow had come to meet us. The bat gave a flap of her wings and put haughty fists at her sides. "Don't you understand what she's going through? She doesn't *trust* him. And she has every right not to. He promised himself to her when they were younger, then neglected to tell her he was engaged after he himself found out, then dragged his feet to make a decision and all but forced *her* to make one for him, then when he finally came around to making his own decision to be with her, he had *horrible* timing and told her the moment *I* decided to leave *him* for Jaq, and now she thinks he only came back to her after he had no other option and…" She lowered her wings, hesitating. "Well… I suppose that last part is also my fault… Perhaps I ought to speak with her?"

Jaq and I exchanged petrified looks.

"That…" I began, clearing my throat. "That was a *lot* to take in…"

Jaq twisted his mouth. "You're weirdly interested in Alex's love-life. Should I be worried?"

Lilli gave a flighty chuckle and wafted a prim hand at him. "I'm sorry, it's simply that, well…" She swooned and clapped her hands. "Oh, it's just so exciting! It reminds me of my favorite drama I used to watch on Screen…!"

Jaq groaned and cupped his face in shame. Then he broke into a laugh.

Willow strode beside me, carrying Lucas in her arms as she hummed, "You seem more relaxed, now that Jaq is here."

I smiled. "Yes… I do feel less panicked, honestly. It was strange to have him gone for so long. He has this way about him that seems to just… ease the tension, I suppose." My smile thinned. "It was something I'd taken for granted… I didn't realize how stressful these last few months had been."

"Agreed," she lamented. "And Bloods, is it relieving to have Lilli back as well…"

"—If their royal Majesties wouldn't mind," Alex called from the other side of the large stream, waiting at the end of the small, stone bridge. "Hurry up! We're nearly there. It's over this way."

Willow hefted Lucas and cast me a sidelong glance. "Should I be impressed or irritated that he knows the way to a Lost Relic so well?"

I rubbed my neck, carefully walking beside her across the stone bridge. "I'm more irritated that *I* don't remember seeing it… Let alone remember the way."

Willow brushed a fallen leaf off Lucas's wolf ear, the pup beginning to fuss. It may have been a risk to bring him with us to the Relic, but neither Willow nor I felt comfortable with leaving him out of our sight after that last demon raid in the colosseum. We decided it was safer *with* us, where we had our own demons to fend off our adversaries that may be lurking out here.

Willow hummed, "I nearly forgot that you've already been to the Willow… Do you find *any* of this familiar?"

I glanced round the woods. The drooping trees swayed in a soothing hush as a crisp breeze rustled the leaves.

"I suppose… some of this *is* nostalgic." I flicked my gaze at Willow. Her long, white hair drifted in lovely curls against the wind. Her silver skull-crown shimmered along with her butterfly marriage-vines. And Seamstress, her azure eyes were mesmerizing under the dim lights floating in Grim's overcasting ceiling mist. I found myself smiling, my nerves calming.

Then Lucas caught my gaze from her arms, and he squirmed like mad.

"Dada…!" He nearly flung himself over Willow shoulder, reaching for me desperately. "Da*da*…!"

My heart melted, and I took him from Willow, holding him tight to my chest in a delirious chuckle. His soul's fire heated my soul's ice, though this time, no steam rose from our contact, since our clothes acted as a gentle barrier.

Lucas nuzzled his face against my throat, and I laughed when his swiveling wolf ears tickled my neck. Virro buzzed down from the trees and perched on Lucas's head in a twitter. Chai came flying after him, my raven alighting on my shoulder as he fussed over Virro's feathers in a fatherly fashion.

I looked up to find Willow was chuckling as well, seeming warmed by the sight. Jewel fluttered to her shoulder and sang to Virro and Chai fervently as we continued through the Weeping Woods with the others.

"Did I ever tell you," I began, keeping a firm hold of Lucas, "why Alex and I were out here in the first place when we supposedly found the Relic of Death?"

"No," Willow said, curious. "Why?"

"I was terrified of exchanging our Ornaments of Endearment in front of the whole country."

Her brow quirked. "Why would that be terrifying?"

"The whole country," I emphasized. Lucas gave mimicking *'Ba Ba Ba's* in response. "Our betrothal was no one's Bloody business but ours. I would have preferred giving you your vines in private…" I lightly shoved her shoulder in a laugh. "But, of course, a Death Princess's business is *everyone's* business, isn't it?"

She chuckled. "Queen, now. So, I suppose you were out here to settle your nerves?"

My head wavered. "That was half of it. I'd also spied a rather large Fallen Light landing out here. I thought it would make for a fair gift for you, along with your vines." I smiled. "But it seems we found the Willow of Ashes instead."

She looked troubled, taking a breath before asking, "Why didn't you tell me sooner…?"

I muttered, "If you recall, I was hence thrown off a cliff and lost my memories. Memories I *still*, apparently, don't have of the finding the Relic in the first place…"

Willow cocked her head. "Do you think… the Noctis Golems could have eaten those memories while they were scattered through Aspirre? As my grandfather explained?"

I grimaced. "Bloods, I hope not."

There was something unsettling about that question. There was no way to know if any memories had been eaten; no way to know if I would ever get them back. But I think the most aggravating question was: what memories had they *been*? What part of my past would always be missing…?

Willow gave me a sympathetic look—

RRRRRRRrrrrrmmmmm…

The ground shook suddenly, making us stagger. Lucas's wolf ears flicked up in alarm, clinging to my doublet with a small whimper.

RRRRRRRRRRrrrrrrrrrrrmmmmmm…

Another tremor came, rumbling all around us as if we were caught in the belly of a growling beast.

Then, like a retreating tide, the tremors faded into soft vibrations… and the caverns were still once more.

Willow cast me a dreaded glance. "A Groundquake…? In the summer?"

I held fast to Lucas, perplexed. "Strange…"

Willow looked troubled, her expression pensive. Then her eyes snapped to my Crest from my left hand.

"Xavier," she hushed. "It's… pointing the way."

I held Lucas with my right hand to look at my left knuckles. The middle diamond of my birthmark was gleaming with a white outline. I waved my hand experimentally around the woods. As it moved, the other two diamonds lit up instead, consistently pointing toward the way we were headed.

Nostalgia swelled again. The memory of the night Alex and I experienced this as children unfurled like a waking blossom. "Just as before…" I murmured, "and with the other Relics…"

Ash fell onto my nose. I glanced round, seeing the soft flakes drifting in the mist. From my arms, Lucas tried to grab the fickle particles, babbling at them as if asking them to stop so he could catch them.

Alex and the others had paused at the base of a mountainside.

My brother stood impatiently outside a thick curtain of willow branches, his plated foot tapping as he waited for Willow and I to approach.

When we stepped before him, I saw that his Crest, like mine, was shining with all three diamonds, the lights brighter than they'd been before.

Alex tossed his head toward the curtain of branches.

Then he disappeared through them, entering a cavern hidden behind those rustling willow leaves.

I held onto Lucas, nodded to Willow, and we stepped through the leaves together.

The wide cavern was far brighter than I'd imagined. Ash danced in the quiet air around us, sparse willows and candle-lilies sprouting around a gentle, crystalline stream that ribboned around the cave and pooled at a pond in the east corner. Iridescent algae radiated from the water with spellbinding blue light. The rocky walls were awash with a subtle, silver filter that brightened the hollow from corner to corner, emanating from the focal point of the cavern which, once my eyes fell upon it, stole the breath from my frosted soul.

The Willow of Ashes…

The Willow was made completely of white crystal. Its long, serrated leaves twinkled melodically in a rhythmic sway, the familiar tune of Death's Requiem singing like angelic bells that graced my unworthy ears. The Relic was enormous, its tallest branches nearly touching the stalactites on the wide cavern's ceiling. The bowing limbs seemed to yawn outward like the cradling arms of a loving mother, its cascading, crystal leaves jingling softly as if beckoning me to step closer...

Willow laid a hand on my shoulder, jolting me out of my trance.

"Well?" She questioned. "Do you remember it now?"

I returned my awed gaze to the Relic, my reply absent. "No... But Seamstress knows I won't forget it now..."

Willow smiled, taking Lucas from me to let me marvel at the Relic longer. She turned the pup toward the Willow and hushed, "What do you think, Lucas? This is where Mama's namesake comes from."

Lucas looked just as entranced as I was, his ashen eyes starstruck. He reached out toward the Relic, babbling and grabbing a lock of his mother's long hair.

Willow chuckled and strode toward the Relic with the baby.

I thought to follow, but my feet were frozen where I stood. Alex came to my side and waited with me, drawing a heavy breath. He stared at his gleaming Crest. I stared at mine.

"So." He said suddenly, hesitant. "This is it, isn't it? The last Relic..."

My reply was breathless. "The reason for our birthmarks... nearly completed."

We stood there, admiring the Relic in silence.

Alex whispered, "What happens after this? What if we stop the End, and everything returns to normal...?"

I yielded to a shiver, a small spurt of fear leaking through the wonder. "Is there such a thing as 'normal' anymore...?"

He had no answer for me. That widened the hollow pit eating my chest, like a beast crunching any surviving hope of returning to an ordinary life.

I held my arms, searching for a comfort that wouldn't come, my breath fogging in the frigid air. "I always thought..." I began, "I thought we would simply return home, once I found my body... that we would go back to our manor in Low Drinelle, greet Mother and Father as our separate selves, find Willow waiting in the palace for me and marry the normal way..." My lungs shuddered, a tangle of emotions unraveling all at once as the unrelenting stress of these past two years suddenly gushed out, and it was all I could do to keep my voice steady. "But none of it happened that way. Mother and Father are gone, we've been on the brink of death in a constant loop, we will never return to that manor, and I..." My claws grew, scratching my arms that I clutched so desperately as the final emotion—the *strongest* emotion—hissed from my twitching lips. "I'm just so *relieved* to be alive… that Willow and my son and *you* are still alive…" Despite it all, I smiled. "I think… all of you are the reason I look forward to the future. To any future. It wouldn't seem worth it, without the right people…"

Alex was quiet, murmuring, "Well… that makes two of us, certainly…"

I let the tension mist away, watching as Willow reached Lucas out toward the twinkling Relic. My son excitedly touched the crystal bark. His hands came away smeared with ash, which flaked off his skin and floated back to the tree where it belonged.

Clattering footfalls came from the cavern's hidden entrance as our armored comrades filed inside, all gawking at the Willow of Ashes. Our Grimish friends dropped to their knees in a prayer while our foreign companions lowered their heads in respect.

Hecrûshou was next to peel back the veiling branches of the cavern's entrance.

—*Thunk!*

Hecrûshou slammed into an invisible wall there, stumbling back as the branches quivered around his shoulders.

"Ocsha!" Hecrûshou cursed, pushing a hand on the rippling barrier. He couldn't get through. "These Bloody Relics and their demon wards…!" He flicked his glower at me resentfully. "I suppose we'll stand guard out here. At least it's comforting to know that the *other* demons won't be able to come near…"

—Aster walked past him through the barrier with an oblivious hum, chewing on his last skewered sausage.

He didn't find a hair of resistance from the demon ward.

Aster looked at me and blinked, swallowing the sausage whole. "What?" he asked, realizing everyone was staring at him.

I hesitated. "You… you just walked straight in?"

"As if you *weren't* a demon?" Alex questioned.

Aster twisted back. He saw Hecrûshou pound a fist on the invisible ward.

"Huh." Aster said, facing forward again with an impassive shrug. "Looks like it… So, this is the tree and whatever?" He leisurely strolled up to join Willow under the holy Relic, as if it were just another boring plant you'd find in everyone's dinky flower garden.

I flicked Alex a perplexed look. "Could he be immune to the ward because he's half the Lightcaster?"

Alex scratched the scruff at his neck. "That's the best explanation we're likely going to have…" He shook his head. "Whatever. Let's do this before Macarius devises a plan to get his own set of this Hallows."

I nodded, following at his side as we approached the Willow tree.

Once under its draping branches, we touched the powdered, crystal bark.

A surge of warmth pulsed over my palm, a calming inferno rolling over my soul and filling my chest with a comforting buzz.

The Mother Goddess is here…

Alex and I whispered soft prayers to the Seamstress.

I turned behind, finding Willow with our son. Aster stood beside her curiously.

"Willow," I said softly, stepping up to my dazzling wife. I cupped her smooth face. Stole the heat from her lips, lingering there in hopes of memorizing the warm touch of her flesh. Whatever happened after this, only one thing was certain: I would *never* accept a future without her.

When I broke away, my voice was a whisper. "Love… it's time. If I'm to protect you both, we can't wait any longer." Our son cooed from her arms, and I stroked Lucas's ashen hair, my soul weighing heavier. "Can you give the Call… and awake the Relic?"

Willow's azure eyes flashed with a strange emotion. She seemed to have a fleeting thought, as if recalling something troubling.

Then she sighed, cradling Lucas… and began to sing.

Kris la vheh weh shae'beahl hu'leigh…

The crystal leaves of the Willow of Ashes trilled with a shuddering jingle. Their notes mimicked my wife's lilting voice as she continued to sing Death's Requiem.

Neschalist p'laven ash kemn mea la shae

Heist e spell du'beahl hu'dohn
Yechet heme kraveshahe trist khon…

The Relic began to glow brighter. Its ash flaked away and drifted toward Alexander and me. The left diamond of our Crests brightened with a white gleam—and, strangely, I noticed a similar light brighten on *Aster's* back through his tunic, where his Crest waited. The demon stiffened, as if shocked by a bolt of static, his breath choking off.

Willow kept to her singing.

A'speles speles la a'hoh hoh

Tatacha veben shelic'u nahohko
Nira veilla ke halaa pievf
Necrotha myel'u dohn la sheft…

The righthand diamond of our Crests gleamed next. Aster fumbled to pull off his tunic, craning to see his own back—which *I* could clearly see was glowing exactly as Alexander's and mine was. All three of our Crests matched. Alex and I exchanged perplexed glances.

O myel heist timbriw lahla'beahl?

Murrderes craw hellacha lola'beahl
Heist craw'u lole fret myel ena…

Aster turned round and round in confusion, desperately trying—and failing—to see what was happening to his Crest. Could it be that… he *didn't* need Macarius here to gain his Blessings…?

Yechet wuw kemn droh la wuw kemn thal

Yechet wuw kemn droh la wuw kemn thal…

The third and final diamond brightened in a flash—
And the cavern vanished.

My eyes peeled open, head throbbing with pain. I was lying on stone, facing an empty, black sky.

A sky that shattered.

Broken shards rained down as the sandy forms of the Noctis Golems poured inside, devouring the screaming shifters who fled for their lives around us.

I shuffled to my feet in a panic.

Here again, I brooded furiously. *Another vision of the End…*

Footfalls sounded nearby. Alex trotted to my side in a heavy pant. "I hope to Gods this is the last time we have to go through this damned vision," he chewed.

"—It's happening…!" cried a different voice to our left.

It was Aster. The skinny Necrofera was gasping for breath on all fours, sobbing like a frightened child as he clutched his head and curled into himself over his knees.

"It's actually happening…!" Aster wheezed. "I-I-I screwed everything up…! I wasn't supposed to be a demon, I-I-I brought it here…! Gods, Herrin was right, I *am* the Ruiner…!"

Yes.

I shocked stiff at the new trilling voice. The sound of it ran through me like static. I hadn't heard that voice through my ears. It had echoed in my thoughts. Aster and Alex were also frozen. They must have heard the voice as well.

The three of us inched our heads to where the voice had vibrated from.

A woman stood there.

No, she *floated* there, her bare feet gravitating over the rubble as her long, white hair drifted around her radiant body as if pulled by a gentle wind, the loose gown she wore ruffling in slow, lulling waves.

For a moment, I thought it was Willow. But the more I focused on the violet-glowing woman, I realized she was far taller than my wife. Her ashen locks were perfectly straight; there wasn't a single, playful curl pulling the strands, and her eyes were not an icy azure. They were a sparkling, colorless white, peering at the chaos in the distance ahead of her as the side-profile of her straight nose and sharp chin was outlined in a brilliant violet glimmer.

Alex and I whispered, "Seamstress…"

Welcome, Champions. Her entrancing voice was a melancholy sigh; a deep, fiery song that kissed my thoughts with every alluring note and warmed my blood like soft embers at the center of a flame.

She finally turned to face us, and my soul froze under Nira's piercing, lamenting gaze.

Long have I awaited your arrival.

33

USURPER

OCTAVIUS

I shivered outside the hidden cave on the mountainside, tugging my fur cloak tight over my numb face. I wasn't sure how, but Grim was just as cold as Marincia's glaciers. Wasn't this supposed to be the realm where fire Hallows came from? You'd think it'd be warmer, with all those Pyrovokers walking around down here… False advertising, I swear to Bloods…

I looked at El, who stood watch next to me in her own armor. Unlike me, though, she didn't look the least bit bothered by the cold. She absently rolled one of her throwing-scythes between her fingers, the small weapon leaving a glowing streak of blue light over her cream-colored knuckles. As if Nira was taunting me, I even saw steam rising off El's skin where her armor didn't cover.

Pyrovokers, I thought, jealous as another cavern wind smacked me like a wall of ice, making me tremble again miserably. My cat ears were already grown to keep my ears warm with fur, but the constant winds kept cutting through no matter what I did.

El saw me staring, and her white cat ears lowered along with her pale-blue wings.

"Tavi?" She asked, taking a worried step toward me. "Are you okay—?"

"El, El, El!" Zyl suddenly chimed as she flapped down from the air and landed between us. The resurrected Sky Princess grabbed El's hand and jerked her away from me, jabbering in Culatian. "<Look, look! One of those Floating Lights is falling over there! Come on, let's go catch it…!>"

As she pushed El toward the falling ball of light some yards away, I saw El crane her head back at me, still looking worried, but sighed and pulled her lips into a forced smile and followed along with Zyl to inspect the Fallen Light.

El... I leaned against the mountainside by the cave entrance, my sigh coming out in a stuttering fog as I scowled at the girls.

Zyl was constantly stealing El's attention ever since she died. And I know that El wanted to spend time with Zyl because of that, but... El was starting to look less enthusiastic about it lately. I was worried if she kept this up, she'd start resenting Zyl... and that wouldn't end well, if she didn't say something to her soon.

But she won't even talk about it with ME.

My plated shoulders hunched noisily, my stomach boiling sick.

I knew it was selfish, but Gardener sow me, it just made me angrier as I shivered so hard, my freezing cheeks hurt. Was she still not comfortable with me enough to talk about what's bothering her? Does she not trust me?

The long branches covering the cave were suddenly pulled back next to me.

Bianca peeked her rabbit-eared head out. When she spotted me right beside her, those ears perked in excitement. "There you are! I need your infections for a sec."

I was still huddled against the mountainside in a crippling tremble. "R-r-r... Right n-now?"

"Yeah, I want to make some more soul-cure vials." She started fiddling through some kind of utility belt around her waist, rifling through the crazy amount of pockets and compartments and getting out a handful of vials half-filled with some kind of weird liquid.

She held out the vials to me, like she was expecting me to fill them up the rest of the way.

"Wh-wh-why?" I stuttered. "W-we... have all th-the Infeciov-v-vokers on *our* s-side now."

"It's a contingency plan." She shrugged. "Given our current track record, Macarius might end up getting his Death Hallows one way or another. Do *you* want to be caught off-guard if that crazy bastard is suddenly imbued with Infeciovoking?"

I tightened my sour expression. "N-n... no... Definitely not..."

My teeth chattered as I snagged the vials out of her hand and stuck my numb finger over their rims, evoking my infection Hallows. Violet light shined from my fingertip before it was blotted out by the crawling infections, which poured into each vial one by one, changing the liquids' colors into bright, glowing violet hues.

I handed them all back to Bianca. "N-n... need any m-m-more?"

"Maybe later," she hummed, putting the vials away in one of her utility belt's giant compartments. "I'll pass these out to the others for now."

"O… o-o-okay…" I gritted my teeth as another freezing gust blew through, my iced bones locking under my fur cloak. "Bloods-s-s I *hate* this c-c-cold…"

Bianca scratched her nose curiously, like she didn't even notice the gust. "What are you talking about? It's the middle of summer. It's pretty warm for Grim."

"But *I'm* n-n-not… a G-G-Grimling-g-g…" I squeezed my arms and wilted over my knees in a groan. "H-How do you *live-ve-ve* here…?"

She rolled her eyes, her long ears draping down in a huff. "Tourists." She looked over to El, who was still busy chatting away with Zyl, annoyingly. "Why don't you get your fire-throwing girlfriend to warm you up?"

My cat ears curled as I muttered, "She's too busy being Zyl's social hostage… again."

Bianca frowned. "What do you mean?"

I shrugged, rubbing a quivering hand over my slightly running nose, which I had the cold to thank for. "When Zyl died, s-s-she's been hanging out with her non-stop… I mean, th-that's fine and all, I g-get it, but l-l-lately, El seems… annoyed b-by it. But she won't t-t-tell m-me anything-g, so…" I hugged my knees, that sickness getting so bad, I thought I'd puke. "D… Does she not t-trust me…? W-why won't she t-t-*talk* to me…?"

Bianca crouched next to me and, after pausing like she wasn't sure if it would help, put a hand on my shoulder. "Uh, well… who cares if she doesn't trust you? It's not like it's the end of the world or anything." She tried to give me an uplifting grin and nudged me with an elbow. "*That's* coming afterward."

She laughed at her own joke, but not very hard. She eventually saw it wasn't working and gave up. "Okay, look. I'm not very good at pep-talks, Tavius, so I don't know what to say. The best I can tell you is that, even if she doesn't want to share what she's feeling with you, it's not because of anything you did. She'll decide when she's comfortable talking to you about it."

"I-I know that," I snapped in a shiver. "I… I'm giving her space to do w-w-what she wants, I just…" I deflated. "I w-w-want to help her through it, I g-g-guess…" I sighed, the breath fogging up. "I don't kn-know… Mostly, I just miss h-h-her…"

"Have you tried *starting* that conversation instead of waiting for her to start it?" she asked.

I blushed. "N-no… it's too s-s-s… selfish…"

Her mouth twisted. "How? Communication is always important in relationships."

I shot her an annoyed glare. "So, I g-guess you talked t-t-to *Alex* about your problems f-f-finally?"

Her face flushing pink.

I muttered, "Th-th-thought so…"

"That's… that's different," she insisted. "Alex doesn't talk about things like that, anyway."

"Y-y-yeah," I grunted, that annoyance bubbling so much, it was actually warming me up, "he's better at showing than telling. So you'd think that, you know, with the world about to end, he'd be focused on *that* 24/7…? But no. While he's juggling the pressure of *saving the world,* he's also trying to prove he still cares about you because you're too busy burying yourself in your work to see that your stupid grudge won't be worth a damn *if we're all dead!*"

She stared at me, shocked silent.

Anger still burned fresh in my throat, and while I was still caught up in the heat, I leapt up and added, "And for the love of Gods, you're literally the only person he's ever gone out of his way to prove anything to! More than he ever did for Lilli, and more than he still does for his *twin,* for Land's sake! If you actually think he ever stopped loving you, you're an *idiot*…!" I stopped, my cat ears folding as she stared at me wide-eyed. I swallowed, my anger puffing into vapor when I realized what I'd just said. And to *Bianca.* "S-s-sorry…" I stammered, pulling my knuckles nervously. "I didn't mean… um…"

Bianca's long ears lowered to her neck. "Okay… wow." She rubbed her arm awkwardly. "I never thought I'd hear you call anyone an idiot, Tavius…" She glanced over at El. "Wait. Is that how you feel about El?"

My face heated. "I… I guess so…" My voice dripped miserably. "Y-yeah…"

Bianca lifted a rabbit ear. "Then you should tell her that, at least?"

My stare flattened. "No way."

"Why not?"

I groaned into my hands. "It's complicated, okay? We've only been dating for a year, and… I-I don't know if telling her that will scare her off, or…" I rubbed my eyes so hard, they stung. "*Ugh,* like it matters anyway… Zyl keeps stealing her attention, so it's not like I've had much time to pull her aside and…" I sighed. "It's just not the right time…"

Bianca pursed her lips. Then she clasped my arm with gentle, gloved fingers. "I know I'm not the best person to offer advice on this, Tavius, but… the world *is* ending. If you don't want to pressure her into talking about how *she* feels, you should at least tell her how *you* feel. Before none of us have any time left, let alone the *right time.*"

With that, she went back into the hidden cave, disappearing behind the curtain of long branches.

I looked back at El. Her yellow eyes snuck a concerned look my way while Zyl chattered on about the Fallen Light she was now playing with. *The world IS ending.* My stomach knotted at the reminder. *You should at least tell her how you feel... before none of us have any time left.*

I sighed. Why did she have to be right...?

—Snap!

A breaking twig made me jolt. Shouts sounded up ahead.

I hurried to get my throwing-scythes ready, and I noticed our Ancient demons were shocked alert, too. It looked like we were all expecting the demon army to run through here any second...

... but it wasn't a demon army. It was just some belligerent, shirtless teenager.

The guy's scarred body was wrapped in bandages, which simmered with steam that seemed to rise off his grey skin like hot coals as he stamped past a very confused Khol and Miranda, casting them appalled sneers.

When he came closer to the cave where I was standing guard, I could finally see his face in more detail.

Wait, wasn't that Willow's cousin? What was his name? Faillen or something? Whatever his name was, he stormed through the woods shouting at all of us as he passed, screaming about how we were tarnishing a holy site and needed to leave immediately.

I lowered my throwing-scythes in confusion. "What the Void...?"

"—Descendant," the purring voice of Cilia rasped by my ear suddenly, making me whip around. She was with Kael. My ancestors' white pupils gleamed bright against the night as neither of them looked at me, but instead scanned the woods with deep scowls. Cilia's throat reverberated. "Something isn't right. The boy prince shouldn't be here."

Kael rumbled next to her, "He shouldn't have known we were here. We told no one."

I swallowed. "You think... Macarius followed him?"

"Likely," Cilia snarled, her cat ears curling as she summoned a burst of fire from her hands. "Be ready, Descendant. If Macarius is here, he is likely planning to slip by us cloaked in an illusion. Do *not* let the princeling pass, if you can stop him."

I nodded, my legs springing forward. I hurried to block the rampaging prince's path in front of the cave.

"N-n... no one's allowed to come in!" I said, trying to stop my hands from shaking. Bloods, I never thought I'd be threatening a Relicblood one-on-one. Then again, I never thought I would stare down a demon before I became a

Reaper—and killed more than I could count. A stupid kid wasn't nearly as terrifying as a Necrofera, right?

That gave me a little more confidence, and I held my ground. "Stay back! O-only the queen can… can grant passage to the, uh… to the Relic…!"

The prince *really* didn't like that. "How dare you speak to a member of the royal family with such disregard…!" He ripped off a scythe-sphere from his neck and had a long scythe materialize in his hands. The prince brandished the weapon while his hands burst with flames over the metal staff and stalked up to me. "I'll have your badge ripped for this if I don't dispose of you now—!"

Cilia sprinted over and shot her own flames between us, forming a licking wall that radiated heat onto my face and forced me to step back.

"If you wish to play with fire, princeling," she threatened. "Wouldn't it be more fun against another Pyrovoker?"

It was hard to see through the wall of flames, but I could see him scowling at her from over the wavering top of the fire.

Then he broke into a sprint *through* the wall, his bandages burning away from his unaffected body as he *shoved* me aside—and vanished into the cave.

BIANCA

When I reentered the cave, the Willow of Ashes was still gleaming with a brilliant white light, its crystal leaves jingling as ash fluttered all around the cave.

Everyone was still here where I left them. Ninumel, Veyazelle and the little Prince Fuérr waited by the glowing pool in the far corner, where Roji and Dalminia's two daughters splashed away happily. Ringëd stood with crossed arms beside his wife, Mikani. The two looked like they were arguing with the pet ferret on Ringëd's shoulder.

Jaq and Lilli sat on the rocky ground mumbling about how much longer this was going to take, while Neal and Matthiel leaned against a regular, boring willow tree that looked more like a bush compared to the Lost Relic of Death.

The rust-haired Dream Queen, Crysalette, held her fox-tailed baby alongside the former Death Queen, Myra, standing under the Willow of Ashes and waiting with shared looks of concern.

Her Highness—I mean, her *Majesty* Willow—held her own baby as she crouched over the three unconscious bodies of Aster, Xavier, and Alex.

The men's Crests were still gleaming with a white light. But they hadn't changed into Death Marks yet, like when they visited the other Relics.

Still no change, I noted, a frown crinkling my face. What gives? They didn't usually take this long to get their Blessings. Did Aster's addition screw up the pattern—?

Something tugged my pantleg.

My head snapped down. Ringëd's pet ferret, Kurn, was standing on my boot and tugging the hem of my pants. He snickered at me in his breathy language, as if trying to ask me something.

"Uh…" I began, "Sorry, little guy. I don't understand ferret…"

"Kurn!" Ringëd hollered from up ahead. The officer noticed Kurn standing on my boot and ran over. "What have I told you about bothering people when we're trying to…!"

Kurn started hopping in circles wildly, giving exasperated *dook, dook, dooks* before stretching up against my leg again. He patted his paws on his furry waist, almost like a gesture. Then he pointed his nose at my utility belt.

Ringëd grimaced at the ferret. "I am *not* asking her to…" He set his jaw as the ferret huffed at him. "That isn't the… why would you need a bunch of…? What are you even going to do with it if…" He smeared a hand over his face and groaned. "*Oscha,* fine! Bloody pushy feral…" He gave me a grudging look. "Kurn wants you to make him a belt, too. But 'ferret sized'… and he wants a ton of Shockvials to put in it, for some reason."

My eyes bulged at him. "Are you being serious?"

Ringëd took out a cigarette and lit it up, pushing it between his teeth. "Unfortunately, yeah… he's serious."

I burst out laughing, bending down to pat the ferret's precious head. "You got it, little guy! Let's get your measurements first thing when we get back. This will be the cutest utility belt *ever.*"

The ferret hobbled around me excitedly, and Ringëd muttered under his breath as he scooped up his pet and went back to his wife to stand guard alongside her.

"A ferret utility belt," I echoed in a dreamy giggle. "That's going to be *adorable.*"

But my cheer drained when I looked back at the Willow of Ashes. Aster and the twins were still laying there, motionless. Nothing had changed, still. I didn't like that.

I hopped over the stream that split through the cave and stalked over to the group under the Relic, crouching beside Her Majesty Willow.

"What do you think's wrong?" I asked her.

Her majesty tucked a lock of her long hair behind a fox ear, bobbing the wolf-eared Lucas over her shoulder. "I'm not sure… Aster is certainly a new factor that may be contributing to the time length, yet… this is *also* the twins' final Blessings. This may have some significance as well…" She cupped Xavier's thinly bearded jaw in a worried sigh, "But I just don't know…"

I hummed. Then I rummaged through my utility belt and took out the handful of Soul-Cure vials Octavius had just finished for me.

"I made more Soul-Cure, by the way," I told Her Majesty, handing one to her. Then I tucked one into Xavier's doublet pocket, doing the same for Alex beside him. "You know. Just in case…"

I looked over at Alex's unconscious face. To anyone else, it probably looked like he was sleeping. But I'd seen Alex fall asleep in his old Academy classes too many times, so I knew better. Alex didn't sleep with his mouth closed. He also wasn't a *quiet* sleeper. Alex could snore like a Flamedragon swallowing boulders. Especially when he was dead tired, like all those times when he stayed up with me when I worked on my lab homework for school, way after Xavier had already called it a night from their psyche and it was just Alex and me, and he would watch me with that stupid smile until he passed out there on the desk and…

My lungs cinched up.

I missed those times… I missed Alex. Why did everything have to change…?

While he's juggling the pressure of saving the world, Octavius's shouts echoed in my annoying memory, *he's also trying to prove he still cares about you because YOU'RE too busy burying yourself in your work…*

The fact that it came from Tavius had been a low blow. *Tavius* for Death's sake! Shy, sweet Tavius called me an idiot. He was probably just projecting because of his own issues, but… well, that didn't make him wrong.

I guess Alex and I do suck at talking about these things. I tucked my knees to my chest. If Octavius was waiting for El to start the conversation… because he loved her… What if that's why Alex hasn't started *our* talk?

I thought he wasn't talking because he didn't care enough… I thought all the gifts and favors were him trying to fix the problem with weak bandages, so he wouldn't *have* to talk… But after what Tavius said, maybe Alex was only doing all that hoping I would *start* the conversation…

But I didn't have an obligation to do anything for Alex. The only person I had to answer to was myself. I didn't owe him anything just because he wants me back.

But you want HIM back.

I pounded a fist to my head. *Shut up, inner-me! Not the time!*

It's never going to be the time. The freaking world is ending.

I grimaced. *Fair. But I thought we agreed we don't need him?*

We don't. That doesn't mean we can't WANT him.

My grimace doubled. *Also fair…*

Bloods, things were *really* bad if I couldn't win an argument with myself. I grumbled and glared at Alex's perfect face, indignantly flipping a lock of his wavy bangs out of his unconscious face.

"Bloody idiot…" I mumbled. "Wake up already…"

"—TRAITOROUS VERMIN!"

Willow and I jumped at the booming voice.

A teenager had shoved through the veiling branches at the cave's entrance. It was that Death Prince who'd challenged Willow to the Duel. What was he doing here?

"You…!" He stabbed a shaking finger at Willow, the rage so thick in the gesture his hands were already brewing fire. "You *dare* stain this sacred Relic by bringing demons here?!"

Willow and I shared a tensed look. Her Majesty's pale face went sheet white as she murmured, "Oh, Bloods…"

34

ANSWERS

XAVIER

I was frozen between Alexander and Aster, breathless as the Mother Goddess stared at us with a mournful gaze, her long hair wavering in an unseen wind.

Only three are present?

Her lips never parted, yet her voice glittered through my mind like a warm breath. She looked between the three of us, her perfect face tilting with sorrow.

Then the Savior of History, again, chooses his own path... A wash of crisp air rolled over my brain, as if She were sighing. She looked to Aster.

Ruiner of Tradition... we have failed you. We had hoped your new vessel could sway your soul-brother to cease his plans... for this, we are immeasurably sorry.

She turned to Alexander and me.

Defenders of Harmony... I am relieved to give you your final Blessings.

"—Wait," Alexander blurted, though his tone was still hushed. I saw him flinch as the Sorrowed Seamstress turned her mystifying gaze at him. He licked his lips, asking, "Why are we getting these Blessings...? What is it all for?"

To save Existence. Her melodic voice sounded as if this had been obvious.

Even I wasn't satisfied with that answer. It was my turn to question, "But *how* are we to save Existence?"

"And why do we need these Blessings to do that?" Alex inquired.

"And what exactly is going to happen?"

"And why are *we* the ones to do it?"

"—And do we really need to keep Macarius alive to save Existence?" Aster piped, interrupting Alexander and my interrogating.

Nira gave that fiery sigh through my mind again, like a ripple of embers puffing over my thoughts.

YES... THE SAVIOR MUST BE PRESENT WHEN THE END COMES TO PASS.

I murmured, "Then, Herrin and Marian were right…"

AS FOR YOUR OTHER QUESTIONS… PERHAPS WE ALL OWE YOU AN EXPLANATION.

Alex and I shared a pale glance. "All…?"

A brightness glared from my right, and I turned to look…

Four new radiant entities had appeared around us. Each gave off their own colorful lights, differing in size and age and skin tone, all staring at us with different expressions painting their perfect faces.

There was a scarlet-glowing man with dark scales and leathery, crimson dragon wings stretching from his back. His electric red hair was spiked and wild like living lightning, his rosy eyes dedicated to the three of us mortals as he cast us a mischievous grin.

It was Ushar. The Archer of Thrill.

Beside him was a towering man with smoother scales than Ushar, an emerald light glittering from his skin. His jade hair was thin and translucent like fins that fell to the small of his back and flowed around him like beautiful waves lapping from the sea. His webbed ears flicked at us and his emerald gaze speared through our very souls with strict scrutiny, as if weighing our worth.

Rin. the Artist of Grace.

At Rin's other side was a small child. The boy's bronze skin gleamed with an ethereal azure light, his curly blue hair glittering like grains of sand twinkling in the hot sunlight. His icy gaze reminded me of Willow's entrancing eyes, but the child's stare held a calming iridescence that no mortal could hope to match.

Iri. the Shepherd of Time.

Lastly, standing tall and poised like the king of the Gods was a muscular, golden man clad in gleaming armor. His hair bounced at his ears like gilded flower petals, his bright stare overlooking the three of us with an intensity that had my spirit tighten and cower.

Shel. the Gardener of Life…

All five of the Gods stood before us. Their many lights radiated against us, their eyes fixed on our every move. Not that we *could* move. Never in my life had I thought I would find myself face to face with the Gods themselves. Yet here they were. And now, it was difficult to remember I had limbs at all.

The Seamstress of Souls was the first to speak.

TO BEGIN… WE OWE YOU AN APOLOGY. WE OWE ALL SHIFTERS AN APOLOGY.

My brow furrowed, and I rasped with a dry throat, "An apology…?"

"An apology for what?" Aster shivered behind Alex and me.

FOR CAUSING THE END.

There was a resounding silence. Then, Alex questioned, "What do you mean? From what we've seen, it looks as though the Noctis Golems will cause the End?"

Nira cast down her gaze.

AND IT WAS BY OUR HAND THAT THE NOCTIS GOLEMS CAME TO BE… IT WAS BY OUR HAND THAT ALL DEMONS CAME TO BE.

"Why…?" Alex demanded quietly. He seemed to be battling between rage and betrayal. "Why would you create the demons at all? If you knew they would bring the End—"

WE DID NOT KNOW, THEN, the smallest God, Iri, whispered. His voice trilled in my thoughts like a delicate bell. He floated into a sitting position, crossing his legs as his glittering azure robes draped beneath him. He spread his hands outward, waving them in a fluid circle.

The scene of the End dripped away. It was replaced with a sky view of various landscapes. It began with a sunlit terrain lush with plant life and roaming lions, which then fell over watery ocean waves and schools of fish and Seadragons swimming freely. Then the view glided upward to show soaring birds and Skydragons racing around jungles that floated on islands high in the air, before finally dipping the view deep underground within rocky caverns where wolves and bats flocked under an overcasting ceiling mist blinking with floating lights.

There hadn't been a single shifter in sight. This must have been a time before shifters existed.

The scene drifted to each Holy Relic. At the Blossom of Gold, a pride of lions gathered round its enormous petals, a glowing lion towering over them in the center of their gathering. At the Phoenix of Scarlet, a radiant, scarlet Skydragon played alongside its mortal kin, the phoenix brewing a thrilling storm with thrashing bolts of lightning and pouring rain. At the Pearl of Emerald, a school of Seadragons slithered into the icy caverns and grew legs, their talons digging into the ice as they gathered round an enchanting emerald dragon five times their size, his gleaming moustache wavering like water.

At the Orbs of Azure, which were nestled into the hidden dirt-tunnels and surrounded by a skulk of foxes, a glittering azure fox sat before them with a sandy tail wavering at its feet. At the Willow of Ashes, a pack of wolves surrounded a brilliant, white wolf with an incredibly long, flowing tail that flaked away like ash.

THIS IS HOW WE BEGAN, Iri explained as he continued showing us these glimpses into the past. OR, I SHOULD SAY, THIS IS HOW WE BEGAN AS YOU CURRENTLY KNOW US. WE EXISTED WITHOUT AN IMAGE IN THE BEGINNING. WE WERE NAUGHT BUT THE LAND ITSELF.

I whispered, "The land itself…"

"Then," Alex sputtered, "You *are* the world…? You're the realms themselves? Literally?"

Nira nodded, continuing for Iri, WE WERE GIVEN OUR FORMS BY THE COLLECTIVE CONSCIOUS OF THOSE WHO LIVED IN OUR DOMAINS. THOUGH, LIKE THEM, WE HAD NOT GAINED MUCH AWARENESS OF OURSELVES. WE WERE CREATED BY INSTINCT, AND SO INSTINCT WAS ALL WE KNEW.

Iri changed the vision around us again. Now, it showed the ashen wolf witnessing the death of a mortal wolf in her caverns. From the deceased wolf's vessel rose a wispy ball of light. The light rose into the overcasting ceiling mist, joining the other Floating Lights that danced in the mist. The glowing white wolf walked up to the new light with graceful, rippling steps that glittered in the air. She touched her long nose to it mournfully, as if assuring it that all would be well again, then pranced down to the grassy cavern floor and sniffed at a Fallen Light that had landed there days before. She took the wispy light in her mouth, as if picking up a pup by the scruff, and dashed upward, phasing through the ceiling, through the crust, then leapt onto the surface lands. There, she met with a golden lion who waited beside a pregnant doe about to give birth.

The ashen wolf placed the Fallen Light on the grass before the golden lion's paws. The lion picked it up and placed it inside the fawn, which was then birthed.

Nira's voice gave a gentle hum in my thoughts. THIS WAS OUR ROLE, WHEN AN OLD LIFE ENDED, AND A NEW LIFE BEGAN.

I stared at the stumbling fawn in awe. "The Floating Lights…" I began. "They're souls…"

Nira nodded. IN THEIR PUREST FORM. THIS WORLD IS MADE UP OF ENERGY. SOME OF THIS ENERGY TAKES DIFFERENT

FORMS—AND THEY CAN BE TRANSFERRED FROM ONE VESSEL TO ANOTHER. WITH EVERY TREE THAT FALLS, A NEW ANIMAL IS BORN... WITH NEW WIND THAT BLOWS, THE SEA IS PUSHED INTO A WAVE, WHICH DIES ON THE LAND... FOR EVERY END, THERE IS A BEGINNING; FOR EVERY BEGINNING, AN END. THIS IS THE EBB AND FLOW OF ALL ENERGY. IT IS A CONSTANT FORCE THAT CONTINUES TO CREATE AND END ITSELF IN AN INFINITE CYCLE. AND ONCE THIS CYCLE STAGNATES, THE ENERGY FINDS A WAY TO CHANGE... TO ADJUST.

The scene changed once more. This time, it showed the birth of a new lion—but this one looked more like a shifter being than an animal. Then Iri showed us a similar scene of a wolf, and a fox, and a Skydragon, and a Seadragon—all born slightly less animalistic than their parents.

And they were all... blank.

They were alive, at least—breathing and open-eyed—but not a single one cried or fussed, or so much as moved their gazes in any direction.

This time, Shel was the one to speak, his voice as solid as stone, yet as gentle as a spring bloom. YOUR CLERGYMEN WERE QUITE CREATIVE WITH THEIR THEORIES, THINKING I SCULPTED THE SHIFTERS FROM CLAY... YET, IT IS NOT TRUE. I HAD NO HAND IN YOUR CREATION. NIRUS ITSELF SAW TO THAT, AS THE EVOLUTION OF A NEW SPECIES CAUGHT US ALL BY SURPRISE.

Iri's vision showed Shel in his lion form, finding each of the newborns and tilting his maned head, puzzled. Nira's wolf form joined him with each one, the two sniffing the babes in experimentation. Nira's wolf ears folded in heartbreak.

The current Nira before us gave a rasping growl. BUT EVERY SHIFTER WAS BORN HOLLOW.

New scenes flashed as the timeline sped up, each babe slowly dying of starvation... and Nira, as a wolf, coming to witness each one mournfully as no souls drifted out of the corpses.

NOTHING SHEL NOR I DID COULD CURE THE SHIFTERS OF THEIR SOULLESS PLIGHT. ANY SOUL I WOULD HAND TO HIM WOULD SLIP THROUGH WITHOUT CONTACT... THE DUALITY OF THE CHANGING FORMS PROVED TOO COMPLEX FOR THE ENERGY WE HAD BEEN USING AS SOULS... SO, I FOUND AN ALTERNATIVE SOURCE.

In the vision, Nira's wolf form wandered an empty, black abyss. I could have sworn it looked like Aspirre, only the emptiness she dashed through wasn't speckled with isolated cities and dreams… it was filled with crystalline lights. Very similar lights, I noticed, to the Floating Lights in Grim. To Soulenergy. Then suddenly the perspective changed within the void—as if I were looking through a lens that had zoomed far, far outward. New crystals of light became visible, so large that my eyes had missed them, as one would ignore the massive walls of Grim's caverns. These larger crystals were in a new dimension… one that, it seemed, only the Gods could slip into.

The wolf slowed to a stop when she found what she was searching for: an enormous, brightly glowing crystal of pure, vivid light.

Nira's voice sang with a small glimmer of triumph. WITH ALL INTELLIGENT LIFE, INSTINCTUAL OR NOT, THEY ALL SHARE COLLECTIVE EMOTIONS, ACCEPTED CONCEPTS, AND MUTUAL BELIEFS. THESE BECOME ENERGY THEMSELVES—WHICH WE CALL CONCEPTUAL ENERGY. AND DUE TO THE NUMBER OF LIVING SOULS WHO CONTINUE TO STRENGTHEN THEM, THEY ARE SOME OF THE LARGEST FORMS OF ALL ENERGY. THESE ENERGIES ARE CREATED FROM THE VERY LIFE WHO THOUGHT OF THEM, AND WHO MANIFESTED THEIR EXISTENCES THROUGH MASS CONSCIOUSNESS. I KNEW USING THE ENERGY FROM ONE WOULD HELP STRENGTHEN THE SMALLER ENERGIES I USED FOR SOULS, ALLOWING THEM TO STAY ATTACHED TO THE SLIPPERY VESSELS OF THE SHIFTERS. BUT I HAD TO CHOOSE CAREFULLY. IF I CHOSE A CONCEPTUAL ENERGY THAT DID NOT COMPLEMENT SOULENERGY, THEY WOULD NOT MERGE, AND WOULD INSTEAD REMAIN DETACHED. I ATTEMPTED TO ATTACH THE SOULS WITH EVERY CONCEPT KNOWN TO EXISTENCE… BUT ONLY ONE WAS SUCCESSFUL. PERHAPS IT WAS DUE TO THE VERY NATURE OF THE DILEMMA I SOUGHT TO RESOLVE, THE CONCEPTUAL ENERGY THAT HELD STRONG WAS ONE EVERY ANIMAL UNCONSCIOUSLY UNDERSTOOD AND FOLLOWED ACROSS THE ENTIRE PLANET:

SURVIVAL.

The scene depicted the wolf ripping her teeth into the towering globe, light splitting through her fangs as she pulled with all her might—and ripped out a radiant thread that hung from her muzzle.

Alex breathed in wonder, "The NecroSeam…"

It was no wonder there wasn't a Necrovoker alive who could create a full Seam—not even me. It wasn't a random magical conjuring of substance. It was *Survival itself.*

We watched as the wolf brought this new Thread, borne of the very concept of Survival, to the golden lion. The lion placed the soul into the new shifter babe, and the wolf sewed Survival into it, attaching it securely to the vessel's heart. At last, the babe blinked into awareness, fussing for milk from its mother.

THE THREAD OF SURVIVAL SUCCEEDED.

Nira's tone lilted with hope as the scene showed the shifters growing into children and adults, creating new societies amongst themselves. The ethereal wolf and lion grew alongside them, taking the forms we knew them as today, and likewise did Ushar, Iri, and Rin change as their own realms grew. Then the first shifter died by the claws of a feral tiger, and Nira's voice curdled with dismay.

HOWEVER... WHILE IT INDEED HELD THE SOUL IN PLACE, THE THREAD REMAINED TIED AFTER DEATH. NEVER HAD WE ENCOUNTERED A SOUL THAT DID NOT RETURN TO MY DOMAIN UPON THEIR EXPIRATION. AS SUCH, WE HADN'T KNOWN WHAT TO EXPECT. BUT WE SHOULD HAVE GUESSED FROM THE BEGINNING WHAT WAS TO COME. AFTER ALL, WE KNEW THAT FOR EVERY TRANSFER OF ENERGY TAKEN, AN EQUAL REACTION WAS ALWAYS DUE...

In the vision, the shifter's corpse began to blacken. Then slithering worms rose out from its skin and slurped over the vessel from head to foot.

UNABLE TO COMPLETE THEIR DUE CYCLE FROM THIS LIFE TO THE NEXT, THE SOULS ROTTED INSIDE THEIR CAGES. THE SURVIVAL CORRUPTED THEIR NATURE AND CONSUMED THE WEAKER ENERGY... UNTIL THEY BECAME THE DEMONS YOU KNOW AS NECROFERA, RULED BY THE VERY SURVIVAL THAT STRENGTHENED THEIR BOND.

The scene became chaos around us, the early shifters running for their lives from the rampaging Necrofera who feasted on their bodies and souls alike.

THE SOLUTION TO THE SHIFTERS' EXTINCTION, IT SEEMED, WAS ALSO QUICKLY BECOMING ITS CAUSE. THAT IS WHEN WE CAME TOGETHER AND GRANTED OUR HALLOWS TO THE FEW SOULS LEFT... BUT THESE SMALLER SOULS WERE NOT COMPATIBLE WITH MORE THAN TWO ELEMENTS AT A TIME. MOST COULD ONLY HANDLE ONE. THESE GIFTS DID INDEED HELP THE SHIFTERS' SURVIVAL AFTER DEATH, AND ALLOWED THEM TIME TO FIND THE CRYSTAL FROM MY MINES THAT COULD MAKE CONTACT WITH THE THREAD OF SURVIVAL, NOT ONLY FORGING WEAPONS TO KILL THE BEASTS, BUT ALSO PREVENTING THEIR CREATION FROM THE START.

A scene flashed with a man slicing a crudely crafted Spiritcrystal scythe into a newly fallen corpse. A wispy ghost drifted out of the soul, still clean and not rotten, taking the scythe-wielder by surprise.

IT WAS RATHER INTERESTING TO SEE HOW THE THREAD OF SURVIVAL HAD SECURED THE BOND WITH SUCH STRENGTH THAT IT CAUSED THE SOULS TO SHAPE TO THE VESSELS AND REMAIN ON YOUR PLANE LONGER THAN THE SOULS BEFORE THEM. WITH THIS NEW WEAPON CAME A SENSE OF RELIEF FROM THE SHIFTERS—AND A SENSE OF CONTROL. HOWEVER, THEY DID NOT REALIZE THAT KILLING THE ROTTEN ON THEIR PLANE…

The vision flashed with a demon being killed by the blade of a scythe, its rotten soul evaporating into mist with a grueling hiss…

And when it disappeared from the physical plane, that mist reappeared into *this* subconscious plane, the rotted droplets congealing into grains of black sand, which poured into the abyss where the young Gods thrashed effortlessly with their gleaming weapons against similar, sandy creatures.

… IT ONLY SENT THE NECROFERA TO OUR PLANE. FOR CENTURIES, WE FOUGHT THE GOLEMS, BUT THE MORE SHIFTERS WHO ROTTED AND WERE KILLED ON YOUR PLANE, THE MORE THEY FLOODED OURS. WE WERE OVERWHELMED. AT THE SAME TIME, YOUR PLANE WAS OVERWHELMED WITH ITS OWN DANGERS, ONES THAT YOUR KIND CREATED YOURSELVES…

Shifters began to fight shifters, civil unrest and international wars erupting from cultural conflicts that raged in all the realms. This must have been the Great Wars—from the Time of Discord.

TO STOP THE KILLINGS, AND STOP THE OVERFLOW OF DEMONS FROM FORMING IN SUCH SHORT TIME… THIS LED TO THE CREATION OF OUR CHILDREN. TO DO SO, WE HAD TO RETURN TO THE CONCEPTUAL ENERGIES, EACH OF US CHOOSING A SOUL LARGE ENOUGH TO HANDLE WIELDING ALL THREE OF OUR REALM'S ELEMENTAL BLESSINGS.

The young Shel floated to one large Concept whose surface twirled with golden flower petals.

SHEL CHOSE THE CONCEPT OF LIFE.

The young Ushar spread his leathery wings and flew to a different Concept, this one zapping and snapping with scarlet lightning bolts.

USHAR CHOSE THE CONCEPT OF THRILL.

The young Rin swam to his own Concept that glistened like green ice around cold fog.

RIN CHOSE THE CONCEPT OF GRACE.

The young Iri skipped to another Concept that swirled with blue sand.

IRI CHOSE THE CONCEPT OF WISDOM.

Finally, the young Nira stepped before a violet Concept flaking with delicate ash, which she raised a hand to like a loving mother.

... AND I CHOSE THE CONCEPT OF DEATH.

Flashes of the first Relic Children's births passed in seconds, and Nira sighed. OVER TIME, OUR CHILDREN DID RESTORE HARMONY AMONG THE SHIFTERS... BUT WE WERE DISTRAUGHT TO FIND THAT IT DID NOTHING TO HELP US WITH THE GOLEMS.

A scream erupted in the abyss of Aspirre. The past Nira had been struck by a Noctis Golem. A blinding streak of light split across her body, and the void rumbled ominously. The scene flashed to the physical plane, showing the caverns of Grim rupturing with Groundquakes as the entire realm *cracked* and fractured in two, the pieces drifting apart in the chilled waters as shifters screamed in terror.

Nira's solemn voice whispered. I WAS WOUNDED IN BATTLE CEN-TURIES PAST... FROM THE DAMAGE I ENDURED, IT TORE MY REALM INTO TWO CONTINENTS. HAD I FALLEN TO THE BEAST, I DO NOT DOUBT THE REALM WOULD HAVE COLLAPSED ALTO-GETHER. IT WAS THEN THAT WE DECIDED TO CREATE MORE CHILDREN—BUT THIS TIME, ONES WHO WOULD HELP US HERE IN OUR PLANE.

Aster peeked his head between Alexander and I, the skeletal Fera gasping, "Oh, oh! That's got to be us!"

Nira nodded.

YES. WE NEEDED AS MANY CHILDREN TO HELP US AS WE COULD CREATE... BUT TO DO SO, WE KNEW THAT THESE CHILDREN HAD TO HAVE THE STRENGTH TO BEAR ALL OUR BLESSINGS. UPON SEARCHING THE CONCEPTUAL ENERGIES, WE FOUND ONLY THREE.

Our perspective of the void zoomed out yet again, farther and farther until the Gods had slipped into a *second* new dimension—one that had us gazing down at the entire planet. Here, three impossibly large crystals encompassed the world, hugging the globe like perfectly fitted gloves. We saw the Gods standing before the colossal Concept crystals—larger than anything we'd witnessed before. The two smaller crystals hugging either side of the center one were of equal size. The center Concept was *double* their stature. All three glittered with vibrant, kaleidoscopic shimmers, like rainbow lights refracted from a prism made of pure energy. Nira gestured to the two smaller Concept crystals and looked at Aster.

THESE, RUINER OF TRADITION, ARE YOU AND YOUR SOUL-BROTHER… AT YOUR PUREST FORMS. THE CONCEPT OF THE FUTURE—OF WHERE WE WILL GROW AND DIE… ALONGSIDE THE CONCEPT OF THE PAST—OF WHERE WE HAVE COME FROM AND WHERE WE WERE BORN. THIS IS THE COLLECTION OF ALL THAT WE REMEMBER, AND ALL THAT WE ASPIRE TO BECOME.

Nira gestured to the largest Concept between the two, turning to Alexander and me.

AND THIS, DEFENDERS OF HARMONY, IS YOUR PUREST FORM. THE CONCEPT OF THE PRESENT… THE COLLECTION OF ALL THAT WE ARE, AS OUR CURRENT SELVES, THE PERFECT COMBINATION OF PAST AND FUTURE SUSTAINED IN A SINGLE, FLEETING TIMELINE THAT ALL SHIFTERS, ALIVE AND DECEASED, ARE MOST AWARE OF. YOU WERE SO LARGE A SOUL THAT I WAS ABLE TO SPLIT YOU INTO TWO HALVES. SEPARATED LIKE THIS, WE COULD GRANT YOU ALL OF OUR BLESSINGS, BROKEN INTO EVEN PIECES THAT, WHEN TOGETHER, WOULD BE WHOLE. THIS WAS SOMETHING WE WISHED TO DO FOR ALL OF OUR CHAMPIONS, BUT YOURS WAS THE ONLY CONCEPT LARGE ENOUGH TO SUSTAIN SUCH A HEFTY BURDEN.

I felt a cold chill run down my spine. Hearing that Alexander and I were created from one of these planetary Concepts was… unsettling. My hands balled, my throat tight as I asked, "But… how are we to help you…? If *you* can barely fend them off as Gods, what could *we* possibly hope to achieve?"

OUR FORMS ARE CREATED FROM THE COLLECTIVE BELIEFS OF THE SHIFTERS INHABITING OUR REALMS. WE ARE CONSIDERED GODS, TRUE, AND DO INDEED HOLD A CERTAIN POWER OVER OTHER ENERGIES…

Nira floated up to me with a warm, glowing smile. She touched Alexander and my faces, her fingers tingling with a heat so intoxicating, it was as if I hadn't breathed my entire life until this moment.

YOU, MY CHILDREN, ARE BORN OF SOMETHING FAR STRONGER. OF RELATIVE TIME ITSELF. YOU MAY FEEL INSIGNIFICANT INDIVIDUALLY, BUT YOU MUST REMEMBER… YOU ARE STRONGEST TOGETHER. THERE CANNOT BE A PAST WITHOUT THOSE OF THE FUTURE TO REMEMBER IT. THERE CANNOT BE A FUTURE WITHOUT THOSE OF THE PAST TO ASPIRE TOWARD IT. AND

THERE CAN BE NEITHER A PAST NOR FUTURE WITHOUT THOSE OF THE PRESENT TO WITNESS THEM BOTH.

As she removed her addictingly warm hands from our faces, Alex struggled to find his voice, his tone strained. "Then… we *do* have to keep Macarius alive…?"

Nira nodded solemnly. YES… THOUGH I DO NOT APPROVE OF THE SAVIOR'S BEHAVIOR, HE IS VITAL TO OUR SURVIVAL. EVEN IF HE WERE NOT TO BRING THE REALMS INTO OUR PLANE AS HE PLANS, THE NOCTIS GOLEMS WOULD STILL CONSUME US ALL, EVENTUALLY. THEY CONTINUE TO RISE. WE WILL NEVER TRULY BE RID OF THEM, WITH THE SHIFTERS NEEDING THAT THREAD OF SURVIVAL, BUT WE CAN, AT LEAST, ACHIEVE BALANCE. AND THERE WOULD BE NO BALANCE WITHOUT THE PAST.

Alex flicked me a conflicting stare. I gave him a nod, both of us exhaling as we hung our heads and sighed, "All right… Macarius will live."

THRRRRRRMMMMM!

A powerful tremor ripped through, causing the three of us to fall to our knees.

THRRRRRRRMMMMM! RRRRRRRMMMM! BRRRRRMMM!

The quakes worsened, the scene around us shivering as if something were trying to break through whatever barrier surrounded us.

The child God, Iri, tensed. His azure gaze narrowed, staring into the distance as if Seeing beyond the scenery he had woven around us. He reached out his hand, and a sudden burst of azure light flashed from his palm. The light stretched and twisted into a shepherd's crook, a bell jingling from the staff.

OUR TIME HAS RUN OUT, he warned, shouldering his crook as the bell gave a flighty trill. THERE ARE TOO MANY SOULS HERE TO ATTRACT THE GOLEMS. MY WARDS AROUND THE RELICS CAN ONLY HOLD AGAINST SMALL NUMBERS. WE MUST HURRY.

Nira nodded, then looked to Aster, Alexander, and me. She held out her arms, and from her hand poured streaks of violet light—which spilled into our chests and clutched my soul with such strength, I couldn't breathe.

TAKE MY BLESSINGS, Nira's mournful voice sang in my thoughts like a fiery kiss. USE THEM WITH HONOR… AND PLEASE. PROTECT MY DAUGHTER.

The void brightened in a blinding white flash… and the Gods disappeared, along with everything else.

35

LOST

WILLOW

When Felix burst into the cavern, Bianca and I shot to our feet, startling Lucas from my arms and causing the baby to wail.

"Felix…?" I stared at the prince in horror. "How did you know where to find us—?"

"You will answer for your sins, heretic!" He sneered, his face contorted in rage. "How dare you bring the rotten to this sacred site? How dare you break our family's ancient code of silence and bring outsiders here? You have no respect for our customs…! And no respect for this nation—*hauchckccrrr…*"

Something long and silver speared through both sides of Felix's throat. It was a blade with no wielder. But once the dagger slid out of the prince's neck, blood pouring from the fresh wound, the wielder of the dripping blade appeared from his shortly-held, invisible cloak like mist.

Macarius fingered the sticky blade with a haunting, fang-filled smile. "The world thanks you, young prince…"

Felix collapsed to the dirt, straining for breath that wouldn't come. His airways had been severed.

The Willow of Ashes flared to life behind me, its crystal leaves jangling with such chaos, I thought they would surely shatter.

From Macarius's exposed chest, I saw his Crest of three diamonds brighten with a white light. Then it shifted into a crowned Death mark. His multi-colored hair bled with new, ashen streaks; his patched eyes added that same white color to his unnatural irises.

His chuckles twisted as his hands ignited in a burst of flames.

"Death…" I cursed, staggering back.

Lucas continued to wail in my grown fox ear. I held my child tight to my chest, cradling him, my instincts screaming for me to run for his sake…

But where would I run? Macarius blocked the only exit. And Xavier was still in the Relic's trance.

I stole a frigid glance toward Xavier lying under the Relic behind me. He still lay unstirred between Alexander and Aster.

"Ah," Macarius hummed, cocking his head at the three unconscious men. "If it isn't the Shadowblood… and, I presume, my soul-brother's newest incarnation?" His tone leaked with venom, his fangs growing long. "Well, Accursius, it seems you wished to make your death a tradition in our family. A shame that it takes so long to gain your incomplete Hallows…" He chuckled darkly, spreading his enflamed hands. "While I, on the other hand, reap the full benefits in a glorious *instant*!"

He slammed his hands to the ground, drenching the cavern with a sudden vortex of green fire.

It raged over the grass and candle-lilies, so hot that it seared the flowers to ash the moment it touched them, skipping over the surface of the stream just long enough to reach the other side where we stood under the Willow. The green flames surrounded the sacred Relic—with us inside.

Smoke poured from the green flames, the confined space of the cavern keeping the fumes bundled and thick. Every breath I sucked in drew in the peppered haze and smothered my lungs, my throat hacking up burning coughs.

I crouched low, trying desperately to keep Lucas out of the smog. I covered his screaming mouth with my hand, seeing that my grandmother Crysa was doing the same for baby Eryn, staying under the smoke alongside my azure-haired mother.

I turned to Xavier's unconscious body, shaking him like a madwoman and screaming. "Xavier! Wake up…!"

No reply spilled from his lips. His eyes remained shut.

"XAVIER—!"

A fiery hand snatched my throat, shoving me to the dirt in a violent jerk. I lost my hold of Lucas, the baby tumbling to the ground and screeching in terror.

"*Mama*…!" Lucas shrieked, his coughing breaths stuttering as his little hands reached for my face that was too far to touch. He rolled to his belly and sluggishly started crawling to me. "MA MA-A-A-A…!"

I wheezed under Macarius's choking fingers, Lucas's screams shredding everything else from my attention. I lifted a struggling hand toward him, gasping, "Don't… Lucas… S-stay back…"

Bianca suddenly crept to the pup, scooping him in her arms and clutching him to her body to shield him from the smoke. She'd removed her gloves, puffing air into his lungs before evoking her remedy Hallows with a golden light and clasped her fingers over his mouth with the utmost care. Lucas's coughs seemed to settle for now. She cradled Lucas with one arm and crawled to Grandmother Crysa and baby Eryn, evoking her remedy Hallows onto the other infant to heal any burn wounds and keep his lungs clean with steady breaths. Bianca's own breath, however, grew worse by the second—

"Dearest, Dearest Death…" Macarius hissed in my fox ear, his fangs dripping venom onto my skin. His fingers tightened around my throat—and his free hand burst into a blackened mass of festering, jagged veins. *Infection Hallows…*

I thrashed, spitting strained expletives as I swiped clawed hands at his face, my own infection Hallows flaring from my palms. I managed to cut shallow claw marks on his cheek, but my Hallows didn't seem to affect him much at all, his new poison-resistance infuriatingly strong. His strangling fingers clenched my throat harder, my vision spotting as I struggled for air.

"Let's hold an experiment, shall we?" His lips curled with a nasty, psychotic smile. "What do you think might happen if we infect the Queen of Death with her own Hallows… and play with her corpse once we're finished…?"

XAVIER

"MA MA-A-A-A…!"

The grating screech of my son ripped my eyes open.

The cries wrenched my muscles alive, instinct blazing as I burst to my feet and searched for the boy in a panic.

"Lu—*Khauch, khoaugh*—Lucas…?!" I hacked, my lungs quickly filling with the burning smoke that had appeared in the cave. Swaths of green fire scorched around me, stinging my eyes as the quivering heat blistered my face. The Willow of Ashes was not affected by the fire itself, but its crystal leaves rumbled and quaked as ash swirled around it in a fierce, green wind.

Alexander and Aster awoke to either side of me. Alex coughed uncontrollably while Aster seemed unaffected by the smog, probably because he was a Necrofera and didn't need to breathe. They stumbled to their feet, shocked alert when they witnessed the raging fires around us.

"What—*Khuah*—happened…?" Alex hacked sorely, his throat scratching painfully. "Gods, it… it's so… *hot…*"

"You're telling me…!" Aster staggered back meekly, sweat already drenching the demon's skin from head to foot. He turned around—and I saw a glimpse of the crowned Death mark on Aster's back.

I noticed Alexander's Crest on his right hand had the same mark. Then, as the two doubled over in agonized yells—fire *blasted* from their hands.

It poured from their palms in furious, violet spirals, bursting into the wall of green flames and vaporizing wide holes straight through them. The edges of the holes dwindled into colder, orange fire, embers popping viciously.

The two panted, seeming to have gained relief from their previous heat, and stared at their hands.

Alex creates the fire, I realized, the pattern of our previous Hallows clicking. *Which means I must control flames that already exist…*

"—MA MAAA-A-A-Ahhhhh…!" Lucas's shriek pierced my grown wolf ears and jumpstarted my blood, panic spurting back to life.

"LUCAS!" I screamed, running toward my son's cries. I batted the fires in wild swipes with my glowing hands, the flames bending at my will and peeling apart to allow me through. I tore through the flames in a mindless fury, trying to find my son in the chaos. The smoke was so thick, I could barely breathe let alone see two feet in front of me.

"MA MAAA!"

—There!

I found the baby cradled in one of Bianca's burn-marked arms, the boy's face mottled red from all his screeching. Bianca's hands were glittering with golden light as she was curled on her side over the cavern floor, keeping hold of Lucas while her free hand was stretched out and clasping over baby Eryn's mouth. She must have been trying to keep the smoke away from their lungs with her remedy Hallows as much as she could.

But Bianca herself didn't look well. Her soot-ridden face had gone purple, wheezing for breath. The rabbit looked to be focusing all her energy on keeping the babies safe… but that energy was quickly fading. Bianca was running out of breath.

Something else was wrong, though. If Bianca was with the babies…

Where was my wife?

"Willow?!" I whirled round, my gaze frantic. I swatted and shoved aside every wall of green fire in my way, coughing the smoke from my hoarse throat. "Will…!"

I stopped, spying something white draped over the grass. Spilling from the thick haze and cascading into the stream of misting water were the long, curling strands of Willow's ashen hair. I followed its trail.

Then found Willow.

She was pinned to the ground and wheezing for breath, Macarius digging his knee into my wife's stomach. His dripping fangs hovered over her jaw. His lips were curled in a thirsty smile as he raised his hand… which festered with black, poisonous veins.

My brain *cracked* like a glass bubble.

I burst into a full-on sprint, my vicious screams splintered as I charged the man hurting the only shred of happiness I had left—hurting the future I swore so fiercely to protect—and *tackled* him to the ground.

My clawed hands squeezed his scaled throat until my knuckles shrieked with pain, Macarius gagging under my merciless grip. I didn't care if we needed him alive. I needed him *dead*.

With my son's screeches grating my ears and my wife's coughs fueling my rage, I squeezed his neck harder, enjoying how every straining tendon and bulging muscle felt under my fingers, his adams-apple looking ripe to *pop*…

"You…" I seethed through sharpened teeth, a prickling wave leaking from my soul and splintering through my fingers as black veins crawled out of me, latching onto Macarius's crushed neck. The infection didn't touch his flesh. It sank into his soul, and I felt the smallest pieces of it hissing away beneath me. "Will *never*… take away… *my family*…!"

All Macarius could do was gag in reply. His limbs flailed around me, bursting with Hallows after Hallows, but in his quickly fading state, none of it was strong enough to overpower me.

Tink, tink, tink…!

Both of our eyes snapped to the lightly thunking sound of the glittering, azure orb that rolled out of the sack from his waist. As if a new thought struck him, his hand flew to the orb in desperation.

He's trying to escape through Aspirre! I realized, my anger blazing hotter.

The moment his fingers touched the Orb, I snatched it as well—

Then the world was sucked away as we were both thrown into Aspirre.

WILLOW

Macarius and my husband blinked out of existence. They had both touched the Orb of Azure at the same moment—and vanished into Aspirre together.

"Xa…" I hacked the smoke from my lungs. "Xav…ier…!"

"—*MA MAAA-A-A-Ah*…!" Lucas's screech made my head and fox ears snap to him with such speed, I thought I felt something tear.

"Lucas!" I stumbled over to him, leaping through a wall of still-blazing fire and not caring that some of my gown had been singed in various patches.

I found Lucas still wriggling in Bianca's hold, her shimmering hand still held over his mouth protectively along with Eryn's. But she didn't last long.

Seconds after I found them, Bianca's eyes rolled back and her hand fell limp beside Lucas. Her dark face was bloated and painted a blotchy purplish blue.

I hurried to pluck Lucas off the ground, cradling him to my chest and cupping his head. He was still whimpering, but at least his screeches had dwindled. My grandmother Crysa hurried to pick up Eryn, sobbing as she held him tight and whispering stuttered *thank yous* to Bianca's unconscious figure.

I crouched to Bianca, balancing Lucas with one arm while I pulled *her* arm over my shoulder and heaved as hard as I could to drag her forward. But I only made it a few miniscule inches, puffing from exhaustion and coughing painfully.

"Alex…!" I screamed, the smoke so thick, I could barely see in front of me. I couldn't even find the exit. "Aster…! Someone—!"

The two men *both* leapt through the wall of flames immediately. They were unscathed by the fire they'd jumped through. Like Pyrovokers. *Now, they ARE Pyrovokers,* I realized. Thank Bloods. The more fire-throwers unaffected by the fire, the more abled bodies we had to help carry everyone to safety.

Alexander found me quickly. Then his gaze split with terror when he spotted Bianca slumped over my back, her legs still dragging on the ground.

"*Bianca…!*" He bolted over to us, lifting Bianca off of me and held her fast to his chest.

Aster waved for me to follow him, and I hurried to his side with Grandmother Crysa, both of us keeping Lucas and Eryn below the smoke a much as possible. Alex clambered alongside us with Bianca.

Around us, I finally spotted the rest of our party. My mother was being escorted out by Matthiel, who parted the walls of fire as fast as he could to let them pass. El had come inside to help Jaq and Lilli, using her own Pyrovoking to banish the fires enough to let them through, and Mikani did the same for Ringëd and his pet ferret.

Good, it seems everyone is being tended to, I thought in relief. *That leaves only…*

When we reached the cavern's exit, I caught sight of a wheezing body at my feet. His ashen hair was blackened by soot, and both sides of his neck poured with blood.

Felix!

Bloods be good, he was alive! I'd thought Macarius had surely killed him, with a wound like that. But here he was, gurgling and gasping for what little air he could get through his flooded passageways.

"Aster!" My head snapped to the demon beside me. I nodded to Felix. "Grab him! He's coming with us!"

Aster gave me a skewed look. "You sure—?"

"Yes!"

I dashed out of the cave with the others. When the smoke finally peeled away from my vision, I slowed to breathe in the clean air of the Weeping Woods. Lucas's cough still clung to his little lungs, and I patted his back soothingly.

"Shhh, shhh, shhh…" I hushed in his folded wolf ear, the pup whimpering. "It's all right… we're safe, now…"

"Dada…" Lucas's cry was heartbreaking. "Dada…"

I looked around the misted forest.

Xavier… where are you?

He still hadn't emerged from Aspirre. Neither had Macarius. Smoke spilled from the cave and peppered the mountainside, embers crackling from the still-burning flames in the Relic's sacred cavern. Whenever Xavier *would* emerge from the Dream realm, I certainly hoped it wouldn't be back in that suffocating death trap while it was still filled with smoke. I may need to send for someone to clear it out after this.

Aster came up beside me, dragging the wounded Prince Felix over the grass in a pant. "So, uh…" Aster began, "What do we do with him? Do we have any healers…?"

I bit my lip, searching among our hacking party.

We had two Infeciovokers: Octavius and Kael… three Pyrovokers: Matthiel, El, Cilia and Mikani… Necrovokers: Lilli and Matthiel… Mother was a Seer along with Oliver… Hecrûshou was an Aquavoker as well as Ninumel; Nikolai was a Glaciavoker; Rossette an Astravoker; Miranda an Arborvoker…

Where were our Healers?

I twisted round, finding Bianca still cradled in Alexander's arms. She hadn't woken. Anabelle was all the way up on the surface, and Sirra-Lynn had stayed at the Death Palace with her husband…

And Xavier was missing.

"Death…" I motioned for Aster to lower Felix to the grass, the demon holding the two holes gushing with blood on the side of the prince's neck. His boney fingers were drenched and stained red.

"Alexander!" I called back to the only *conscious* Healer we had left. "We need your help!"

Alex clutched Bianca's limp body and trotted over, his face horrified as he saw all the blood pouring out of Felix's throat.

"I…" Alex's breaths heaved, panicking as he knelt beside Aster, holding Bianca tight. "I can't do anything to *start* the healing… I can only amplify what's already there, I…" His breathing worsened. "I need *Xavier*…"

"—then don't use healing," Kael blurted from the side. The Infeciovoking demon rushed over to us, crouching over Felix and rolling up his sleeves. It seemed his years as a trained surgeon had taken over by habit. "Turn him on his side, quickly! We don't want him choking—and both of you have fire Hallows now, don't you? Cauterize the wounds immediately, before he loses any more blood!"

Aster quickly burst his fire Hallows over one of the entry points, and Alexander gently laid Bianca over the grass to do the same for the other side of Felix's neck.

Kael checked over their work with a grim hum, "That's the best we can do for now… Come, we must bring him to a hospital immediately. He'll need an emergency operation to tend to the wounds *inside* his neck, not just outside it, and…"

Kael went on as he lifted the prince by the arms, Aster pulling up his legs as the two carted Felix out of the woods.

Alexander ran a hand through his soot-coated hair and pushed out a hard breath, hurrying back to Bianca. He scooped her up again, hefting her delicately…

But he froze, his gaze sharpening at her. I saw his Crest gleam with an azure light from his right knuckles, shifting into a Dream mark, and his eyes lost focus. *He must be having a vision.*

"Bianca…?" his voice shivered.

I hurried to his side, worried. "What's wrong?"

He didn't reply. I doubted he'd even heard me.

—He dropped to ground and laid Bianca down again, prying her mouth open to breathe air into her lungs. He worked like a possessed man, alternating from breathing to shoving chest compressions over her.

"Kael!" Alex screamed into the woods. *"Kael, come back…! I-I need help…!"*

Up ahead, Kael cursed and handed Felix's arms to Matthiel who stood nearby, the doctor sprinting back to crouch over Bianca.

"What's happened?" Kael panted, waving his hands over Bianca, probably to feel her injuries with his Infeciovoking.

Alex was shaking like a rabid dog, his voice a tight whimper. "S-s-she's not breathing…!"

Kael took over the chest compressions, the doctor's form more experienced. Alex started biting his knuckles bloody as he sobbed with such terror, I hardly recognized him.

We all came round, watching them with anxious murmurs…

Then Kael stopped at last, panting over his knees.

He hung his head, his whisper so, so soft. "I… I'm sorry…"

36

COMPETING PLAYERS

XAVIER

The moment Macarius and I were transported into the empty void of Aspirre, I lost my hold of his neck, and he kicked me in the stomach, splitting us apart.

He steadied himself in mid-air, floating in the abyss and gasping to regain his breath.

I did the same, willing myself to hover in place, my claws still grown as I set my sights on the bastard and…

… The Orb of Azure floated between us, glittering brilliantly with its own, ethereal light.

My gaze fixated on the Orb. As did Macarius's.

We dove for it at once, grabbing it together—

—We fumbled out to the physical plane and slammed onto a steep, angled mountainside far above the cavern where we'd begun. We tumbled down the sloped terrain, the Orb of Azure bouncing down between us with shimmering *tink, tink, tinks!*

My shoulder rammed against a tree. Macarius's back hit a boulder, the landscape keeping us afloat while we struggled to find a stable footing.

He glared at me across the slope, raising his hand to summon a swath of fire. I did the same for my ice—

Tink, tink, tink…!

The Orb clunked past us down the slope.

Our eyes snapped to it, hesitating. We exchanged furious scowls. Then broke away from our boulders and fumbled after the Orb.

It clinked over stones; it clanked over dirt; it thunked against trees and rolled through the shrubs…

Then hurtled over a cliff, spiraling down toward the Weeping Woods below.

We leapt off the cliff after it, both grabbing it desperately—

We were thrown back into Aspirre, the Orb still clutched in our entangled fingers. He pulled and I tugged, he kicked and I shoved, pushing ourselves in all directions through the empty abyss of the Dream realm.

He gave a ripping scream and pushed us downward, spiraling toward a small, miniature city that grew larger and larger the closer we drew.

We were inches away from slamming against the cobblestones—

—the Orb transported us back into the physical plane, this time in the middle of Low Rastiria's bustling market square.

My back hit the ground in a winded cough, the cobblestones bruising my spine and prying a pained seethe between my teeth. Macarius fell on top of me like a flailing crab, his weight crushing the air straight out of my lungs— and from the sound of it, *his* lungs as well.

Shrieks blurted around us from the crowd of civilians, our sudden appearance startling them.

Tink, tink, tink!

I spotted the Orb clinking away from us yet again, the thing getting lost in the mass of Grimish shifters and drifting ghosts.

Macarius and I fumbled after it, pushing and shoving.

His hands shimmered with gold light suddenly, and he slammed them over the cobblestones. The stones fractured and split apart from the ground, cracking toward the retreating Orb and forming a ramp underneath it. As the ramp's incline grew taller, the Orb slowed, stilled, then rolled backward and headed for Macarius.

I growled and evoked my own rock Hallows, breaking his ramp right under the Orb, which dropped to the ground again. A running shifter's panicked foot kicked the Orb sharply to the left, and I sprinted after it, Macarius close behind and shoving aside the crowd of screaming citizens.

He threw blasts of fire at my feet, which I quickly hopped over. I shot back a spear of ice at him. He lunged away, the ice shattering in front of a fleeing group of startled Grimlings.

The Orb *clunked* over a trash bin and arched upward, *splashing* into the pool of a trickling fountain and bobbing in place with chaotic ripples.

I summoned my Aquavoking, my hands gleaming with emerald light as I took control of the pool's water and *pulled* it out of the fountain. The Orb was cradled in the airborne water, floating in the giant droplet like a marble suspended in gelatin. I stretched the liquid into a long archway, and the Orb rolled down its slippery path toward me.

Macarius froze my water with his Glaciavoking, steering the archway toward him instead as the Orb rolled away from me.

I used my own Glaciavoking to add another branching pathway on the ice, the Orb popping onto *my* track once again.

He evoked his fire to melt the ice altogether.

The Orb *clunked* between us.

We dashed for it, both of us phasing through ghosts and shoving past frightened shifters.

We met in the middle and grabbed the Orb—

—*We tumbled back in the abyss of Aspirre, the miniature city now crowded with hooded shifters, all of whom hid their faces with veiling masks.*

Macarius and I were still crouched on our knees over the ground, trying to pry the Orb out of the other's hold.

I yelled and yanked it out of his grasp—but put too much force in it. The Orb slipped from my fingers and flew so high, it crested the miniature city's spired roof-tops and hurtled into the abyss.

We sprang up, pushing off the ground to launch ourselves over those rooftops to soar after the elusive Orb. Neither of us were bound by the construct of gravity here. We were free to fly in this realm without resistance.

But as I glared at Macarius across from me, I noticed something strange was happening with him. He was slowing. His face was red from exertion, sweat drench-ing his skin as he wheezed for breath.

He's losing stamina, I realized. That's right—Dream had mentioned this would happen if one shifter had all fifteen elements. Macarius had too many Hallows packed in his soul… he couldn't last very long while evoking them like this. I suspected the only thing keeping him going was his determination to retrieve the Orb.

I grinned, keeping my sights locked on the incoming, azure globe. As we reached the Orb, we both clasped our hand over it—

Pain splintered through my ribs.

Macarius had summoned his Glaciavoking to form a sword of ice… And pierced it straight into my chest.

I tried to breathe, but only a strained wheeze burned—

—the ice still numbed my muscles as we were transported back to the physical plane, lungs shuddering and locked. We were back on the mountain, higher than before, on more stable footing.

Macarius shoved his frosted sword farther into my chest. I felt the skin on my back *split* open, my spine screaming as warm blood dribbled down my back and chest.

My vision blurred, black splotches patching Macarius's livid face in front of me. Breathing was agony. Moving was even worse, my legs turning to rubber under me as I lost the strength to keep myself standing—which caused the ice to dig into my muscles upward, prying an excruciating scream from my punctured lungs.

"Finally…!" Macarius panted furiously, grabbing the Orb with his free hand. "I grew tired of that… *irritating* game…!"

A rusty taste washed over my tongue, blood gurgling up my throat and gushing down my lips.

Black, spidering veins crawled from Macarius's hands, leaking onto his sword of ice—and they rooted into my open chest.

He hissed in my wolf ear, "Now, Shadowblood… do me a favor, will you?" He shoved me back, his infected sword *tearing* out my chest. My feet slipped over the ledge, and Macarius's face fell away as I began to drop, his snarl dimming through my fading ears. "And *stay* dead this time…!"

Not… yet…!

With the last of my strength, I reached out—and snatched the Orb from his grasp.

His shocked yells faded as I spiraled down with the Orb in hand, the Weeping Woods flying closer every second.

In a desperate holler, I squeezed the Orb—

—Aspirre's abyss slammed into existence around me, my fall halting as I floated calmly in midair.

But I still couldn't breathe. I could barely move, the gushing holes in my chest and back thrashing with pain. The black tendrils of Macarius's infection Hallows writhed within me, tearing at my soul at an alarming rate, my vision spotting faster now.

Blearily, I evoked my remedy Hallows, my hand glowing with a golden sheen as I pushed it over the veins, hoping like Death it was enough to banish the acidic plague eating through my soul.

But without Alex here to speed up my Hallows, my Healing was dangerously slow, the veins spreading faster than my sluggish Hallows could handle... I needed to find help, I needed to...

Something floated before my nose in the abyss.

I went cross-eyed. There was a vial filled with glowing, violet liquid twirling before my face.

Was that... a Soul-Cure vial? Where had it come from?

I weakly grabbed it, pouring it over my chest... a stinging hiss came as it touched my wound, and I seethed a wince...

Then the infection sizzled away from my soul, sparing my spirit from destruction.

But it did nothing for the physical wound. I needed a new plan, else I would die in here.

I drifted forward, concentrating on floating through the abyss. I didn't know what waited there in the physical plane, yet I didn't care. I had to gain enough distance from the mountain—from Macarius.

I kept my goal firmly in mind. He could NOT get his hands on this Orb again. Regardless of what happened to me.

I was running out of air and blood, my head sloshing—

—The Orb brought me back to the physical plane.

THMP!

My pulse exploded with an agonizing ache. I dropped to all fours, trying to gasp, but nothing escaped. My lungs shriveled closed, throat straining to push anything out save for a weak, blistering gag.

THMP!

My pulse struck again like a sledgehammer, nearly bursting out the wound in my disfigured chest. Blood dripped onto my fingers, the gash warm and sticky like a gushing orange *crunched* by rusty fangs.

THMP-THMP!

I lost my grip on the Orb, and it rolled away.

The... The Orb...

I reached a shivering hand toward the azure globe.

THMP!

Another shooting pain ripped from my chest. I collapsed and spit up blood over the grass. I curled on my side, my muscles seizing, vision crawling with silver shimmers.

At least... he can't... use the Orb now... The thought evaporated like mist, churning in a numbing fog that swallowed me whole.

Until the numbness died as well.

37

CASUALTIES OF WAR

ALEXANDER

*T*HMP!

Pain split through my chest, as if my heart were erupting.

I screamed, my voice echoing through the woods as I clutched my chest, dropping to the grass beside Bianca's limp body. Chai and Mal began screeching alongside me, the ravens fluttering in a rage.

I writhed and sputtered on the grass, my muscles convulsing as that constant pounding struck my chest.

"Alex?!" Willow shouted above me, holding her baby in fright. "What's happened?!"

—THMP!

"ARGH…!" I curled to my side, that pain splintering in my chest again. But there was nothing wrong with my chest… which meant the pain wasn't mine.

It was Xavier's.

—THMP-THMP!

"Rrrrrargh…!" I pushed past the agony and rose on all fours, my arms quivering as sweat rolled down my nose. "Xavier…!" I heaved for breath, my voice hissing like acid. "No…! Please, *no*…!"

This pain, this torture… it was too familiar. Only once had Xavier's pain been this intense. Only once had his suffering been so powerful that it echoed through our connection and reached me with this much clarity. Only once…

When we thought he'd died.

—THMP!

I gagged, my twisting heart threatening to burst.

My vision spotted as I collapsed to the grass. But in that moment, I spotted Chai launching into the air and soaring over the trees past the mountain, his screeches an echoing, wounded cry… until the blackness swallowed my vision.

"… don't know what's wrong with him," I heard Willow's terrified voice shaking above me in the darkness. "He-he was screaming like a madman, he said something about Xavier, and…" I heard a sob spill. "I-I think something's happened to Xavier. They've always sort of… *felt* each other's ailments, like-like some connection. And Xavier is still missing, Chai flew off suddenly, and now Alex is acting like this and—"

"Willow, be calm," I heard Lilli's voice hush sternly. "We don't know if his behavior is about Xavier or Bianca. And if you recall, the twins' connection echoed *general* pain as well, like when Xavier was stung by a Poisondragon. He was fine then, I'm sure he's fine now. But we can't stay here much longer, if the Necrofera find us, they'll…"

Their murmuring voices wafted in my ears. The blackness swam, and I vaguely felt someone hauling me up by the arms. My eyes peeled open. The darkness was flooded with the new light, but my vision stayed blurry and splotched.

The person hauling me slung my arm over his shoulder in a deep grunt. My head rolled toward him, willing my vision to focus on his scaled face.

It was Jaq. The viper's face was drenched with stale tears, causing his eyeglasses to slip down his nose as he struggled to keep me up.

My throat burned. "Jaq…?"

"I've got you," Jaq assured, hefting me over his shoulder. His peasant persona had completely vanished as he murmured, "Don't strain yourself… We'll see you to a clinic. Octavius—come help me with him!"

"O-okay!" Octavius piped off to the side, running over and slinging my other arm over his shoulder to match Jaq. The cat waved a hand over my head, wincing. "Bloods, his head is throbbing… but he seems fine, otherwise. What happened to him?"

"We're not sure," Jaq said. "Willow's worried something happened to Xavier. But it might be shock from… from Bianca…" Jaq gritted his teeth, more tears leaking.

My voice was bleary, "B… Bianca…" The world spun, and I rolled my head forward.

Bianca's corpse still lay on the grass.

"Bianca…!" I wriggled out of their hold, stumbling over to Bianca. I cupped her face with shivering fingers, touching my brow to hers as another stab of agony drilled through my heart. "Bianca…"

"—Uh, C-Captain?" Neal called awkwardly above me. He rubbed his neck, his plate clattering noisily. "They're saying we have to, uh… *go*… Do you need help with, uh…" Neal's green eyes lowered to Bianca. He didn't need to finish.

I squeezed my eyes shut, burying the pain as far down as I could shove it. Then so, *so* tenderly, I lifted Bianca in my quaking arms.

"N-n-no…" I whispered, my voice weak. "I… I will carry her… alone…"

I drew in a sharp breath, hefting Bianca against my chest… and ordered my feet to move.

WHERE YOU BELONG

OCTAVIUS

Kck, kck, kck!

I rapped my knuckles on the huge, oak doors of Alex's room in his old manor. The ghostly servants downstairs told me Alex had locked himself up in here since we got back from the Willow of Ashes hours ago. It was already morning, and none of us had slept a Gods damned wink.

"A... Alex?" I called.

No response.

"Alex, u-um... Lilli wants to know if you, um... need help with Bianca's reaping in there...? She's worried about you. W-we're all worried..."

Still no response. Which meant *no*.

He'd already told us he wanted to conduct her reaping alone. I wasn't surprised he didn't want to talk.

I sighed and walked off, heading downstairs to the foyer. Ghosts floated all over the place, phasing through walls and furniture and muttering between themselves about what was going on with Alex. They said he was just sitting in there, in silence. Not even moving.

The only *living* shifters in here were the Alchemists from Bianca's guild. They all occupied the couches and chairs, since the ghosts weren't using them. Their postures practically melted into the upholstery, a lot of them sniffling and rubbing at tears.

Bianca's right-hand man, Red, looked like he was all out of tears, though. He sat hunched in a chair with his arms and legs crossed tight, his eyes rimmed red and wearing a glower so dark, the skin under his eyes dragged down his lids with deep circles.

I skittishly passed him to meet up with the twins' grandfather, Edric Devouh. Edric puffed on a thick pipe, wearing a soul-seeing mask over his eyes while he busied himself by assigning jobs to the huge crowd of ghostly servants drifting all over this manor. Apparently, this place used to be the same manor the twins grew up in when they lived on the palace grounds. Now that their parents were dead, and Xavier was obviously going to live with Willow in the palace—well, when we find him, at least—Alex didn't have a reason to go back to their old manor in Low Everland. So, Edric had brought all their spectral servants over here. All of them were glad to take up a vassalship with the sons of their former *Da'torr.*

Well, they *will* be glad to take up a vassalship. Right now, with Xavier still missing, Alex couldn't form a Bloodpact with any souls. You can't exactly share your blood with a spirit if you can't *touch* any spirits. But they were happy to wait, from what Edric told me.

When the stately old man noticed me walking up to him, he stopped puffing on his pipe and hurried over.

"Any word?" He asked hopefully, his curled moustache rising along with his smile.

My cat ears grew, shaking my head. "Alex isn't talking. And the door's still locked."

Edric's expression sagged. "He won't even speak to the ghosts when they phase through the walls in there… He isn't acknowledging anyone, it seems."

I offered a twitching grimace. "Sorry… I'll go see if the others have heard from Xavier. It's been a few hours, maybe his vassals have made contact?"

Edric nodded and chewed on his pipe broodingly. "Yes, yes… do tell me what you learn, will you…? It's… inconsiderate of him to make his grandfather worry over him like this a second time." He breathed in a shuddering breath, collected himself, then went to talk to the hovering ghosts around him again, keeping up a pretense of 'business as usual'.

I rubbed my nose and blew out a heavy sigh. Since there wasn't anything left for me to do here, I walked outside to the palace grounds.

A crisp breeze crashed over my face the minute I stepped out, and I hurriedly tugged my fur cloak tighter around my shoulders. I pulled the hood over my head and gritted my teeth against the cold, running through the grounds to keep warm—

RRRRRRRrrrrrrmmmmm…

I almost tripped from the sudden Groundquake, flailing to keep balanced. It took a few minutes for the tremor to die down, and when it did, I exhaled and kept walking with a more cautious step.

"Blood-d-dy Groundquakes-s-s," I chattered in a shiver. "I d-d-don't like how f-f-f-frequent they're g-getting…"

Craaawww!

The familiar croak of my white-cheeked raven, Shade, soared down to follow at my side. He lost a black downfeather as he flapped to keep up with me, staying close. Our Bond pulled at my soul with worry. Shade must have been extra on-edge because of all the crazy stuff that's been happening in the last few hours. And Land, I didn't blame him. That latest Groundquake was just another thing on the list of 'things to freak out about'.

When I reached the royal markets, I rounded the next left where the hospital waited. Shade flew to a lamppost and perched himself there, biting at his wing as I shuffled inside the hospital's lobby, letting the warm air from the heater on the ceiling wash over my skin.

I crossed the floor and waved to the receptionist behind the front counter. "I'm back," I announced with a smile.

The man behind the counter seemed to recognize me—and he backed into the wall, his coned fox ears growing in terror. "S-S-S-Sir Oct-t-tavius…!"

My smile turned into a glower. *Gods damn it.* I had no idea how word spread so fast, but pretty much everyone in the palace grounds knew who I was—and *what* I was. I guessed being a non-royal with Infection Hallows wasn't something these Grimlings saw every day… not that Everlanders saw much of us, either, back home.

I sighed and tried to keep a friendly face. Maybe if I was nice enough, people would ease up. "Hey, um, do you think you can buzz me in again?" I asked. "I need to report to the Queen's Hand… and my squad's Lieutenant." Because Gods knew I tried and failed getting our Captain back on task.

The receptionist stuttered. "Y-y-y-y-yes…! Yes, of course…!" He quickly pushed a button from behind the counter.

A loud *BZZZZ* vibrated from the double-doors, followed by a soft *click* to signal the locks were off.

I waved to the man and called, "Thanks!" before opening the doors and walking down the labyrinth of hallways in the hospital.

I remembered which turns to make and which stairs to take to the second floor. My armored steps clattered like Void, but I was too exhausted to care about how much attention I was drawing from the nurses and other patients. From what I understood, this hospital only saw the people who lived on the palace grounds. And right now, Willow's cousin was being operated on in here.

I finally found Jaq standing guard outside the door to the private waiting room. We traded nods, and I took a quick breath before cracking open the door.

"… not sure I'm comfortable having a demon of his history operating on my son…!" the shrill voice of the councilwoman cried. When I peeked in, I saw her arguing with Willow, Felix's dad looking just as pissed next to his shouting wife. "We should have been informed the *moment* he was admitted! We have a right to refuse any doctors—"

"—and I have a right to ensure that your son lives through a fatal wound *to the throat*," Willow clipped, barely keeping her tone calm. "I understand your concern, Councilwoman, but believe you me, Kael is the best chance your son has at surviving right now. He is a trained surgeon from the Land King's ancient palace—"

"—ancient enough not to know how our modern practices have changed—!"

"—is an Infeciovoker of great skill who can sense his injuries better than any of us—"

"—can't perform a miracle even with an extinct Hallows—!"

I cringed away as they kept up their shouting match, the two trying to drown each other out and getting nowhere.

Lilli was still in there, too, making damn sure to stay out of the argument. She stood at attention in the corner like a statue, her bat wings tucked behind her back while her jet-black hair had been tied in a frazzled bun since I left.

When her chartreuse eyes found me at the door, she slipped out to meet me in the hall with Jaq, clicking the door shut.

"Did you get through to him?" Lilli asked. "How is he?"

I shrugged, my pauldron clanking against my breastplate. "Still not talking. Bloods, Edric said he's not even talking to the ghosts who phased in there."

Jaq let out a long, rumbling sigh through his nose, too depressed to bother putting up his peasant persona. "I don't blame him," Jaq said. "We all grew up together, the four of us… I can hardly believe it myself. But Alex is taking it harder…"

Lilli scowled at him. "Of course he is. I know she was your friend, but she was *everything* to Alex. With her gone, and his brother missing, I just knew he would shut himself off from the rest of us. This is exactly how he acted when Xavier first went missing when we were children—"

"Pardon," a deep voice suddenly said, making all of us jump.

It was Kael. He was dressed in blood-stained surgeon scrubs, and his white pupiled, yellow eyes peered down at me from above his medical mask.

He pulled the mask down and asked me, "Have the boy's parents arrived yet, Descendant?"

I nodded. "Yeah… but you might want to ease in carefully. They're seriously pissed."

He grunted. "Rightfully so."

"Did…" I began queasily, staring at all the blood on his scrubs. "Did he make it…?"

Kael hummed, "Yes. But with an injury that severe, I'm afraid he'll never speak another syllable again."

I gripped my throat. "Damn… Well… good luck giving the news…"

He gave me a thin smile. "Thank you, Descendant… I'm certainly going to need it."

With that, he knocked lightly, the shouting voices on the other side hushing as he walked in and closed the door behind him.

I rubbed my neck, looking at Jaq and Lilli. "So, um… I-I guess I'll just… find Neal and keep patrol around the palace?"

Jaq cocked an eyebrow. "Why are you asking me?"

"Who else am I supposed to ask?" I threw up my hands. "Our Captain's locked himself in a room, the Death King is missing, and the queen is busy fighting with family. Since you're Alex's Lieutenant, you're the only one here who's allowed to give me orders and *isn't* broken."

Jaq scratched his scaly jaw, tilting his head to consider that. "Ah… I suppose you've a point, there." He crossed his arms. "All right. In that case, your brother and Matthiel are already on patrol with our Ancient demons, so don't worry about that. Have you found a place to stay yet? You're going to need rest, after all that's happened."

"Yeah." I rocked my head. "Edric said the Howler's Inn was open to any us, if we wanted. It's farther in town outside the palace grounds, but it's better than nothing. You guys should probably ask if there's room for you before it's filled up."

Lilli shook her head. "No need. My father and I still live in our manor here on the grounds. The servants are moving my belongings into a larger bedchamber to accommodate Jaq and Oliver's addition, but otherwise, we have everything in order."

"Oh." I paused awkwardly. "Uh… okay. I guess I'll just… check into the Inn…"

I unceremoniously left, leaving the hospital. Once outside, I whistled for Shade to fly down from the streetlamp he'd apparently perched on, and my raven settled on my shoulder as I flagged down a hover-coach to take me into town.

As the coachman whipped the horses forward, I groaned and sank back into the cushioned seat, rubbing my eyes. They were still dry from the smoke in the cave last night. Well, I guess it was this *morning?* Bloods, the night flew by so fast, my inner-clock was getting blurry. The Floating Lights weren't helping either. They were paler than sunlight, so it was hard to tell if it was actually morning yet. Everything was so much darker than the surface down here. I massaged my eyes harder, trying to force them to adjust.

Now I knew how Jaq and the twins felt when they first came to the surface on my beach… Though, the lights were getting brighter by the minute, so I guessed it wasn't so bad anymore. When *they* were getting used to life on the surface, I told them to give it time. Guess it was my turn.

"Well, Shade," I mumbled, scratching under Shade's beak as he gave a soft coo. "Just us, again…"

I was pretty used to having a room to myself now, after months of traveling to Marincia, then to Grim, without Neal and the guys there. When we first left the group, it felt a little unnatural, but now I was actually looking forward to some time alone. Tonight had been non-stop *awful*. I just wanted to get to a room, curl up in five-hundred blankets by a fire and have a pint of the strongest ale the Inn could offer.

As we entered the city, I stared out the window with Shade.

Low Rastiria was way different from the surface cities I grew up around. Instead of flat-roofed, yellow stonework, Grim's buildings were all made with faded grey brick and black stones, topped with sharp spires and curling shingles—some of which were so tall they vanished into the ceiling mist, those weird, Floating Lights weaving around them like water parting around boulders in a river.

There were *tons* of black birds flying around, too. Shade croaked and fluttered his wings as each one passed our hover-coach, our Bond pulling with excitement. He tapped his beak against the glass window, and I unlocked the latch and slid it open for him, letting him fly out to socialize. I smiled after him, tucking an arm out the window in a small chuckle.

But another freezing cavern wind blew through, the cold air leaking into the coach, and I hurried to shut the window to keep it out. Bloods, I did *not* like this cold weather…

The coach finally pulled up to the entrance of the Howler's Inn. It looked pretty similar to the ones in High Everland with its metal and glass structure and giant silver letters that read *Howler's Inn*. The only difference was how the roofs pulled into tall spires at each corner. I hopped out of the coach, paid the coachman two silver coins for the fare, and trotted up the steps to walk into the lobby.

This place was full of Grim-haired nobles. I only saw a few familiar Landish faces in the crowd, and they were all from *my* family. My parents were eating in the fancy dining area in the corner while Ringëd and Mikani walked over to the lifts, keeping a strict eye—and a stricter hold—on Kurn. I had a hunch the ferret had gotten himself into trouble in that dining area. Probably stole someone's sandwich again.

I went to the front desk, leaning over the counter to get the clerk's attention. The sheep-horned Grimish woman noticed me and smiled. Thankfully, she didn't seem to know who I was, unlike the people at the palace grounds.

"Do you have a reservation, Sir?" She asked in a pleasant tone, her vowels curled in the same accent that all the locals had here.

"Um, yeah," I said. "I'm with, um, Howllord Edric Devouh's party. He said there was a block of rooms reserved for all of us."

"Oh!" She said cheerfully, picking up a ledger that was off to the side. "Certainly, Sir! Could I have the name he would have registered you under?"

"Octavius Treble."

She scanned the list of names in the ledger, then tapped on my name and chimed "There you are! Sir Octavius Treble." She got a key off the wall-hooks behind her and handed it to me. "Room 206. Please enjoy your stay!"

I smiled. "Thanks. I will."

As I walked over to the lifts, I already felt the stress of the last few hours leaking out. *I guess Jaq was right,* I thought as the lift doors opened up, and I shuffled inside next to the liftman controlling the levers. *I do need a good rest—*

"Wait!" a familiar girl's voice shouted—and *El* squeezed inside the lift right before the liftman closed the doors on her feathers.

"E… El?" I blinked at her, too surprised to move. Not that I *could,* anyway. The liftman had already rolled his eyes and got the lift moving upward. I swallowed, giving a nervous cough and asked, "What are you doing here? I thought you were going to stay with Zyl?"

She had to pant over her knees before she could answer, and I wondered if she had flown over here in a rush. Her wings sure looked tired enough, the way they sagged to her feet in exhaustion.

"I…" she puffed. "I, um… asked Edric to put me in the same room as *you* here…" Her cat ears folded down in a guilty blush. "I… may have told Zyl he made the reservation in advance and couldn't change it…"

I frowned. "You lied to Zyl?"

"What else was I supposed to do!" She threw her hands up in a groan, her wings mimicking the action and smacking the liftman's hat off. She winced and picked it up for him, offering a meek, "Sorry…"

The man scowled at her and snatched his hat back without a word.

Ding!

We reached our floor, and the liftman shot El an annoyed glare as we walked out and started down the hall.

I rubbed my eyes. "El… you shouldn't lie to her like that."

"But I have to," she protested miserably. "She's being so… so *clingy*. I barely have time to myself anymore, let along time with you." She grabbed my arm and practically melted into it was a tired sigh. "I miss you…"

I blushed, my chest fluttering as her Pyrovoker's heat warmed me up. I pushed a breath through my nose and murmured, "Yeah… me, too."

I found the right room and unlocked the door, walking in with El.

The room wasn't as big as the penthouse suite the guys and I usually stayed in at these inns, but it was still huge. The outside wall was nothing but wide windows, one of which was actually a door to an outside balcony with a stone railing, there was a fire already crackling in the hearth, the wet bar was lined with a variety of liquor around cushioned seats and couches…

And in the center of the whole room was a single, king-sized bed.

Wait. The minute I saw the bed, I belatedly realized something I should have thought about earlier. El was going to stay with me. In one room. With one bed.

My face blistered unbearably hot.

El didn't seem to notice and went to open the balcony door. Shade had apparently flown up here and perched on our railing, and El's albino raven, Salfwy, flapped next to him. When El opened the door, they flew in, a freezing gust blowing inside until El shut the door again and flopped onto one of the couches.

"*Skrii*, it's been a horrible night," she groaned and started taking off her armor, dropping her holster of throwing-scythes and peeling off her gauntlets. "Any word on Alex, yet?"

The question distracted me a little, thankfully. Though not by much. I wasn't sure if she expected anything to happen, but I also didn't want to give her the impression *I* expected anything to happen… But I was seriously itching to take off this armor after a full day of it weighing me down.

Yeah. That was probably all *she* wanted, too.

I went ahead and started taking off my armor, setting it aside as I went to the wet bar to pour myself a drink, hoping it would get my mind off how awkward I felt.

"He's locked himself in a room with Bianca," I told her. "The ghosts say he's just sitting there. He probably hasn't gotten around to Reaping her soul yet, from what I gathered."

She hummed. "And the Death Prince? How did the operation go?"

"Felix will live." I shrugged, taking a shot of my drink. "But Kael says he'll probably never speak again. Had his voicebox damaged beyond repair."

El grimaced. "I guess that's better than being dead."

"Yeah. Seriously."

It got really quiet, then. My nervousness flared back, and I hurried to take another shot. Maybe I needed three.

El took another breath and asked, "What about Xavier…?"

Make that *four* shots.

I chugged down two more gulps and *clacked* the glass down, leaning over the counter heavily.

"No one's heard from him," I said, my throat tight. I'd spent these last few hours trying to ignore the festering nausea, but with my nerves already shredded to Void and the reminder of our missing Death King being shoved back to my attention for the billionth time tonight, my panic rushed back as my voice started shaking.

"We haven't heard a Gods damn word from him—not even his vassals can get through." I slammed a fist on the counter, the glasses clattering. "Damn it…! Alex is broken, Macarius is still on the loose, Xavier's probably lying dead in a ditch somewhere, and the only hope the world has at surviving is in the hands of a newborn demon who only has *one* set of Hallows…!"

RRRRRRRrrrrrmmmmm…

Another Groundquake rumbled around us, the glasses clinking and rattling along with my unraveling nerves. Even after the tremor died off, my heart was still hammering out my grown cat ears. Tears hit, and I squeezed my head and broke into a trembling sob over the counter. "I… I don't know what to do…! The fucking world is ending! We're all going to die at *any second*, and I…!" My voice cracked. "I'm really scared, El… and-and I don't have anyone to talk to about it because everyone's too busy trying to fix it, and… and *you're* constantly with Zyl, and…"

Her warm hands suddenly slid around my chest, and soft feathers brushed around my arms as she wrapped her wings around me.

"I'm… I'm sorry…" She hiccupped, sounding like she was also crying as her grip tightened around me. "I'm *sorry*… I didn't spend enough time with Zyl before she died, and-and I wanted to make it up to her, but… n-now I'm not spending enough time with *you*, and that's all I *want* to do, but I…" Her voice cinched up. "I don't want to hurt Zyl again, either…"

I turned around and hugged her close, letting her cry into my chest while I cried into her hair. Her familiar warmth was something I'd missed these past few months… I couldn't even describe the flush of relief it brought, to finally have it back. To have *her* back. For the first time in way too long, it didn't feel like everything around me was falling apart.

I leaned my cheek on her hair. "Don't let Zyl *or* me keep you from doing what you want… We'll both get over it."

She sniffed and rubbed her eyes to look at me. "You… you don't think… she'll hate me…?"

I groaned. "She's not going to hate you just because you have a life outside of her. She'll adjust."

"What if she doesn't?"

I choked on a thin laugh. "El, she loves you. She'll understand. I mean, you've basically been ignoring *me* for months, and I'm sure as Void not going anywhere, because…" I held my breath, touching my forehead to hers in a sigh. "Because *I* love you."

Her cat ears perked straight up, and she froze in my arms.

I swallowed, not sure if I just screwed everything up… but it was already out there, so I kept going. "And-and unless you break up with me, I'm *really* sorry, but y-you're stuck with me. S-so if you don't want that, you need to tell me now so I can leave you alone and—*mmnff!*"

She kissed me so hard, I thought the burn of her lips would melt my face off. In a good way.

"Don't—*hic!*—don't you dare leave me alone…!" she hiccupped and rubbed her eyes dry. But they got drenched again when another wave of tears streamed down, and she smiled. "I love you, too."

Gods, hearing her say it made me drunker than the shots ever could.

So what if I couldn't stop the End from coming? So what if it happened any second? I was exactly where I wanted to be, if it came.

And I was happy for every one of those Gods damn beautiful seconds.

39

MOURNING

ALEXANDER

I am calm.

My lungs drew in a breath, then banished it in a slow, even stream.

Darkness graced my sight. I hadn't opened my eyes since I shut myself in my old bedchamber. We'd returned from the Willow of Ashes hours ago, and the twitters of cheerful songbirds outside told me it was morning already. I didn't care to occupy the finely upholstered chairs, and instead sat cross-legged on the lush carpet. My posture was pristine; my hands relaxed and lightly gripping a long-staved, Pure Crystal scythe that lay across my lap.

I am calm.

Another long, deliberate breath, holding it there like a weightless waterskin.

I am… c-c… calm…

My breath broke into a shudder, my fragile bubble of peace teetering on the edge of a fractured ledge—

CALM.

My eyes flew open in defiance, my cool expression quivering as I pried my lids so wide, I didn't care if they never shut again.

"I…!" My blistered throat burned furiously, and I shoved to my shaking feet, using the scythe to steady myself. "Am…! A *Reaper*…! This is my *duty*…!"

Before the surge of determination could puff away, I raised the scythe overhead and spun round to face the feathered bed—

My bones locked.

The rabbit eared corpse still lay exactly how I'd left her on the mattress: her arms folded politely over her chest, her serene face tilted to face me as her silken, orange hair fanned over the soft comforter like satin ribbons made of the surface's enrapturing, rustic sunsets…

The pain came raging back, my heart ripping off its valves and twisting to miserable shreds—

"*This is my DUTY!*" I screamed and *sliced* the brightly glowing scythe over her chest. The misty blade cut her blouse, yet phased though her skin untouched.

I felt the vibrating *snap* of her NecroSeam twinge over the sharp Crystal.

I pushed out a choked sob, flung the scythe against the wall with a deafening *CLANG,* and jerked away before I had to watch her ghost rise from her body. Pain devoured me again, and I fell to my trembling knees, gasping through a closed throat and clutching my face so desperately, I didn't care that my claws dug into my shrieking scalp.

For what felt like hours, the chamber was silent of all but my wheezing sobs.

Then, as soft as a droplet plinking into a cavern pond, Bianca's voice whispered through my wolf ears. "Alex…?"

The sound shook every hollow bone I had, and my sobs worsened. I didn't dare turn to face her, keeping my wet lids shut.

"Alex…"

Don't look, I commanded in silence, my breaths shuddering.

Her voice drew closer behind me. "Alex."

Don't look, I warned again, wrapping my arms tight over my face.

"Alex!"

—Her voice barked in *front* of me now, catching me off guard as I opened my eyes.

Bianca's pale, translucent spirit crouched before me. Her rabbit ears were draped down her neck. Her face was marred with despair as she reached for my face with her wispy fingers…

They misted over my skin without contact. I didn't even feel so much as a cold breeze.

I desperately reached for her hand, but only felt my own face, my vision blurring as more tears flooded.

"I-I-I…" My voice could barely push through my swollen vocal cords. I lost control of my body and flung my arms around her—the soul puffing away from my skin like before without a sound. I flopped back, defeated, and whispered. "I'm sorry… I-I can't… c-can't touch…"

She released a solemn, though accepting breath. "I know… That's Xavier's department." She paused, glancing around the room as if only now noticing where we were. "Wait… where *is* Xavier?"

My answer came out in a hollow croak. "He's dead."

Silence followed. Then she hushed, "Wh… what?"

"He's dead," I echoed, strained as I cast her an empty stare. "We haven't found him since he vanished in Aspirre with Macarius, but… I felt it. He isn't coming back. Not this time…" My tone dimmed further. "Xavier's dead. My parents are dead. And now, you're dead along with them. Macarius got what he wanted. He killed *everyone* I loved…"

Her spectral knees folded to her chest, and she hugged herself across from me as though taking her time to let it all sink in.

Then she took a breath, trying to keep her rasping voice cheerful. "Well… at least… at least my soul wasn't destroyed…? Maybe I can form a vassalship with you—"

"*I can't touch you, Bianca!*" I shouted, my teeth sharpening. "Even if I wanted to form a contract with you, I need *Xavier* to make the Bloodpact at all…! And don't you *Gods damned dare* make light of the fact that I just watched the only woman I've ever loved die *right in front me…!*"

Her ghostly lips twitched in a start. She couldn't weep as a ghost, but the sorrow wrenching her features made it clear she very well would have been now.

I sucked in a tremulous breath and cupped my eyes, whispering, "Bianca, I… I'm sorry. For everything. I wasted so much time worrying over trivial things, and I… I should have called off my engagement to Lilli the moment I learned of it. I should have put you above everyone else—ignored what my parents wanted, ignored what Lilli wanted, told them to shove their arrangements up their arses, but I…!" I slammed a fist on the floor. "I didn't fight for you enough… I couldn't decide what 'the right thing to do' was until it was too late—and now, because of my sheer stupidity, I lost you along with everyone else…" I squeezed my eyes shut. "I treated you so horribly… I'm so… so sorry…"

Her voice was soft, sniffling. "N-no… *I'm* sorry." She deflated over her knees. "I'm the one who treated you horribly… I thought you waited so long to call off your arrangement because you didn't care about me." She sniffed, her lips twitching with a weak grin. "But you were just doing what you always do and taking care of the people closest to you. You weren't having trouble choosing what you wanted, you just… couldn't bring yourself to put your needs first."

I rubbed a heavy arm under my nose, muttering, "You're certainly one to talk… you died saving your Spirit Son from suffocating." I attempted a fragile smile. "You've been warned. Willow is planning an award ceremony in your honor. Well… If the world isn't destroyed by then."

She snorted. "I think I'll pass, thanks…" She seemed to have an afterthought, then lifted a rabbit ear and asked shyly, "But if you wanted to ditch that *with* me, I… I guess I wouldn't mind a tour of the royal capital…" If her ghost could blush, she would have.

Despite it all, I shuddered a thin laugh. "A-a tour, eh…? Well… I'm not one to be persuaded into something so frivolous while I should be on duty as Captain of the Royal Guard…" I smiled, reaching for her hand—not caring that our fingers couldn't touch. "But for *you*, from now on… I'll always make an exception."

She yielded to a chuckle at that. "You don't need to. But thank you. I can wait until you make sure the End of Existence is stopped so we don't *all* die." She shrugged. "That kind of takes priority."

I scratched behind my wolf ear, grumbling. "I suppose…" I stopped, a cruel reminder creeping its way to the back of my mind. "Then there *is* something I need to do, first…"

Her spectral brow knitted. "What?"

I pushed to my feet in a heated growl. "I have to find my brother."

40

ACCEPTANCE

WILLOW

I paced the royal library with panicked steps, circling the ebony rug Lucas and Eryn played atop for the fiftieth time round the cluster of couches and chaises. The infants babbled to one another, Lucas sitting up and grabbing Eryn's azure fox tail while Eryn crawled after me excitedly.

Occupying the seats were our slumbering Dreamcatchers. Jimmy and Yulia sat along two separate chairs, their faces serene as they slept soundly before the hearth's fire, their azure Dream marks gleaming bright. On the shared chaise were my azure-haired mother and rust-haired grandmother Crysa, both asleep like the first two with their own Dream marks shining.

They were all searching Aspirre for any traces of Xavier. They'd been at it since we returned from the Relic, and it was nearly noon. Which had my nerves shredding at the seams. What in Death was taking so long? If I hadn't agreed to watch the children, I would be in there myself—I probably would have found him by now!

My pacing grew angrier.

From the rug, Lucas's wolf ears swiveled as he tried to keep watch of me during my circling. He found it amusing, laughing and babbling *Mama* over and over, thrilled to have learned this new word. As if he'd already forgotten he and Eryn had been moments away from suffocating in the cave. As if he'd forgotten how that lunatic almost killed his mother…

And disappeared with his father.

Panic flushed back, my claws digging into my crossed arms. Why did this keep happening? Why was it always Xavier who vanished? Could that man spare me the constant grief of losing him for *one Bloody day?*

"No, no," the voice of Matthiel caught my attention from the nearby nook of bookshelves, and I flicked my gaze at him.

He and Aster were seated at a squat coffee table cluttered with toad bones. Aster's hands gleamed with violet lights as he attempted to assemble the bones piece by piece with his newly gained Necrovoking, squinting at the instructional text as Matthiel gave him direction.

"That is the *left* femur," the sienna-eyed Howllord corrected, using his own Necrovoking to lift up the proper toad bone and hover it over the picture in Aster's text. "You see? The curvature is arching this way and—"

"How in Bloods am I supposed to remember which tiny twig is which?" Aster moaned and dropped the bones, dismissing his Hallows to *thunk* his head on the table and rattle the scrambled skeleton. "This is hard! I don't have to memorize puzzle pieces with *fire*, can we just go back to that?" He threw up his hands, which burst with blue fire, his grin stretched wide like a child who'd learned how to walk on his hands for the first time.

Matthiel evoked his own fire Hallows and clapped his hands over Aster's overzealous flames, snuffing them.

"No," Matthiel muttered, thin smoke dissipating from his hands. He took in a patient breath and smoothed back his raven-black hair. "You're already adept enough with your Pyrovoking. Yes, it *is* easier, but that's precisely why you must focus your efforts on Necrovoking. It takes far more study and memorization than perhaps *any* other element." Matthiel cocked an eyebrow at the demon. "You say you're one of the Gods' Champions, yes? I should think they gave you *all* your Hallows expecting you to learn each and every one. Do you want to save Existence?"

Aster puffed up his cheeks in a mumble. "Yeah…"

"Then you will cease your complaining and resurrect this toad." Matthiel stabbed a strict finger at the page in Aster's text, prompting him to grudgingly return to his lesson.

Across from them, Herrin and Marian sat on the rug with ruffled wings, the two Enlighteners having a field day as they scribbled down frantic notes in their ledgers, like their trembling quills had minds of their own.

Herrin didn't pause his writing when he questioned Aster, "Now, you said She called you *and* Xavier the Ruiners of Tradition?"

Aster dropped one of the bones as he answered, "Uh, yeah… and Macar and Alex are the Saviors of History. But Xavier and Alex are two halves of the collective Concept of the Present, so She also called them the Defenders of Harmony."

I scowled at them as I continued my pacing around the babies. '*She*' was supposedly the Seamstress of Souls herself: the Mother Goddess, Nira. According to Aster, he and the twins had spoken with Her—along with the rest of the Gods—and learned of their purpose. Aster and Macarius were apparently a Concept of the Past and Future, created from the minds of us shifters since shifters first evolved.

It was utter nonsense.

He claimed that *I* was even the very Concept of death—the shared belief of it, at least. I supposed it could have made sense to a degree, since it was widely accepted that Nira was my Soul-Mother…

But Xavier and Alexander? A Concept of time itself? Ridiculous.

Even so, the Enlighteners devoured the ludicrous claims like a five-course banquet on Death's Festival, continuing their interview with twitching feathers and spastic quills.

I rolled my eyes.

A tiny hand grabbed my ankle, then. I glanced down and found baby Eryn. The kit used my leg to pull himself up to his wobbling feet, cackling at his success. His azure tail swished to keep balanced, and his fox ears flicked toward his slumbering mother: my grandmother Crysa.

She and the other Dreamcatchers were still asleep. Still searching for Xavier in Aspirre.

Lucas was still where I left him on the rug, Virro buzzing around his head as the boy's babbles changed from *'Mama'* to *'Dada'* now. I sighed and slowly made my way over to the pup—allowing my little Uncle Eryn to step with me as he still held my leg—and picked up Lucas. He nuzzled my neck, his wolf ears brushing my jaw and easing my worries slightly.

Very, very slightly.

Creee…

The library doors creaked open, and my head whipped about so fast, my neck muscles screamed.

Alexander stepped in.

He looked absolutely awful. His eyes were bloodshot and rimmed red, his lids were sagging with dark rings, his hair was tousled and unkempt while his face was still blotched with soot from the cavern's smoke.

I blinked when I noticed he wasn't alone. At his side floated the ghost of Bianca. And in his arms was her limp body.

"Bloods be good!" I set down Lucas again beside Eryn and hurried to the newcomers, looking from Alex to Bianca frantically. "You've finally finished…! Oh, Bianca, I wanted to thank you for keeping Lucas and Eryn from—"

Bianca's ghost held up her hands in an 'x' shape. "No, no, no! That's okay…! One of them is my Spirit Son, so it was my job. Please don't make a big deal out of it."

I stared at her. "Make a big deal out of…? Bianca, you saved the next heirs of Death and Dream!" I pulled her ghost in for a strong embrace, her misty skin rippling under my touch like chilled water droplets. "You saved *my son…!* You may not think much of it, but it means *everything* to me…!"

When I drew her at arms' length, the specter looked ripe to blush, and I didn't doubt she would have, had she been in her vessel.

I paused, looking at Alex. "Hang on. You haven't resurrected her yet?"

Alex's eye twitched as he glared at my soul-touching hands, which still held Bianca's arms. He looked down at Bianca's body that he carried, envy burdening his features. "I… need Xavier to attach her soul…" His lips pulled into a grimace. "And… I don't think I'm quite ready to… to use my Hallows on her and…"

Bianca's ghost peeled away from my hold and floated beside him, motioning to touch his shoulder. The action phased through without contact.

Alex looked at her, his gaze sorrowed. Then he cleared his throat before nodding to me. "I… I'd hoped you could help resurrect her instead… since Xavier is…" His eyes misted. He squeezed his lids shut and drew in a calming breath. "Since Xavier is gone."

The reminder had my fox ears grow. "We'll find him," I assured, gesturing to our Dreamcatchers on the chairs. "They're searching for him in Aspirre, in case he's been trapped in there and can't get out. We can't find Chai, so following *him* is out of the question, so the best we can do is search the Dream realm. There's no telling what happened after he and Macarius vanished in there, we need to find him before something *worse* happens and—"

"That's not what I meant, Willow."

His gruff tone made me pause. I glanced back at him, puzzled. "You think he made it back out to the physical plane?" I asked.

He looked at Bianca, hesitant. My nerves screamed at that look. Why was his expression so pale…? What did that mean?

After a long, tortuous moment, Alex laid Bianca's body gently over the rug. Then he hung his head. "Willow…" He tried to go on. Pursed his lips as if pained. Then sighed. "Xavier is dead."

The entire library fell silent. Matthiel and Aster ceased their Necrovoking lesson to turn to us. Herrin and Marian stilled their quills, their wings falling to the rug. The warmth of the hearth chilled.

"Wh… what…?" My voice was so detached, I could scarcely believe it had spilled from my own lips.

Alex chewed each word with guttural care as he repeated, "Xavier is dead." He wiped a quick arm over his eyes when they yielded to fresh tears. "I… I'm sorry. I felt it after we fled from the Relic. I didn't know how to tell you, I…" His voice fell to a whisper, "I'm sorry…"

My body was ice. It didn't belong to me anymore. In the choking silence, the grandfather clock along the wall chimed the night's third hour, its soft rings deafening in the dense quietness.

"But." Alex sniffed and went on, "There's still a chance Macarius didn't destroy his soul. If we can find his body out there somewhere, we'll know for certain if we can save his soul—"

SMACK!

I struck his cheek with such fury, his head ripped away in a startled jerk, and I didn't care that my fingers stung like Void.

"*He. Isn't. Dead.*" My throat clicked, gaze curdling with such hatred, I thought my soul's fire would roast them to ash in their sockets. I hissed, "Do you take me for a fool…? Have you already forgotten the years you and I *both* spent listening to everyone who insisted Xavier was dead the last time he disappeared—only to learn that he was alive?"

Alex ground his teeth, holding a tender hand to his reddened cheek. He kept his tone even. "This time is different. I know what I felt—"

"Then you're disgracefully mistaken." My tone twisted vindictively. "Xavier *always* comes back. Alive. Were I you, I'd focus my efforts on keeping watch for his soul *inside* you again—"

"*HE IS DEAD, WILLOW!*" Alex roared, and his hands burst with green flames. They only lasted seconds, but it was enough to heat my face before they puffed into wavering smoke between his clenching fingers. He puffed hard, shutting his eyes and trying to calm again. Then, after several moments of deep breathing, he hushed, "It doesn't matter if you believe me or not. It won't change anything… either way, I have to find him." He opened his eyes again and looked at me with a new, heartbreaking expression. "Will you help me bring him back?"

My eyes welled. I blinked them away quickly, shoving down the twisting pain strangling my heart and gave a defiant growl, "Of course I'll help bring him back… *alive.*" I whirled away and went to pick up Lucas from the floor, cradling him with quivering arms. "I'll just have to prove it myself when we find him… you'll feel like such a fool…"

Alex said nothing behind me.

I held Lucas tighter, hoping to squeeze away the fear pulling at my lungs. The pup giggled and nuzzled my throat, blissfully unaware of the foreboding situation that surrounded him.

"—Willow?"

I nearly yelped in fright when my mother's hand suddenly clasped my shoulder. She was standing beside me now. When had she awoken?

"Willow," my mother said, concern tugging the crow's feet at her sharp eyes. "We've found something in Aspirre."

Hope swelled, and I set down Lucas at my feet. "Something of Xavier's?" I asked. "Can we use it to Scry his whereabouts?"

"We hope so," Mother agreed. "We found his crown. But because it came into Aspirre with him physically, we cannot return it to this plane without the Orb of the Present. My attempts at any Scrying have proven useless, also. I can't get a single vision out of it."

From my peripherals, I noticed Alex glance away. But he knew better than to say a Gods damned word, it seemed.

Mother nodded past me, looking at Aster. "We wondered if Aster would be willing to come into Aspirre and try his hand at Scrying…? Considering his specialty is prophetic Hallows…"

Aster's meercat ears folded to his neck meekly. "M… me?" He asked, pointing to his chest. "But I'm a Necrofera… we can't enter Aspirre?"

Mother's head wavered. "You can, actually. But only if a Somniovoker brings you there." She waved for Aster to come. "If you wouldn't mind? It will only be a few moments of your time."

Aster sheepishly rose to his feet and made his way over. "U-uh… sure. Okay…"

Alexander left Bianca's ghosts to join Aster, announcing gruffly, "I'll come as well. My prophetic Hallows may not be as strong, but he's *my* brother. I might have a better connection to his corpse."

My anger flared back tenfold. "He is *not* a corpse!" I sneered, stepping beside them. "That's it! I'm coming in there as well. Matthiel?" I whipped my gaze at Matthiel, who promptly fumbled to salute from the short table beside the Enlighteners as I said, "Please watch the children while we're gone. It won't be long."

Matthiel's grey face blanched, but he managed to sputter an affirmative, "Y-yes, Your Majesty…!"

Alexander and I exchanged sharp glares, then joined my mother in taking a seat in whichever empty chairs we could find around the hearth. She herself sat beside a skittish Aster, keeping her hand around his as we all evoked our sleep Hallows, our hands glittering with azure lights that we brought to our brows…

And the crackling embers dimmed into silence as we put ourselves to sleep.

My eyes pried open.

I was in a very different version of the royal library: the version I knew to be Aspirre's parallel. My grandfather and his knights had spent two thousand years creating structures that matched the physical plane, but I was well acquainted with how difficult it was to keep each and every room updated with the constantly-changing architecture.

There were still bookshelves here, and an empty hearth, tables and chairs and couches scattered about...

And surrounding one of those tables were the familiar faces of Yulia, Jimmy, and my grandmother Crysa.

Bright, azure lights suddenly gleamed around me. Then the others from the physical plane appeared. Alex was the first to solidify, opening his eyes and finding me beside him. My mother came with Aster—whose white-pupiled eyes bulged as he looked round this eerily quiet library. I presumed this must have been the demon's first time being conscious of his residence in Aspirre. Most shifters weren't aware of their soul's visitations, since they were typically dreaming. This was different—we had entered with the intent of wandering this plane. It gave us the means to dream lucidly.

Once we were all present, we joined the others around the table.

Xavier's silver skull-crown lay on its surface like a shimmering centerpiece. He'd been wearing it when he vanished here with Macarius. I could only assume it had fallen during whatever struggles they engaged in.

I picked up the crown and hesitated before handing it to Aster.

"Find him," I pleaded, then stepped back to give the oracle space.

Aster held the crown with care, gripping the headpiece with one hand while he seized Alexander's shoulder with the other.

"Okay..." Aster began. "Here goes nothing..."

He drew in a long, slow breath.

Then he became the epitome of absolute stillness. The Crest on his back gleamed with a blue light, and his eyes glazed over distantly.

I waited with splitting nerves, the silence fueling my anxiety the longer Aster stood there, utterly motionless.

Then, at long, long last, Aster blinked.

I could barely contain my impatience. "Well? Have you found him?"

Aster licked his lips. "Sort of... He was able to steal the Orb of Present back from Macarius before escaping outside to the physical plane. I don't know where he is exactly... but it's somewhere east of the mountain where the Relic was."

I blew out a relieved breath. "Oh, thank the Seamstress and Her holy spindle...!"

"—uh, well, hang on," Aster interrupted. He ducked his head and fiddled with the crown as if to distract himself. "There's something else... at the last place I See before everything goes dark is... um..." His tone drained. "He may have gotten the

Orb away from Macarius, but…" He cast me a pitying, sorrowed gaze. "I'm sorry. Alex was right."

My cheer snuffed into smoke. "No… No, please…"

Aster shook his head and sighed, "Xavier really is… dead."

41

THE CORPSE OF A KING

ASHYA

In the jaws of the fire, laid across the Death Palace's spired rooftops that suffocated with smoke, my sister's corpse hissed with black mist. It rose from my sister's scaled pores, her skin dissolving as her rotted soul was sent to Nira.

I hid behind one of those spires atop a nearby tower, glaring at her killers: The azure-haired princess... and the ashen-haired prince.

"Charra..." I hissed as my vision flecked with tears, my sister's corpse flaking away and turning to bare bones over the rooftop. The two royals shared a loving embrace over their victim's remains, and my fangs dripped with venom.

I was stirred awake within my gleaming, Crystal Caverns by the hefty Weight of a fellow Ancient Necrofera.

"La'Lunaî the Little?" I greeted curiously. I found the little Seadragon girl standing behind me, her scaled hands on her hips as if she'd waited for me to awaken for some time. "Why, it has been some time since you graced my caverns... to what do I owe the pleasure?"

"No pleasure," La'Lunaî dismissed, getting right to the matter. "I am in need of the Grim Sisters' assistance... where is Charra?"

The mention of my sister's name made my fangs unfold in a vicious hiss. "She was slain..." Venom leaked from my glands. "By the royal Death family."

La'Lunaî's face wrenched with shock. "Charra...? But she was always so careful—especially after our last revolution?"

My tone curdled into a sneer. "She thought she'd found a way to kill them without raising their alarms… but she let her ambition blind her." My hands balled with fury. "One day, La'Lunaî, I *will* see the Death family exterminated. As they continue to exterminate *us*."

La'Lunaî's lips rolled with a pleased smile. "Well, Ashya, I do believe that day has come. I descended to your caverns to ask for your assistance in bringing down that very family. But this time, I've made a few allies…"

She reached back a hand and curled her fingers—and with the motion, a golden-haired viper woman came hurtling *into* her hand by the throat.

This new woman's eyes gleamed with white pupils. It was a newborn Necrofera… and a *Relicblood* of Land, at that?

La'Lunaî tossed the bright-haired viper before her feet, the Seadragon's smile stretching hungrily. "And those allies have gifted you a most curious welcoming gift."

TAYMEN

As the Floating Lights glittered overhead in these weird cavern mists, Syreen and I crept down the east mountains of Low Neverland. It took three Bloody days after the clash at the colosseum to find an opportunity like this, but we finally had time to sneak away from the rest of the nest after they'd gone to sleep for the morning.

Well, I assumed it was morning. It was hard to tell without a sun, but Grim's Lights went through different stages of brightness, so I've been able to tell the difference through that. At night, they fall to a dim bluish glow. In the morning, like now, they started brightening to a slightly whiter gleam. They were actually really pretty, to be honest. Wish I could have appreciated it more, if I wasn't scared out of my damn skin right now. I hoped to Gods La'Lunaî's Mark in my head wouldn't tip her off that Syreen and I were going all the way out here.

But we had to risk it.

We'd been so close to meeting with the Death King in person—so close to Syreen's brother, Hugh—but we hadn't been fast enough. La'Lunaî gave the order to retreat before we could find them again… and before those other Ancients could extract her Mark and free us.

If we could find them before La'Lunaî woke up and noticed we were out here, maybe we still had a chance at freedom.

As we stepped into a thicket of willow trees, I twisted back nervously, checking for the dozenth time to make sure none of the other demons followed us.

"A-are you sure we can make it all the way back there fast enough?" I asked Syreen, my lion ears folded down shakily.

Syreen kept her eyes forward, her scarred face set in a deep snarl. "Rumor has it, La'Lunaî is busy meeting with another Ancient miles off from the nest. Even if she does notice we're gone, she should be too preoccupied with that to care about two newborns. If we're dragged back, we'll tell her we were hungry and went searching for food."

The reminder of hunger made my stomach growl miserably. I groaned, "Bloods, I haven't eaten since we left the colosseum… If we're going to get our freedom and find your brother again, let's hope they'll let us have some actual food and…" I trailed off, my nose picking up a scent.

A *delicious* scent.

Syreen must have smelled it, too, because her head perked just like mine did.

"No way…!" My mouth watered, and we both drifted through the forest toward the source of the smell. It was the irresistible scent of decaying flesh and rotting meat. "It's… it's got to be a corpse…!" I said, already drooling as we got closer. "Oh my Gods, someone must have hiked out here and keeled over…! We lucked out—!"

Craaaaw!

We flinched at the grating croak. Our heads snapped down.

There was a raven there. It had a scar running down its right eye, flapping its wings at us threateningly as it balanced itself on a glittering, azure ball.

"Ba-*ck!*" the raven screeched at us and flared its neck feathers in warning. "Ba-*ck!* Aw-*ay! Mine! Mine!*"

I frowned. "A raven?"

Syreen's brow furrowed. "Then… it was a Reaper who died out here?"

"Why would a Reaper be way out here?" I questioned. Then I thought about it and muttered, "actually, why would *anyone* be way out here? We're still miles off from the nearest city."

The raven kept shrieking at us, wobbling on the azure ball protectively. Weird bird. Did it think that thing was its egg or something—?

"Land's Blade…!" Syreen gasped beside me, throwing a hand in front of me to block my way.

"What?" I asked, following her shocked gaze.

Behind the raven, I barely saw the source of the scent: a slumped over corpse curled on its side.

The brightening lights overhead speared through the forest's canopy and speckled the body's grey skin and silken, ebony clothing. There was a huge hole jutting from his ribs, crusted with dried blood and festering with squirming maggots. Flies zipped around him as ants marched over his face, the bugs crawling in his shoulder-length, shadowy hair that was tangled over the dirt. I had to stretch to my toes to get a look at the man's face, his long bangs tossing and turning in the cavern winds.

It was a face I knew.

"Bloods!" I cried, running over to the corpse—ignoring the screeching raven who fluttered its wings at me furiously.

I turned the body over, examining him frantically.

It *was* him! The Death King I saw in the colosseum…!

"What in Land is *he* doing here?!" I demanded and hurried to grab his stiff arms to drag him out of here. "Shel Almighty, we have to get him back home…! His wife better not blame us for this, I swear to Bloods…!"

—Something squirmed under my fingers, making me yelp and drop the king on the forest floor with a *thump*. Syreen and I stood over him cautiously.

His skin leaked with throbbing, black veins. They pulsed and quaked over his flesh, squirming like worms from the hole in his chest—frightening the maggots out of there—as they trickled up toward his face and poured into his closed eyes. With a disgusting slurp, they vanished under his lids.

Lids which cracked open to show two shining, white pupils.

42

AWAKENING

XAVIER

My eyes split open.

It was unbelievably painful. My lids screamed the wider they unfastened, and my blurred vision twirled along with my churning stomach.

I groaned, feeling for the ground under me and pushed to sit up. But that only made my vision spin faster, and the sloshing sickness bubbled in my gut, spiked up my throat and…

I lurched on all fours. Vomited in a burning retch. The bile was a horrid mixture of maggots, writhing centipedes, and rancid stomach acid. I panted over the mess, thankful the sickness had dwindled—

The stomach acid suddenly blackened over the wriggling insects between my hands, like boiling tar. Then the tar dripped off the insects and slithered into a single mass over my fingers, creeping up my arm. I gave a disgusted yelp, trying to fling the muck off, but it clung to me like a living creature all its own.

Then it crawled over my lips and seeped between my teeth—pouring back into my throat.

As it slid down my esophagus, I gagged, the taste as grotesque and sour as the first time. Nothing I did ejected the wretched bile. It didn't cease its course until the muck was back where it had come from, safely bubbling in my stomach and leaving me clutching a hand to my mouth in moaning agony.

Then a line of ants crept over my fingers. I hurried to wipe them off. There were apparently *more* ants scurrying over my face and I slapped them away in disgust, desperately ruffling them out of my tangled hair. Some of them managed to sneak into my mouth and nose, and the muck in my belly lurched out of me a second time—only to slurp back *into* me as it had done the first time, prying a squelching air bubble from my scratchy throat.

"—that'll pass in a bit," a young man's voice sounded over me. "It takes time to get all the bugs out."

I flinched back, nearly falling over before I slammed my elbows on the dirt to catch myself.

The young man looking down at me had blond hair and glowing, white pupils. He raised pacifying hands and said, "Take it slow, okay? The Change can be pretty rough for some of us. I know *I* had a hard time when I first Changed myself."

I gulped down breaths, my voice a pained rasp. "Ch-Ch… Changed…?"

He gave a nervous laugh. "You'll get used to it. Trust me. But right now, we should hurry and bring you home."

"—We can't bring him back like this," a woman's voice crunched behind me.

I whirled, finding the lion-eared woman with cropped, blonde hair. She had a scar running down her lips and chin, her piercing olive eyes casting me a vile glower.

There was something familiar about her. Something *dangerously* familiar…

—I tried to pull away from her invading lips, but the vines strangling my neck pulled me back to her face like elastic, my skin flinching as her unwelcomed fingers traced my chest, my shouts drowned by her exploring tongue—

"Y-y-you…!" I scuttled away from her, my wolf ears growing, memory racing back the longer I looked at her face. "You're that… that insane queen…!"

The woman—Syreen, as I suddenly remembered—rolled her eyes. "I was *ambitious*, yes, but I should think 'insane' is a bit of an exaggeration."

The young man beside me furrowed his brow at the woman. "What exactly did you do to him when you were alive?"

Syreen wafted a flippant hand in the air. "I may have tried to make a consort of him and his brother. I was in my rights to do so, as queen, but they weren't very accommodating."

I gawked at her, anger flaring. "Accommodating?! You tried to *rape* us! I was engaged…!" I stopped.

Engaged? That did feel right… and yet…

"Who was I engaged to…?" I murmured broodingly. My head throbbed with an ache, and I clutched my brow. "Why can't I… remember…?"

I strained to pull the memory out of my foggy mind, but all that came were fragmented pieces. A flash of long, ashen hair… marble skin as soft as a lily… a warm chuckle from lips that burned over mine, steam rising between our shared flesh as I held her and whispered in her ear…

Myel Ma Amya, Willow…

"Willow…?" The name danced on my tongue as naturally as a breath. That must have been her name. It felt right, my heart filling with unrivaled bliss to merely speak it.

But why couldn't I remember her face…?

The young man bent to offer me a hand. "Don't worry about it too much. I can go into Aspirre and look for some of your memories, but it might be faster if you see your family directly."

"I… I have a family…?" I dazedly took his hand, allowing him to pull me to my wobbling feet.

The faint giggle of a baby hit my memory. Then that giggle changed into terrified screeches, the baby crying for its mother, smoke and green flames raging around us. An azure Orb rolled beside my field of vision, and I reached for it the same moment a scaled hand grabbed it and—

"The Orb…!" Panic flooded, and I whipped my gaze around the terrain. "Seamstress Cleanse me, where is the Orb—?!"

Craaaww!

I turned toward the low croak.

A raven with a scar running down its right eye was staring at me. It flapped its wings and screeched, but never once moved from the azure Orb it was perched atop.

"Chai…!" I hurried to the raven—who I instantly remembered when my soul pulled tightly, our Bond pulsing as I knelt to my messenger. "Oh, thank Death you're here…"

Chai nuzzled my thinly bearded jaw with his beak, croaking in saddened whines. He hopped off the Orb and alighted on my shoulder, his talons' grip light and gentle.

"Were you protecting this for me, Chai?" I asked, scratching under his beak appreciatively. I plucked the Orb from the dirt and rose to my feet, examining the glittering sphere. It didn't have a scratch on it. This was a resilient little thing, wasn't it?

I paused when the Orb reflected my chest.

My grotesque, *blood-caked* chest, my scarred flesh coagulated and shredded around a hideous wound that gleaned through a tear in my silken doublet.

I dropped the Orb with a *thunk!*

"What in Death…?!" I feverishly touched the scarred wound. The memory of an icy blade piercing through my ribs came surging back, infectious veins pouring into my chest… I had gotten away, escaped through Aspirre and came out here in this forest…

Where I died.

"I…" My weak legs gave way and I sank to my knees. Chai hopped off my shoulder and fluttered onto the Orb again protectively. I clutched my ripped-up chest, a hollow pit twisting my soul. "I'm… dead…"

Yet I was still here. Which meant… I'd become a Necrofera? A demon…?

I was sure the infection would destroy my soul, I thought with shuddered breaths, *Had I Healed it in time after all…?*

Wait. Healed? That didn't seem right. I was a Necrovoker, wasn't I? At least, that's what I remembered… half a Necrovoker.

I turned my left hand, staring at a Crest of three, black diamonds under my knuckles. *My Evocator's mark…* Hesitant, I experimentally evoked an element of Hallows that *wasn't* Necrovoking. My hands glittered with emerald light, my Crest changing into a crowned Ocean mark. My frosted soul suddenly warmed as the coldness poured out of my hand, crystalizing over my palm in the shape of an icy candle-lily.

"Bloods…" I dismissed the Hallows, and the ice-lily dropped into my palm. "How did I…?"

"What do we do with him now?" Syreen demanded behind me. "We can't bring him back like this. Do you have any idea what his wife would do to us if she thought we were responsible?"

The young man protested, "W-Well, he can just explain it himself! What if she rewards us for bringing him back?"

"Yes," Syreen drawled in a sarcastic growl, "I'm sure the Queen of Death, whose duty is to exterminate all demons, will shower us with a hero's medal and a fine banquet for delivering a *demon Death King.*"

"But she's giving demons citizenship now…! Things will be different—!"

"Wait," I interrupted them, twisting to the two in confusion. "What do you mean 'Death King'?"

Syreen clapped a hand over her eyes with a groan. "Oh, we're doomed. He doesn't even remember who he is."

The young man sputtered, "H-he will! He just needs a reminder!" He shuffled over to me, crouching to meet my gaze. His smile was desperate. "H-hey, so, um! Do you remember your name, at least?"

I frowned. Oddly, I did not. As much as I strained to think of it, the syllables slipped away each time.

"—*Xavier!*" Chai suddenly blurted in a scratchy croak, wobbling on the Orb at my feet. "*Craaaaww! XAVIER!*"

I scratched the thin hairs at my jaw—grimacing when I pulled out an ant carcass. "Ah, right… thank you, Chai." I turned to the young man. "It's Xavier."

He let out a relieved laugh. "Okay, good! My name's Taymen, by the way. We kind of met a few days ago, but um… well, you probably don't remember that either." The young man, Taymen, turned to Syreen with a smug grin. "See, Sy? He remembers enough."

My gaze narrowed at Taymen. "What did you call her…?"

Taymen looked puzzled at me. "Huh?"

"That nickname, what you called her…" My head throbbed with nostalgia. "*Sy*… I think… I think I knew someone else who called her that—*huah*!"

Syreen grabbed my doublet's collar and yanked me up, bringing me face to face with her enraged scowl. "Do you speak of my brother?!" She demanded. "My Hugh?! Was he your vassal?! Do you remember him—?!"

"Stay away from me!" I shoved her back, my Hallows igniting on instinct.

Violet lights glittered from my hands as they *slammed* into her chest, causing her skin to squirm with black sludge, her body locking in place as the tendrils quivered and writhed in fright.

When I was free of her, I scuffled behind Taymen, *not* comfortable being so close to her after what she did to me.

She stood there, rigid, until the black worms slithered back into her skin and disappeared. She stared at me, her eyes pried open in utter shock.

"What…" She began breathlessly. "What did you just…? I-I couldn't move… Only La'Lunaî has ever…"

"—Oh, my," a husky voice purred from the misted forest suddenly.

We all turned to the woman who hid in the shadows. When she stepped into the slitted rays of the brightening lights above the forest canopy, I found myself staring at a thick woman with reptilian scales. Her long hair was braided in a multi-layered plait that wavered at her ankles, and long fangs bowed from her mouth as she gave a playful smile.

"Three little newborns, wandering my territory?" She hissed, her white pupils gleaming with delight. She lifted a hand, clenching it into a fist.

—An invisible weight crushed me to the ground, like a boulder slamming over my chest and forcing my legs to buckle and collapse.

I was pinned on my back, my ribs cracking in agony. My flattened lungs ripped a horrendous scream as black sludge trembled from my skin. The pain squeezed every inch of my writhing body, the worms tugging at my rotted soul without mercy.

Syreen and Taymen had dropped to either side of me as well, struggling to get free. After a few moments, however, a sliver of black sludge glopped from their brows defiantly, and the two stopped their struggling. They were suddenly fine, and scrambled to their feet and cowered behind a drooping tree.

Why are THEY suddenly unaffected? I thought bitterly, a scream tearing from my choking throat again, the Weight crushing me harder as the viper woman stalked toward me.

"How intriguing…" she cooed. "Two of you have been Marked already…" She cocked her head and glanced over a shoulder. "Are they yours, La'Lunaî?"

A second figure stepped into the spotted light. It was a little girl with webbed ears and smooth scales, her emerald hair holding the texture of fins as she flipped it with a scoffing hand and huffed, "Yes, these two are mine, Ashya. What they're doing here, however, is another question."

Taymen and Syreen cowered behind their tree.

Taymen quaked with fright. "W-w-we were just… u-um… hungry, Mistress!"

"Yes, starving!" Syreen agreed in a squeak. "W-we smelled a corpse out here and-and-and… and we found, um… this newborn…"

The little fish girl, La'Lunaî, crouched over me with an inspecting hum. Every cell in my body shrieked for me to flee—but I couldn't move. The Weight of that viper woman pinned me like a feral crab under a mountain, my rotted insides crumpled as I wheezed in pain.

La'Lunaî snatched a tuft of my bangs and *yanked* them upward so hard, I was shocked they didn't rip off my scalp. Her scrutinizing gaze narrowed as she inspected my eyes—then she gasped.

"It's *you*…!" She quivered with entertained cackles. "Artist sink me…! It's that *freak* twin with all the Hallows…!" She released my hair, causing my head to *thud* back to the dirt with a dull ache. "Oh, the Gods have smiled upon me this day…! Where is your brother, freak twin?! Not here to save your corpse from rotting?! What a shame…!"

She fell into a fit of uncontrollable laughter. The viper who had me pinned cocked an eyebrow at the little demon girl. "La'Lunaî, do you know this newborn?"

"Oh, do I know him!" La'Lunaî's teeth were sharp when she smiled. "And you'll simply adore this, Ashya. Our lost little corpse here?" She kicked my skull, pain spearing at my temple and pulling a yell from me. "He's the Bloody *Death King!* Oh, I couldn't ask for such divine poetry…!"

Ashya tilted her head, looming over me with more interest.

"Is he now?" Her fist squeezed tighter, and the Weight crushing me mimicked the action. She purred a chuckle. "Well, well, well… quite the luck we've run into, haven't we?" She crouched down and reached a hand to my head—

Then she *skewered* her finger into my skull, digging deeper until her knuckle touched my forehead.

Agony splintered as a thick glob of black sludge poured out of her finger and rooted into my brain. I thrashed to get away, powerless under her as I screamed until my throat went raw.

"You will be a most useful toy in this war…" The viper woman traced my jaw with a tender finger. "Oh, but I cannot wait to see the Death Queen's face when she sees you…" Her lips tugged with a fang-filled grin above me, her chuckles curdling. "Before you kill her."

43

SEARCH PARTY

WILLOW

The Weeping Woods had never been so loathsome.

My white-and-grey spotted mare sluggishly clopped through the fog, dragging me under a veil of drooping branches.

To either side of me, Alexander and Aster rode on their own horses, their gazes turning in every direction as they searched the woods with ferocious intent. On Alexander's shoulder was his messenger raven, Mal, who turned his beak just as determinedly as his Reaper, keeping alert.

Only three Ancients accompanied us today. Cilia walked on foot ahead of us, Hecrûshou behind, and Thörd soared above us to search from a higher vantage.

Three of the twins' vassals, Hugh, Vendy, and Dalen, all rode on a soaring Flamedragon above us. The dragon was slender and long, his scales a marbled red-and-black. His serrated snout was as long as a swordfish and his leathery wingspan as wide as a small tree, his barbed tail dragging beneath him limply.

This was my father's Flamedragon, Raavith. The poor dragon hadn't been himself, since my father's passing. We brought him back with us to Grim, but he never seemed quite in a mood for flying anymore. I thought taking him out here would help his mood. Thus far, it wasn't helping mine.

From atop my mount, I spotted a large boulder by a nearby stream. It had the potential of hiding a shifter, I supposed. I steered my horse toward it, my heart pounding.

But after peering behind, I was disappointed yet again.

I loosened my breath and pulled the horse's reins away from the boulder, resuming the search.

As a child, I remembered many days spent venturing this mystical forest with my father in the Bright Light hours of autumn. In my adolescence, I would ride beside Lilli, Alexander and Xavier on horseback, wasting the day in the streams that latticed through the woods...

Streams that my horse now crossed with cold splashes, their once cheerful nostalgia now replaced with bitter resentment.

These were no longer the woods of my childhood.

These were the woods where my husband died.

My grown fox ears curled, tears threatening to sting again, but I blinked them back. *Dead or not,* I reminded ruefully, my heart twisting into a sickened pit of misery. *I will find him.*

It had been three days since he disappeared; since Alex told us of his death. There was a chance Macarius didn't destroy his soul, though. If that was the case, then today would be the day Xavier would Change into a Necrofera... if we didn't find him in time to reap his soul.

Xavier, if you've rotted, I don't care anymore. The thought weighed down my soul. *Just come home...*

"Are you certain it was this far out?" Alexander questioned to my left. I turned to see he was looking at Aster, his tone impatient. "We're miles from Low Rastiria already. Are you sure we aren't lost?"

Aster ducked his head. "We're not lost. It's just, you know, all these trees look the same so it's kinda hard to tell which section to look in and..."

Rrrrrrrmmmmm...

The ground shivered under us suddenly. It was a deep, hollow vibration, causing our horses to chuff nervously.

My teeth sharpened. "Another Groundquake..."

RRRRRRRRRrrrrrmmmm...

Another tremor rumbled beneath us, the horses whinnying with growing fright. I patted my mount's neck, and Alexander pulled on his stallion's reins to steady the beast.

When the quakes dimmed at last, Alex seemed disturbed as he growled, "This many in only a few days is worrying."

My own fears bloomed, and I shushed my horse with a worried breath, "Could it be the Gods...? Could Nira be sustaining damage from the Noctis Golems, as She explained...?"

—Mal suddenly perked from Alexander's shoulder. The raven fluttered its wings, screeching and taking flight, veering left.

Alex kicked his horse after him. "He feels something...! Follow Mal!"

My pulse raced with hope, whipping my horse into a gallop to keep pace with the raven. Mal flew to a tall, hollow tree stump. His talons gripped the bark's ledge, pieces flaking off as he croaked down into the hollow.

A replying screech answered him from within.

"It must be Chai!" I cried, dismounting and running over to look inside the hollow.

As I suspected, Chai sat in there, fluttering his wings when he saw my face peering down at him.

"Chai…!" I reached in to pick him up gently. "Thank Death, at least we've found *you*…" I trailed off, seeing something glint in the hollow. Chai had been hiding something. That must have been why he didn't simply fly out. After setting Chai over my shoulder, I reached inside once more. "What is this…?"

My fingers pulled out a glittering, azure Orb.

I gaped at it. "The Orb of the Present…!"

Alex trotted over, allowing Mal to perch on his shoulder, and his brow knitted at the globe I held. "Then, Xavier *did* steal it back from Macarius. Why didn't Chai bring it to us the moment he found it?"

I examined the Orb while turning it over, my hum brooding. "It must have been too smooth for his talons to grip…"

Chai gave an urgent croak from my shoulder. My own, tiny messenger, Jewel, fluttered down from the air and hopped onto Chai's back, twittering frantically at her larger mate, who croaked back in response. My Bond with Jewel suddenly pulled tight. She was worried. No, she was beyond worried—she was downright panicked.

"What is he telling you, Jewel?" I asked my Songcrow, dread festering as she kept our Bond taut with anxiety.

Alexander's face twisted into a scowl as Mal, too, flared his neck feathers the longer Chai croaked at them. "Something isn't right," Alex said, his wolf ears growing as he looked at Chai. "This isn't simply about Xavier's death, is it?"

"Was his soul destroyed?" I asked Chai desperately. "Did Macarius use his Infeciovoking…?"

"Wr-*ong*…!" Chai screeched from my shoulder. "Wr-*ong*…! Demon! De*mon! Wr-ong…!*"

"Demon…" I whispered in a breathless echo. Tears hit so suddenly, I hadn't time to will them back. "Nira be praised… I-I can have him back…"

Never in my life had news of a demon brought me such absolute joy.

"—So, where is he?" Aster questioned, bursting my brief moment of relief. The skeletal Sentient scratched his head, glancing round the forest. "If he's already Changed, and his raven's here… shouldn't *he* be here, too?"

He had a point. I searched the terrain, hoping to find his shadow hiding behind one of the veiling branches of willow trees surrounding us. Could he be watching us now? If he was a demon, he surely lost his memories. Our presence here may have frightened him.

"Xavier!" I called into the mist. Nothing stirred save for a stray butterfly that fluttered over a grove of candle-lilies. "Xavier, are you out there? It's your family…!"

Chai suddenly flew off my shoulder. He flapped farther down and croaked, as if telling us to follow him. I hurried after the bird, Alexander and Aster at my heels.

Chai flapped down to a patch of dirt, bobbing his beak over a wide, splotchy pool of what could only be dried blood. Strangely, a cluster of squirming maggots and centipedes writhed over the crusted patch. Half the insects were curled up dead, and the others seemed to be on their way shortly.

"Aster!" I shouted back.

The demon ran beside me and crouched over the patch of blood. He grimaced at the scuttling insects. "Gross… Is this where he died?"

Alexander shot him a flat glare. "Why don't you tell us, *oracle*?"

Aster gave a disgusted look. "I'm not touching that—"

"Oh, yes you are!" I snatched his wrist and shoved his hand into the blood-stained dirt and insects. He gagged, but I kept a firm grip of his wrist, snarling, "*Where is he?*"

Aster shuddered, shutting his eyes. "U-Um, okay…! Let's see… He woke up… had some serious Changing sickness… Man, I feel you, buddy—oh, *gross!* He threw up the bugs! Ew, ew, ew, ew, ew—!"

"Get on with it!" I snapped, pushing his hand down harder and squashing the insects under his palm. "Where. Did. He. *Go?*"

He whimpered, his meercat ears growing and folding to his neck. "All right, all right… uhm, so after that… He ran into two other demons—wait! I know one of them!"

My blood ran cold. "Was it La'Lunaî?"

He hummed, keeping his lids closed as he concentrated. "No. It's that kid from the colosseum. The Somniovoker."

Alexander's brow scrunched. "The one who asked about Hugh?"

"Yeah, him. And there's some lioness there with him. Short hair, a scar on her lips. Oh—Xavier knows her! He called her Syreen."

My expression soured. "Of course *she* would be the one to find him…" I pushed my thumbs into my lids with a long, exhale. "Wonderful… I suppose she stole him, then? It wouldn't be the first time…"

That bitch had tried to claim the twins as her consorts before the war in Neverland broke. I fondly remember burning an entire wing of her palace to a crisp when I caught her tongue-deep in Xavier's suffocating mouth.

My soul's fire crackled at the memory. "I swear to Bloods, if I she's taken advantage of him as a newborn, I will *not* have mercy left to spare her rotten soul…"

Aster frowned, his eyes still closed. "No, wait. They're talking about bringing him back home. Sounds like they're trying to run from La'Lunaî. Syreen's asking about… Hugh."

"—Who's asking about me?" the voice of Hugh called from above.

My father's Flamedragon soared down to us, landing on his haunches as he allowed the three vassals of Hugh, Vendy, and Dalen to hop off. They were all resurrected still, though we knew that, without Xavier, their revival would end in a matter of weeks. They decided to use the time they had left to help find their missing *Da'torr*.

As Hugh ran over, his messenger crow, Lady Lilac, flapped after him and latched onto his head. Hugh crouched beside me, his lion ears growing in concern. "What have you found?"

I shook my head. "Xavier's Changed into a Necrofera. Your sister seems to have found him."

Hugh's eyes widened, and Lady cocked her head atop his blond hair. "Sy…? She's with Master?"

I rumbled, "It would seem so… though, the question now is where did they go?"

Aster's face wrinkled. "Oh, Bloods… that isn't good."

"What?" I asked. "What do you See?"

"The three of them were found out by La'Lunaî. There's a new Ancient woman with her, some viper lady named Ashya." He finally opened his eyes and looked at me, a flash of terror overcoming his features. "She… she Marked him."

The warmth fled from my cheeks. "Great Mother Below…"

44

THE CRYSTAL CAVERNS

XAVIER

Rrrrrrrmmmmmm…

The Groundquake made me pause my forced trek through the woods. The Demon Queens and two newborns stopped as well, the lot of us staring at the dirt under our feet.

I twisted back toward the distant mountain range where I'd first Awakened. The tremor hadn't been terrible, but it was strong enough to cause a piece of the mountain's ledge to chip away and crumble into the forest.

"What in Bloods…?" I panted, my fogging breath curling from my lips—

"Keep moving, little newborn," the viper woman, Queen Ashya, huffed with a twirl of her scaled finger.

Crack went my knees as they buckled and snapped out of place, prying a scream from me as the limbs hurried to obey the command and marched themselves forward—bringing me with them.

I was forced to follow her through the forest for *hours.* Ashya shoved me into freezing streams, knocked me over rough boulders, kicked me up the jagged mountain pathways, and forced every limb in my body to bend to whatever new fickle desire crossed her cruel mind. My muscles ached. The trek had been treacherous. Any living shifter would have died from attempting it.

But I was no living shifter anymore, was I…?

Those two other demons followed us. Taymen and Syreen. The pair kept pace with us and cowered under the strict gaze of the little girl, La'Lunaî, who strode beside Ashya in blithe conversation.

The queens were speaking of some upcoming war against the Death family. They were still convinced I was the supposed king, but that couldn't be right. I certainly didn't feel like a king. It had to be a mistake.

"Great…" I heard Taymen hiss under his breath to Syreen beside me. "We spent all morning getting out of the nest, and now we're back where we started…"

Syreen chewed through clenched teeth. "Will you shut it? If they hear you, we'll be lucky if they don't shred our Seams into ribbons for sneaking off…"

We crested the mountain's next hill, and Ashya forced my legs to enter a wide cavern. I fumbled inside, nearly falling over the ledge of a steep drop as my feet slipped over…

Were these crystals?

Yes, where there should have been dirt and rock, the cavern was made of enormous, glowing-blue crystals. They jutted from the walls, they speared from the ceiling, they cascaded into natural pathways and bridges all through-out the entrancing hollow in sharp, jagged spires and glistening facets. The colossal gemstones under my feet were also lined with smaller crystals that were sharp enough to slice your finger open with a single touch and beautiful enough to entice you to try.

Spiritcrystal, I realized. *Pure, raw Spiritcrystal.*

Yet, despite the mesmerizing beauty of the hollow, much of their gleam-ing pathways—which spiraled down the entire length of the mountain—were blotted out by an uncountable horde of rotted, squirming Necrofera.

The enormous horde was scattered about the sparkling hollow. Although there were a knee-quaking number of demons below, none stirred from their slumber. Most were black-infested mongrels, all sleeping in stacked huddles along the larger crystals while only a few handfuls of the masses were snooz-ing Sentients.

So many demons… I knelt to the sparkling floor and cautiously gripped the ledge of the cliff. It was cold under my fingers. My flesh began to sink through it, misting like smoke into the ethereal Crystal.

Then my skin boiled into black globs around my fingernails. The tendrils peeled away from the Crystal and sent a chill running up my arm. My hand stayed atop the surface now, the Crystal resisting my touch this time.

But why? My long-term memory recalled how pure Spiritcrystal couldn't touch skin of any kind—living *or* dead.

But it can touch a soul, came the dawning afterthought. I stared at my hands with a gruesome understanding. *I'm a Necrofera. We're a merging of both vessel and soul…*

The Crystal may have wished to pass through my corpse, but the rotted soul alloyed with my flesh wouldn't allow it. That must be how the other demons could walk upon it without a problem. Any living shifter would fall through without footwear to serve as a barrier.

"Death…" I whispered, staggering back so I wouldn't fall over the ledge into the bright depths of the hollow. "Where… where are we…?"

Ashya clapped a scaled hand on my shoulder, spiking my rotten blood in a panic.

"Welcome to the nest, my newborn king." Ashya hissed in my ear. "Do make yourself comfortable."

She *shoved* me over the ledge.

I screamed as I dropped, my stomach lurching sick, the gleam of the crystals streaking my vision with blinding glares—

ShhhKTCH!

I landed on a thin, sharpened crystal, the spire piercing through my gut like a lance, a spurt of black blood spraying as my cries doubled.

Crack!

The spire broke apart under my weight as the sharp end was still lodged inside me, and I dropped farther—

Clunk! Crack! SPLICKT!

I rammed into every bulging crystal in my path, my skull crushed, my face scraped clean, my leg skewered and ripped off, until—

Crrrrriiiccccshh-CRUNCH!

I splattered onto the mountain's floor in a thousand mulchy chunks of meat. The Crystal spire still wedged in my gut shattered into smaller fragments. For what felt like a hundred lifetimes, I knew nothing but pure agony. My scattered chunks took their wretched time to slither back to me, every glopping worm latching onto my maimed joints in a slurp, snapping and squirming and breaking and cracking back into place as my broken skull crinkled back together with ripping throbs.

By the time I was whole again, the vibrant gleam of Spiritcrystals swirled nauseatingly. Above me were the bright, layered pathways where I'd dropped, the glare too blinding for me to see past them.

I groaned and pushed to all fours over the rough crystals, my sliced arms licking with blackened tendrils to heal. Bloods, that was torture… I was lucky as Death my Seam wasn't sliced on the way down. But at least it's over—

"Who's there?" A woman's voice called shakily behind me.

I scrambled back in a start, frantically searching for the source of the voice.

Then a scaled woman peered from behind a tall crystal jutting upward from the cavern's floor. I had to squint to see past the crystal's glare, but was able to spy a pair of gleaming, white pupils.

The woman blinked at me, her voice hushed. "You… I know you…"

I rubbed my eyes, trying to force my sight to adjust to the brightness of the Crystal cavern. Finally, after she had stepped out from behind the pillar, I could make out the woman's familiar, scaled figure, her golden hair wild and tangled.

That hair…

Memory leaked back in a tiny spurt. I knew someone with hair like that… but it wasn't this viper, was it? I remembered a golden-haired *lioness*, waiting beneath a colossal, glowing blossom in the center of a jungle… and I remembered her throat being slit by the viper woman now staring at me with shining, gold eyes.

I staggered back in a yelp, her name pushed from my lungs, "Genevieve…!"

Her breath stilled. "Yes… yes, that… that is my name, isn't it…?" She didn't sound sure.

It seems I'm not the only one who's lost their memory.

Her white pupils turned to slits as her lids narrowed at me. "You're… the Death King?"

I clutched my still-throbbing head in a moan. "I am *not* a king…"

—Master?

I leapt to my feet, searching the terrain for the boy who'd spoken. There was no one else in sight. Was he hiding behind another crystal?

I panted heavily, calling, "Wh… wh-who's there…?"

Master! The voice chimed again. He sounded so familiar, his words fuzzing like static in my head as if I were hearing him through my thoughts rather than my ears. *Master, it's me…! It's Hugh!*

"Hugh…?" The name did strike my memory. I think I may have had an apprentice with that name? And hadn't Syreen made mention of it earlier? I licked my lips, questioning, "Come out where I can see you."

I'm using our mental connection, the voice of 'Hugh' explained. *Do you not remember—?*

—Where are you, Da'torr?! A girl interrupted suddenly. Her voice split through my thoughts in a similar wave of static as the boy's. *It's Vendy! Remember? Your first vassal—!*

—Hey, don't ya forget about me, Da'torr, it's Dalen here, too—

—And ye can't tell me ye don't 'member ol' Nathaniel, Lad—

—Nor your favorite new vassal, Aiden, Young Sir—!

—Well, you might not have much reason to remember this old snake, but you surely remember my grandson, Jaq—?

"For the love of Death, will you all shut it!" I shouted over the voices, clutching my swelling head. "Bloods, how am I supposed to think with all of you speaking at once?"

Where are you? The voice of the girl—Vendy—questioned hurriedly.

Hugh asked after her. *We're trying to find you, but Aster can't See past your Awakening.*

I hadn't a damned clue who Aster was or what any of that meant, but I looked up at the Crystal cavern's maze-like pathways and bridges, shielding my eyes with a hand as the bright glare from above stung my retinas.

"I'm… in some sort of cave…?"

SLAM!

The ground behind me *cracked* with a vicious echo, crunching into a dense crater.

Within that crater rose Queen Ashya, whose white-glowing eyes stared at me in a crazed smile. In both hands, she clutched two *living* shifters by their necks, one man and one woman. They quaked under Ashya's grip, trying to squirm free, but nothing they did made her leaden fingers yield.

"Speaking to your vassals, Your Majesty Death?" Ashya hissed in a chuckle. "La'Lunaî warned me of your Hallows… And I do hate to interrupt your conversation, but I'm afraid I can't allow you to give our location away just yet."

Pain suddenly splintered in my brain. The Mark Ashya had latched in my head began to writhe, prying a scream from me.

Master?! The voice of Hugh shouted in my thoughts, but his words began to dim. *Master, can… hear…?*

My mind was filled with silence once more, and the Mark ceased its wriggling.

"There," Ashya sighed pleasantly. "Now we won't be rudely interrupted by any unwelcomed guests."

She tossed one of her captured shifters—the terrified woman—on the glowing floor in front of Genevieve. The frightened thing yelped when she fumbled on all fours like a feral crab, cowering under Genevieve's tight stare, frozen with fear.

"Breakfast, deary," Ashya sang to Genevieve.

Genevieve staggered back, sliding behind a crystal pillar in a shiver. She shook her head desperately.

Ashya quirked a black eyebrow. "No?" She stepped toward Genevieve, her fangs unfolding and grey scales growing prominent. "Dearest Genevieve… Must we continue this defiance even still?"

On her way to Genevieve, Ashya grabbed the frightened 'meal' by her hair and yanked her over the vibrant ground.

Ashya's tongue slit as she hissed, "Your mother did not gift you to me so you could starve yourself into weakness."

Ashya *ripped* off the living woman's arm in a gush of blood, screams tearing through the cavern. I cringed back in horror as Ashya shoved the dripping arm down Genevieve's protesting throat. "I am building an army," Ashya emphasized, "and I need my Sentients well fed in time for battle… I will not have you fall because you wouldn't *eat*."

Genevieve gagged and sobbed as Ashya fed her the rest of the woman, the grotesque pops and cracks and squelches forcing my wolf ears to grow and fold down in disgust. She pushed her Weight over Genevieve to force her to eat the woman's screaming soul last.

Then Ashya's gaze snapped to me. She tossed the living *man* she still held onto the crystal at my feet.

"Your turn, newborn," Ashya sighed.

Horrified, I craned my gaze to the tear-ridden man beneath me.

"P… p-p-please…" He squealed in a sob, the scent of urine swelling. "P-please, no… Just… just kill me first, please… I-I don't want to feel it…" He cupped his face in his shaking hands, blubbering. "I-I don't want to feel it…!"

My abhorrence had my face wrenched so drastically, I felt every muscle pulling out of place.

"I…" A furious growl clicked from my throat, my teeth sharpening as I glared at Ashya. Then, as if instinct had taken over, my hand flew toward a thin spire of Spiritcrystal, and I snapped off the sharpened tip and darted straight for the queen. "… will *not* kill a single shifter…!"

I hurled the broken crystal at Ashya's chest—

An invisible force knocked me back like a boulder, and I fumbled to the ground in a winded cough.

"You Reapers are always the most amusing to break," Ashya hummed.

I tried to push upright, but the Weight was too heavy. I was pinned in place, my head could hardly pry itself off the glowing floor.

Ashya strode toward me. She snagged the cowering man's neck and dragged him over. Then she reached out a hand and curled an egging finger at me.

My bones moved on their own, cracking out of their joints in a surge of black sludge, the pain searing as every tendon and ligament peeled at unnatural angles, forcing me to rise to my knees.

Ashya threw the man in front of me.

"Feast," she commanded, clenching her fingers to pry my head forward and forced my teeth to sharpen. She pulled her fist in a slow draw toward her own chest—prompting my teeth to hover over the man's neck. My tongue tasted his flesh, his pulse throbbing so intensely from his neck, I could feel every beating quiver.

And it tasted *delicious.*

Something deep within me yearned to taste the rest. The fragrant scent of a terrified soul filled my nostrils, so intoxicating, my mouth watered over the man's exposed throat, and I barely noticed my teeth closing in on their prey—

No...!

I pulled away from the man, feeling something in my rotten soul tear apart from Ashya's invisible hold, and scrambled backward.

Ashya's head cocked curiously. Then her eyes narrowed. "That's certainly new..." She grabbed the man's arm and yanked him toward me once more. "No matter. I can do it myself—"

"Stay *back!*" I shoved her away, evoking my death Hallows on instinct as violet lights poured out of my hands.

The lights hit Ashya with a shocking tremor, causing her to falter as she gasped and went rigid. For barely a second, she was stone-still, black sludge wriggling out of her skin in fright.

Her wide glare curdled at me, fangs dripping with venom as she gave an enraged hiss, "What *are* you?"

She stormed toward me again, and I shuffled back, scuttling behind a crystal pillar in hopes of shielding myself—

I slipped over the ledge of a deep pit that waited behind the pillar, and I tumbled down, *cracking* against the glowing floor, my neck breaking on impact. It took several dizzying moments for the bones to mend themselves with painful, slurping tendrils.

THUMP!

Ashya dumped the terrified man into the pit with me. His head splattered on the ground in a mess of crimson that stained the crystal's flawless gleam. The scent of blood permeated like sweet honey. My stomach moaned encouragingly, my teeth sharpening as I hovered over the fresh corpse with a dripping tongue that gravitated toward the promising meal...

I clamped my teeth shut, my gums shrieking in protest, and slapped a hand over my mouth as I backed against the smooth walls of the pit.

Ashya's melodic voice reverberated far above me, "Interesting... whatever you are, at least there is one thing you share with your fellow newborns." Her chuckles were an angelic sonnet, her smile peeling across her scaled face. "You can barely control your Soul Thirst."

She clenched her fist.

Her Weight crushed over my bones again, throwing me atop the corpse. The scent drove me insane, my breaths tight and wild as my vision hazed, my thoughts spiraling into a distant void of mist as the only thing I knew was the strangling Thirst...

Her Weight pushed my mouth over his throat, as if her own fingers were shoving down my skull, my neck straining to stay lifted. It took everything in my power to resist her Weight. But in doing so, I had nothing left to resist the crippling *Thirst*. The desirable scent was so strong, my thoughts barely clung to my dwindling mind, the world spinning like mad until...

... Until a delicious flavor suddenly washed over my tongue. My mind blanked. My vision dimmed and blurred. What was that *taste*...?

I was caught in a dazed euphoria, the world slipping away as I let the wave pull me into its pleasuring current, that same taste hitting again and again and again and...

Suddenly, it was gone.

My vision sharpened as I sobered, the glowing pit of crystals so bright, I had to block my stinging eyes with a hand.

A hand that was dripping with blood.

I flinched and snapped down my gaze. The corpse was gone. In its place was nothing but crimson smears spattered over the crystals...

And all over me.

"N-n-no...!" Tears stung, sickness churning. I fell to my knees. "No...! I-I... I didn't... I *didn't*..."

—THUMP!

Another body crashed into the pit with me, blood spurting on the crystals and dampening the light.

Ashya had fetched another shifter for me, like feral mice dumped into a viper's tank.

"Nira..." I broke into an anguished sob, the scent of the new corpse so powerful, I felt the Thirst shrouding my mind again. "Forgive me..."

—The taste returned, and I floated on a new wave of morbid euphoria all over again.

MACARIUS

Rrrrrrrrmmmmmm...

The latest Groundquake rumbled through Grim's detestably chilly caverns, causing this manor's corridors to quiver, chandeliers jingling in protest above me.

Even more Groundquakes, I brooded, my fangs unfolding as venom swelled in my glands. *They're worsening by the day...*

I paced the carpeted hallway feverishly, my legs sluggish and wobbling from fatigue. It had been three days since I gained the last of my destined Hallows. Three whole days. Yet I still hadn't fully recovered from overexerting myself with them.

My soul roiled harshly within me, expanding and bloating so much I feared I would burst. I doubled over in pain as I clutched my chest, wheezing for breath. The cacophony of Blessings inside me gave another aching swell, ice and fire and electricity thrashing against the tangle of water and poison and pressure and… and so much *more…*

Crck!

A glowing crack split across my scaled hand suddenly. The crack gleamed with multiple radiant colors, pulsating along with the painful buzz rupturing from my over-encumbered soul.

Dream was right… the thought sent a flush of panic through me, the lone crack in my scales slowly branching into other tiny, iridescent fissures. *No single shifter can bear so many elements at once… Not without sacrifice.*

But it was a sacrifice I was willing to make, if it meant the world would be spared.

Though, perhaps it was best to reserve my strength. If I had any hope of weaving enough cities in Aspirre for the world's housing, I would have to limit use of my other Hallows. That also meant my phantom copy's visits to our Demon Queen allies would need to cease. And I Bloody well wasn't fool enough to meet with those beasts in the flesh…

My wife's muffled screams split behind the door of the bedchamber where she lay in the throes of labor. This was the manor of a minor Headmaster in Grim's Lysandre Academy. *Our* academy. They knew of our cause and agreed to hide us, should the Reapers come looking on the schoolgrounds. We knew it was a risk to come to the school bearing my name, but… it was the safest place for us. We had allies here. And with Lannyse about to birth our child, *safe* was the only concern echoing in my tumultuous mind.

RRrrrrrmmmm…

A second Groundquake shook the manor.

It is a sign. The thought had me resume my terrified pacing. *A sign that the End is approaching.*

I scratched at my cracking knuckles as the glowing rash split over my scales next. Bloods, look at me—I was falling apart at the seams. And any moment now, my son would be born. According to my Third Eye, the End would come in three months' time. I had planned to finish building Sanctuary in Aspirre before then, but now…

The Orb of the Present was gone.

I glanced at the velvet pouch strapped to my belt. The two remaining Orbs of Azure were housed inside: the Orb of the Past, and the Orb of the Future. They still created the Relic of Dreams, true… but without the Orb of the Present, I could no longer bring myself, nor anyone else, into Aspirre physically. It was the *one* Orb that held that feature.

And that damned king stole it from me.

I sank to my knees, trembling as my wife's agonized screams shredded my tattered calm, blooming a fright so devastating, I succumbed to tears.

The End of Existence was coming. The prophecy had been true—the *Shadowblood* would cause it…! The fool had stolen our only chance of survival, and now, with my Hallow's stamina fractured so easily, we would all be left to die at the mercy of our bleak, gruesome futures…!

Lannyse's screams dimmed behind the doors.

My lungs clenched. I fumbled to my feet and threw open the doors.

My wife lay on the cushioned bed, horribly exhausted. She was surrounded by nurses, all of whom were busy collecting dirtied towels and sheets, one stoking the fire at the hearth to keep the chamber warm.

In Lannyse's arms was a large, round egg. An egg that wobbled in her hold.

I rushed over, hurrying to her bedside and clutching her shoulder anxiously. I knew that for a reptilian shifter, the egg would hatch soon after it emerged.

Creeee…

A small crack split across the egg.

Cr-cr… crick!

The crack widened and branched into many fissures, until a tiny, scaled hand broke through the shell, sticky membranes and fluid dribbling over the egg.

Auwahh…

The tiniest cry spilled from the broken egg, another flush of tears ailing me.

Lannyse and I peeled away the rest of the shell, and I found myself staring at the brown eyes of a dark-scaled newborn that bore my face.

I touched the precious boy's cheek, a joyful sob catching me by surprise. Lannyse wettened my brow with her lips, and we cradled our son together.

I will build our Sanctuary, I swore in silence, ignoring the sting of another gleaming crack that split over my cheek and caused a glare in my vision. *For you, my son… I will never let the future come to ruin.*

These next three months would not be spent in vain.

45

WORLD TOUR

ASTER

THREE MONTHS REMAINING

"*D*un! *Dun, dun, dun! Dun, dun, Dun! Dun, dun dun, d-d-d-d-dun!*"

I drummed my fingers against the tiny ship's railing as our team glided through the empty abyss of Aspirre at an urgent speed. The vessel was like an Airship, but in the Dream realm. A Dreamship. How 'bout that? I kept to my drumming, ignoring the thousands of Noctis Golems squiggling around our ship's protective bubble, and raised my voice to sing over their freaky screeches.

"DUN! D-d-d-DUN! D-d-d-DUN! D-d-d—"

"What are you doing?" the curious voice of Yulia interrupted beside me. She was wearing her azure Dreamcatcher cloak with her hood drawn up, her head cocking at me.

I shrugged and kept to my finger-drumming on the railing. "Those guys up there are giving me the creeps, so I'm distracting myself with some ambiance."

Her delicate lips pulled into a confused frown. "Ambiance?"

"Yeah, you know—some energy! We're on a mission to get to the other Relics so I can help save the world. Every world-saving mission needs theme music, right? DUN! D-d-d-DUN! D-d-d-DUN!"

Yulia gave a soft hum. "You are a very strange holy Champion, Ruiner…"

"—no, he's got a point, there," Jimmy agreed to my other side. The elk shifter wore his own Dreamcatcher's cloak, but his hood was collapsed at his shoulders to make room for his long, spiked antlers bowing behind his head. Jimmy rubbed his goatee and leaned back against the rail beside me, considering, "This is some pretty important stuff we're doing. Totally theme-song worthy."

I lightly punched him in the shoulder with a laugh. "He gets it!"

"—If the Champion wouldn't mind," the blue-haired Myra said as she and Crysalette floated up to us from the other side of the railing. They both held shepherd crooks over their shoulders, their bare feet hovering in the abyss as they followed our ship's pace. Myra crossed her arms in a sigh. "I don't mean to interrupt, but we're nearly upon Queen's Treasure. It's this way." She waved a hand toward the abyss, where I could just barely see a floating cityscape in the distance. "We'll weave a road for you to cross and—"

"I'm good." I hopped onto the railing, then skipped off to float between the two women. I put fists at my sides with a grin. "Let's go."

The four of them stared at me.

"We gonna go?" I asked, pointing up at the screeching Golems trying to break through our barrier with their sandy figures. "The longer we wait, the more these guys build up. What's the holdup?"

Myra squinted an eye at me. "You... you're able to float? Like my family?"

Crysalette added, "Without being a Somniovoker?"

I flicked down a meercat ear. "Well, yeah. Alex can do it, and he can't weave anything. He said traveling in Aspirre isn't really about casting an Evocation." I tapped my head. "It's about perspective. As long as you understand gravity doesn't exist here, you don't have to follow the rules of the physical realm."

Crysalette raised a hand to her lips in wonder. "Well... well, yes, but... it took a whole century for my husband to teach me how to master it..."

I jabbed a thumb at my chest. "Hello? Champion, here? If Alex could figure it out in a few weeks, why would I be any different?"

They didn't have an argument for that.

Myra sighed and gripped her shepherd's crook. "Very well... let's be off, then. But stay close to us." She lifted her crook, and an azure light spilled from her hand and shot up the crook, pouring upward as it bloomed out and flowed into a clear, protective bubble around her, Crysalette, and me. She growled, "If you don't want to be eaten, don't leave the barrier."

I grimaced at the sandy monsters screeching around our ride. "Noted."

We peeled away from the ship and drifted through the abyss, leaving Yulia and Jimmy behind to watch the vessel.

It didn't take long to reach the floating city. Our small bubble plinked *into the larger bubble surrounding the buildings, and when we touched down on the cobbled streets, Myra's bubble popped. Crysalette wove us all azure cloaks and fox-masks to hide ourselves, blending in with the hooded crowd bustling around this weird replica city.*

We walked for what felt like an hour, only stopping when we reached the huge castle up the hill. Then Myra had us gather around, and she pulled out the glittering, Azure Orb of the Present.

There was a blinding FLASH—

We were thrown out of the Dream realm, gravity slamming over my muscles again in an annoying *yank* as I fumbled to keep my balance on the *real* ground.

It was night out here, apparently. The stars glittered in the dark sky as the half-moon smiled down at me, crickets whining from the grass and toads croaking from a nearby pond. We were in the royal gardens on Queen's Treasure—the new Grand Capital of the Land realm.

There was a huge *crowd* of people surrounding me now, their attention snapping to me all at once and whispering to each other anxiously. It was like the whole Bloody island decided to show up for this. But I guessed that made sense, since the Relics had officially 'come out of hiding'. Some shifters were commenting about my glowing pupils, others were cringing at my shriveled limbs and hollow face, some were skeptical about whether or not the rumors of my Hallows were true…

I gulped, the audience making me skittish as their souls gave off an addicting scent all around me. My vision was starting to blur.

"—Welcome, Champion Aster," a woman whispered behind me, making me flinch. She was so quiet I hadn't noticed her sneaking up on me.

She had metallic, golden hair that fell to her shoulders in flowery curls, her gilded eyes as bright as the jeweled crown on her head. A violet ribbon was tied around her neck, her matching dress tailing behind her in a frilled train. She rested her delicate hands on the hilt of a thin sword, which was dug into the ground at her feet, and cast me a sweet smile.

Standing beside her was a contrastingly burly man with arms as big as my Bloody skull. His face was covered in puckered scars, a Shelic coin dangling from his thick neck. He wore a deep purple doublet with golden embroidery, standing tall with his arms folded behind him as the moonlight glinted over his own crown. His amber eyes sharpened at me, and he lifted an eyebrow. I probably wasn't what he expected, judging from that look.

The golden queen leaned on her sword's hilt and lifted her chin with a hum. "My name is Anabelle Goldthorn, Queen of the Land realm. I have heard much about you, Ruiner of Tradition."

"Uh, hiya…" I waved with two weak fingers as I looked around the packed crowd of faces. The delicious scent of souls all but swallowed me, my stomach rumbling as the Thirst started creeping up. Bloods, I didn't think there would be this many people here. This wasn't good. I didn't eat enough before we went into Aspirre, and now that we were back in the physical realm, my hunger came back with us. There were townspeople and nobles and merchants and servants and…

My head snapped to a whole bevy of servants holding golden platters of food. There were enormous grape bunches cascading with plump fruit, vegetables of every color decorating cheese wedges, glistening turkey legs and a honey-glazed roast—

"Aw, *sweet!*" I bolted for the platters in a drooling frenzy. The servants abandoned their posts and scattered away as I ripped my teeth into the turkey legs and glazed roast, *popped* off every grape from their vines, gnawed all the cheese and vegetables to splinters…

Until the last of it *thunked* into my stomach, every platter licked clean in a satisfied belch.

I froze when I saw the Queen and King were staring at me in shock.

My meercat ears lowered, and I wiped off the crumbs and juices dripping from my chin. "Uh, sorry… Got a bit carried away."

The king grumbled awkwardly, "Well… Tradition is thoroughly Ruined, indeed…"

Queen Anabelle chuckled behind a polite hand, her curly hair bouncing over her shoulders. "Not to worry, Champion," she assured. "Her Majesty Willow warned me of your impressive appetite. We thought a banquet would benefit all of us, since you require nourishment to stave off your Soul Thirst."

I exhaled in relief. "Cool, cool… So, uh, what now?" I looked around again, seeing I was standing right between two hollow trunks. I pointed at each of them. "Is this the Relic they mentioned?"

Anabelle nodded. "Yes. Welcome to the Blossom of Gold, Aster Sorelles. It is my honor to grant you the Blessings of Land."

I scratched my chin, frowning at the tree trunks. "Huh… I kinda thought it'd be… *bigger.*"

Anabelle's smile widened.

Then, randomly, she started to sing.

Breathe ye child your life begins,

Cherish thine hallowed garden again

As she sang, the hollow trunks *cracked* alive with twisting branches, making me shuffle back. They grew and stretched and creaked and groaned as the bark thickened and shimmered golden, vines and flowers of all kinds ruffling in an arch over my head, gigantic petals unfurling like a colossal rooftop.

The radiant Blossom of Gold towered over all of us, its gleam brightening until I was blinded by a flash—

The Blossom was gone. Now, I was back in Aspirre, floating in the familiar, black abyss.

WE MEET AGAIN, RUINER, a stony voice rumbled in my thoughts behind me. I whirled—and found myself staring at a glowing, golden lion. It was the Father God of Life… Shel. The lion's glittering tail flicked around His paws, and His maned head tilted at me.

I AM PLEASED YOU CAME TO MY RELIC FOR YOUR NEXT HALLOWS. BUT YOU HAVE MORE YET TO RECEIVE—

"Yeah, yeah." I snapped my fingers impatiently. "I got some catching up to do, I get it. After this, I need to go back to Grim to grab Roji, get my Blessings from the Phoenix of Scarlet, go back to Grim to drop him off and then get Fuérr to take me to the Pearl of Emerald, blah, blah, blah—old news. We're on a tight schedule here, so could you wrap it up, pops? We've only got three months to work with here."

The lion's sigh rolled through my brain like tumbling boulders. VERY WELL.

His fur glittered with golden light, which shot into my soul and squeezed me tight, pushing a laugh out of me.

TAKE MY BLESSINGS, *he rasped in my head.* THOUGH, AS THE RUINER, YOU CAN ONLY SUSTAIN TWO ELEMENTS. I PRAY YOU USE THEM WITH COURAGE…

I felt the Hallows of rock and plant tangle and crunch inside my spirit, and my face pulled into a toothy smile. But I had an afterthought, and frowned.

"Oh, hey, pops?" I asked, turning to the glowing lion. "So, I know we're sup-posed to help fend off the Noctis Golems, but… you didn't actually say HOW we

were going to do that? Nothing Alex does so much as touches those things, and he has ALL his Hallows…"

The lion growled. THE DEFENDER OF HARMONY HAS BEEN SEPARATED. THEY CAN ACHIEVE NOTHING UNTIL THEY ARE WHOLE AGAIN… *He lifted a heavy paw toward me.* LIKEWISE, NEITHER YOU NOR THE SAVIOR OF HISTORY CAN ACCOMPLISH THE TASK ALONE. BOTH THE CONCEPTS OF THE PAST AND FUTURE MUST FIRST BE UNITED.

I rocked my head back in a groan. "UGH, great… one more impossible thing to add to the list…"

The lion dipped his head apologetically.

Then the void vanished around me.

TWO MONTHS REMAINING

I desperately clung to the slippery rim of the stone goblet in the Sky realm's colosseum, sobbing in terror as the rain drenched me from head to foot, the wind threatening to pull me right off this damn pillar and splatter me all over the Land realm's rocky ground below the floating islands.

Thunder crashed, the crowd of spectators in the benches cheering wildly and almost drowning out the booming voice of King Roji as he flew inside the thrashing storm and sang his Culatian song through the microphone hooked to his ear, treating this like a Bloody rock concert.

Strü aero!

Fregĕcht necrogo!
Shwaw Kegtcha Mot Gobovgo!
Strü Kôkô!
Shwiw pa Glactîc!
truftô Zǎ Kegt Mot necro!
Astrabôv Mot Aero!

Lightning zapped into the stone goblet right under my clinging fingers. The scarlet sands in front of me were blasted into glass fragments with each spark of electricity. Piece by piece, the glass clinked together and became an enormous, phoenix made of glass feathers, spreading its wings over the floating arena in a blinding flash of lightning that *crashed* over me.

The rain vanished, and I unclenched my muscles in relief. "Thank Bloods…"

A streak of scarlet light suddenly zipped around me, a laughing voice thundering in my thoughts, RUINER! GOOD TO SEE YOU AGAIN! I'VE BEEN WAITING AGES TO GRANT YOU MY BLESSINGS!

The red streak spread its leathery wings, floating to a stop in front of me until I found myself staring at a huge, glowing Skydragon.

"Sup, Ushar?" I tossed my head at the God of Thrill in greeting. But I paused, noticing his scales were dripping with radiant blood. His wings were torn in some places and holding glowing scars. "Hey, man, you okay? You don't look too good…"

It was hard to tell with the reptilian face, but it looked like his scaled snout pulled into a thin smile. DON'T WORRY ABOUT ME RIGHT NOW. WE'RE ALL TRYING TO GIVE YOU AS MUCH TIME AS WE CAN.

I nodded. "Right. Ready to get this show on the road?"

The dragon chuckled. LET'S DO THIS! TAKE MY BLESSING! *His scales gleamed with sparking light—which zapped my soul and filled my reserves with a single, electric element.* HAVE FUN!

I saluted with two lax fingers. "Will do, 'Shar! Hang in there!"

The void blinked away, his rumbling laughter choking into a coughing wheeze in my ears.

ONE MONTH REMAINING

I shivered in the glacier's frozen caverns of Marincia, the humungous, Pearl of Emerald floating over its chilly pool inside the giant ice-clam and thanking Land I'd gotten my fire Hallows before diving into that freezing lake to get here.

The refined fish-shifters of Marincia had come with us and gathered round, offering polite applause and adoring compliments as the little Prince Fuérr danced in front of the Relic with glowing-green hands, causing the hollow icicles poking up from the floor to whistle in a beautiful melody that accompanied the prince's lilting voice.

Jeaux chad'naît faquer'joul

Jan'nasch trët Oscha
Ma'tu aqua goul'joul na min
Foi min lül ga'jin
fëttscha min Söl praul nawhil
Min ma'tu M'älmerre
Ît Tët Fae Pas Flouflusé
Jan'nasch trët Oscha…

The enormous pearl gleamed brighter and brighter, and I gave a defeated sigh, bracing for the blinding flash I knew was coming—
FLASH!
Yep. There it was. Man, this was getting old.

The usual void dripped back into view again, and I crossed my arms while floating cross-legged in the abyss.

"Hey, Rin, you there?" I called in a yawn. "Home-stretch here. Let's hurry it up."
SUCH RUDENESS, *grumbled a watery voice in my thoughts. An emerald light blossomed from the abyss, and a serpentine Seadragon slithered in the darkness toward me, its long whiskers wavering gently.*

He coiled in front of me and cast me an emerald glower, rumbling, THE DEFENDER AT LEAST HAD THE SENSE TO PAY THEIR RESPECTS IN MY PRESENCE.

"Look, we've got a month left before everything falls apart. I mean, look at your scales, dude." I shot a hand toward the Seadragon, drawing attention to the patches of glowing scars and dripping blood. "You gonna deal with some rudeness and live? Or be stingy about manners and die?"

Rin's snake-like face pulled into a scaly grimace. VERY WELL... TAKE MY BLESSINGS. *His tone curdled into a pretentious scoff.* USE THEM WITH GRACE... IF YOU CAN MANAGE.

Emerald light peeled off his scales and misted into my soul, freezing me with icy Hallows and watery magic.

As the void faded for the third time, I heard the Seadragon huff. UNGRATEFUL WHELP...

THE EVE OF THE END

46

EVE OF CALAMITY

WILLOW

*R*RRRRRRRRRRRRRRRRRRRRrrrrrrrrrrrrrrrrrmmmmmmmmm....
The Groundquake shook the palace corridors, ceiling debris dusting over my head.

My boots faltered mid-step, staggering to keep balance until the quake died into silence once more.

Beside me, my First Fangs, Matthew Inion, readjusted the com hooked to his ear and brushed the dust off his armor. "Bloody quakes," he muttered, his sienna eyes sharpening at the floor as if the marble were to blame. "Seamstress knows these quakes speak ill of the coming battle…"

I sighed and patted the dust off my velvet sleeve, smoothing back my long, ashen hair. "Yes… I'm growing tired of them. Three months of these tremors, and they've yet to weaken. They keep growing stronger…"

It wasn't a comforting sign. But I did my best to push that worry down, deciding it wasn't the priority right this moment.

"Is everyone evacuated?" I asked Fangs Matthew as we strode through the palace corridors, continuing our discussion from before that Groundquake so rudely interrupted. I nodded to the masses of Reapers and spear-wielding Footrunners bustling all around us, carrying out their tasks before their quickly-closing deadline.

Matthew folded his arms behind his back with a stately posture, inspecting each passing knight with strict scrutiny while his messenger raven puffed out her chest feathers with pride.

"All civilians have been relocated to a safe location," Matthew reported.

"And our knights are stationed accordingly?" I asked.

"At every street and lookout post we constructed around the city's perimeter over the last three months." He sounded pleased with that. "Flamedragons have been assigned, Shotri ammo well-supplied, scouts fully equipped and ready to report the first sightings they should find." He lifted a hand. "Our Reapers have been deployed, and I've spoken with the generals of Land, Sky, and Ocean to confirm that their knights are prepared and posted at their assigned posts as well. The Wavecrashers are guarding every river and strait surrounding us, the Stormchasers are patrolling the ceiling mists as we speak, and the Bladesworn—once they arrive with their queen any moment—will double our Reaper guard in the streets."

I nodded. "And *all* these knights have been given their Crystal weapons?"

While it was usually against the Fourth Law of Death for anyone except Reapers to wield Spiritcrystal weapons, we were preparing for a Necrofera invasion. You very well couldn't fight demons with normal steel and iron. It may have been unorthodox, but damn me, I had a duty to protect my realm and its people. And I intended to do so at any cost… Especially when all our Seers have foretold the End was due.

Tonight.

Matthew grunted his affirmation, "All Crystal arms have been granted, last I was told. And they have agreed to return those weapons after the battle is over."

I nodded. "Thank you, Matthew…"

"Your Majesty!" A frantic voice cried behind me. I whirled, finding my Master Servant, Morice, fumbling after me, drenched in sweat. He held a stack of loose papers in his hands, thick enough to be a full volume of the Grimish dictionary. "Your Majesty! I've j-j-just seen Regent Hecrûshou! More requests came this morning for you…!"

I took the papers from him in a hum. "And they've agreed to fight for us tonight if their requests are granted?"

Morice's cheeks flapped as he nodded vigorously, dabbing at his sweaty brow with a kerchief. "His Regency pre-approved their applications himself. He only sent those who were willing to aid us tonight."

I nodded. "Thank you, Morice. I'll sign these immediately… and do send word to me once Her Majesty Land arrives with her army."

He bowed low. "Yes, Your Majesty."

I bid him and Matthew farewell until tonight, and strode to the royal study to sign these citizenship papers with a weary sigh.

—A small child suddenly popped into existence in front of me, nearly making me stumble to avoid tripping over him.

I gasped, "What in Death, Eryn…!"

My voice died on my tongue. The azure-haired toddler had no fox tail. Nor did he have primary ears. I drew in a soundless breath, whispering, "Grandfather…?"

The toddler looked quizzical. He frowned up at me with curious azure eyes. "Death? What happened to your corridors?" He looked from one end of the hall to the other. Then his brow furrowed at me. "And why are your eyes different? They look like mine, now." He squinted at my face, his confusion doubling. "Wait. Your entire *face* is different! And why are you so much shorter?"

He snapped his fingers, as if having an epiphany. "Oh! I see. I must have slipped off to sleep after that last meal and am stuck in a dream. Silly me. I suppose I'd best familiarize myself with *actual sleep* in the physical plane now, hadn't I?" His hands began to gleam with azure lights, and he waved them around in the air with an amused chuckle. "Let's see if I can take a look around your subconscious first and…"

He paused. His Hallows did nothing to change his surroundings.

"Wait…" The toddler hopped up and down, as if the gravity confounded him. "Why can't I…" He groaned and ruffled his curling locks desperately. "This isn't a dream?! But—but if I'm still in the physical plane… where am I?!" He peered up at me, his blue fox ears growing. "And who are you?! You're not Death!"

I blinked at the little child. My, he was so small. He spoke like an adult, but he looked no older than three.

"I *am* Death," I chuckled and knelt to meet his eyelevel. "I'm simply a different incarnation. In the future… I assume this is your first Shared Vision, is it?"

His brow furrowed drastically low. "Shared what?"

"Shared Vision," I explained again. "*I* am having a vision of you in the past, and *you* are having a vision of me in the future. It's a simultaneous Scrying, between two Seers."

He looked bewildered. "But if you're a future Death, you wouldn't be a Seer. That's *my* Hallows."

"Yes," I said with a smile. "My name is Willow. I'm your granddaughter."

He scowled at me. "I don't have a granddaughter. I'm not even married."

"Not yet," I hummed. "You don't meet my grandmother for quite some time… when you're older."

He scratched his head. "So, then… are you suggesting I'm going to marry someone from the Death Bloodline in the future?"

"No, no." I held up a correcting finger. "Your *daughter* will. You marry someone from the Land realm—well, not Land's Bloodline, just a normal citizen from that country."

He scratched his head. "You're confusing me."

I put fists at my sides in a huff. "Well, it's about time I returned the gesture. I was in your shoes when you first explained this very same thing to me."

He glanced down at his bare feet, wiggling his toes. "I'm not wearing shoes?"

I sighed. "It's an expression, Gran—"

He vanished.

I had to take a moment to realize that his vision had ended, slow to rise to my feet in a mutter, "Well, that was the shortest vision yet..."

I shrugged and patted my stack of papers as I continued on my way to the royal study. But something about that encounter didn't sit right with me. It had been months since my last Shared Vision with Grandfather... Since we'd left the Blossom of Gold on the surface. If tonight was to bring the End of Existence, why did I have a vision *now*?

That question weighed heavily as I entered the study. I found two other royals were already here at their separate desks, signing their own papers. It was Sky King Roji and Ocean Queen Veyazelle.

The two greeted me when I entered, and I nodded to them as I crossed the carpeted floor to the main desk at the back of the study. I sat, picked up my quill, and began my last-minute paperwork.

Skritch, skritch, skritch...

I signed my name on the newest certificate of citizenship that Hecrûsou had approved.

Thump!

I stamped it with the Death Bloodline's royal seal, the ink pressed into the shape of an encircled, crowned Death mark. Once done, I set the certificate into the 'finished' bin on my desk, then plucked a new document from the 'pending' stack.

Skritch, skritch, skritch.

Thump!

Skritch, skritch, skritch.

Thump!

I was a machine at this point. We'd passed the bill of laws for all Sentient Necrofera to be granted citizenship three months ago, and now hundreds of Sentients had flocked down here from all over the Bloody Death realm to get their citizenship approved and officiated.

Roji and Veyazelle were filling out similar requests that flooded down here from their respective realms. It seemed word of Grim's new law had made it to the other countries across Nirus. Even Anabelle called to inform me she'd been undergoing the very same requests on the surface last month, thus why her descent down here was delayed until today.

Once the final paper from this morning was signed and stamped, I set down my quill with a long sigh, running my hands through my hair as I *thunked* my elbows on the desk. My gaze drifted to the large map of Low Neverland. Every known cavern and nook on this side of Grim were circled in red ink. Only a third of them were crossed out with opposing black ink.

It had been three months since we learned Xavier had Changed. One-hundred and eighty days since he was held prisoner by the Ancient Necrofera queens who sought to kill the rest of us. We'd searched tirelessly through the Weeping Woods, scoured the mountainous crevasses and plateaued pillars for miles out, but we always came up short. I could only imagine what they were doing to him.

Xavier, I thought dismally, my heart twisting. *Please hold on. We'll find you and bring you home… before the End comes tonight…*

A knock came at the door.

My bat-winged Hand, Lilli, peeked inside.

She was dressed in her finest armor today, her silver helm snug around her head and glinting in the lamplight. Only a few stray strands of her sleek, black hair escaped from the ear-slits on each side and through her open visor, the freed bangs wavering at her chin.

"Your Majesty?" Lilli called gruffly. "My apologies for the interruption… but Morice asked me to inform you of the Land Queen's arrival."

I rose to my feet and blew out a breath. "Thank you, Lilli. Have her generals meet with Fangs Matthew. The rest of us will meet the queen ourselves in the dining hall."

Lilli bowed with a fist to her chest, then took her leave.

I stretched my back, audible *cricks* sounding with the motion, and I saw the others do the same.

"*Skrii,*" Roji stretched out his wings, his feathers flaring. "Who knew this many Sentients were flying around my islands? I thought Thörd was an outlier."

Veyazelle agreed, "I shuud have expected eet. We have *tuu* Ancientz from ze Ocean realm on our side and anozer trying tu kill uz."

They left before me, and I lingered in the room for a moment longer, going to the map along the wall and dragging my fingers across all the un-marked caverns. *Where are you, Xavier?*

"—Willow," the voice of my mother blurted suddenly, making me flinch.

My azure-haired mother now stood beside me, the Orb of the Present glittering from her hands. At her side were Grandmother Crysa, Yulia, Jimmy, Little Fuérr… and our skeletal, undead Ruiner: Aster.

They hadn't been there a moment ago. Which meant they'd come from Aspirre—which also meant they'd returned from their mission to take Aster to the Pearl of Emerald to receive his final set of Hallows.

"Well?" I asked, looking at Aster. "Was it another success?"

Aster yawned and raised two glittering, emerald hands. The air over his palms suddenly quivered, crystalizing with ice over his right hand and sloshing with water over the left. "Ice and water," he announced, sounding jaded. "That's the last of it. I'm all set to go—Ruiner locked and loaded."

I blew out a relived breath. "I suppose that's one worry I can cross off the list…" Still, the looming reminder that tonight would mark the End still bit at my nerves. I questioned, "Are you prepared for our next mission…?"

Aster slapped his face, as if trying to wake himself up, and chuffed, "Right, right—I'm good. It's time to get the other Ruiner back and save the world."

My nod was dismal this time. I turned to the Dreamcatchers. "Did you find any more of his memories while you were traveling in Aspirre?"

Yulia gave a small smile as she stepped forward. "Quite a bit more, yes."

She held up a mirrored, spherical container, my stretched reflection staring back at me. It was the memory holder they always brought with them during their multiple journeys to the Relics. Now that Xavier was a Necrofera, we knew his memories were lost and scattered in Aspirre, like all demons.

I took the sphere and slid open the lid, peering at the new collection of shining, bright wisps of light. I scooped one up and brought it to my brow, letting it sink into my skin.

Visions of my own laughing face appeared, my ashen hair bouncing along with my marriage-vines while twirling hand in hand with the narrator as we danced within our celebrating circle of friends round the camp's bonfire, lively music playing in step with us…

The memory faded, and the ball of light emerged from my brow and settled back into my palm.

Our wedding… He doesn't even remember that? Why did it feel like I've played this game with him for a Gods damned eternity?

I dropped the light in the mirrored sphere and gave it back to Yulia. "Thank you… Please look after them. I'll be damned if we let the Noctis Golems devour these before we rescue him."

Yulia nodded dutifully. "Yes, Your Majesty."

"Now." I went to the door, the others following me out to the corridors. "Anabelle has arrived. We're to meet her in the dining hall… I suggest we take this time to enjoy what very well may be our… final meal…"

My mother tucked the Orb of Present in the velvet pouch tied to her silvery, chained belt. "I'd say that's a splendid idea. Ana and Kurrick certainly took their time, didn't they?"

"They would have come sooner, but they first had to stay with the Blossom of Gold to give Aster his Hallows months ago."

She hummed. "I'm glad traveling through Aspirre is far quicker than in the physical realms, at least. Could they not have traveled back with us that way, though?"

"Their hands were tied, unfortunately. They've been busy managing an entire realm of two continents while building a Grand Capital. And they also couldn't very well bring their entire military force into Aspirre with them—and let's not forget they've *also* been dealing with immigrating Necrofera like the rest of us."

Grandmother Crysa tilted her head. "It's quite fascinating how quickly the world is changing. How are the living citizens taking it?"

My head wavered. "They have… mixed feelings, from what I can glean. There are some who have watched the recordings of the Sentients' stories and welcome them fully, yet there are others who are still hesitant to trust them." I grimaced. "And then, you have the pocket of shifters who are fully opposed to it and have sent me many a death threat."

My mother intoned neutrally, "Ah, I remember the death threats. These must be the same shifters who hated your father and I for mixing the Bloodlines. Don't let them pester you, dear. They've been screaming into the wind for so long, they merely seek recognition."

I snorted. "You forget, I was the product of that very mixing, mother. I've received threats like that since I was a girl." I laughed. "I find it amusing, actually. Sending death threats to Death herself? Bloody ridiculous."

We climbed down the curling stairwell down to the first floor, then strode to the dining hall's arching doorways. With a creak, I pushed them open.

—But the dining hall I entered wasn't the one I knew.

The décor had changed.

Instead of the silver, reflective chandelier with electric bulbs that used to hang over the blackwood dining table this morning, it had been replaced with an obsidian chandelier full of flickering candles instead. The brightness of the hall was now filled with dim gleams of firelight and Fallen Lights that nested in lanterns along the walls, which were dressed with an old-fashioned black-and-white wallpaper ornamented with curling vines.

The strange dining hall echoed with chatter and scraping dishware, the gentle sounds echoing in the arched ceiling which, I noted, was still *shaped* the same as I was used to, at the very least.

But what snagged my attention most were the teenaged shifters dining at the table.

One was a quiet, lion-eared young man with golden hair and coin-bright eyes. A crowned Land mark burdened his brow. He sat at the foot of the table with his head ducked while he delicately cut into the lamb flank on his plate, his velvety bronze cheeks flushed pink as he watched the other diners conversing jovially amongst themselves. He seemed far too flustered to join them anytime soon.

In the adjacent seat to his right sat a scarlet-haired adolescent with leathery, scaled wings. This one had a crowned Sky mark on his forehead. He guffawed with a mouthful of grilled carrots, laughing at some jest he'd made and jabbering in Culatian as he slammed an entertained fist on the table with loud *bang, bang, bangs!*

His knocking caused a silver goblet to topple onto the table, his wine spilling onto the lap of the web-eared, emerald haired teen who had previously been enjoying his meal with an air of sophistication and poise. Now, with the wine staining his robes, he frantically grabbed the nearest napkin and dabbed at the clinging liquid, sputtering a string of obscenities in Marincian. *His* brow held a crowned Ocean mark.

Squeeeeee…

The eastern, arching doors suddenly squealed open. The three teenagers all turned to the newcomer under the sharp doorway.

"Thank you all for coming," said the young girl with long, ashen hair cascading over the floor at her feet in perfectly straight strands. Burdening her forehead was a crowned Death mark. She looked no younger than the three teens at the table, and her colorless white eyes swept over them all in turn. "I'm sure you're all curious why I've invited you to my caverns out of the grey. There is someone I would like you all to meet."

She twisted back, her gaze craning down. "It's all right," she hushed encouragingly. "You can come out, now."

At first, nothing happened.

Then a tiny voice grumbled behind her, "No."

The girl seemed surprised by this defiance. Then irked by it. "No? What's wrong? This is what you asked for, is it not?"

"I asked to meet them," a child's voice muttered. Then the sound of jingling bells trilled. "I didn't expect to be put in a *jester's* uniform for it…"

She rolled her eyes. "It is hardly a jester's uniform. Besides, I find it quite charming. One of royal blood ought to wear royal garb."

"And who exactly decides what 'royal garb' should look like—?"

"Oh, will you just come out? Your entrance is properly ruined now. I hope you're satisfied."

There came a small sigh. Then a little hand grabbed her skirts from behind her legs.

An azure-haired child peeked his head out.

His grown fox ears twitched with annoyance, his round face set in an indignant pout as he shuffled out from behind the girl. He wore a miniature vermillion cloak that draped to his bare feet, and atop his head was a white-gold crown with jingling bells glittering from the curved brim. In one hand was a small, polished shepherd's crook that dragged on the floor as if he'd been reluctant to hold it at all. His icy, blue eyes were wide with fear as he stared at the three strangers along the table. A crowned Dream mark was displayed on his brow.

"This," the girl announced as she pinched the rim of her nose in irritation, "Is King Dream of Aspirre. Fourth Relic Child and ruler of the subconscious realm of Dreams…" She waved to the child in a light gesture. "Please welcome our lost Soul-Brother. Dream Sandist."

My face drained into a grimace at the little boy. *Grandfather.*

I buried my face in my hands with a groan. "Not another Shared Vision…"

MYRA

The moment Willow opened the doors of the dining hall, she froze. Her gaze staled over.

I quirked an eyebrow at my daughter. "Willow?"

She didn't move an inch, as if she hadn't heard me. Her azure eyes were fixated on the eastern doors of the hall. Which was odd since those doors were closed and void of anything interesting.

I waved a hand before her face. "Dear? Is everything all right?"

She was silent, still obsessed with those doors. Then, at last, she buried her face in her hands and groaned, "Not another Shared Vision…"

I glanced back at my rust-haired mother, Crysa. "What is she on about?"

Mother's head cocked curiously, her hum flighty. "Perhaps she's finally cracked?"

"—Mother," Willow suddenly said. Her eyes were still plastered to those doors. "If you're there, listen carefully. I'm having a Shared Vision with Grandfather. I cannot see you, and I cannot hear you. I'm in *his* time… with the first Relic Children."

I stared at her. "What?"

"I have to allow the vision to play as it wills," she said bitterly, taking a deep breath and pushing it out in a steady stream. "Typically, I'm brought here when I must learn something. If you hear me speaking to myself, I have not gone mad. I am talking with Grandfather. Please inform the others so they don't worry over my sanity."

"Erm…" I fanned a hand over my chest, perplexed. "Very well… I suppose."

She shut her eyes, blushing. "And… could you do me a small favor and make sure I don't run into anything in *our* time? I can only see the furniture in *his* time…"

"All… all right…" I hesitated, then remembered she couldn't hear me. Any confirmation I made would go unnoticed. Instead, I gripped her shoulder, hoping this would signal that I'd heard her.

It seemed to work, and she sighed in relief. "Thank you, Mother."

"What a strange vision…" I murmured, exchanging a concerned glance with my mother.

"—Myra?" the familiar, quiet voice of Anabelle called from the somber dining table in the center of the hall. "Crysa?"

My golden-haired sister waved from her seat beside Kurrick, the two rising to meet us under the door. She stopped before my blank-faced daughter. One of Ana's lion ears flicked at Willow.

"Sister Death?" Ana whispered. "Is something wrong?"

"She can't hear us, Ana," I informed, "She said she's having a… 'shared vision' with Father."

Beside her, Kurrick's brow furrowed with deep creases. "With Dream? But he's…"

"The *past* Dream," I corrected, still uncertain of the whole thing myself. "She claims to be Seeing something during a time when all the first Relic Children were together."

Ana waved a hand in front of Willow. "How very odd…"

"My liege!" a chuckling man's voice bounced through the hall.

Striding through the open doorway was Cayden—Ana's appointed Regent of High Everland. The lion-eared man came trotting in, fully plated alongside his lover and new general, the goat-horned Linus. Following them was an armored woman I recognized as Vanessa, Ana's appointed Regent of High *Neverland*.

"Ah, Cayden!" Ana broke away from us to greet her regents with a warm embrace. "Linus! Vanessa…! I was worried you wouldn't make it in time."

Cayden laid proud fists at his sides, his lion ears perked as he laughed, "Well, it did take longer than expected, I admit. But it was worth every second." His lips rolled into a grin. "Linus and I brought Sir Alexander a little gift from High Everland."

Linus folded his arms and chuckled. "It took some time to bring all the pieces down here to Grim."

Regent Vanessa grumbled. "And longer still to put it all back together outside the city where the troops are deployed."

"But it's here," Cayden declared and rubbed his hands eagerly. "Oh, I cannot wait to see the look on Alexander's face when he sees it. I've always wanted to break that stubborn scowl of his."

I was puzzled, about to ask what they were on about with this supposed 'gift'.

But Willow suddenly strode forward. I quickly followed her, determined to keep to my promise and steer her away from any obstacles she couldn't see, and left Ana and Kurrick with the new arrivals.

The dining shifters haunting the table seemed far too obsessed with their meals to notice anything strange was happening with Willow. Either they were too morose from the looming threat of the End, or they assumed *I* was speaking with my daughter.

That may be best, I decided, keeping my hands cupped before my skirts casually as I walked alongside Willow in a feigned smile.

"—Your Highness."

I yelped at the growling voice behind me.

It was Alexander. His glower was expectant as he folded his plated arms over his chest. His heterochromic eyes flicked to Willow beside me. He questioned, "Why is she staring off into space?"

"She's having a Shared Vision with my father," I explained. "Supposedly, she can neither see nor hear us in this time. She claims to be viewing this very hall far in the past."

Alex looked quizzical and waved a hand in front of her face. When Willow didn't so much as blink, he gave a hum. "Curious. Well, if she isn't aware of us, I suppose that's all the better right now. Did you bring it?"

I nodded, untying the velvet pouch at my hip; the pouch that held the Orb of the Present.

"I'll pretend I still have it," I said, handing him the pouch. "I don't want her to worry during the battle tonight… And Macarius will likely assume my mother and I will keep it in *our* possession. It's a grand diversion, I think."

He nodded. "Thank you… And Willow still doesn't know we're leaving without her?"

"No. I'll distract her for as long as I'm able. I'm worried if she discovers you've left already, she may chase after you anyway."

He shook his head. "She has obligations here. We need her to keep the palace secure with the other Relicbloods… as well as keep her oath to Hecrûshou."

With the hidden Orb in hand, Alexander bowed to me, then turned to leave. "And *I* have an oath to keep with my brother."

SUIT UP

ALEXANDER

I left Myra with the distracted Willow, crossing through the palace corridors and heading outside to the courtyard.

Jaq and Aster were still leaned against the awaiting hover-coach where I left them, the feral horses chuffing impatiently. The viper spotted me and pushed off the royal coach's black-painted walls, the stabilizers hissing in relief without his weight as he trotted up to me.

"Henry called," my scaled lieutenant reported, his armor clinking as he put fists at his sides. "He said everything's ready. Got Bianca and Red fitted and good to go. They're finishing up now."

"Good." I climbed into the hover-coach. He and Aster followed, the demon shutting the door behind us. As the coachman whipped the horses toward the royal markets, I removed the Orb of Present from the velvet pouch Myra had lent me. I stared at my bulbous reflection in the glittering azure sphere, its contents swirling like ethereal smoke beneath its pristine surface.

"We've waited too long," I said, putting the Orb back in its pouch with a sigh. "This plan had better work."

"It will, mate," Jaq assured with a fang-filled grin. But his confidence faltered, and he added, "But, uh, if it doesn't go so well… could ya keep this little insurrection between us? Lilli's gonna kill me for not includin' her in this, if we come back empty-handed. Why can't we just bring her along again?"

"Lilli's place is with Willow, as the queen's Hand," I emphasized. "We also need Matt, El, and the Treble brothers to stay behind to keep Willow guarded. I still have a job to see to—I can't just bring the entire royal guard with me and leave the one person we're *paid* to protect exposed on the eve of the End."

Jaq scratched the reddish goatee hugging his scaled chin. "You sure it's happening tonight?"

Aster gave an affirmative hum beside him. "Yep, super sure. Even Myra Saw it in her visions. It happened in every vision us oracles had."

I cupped my hands broodingly as we entered the royal markets, the crowd of shouting soldiers buzzing outside the coach. "We have to act now... we've run out of time. We have three futures ahead of us that involve freeing Xavier before the march. If we don't hit at least *one* of them, the kingdom will fall—"

RRRRRRRRRRRrrrrrrrrrmmmmmmmm...

The coach suddenly shook, Grim's caverns trembling.

A Groundquake surged through the kingdom as startled yelps split from the markets outside.

Thankfully, the tremors lasted only a few moments, quieting as the shifters around us went back to their busy day with more hesitation and concerned murmurs.

I rubbed my eyes. "Bloods... They're getting worse."

Jaq grimaced out the window. "Why's it happening at all? Talk around town says these things didn't start until earlier this year down here."

"It's been happening in every realm," I said. "Roji and Veyazelle have been receiving similar complaints... and we'd already experienced a few during our time in High Everland. They're getting more frequent. And stronger..."

It was a concerning statistic. It must have something to do with the Noctis Golems... They were the aftermath of the demons *we* reaped, here in our plane. They were our mess. If the Gods were the very manifestations of the realms themselves, could the increasing tremors be linked to them? They claimed our continents had split because of severe injuries they'd undertaken in the past... And according to our Dreamcatchers, the Noctis Golems had been increasing at an insane rate.

Though, oddly, the number of Aspirrian cities had increased as well. Word had it, a sudden plethora of locations had been constructed every night and morning. As if someone were preparing to house a sudden influx of shifters there.

And I know exactly the Somniovoker who'd be quite keen on doing so.

My teeth sharpened, wolf ears growing. There was still no sign of Macarius. Not surprising. Despite the countless Wanted posters we pinned up all over the country—in both continents—his Decepiovoking could easily hide him. Pair that with an ever-growing following of anti-Relicblood extremists more than willing to house him, and he was perhaps the most impossible man to find in all of Nirus.

Clack! Clack! Clack!

The coach's window beside me rapped noisily, catching my attention. My raven, Mal, pecked his beak against the glass. I opened the window and he climbed inside to settle on my armored shoulder. Jaq's crow, Bridge, came flying in after Mal and fluttered to the curtain rail beside Jaq, her tattered feathers fluffing dutifully.

Mal rubbed his beak against my jaw. He must have felt my anxiety through our Bond. *Only three futures…*

And all but one of those chances would still lead to the End.

One devastation to fix at a time, Alex, I reminded myself.

The coach floated to a stop outside the royal Blacksmith's forge—Henry's new armory—and Jaq and I climbed out with our messengers perched on our shoulders, paying a tip to the coachman and walking into the forge.

A wave of heat wafted over me from the blazing firepit, smoke rising through the chimney and perfuming the armory with a peppery scent.

Henry was at his grinding wheel, sharpening his latest prosthetic tool currently attached to his wrist-stub: a Spiritcrystal hook. He greeted the three of us with a nod when we entered, and I found the rest of our covert party preparing themselves for the task ahead of us.

Aster went to poke at a set of armor suitable for a starved demon such as himself that hung on a wooden mannequin. He didn't seem sure what to do with the plate. As if the Bloody Sentient had never encountered something so well-polished that it showed his reflection. Either that, or he was debating whether or not he could eat it.

The ghosts of Aiden, Nathaniel, Apson and Dalen were wearing the Blacksmith's latest creation:

Armor made entirely of pure Spiritcrystal.

The glowing plate curled and spiked in graceful shapes, their helms fitted snuggly to each specter. They looked like elite soldiers now. Even their weapons were made of pure Crystal. Aiden had a crossbow and quiver of bolts; Apson, a sword; Nathaniel, a saber; Dalen, twin daggers, which he experimentally sliced in the air with a thrilled grin.

After three months without their vessels—three months without their other *Da'torr* to tie their intangible souls to the corpses I raised—at last, they looked prepared for war.

At the back table, I found Bianca with her back facing me. I had been resurrecting Bianca for the last few months, now. Enough time had passed since her death and I was more comfortable with it, trying to instead think of it as 'Healing' instead of 'reviving'… but I still needed Willow or the other

Necrovokers in our party to attach her soul every time. It was getting aggravating, having to find someone available every few weeks to do it for me.

It will be far easier when Xavier is back, I thought, *then we can form a Bloodpact with her.*

Bianca's long ears were folded down in concentration, fixated on her current task of carefully coating a dagger in a strange, blackish-green tonic before sliding it neatly into its holster. She then began tinkering with vials and fist-sized Flameglobes and Poisonglobes beside her assistant chemist, Red.

Now that Bianca was dead, Red had been declared as her successor as Master Chemist in the Alchemist Guild. He'd struggled with the new role the first month after her death, but he now seemed more at ease with his duties, and was determined to help the former Guild Mistress with her latest mission.

Scampering on the center of the table was Kurn. The ferret wore his very own *tiny* armor and little helm, looking quite pleased with his miniature utility belt featuring multiple pockets and compartments filled to the brim with little globes.

The two Alchemists wore armor as well, though theirs, like the rest of us living shifters, were made of polished olium.

The sight of it made me stagger. I knew Henry had been fitting Bianca for armor, but this was the first time I'd seen her in *any* plate. Before then, she'd only ever worn non-fitted, standard leather armor—or, more frequently, loose clothes and overalls that never showed even the slightest impression of curves. But with this, Henry had acquired her exact measurements for the most optimal fit. And I'd forgotten just how enticingly small Bianca's waist was…

Red was the first to notice I'd arrived. He snorted a laugh and nudged Bianca's shoulder. "I think you just broke your knight, Boss."

Bianca's ears lifted, and she twisted back, spotting me by the door beside Jaq.

"Hey guys!" Bianca greeted as she slid off her seat and came to meet us.

I swallowed. Seeing her armored figure from the back had been devastating enough. Seeing it from the front was so much worse. *Delightfully* worse. Granted, there was nothing out of the ordinary, as armor went. There were no ridiculously added curves to her slope-less breastplate, there were no useless designs curling around her stomach… but even still, there was something about seeing her in *any* plate that set my pulse blazing.

Bianca must have noticed me staring. She grinned and put a gauntleted hand on her accentuated hip. "You like it?"

"Erm…" I was sure my face had gone pure scarlet. I coughed into a fist and muttered, "I… I'm realizing I may have a 'type'…"

She chuckled. "Noted. So are we ready to…"

RRRRRRRRRRRrrrrmmmm…

The ground shook again, just like earlier, swords and scythes and axes clattering off their mounts around the forge. The tremors strengthened, throwing all of us to the floorboards in startled yelps.

It took several moments for the quakes to die this time.

When they finally faded, I pushed up and muttered, "Bloody quakes…"

The others hauled to their feet, though Bianca was still on her knees. She looked woozy.

"Bianca?" I asked, crouching to her and inspecting her face. "Still dizzy from the tremor?"

"I, uh…" she began uncertainly. Her skin was turning grey now, her cheeks hollowing as her gaze staled. "I… think I might need… an extension for…"

She started to drop backward, and I hurried to catch her in a curse. "Death!" I pulled her upright as her breaths grew ragged. Her dark skin continued to pale. I sighed. "Is it that time already…?"

I cupped my hand against her cool cheek, evoking my Death Hallows. Violet lights spewed from my palm and seeped into her skin, wrapping around her figure beneath her alluring armor. As my Hallows rejuvenated her vessel, and her sweetened breath was freed from her restarted lungs, I exhaled in relief and took her gentle lips.

"Sorry," I said with a thin smile, still holding her face. "I should have noticed you were about due. The rest of you distracted me."

She clasped my hand over her cheek with a chuckle. "We can have more distractions later… We've got a future to secure, first."

I loosened a long, hollow breath. "That, we do…" I pushed to my feet, then helped Bianca to hers.

"Ruiner," I called to Aster, turning to him.

The demon was hesitantly pulling on his personally-fitted armor and poking at the spiked ailettes. He flicked his gaze up at me when I called him, pointing at himself in question. "Me?"

"Obviously you, idiot. The only other Ruiner is missing." I reached for a Storagecoffin strapped to my belt. "Come here."

Aster waddled over, very clearly not familiar with the weight of his new armor—despite the fact Olium was among the lightest of durable metals. "What is it?" he asked.

I evoked my violet Hallows and pulled out the skeleton that waited in the Storagecoffin, setting the pile of bones at his feet.

"These are the bones of Nathaniel," I said. From the back, Nathaniel nodded his approval to me, knowing this test well. We'd done this with Aster every month after he returned from each Relic, to see how his Necrovoking was progressing. I cleared my throat and said, "Piece him together."

Aster grimaced, but blew out a breath. "Okay… here goes."

Violet lights streamed from his fingers, leaking in the air like smoke and engulfing the pile of bones. It was a slow and grueling process… but after thirty minutes, the last spinal disc was connected, and the morbid puzzle was finished.

Aster beamed at his achievement. "I did it!" He glanced at me for acknowledgment. "See? See? It's all there…!"

I gave a commending hum, inspecting his work. "Very good… and it only took three months to get to this point. It normally takes years to get this far… well, save for me." I shrugged. "It took me three weeks."

Aster pouted. "Yeah, well, I didn't *start* with Death Hallows… I also don't have mine *halved*, Defender, so obviously it's not as strong."

I reached out my hand. "Now that you've gotten a fair grasp of vessel assembly, let's see how your sensory-illusions are."

He licked his lips and clasped my offered hand. He gave a sly grin as he evoked his Hallows, violet lights pouring out of his palm and into mine, and the gnawing feeling of ravenous hunger crumpled my stomach.

I grimaced and freed my hand. "Annoyingly convincing… well done."

It wasn't nearly the same caliber as Xavier, but I supposed I couldn't expect *anyone* to match his level of soul-Hallows. He was the only man in history to have been born with only that half—as I was the only man born with *mine*.

I rubbed my chin in thought. "Now… for *my* test." I cracked my knuckle, shaking them out in a preparing breath.

Then, I evoked my Hallows, hands gleaming once more—

And *shoved* them against Aster's chest.

Aster jolted, caught by surprise as I tried to grab his rotten vessel with my gleaming Hallows. But Death, was it slippery! His skin was only *half* physical, merged with his rotten soul which I couldn't touch, wiggling and slithering out of my grasp every chance it could, instinctually resisting my pulls and shoves as I tried to order his bones to move against his will…

I ripped a determined growl and braced my footing, yanking as hard as I could.

Aster finally stepped forward to keep his balance. Then his bones slipped out of my Hallows' grasp for good, and I fell over my knees in a winded pant.

"Death…" I puffed, wiping sweat from my brow. "It's *still* like grabbing soap with oily hands…" My lungs quivered a laugh suddenly. "But it's something. Which means it's possible… Just as it was for Xavier, as we saw in the visions."

Aster frowned at me. "Did I miss something? What are you trying to do?"

"I'm trying to control rotten demons with Necrovoking," I explained. "No one's ever been able to do it before. Not even Xavier and I. But… now that he himself is a rotted soul, it seems he may have gained a… a better *grip* on your kind. At least, that's the theory." I gave a toothy grin. "And with some practice, it seems I may be able to control your kind's vessels."

Aster held back a snicker. "If that's what you were trying to do, better get a *lot* of practice in—*ow!*"

I punched his shoulder, making him whine in a pout.

Red picked up the armored Kurn from the table and set him on his shoulder in a grin. "He's got a point, you know. If you don't have control of it just yet, probably not a good idea to try it on this mission."

Bianca rubbed her hands excitedly. "But when we get Xavier out, you bet I'm going to run both of you through some tests to get new data…!"

I smeared a hand over my face and groaned. "Let's just hurry up and retrieve Chai…"

48

HONORING VOWS

WILLOW

The trio of colorful teenagers at the ancient table stared at the blue-headed toddler who'd slid out from behind the ashen-haired girl.

Not a soul spoke.

I walked closer to them, hoping to get a better look at my young grandfather. He was just so *small*… He looked barely older than his one-year-old son in my time. It seemed baby Eryn took after his father more than I originally thought.

Little Blue King indeed. I stifled a chuckle. Grandfather often told me of his old nickname in previous centuries. *You were even smaller than I imagined, Grandfather.*

The silence broke when the scarlet Skydragon—whom I could only assume was Skrii, the original Relic Child of Sky—blurted in stilted Landish from the table. "Ees being King of Aspirre? Rumor being the true one?"

The emerald Seadragon across from him, who must have been Oscha, scratched his scaled head with a frown. "Eh? Fourth king eez real? Oscha thought eet waz myth."

"—Oh, how absolutely adorable!" The golden lion, no doubt Land, swooned, clapping his hands as he all but floated out of his seat to meet the child. He pinched the boy's round cheeks with a smitten giggle. "Such rosy cheeks…! And a tiny crown for a tiny head! I have never seen anything more precious than a little baby king—!"

"*I'm fifteen,*" the toddler chewed, pushing Land's hands away in an annoyed pout. "I'm not a baby. I'm the same age as you all—I'm even a month older than Death." He threw a little hand at the ashen haired girl behind him.

Land blinked, his golden eyes perplexed. "Fifteen…? But—but how are you so small?"

"Time doesn't exist in my realm." Dream muttered, using his polished crook to scratch at an itch under his jingling crown. "That's where I live. Do the math… Is this my seat?"

Dream hobbled to one of the empty chairs, struggling to climb atop. He couldn't quite reach it, the bells on his crown jingling with each futile hop. The boy muttered, "Blasted physical plane and this irritating gravity… Death, could I trouble you for some assistance? I'm not able to float in your realm."

Death gave a sigh and went to pick him up, setting him on his bare feet over the chair so he could see over the table. He unceremoniously discarded his crook beside his dinner plate. Death sat at the head of the table, a grey hand cupped over her eyes in a grimace.

Land skittishly lowered back into his own seat at the foot of the table, and Oscha's gaze narrowed at the blue-haired child, the Seadragon looking confused.

"If eet haz been fifteen yearz," Oscha began, "why haz ze baby king not shown himself until now—?"

"*I am not a baby*," Dream emphasized, slapping his tiny hands on the table. He calmed in a puff, still seeming peeved, but kept an even tone. "As for why I've been in hiding for so long… truthfully, it was due to the wishes of my Dreamcatchers."

Skrii flapped his leathery wings in question. "What being a Dreamcatcher?"

"They are the knights of my realm," Dream explained. "I was raised by them… or, a cluster of them, rather. I have knights in *all* your realms. Much like how Death has her Reapers to fight off the Necrofera in your cities, I have my Dreamcatchers to fight off the nightmares in your sleep."

Land frowned. "But we have our own hired Somniovokers for such matters. How can we trust perfect strangers to toy with our dreams?"

"Because those perfect strangers have been handpicked by *me* and were deemed to be trustworthy souls," Dream growled, his fox ears twitching. He flicked Land a sharp glare. "And were I you, Land, I would fire my current Somniovoker immediately upon your return to the surface. He plans to sell information regarding your lover to the Shelic church for a hefty sum."

All heads turned to the gold-haired lion with quirked eyebrows.

Land's face turned bright scarlet. "Erm… uhm… I-I don't know what you're on about, but, erm…"

Dream waved a dismissive hand. "Oh, save it. I've seen your dreams countless times already, and plenty more visions. I'm more concerned with the events that will happen if your affair comes to light in your kingdom, Land. I'd rather like to keep you alive, as my Soul-Brother, so I tell you now, have the man imprisoned for treason. Else you'll find yourself at the noose, along with your lover."

Land's bronze face paled in fright.

Dream hummed in assurance, "Not to worry, though. As I said, I wish to see such a disaster averted. I've already selected a team of my knights to watch after your dreams in his stead—and they are five of the most tight-lipped Catchers in my charge. Your secrets will be closely guarded, I guarantee."

Land blinked dumbly at the child. "Er, uhm… th-thank you…?"

"You're welcome," Dream said neutrally. "As for the rest of you, I have other Catchers selected in your realms to watch over you. I don't trust any Somniovokers who don't pass my tests, so I'll be far more at ease to know you're all well looked after in your sleep. I can't be everywhere at once, after all, otherwise I would do it myself. Now, as for their payment, I think taking a small portion of your countries' taxes should suffice, since the rest of the Dreamcatchers overlook your citizen's dreams regardless, so they're really doing a public service for your people anyway. I can come to collect the payment from your treasurers myself and distribute it amongst my knights—"

"Baby king being the waiting one!" Skrii interrupted. Dream shot the Skydragon a grizzly look at the mention of 'baby king' again, but he held his tongue as Skrii protested, "Skrii no say if he be the agreeing one, yet!"

Oscha muttered his agreement as well, the two sputtering their protests at once—

"You *will* agree to this!" Dream shouted, slamming his little hands on the table again. The toddler was the very image of livid. "Do you want to know why my knights have kept me hidden from your realms for so long? Why none of you knew I even *existed* until today?"

There was silence.

Dream's voice shook with rage. "It is because your people have slaughtered my kind for centuries—and continue to slaughter them to this day. *Without* trial. *Without* hesitation. *Without* mercy."

Land held an aghast hand to his chest, whispering, "But… We've all banned the killings of Somniovokers in our countries. To execute anyone over their Hallows element is illegal—"

"Making something illegal isn't enough!" Dream barked. "It is still happening! The shifters you've put in charge of your military and civil officers are the ones allowing the continued extermination of my people…! Of my *family*…!" His eyes began to well, voice tightening. "My Catchers don't know I've come here to the physical plane… I… left their watch, despite their warnings. Because I had to do something—I needed your *help*…" He let his tears crawl down his rosy cheeks. "Please… if you really are my Soul-Siblings, as everyone says… Will you *help* me? As you've all helped each other…?"

The four Relic Children glanced round the table. Then, with heavy heads, they all nodded.

Death stood from her seat and announced with pride, "Then, we are in agreement. Brother Dream of Aspirre, we recognize your plight and offer our services to help your people, to the best of our ability."

"Aye," the others declared with thick voices.

Dream seemed relieved as he slumped down in his chair at last—his head barely peeking over the table before his meal—as he wiped his eyes dry. "Th… thank you, brothers… and sister… thank you…"

His eyes flicked up suddenly. He spotted *me* by the doorway.

He hesitated, waiting for the others to be well into their meals before excusing himself from the table and hopped down, making his way to me with hurried steps.

"Granddaughter," he said, sounding urgent. "Thank Iri's sands, I have something to ask you, of the future." He looked terrified suddenly. "I… I've had a vision, last night. Of the End of Existence. There were three shifters in its wake, a man with hair of every color… and a pair of twins, with shadowed hair. I-I do not know what it means. Do you know, in your time…?"

I pursed my lips. "I do… in fact, today is the eve of that End."

His azure fox ears folded to his neck in a shiver. "Which of the three will bring it…? How do I stop it?"

I gave a brooding grumble. "As for how to stop it… I'm afraid I don't know either, Grandfather. We are in the midst of trying to prevent it now. But I *can* tell you that the man with the colorful hair… the Lightcaster…" I closed my eyes with a long breath through my nose. "He will betray you. And accelerate the End to come. If you remember anything in your life, grandfather…" My gaze was pleading. "Remember the Shadowblood is your rightful Champion."

The dining hall suddenly slammed into the present time again.

The electric chandeliers shined brighter than its candled predecessors, the gaudy wallpaper was stripped away and replaced with solid white paint, and the dining shifters at the table blurted with darker chatter and somber tones.

Rrrrrrrrrrrrrrrrrr…

The familiar rumblings of weaker Groundquakes shivered the chandeliers on the arching ceiling, vibrating the floor under my boots with a low hum. The constant tremors further dampened the spirits of the shifters haunting the dining hall, their voices quieting with fear as they shakily ate their meals.

"Willow?" the voice of my mother called right beside my ear, making me jump.

The sight of her concerned, aging face eased my nerves. "Oh, thank Bloods. The vision is over…"

"Oh, good," Mother rubbed her cheeks tenderly. "My face was growing sore from all the smiling… So, then. What exactly did you See in this vision?"

I murmured, "Grandfather's first introduction to the other Relic Children. He was pleading for them to help stop the killing of the Dreamcatchers…" I pinched the rim of my nose. "It was exactly like Hecrûshou's plea to stop *our* killing of the Sentient Necrofera…"

Mother seemed unsure of what to make of that. "I see… then, what did you learn from it?"

"Nothing I didn't already know, honestly… except…" I stifled a giggle that threatened to burst. "… that grandfather was *adorable*."

That made Mother cluck with a laugh, and she drew me toward my seat at the head of the table beside her. "Oh, I've seen the portraits, dear—despite my father's efforts to keep them hidden."

I chuckled. "He looked remarkably like Eryn, save for the tail."

"Oh, goodness, yes, and the same age as well."

We shared a laugh at that—

RRRRRRRRrrrrrrrmmmmmmmmmm…!

Yet another Groundquake ravaged the dining hall, knocking over goblets and shattering plates that fell off the table.

When it finally died into quietness, I pushed out my tension in a hard exhale. "They're happening more frequently… and getting worse."

Is Nira taking damage against the Noctis Golems…?

I didn't want to believe what Alexander and Aster told me had happened at the Willow of Ashes. I didn't want to believe that our fate hung on their shoulders—on the shoulders of the Gods, whose livelihoods were directly linked to the fate of the realms themselves. If it was true, and Nira were to meet a fatal blow from the Golems at any moment…

I tried to push down the thought, knowing it was out of my control right now, and instead attempted to focus my attention on the meal in front of me. It would likely be my last.

—then two ghostly heads popped up through my roast like translucent weasels. One was a rabbit-eared teen, and the other a familiar lion boy.

"Vendy," I huffed. "Hugh. What have I told you two about surprising the living from inside their long-awaited meals?"

Vendy gave a crooked-toothed grin as she recited, "That it gives them 'quite a fright'. Why do you think it's so fun?"

I rolled my eyes, wafting my hand to signal the two specters to come out of the table. They complied, floating at my side. I propped my chin up with a fist. "So, then? Is Alexander prepared for our rescue mission to find Xavier?"

Hugh shook his spectral head. "He's still in conference with Aster... they're not gleaning much else from their combined visions other than the Spiritcrystal cavern we've been seeing for months. But that shouldn't matter if we use Chai to lead us to him."

Vendy set fists at her sides. "But *Da'torr* says there's thousands of demons in whatever cavern he's locked up in. Even if Chai does find him, we'd be out-numbered like crazy."

I bit my knuckle, my mood souring all over again. "Perhaps... perhaps I can speak with Fangs Matthew again. Now that Anabelle has brought her reinforcements, if we deploy a portion of our troops to storm the nest, we could eliminate them while rescuing Xavier at the same time and..."

"—and murder more of my people without trial?" came the rumbling voice of Hecrûshou behind me. The shark shifter had come with more scrolls of citizenship requests in hand. His glower was long past disapproving. Now, he was on the brink of looking... betrayed.

His voice crunched as he flapped the scrolls at my nose. "You gave me your word, Death. Those Sentients are in need of rescuing just as much as your king. To kill them in favor of saving your husband would mean admitting that you think your selfish desires outweigh our struggle for survival from *your own kind.*"

My lungs tightened, a new sickness shriveling my appetite. Grandfather's words from our shared vision rang in my memory. *Making something illegal isn't enough...*

"I... I'm sorry," I whispered, shame squeezing my throat. My head felt like granite as I shut my eyes. "And you're right... we'll come up with a plan to... to rescue *all* of them." I cast Hecrûshou a determined gaze; one that held a promise. "And once they're free, we will be sure to *enforce* the ban on Marking."

His brow lifted, either surprised or skeptical. "We shall see... such a thing will be difficult to enforce, without a strong means of ridding those Marks in larger numbers..." I caught his lips cracking with a small smile. "But we can try, nonetheless... I suppose all we *can* do is try."

HUGH

Her Majesty Death had turned her full attention to the Ancient demon now. They were speaking of delaying *Da'torr* Alexander's plan to have Chai lead us to Xavier, in favor of a better plan.

A plan we didn't yet have.

My impatience bubbled, and I floated away. Lady Vendy noticed me leave and drifted after me.

"H-hey," she protested. "Where're you going?"

I gritted my incorporeal teeth. "To find Chai."

As we phased through the wall and popped out to the palace corridors, Lady Vendy's features pulled into a misty grimace. "You're just going to those Crystal caves alone?"

"If we wait any longer, it may be too late," I growled, phasing through another wall and exiting into a curling stairwell that I knew led to the aviary. "He was with Sy in the first vision Aster had of him. With my sister…" I clenched my spectral hands. "We need to get both of them out before anything else happens. We've waited long enough already!"

Vendy snatched my shoulder, the touch rippling like water. "Hold up," she said. "You're just a *soul*, Hugh. *Da'torr* Alex can resurrect our vessels, but he can't tie us into them. What are you going to do, just walk through the front door of a *soul-eating demon nest?*" She threw up her hands. "You'll be eaten in seconds!"

I bit my lip. "I… I don't care. I have to try…!"

I shoved past her and floated up the rest of the stairwell, Lady Vendy calling after me in protest, "Hugh…!"

I reached the aviary to find Chai… But stopped.

Da'torr Alexander stood in the center of the aviary alongside Sir Jaq, both fully plated as *Da'torr* held a croaking Chai in his arms, Mal perched on his shoulder.

Henry was by the open window, the rabbit-eared Blacksmith sharpening his newly equipped Spiritcrystal hook he'd attached to his stubbed wrist. To Alexander's left stood Aster, who was fiddling with newly acquired chainmail. To his right stood Bianca and Red, the Alchemists clad in silvery armor with numerous vials and tonic globes strapped to a plethora of pockets and compartments on their matching utility belts. On Bianca's shoulder was Kurn the ferret, who wore a miniature armor and a utility belt complete with numerous Shockvials.

But what I found most intriguing were the ghosts of our fellow vassals who surrounded *Da'torr* Alexander.

Aiden, Nathaniel, Apson and Dalen all wore gleaming Crystal plate and helms, the wispy specters hefting equally gleaming shields as tall as their misty bodies.

All heads—solid and translucent alike—gazed at Lady Vendy and me expectantly.

"Ah," *Da'torr* Alexander hummed gruffly. "There you two are. Grab a shield and plate set. You both have yours specially made for each of you, thanks to Henry."

Lady Vendy looked at Henry with wide eyes. "Uncle! You made all this? Out of just *Spiritcrystal?*"

Henry guffawed and gave a smug grin. "Had to see that my niece was well protected somehow, since you can't be sewn into your vessels right this minute."

Lady Vendy picked up the armor set that looked to fit her best. "But this must have taken months to make…!"

"Three months," Henry grunted, crossing his burly arms. "Been working on it since your other *Da'torr* went missing. Why do you think we all waited this long to go find him? I'm not letting you infiltrate a demon nest without the right precautions, that's for damn sure."

Vendy squealed and threw on her armor, turning experimentally and rotating her arms with excited twirls. The spiked ailettes didn't so much as clatter or squeak with the motion. The only noise they made was a soft breathy sigh.

Vendy cackled. "Awesome…! Thank you, Uncle!" She ran up and hugged him—*actually* hugged him, now that she had the gleaming armor to serve as a tangible medium between her ghost and him. The armor phased through his exposed arms, but she was able to settle on his metal breastplate firmly as he hugged her back in a chuckle.

Then he seemed to remember something. "Oh—don't forget your sword."

He craned back and picked up a glowing sword. Even the hilt was made with Spiritcrystal, its sharp double-edges glinting in the outside light with rainbow glimmers.

Vendy took it with absolute glee. "Oh, this is *so* much cooler than my first one…!" She turned to me with her famous crooked-toothed smile, showing me the beautiful blade excitedly. "Look, look, look! I can actually hold this one…! And it's a *lot* lighter!"

Henry used the tip of his alloyed Crystal hook to scratch his beard thoughtfully. "Without your vessels, you ghosts wouldn't be able to hold any alloyed weapons. Since you can't be resurrected yet, we had to only use the Crystal outright."

I bent to pick up the last armor set, examining it before donning it. It fit snuggly, the shining plate barely weighing more than air itself. "Fascinating…"

"Hugh," *Da'torr* Alexander said, then pointed his chin at two Crystal dual-scythes waiting on a stone bench. Their handles were also made of pure Spiritcrystal, perfect for my spectral fingers to hold. "Those are your new scythes," *Da'torr* informed. "At least until we retrieve Xavier and properly resurrect you."

"Th-thank you, *Da'torr*…!" I hurriedly grabbed the scythes and tucked them into the scabbards at the sides of my armor. "Then, um… are we leaving now? To find him?"

He nodded. "Obviously. Unless you'd prefer to wait for him to come to *us*, along with the rest of the demon horde?"

I vigorously shook my head.

"Good." *Da'torr* nodded to a pile of tall, brightly-glowing shields that could only be made of pure Spiritcrystal as well. "Now grab yourself a shield. And you as well, Vendy. And whatever you do…"

He stormed over to the pile himself and grabbed a glowing shield by its padded, leather straps, slinging it over his back as a low growl slipped from his throat. "Don't tell the queen."

49

CRYSTAL CAGE

XAVIER

RRRrrrrrrmmmm…

R The bright glow of the Crystal pit quivered as another Groundquake shook the mountain's hollow, the radiant walls pulsating around me. Bits of Crystal broke off the walls and *plunked* over my head, debris dusting my tangled hair until the quake settled again.

My heavy skull rolled back and knocked against the beautiful prison, the dull pain barely distracting me from my shriveled stomach.

I didn't know how long I'd been trapped down here. It felt like months. Maybe years. The constant light made it impossible to know what day and night was anymore.

My stomach groaned hideously, and I clutched my belly in a whimper. Queen Ashya had spent Gods knew how many weeks chucking shifters down here for my feast… most of it, I didn't remember. It was always a blur, when the Thirst took over… proving that I truly was, now, nothing more than a ruthless beast.

My stomach groaned again, and I seethed in agony, tears burning as I yielded to a sob.

All those people—all those souls, forced to spend their afterlives as my *fuel*… And I let it happen. I may not have been the one to kill them, but *my* teeth had torn out their specters, *my* tongue had relished their entrancing, honeyed, *glorious* taste…

My belly snarled, craving that sweetness after such a long deprivation.

Despite how many victims I'd eaten the first few weeks, there hadn't been a single shifter tossed down here in what could only be months. I couldn't die of hunger, but *Death* how I wished I could…

"—Death King," a familiar voice hissed above me.

My groggy eyes drifted up the tall, glowing walls. A golden-haired viper woman was peering down at me.

Genevieve. She'd been sneaking a look down here since I was first imprisoned. We knew each other when we were alive, of that we were both certain. But it seemed neither of us could exactly remember any details as to how and when. We both only remembered flashes of the other. Impressions. Feelings… hatred, mostly. All I knew was that she was my enemy. She'd nearly killed a friend of mine, I was sure of it. I just wished I could remember which friend that was.

Though, Genevieve rarely ever came to talk. She was Queen Ashya's prisoner also. I wasn't the only newborn Ashya had been force-feeding… and then starving.

My scratchy voice blistered as I croaked up at Genevieve, "What do you want…?"

The viper hesitated. "I… I remembered something, I think… Something about you."

I rubbed my stinging eyes, the glaring afterimages of these ceaselessly bright walls still shining through my lids. "Have you now…"

"Yes." She craned to look over her shoulder, as if to be sure Queen Ashya wasn't coming. I thought it was useless paranoia, since the queen hadn't appeared in months. I didn't expect her to break that routine of absence anytime soon. Regardless, Genevieve made certain we were alone before she peered down at me again and continued, "You are what they call the Shadowblood… or, half of him."

I sighed. "Genevieve, I don't know what that means."

"It means…" Her voice grew into a dark hiss. "You will bring the End of Existence…"

I rolled my eyes. "Well, wouldn't that be lovely? Maybe then, I'd have no trouble at all escaping from this pit."

"What if you can?" she questioned.

My tone flattened. "You don't think I've tried?"

"What of your Hallows? You have many, I… I remember that. You recently gained the Hallows of Land. You're a Terravoker…" Her next whisper sounded more for herself than for me. "And I… I am, as well…"

I loosened an aggravated breath. Then evoked my rock Hallows, hands glittering with golden light as I pressed my hand against the Spiritcrystal walls and *pulled* with all my might.

The Crystal *cracked* loudly and slid out of its place in jagged, sharp edges, dropping with a *thrump* into the tall pile of similar rubble that glittered uselessly beside me like brittle mica.

"Terravoker or not," I muttered. "I've been trying to pile these damned fragments ever since I came here… I can only pull out as much as I can carry. And it's all just loose ore—I can't seem to connect any of them to provide a stable footing. I just sink back to the bottom every time. I've even tried pulling myself onto the walls and *walking* up there, but… I only get so far before the Thirst comes again and…" I gripped my aching stomach, which moaned in protest, weakening my breaths. Then an afterthought struck me. "Wait. If you remembered my multiple Hallows… You weren't babbling nonsense? About the End of Existence…?"

She ducked her head so I could only see her eyes over the mouth of the pit. "Yes… You will bring it. Alongside your brother."

"My brother…" Something about that did sound familiar. I called up, "Genevieve, how do you know I'll… *we'll*… bring the End, exactly? Who told you this?"

"My mother," she said. "And… my step-father. He is your opposite. The Lightcaster…"

I scoffed. "And I suppose they are the same mother and step-father who 'gifted' you to Queen Ashya?"

Her tone dimmed. "I… suppose…"

"Yes, well… forgive me if I distrust anyone who throws away their child like table scraps. If it were my son, I'd…"

My son.

The face of a wolf-eared baby punctured my memory. I was cradling him in my arms. He had just been born. His lids peeled open so, so slowly, and I found myself staring at a pair of colorless, white eyes.

"Lucas…" Tears stung as his name flooded over my lips. "I-I had a son…! I had a—!"

THUNK!

THUNK!

The ground above me rumbled, two figures having landed up there beside Genevieve. She flinched and shuffled back, and for a moment, I feared it was Queen Ashya and La'Lunaî again, scrambling to my feet and backing against the wall…

But then, suddenly, a small ball of light tumbled down the pit.

It drifted and spiraled lazily overhead. Then it hit my brow… and sank into my skin.

"—*Come on, Alex!*" a younger version of my voice called. Then the bright gleam of the pit fell away, replaced by images that flickered behind my eyes…

I climbed down the stone staircase of the Devouh family crypt, following the ghost of my Ancestor Jilluh. She said our other Ancestors were holding a small celebration, for Ancestor Bathesda's Rae'u Necros—her Day of Death.

I hopped down the steps after Ancestor Jilluh. In my hand quivered a lantern, which housed a single Fallen Light that shined through the fogged glass in a bluish gleam. This was to be my gift for Ancestor Bathesda. It wasn't much, but the Lights were one of the few things ghosts could touch, so I didn't have many options to choose from. I twisted back and paused on the steps, waving for my slow brother to follow me down.

"Come on, Alex!" I called, my voice echoing up the tunnel. "We're going to be late!"

He didn't move from the top of the stairs. He wasn't even facing me, all I could see was his back.

"Alex?" I climbed back up the stairs to meet him. "What's wrong?"

I clasped his shoulder, coming around to face him.

My brother's blue-and-clear eyes didn't pay me the slightest mind. They were fixed on the lantern in his hands. The single ball of light inside it was flickering. It blinked thrice, held for a moment, then dimmed into nothing.

His lantern was now empty.

"I…" he began, his voice tight as his wolf ears grew. "I can't go, now… my gift just faded…"

I looked down at my own lantern, pursing my lips. Then I held it out to him. "We can just share mine. It'll be from both of us."

He scowled at me, wolf ears curling in annoyance. "That doesn't count. We're two people, so we both need one."

I held up a finger with a grin. "Ah, but that rule only applies for non-twins. We have the same blood—so we're basically the same person." I lightly nudged him in the ribs. "We're just two versions of that person."

He gave me a flat stare. But I saw his lips twitch in a reluctant smile, and he broke into a laugh.

"That's the daftest thing I've ever heard, Xavier," he said, but gripped my lantern's looped handle beside my fingers nonetheless, and we climbed down together, catching up to Ancestor Jilluh's ghost.

The memory dripped away, and I was staring up at the gleaming mouth of the pit again.

My voice was hoarse. "Alex…?" My stomach boiled sick. "*Alex*… How could I have forgotten…?"

Another ball of light sparkled down the pit. When it floated close enough for me to reach, I snatched it out of the air and shoved it into my brow—

"—You shouldn't have yelled at her," I chided Alex beside me.

We were standing with our parents on the blackwood stage in the center of the town square. Father was giving a speech for Death's Festival at the podium, his voice amplified by the surrounding speakers to allow all the terrified shifters in the crowd to hear him.

My brother and I stood off to the side of the stage, waiting for Father to hurry and finish his speech.

Alex snorted beside me and folded his arms. "What was I supposed to do? Let her continue to lie about Father to everyone?"

Earlier this morning, one of our classmates accused Father of enslaving the souls of his current vassals. But that was hardly the truth. We'd heard the OLD Eyes of the Death King had committed such crimes, but it seemed the rest of the world thought our father was just as guilty.

But while the young Howless had no right to speak of Father that way, true, that didn't mean Alex had the right to scream at her.

"You only gave them more reason to think the rumors were true," I grumbled. "You scared her, Alex. You scared all of them. Now none of them will want to go near us and… where are you going?"

Alex had stormed off the stage. He offered no reply, then disappeared around the corner without anyone's notice.

I rolled my eyes, turning back to Father at the podium. "Fine," I muttered. "Throw a tantrum…"

That memory faded as well. Light after light fell down the pit toward me, and I eagerly snatched them out of the air, my blood rushing with such thrill, I feared I would burst if I slowed even a little.

I still waited on that same stage in the town square, Father's speech having droned on and on since Alex left. He'd been gone for a long time. Longer than usual. I was beginning to worry.

Thmp!

A sharp pain suddenly struck my stomach, making me double over, dropping to my knees on the stage.

Confused, I rubbed my belly. But the pain didn't seem… physical. It was faint— almost like an echo.

Thmp!

It struck again, and I yelped. Then a barrage of strikes continued, moving to my ribs and my arms, my face and my nose, the echoes of agony crashing like a volley of blunt arrows that I couldn't see…

"Alex...!" Somehow, I knew this was Alex's pain. Not mine. It was an instinct, an impression that screamed at me with every strike of pain that split through my soul.

He was in trouble.

I gritted my sharpening teeth, then dashed off the stage and sprinted through the streets where I'd seen him leave.

After turning two corners, I found him in an alleyway.

He was surrounded by a group of children our age—young Howllords I recognized from the Academy—who were kicking and beating him to a Bloody pulp on the cobblestones. Each strike they made caused that phantom echo of pain to split through my stomach again.

Alex's blood-stained face was so drenched with crimson, it was hard to see his grey skin. The sight set my pulse into a blind, crazed rage. I screamed, my claws growing as I barreled toward the nearest classmate and tackled him to the ground. I scratched and I hit as hard as I could, the boy retaliating under me, but I had higher ground—

The two other boys hauled me off him and threw me to the ground beside Alex. My ribs splintered with pain under their kicking feet, my world a flurry of agony...

But that didn't matter anymore. When I looked at Alex, he wasn't moving. I couldn't see if he was breathing.

"Hey!" an adult's voice barked from the mouth of the alley. Armored footsteps clattered toward us, and through my swollen eye, I saw a patrolling Reaper running for us. "What in Death is going on here...!"

Our classmates scattered. They were gone when the Reaper found Alex and me. A second Reaper came up beside him, the two cursing under their breaths as they lifted us off the ground and hurried us to the nearest hospital.

—I was thrown out of that last memory, and quickly grabbed a new one that floated down the pit—

It took hours for Alex to wake up in the patient bed beside mine.

He was wheezing when his head turned toward me, and he croaked. "Xavier...?" He sounded disoriented, his hand fumbling to reach over his bed toward mine. "What happened...? I thought... I thought I was dead..."

Tears hit again, and I blubbered, "I-I thought you were too... I thought—I thought you l-l... left me..." I reached for his hand, squeezing his fingers as tight as I could. My voice broke. "Don't ever leave me... I-I don't want to be alone..."

Alex sniffled, his own tears draining down his face. "M-me either..."

—Another memory—

"How did this happen...?!" I panted in a panic, patting my soaked clothes and shivering from the cold water clinging to my skin. But this wasn't my skin, was it? This was Alexander's. Why was I in Alex's body? How was I here? What happened to mine...?

—Another—

"Guys...!" Bianca all but shouted through the fuzzing com-screen. "I think I might have a lead about Xavier's body...!"

—One memory left—

"... Welcome back to life, Xavier," my brother said with a toothy grin, clasping my skinny fingers for the first time in six Bloody years. "This time, we'll do it right. Born together..."
"Die together," I finished with a warm, relieved smile.

... The last of the memories dissolved.

I was somehow lying on my back now, staring up at the mouth of the gleaming pit.

"Alex..." A laugh bubbled out of me. "How could I forget Alex...?"

"—We all forget our family for a while," a voice called down from above the pit. A young man's head peeked down at me. I recognized him as that demon teenager who first found me when I'd Changed. Bloods, I hadn't seen him in months... Taymen, if I recalled.

Beside him was Syreen, who peered down at me with annoyance. "Do you remember anything about *my* brother now, Shadow-half?" she called down.

I grimaced up at her. She was a face I'd hoped would *remain* absent. "No," I growled, pushing to my feet.

She scowled down at me, but sniffed.

Taymen sounded apologetic. "This was all I could find over the months... it's hard to sort through all the memories scattered around the Horde."

My brow furrowed. "You can find memories? How?"

"I'm a Somniovoker," he explained with a shrug. "I can put my soul into Aspirre and look for memories there."

That did sound familiar... Hadn't I done as much myself, before...?

"But," I began skeptically. "We're Necrofera. Rotten souls can't enter Aspirre. We only dream of memories."

I vaguely recalled someone telling me that once. Though, I couldn't quite remember who. Still, the rule was there in my mind, the same way I knew that I breathed with my lungs and not my toenails. It was simply a fact.

Taymen hummed. "Guess I missed the memo. I just tried it once after I'd Changed and *bam*. I was in. I've been collecting memories for the Horde ever since. Well—they don't actually know that though. I just pass them on in their sleep. The last time I gave someone a memory while awake, she almost tore out my Seam and—"

"I apologized for that," Syreen huffed. "I thought we agreed to put that behind us?"

"We did," he muttered, "but that doesn't mean I'm going to make the same mistake twice with someone else who might *not* apologize for it."

She massaged her temple. "Oh, for the love of Shel… Shadow half: Catch."

Syreen tossed down a rope made of thick, braided willow branches, the serrated leaves unfurling before my nose.

"Well?" She said testily. "We gathered these and sealed them with my Arborvoking. Don't spit on our efforts by staying down there."

My limbs were frozen. I stared at the rope in disbelief. It was a way out… An actual, stable, *reliable* way out of this Gods forsaken pit—something I'd started to think I would never see.

I reached for the rope, hope pounding for the first time in a long, long time. But I hesitated, my fingers halting just before a serrated leaf. I squinted a suspicious eye at Syreen. "Why are you helping me?"

Her teeth sharpened. "Because my brother is *your* vassal. And I'll be damned if I be involved in his death for a second time."

Taymen corrected with a helpful finger, "Well, third time, actually. Remember the Battle of Aldamstria—?"

"—We aren't counting that!" She snapped, then glared down at me. "Are you climbing out of there or aren't you? I need you to find my brother!"

I considered that, murmuring, "I suppose I need the same of you… fine. It's a deal." I took the thick, braided branches, the rough bark scratching my palms and causing the scrapes to mend with slithering, black blood.

CRACK! CRACK!

The pit vibrated as something hit the floor on their level above me, knocking me off my feet and onto my back. My stomach moaned painfully, the Thirst gnawing my belly again.

The braided branches suddenly fell over me in a thumping tangle, their entire length slipping from Syreen's hands.

Then her throat was snagged by an enflamed hand.

Queen Ashya.

"Plotting to escape with our resident Death King, are we?" Ashya cooed, her flames scorching Syreen's black-squirming throat. The queen's gaze flicked to Taymen and Genevieve from up there, the two cowering back. Ashya's tongue gave chiding *tsk, tsk, tsks.* "Poor little newborns… such hope. Such inspiring determination." Her grip tightened on Syreen's neck, making her squeal. "We must correct that ill behavior… La'Lunaî?"

She tuned behind her. And from my vantage in the pit, I saw the little Seadragon girl step beside Ashya merrily.

Ashya purred, "These two are *your* Underlings, yes?"

La'Lunaî folded her arm. "They are. And this isn't the first time I've found those specific newborns attempting to flee."

Ashya hummed. "I see… Then perhaps they'll enjoy time in isolation from the rest of the Horde." She peered down at me with a sneer. "And away from my prized possession."

My head suddenly throbbed with agony, the Mark in my skull writhing.

Ashya's voice echoed down the pit in a low rumble. "You'd do well to remember who you belong to, Death King… I hope your Thirst is at its peak." Her lips curled in a smile. "We march tonight."

They all vanished from sight at the mouth of the pit, leaving me with naught but the gleaming Spiritcrystal walls.

And the shriveling pain of Thirst crunching my stomach.

50

RESCUE MISSION

ALEXANDER

The cavern winds licked over my face as we soared through the churning ceiling mist, Floating Lights gliding past us as we flew on the backs of Flamedragons over the rocky peaks of the mountains.

Chai flapped ahead of us as fast as his wings could take him. Mal flew behind him determinedly, alongside Bridge and Lady Lilac taking up the rear of their formation.

The Flamedragon I rode had no trouble keeping pace, the reptile's wingspan far larger than a raven's. Bianca rode with me, keeping hold of my ribs to keep from falling off while Kurn had fastened himself to her shoulder-guard. Bianca's and my tall, Crystal shields were strapped to opposite arms and hanging horizontally at the dragon's sides, so as not to disrupt its wings.

Similarly, Henry rode on a different Flamedragon with Jaq clinging to him for dear life. The viper had never been keen on heights, but did his best to keep hold of his Crystal shield just as well as the Blacksmith.

The armored ghosts of Vendy, Hugh and Dalen rode on their own Flamedragon, and Nathaniel, Aiden, Apson and Red had one for themselves. The lot of them had the same tall shields as the rest of us.

After hours of flying, Chai finally descended from the ceiling mists.

Our Flamedragons followed him down to a particular mountainside, and we dismounted after landing in a sparse forest.

Chai perched on a tree branch and fluttered his wings, his head dipping anxiously at us.

We tied the Flamedragons to the trees, keeping them away from any Necrofera. If our current plan failed, we needed to be sure a contingency plan was in place.

My boots crunched under pine straw as I followed Chai, the raven flying from branch to branch along the mountainside.

This path was thinly beaten, which meant not many shifters had traversed these mountains. But *some* had certainly done so, and recently. The likely suspects were the Necrofera hordes. Which, hopefully, meant we were drawing near.

Chai led us to the small mouth of a cavern. He didn't enter. Instead, he flared his neck feathers and screeched wildly, his sounds a warning tone.

I crouched to the raven and let him flap to my shoulder alongside Mal, my throat rumbling, "It's here."

I evoked my fire Hallows, letting the heat in my soul pour out of my palm in a jet of orange flames for light, then led the way into the cavern, the others' armored footfalls clattering behind me. Feral bats screeched awake at our intrusion, flying past us in an enormous cloud as we braced. When they receded, we shook ourselves to regain our wits and continued into the darkness.

Aster lit his own fire beside me, providing more light over the dirt floor and rocky walls. The ghosts' Crystal armor was bright enough to give the rest of our group light, so we had little problem stepping over sharp stalagmites and loose stones.

A blue glow spilled from a conjoining tunnel up ahead.

I snuffed my fire. Aster did the same. Then I pulled my Crystal shield in front of me to hide my visage from any stray demons that may be lurking in that bright tunnel. The others followed my example and readied their own shields.

Now we all resembled moving pillars of Spiritcrystal. Which was the plan.

I signaled for everyone to cluster against me. We were shoulder to shoulder and back to back, forming a circle to hide every crevice of living—or dead—body in our party.

To my left, Aster muttered, "You know this isn't going to do anything for the scent, right?"

I growled, "I know. But I can't control that. So, I'm choosing to ignore it."

Aster rolled his eyes, but raised no protest.

I took a breath, held it, then stepped into the gleaming tunnel. I was glad we were wearing boots so we could traverse the mystical floor at all. The Crystal cavern hadn't even a speck of dirt or dull rock in it. The glowing stones sprouted from every angle, dipping and twisting and shooting with sharp buds of razor-like ores that glinted with rainbow sheens under its bright blue radiance.

It was absolutely *breathtaking*.

This wasn't nearly the same look as the refined Crystal we wielded. Our weapons and shields did have a similar blue radiance, yes, but... This was

Spiritcrystal in its rawest form—untouched by any miners or smiths. It was jagged and uneven, natural and spectacular…

Though, the constant light was stinging my eyes.

Skritch-skritch-skritch-skritch…

I tensed at the sound of scratching.

Skritch-skritch-skritch-skritch…

I peeked round the edge of my shield. Bianca was scraping one of her daggers over a Crystal mound. She was collecting the rainbow flakes in a glass jar, grinning like a maniac as she also began pocketing smaller Crystals with metal tongs and tucked them away in her utility belt's many compartments.

"Bianca…!" I hissed, twisting back to see everyone else in our formation was just as confused by her sudden absence. Red was desperately trying to fill the hole she'd left in our disguise. I broke formation, snagging her arm. "Bianca, *what* are you doing?"

She didn't look the least bit ashamed with that delirious smile. "I had an idea and wanted to try something when we get back—"

"This is *not* the time for…!"

"—D'you smell that, Jace?" a woman's nasally voice echoed from around the tunnel's glaring bend. The sound of someone sniffing the air followed. "It almost smells like… Clean souls…"

I bit back a curse and swept an arm in front of Bianca, shoving us both against the bright wall. We tucked our shields against each other, and I barely saw the rest of our party doing the same with their shields across the tunnel before our view was blocked entirely.

Footfalls pattered toward us.

This time, a man's voice rumbled, "It's coming from over here…"

The footfalls grew closer. They stopped between our two hidden groups. I heard a pair of boots crunch over the loose shavings Bianca hadn't caught with her jar, and we tightened our huddle against the wall.

"What the Void…?" The man's voice sounded directly in front of me. My pulse quickened as he questioned, "Never seen this before… looks like someone was scratching at this."

The nasally woman snorted near our other group. "It's a bunch'a rocks, Jace… but *Bloods* it smells so good over here…"

"—Wow, uh, hey!" A new voice piped cheerfully, interrupting them. "What's going on over here…!"

I grimaced, recognizing that voice.

It was *Aster.*

I dared a peek through the crack of Bianca's and my shields. The man, Jace, had turned away from us to look at Aster. The idiot demon had removed his armor and snuck out of the other group's formation, leaving his shield stuck in the ground. He was now pretending to be strolling into the tunnel for the first time, his posture drastically casual.

Jace glowered at the intrusion. "What are you doing over here, Newborn? The Queens wanted all of you to form up for the march."

Aster laughed, his unnecessarily loud voice echoing through the tunnel. "Yeah, well, uh…! I could ask *you* guys the same…! Hah, hah…!"

What is that idiot doing?

A sudden roar of more footfalls came from around the bend, and eager voices buzzed about.

"What is that *smell*…!"

"… has to be new Clean Ones!"

"—They're finally letting us eat again?!"

"Thank Bloods, I've been *starving* for months…!"

Death, I cursed in my thoughts. *Death, Death, Death, Death, Death…!*

"—What…" a new girl's voice boomed testily, cutting through the noise and silencing them all. "… is all this commotion about?"

No one spoke, despite their previous glee. It seemed that had been snuffed and replaced with whimpering fear.

Jace was the only voice who didn't seem affected by the frightening tone, reporting dutifully. "We smelled Clean Souls over here, Mistress. Was it intentional, or do we have intruders?"

I looked past my shield again to get a glimpse of what was happening.

Among the mass of Sentient Necrofera cowering in the tunnel, a little Seadragon girl with emerald hair and eyes stood before Jace.

La'Lunai!

Damn it! And that thick viper woman was with her. That Ashya Queen. This one had grey scales and long, plaited black hair, her small nose thin while her face was rounded.

La'Luna glanced at Ashya with a raised brow. "I hadn't sent for new Clean Ones."

Ashya's gaze narrowed. "Nor had I… Search the caverns. I don't want any of you to feast until we reach the Death Palace—"

"Oh, hey!" Aster chimed suddenly, backing up toward my shield with a merry hum. "Look what I found!"

He reached for my shield—and yanked me out into the open. My heart stopped, all the demons' glowing-white pupils fixated on me.

I clenched my teeth in a panicked mutter, "Aster, *what* are you doing?!"

He hissed under his breath, "Sorry. We only have three futures that lead to what we want. You sort of… get discovered in all of those. I thought it'd be easier to speed things up a bit."

A seething rage burned my throat. "And I survive in all of them?"

He coughed nervously. "More like one."

"Gods damn it, Aster—"

"Oh, look at that!" Aster announced with an overdramatic look of shock. His meercat ears perked as he pointed at my face. "Isn't this the Death King's *twin brother?* Man, what are the odds he'd be here, where *his brother* is being held prisoner! Did I mention it's his brother?"

The queens grew still as they studied my face. More particularly, my eyes.

Ashya's lips split with a conniving smile. "The king has a twin…?"

La'Lunaî folded her arms ruefully. "Regrettably, yes. I had the misfortune of facing them in High Neverland. This one also has those unnatural collection of Hallows."

Ashya snatched my chin and inspected me eagerly. "Lost, are we, little knight? Thought to return your dear brother home to mother and father—?"

I spit in her face.

Her smile drew into a thin line, her tone souring. "Well… I suppose I'm feeling quite generous today, little twin… Why don't we reunite you with your brother?" She grabbed my throat and dragged me through the tunnel. "I will enjoy watching our starved Death King feast upon his dearest brother… *alive…*"

I inched my gaze back at our hidden group. I glared at Aster, who gave me an encouraging thumbs up.

Aster, I thought angrily, letting the queen drag me through the crowd of hungry demons. *If I live through this, I'm going to Cleanse you myself…*

HUGH

From behind our shield, we watched as *Da'torr* Alexander was dragged out of the tunnel, disappearing around the bend. The other queen, La'Lunaî, ordered the others to get back in their formation. When they were gone, save for Aster who stayed behind to signal that it was safe, we all loosened our lungs and lowered our shields.

Bianca was the first to shout at Aster, "What in Death was that for?! They just took Alex because of you!"

Aster held up pacifying hands. "Hey, I was just speeding things up. It was going to happen eventually, no matter what we did."

Bianca groaned and buried her face in her hands. "Now I see why Alex hates Seers…"

Red scratched behind an ear uncertainly, making the armored Kurn scamper to his other shoulder. "So, uh… now what?" Red asked. "We were kinda followin' *his* lead, so…"

Bianca's long ears folded back in annoyance. "Aw, who cares? He didn't have a solid plan in the first place." She went over to Mal and Chai, who had taken shelter under a cluster of Crystals. She scooped them both up in her arms and huffed. "We were just going to follow Chai's direction anyway. But since it sounds like they're taking Alex *to* Xavier, even Mal should be able to find him now." She twisted her mouth at the twin ravens impatiently. "All right, guys. Throw me a bone here—where are we going?"

Both ravens pointed their beaks down the tunnel where the demons had left.

Bianca chuffed smugly. "Good start. Come on, everyone. Keep your shields going. Hopefully, Alex's disruption will throw off the whole 'Clean Soul' scent or whatever."

We all moved out, following Bianca and the ravens.

With Lady Lilac ducking her head from my glowing shoulder-guard, I was the last to chase after them alongside Lady Vendy, the two of us raising our Crystal weapons at the ready while keeping watch of the rear, in case any more demons decided to come down the opposite way.

But when we passed a narrow crevice, the echoing voice of a girl caught my spectral ears.

"…do you think is all that noise about?" the voice questioned. She sounded irritated.

She also sounded familiar.

"Sy?" I whispered, my soul stumbling to a cold stop at the crevice. It was too deep to see through the other side… but it was just big enough for me to squeeze through, even with my radiant armor.

I turned to the others, who hadn't noticed I'd paused and were still moving ahead.

Only Lady Vendy beside me stopped. One of her brown rabbit ears lifted as she questioned me, "Something up, Hugh?"

I had my soul grow one of my lion ears to better hear, pushing it against the crevice. "I… I think I hear Sy…"

Lady Vendy mimicked my posture, swiveling her long ear toward the gap. "Your sister?"

There were two more voices murmuring in there, alongside Sy. One boy, and another girl, by the sound of it. It was difficult to hear any distinct words, but a few slipped through clear enough. They seemed to be discussing the recent commotion. Though, they didn't sound sure of the details behind it.

I licked my lips. Then squeezed through the crevice.

"Hugh!" Lady Vendy hissed. "Where are you going?"

"To see Sy," I called back quietly, pushing onward through the crevice.

I heard Lady Vendy chew on a string of curses... then she followed me inside.

We sidled through the narrow tunnel, curling around two bends, then finally found the opening into a small, isolated cavern of brightly glowing Crystal.

When I squeezed through, helping Lady Vendy out after me, I found the source of the three voices. The boy, surprisingly, was someone I recognized. He was the one who told me of Sy at the colosseum months ago, wasn't he? The Somniovoker?

The scale-skinned girl beside him was none other than the traitor: Genevieve. What in Land was she doing here?

But my eyes stopped on the teenaged girl sitting cross-legged between them both, her back facing me. I knew that cropped hair anywhere.

Sy...!

I absently took a step forward.

All three heads suddenly jerked to a stop. Sy's lion ears perked straight up, along with the boy's.

The trio had gone eerily still. Then, Genevieve whispered, "Do you smell... souls...?"

The three twisted their gazes straight at Lady Vendy and me.

Their white pupils were dilated so wide, I couldn't see even an inch of their irises. Not even my sister's. Her wild stare was blind to me.

I swallowed. "Sy...?"

51

THE LORD OF SOULS

ALEXANDER

Ashya dragged me through the massive nest, descending each level of the Crystal caverns until we, at last, reached what I hoped was the mountain's gleaming floor.

The horde of shouting demons reluctantly parted to make way for us, their mouths dripping with saliva and white pupils dilated so wide their irises were hidden. There were even mongrel Fera in the mix, the beasts snarling and snapping their jaws at me.

Ashya pulled me over to the mouth of a pit—and shoved me over the ledge.

I screamed as I tumbled down, quickly evoking my rock Hallows to shove the jagged edges of Crystal spires away from my chest, then used my wind Hallows to puff a strong gale under me just before I hit the radiant, blood-stained floor. The wind cushioned my landing, and I was able to safely stumble over my knees in a heavy pant.

Ashya's chuckles reverberated down the pit, her round face peering from the mouth above me with pure amusement.

"Oh, little Death King…" She sang down. "I've brought you a special treat…"

I looked around the pit, my pulse thundering.

A slumped body was splayed on the floor, curled on his side. His shadowy grey hair was a tangled mess as it hid his face from me.

"Xavier…?" I hushed, pushing to my feet in a thrill. "Is it really…?"

The body twitched. His head lifted, staring at the glowing wall. Then, so, so slowly, he craned his gaze to me. His white pupils were so dilated, they hid his heterochromic irises. Like a machine, he rose, creeping toward me with blind hunger. His mouth and bearded chin were stained with dried blood. And given its crimson hue, I doubted it was *his* rotted blood.

"X…Xavier…" I warned shakily, reaching for the scythe-spheres dangling from my neck.

No. I lowered my hands, my breaths quivering. *It won't come to that. He'll know it's me. He'll know…*

Xavier crawled closer, his sightless gaze unnerving. A deep, guttural click rumbled from his throat, his teeth sharpening and wolf ears growing. He was more wolf than shifter, now. And that wolf was hunting me.

My throat dried. "Xavier… I need you to snap out of—"

He lunged for me in a crazed snarl, teeth diving for my throat.

I panicked and ducked away from his bite, but he thrashed his claws at me, aiming for my face. I caught his wrists, struggling to keep him back. He shoved me against the glowing wall and snapped at my throat like a feral beast, his skin squirming with black sludge.

I kept a firm grip of his wrists, leaning my face away from his sharp teeth and scraping my scalp against the Crystal wall.

"XAVIER!" I shouted with all my might, so loud that it caused the Crystals to shudder above us. "IT'S *ALEX*…!"

Xavier froze mid-bite.

His teeth retracted along with his claws. "Al… Alex…?" His gleaming pupils quivered, fighting to regain his sight. At last, they shrank to a docile size, his heterochromia visible again.

Xavier finally saw me.

Then burst into tears.

"Alex…!" He collapsed into me, crushing my ribs so hard, they were sore even under my armor. He broke into a trembling sob. "It's you—it's really you…! T-t-t-they've kept me trapped down here for so long and… and I… I-I ate *so many…*" He couldn't finish, his throat squealing shut as his sobs consumed him, so powerful all he could do was weep into my chest. "I'm a *monster…*"

Bloods. I grabbed him in a stubborn embrace, my own tears stinging as I ground my sharpened teeth. *What have they done to you?*

"You're not a monster," I growled, his grueling sobs puncturing my fury. I strengthened my hold of him. "You're my *brother.* I don't care what you are or what you've done. I only care about getting you home… where you belong."

His sobs heaved deeper, his lungs shuddering. "H-h-h… how can I… belong anywhere now…?"

"You have a family waiting for you." I snatched his head so he couldn't pull away from me, determined to let him know I was here for him. "We… we knew you'd Changed. None of us cared. We've been trying to find you every Gods damned second you've been gone. I need my brother, Xavier. Your wife needs her husband… and your son needs his father."

"My son…" His voice was a distant murmur. I eased my grip from his head, and he quivered while rising slowly. He took a deep, calming breath. "My… wife… I can't remember…" He drew in another long inhale.

—then clapped a hand over his nose in a sudden shock.

"No, no, no, no, no…" He scuttled away from me, covering his nose. His pupils were flickering again, but he fought to keep them focused on my face. "I-I… I can't… I can't be near you… You have to leave. I haven't eaten in months, and you smell so…" He sank his teeth into his own hand, stifling a sobbing scream as black blood surged from the puncture wounds, and tears streamed down his face all over again.

Ashya's voice *tsked* from above us, startling me. I'd nearly forgotten she was still up there. "Ah, ah, ah," she sang. "I didn't come here for a happy ending, little king…"

She curled her fingers—and Xavier's body lurched forward on its own, tackling me to the floor.

I desperately shoved his face away from me, but his sharpened teeth still hovered over my throat.

"Go on," Ashya cooed. "I'm waiting…"

Xavier's pupils flickered violently, his snarls deathly resistant. "N… No…!" he growled, his breath hot over my neck. Then he tore himself off me and screamed up at the queen. *"I will NEVER eat another soul…!"*

His fingers glittered with violet light—and he *jammed* his claws into his own skull, digging deep and shrieking in pain, but he didn't stop.

I watched in horror as his fingers plucked out a small, wriggling worm. His hands glimmered with more violet light, which dampened under a flurry of black veins. He squeezed his fingers around the worm.

Splikch…!

He crushed it into oblivion, the poisonous veins he evoked disintegrating it.

Ashya's grey scales drained to a ghostly white above us.

"Alex," Xavier growled, his white-pupiled gaze snapping to me. "I've been starved for months and I don't have much strength by myself… I need a lift."

I nodded, evoking my rock Hallows over the pit's walls.

Crunch!

I forced a piece of the Crystal walls to jut outward in a large, sturdy platform, still connected to the wall itself and adding to its stability like a large, natural stairstep.

Crunch! Crunch! Crunch! Crunch!

I pulled and yanked and ripped at the wall, molding more steps to form a spiraling, Crystal stairwell.

Xavier darted up the steps without a wasted moment, and I rushed after him. He seemed to struggle the higher we climbed, though. His legs wobbled and swayed, repeatedly collapsing into the jagged walls in heavy pants. His months of hunger must have weakened him.

Then I'll have to give him an extra boost, I decided.

I switched to Aerovoking, my hands glittering scarlet—and I thrust a dense gale up at Xavier. My wind was so strong, it lifted him off the Crystal steps, and he hovered in the air for a startled moment.

Then he snapped his gaze down at me, and seemed to understand. He evoked his own Aerovoking and took control of my created gale, swirling it around him and churning it at a rapid speed. It spiraled into an isolated twister, which sucked me in alongside him as he ripped a determined growl and propelled us out of the pit's mouth.

We landed in a crouch with a hard *crack,* standing before Ashya and La'Lunaî both.

The queens cowered back. Not even the countless mass of Sentients around us dared to approach, keeping a wide perimeter away from Xavier and me.

La'Lunaî staggered back, fear wrenching her scaled features. "I-I-I told you they were *freaks*…!"

Ashya was frozen with terror, the viper's face riddled with disbelief. "What *are* you…?"

"A Concept," Xavier and I answered in unison. I held out my hands, one bursting with fire and the other sloshing with water. Xavier's sparked with zapping lightning and crystallizing ice. "A *dangerous* Concept."

We slammed our hands on the ground.

A vortex of purple flames, streaking lightning, flooding waves, and showering ice exploded around us. The mismatched inferno swirled outward over the mass of screaming Necrofera, leaving a wide perimeter of bodies in its wake.

Including the two queens.

The horde was slow to recover from their injuries. Ashya and La'Lunaî healed faster, their skin crawling with black blood as they backed away from us with trembling limbs.

"K… K-kill them…!" Ashya shrieked to the horde, curling her fingers in the air—and pulled the entire nest down to this floor in a hail of demons. "All of you—*any of you*—KILL THEM!"

Her commanding hand sent the demons hurtling after us against their will. I prepared my fire again, bracing for the onslaught heading straight for us…

But Xavier stepped in front of me. He drew in a deep breath, let it out in a smooth, even stream as he closed his eyes and outstretched his violet glowing hands… then jerked those hands toward his chest.

Splikch! Splikch! Splikch! Splikch! Splikch!

All at once, the first row of fifty demons had their Marks *yanked* out of their skulls by his Necrovoking. The blackened worms flew to his hands—then *squished* between his fingers. He summoned his Infeciovoking next, and the Marks sizzled into vapor as he destroyed them with his poisons.

That row of demons staggered and fell to their knees in confusion, testing their newfound control of their limbs in wonder.

Xavier evoked his Hallows again, his fingers glittering with violet light as he gave another effortless curl of his fingers.

Splikch! Splikch! Splikch! Splikch! Splikch!

Row after row, all who dared to near us at a ten yards radius had their Marks extracted with little more than a flick of Xavier's wrists. By the time Ashya and La'Lunaî had their minions stop the pattern, Xavier had freed hundreds of Sentients.

I stared at my brother in awe. Xavier's long hair drifted at his shoulders as a light breeze ran through the Crystal cavern, the glowing walls shining around him as he held himself high, his gaze menacing.

The army of Fera he'd freed now regarded Xavier with an all-too familiar look. The last few years of traveling with every Relicblood on Nirus gave me a first-hand view into the transformation of any society—of any culture whose hierarchy shifted because of a single, crucial moment that marked the dawn of a new era.

They looked to Xavier like a true King of Demons.

"All those newly freed," Xavier roared to the crowd of mesmerized Sentients, his booming voice rumbling through the Crystal caverns—and even shaking my own belly. "Go home to your families. Your torture is over." His tone crackled like embers. "There will be no more Marking of *any* demons."

The free Sentients were silent, as if in disbelief. But one web-eared man suddenly burst into tears and broke away from the rest, rushing to stand behind Xavier. The man's scaled hands glittered with green Hallows, and a surge of water sloshed in the air above his palms.

"I… I don't have a family to go home to." The man stammered in a light Marincian accent, tears still streaming as he looked at Xavier with unbreakable gratitude. There wasn't an ounce of doubt in that gaze, which curdled when he looked at the two Demon Queens. "They killed my family when they killed me. I will see them *Cleansed…!*"

The rest of the Sentients followed his example, clambering with their own Hallows and surrounding Xavier and me, glaring at the two queens with pure, seething hatred.

Ashya and La'Lunaî shuffled back against the remaining horde of still-Marked demons.

"Very well…" Xavier cracked his neck, making the queens flinch. His snarl was a deep, guttural hiss. "Cleansing granted."

BIANCA

Rrrrrrrr…

A low rumble shook the Crystal caverns. At first, I thought it was another stupid Groundquake, but then I heard shouts ahead in the bright tunnels, getting closer by the minute. It almost sounded like a stampede was headed our way.

"Hide!" I yelped to the others behind me.

Our team backed against the glowing walls and put up their shields. I did the same, passing Chai over to Jaq while I cradled Mal with one arm and hoisted my tall shield with the other.

The horde burst past us in a frantic mob.

I struggled to keep my shield up, demons accidentally shoving into me in their hurry. I peeked past the edge of the shield to see what in Bloods was going on.

The Fera poured through the tunnel like a chaotic river, shoving past each other as if their limbs were moving on their own, some tripping to the floor and being crushed in a gush of black blood under the trampling boots of their fellow demons.

But there were others, I noticed, who clung to any Crystal pillars their claws could snag, scratch marks digging trenches in the radiant rocks. It looked like they were pulling against *themselves*. Their legs strained to continue forward, but their arms kept hold of the pillars for dear life, clamping down with sharpened teeth, even.

When the stampede finally disappeared around the bend, the few straggling demons were *still* stuck to the pillars.

I hesitantly lowered my shield. "What in Bloods…?" I pursed my lips, then sidled up to one Sentient who straddled a thick spire on all fours, his claws determinedly wedged in the Crystals. Bloods, he *really* didn't want to go wherever he was being forced to go.

"Uh…" I began with a perked rabbit ear. "Do… do you need help?"

The Sentient barred his teeth. "Please… Don't let me… leave…" His claws dragged down an inch, and he panicked. "I-I-I want my freedom, too…!"

I blinked. "Huh?"

Jaq trotted up beside me, his chain-scythe out and ready as he questioned, "What's up with this one?"

I shook my head. "I don't know. He says not to let him leave—"

Something black and slimy shot out of his forehead suddenly.

It flew across the tunnel, and the other Sentients had similar slimes split from their heads and fly across the cavern—

Splikch!

The blobs of slime were crushed by the thin fingers of a man with shadowy grey hair. His hand glowed violet, and the slimes disintegrated to mist. He lifted his blue-and-clear eyes, pupils shining white like burning stars.

My rabbit ears folded down in shock, Jaq and I shouting, "Xavier!"

—The Sentient next to us suddenly unlatched himself from the pillar and nearly knocked me over as he rushed to grovel at Xavier's bare feet alongside the other Sentients. They sobbed and thanked him over and over, their voices tripping over one another as they swore to follow him wherever he asked.

I looked over at Jaq and the others, who all lowered their shields and scratched their heads. Jaq only shrugged at me, not sure what was going on either.

Behind Xavier, I spotted Alex. And behind *Alex* was an entire army of demons. This horde was different from the first wave, though. They weren't desperately trampling each other to leave the tunnel. Their limbs weren't moving without their permission. *This* horde stayed right where they were, behind Xavier. And it looked like that's where they wanted to stay.

Alex found me with Jaq and trotted to us, panting, "Good, there you all are. Any injuries in need of Healing?"

I absently shook my head, still staring dumbly at Xavier and the horde of demons as I muttered, "All good here…"

Jaq circled a finger at the confusing scene. "But, uh, what's going on with *this?*"

Alex's lips tugged with a proud grin as he glanced at his brother. "Exactly what you'd expect of *Xavier, the Lord of Souls.*" His grin curled into a laughing smile. "Our demonic Death King is enforcing his new law… and accidentally gaining himself a horde of adoring subjects in the process."

"Woah…" I breathed, impressed.

I watched Xavier crouch to his newest followers and gently tell them they didn't have to bow. He encouraged them to go home, to see their families. A few of them took the offer and ran out of there as fast as their stumbling legs could take them, but most stayed behind, offering their Hallows for the battle against the Demon Queens. Xavier tried to talk them out of it, but they scrambled into the ranks, leaving him shaking his head in a sigh.

Then Xavier noticed Jaq and me.

"Bianca?" he called, as if he only just remembered my name. "Jaq? Bloods, what are you both doing here?" He came over to meet us, but paused when he squinted at me. "Wait… Since when do you wear armor, Bianca?"

I punched his shoulder. "Since I infiltrated a mountain full of demons to rescue your undead arse."

He rubbed his neck with an embarrassed laugh. "I suppose that's sensible—*Hgh…!*"

He was jumped by the armored ghosts of Aiden, Nathaniel, Apson and Dalen, all of whom found some part of him to hug as tight as they could and cry happily, "*Da'torr!*"

Xavier's shining pupils started flickering. His face wrenched tight, and he pulled away from the ghosts, plugging his nose.

"Keep your distance…!" Xavier warned, clutching his stomach when it gave a hollow rumble. "I… I haven't eaten in months…"

I clapped my hands. "Oh, right! One sec." I opened one of my utility belt's compartments, pulling out a Storagebox. I tossed it to Xavier, and he fumbled to catch it.

"What's this?" he asked, squinting at the box to look at its shrunken contents.

"It's food," I explained. "*Normal* food. We knew you'd been starved, so I packed as much as I could stuff in there."

He stared at the box with wide, longing eyes. But he stopped and twisted to the equally hungry gazes of his new subjects behind him. He frowned at me. "Is there enough for everyone?"

I lifted a finger, but it went limp as I clicked my teeth shut. "Mm… probably not… But we can get more at the palace. Can you guys hold off long enough till then?"

They all muttered their agreements, though most of them sounded unsure. Still, it was better than a solid 'no', I guess.

Xavier handed me back the Storagebox. "I'll wait as well… I'm not the only one starving."

I grumbled while putting the box back in my utility belt's compartment. "If you're sure… Just do me a favor and *please* don't eat us?"

Xavier's face soured. "I won't... Alex woke me enough for that much, at least. If I see anyone back there coming for you, I'll snag them with my Necrovoking. Sound fair?"

I sighed. "Whatever you say, *Lord of Souls...*" I stole a glance at Alex. Mal had fluttered on his shoulder, just as Chai perched on Xavier's cheerily. But while Alex was looking over our team, he frowned.

"Where are Hugh and Vendy?" Alex asked.

I twisted behind me. Everyone was here... except for those two. My nose scrunched. "What the Void? Weren't they just behind us?"

Mal and Chai started screeching. The ravens flew off their Reapers and flapped through the tunnel down the way we came.

"Death," Alex groaned. He plucked his scythe-spheres from his necklace and had his weapons materialize. "Why don't I have a grand feeling about this?"

HUGH

The three Sentients of Genevieve, the Somniovoker teen, and my sister all stared at Vendy and me with dilated, white pupils.

I shuffled back toward the crevice in a tight swallow, my voice trembling. "S-s-s... Sy...?"

My sister was the only demon to pause. Her pupils flickered, her gaze narrowing at me. "Hugh...?" She whispered. "Bloods be good... Is it truly—?"

Genevieve and the Somniovoker bounded for us.

I cringed, raising my scythes over my head, but my arms were too slow to cut—

Sy tackled them both to the floor.

The Somniovoker's head speared against a spire of sharp Crystal, black blood spurting until he pulled himself off the spike. His wound mended in a surge of blackened worms. He blinked sober again as his pupils shrank dizzily.

Genevieve, however, still thrashed like a feral beast under Sy. The viper bit my sister at every chance she could, but Sy ignored her puncturing fangs, injuries mending after each attack, the viper's venom useless on the undead.

"Hugh!" Sy shouted at me. "You shouldn't be here...!"

I swallowed, raising my scythe blades again. "I... I've come to get you out, Sy! I'm not leaving without you!"

A growl vibrated her throat. "Just get out of—!"

Splikch!

A squirming black tendril shot out of her forehead suddenly. The same thing darted out of Genevieve and the dazed Somniovoker. The tendrils whistled past my ear. I twisted to watch the pieces of sludge *squish* into the violet-glowing hand of a man with long, grey hair and shining, blue-and-clear eyes.

"Hugh," Master Xavier growled testily. "Vendy. Behind me."

Our exposed souls quivered with the direct command, and we rushed to obey, falling behind Master Xavier. I stole a glance at the crevice we'd entered through, and saw that it had doubled in size, as if pushed away to fit Master Xavier. The sight confused me for a moment until *Da'torr* Alexander came trotting through the new entrance, using his Terravoking to shove the narrow walls away even more before coming to stand beside us.

"So," Master Xavier sighed a long breath, his tone dwindling down to a softer, more curious tone as he regarded the three confused Sentients. "This is where they sent you three… Syreen. Taymen." He flicked his bright-pupiled gaze at my sister and the Somniovoker. "You tried to help me escape before. Consider us even, now. You no longer belong to anyone." He tossed his head back in a gesture toward the crevice. "I'm going home before it crumbles to dust. You can either come with me or go about your way elsewhere."

Taymen squeaked with welling eyes. "I-I'll go with you, for sure! I just wanted citizenship…! Can't get it if there's no Death Queen to grant it, s-so…" He sniffed and rubbed his running nose. "I don't have anywhere else to go anyway…"

Sy stormed toward us, jerking a hand at me. "Obviously, I'm going to follow my brother. If he's going to follow you into danger, then I need to be there to be sure he's safe."

Master sneered at her. "Even from you?"

Sy's gaze darkened. "I… made many horrific mistakes, I know…" She shut her eyes in a hard exhale. Then kneeled and looked to me with a saddened gaze. "Hugh… I deserve no forgiveness from you. I was an obsessive fool, and it cost me the very thing I was trying to protect. Shel will damn my soul for eternity for what I'd done to you…" Her hands balled. "But I swear on my soul, I *will* redeem myself to you. This time, there will be no conquering to distract me. My only place in this world is with you. Always."

If I could produce tears as a ghost, I would be weeping. I broke away from Master's shielding back and squeezed Sy's ribs as hard as my spectral arms would allow. She was *tangible*, even if I hadn't been wearing this Crystal armor. Here, we were both dead. She rotted, and I clean, but…

We were equal, despite it all.

She burst into a sob and wrapped her arms around me, relaxing under my hold.

Master gave a reluctant sigh. "I… suppose you may come, then… But we must hurry. There isn't much time left."

He turned to leave, and we all followed behind.

"—wait…!" Genevieve blurted suddenly. I'd nearly forgotten she was still there. The viper girl shook on her knees, stammering, "What… what of me…?"

Master Xavier halted so abruptly, I nearly ran into his legs.

"You can go wherever you wish, Genevieve." He didn't so much as face her, his voice a deep, cold rumble. "*Except* with us. I remembered what you did. You betrayed us… Lied to us, pretended to be our ally. Then you tried to kill Anabelle—and stole her Hallows. I will spare you for now, out of respect for your imprisonment, but if I *ever* see your face in my domain again…"

He gave her a dark, twisted look with those shining eyes of his, and his hands leaked with poisonous tendrils. "I *will* kill you."

With that, we left Genevieve in the cavern, alone and hugging herself while she wept in isolation.

52

ON THE CUSP

WILLOW

RRRrrrrrrrrrrmmm…

I steadied my nervous Bonedragon under me, pulling the reins taut to keep my mount at bay as another tremor rumbled the caverns. The dragon's claws clattered over the blackstone ground where we waited outside the city of Low Rastiria. Many bubbling geysers peppered the chilled air with warm swaths of steam, their grey rivers flowing between rocky pillars that jutted from the cavern floor to the misted ceiling. The pungent scent of sulfur thickened. Wild Flamedragons bathed in the larger geysers atop rocky mounds, their amber eyes glinting at our vast army from the geysers' lips. They were like horned spectators awaiting a grand show. I envied their oblivious leisure.

Behind me, I could hear the thousands of soldiers murmuring in their ranks, struggling to keep their attentive formations under the ever-growing Groundquakes.

Jewel twittered from my shoulder in concern. My Bonedragon shuddered under me, chuffing as its boney armor rattled with fright. I patted the creature and calmed him, twisting back to inspect our ranks.

The sharp rooftops of the kingdom pierced up from behind its defensive, stone wall wrapping round its perimeter. Soldiers patrolled that wall from above *and* below, the city gates guarded to the best it could be. We knew the Demon Queens wanted the kingdom itself—and wanted me dead along with it—and although I doubted we could stop them from pushing into the city, I'd be damned if I gave it to them without a struggle.

To my right, the bat-winged Lilli rode her own Bonedragon beside her father, Daniel Tessinger. To my left was Fangs Matthew and his son, Matthiel, who both sat atop separate Flamedragons. Beside them on horseback were Octavius, Neal, and El, their throwing-scythes strapped to every part of their armor and saddles they could occupy.

What was troubling, though, were the missing members of my royal guard. Alexander and Jaq were absent. No one had heard a word from them. I could only assume they'd left on their own to retrieve Xavier… but I didn't know if they succeeded.

Xavier, I thought anxiously, my grip tightening on the reins of my Bonedragon. *Please come home… before there's no home to return to.*

I double-checked our ranks, spotting the faces of Roji, Anabelle, and Dalminia scattered in their respective posts amongst the multi-colored army. The trident-toting Wavecrashers wore emerald plate while Dalminia had donned crimson armor at their frontlines. The Stormchasers readied their crossbows wearing scarlet armor while Roji wore jade plate. The sword-brandishing Bladesworn wore gold armor while Anabelle wore violet mail beside Kurrick on horseback.

And, of course, my scythe-wielding Reapers wore silver plate while *I* wore royal black.

I even spotted our Ancient demons keeping their newly recruited Sentients in check. They looked like true soldiers themselves, having been granted armor and weapons for this battle. They would certainly need it.

Rrrrrrmmmm…

The ground shook again, though this was far lighter than the last one.

"Bloods," Lilli cursed beside me. She lifted her visor with a sliding scrape to unveil her chartreuse gaze and indignant scowl. "When will these blasted Groundquakes end?"

Octavius winced when he looked ahead. "Um, I don't think this one's a Groundquake." He pointed at the dimming horizon toward the east. "It's probably *that*."

There in the distance, a black mass poured through the forests and mountain peaks, like a festering wound oozing from the rocks.

Bloods, it was larger than any army I'd faced yet.

My wolf ears grew, a growl rippling as I pulled my hair-stick from my bundled, ashen locks, had my scythe materialize, and *clacked* my helm's visor shut.

"SOLDIERS, TO ARMS!" I roared and lifted my gleaming scythe. *"FOR NIRUS…!"*

"FOR NIRUS!" echoed the wave of shifters behind me, banging their weapons on shields and breastplates.

I kicked my Bonedragon forward through the geyser field, my lungs tearing with a vicious command, *"TO VICTORY…!"*

XAVIER

I straddled the speeding Flamedragon's leather saddle as tight as my legs would allow, my hands glittering gold as I used my Terravoking to keep hold of Alexander's armored ribs.

The sharp wind stung my watering eyes, Floating Lights bouncing off me like gentle bubbles until Alex brought our Flamedragon down to a lower altitude to survey our new army's progress.

My rotten followers weren't too far behind. The freed Necrofera were now pouring out of the Weeping Woods and funneling into a rocky geyser field littered with bubbling pools and sulfur-scented steam.

Alex steered our Flamedragon forward again, soaring toward the spired rooftops of the city. Mal and Chai beat their wings as hard as they could to keep pace with us, and as Low Rastiria grew closer…

"Wait!" I hollered, reaching past Alex to snatch the Flamedragon's reins. I pulled the beast to a stop, the dragon flapping in place, and my face cracked with horror as I overlooked the rocky field beneath us.

The Demon Queens' horde had already attacked.

Mongrel and Sentient Fera swarmed the geyser fields, the pools bursting alive when demons and shifters alike fell into them with scalding splashes.

It wasn't just in the field, either. The buildings of Low Rastiria clashed with every type of soldier you would ever see in every realm on Nirus. Bursts of fire and electric explosions bloomed all over the terrain, bricks spraying and crumbling into rubble as smoke blanketed the air.

"Death," I cursed, gesturing for Alex to pull our Flamedragon over the horde of *free* Necrofera beneath us. "The others need to be warned…!"

There were so many Sentients in our charge, I wasn't sure where to start except for those in the frontlines. Every demons' white pupils snapped to me when we glided over each of their heads, and they shouted up at me eagerly, the name *Lord of Souls* spouted like an undying prayer… like I'd suddenly become their messiah.

I shuddered. That was *not* the intention. Even so, if they listened to me, perhaps they would flee to safety now.

Alex had our Flamedragon glide over the frontlines to match their pace. They shouted up more adorations, making me cringe, but I steeled myself and bellowed over their voices, "The Queens have already invaded…! Anyone who does *not* wish to fight, turn back now! There is no need to risk your Afterlives now that you have your freedom!"

"NO!" They shouted up at me, making me wince as they began hollering their protests over each other.

"—I'm not going anywhere until those bitches are dead—!"

"—Really think I have anywhere else to go—?"

"—Follow you anywhere, my lord—!"

"—You're the only future I've got—!"

Alex snorted a laugh, amused with it all. "Sorry, Xavier. Looks like you've got yourself a loyal demon horde."

I pinched the bridge of my nose and groaned. "Gods damn it, these reckless fools… All right! Fine! If you're going to stay, don't get yourselves Cleansed! If you run to the aid of any living shifters, tell them you're with Xavier! That should be enough to stay their blades!"

At least, I hoped it would be enough. Alex told me the kingdoms had been looking for me while I was imprisoned. I presumed the name would catch their attention.

The horde gave a resounding flurry of determined shouts, charging into the field at full speed—

"Hang on!" Alex tugged the dragon's reins so hard, it reared back and nearly caused us both to fall off. I called over the mount's beating wings. "What is it?"

My brother's eyes were fixated on something down below in the steaming battlefield. His face was disbelieving. Then mischievous.

"I'm taking a little detour!" he announced with a wild grin. "Down *there!*"

I followed his gaze to the object of his obsession:

The colossal, terrifying skeleton of a Stonedragon.

My gaze widened at the perfectly arranged pile of bones. It was all in place. As if it had been planned as a surprise gift for someone. And if my new, sparking memory was any indication, I had a feeling it was a gift for *Alex*. This had been the very same colossus he'd resurrected in the surface canyons of Tanderam Prison two years ago.

Alex laughed and kicked the Flamedragon down to the enormous skeleton, lowering close enough to the huge skull so Alex could hop onto the gigantic brow, leaving me fumbling to take the reins instead.

As my brother's hands gleamed with violet light, I watched his grin pull all the way to his ear. "*Chanerr*, my old friend!" He cackled.

Then slammed his glowing hands over the Stonedragon's thick bones.

The violet lights wrapped around each piece, connecting them like radiant joints as the skeleton trembled to life. Its head *cracked* upward, shooting Alexander up with it. I steered my Flamedragon upward to match his altitude.

Alex's laughter was wicked with thrill as his enormous beast took a step forward—crushing a flurry of mongrel demons underneath its mountainous feet. One of its claws punctured a geyser pocket, causing a gout of liquid to gurgle up in a sloshing *plunk!*

"Sir Alexander!" a voice sounded from down below. It was so distant, it was almost lost to the wind.

I looked down, as did Alex. We spotted a familiar face below the skeletal colossus. It was the lion-eared Regent Cayden. Beside him was the goat-horned Linus, slicing into the scattering mongrels with a Crystal sword.

"I hope you like your gift!" Cayden hollered up at Alex. Then he grinned up at me from my Flamedragon. "Good to see you're still with us, Your Majesty Death! In some manner, at least!"

I waved down to him and Linus, my smile thin.

Skririririririiii…!

A winged mongrel screeched for my head, and my Flamedragon dipped out of the way. I shoved a violet-glowing hand at the mongrel—

But I didn't have to, apparently. Something else projected out of me, like an echo rippling from my rotten soul. It was intangible to Alex, but beside him, the mongrel was shoved away as if by some invisible Weight.

That was interesting, I mused, keeping note of that for later. That would surely come in handy in this battle. Though, I had something to tend to first.

I glanced at Alexander. "Will you be all right if I fly ahead? I have… someone to find."

Alex was still evoking his violet Hallows on the Stonedragon, crushing another group of mongrels beneath him while making sure to avoid our allies. "Oh, I'm set!" His lungs rolled with thrilled laughs. "Now go find your wife already! You've made her wait long enough!"

I nodded. Then hesitated. "Erm… what does she look like, again…?"

I was ashamed to even ask, but those memories still hadn't returned. I only had impressions of my wife. Of Willow. They were vague flashes; feelings rather than images. But if there was one thing I *did* remember, if nothing else, it was that Willow meant *home.* And Bloods, I'd give anything to see her again.

Alex tossed his head in a flippant gesture. "Just look for a *lot* of white hair! You can't miss her!"

That did sound familiar. And it was certainly easy enough to remember.

I blew out a breath and gripped the reins tight. "All right… a lot of white hair. A lot of white hair. A lot of white hair…"

I kicked the Flamedragon forward, speeding through the geyser field.

KURN

WARNING: KURN'S DANGER LEVEL HAS INCREASED, the nanite woman's voice alerted in my thoughts. *SUGGESTED ACTION: GET THE HELL OFF THIS THING.*

"That's the plan, woman!" I shouted over the wind, clinging to Red's ailette and peering down below our soaring Flamedragon.

The battle raged beneath us. I caught sight of a familiar colossus of dragon bones lifting high off the ground ahead of us, violet lights connecting its moaning joints together as it smashed mongrel demons under its boulder-sized feet. Knights from every realm clashed against mongrel beast and Sentients alike, black and red blood spattering equally down there. So many were falling—on both sides.

I have to help…! My round ears curled. Now that I had this trusty armor and utility belt the Lady Bianca had commissioned for me—and Henry had fitted me with—I had the *proper* tools I needed to be of help here.

I rose on my haunches and pulled up the utility belt over my furry waist. Then I snatched up one of the many rows of Shockvials strapped there. The electricity poured out of the vial and shocked the nanites in my blood to life. My body hummed with the soothing vibration of technology enhancing my muscles, accessing a protocol I hadn't had enough power—nor a reason—to summon.

"Activate Royal Emperor System Protocol 5!" I proclaimed and spread my armored paws out. "Cry havoc! And let slip the *ferret of war!*"

ACTIVATING PROTOCOL 5, the nanite's voice fuzzed in my thoughts. *KURN IS NOW READY TO INITIATE COMBAT DEFENSE SYSTEM.*

The power surged in my enhanced blood—and I plunged head first into the fray.

Winged mongrels dove for me from every direction, screeching their hideous war cries.

The blood in my veins heated to a scalding temperature, leaking their way to my eye sockets as the pressure balled, my vision burning red until—

SPEWWWWWWW!

My system's phasers exploded out of my enhanced pupils and streaked round the cluster of Fera coming for me. They were all vaporized in half.

I blasted the grounded beasts with my phasers during my descent, creature after creature blown back from our allies to let them recuperate. When my energy levels drained, I quickly snatched another Shockvial from my utility belt and recharged, activating my levitation defenses at full force.

My fall stopped six feet before hitting the ground, allowing me to float in place safely and…

I jolted.

Ringëd was standing right in front of me. His face was contorted with such confusion, I was worried I'd broken the poor thing.

"Kurn…?" Ringëd didn't even blink as I floated before his face. "Were those… were those *laser beams* coming out of your eyes?"

I rubbed my paws bashfully. "Er, um… technically, they're called phasers on my planet…"

"And how are you floating?!" he demanded.

"N… now's not the time to explain, butler—*huah*…!" My power had drained again, and I dipped down a foot before quickly recharging the nanites with another Shockvial on my utility belt, letting me float back to Ringëd's eye level.

Ringëd's confusion dripped into an angry scowl. "Wait a minute. Is *that* why my Com is always dead—?!"

"Oh, look at the time, Ringëd!" I piped, flying away to blast another cluster of mongrels with my eye-phasers. "No time to waste! The battle is afoot and all that…!"

"KURN!" He hollered after me as I floated away. "You are going to tell me what is going on when this is over…!"

That I will, butler, I thought as I blasted another cluster of Fera, zipping by the startled faces of our Ancient demons and allying soldiers. *But this time, perhaps you'll believe me.*

ANABELLE

Kurrick and I danced together in the heat of battle, our Crystal swords cutting down the mongrels and Sentients who dared to attack us. Fighting around us were Regent Vanessa, Regent Cayden, and General Linus, all armed with similar Crystal swords and handling them like the master Bladesworn they were. Black blood sloshed and spurted around us all, NecroSeams severed as their rotted souls hissed into the air and disappeared in a hazy mist—

RRRRRRRRRRRMMMMMMM…

Another Groundquake trembled through the caverns, debris flaking off from the hidden ceiling and spiraling down to the battlefield. We'd noticed the pattern moments after the war had started: with each bundle of Fera defeated, a new Groundquake would erupt.

To keep steady, I touched backs with Kurrick, panting, "It seems each victory comes at a cost… Our survival out here means more danger for the Gods in their plane."

Kurrick's deep voice rumbled, "The Gods will just have to hold their own—if they truly are the realms and their cultures, they'll die quicker if *we're* all dead out here. A culture cannot exist without those to uphold it."

I wiped the sweat dripping from my chin. "Yes… I suppose you're right—"

Phweee…!

Something small and furry zipped past my nose.

Kurrick and I stared after it. Had that been… Kurn? Yes, it *was* the ferret! He was floating in the air and blasting clusters of mongrel Fera with pinpointed beams of red light through his eyes.

Kurrick and I exchanged perplexed looks.

RRRRRRRRRRRMMMM!

Another Groundquake ruptured through the caverns, so strong we were all knocked off our feet. I hit my back in a winded cough, then spied an enormous stalactite plunging down from the cavern's misted ceiling straight for me. I hurriedly threw my hands up and evoked my rock Hallows, hands glittering with gold light as I caught the jagged spire in mid-air just above my head. I heaved and threw it away, the spire crunching over a geyser pocket with a *splich* of scalding liquid—

A pillar of ice shot past my face, grazing my cheek. The new cut stung with blood, and I hurried to find who had thrown the ice.

It was a little web-eared Seadragon girl. Her fin-like, emerald hair wavered in the cavern winds, her green eyes boring into mine with a look of pure hatred.

La'Lunaî the Little.

She evoked her ice Hallows, gripping a new trident of ice. "I remember you, golden-hair… you're that lost Relicblood of Land."

My throat clicked, lion ears curling back. "And you're the demon who kidnapped the old queen's corpse." I swept my blade in front of me. "How convenient for me. I have a chance to dethrone *you*…!"

I charged for her, my sword ready to strike as she came for me, her icy trident cocked back and ripe for throwing like a javelin—

"*NO!*" A different woman's voice ripped through the clamor.

A girl with brown scales and wild, golden hair hurtled out from a geyser's peppered steam, her bare feet skidding to a stop between the Ancient and I.

Genevieve?

I staggered, startled by the newcomer. My teeth sharpened, the scar across my neck pulsating under its satin ribbon as memory heated my fury. What was that *traitor* doing here? Had she come to finish me off? Had Macarius sent his vile step-daughter to complete her task—?

Genevieve darted toward the Ancient demon so swiftly, La'Lunaî didn't notice her until Genevieve evoked her rock Hallows over a fallen soldier's Crystal sword, making the weapon fly to her hand.

And thrust the glowing blade into La'Lunaî's ribs.

Snap!

Genevieve twisted the blade over La'Lunaî's heart, severing her NecroSeam.

"You will not…" Genevieve panted hoarsely, "… *touch my queen.*"

I stared at the viper, shocked stiff. She wasn't here to kill me…? She was… protecting me?

La'Lunaî stared beguiled at the viper woman, her black blood hissing away as her skin began to deteriorate.

"You…" La'Lunaî's enraged stare blazed at the girl who'd finally struck a fatal blow to the Ancient queen. "You… traitorous… *Vermin!*"

—Splickch!

La'Lunaî's hand drove into Genevieve's chest. Then she jerked out the viper's soaking, black heart.

Squelch! Snap!

La'Lunaî crushed the grotesque muscle in her claws, tearing Genevieve's NecroSeam in the process.

Then La'Lunaî the Little, Ancient Demon Queen of the Southern Seas, deteriorated to bones. Her skeleton clattered down, half of it tumbling into a bubbling geyser's pool that hissed with steam.

She was dead at long, long last.

And, as Genevieve turned to me, tears fresh on her cheeks and black blood pouring from the open wound in her chest, she whispered, "I… am sorry… For everything…"

Genevieve held her shivering head high and shuddered toward the geyser's crumbling cone, determined to see through one last mission.

I could only stare beside Kurrick as she leapt into the scalding pool, her screams shattering my lion ears as her rotted soul hissed into the air…

And vanished alongside her flesh.

53

REUNITED

XAVIER

The smoke spiced my lungs as I steered my Flamedragon over the burning city, Chai flying at full speed beside us, my head whipping over the chaos like a madman.

White hair, I reminded in an obsessive mantra. *White hair... white hair... white hair...*

Blast it, why couldn't I just remember her Bloody face? The sound of her voice? Anything! All I had were the vague memories of her lips on mine, the touch of her warm skin, the sound of her entrancing laughter... the way my pulse twisted and fluttered when she was with me...

White hair, I reminded again, bitterly resigned to looking for the only physical descriptor I had. *White hair... white hair... white...*

Wait.

Among the colorfully-plated soldiers, I spotted someone riding a small Bonedragon who was clad in polished, black armor. I hadn't seen that color on any other soldier down there. And this one had a silver crown attached to her closed helm.

The warrior swirled a glowing, long-staved scythe round her shoulders, ripping open the sticky chests of every mongrel demon who dared to near her. The warrior was ruthless and unwavering, black blood swirling around her as she leapt off her Bonedragon and sliced into another cluster of mongrels, rolling away from a Sentient's lightning strike before ripping into *his* chest without so much as a wasted breath.

That form... it's so familiar...

A new Sentient scrambled behind her, swiping at her head with enflamed hands. The warrior ducked and rolled away—but her crowned helm was knocked off, the thing clattering to the crumbled stones.

A drapery of long, white hair flared around the warrior's figure, falling past her feet like curling ribbons of ash. The cavern winds swept the strands away from her face… and revealed her icy, azure eyes.

Everything slammed back.

WILLOW

My helm was knocked off by the fire-throwing Sentient, my hair fanning around me. I roared and charged for the Pyrovoker, slicing into his chest and *snapping* his NecroSeam.

My royal guards clashed with the enemy demons around me. Lilli sliced her dual scythe into an ice-thrower while Neal, Octavius, and El flung their throwing-scythes at distant foes and cut into the Seams of nearby threats. Matthiel swirled his long-staved scythe round his neck to peel open a mongrel's chest, and the resurrected Zyl shot her Crystal arrows into another.

My three vassals fought around me as well. Rosette soared overhead alongside Zyl and Lilli, using a crossbow with Crystal arrows just like Zyl to shoot down the beasts. Nikolai and Ninumel worked as a dangerous team as the two froze any mongrels vying for us with their ice Hallows before cutting them down with Crystal tridents.

Four mongrels sprang for me with dripping muzzles, and I spun with my scythe, my long hair flowing after me, and sliced into their sticky chests one by one.

CRACK!

A new Sentient dropped from the sky behind me, fracturing the stones under my boots.

I wheeled my scythe around to kill the new enemy—

The Sentient snatched my staff with resistant fingers, pushing against my swing.

"Mal Aschay…!" The Sentient panted for breath, straining to keep my blade away from his throat. "Willow…! It's… me…!"

I stopped cold. My gaze drifted to the man's face.

He had Grim-pale skin and a thin beard lining his jaw, his cheeks slender and nose handsomely sturdy. His tousled grey hair fell to his shoulders, his ratty clothes tattered and stained with old blood…

And his mismatched, blue-and-clear eyes gleamed with shining, white pupils.

—Clank-clank-clank!

My fingers lost hold of my scythe, and the weapon clattered to the stones at my feet.

"Xavier…?" I could hardly breathe the name. My hands trembled as I reached for his face. My hot fingers hissed with steam under his ice-cold cheeks. That familiar, numbing prickle came—the one that always bloomed when we touched.

Tears stung, and I squealed a joyful sob. "Xavier…! *Mal Aschay…!*"

"I'm sorry for making you wait," he hushed, running his fingers through my hair and giving his usual, signature smile. Bloods, I didn't realize how much I missed that smile. His beautiful shining eyes softened as he took my face and pulled my lips to his in a deep, addictive kiss. The hiss of our contrasting flesh was a welcomed sound; the refreshing coldness of his lips was a touch I never wanted to be without again.

When we finally parted, he wrapped his arms around me in a long, relieved sigh. "Thank Death, I'm home. Finally, *home…*"

I leaned into him, his dearly missed scent calming. "Welcome home, Xavier…"

Wait.

My eyes snapped open. I realized something I should have noticed sooner. Our guards were staring at us. Jaq had even appeared out of the grey, dismounting a Flamedragon and casually leaning against the reptilian mount. Lilli gasped when she saw Jaq, reprimanding him shrilly for making her worry. But their stares weren't what had me concerned.

It was the sudden lack of Necrofera.

The clamor of demons against soldiers still raged through the smoky city, so I was sure the Fera hadn't retreated… But they were nowhere on *our* current street anymore.

"Xavier?" I asked, dread snuffing my previous calm. "Why did the battles stop around us?"

Xavier hummed in an afterthought, withdrawing from our embrace to throw a thumb over his shoulder. "Oh. I forgot to mention. I've come with aid."

I glanced to where he directed. There, in an adjacent street, was *another* horde now fighting against the mongrels and enemy Sentients. But unlike *our* Ancients' hordes, these had no armor. They looked more like the enemy horde the Demon Queens had brought.

My brow knitted at Xavier, and I questioned. "They aren't fighting for the Queens?"

Xavier rubbed his neck in a reluctant mumble, "No. This is, er… *my* horde, I suppose…"

I wasn't sure I'd heard him correctly. "What do you mean your…"

"One moment, love." He broke away from me, evoking his violet-glowing Death Hallows—and pulled out squiggling, black worms from the heads of every Sentient Fera within a ten-yard radius. The worms, which I knew were the Marks of either La'Lunaî or Ashya, flew into Xavier's outstretched hand. Then he *crushed* them as he evoked his Infection Hallows to disintegrate the Marks into vapor.

The newly freed demons turned round and began attacking what *had* been their own horde.

Xavier trotted back to me in a pant. "Sorry. I'm glad as Death to be back, but we *are* in the middle of a battle, aren't we?"

I stared at him. "How did you…? What just…?"

VRRRRRMMMM!

CR-R-R-ACK!

The ground shook, but not from a natural quake this time. An enormous shadow splashed over us, and I craned my gaze upward.

Far upward.

A colossal Stonedragon's skeleton clattered amidst the spired buildings. And riding atop the skeleton was Alexander.

Xavier hollered up at his brother. "Careful up there, Alex! Don't forget the rest of us are still down here!"

Alexander's distant figure shrugged, but waved a confirmation.

"—Lord of Souls!" a Sentient man shouted suddenly, making me whirl as he came sprinting over to Xavier.

My stare widened at my husband. "'Lord of Souls'?"

"It's a long story." Xavier grimaced, turning to address the new demon. "What's wrong?"

The Sentient saluted. "La'Lunaî the Little has been reported as Cleansed, my lord! Ashya the Ravager is still alive and was seen heading for the Death Palace!"

My Pyrovoker's heat chilled. I looked at my husband with a sagging face. "Oh, no…"

Xavier looked concerned at me. "What is it?"

"My mother and grandmother stayed behind there," I growled, swiping my scythe off the ground as my ears curled tight to my head. "With our son."

Xavier's teeth sharpened. "Can you ignore your fear of heights and get on my Flamedragon?" He pointed his chin to where a lone Flamedragon had landed and was now waiting beside Jaq's mount.

"What sort of mother would I be if I couldn't?" I snapped. "We've no time to waste—"

"My lord, wait!" That same Sentient stopped us. "There's something else…! There have been reports of another man joining Queen Ashya…" The demon sounded unsure as he said, "They say he has… multi-colored hair?"

Xavier and I exchanged pale glances.

Which curdled into murderous snarls.

54

BROTHER OF THE PAST

MYRA

The palace saferoom rumbled as another Groundquake ruptured the caverns. My rust-haired mother and I huddled together, baby Lucas in my arms and little Eryn in hers. Behind us was Veyazelle who crouched with a shivering Prince Fuérr. Yulia and Jimmy guarded Oliver and Princess Milann to our right. To our left, Herrin and Marian sat against the wall and fidgeted nervously.

Our assigned Ancient demon, Khol, was riddled with anxiety as he paced around us with twitching, webbed ears. He was tasked with guarding the lot of us: the few non-warriors left. We were deep within the walls of the palace itself on the third floor, which was the most secretive room in the whole structure. But that meant nothing. Macarius's visions had already exceeded even that of my father's.

And he'd *killed* my father.

I held Lucas tighter, the pup nuzzling against my chest as another Groundquake rumbled the palace and caused the children behind me to whimper.

They shouldn't be here. Every maternal instinct in my body screamed the logic, but… Aster's visions claimed they had to be here, to reach the future we wanted. I had to admit, even my own visions were showing the same outcome. I only prayed the cost of that future wasn't in the form of their deaths—

K-BRRRRMMMM!

The saferoom's walls exploded in a burst of purple flames, stones and dust crumbling to rubble.

Through the residual smoke, a plump, scale-skinned woman stepped into the saferoom. Her black hair was long and braided into a thick plait, her shining white pupils gleaming through the smog.

And her gaze was dedicated solely to me.

"Ah," the viper Sentient hissed, tilting her head. "So, the cobra was correct… I would indeed find the woman who killed my sister here." Her tongue slitted and forked loathingly. "I recognize that freakish blue hair anywhere."

Bloods be good. Despite the thickness of her figure, she looked remarkably similar to the Sentient Serdin and I killed years ago…

I quickly handed Lucas to Yulia, who herded the children to the far corner alongside Veyazelle and Jimmy. My mother sent Eryn to stand with them as well, the two of us blocking the Ancient woman's way.

My mother plucked a glowing, curved pendant from her magnetic necklace—similar to a scythe-sphere, but it was thinner and oblong, hooked at the end. As she pressed the sealing-rune engraved on the pendant, it rippled and melted in her hand, stretching into a long staff and curving into a sharpened, Crystal shepherd's crook. It solidified with a clash, and she held the crook at the ready before her.

I had the same sort of pendant on my own necklace. Henry had crafted these weapons for all the Dreamcatchers—Jimmy and Yulia included. The two Dream Knights behind us had their Crystal crooks materialize as they guarded the children, and I summoned mine as well.

The weapon's weight felt familiar in my fingers. It was akin to the crook I once wielded in Aspirre, when I was Father's heiress. But it had been ages since I'd touched the thing. After I'd married Serdin, I hadn't been a Princess of Dreams for over twenty years.

But now, Serdin is gone.

The reminder squeezed painfully, but I molded that sorrow into anger, gripping the crook that, despite how long it had been, felt so *right* in my hold.

"You must be Ashya the Ravager," I said, stepping in front of the group I was charged with protecting. "It's a pleasure to finally kill you."

The Ancient Queen didn't respond to the threat. Instead, she flicked her eyes to the bald demon who stepped beside me with shuddering legs.

She purred in amusement. "Khol the Kindhearted? I never thought I'd see *you* down in my caverns after you refused to join our last rebellion." She sneered. "And conspiring with Clean Ones, like the other Surface Ancients, no less… Your stupidity never ceases to disappoint."

Khol cringed, but held his ground. "Y-y-you… w-w-won't lay a hand on these Clean Ones…! Th-Th-they're under m-m… *my* protection!" His voice cracked with 'my'.

Then he brandished an overly *long* pair of glowing, Crystal crochet hooks. Their curved ends were sharpened so thin, a single touch would cut even the most calloused skin.

Ashya stared at him.

Then she burst into laughter. "You *must* be jesting…!" She clutched her ribs as if pained, her chuckles worsening. "Oh, dear me, what shall I do?! Khol the Kindhearted is going to *KNIT* me to death!" She cackled and wheezed for breath. "What will you knit me into first?! A Bloody scarf—?!"

Khol slashed one of the hooks over her throat—which spurted with black blood. She was startled out of her laughter and staggered back, letting the wound heal with a slurp of black sludge.

Khol gained a little more confidence and lifted his long hooks in front of him, puffing out his chest. "These…!" he said a little less shakily. "Are *crochet* hooks…! I do both, you uncultured Neanderthal!"

He barreled toward her, and I hurried to join him, my mother right at our heels. We all traded blows, slashing at the viper and hooking her limbs to disrupt her attacks—

"Enough!" She shrieked, evoking her fire Hallows in a bubble of flames around her, exploding toward us.

Khol slid in front, taking the fire at full force and sparing the rest of us from being roasted. His scaled skin was burned to a crisp, peeling away from his muscles and bones with rippling, black sludge that danced over his disfigured visage. But demon that he was, it took mere seconds for his burnt skin to boil black and mend with wiggling, sticky tendrils, his scales regenerating back to normal.

Khol lifted his crochet hooks once more, shivering only slightly as he panted. "Y-y-you… Will *not* hurt… these Clean Ones—!"

Khol was thrown back by an invisible force suddenly, slamming against the wall beside the shrieking children and their protectors, who scrambled away. Khol hung there, pinned against the stones with the painful sound of cracking ribs snapping under the invisible Weight holding him there.

Ashya stepped toward him, causing the Weight to push him farther into the fracturing wall.

"Of all the time for you to grow a Bloody spine…" Ashya's hands burst with flames. "You should have stayed a mongrel, Khol. Perhaps you would have eaten enough souls to match me, then—"

Ah! Ahhh!

The sound of a babbling baby made Ashya halt. Her gaze dropped to her feet.

Clinging to her scaled leg was little Lucas.

Panic split my pulse, and my eyes snapped to Yulia and Jimmy in the back corner. The two Dreamcatchers looked just as baffled as I was by the baby's absence. The blue-haired Eryn was still behind the other children as he should be, but it seemed Lucas had crawled over to Ashya while everyone had been distracted with Khol's struggles.

Ashya's brow puckered at the wolf-eared baby attached to her leg. "An ashen haired pup? And white eyes…?" Her glowing gaze widened with interest. "You must be a Relicblood of Death…" Her lips peeled into a grin, and she lifted her enflamed hand toward Lucas, raising her leg and lifting the baby along with it. "Well, my dear boy, if you insist on being the first of the Death family to die, I suppose I've no room to protest…"

I rushed forward. "Lucas—!"

Ashya let loose a gout of orange fire over the baby, engulfing him in flames, my screams drowned by crackling explosion bursting from the Ancient queen's hand.

Yet, within the vortex of fire, giggling sounded.

Ashya frowned and dismissed her fire. Smoke twirled away from her leg and revealed an unharmed baby. A very *naked* unharmed baby. Her flames had scorched the child's clothes to ash, but left his skin perfectly unmarred.

Ashya grimaced. "Ah. Right. The Death family has fire Hallows… even fledgling Pyrovokers are resistant to fire, I suppose…"

The naked baby giggled from her leg.

Then his tiny hands fizzled with black, jagged veins.

"Death!" Ashya yelped when the veins squirmed over her scaled leg, burning her flesh as her blackened soul raced to heal itself. She desperately tried to kick Lucas off, but the baby clung to her calf with entertained chuckles. "Get… Get it off…! Get it off—!"

A new baby's giggles echoed all around her suddenly. The blue-haired Eryn had toddled over to her and cast his Somniovoking, creating several copies of himself as they all surrounded Ashya while clapping in a thrill as he watched Lucas's Infection Hallows crawl up Ashya's leg.

Ashya's head whipped from toddler copy to toddler copy, one hand keeping Khol pushed against the wall with her invisible Weight and the other bursting into flames again. "Bloody pests…! Which one of you is the real—"

A sudden gush of water spurted over her, dousing her flames.

The young Prince Fuérr had stepped out from his protectors' guard, his scaled hands gleaming with emerald lights. The Ocean Prince flicked his webbed ears angrily, his green glare sharpening at the Ancient Queen.

"Yuu will leave ze babiez *a*-lone!" Fuérr shouted. Ice crystalized over his hands, the frost shaping into a small trident, which he twirled over his head and regripped with the sharp fork pointed at Ashya. "Dem-*on* hurt ze friends of Fuérr—Fuérr hurt *yuu!*"

Fuérr charged Ashya with his icy trident, Veyazelle screaming after him in protest—

Oliver and Milann suddenly broke past her. Oliver had armed himself with a candelabra, and Milann had her long-staved scythe materialize, cocking it back as she and Oliver rushed Ashya alongside Fuérr.

Fuérr swung and stabbed the queen with his trident, Milann ripped her scythe into any limb she could reach, Oliver shouted egging heckles to distract the demon before ducking and evading Ashya's irritated swipes, using his foresight to predict where she would strike and *clunking* his candelabra over her toes.

For a moment, I was too dumbstruck to move, watching as the children were, surprisingly, proving formidable with their chaotic teamwork. Fuérr had used his Aquavoking to summon a serpent made of water to wrap around the demon's limbs, snuffing out any attempt she made at throwing her fire Hallows, and as he used his Pregravoking to increase the water's pressure—cracking Ashya's bones in the process—Milann leapt up, cocked her gleaming scythe over her head…

And *sliced* into the Ancient's ribs.

Snap!

Ashya's NecroSeam was severed.

Fuérr dismissed his Hallows, the water splashing down and soaking the carpet as he dropped on all fours and panted in exhaustion. Oliver went to help the prince to his feet, letting Fuérr lean on him for support.

Milann swirled her scythe and flicked off the blackened blood dripping from the blade, which hissed into the air and vanished.

Eryn's phantom copies disappeared in a puff of mist one by one, until the original toddler was revealed, his fluffy fox tail swishing happily behind him. My rust-haired mother hurried to Eryn and plucked him off the floor, checking him for injuries and sighing in relief when she found none.

Lucas dropped on his bare rear over the burnt carpet, laughing and clapping his hands in amusement. Milann hurried to pick up her naked stepbrother, grumbling at the baby in scolding tones as her free hand still gripped her scythe tight.

Ashya's corpse lay strewn on the carpet. Her scaled skin cracked and flaked, deteriorating into ash… until all that was left of her was naught but bones.

Khol was released from the wall, thumping to the floor in a wheeze. Oliver and Fuérr hurried to the demon, catching him off-guard as they threw their arms around him in a relieved embrace. Khol's webbed ears flapped bashfully, but he couldn't help his heartwarming smile from splitting, and he hugged the children tight.

Milann still held her blade with a scowl while bobbing Lucas gently, glaring at the queen's remains as if disgusted.

A Death Princess certainly worthy of the title, I thought, pride swelling. I remembered thinking the same for my own daughter. Willow was much like Milann at that age, wasn't she?

I knelt to Milann and kissed her head, ruffling her copper hair between her sheep horns. "Well done, Milann," I praised, checking over Lucas and exhaling in relief to find him unharmed. "Your mother will be *incredibly* proud."

Milann blushed, glancing away with a pursed smile.

Then her eyes shot past me. And her sheep ears grew, grabbing her scythe again in a panic. "Nana Myra…!"

I twisted back and shuffled away, keeping Milann behind me in case another Necrofera decided to attack. But it wasn't another Necrofera. Through the hole in the wall, a man stepped over the rubble. He didn't have white pupils.

He had splotchy, colorful hair and eyes.

"Well, well…" Macarius hissed, his fangs growing long and dripping with eager venom. His rainbow eyes drifted between my mother and me, and he pushed up his half-moon spectacles. His dry voice ground like sandpaper. "What have we here…? Little Myra and dearest Crysalette… My, but it's been ages since I've seen either of you…"

RRRRRRRRMMM…!

Another Groundquake shook the palace, and we all teetered.

Macarius wasn't fazed by the interruption. His bare feet gleamed with golden lights, using his Terravoking to keep himself firmly on the stone floor that hid under the carpet. Something was horribly unnerving about his visage. His bronze scales had grown pale and weary with fatigue, colorful cracks splitting across his flesh and pulsating like a disease made of brilliant lights. It was as if his soul was overflowing with power—and his mortal body was a fragile waterskin ripe to burst.

RRRRRRRRRRRRRRRRMMM…!

"What a glorious reunion, is it not?" He stepped forward at a sluggish pace as the quakes worsened. "Here we are, at the dawn of the world's salvation…" He reached out a hand, and his voice dimmed to a wheezing croak. "It will be most fitting for Dream's family to provide me with the doorway to our Sanctuary…"

RRRRRRRRRRRRRMMMM…!

Ceiling debris plunked down, dust puffing over us as the caverns were burdened with constant, sporadic tremors. Baby Lucas and Eryn began wailing in fright, Oliver and Fuérr huddled against Khol. Milann slipped to her knees, keeping hold of Lucas. My mother crouched beside her protectively with Eryn.

I was the only one still standing. But only just. I dug my crook into the floor, using it to keep me steady under the barrage of quakes.

"The time has come," Macarius hissed, his hand still stretched out before him as he stopped in front of me. "The End has come for us. You wish to protect your family, little Myra?" He snarled, the radiant cracks that marred his skin flaring brighter, *"Give me the Orb of the Present."*

I kept hold of the crook, the tremors shuddering harder. "I don't have it," I said, my grown fox ears curled.

He was not amused. "The Orbs of Azure are the Relics of Aspirre. You would never entrust them to those outside your family—"

"Yeah, that's probably right," a new voice suddenly piped behind him. "But this time, I told her to do something different."

Macarius turned. I peered past him to see who in Bloods had entered through the rubble.

It was Aster. The meercat shifter hopped off a pile of stones and landed before Macarius, using *his* Terravoking to keep his bare feet stuck to the floor, just as the cobra was doing.

"Hey, bro," Aster greeted cheerfully, sliding his hands in his pockets. His glowing eyes shinned in the dimness. "Long time, no murder, am I right?" He winced in sympathy as he gazed at Macarius's fragile state. "Man, you don't look so good. Guess all those Hallows aren't sitting well with your soul, huh?"

Macarius's glare curdled at him. "Ah… you're the one claiming to be Accursius's new incarnation."

"I know, I know." Aster gestured toward his skeletal figure with a toothy grin. "You didn't think I could be *more* gorgeous than my last vessel, did you?"

Macarius's throat clicked. "You certainly sound like Accursius, I'll give you that…"

Another Groundquake tore through the palace, the rest of us fumbling for balance while the two soul-brothers remained standing with their shared Terravoking.

"So, here's the thing," Aster began, clicking his tongue. "We know how to stop the End. And it's *not* through your Sanctuary in Aspirre."

Macarius's brow twitched. "Is that so? And I suppose you had a vision of it, did you?"

"Naw." Aster stuck a finger in his meercat ear and turned it as if getting an itch. "The Gods told us."

Macarius stared at him flatly, his exhaustion accentuated with dark circles under his lids. "And I was beginning to think you were capable of saying something believable…"

"No, seriously," Aster insisted. "I talked with them—so did the Defender twins. Dream was wrong about everything. The End isn't caused by any of us. It's the Noctis Golems."

Macarius sneered, "The Noctis Golems are easily avoided. All it takes is a simple barrier—"

"That's the thing, though," Aster interrupted. "There's too many of them. The Gods have to kill each one before they devour the world itself—and the world *is* the Gods. But the more we kill the Necrofera out here in our plane, the more Golems that form in Their plane. It's all connected." Aster spread out his hands in a welcoming gesture. "And they need *all* of us to keep them at bay. That includes you, little brother. Will you help us save the world?"

Macarius was silent for some time, his glowing cracks pulsating with colorful light. Then he sneered, "If you actually think I'm fool enough to believe something so ridiculous…" His hands burst with a flurry of static bolts— which he shot at Aster, the lightning streaking across the room. "You would still be *Accursius!*"

As the bolt came for him, Aster lifted pacifying hands—and he snatched the lightning out of the air.

Macarius's face shattered with furious shock, the band of jagged electricity sparking between the two men like a living rope.

"Sorry, little brother." Aster's lips rolled into a grin. "This time, I'm already dead."

FINAL CONFRONTATION

XAVIER

Willow clung to my waist as we sped toward the Death Palace atop our speeding Flamedragon, Chai and Jewel soaring alongside us.

My wife squeezed me with shivering arms, keeping her eyes shut at all costs and trying like Death to ignore her fear of heights. I felt her claws digging into my skin, puncturing holes that writhed with black blood, my flesh quickly mending around her nails in ugly slurps. Her fingers flinched at the squiggling tendrils rising out of me, and I bit down a wave of shame. Did my new form disgust her…?

That can wait, I decided, kicking the Flamedragon faster. *Get to your son, first.*

Beside us, Alexander rode on his enormous Stonedragon skeleton, stomping away at the mongrel demons who tried to scour the palace grounds beneath us. His raven, Mal, had hitched a ride on the monstrosity's horned snout, croaking excitedly as my brother looked a little too enthralled with his reunited pet, smiling like a child who'd been given an adult's Shotri to play with.

"Where will they be?" I asked Willow over the wind, guiding our Flamedragon down to perch on a spired roof of the palace.

She still didn't open her eyes. "They were in the Saferoom! Third floor, between the halls of the East wing—!"

SMASH!

Alexander's boney puppet shoved its horned snout into that very place. Mal was startled off the horn and went to flap in the air next to Chai and Jewel, the three black birds screeching testily at Alex.

I winced at the crack he'd made in the roof, cupping my mouth to shout, *"ALEX!* Be careful, you reckless bastard! My son is in there!"

Alex tossed dismissive hands at me. "I can See them with my visions! He's well protected! Now come on!"

I pulled the Flamedragon over to the giant skull, helping Willow off the Flamedragon as we all held onto the horn of the skeleton's snout.

"Hang on tight!" Alex ordered, then evoked more of this violet-glowing Hallows onto the skull.

The bone-dragon *chomped* into the roof, ripping it off the bricks and hurling the chunk away with a rumbling *smash!* The skull crashed into the newly-opened roof and we all tumbled inside, the skull stuck between the floor to the holed ceiling. We hurried to our feet…

I paused. Those occupying the room were all staring at us. Including Aster and Macarius. The two clung to either end of a string of lightning, as if we'd caught them in the middle of fighting over it.

Macarius was riddled with horrifically radiant scars, their lights pulsating every color imaginable as they seemed to steam with raw energy. The cobra didn't seem to be taking the new power well. He seemed on the brink of combusting out of his mortal flesh, one sagging eye twitching as though in massive pain as he snarled with dripping fangs, "What in Land…?"

RRRRRRRRRRRRRRRRMMMMMMMMM!

The caverns trembled under another Groundquake, this one rising in strength with no sign of ceasing.

Alex stumbled to the ground beside Willow, and I hurried to summon my Terravoking, feet glittering gold to keep myself stable over the covered stones under the ruined carpet. But even that was proving useless as the stones started crumbling under my feet. I hurried to hop onto a different section, grabbing Willow and Alex off the ground and pulling us all to the corner where Veyazelle and the Dreamcatchers were huddled with the children.

"Dada…!" Lucas wailed in Milann's arms, wriggling toward me. "Dada…!"

The baby's cries blurred my vision. "Lucas! Milann…!" I barely had the breath to whisper, rushing to Milann and hugging her close, taking the wolf-eared baby from her and holding him tight. Lucas clung to my neck and nuzzled me, whimpering. His warmth a Gods damned relief after months away from him. "Daddy's back, Lucas, Daddy's here… Bloods, thank you, Milann… I'm relieved you're both all right…"

RRRRRRRRRRMMMMMMMMMM!!!

Through the crumbled hole in the ceiling, I watched two of the palace towers break apart and *crash* down, rubble tumbling after them along with large spires of fractured stalactites from the cavern's hidden ceiling.

The quakes grew so violent, Macarius and Aster had to dismiss their shared lightning bolt, their own Terravoking rendered useless on the crumbling floor.

"All right, Alex!" Aster shouted over the deafening rumble. "We've got the Savior with us! We're all here! It's time for the four of us to go!"

Alex nodded to me, and I reluctantly handed Lucas over to Willow. As much as I never wanted to let go of him again, I knew if we didn't take care of this, there would be no son nor step-daughter for me to hold.

Beside me, Alex frantically reached for a velvet pouch that hung from his belt. From the pouch, he pulled out a glimmering azure orb.

The Orb of the Present.

Macarius's gaze widened at the Orb, the scales around his eyes cracking with rageful splinters of colorful light. *"You dare hold our salvation in your destructive fingers?!"* Macarius sprang to his feet, stumbling toward my brother. He snatched the Orb alongside Alex's hands, the two tugging against it desperately. I grabbed hold of it next, and Aster snatched as well, the four of us struggling to pry it from each other's grip.

Macarius wheezed for breath as he sneered, "I… will *not*… allow you to *destroy us all…!*"

"Wake up, you daft lunatic!" I barked, keeping my grip on the Orb for dear life alongside them.

Aster hollered, "Only the *four* of us can go to Aspirre!"

"We have to kill the Golems…!" Alex growled, pushing his clawed fingers under all of our palms and gaining the best leverage. He'd almost pried the Orb out. "Not bring… the whole Bloody world to them… as a gifted banquet—!"

Macarius screamed, and his hands *exploded* with an enormous blast of lightning, throwing all four of us away from the Orb in an electric burst.

Alex crashed into Jimmy and Yulia, who quickly righted him. Macarius stumbled over a pile of rubble and had difficulty steadying himself as the tremors strengthened. Aster and I slammed into opposite walls, which cracked behind us, shattering my spine. I dropped to my knees in an agonized shriek and waited for the black tendrils of my soul to mend the discs again. It looked like Aster's sludge was doing the same.

"Xavier…!" Willow hurried to crouch beside me wile clutching the wailing Lucas, Milann hurrying at her heels in concern. "Are you all right?!"

"F… Fine…" I wheezed, the last spinal disc *snapping* into place with another spurt of black blood. The squelching sounds made Willow wince, and I gritted my teeth, wishing she hadn't seen that.

Clunk, clunk, clunk…

The Orb of the Present knocked against the rubble, rolling toward the crumbled hole in the wall that lead to the distant ground outside.

"Death!" I fumbled on all fours, the ground rupturing and trembling under my limbs and rolling the Orb faster toward the hole.

Alex suddenly snatched the Orb, breathing in relief—

Until Macarius tackled him to the ground, the two men skidding halfway over the broken ledge. Alex pushed and shoved under the cobra, keeping a firm hold of the Orb as the two tried to yank it out of the other's hold. Alex tore the thing out of Macarius's brittle fingers at last—

But Macarius shoved his glowing palm over Alex's eye.

Shhrk!

A shard of ice speared through my brother's socket, *cracking* out the back in a splash of blood.

Alex went limp. His head rolled back over the ledge, his only remaining eye gazing at the Floating Lights with an empty, hollow stare.

—THMP!

My ribs burst with a sharp, choking pain, suddenly strangling my lungs.

"A… Alex…?" I couldn't feel my face. My vision tunneled. Everything went black—except my brother's slumped figure under Macarius.

THMP!

The pain blasted my pulse again, but I couldn't move. I couldn't even scream. All I could do was whisper, "A-Alex…?"

My brother's grip slacked from the Orb, allowing Macarius to rip it from his lax fingers. The cobra pushed to his feet in a furious wheeze, kicking Alex further over the crumbling ledge until Alex slid off entirely, dropping toward the rubble below.

My lungs peeled with a grueling scream. *"ALLLEEEX…!"* I dove for the ledge and snagged my brother's wrist to keep him from falling. He didn't respond. He didn't move. The shard of ice was still jammed in his socket and skewered through his bleeding skull. I hauled him back to our shaking floor, my voice quivering, *"Alex…!"*

A sudden, bright light spilled above me, casting a harsh glare over the room. I hovered over Alex protectively and held a hand to my eyes, squinting to see where that light was coming from.

I found Macarius raising the Orb of the Present. The light swelled and grew from the globe, pouring over the room, the palace, the *air…* It swallowed everything.

Then it blinked out in a burning flash so bright, it stung through my lids, blinding me and making my eyes water. When the light finally dimmed, I was still rubbing the pain away… then opened my eyes.

My brother's corpse still lay beneath me. His wound was sticky with fresh blood, the icicle still skewered through his eye socket. I reached for his face, my fingers stained with his dripping blood. The alluring scent of death stung my nostrils, but I barely noticed. My ravaging hunger was destroyed by the grisly hollowness now shriveling my chest. My brother's single, sapphire eye stared up at me. His clear eye had been pierced through.

"Alex…" My sobs tasted like bile, agony roaring back and rattling my already shredded sanity. "Not you. Please…"

"—oh, Land." Aster blurted behind me. "Uh, Defender? You might want to take a look at this."

I didn't want to look anywhere else. All I could focus on was my brother's face; the face who was always there for me, from the beginning… Always, always, always, always, always—

"Xavier!" Aster barked, startling me out of my trance. "I'm serious! Look!"

I shuddered and sucked in a pained breath, prying my gaze from Alex to twist back to the skeletal demon furiously. *"What?!"*

Aster stood beside Khol, the two Necrofera looking around the broken saferoom.

The newly *empty* saferoom.

"What…?" My voice shook, looking all around me. "Willow…? L-Lucas…?!"

There was no reply. My wife had vanished with our child, along with the others. Even the messengers were gone.

I snapped my gaze out the broken wall in front of me, peering at the cityscape. The clamor of battle had faded to silence. The Necrofera hordes shuffled along the roads and palace grounds in confusion. Both the enemy queens were dead, and all were now free…

But the living shifters had disappeared. All that remained were the dead and the rotten.

RRRRRRRRMMMMMMM!

The tremors thrashed the caverns again, more pieces of the palace breaking apart along with the misty ceiling above. I was thrown on all fours over Alex's body, realizing what had happened:

Macarius had taken everyone into Aspirre.

And we, the three souls he needed to help stop the End, were trapped out here in the physical plane.

Watching the world fall to dust.

56

THE END OF EXISTENCE

MACARIUS

*T*he blinding light faded around me, the Orb of the Present dimming back to its normal, glittering state.

I collapsed to the ground in an exhausted wheeze, sweat drenching my skin as my limbs quivered to push me up on all fours. My entire body pulsed with those damnable, glowing cracks. They festered like veins, stinging with every beat of my racing heart as they split across my scales wider, barely leaving any room for my flesh.

Feeling ill, I focused on the swimming cobblestones beneath me, struggling to regain my equilibrium.

Bloods, that had taken too much of my stamina… Dream had once told me the Orb itself couldn't bring the entire world into Aspirre, so I'd used however much of my Somniovoking I could muster to amplify the transport. Thank Bloods Somniovoking was one of my original elements—had I been less practiced with it, like my more recent Hallows, I may well have burst from even attempting such a feat.

The sound of shocked gasps and questioning voices filled my ears in all directions, giving me hope. Iri, please, tell me it worked…!

I dared to peer up, searching my surroundings. The crumbling palace was gone. In its place was a garden within the palace grounds—of a similar, yet slightly different palace. Among the flowers was a trickling fountain, the fake sky above us drifting with cheerful clouds and false sunlight.

My lips peeled into a victorious smile, a laugh escaping. "I've done it."

My chuckles grew, catching the attention of the crowd of perplexed shifters surrounding me. Among them were the familiar faces of the ashen-haired Death Queen with her wolf-eared baby, Crysalette who held her fox-tailed child, her daughter Myra, the two Dreamcatchers, and the Ocean Queen with the three children from *the tower. Even their flurry of black birds had come to join them, as I'd intended. The goal was to preserve all life on Nirus—including the feral wildlife.*

It seemed that none of the demons had entered with us. Neither had any useless ghosts—their time had already expired. It was time for the world to prioritize those who were already living.

Exactly as planned. My laughter grew hysterical, relief dousing the rattling pit of panic that had held me captive for so many centuries. I felt weightless; drunk, even. At long, long last, we were safe. We were free from destruction—free to live.

And it had been I who freed them.

With immeasurable pride, I ignored my ever-growing agony and stepped onto the fountain's ledge. Then I lifted the Orb of the Present triumphantly, declaring, "Shifters of Nirus, rejoice! You have all been spared from devastation…!"

RRRRRRRRRRRRRMMMM…!

The sudden tremor was so powerful, I stumbled into the fountain's pool with a cold splash.

I blinked away the irritating water, befuddled.

RRRRRRRRRRRRRRRRRRRRRRRRRRRRMMMMMMMMMMMM!

The tremors shook and shuddered the floating city, and the fake sky above began to vibrate.

Screeeee…

Crack!

A hairline fracture split through a cloud.

Crack! Crack, crack, crack!

The fracture grew longer, branching off and crawling along the entire bubble the sky was painted onto.

From between the cracks, I spotted tiny grains of black sand dripping down to the gardens.

CRASH!

The sky shattered, shards of blue and white raining down as thousands upon thousands of sandy beasts poured inside…

And began to slaughter the civilians in a sea of blood.

"Wh-wh… What…?!" I staggered to my feet, not caring that I was soaking wet from falling into the fountain's pool. The terrified shrieks and agonized cries haunted my ears.

The Death Queen handed off her infant son to the sheep-horned girl behind her and roared, "Dreamcatchers!"

All at once, the Somniovokers of their party—Crysalette, Myra, the antlered man and fox-tailed woman, and the Death Queen herself—evoked their dream Hallows, hands glittering with azure lights as they combined their efforts to weave a thick, sparkling barrier around us, catching as many helpless civilians in their bubble within a thirty-foot radius.

But just outside the barrier, I saw Lannyse—my beloved Lannyse—torn apart among the butchered crowd. Her blood spattered the translucent wall before my nose. My stomach twisted as our newborn child was devoured by the beasts alongside her pieces.

"H-h-how…?" I quivered in horror, tears hitting as I heaved a thick gout of bile and vomited over the cobblestones. My sobs were weak and strained, my radiant plague splitting all across my skin and swelling farther than it ever had before. "This was our salvation…!" I cried. "This was Sanctuary…!"

THIS IS THE END.

The voice trembled in my thoughts so clear and forlorn, it shook the very being of my mortal soul. I inched my gaze back.

Five gleaming figures had appeared behind me. They were towering and magnificent, clothes and hair drifting in an unseen wind as they floated in the air.

They were also riddled with scars made of pure light. They each had radiant weapons in hand, and as the Noctis Golems scoured the square of dying shifters, the glittering beings sliced into them as swiftly as they could, eliminating them with each fatal blow. In each Golem's place, a ball of wispy light appeared.

SAVIOR OF HISTORY…

The white-glowing woman with long, flowing hair was the one who'd spoken in my thoughts. She twirled her brilliant scythe over a rash of Golems before turning her light-scarred face to me, freezing my limbs.

YOU'VE SEALED OUR FATE.

57

STRANDED

XAVIER

*R*RRRRRRRRMMMMMM!

The caverns trembled at the cusp of the End.

I was still on my knees above my brother's corpse, my useless body a flimsy shell waiting to flake away along with the caverns. Beneath the crumbling palace, the Necrofera were still scattered around the city, crying out in a unified panic.

"Land," Aster cursed behind me. The sound of his footsteps barely filled my wolf ears. "Land, Land, Land, Land, Land…"

Khol was sobbing behind him, blubbering that he wasn't ready to die again.

My placid gaze stared aimlessly at the rumbling cityscape. Fire raged the spired rooftops, and I watched as the long tower of a Harmonist Temple's clocktower split in two and crashed to the street, crushing the scrambling Necrofera underneath. Khol's sobs and Aster's cursing were muted in my ears. All I could hear were the Fera's echoing shrieks, as if the caverns themselves were screaming in terror. Smoke and debris filled the air, rising into the ceiling mist and blotting out the dim, Floating Lights.

And all I could do was sit there. Stare. Waste away, until everything Ended… It wouldn't come soon enough.

A cluster of Flamedragons suddenly soared down from the blotted mist. On their backs were the armored ghosts of our vassals: Dalen, Nathaniel, and Aiden on one dragon, and Apson, Vendy, and Hugh on another. On a third dragon were the three *resurrected* vassals of Willow's: Ninumel, Rosette, and Nikolai.

Then, riding her own, fourth dragon was Bianca. She led their small flock and soared toward us, having the dragons perch on a barely-intact spire over us. Their wings beat heavily and caused a gust that snagged my hair, tangling it every which way.

But I didn't care. I kept my gaze fixed on the burning city, the Groundquakes continuing their devastating tremors.

"Da'torr!" Vendy called behind me, frantic as I heard the sound of her Crystal armor clattering across the tower's broken floor. "Oh my Gods, is he…?"

"Alex!" Bianca's voice splintered, and I heard her clambering toward us. She crouched over Alex's corpse beside me, her rabbit ears draped drastically low as she witnessed his lurid state.

The others began to shout at one another, desperate and frantic. The fact they were here meant Macarius had excluded *all* the dead from Aspirre—clean and rotten alike. He probably didn't see a point in bringing us with the living. Our fate had already come to pass. Theirs, in his mind, were the only souls worth saving.

And now even *they* would soon join the rest of us.

The vassals' arguing buzzed in my wolf ears, tangling and knotting as they each fought to be heard. They were debating the next course of action. Why? It was already over. There were no choices left to make. They could waste their breaths shouting at one another, but it was pointless now.

We were all about to blink out of existence at any second.

"What do we do now?!" Aster demanded behind me. He sucked in heavy breaths, as if trying to calm himself, pacing the cracked floor behind me. "We aren't supposed to be out here! We need to be in there!" He stomped over to me, hollering right in my wolf ear. "Well, Defender?! Any ideas…?! How do we get in Aspirre?!"

My voice was a dim whisper. "We don't."

Aster paused. Then he clipped, "What do you mean we don't?!"

"Macarius brought the Orb of the Present with him," I said, hushed. The crisp breeze was stained with the haze of smoke as it ruffled my hair, numbing my face. All I could do was stare ahead at the blazing city. "We can't enter Aspirre without it."

"Sure we can," Aster disagreed. The poor fool clapped his hands together in a show of misplaced positivity. "We just… we just gotta get our *souls* in there! Yeah, we can put ourselves to sleep! Or—uh, *you* can! I don't have any Somniovoking, but you've got half of it at least! You can put us to sleep and force our souls into Aspirre and—"

"I don't have that half," I said distantly. "I can only wake others from a deep slumber. Alex was the one who…" My throat closed, and I forced myself not to look down at Alex's body beneath me. Instead, I focused on the breaking caverns, trying like Death to block out Bianca's whimpering sobs beside me.

Aster snapped his fingers. "Oh! Alex did that half? All right, cool—I can work with that!" I heard a zipper of cracking knuckles.

My gaze absently drifted to the skeletal demon, puzzled. I saw Aster's hands gleam with violet lights.

Lights which wafted past Bianca's sobbing figure and crept toward Alexander's corpse.

My calmness shattered.

"DON'T YOU FUCKING DARE!" I screamed and threw myself over Alex protectively, startling Bianca. My wolf ears curled, teeth sharpening as I snarled at Aster. *"Not to my brother…! NEVER to my brother!"*

"Why not?!" Aster demanded, throwing up his hands. "Because he's dead?! Guess what, genius—*we're* dead! Everyone left on the Gods damned planet is dead! Now get over it so I can wake *his* dead ass up and get us in Aspirre so we can do our job!"

His glittering hands shot toward Alex defiantly, the lights leaking under me and seeping into my brother's skin.

One of Alex's hands twitched.

Then dropped like a stone.

Aster blinked. "Huh?" He tried again, evoking his Hallows into Alexander's corpse, but all that came of it was a useless twitch. "What gives?! Am I supposed to make *all* of him move or something?!"

He blasted Alex with Hallows again and again and again—

"STOP!" I demanded, trying like Death to shield Alex better. But I could do nothing to block the purple lights from sneaking under me and violating my brother's lifeless limbs. My rage simmered tenfold. *"Stop…!"* The Seamstress Cleanses anyone who carelessly toys with the freshly fallen…!" When Aster refused to stop, my voice cracked into a desperate whimper. "Please…! You disgrace his vessel…!"

Bianca sprang to her feet and pushed Aster back, interrupting him. "Shove off!" She snapped. "You can't do it, all right?! You're not experienced enough with your Necrovoking, and you're breaking Xavier! Let it go!"

Aster scowled. Then he snorted, finally ceasing his cruelty, and muttered, "Well, what else are we supposed to do? All the better Necrovokers are in Aspirre… I had to at least *try.*"

I gritted my teeth, eyes stinging with bitter tears. I looked at Alex's blood-spattered face. His left eye socket was caved in, a soaked mess of gore. His right, sapphire eye stared at the hazing ceiling mist emptily.

"No…" I rubbed my eyes dry, clearing my vision as I inhaled a deep, deep breath. "Not you… Not anyone. Alex would never trust *any* Necrovoker with his vessel…" My lungs froze. Then an idea sparked. I whispered, "Except himself…"

Aster's gaze flattened at me. "And how exactly is he supposed to do that if he's dead?"

I shut my eyes, banishing the sight of Alex's gruesome face beneath me. "Because I can do something no one else can… with *my* half."

I evoked my death Hallows. The familiar tingle of magic swelled in my soul like fluttering smoke, pouring out my hands and sinking into Alexander's chest. A vibration came to my hands. I could feel his NecroSeam tethered there.

With a long inhale, I drew my hands upward, lifting that Seam… and peeled my brother's soul out of his vessel.

When my eyes opened again, I was face to face with Alexander's pale ghost. His NecroSeam gleamed from his chest, fully intact. His wounded eye was unscathed in this form, his colorless eye unharmed right beside his sapphire eye, staring at me in confusion.

"Xavier…?" His voice quaked. He glanced down at his corpse. "I… I'm…"

"Alex," I croaked. "We need you. Macarius took everyone into Aspirre… except the dead."

Aster blurted behind me, "You have the sleep-half of your Somniovoking! Can you try bringing our souls into Aspirre or something?"

Alex took a panicked moment to process everything. And there was *much* to process. "That… no, that… that won't work," Alex said at last. "We need to *physically* be there with Macarius. Otherwise, our sleeping bodies will be at risk out here… and we'll be forced back out, if anything happens to us."

I sniffed and wiped a hand over my running nose. "Like… like the world ending?"

He grunted. "Like the world ending…" His ghostly eyes flicked away suddenly, as if a new thought struck him. He craned his gaze to the sky. "Mal?"

There was no croaking reply from his raven.

I shook my head. "He was taken to Aspirre with the rest of them. As was Chai… I suspect *all* ferals were."

Alex rubbed his spectral chin. "I wonder…"

My brow knitted, still rattled as the world trembled around us. "Wh-what is it?"

His lips pursed. "Well… the messengers are said to be an extension of a Reaper's soul, yes? Like they were a… a *piece* of us, broken off and placed into the vessel of a feral black bird?"

"That's the theory…" I agreed skeptically. "Where are you going with this?"

He pressed his hands together and pushed them to his pale lips. "If Mal and Chai are pieces of *our souls*… and they're in Aspirre while *we're* out here…"

I drew in a breath. "You think you can use them as some sort of bridge? To let us cross over physically?"

"That's the theory." Alex reached out a ghostly hand to me. "Xavier, put me in your vessel. I need to…" He shuddered. "Resurrect myself…" The words sounded uncomfortable on his tongue. Nevertheless, he looked resolved in his decision.

I nodded. "That's what I thought you'd say."

I evoked my violet Hallows and seized his glowing NecroSeam, dragging it—and his soul—into my chest. I felt a strong vibration thrum in my blackened heart as the Seam latched itself there securely.

Alex's voice bounced in my thoughts, *"I'm coming out…"*

I sighed and closed my eyes, feeling that old, familiar tug at my soul. I let myself sink back into the numbing void of nothingness, every sensation of touch and taste and smell growing fainter and fainter… until it vanished entirely.

My eyes flew open. I found myself in a black abyss, naught but a circular window spilling with light to the outside world… through Alexander's vision.

No, it's MY vision this time, I realized. After six years of my own soul being trapped in Alexander, it seemed he would be trapped in *me* from now on, when he needed to be resurrected. We'd had a select few instances of sharing my vessel since we returned to normal, but now, the permanence of it was daunting enough to leave my floating soul shaking inside the psyche.

Even if we survived the End, nothing would ever be the same again.

I watched through the psyche's window as Alex raised my borrowed, right hand, his Crest of diamonds gleaming into a white Death mark as he evoked his half of our Hallows. Violet lights strung from his fingertips and curled around his own corpse, his skin slowly beginning to regenerate, the wound at his eye sealing and returning his usual heterochromia. He gave a final push— jumpstarting his heart, and his lungs filled with air in a shuddering gasp.

He dismissed his Hallows and shook his hand in a wince, as if detesting what he'd just done to his own body.

"All right," he said shakily. "Your turn, Xavier…"

I pulled myself through the psyche's window, the clear surface rippling as I sank inside.

—and felt the cold winds lick past my face, the peppered air spicing my nostrils once again.

I evoked my Hallows a second time and peeled Alexander out of my body, bringing his NecroSeam with him, then sank him back into his awaiting vessel.

Alex gasped to life, his eyes flying open.

I reached a hand down to him. He clasped it and let me haul him to his wobbling feet.

RRRRRRRRRRRMMMMMMMMMMMMMM!

Another Groundquake ravaged the caverns, and we all fumbled to grab a stable wall that hadn't yet crumbled.

RRRRMMM!

RRRRMMM!

RRRRMMMMMM!

Tremor after tremor pounded the caverns, as if the realm itself was being beaten with a planet-sized battering ram.

RRRRMMM!

RRRRMMM!

RRRRMMMMMM!

"Stay close to me!" Alex quickly grabbed my arm, sinking his claws in my skin and drawing black, squiggling blood. He flung his other hand out at Aster nearby, snatching his arm as well. Azure lights sparkled from Alexander's palms over our skin. "Get ready…!"

"Wait!" Aster shrieked over the chaos. "I-I don't have a messenger! What if I get left behind?!"

"We don't have time to worry about that!" Alex shouted. "Just keep hold and don't let go!"

Alex ripped a determined roar, the azure lights spilling around the three of us and swallowing us whole, blotting out the others on the tower—

The lights blinked out.

58

A WORLD IN CHAOS

WILLOW

I poured my quickly draining Hallows over the barrier, protecting as many shift-ers as I could, the other Somniovokers doing the same around me to keep the walls thick.

The Noctis Golems ripped into whoever had been unlucky enough to be outside of our barrier's reach. Other Somniovokers scrambled to put up their own barriers amongst the crowd, but not everyone could be protected.

There were just too many… It was an absolute slaughter…!

—My vision suddenly bloomed with a brilliant, colorful light.

"What in Bloods…?" I grunted, keeping my Hallows pouring over the barrier while searching for the source of the strange, radiant gleam. The light spiraled and swirled from only two small, familiar figures.

It was Mal and Chai. The twins' ravens had been trapped here with us and were perched atop the fountain's stone statue.

Their feathers were emanating that beautiful light, swelling and sparkling in a kaleidoscope of violet, azure, emerald, scarlet, and gold. The lights crystalized and pulsated, spreading outward and washing over us all until—

They burst into a blinding flash of light, forcing me to look away to spare my stinging vision.

When it finally dimmed behind my lids, I dared a peek.

My breath fell away.

Floating high above us alongside the two ravens, outlined in those gleaming, colorful shimmers with skin like refracting crystals…

Were Xavier and Alexander.

"Bloods be good…" I whispered, hypnotized.

The twins looked otherworldly, as if made of clear-cut gemstones. Their ravens had taken the same forms, their feathers glinting with an obsidian sheen and radiating the same crystalline lights of every color. The glowing ravens hovered gracefully beside the two brothers' heads, suspended there as if the black abyss was as solid as the stones beneath me. With the twins and their ravens sharing that ethereal, crystalline light, it was as if their Bond had become visible to us all—like a drop of pure energy had splashed over them and soaked into their very being. They were scarcely like any mortal to ever grace Nirus.

They were like Gods themselves.

59

DEFENDERS OF HARMONY

XAVIER

I was the very essence of pure energy.

Every breath was a flush of reviving static; every beat of my pulse a steady hum burning with power as a flight of laughter fluttered from my sweetly prickling lungs.

Alexander and I floated high above the Aspirrian palace grounds, our skin crystalized and sleek like perfect, geometric gemstones that sparkled with refracting, rainbow glints and trickled with vibrant sparkles.

Our ravens hovered beside us, sharing our geometric forms and colorful shimmers. My Bond with Chai had never felt so strong—so in tune and tangible—as if here, with he, Mal and Alexander beside me, our souls bursting with every elemental Hallows on Nirus…

We were whole.

I turned to Alex, and his shimmering head twisted to me. It was strange to see him and Mal so… celestial. And judging from his equally breathless state, he must have thought the same of me and Chai.

RRRRRRRRRRRRRRRRMMMMMM!

A powerful tremor ruptured the abyss, shaking the air itself.

Our heads snapped down.

Scouring the Aspirrian version of the Death Palace were millions of sandy, nightmarish Golems. They tore through the crowd of trapped shifters in a sea of blood and death. Bubbles of frantic barriers were woven in small pockets within the crowd by desperate Somniovokers trying to protect as many lives as they could.

But there was one bubble that stretched farther than any other. A handful of shifters kept that bubble thick and strong, the Golems thrashing against it like mad and chipping its surface.

Through the veil of black sand, I caught sight of a familiar, frightened woman under the barrier, her arms shaking to keep her azure Hallows flowing into the protective bubble.

It was Willow.

Anger sparked like a match, my wolf ears growing as I growled with a voice like buzzing energy. "Alex."

He knew what I was going to ask. I could feel his emotions—and knew he felt mine. It wasn't a mere guess, nor even a thought. It simply… was.

His throat rumbled, his own voice the sound of power. "I'm ready when you are."

I nodded.

Then we blasted downward. Our movement was as smooth as a river, flowing and weaving in a radiant spiral alongside our ravens. Refracted glints of rainbow light trailed in our wake and streaked through the void around us.

My anger twisted as we descended, melting into an absolute thrill that thrummed in my crystalline blood. My heart pumped as a smile peeled across my face in an uncontrollable burst of elation that blossomed deep in my soul.

And from that elation sprouted a new feeling. It was indescribable, a mixture of every emotion blending into a whirlwind of controlled chaos that prickled my chest and poured down my arms, leaking from my hands until…

Until a stream of mist poured from my fingers like smoke. The smoke spewed forth, growing long and stretching into a tall staff, shimmering with rainbow light as the brilliant haze solidified into radiant crystals that matched my faceted skin.

The crystal staff grew a large, crooked blade. This new, sharp joint curled over my head in a long arch, refracted light shimmering from its polished surface as the scythe loomed above me and pulsed in my grip like a weapon of glorious majesty.

Beside me, Alex had formed his own celestial weapon, matching mine in perfect unison as we spiraled toward the mass of Golems swarming Willow's protective barrier. Alex raised his gleaming scythe overhead, and I drew mine downward behind me.

SLASH!

Our strikes cracked the abysmal air in a screaming whisper, the odd sound echoing in the void as glittering light streaked out of our blades and split across the gardens in a cross shape. Their wide paths left enormous trails of rainbow lights that rose from the ground and speared through Willow's barrier—and Willow herself—towering far over the mesmerized shifters' heads like beautiful tsunamis. Willow and the others were unharmed by our weapons' strikes.

But the Noctis Golems were vaporized the moment the lights scorched their grains. And in their place rose balls of white lights.

They were the Golems' Cleansed souls… along with the newly freed souls of those they had devoured.

Two crossing lines had been cleared of Golems entirely, leaving them bare of any black sand.

Willow dismissed her exhausted Hallows from the barrier, leaving it to the stronger Somniovokers of her party as she gazed up at me in awe.

"Xavier…?" she called, almost breathless.

I twirled my large scythe behind me and left Alexander's side to glide down to her, phasing through the barrier without contact. Once my feet touched the grass before her, I cupped her jaw with a warm smile.

Then pressed my lips to hers.

My crystalline flesh blazed through her dazed soul like vapor, so sweet she leaned into my touch, her hands drifting to my face…

Until I pulled away, gripping her hand with a gentle chuckle. "I'll return in a moment, Mal Aschay." My new, resonating voice seemed to leave her mute, her azure eyes wide and welling with overwhelming love. I kissed her fingers. "I have a world to protect."

Tears leaked down her face. She didn't seem to notice, her voice quivering. "Myel Ma Amya, Xavier…"

I smiled, my heart swelling as I echoed, "Myel Ma Amya, Willow."

I released her fingers, gliding back up to Alexander's side with Chai hovering beside me.

RRRRRRRRRRRRRRRRRRRRRRRRRRRRRMMMMMMMMMM!

Another tremor quaked the abyss.

Then a scream of agony trembled through our thoughts.

We cast down our crystalline gazes to the terrain. The cross-shaped path we'd made with our glowing blades had faded, and the surrounding Golems had filled in the gaps as they swarmed the grounds.

But the haunting scream that had erupted didn't belong to them. It belonged to the cluster of five, glowing beings who flew over the crowd with their own weapons, slicing through the Golems one by one.

It was the Gods.

The Gardener thrust his blade of golden light over the sandy creatures, their grains puffing into mist as glowing balls of Cleansed souls rose in their wake. The Archer shot a volley of gleaming, scarlet arrows over the mass, felling Golem after Golem with his holy bow as he soared overhead with his leathery dragon wings. The Artist speared through the beasts with his radiant, emerald trident, twisting the sharp fork within their grains until they too were Cleansed into floating lights. The Seamstress glimmered with violet light as she twirled her scythe over the sandy creatures mercilessly, reaming through them with such fury, her wavering ashen hair swirled around her like a ribbon of thrashing wind.

But the smallest, azure-glowing God was not faring well. The Shepherd was all but drowned in the sea of black sand, his radiant skin dull and cracked as he was slashed and bitten ceaselessly.

RRRRRRRRRRRRM!

RRRRRRRRM!

With each injury Iri endured, the tremors strengthened.

He was dying… and so were the rest of us, trapped inside his domain.

RRRRRRRRRRRRRRRRRRRRRRRRRRRRM!

—Alex and I blasted toward him. We sped at full speed, reaching Iri in a blink, refracting glints of rainbow light streaking behind us. We cocked back our large scythes again.

SLASH!

Our simultaneous slices ripped over the infestation that mauled the child God, blowing them into mist and clearing the way in a wash of light. Thousands of glowing soul-lights appeared in their stead, drifting away in a gentle flutter.

Alex and I glided down to the broken Shepherd, and I scooped him up. His little figure was creased and cracked all over, his sandy blue hair pouring with dull grains.

It hurt to see the child like this. He was falling to pieces in my arms, his shifter form dripping into an azure fox. He had lost the energy to keep his other shape.

I sank to my knees and tenderly laid the kit on the disheveled grass, evoking my dream Hallows to weave a crystalline barrier around him, thick and resilient that no Golem could penetrate.

"You've done your part," I said in unison with Alex. "Leave the rest to us."

The fox inched his pained gaze at us. Then gave a weak nod in thanks, his coned ears folding down in exhaustion.

*D*EFENDERS OF HARMONY, *A woman's trilling voice said above us. We turned, finding the Seamstress waiting with her scythe cocked behind her. The other Gods surrounded her expectantly, their expressions tight with determination. The Seamstress reached her hand toward us in a welcoming gesture.*

*I*T IS TIME.

MACARIUS

"What…?" My breath shuddered, gazing upon the beautiful beings who shimmered like crystals with rainbow glints alongside their equally shining ravens. They hovered in the air like celestial beings, gliding alongside the Gods as they raked through the swarming demons with an insatiable fury.

Fire and ice spewed from their hands, blasting the Golems into oblivion with such precision, not a single civilian was hit. Lightning thundered all around, water flooded the sandy beasts, the cobblestones and shredded trees ripped out of place and tore through the Golems mercilessly.

As one, they dipped and bowed and twisted and wheeled, trading blows and shining Hallows… and each time they themselves neared a cluster of Golems, their hands would gleam with that same crystalline, rainbow light, stretching and pouring outward into two long scythes with impressively large blades.

They lifted these ethereal weapons over their heads and thrust them down in a wide arc.

SLASH!

Their shimmering slices cut through reams of the Golems, rolling a mile long and tearing through their gelatinous grains like hot steel through paper. The path of those slices left a trail of colorful light that split through the terrain and rose as tall as tsunamis. But while the attacks had devastated the Golems, they phased through the living civilians without a single threat of friction.

Their ravens croaked and guided the celestial twins to another cluster of civilians in need of saving, and the men glided through the air to follow, shooting past me with such speed, I fell backward into the fountain's pool again, the cold splash completely lost to my transfixed attention.

"Wh-wh-what…" I stuttered, clutching my aching chest in hopes of keeping my swelling soul from combusting. "What are they…?"

"—They're the Defenders."

My gaze snapped to the new voice.

Perched on the fountain's ledge and crouched beside me was that meercat shifter with glowing, white pupils. The skeletal demon who claimed to be the incarnation of Accursius.

"We can be like that, you know." The meercat scratched his neck. "But they needed each other to reach that potential… and so do we." He offered his hand, his look pleading. "Come on, Macar. I know you hate me—and I probably deserve it—but I need you. And the world needs both of us."

Tears stung. The scales on my face split and cracked like a maelstrom, my glowing blight flaking away the last of my skin. I glared at the meercat's bronzed fingers. Then, ruefully… I reached for them.

"This…" I wheezed, bracing as another wave of agony swelled through my bursting soul. "This changes nothing, Accur…"

He smiled. "In that, we agree."

I clasped his hand.

Like a cool breath, my painful blight dissolved. My soul calmed, the excess Hallows ripped from my soul like diseased limbs, salvaging the correct amount of Blessings I was meant to bear instead.

Now, with my hand joined to the meercat's, our fastened fingers radiated like shimmering crystals. The beautiful wash spread up our connected arms and enveloped us with such power, it felt as if we breathed time itself.

But then, if Accur was to be believed… we WERE time itself.

I watched as his white-pupiled gaze twinkled into crystals, and from his free hand sprouted a large, crystal shepherd's crook. He shouldered the crook as his glossy lips peeled into a thrilled grin. "Come on, little brother. Let's save the world… together."

This time, I let the tears spill from my lids. "Yes… it is time."

60

REGRETS

XAVIER

*A*lex and I slashed through thousands of Golems at a time, each blow streaking with a wall of wavering light. We glided toward a new cluster of shifters who screamed as the beasts came for them—

A crystal barrier suddenly bloomed around the shifters, pushing away the Golems with a flurry of refracted glimmers.

A new pair of crystalline men soared beside us. Aster and Macarius.

They both wielded large shepherd crooks akin to our scythes, slashing away the nearby Golems in a similar streak of light.

Alex and I glared at Macarius. The cobra glared back. Then he sighed and lowered his gaze. It seemed he had resigned himself to helping us with the task at hand… despite how much we loathed one another.

Macarius turned his gaze to the small bubble on the grass; the barrier that guarded the tiny, wounded fox.

His face twisted with guilt at the injured creature. He descended beside Iri, taking my woven barrier and expanding it, strengthening its walls and prying the bubble wider and wider, stretching as far as the eye could see in the abyss as if to swallow a dozen cities at once.

The shimmering walls pushed out the remaining Noctis Golems, leaving the living shifters unaffected within its protective shield. This barrier was nothing like what I had created. It was thick and pristine, radiant and impenetrable as every polished facet shined like a thousand blazing stars.

For now, the shifters in this continent were shielded from any more outside Golems.

But this was only half of Grim… and the Death realm was not the only kingdom at stake.

As the Gods of Shel, Ushar, Rin, and Nira floated around us, the violet-glowing Seamstress swept her scythe down toward the awaiting crowd of anxious subjects.

THIS AREA IS SAFEGUARDED FOR NOW. She said in her sorrowful voice. BUT THE OTHERS MUST BE HELPED IN THEIR REALMS AS WELL… THE GOLEMS FEAST ON ALL SOULS THIS DAY.

We all nodded.

… But Macarius hesitated, his attention turned back to the injured fox that was Iri behind us. I noticed a strange flicker of emotion welling in the cobra's eyes as he looked upon the wilting fox. It was an emotion I hadn't expected the man was capable of feeling.

It was incredible, crippling remorse.

So softly, I heard Macarius whisper, "I… I did this…" Tears spilled over his crystalline face suddenly, a rampage of anger festering his tone as he knelt beside the injured fox. "What have I done…? I was supposed to… to help you…" He reached a gentle hand toward the fox, but retracted it, his fingers balling into fists. "And all I've done is put you in greater danger… Put us all in greater danger." He pulled out all three Orbs of Azure from his robe's long sleeves. "I… I'm sorry. I don't know if I can heal you, but… I will try. I must fix my mistake. I only pray you can forgive me…"

He cradled the Orbs, inhaling a deep, hollow breath, then raised the Orbs over his head.

And began to sing the Relic's Call.

Sleep

Dreamest thou of me

The Orbs began to shine a bright, azure light.

Breathe

Mine ears beg thee to sing

The light grew swollen and radiated outward like pure sunlight, washing over Iri's broken figure.

May 'ere mares be repelled from thee

Pray sleep, and dreamiest thou of me

The Orbs burst with a sudden, blinding flare, the abyss turning white for all but a blink—

Then it dimmed as fast as it came.

When I glanced round, the living shifters who had been trapped in Aspirre had vanished. I couldn't even find Willow anymore.

Macarius had returned them to the physical plane.

The fox was standing before him, its azure glow radiant once more as its sandy tail shimmered in an unseen wind.

COME. *Iri's childish voice beckoned him.* Then he turned his snout up at all of us. THE REST OF THE WORLD AWAITS ITS CLEANSING.

61

SAVE THE GODS

WILLOW

The blinding flash blinked out so suddenly, I had to rub my stinging eyes to regain my speckled vision.

"What happened…?" I asked, dazed.

Then I stopped, realizing the black abyss of Aspirre had vanished. Grim's familiar, misty ceiling had returned, smoke and ash tainting its usual soft grey hue. I stood on the broken tower of the crumbled saferoom from the Death palace, where I began *before* being trapped in Aspirre. The ghosts of our vassals surrounded us, and many Flamedragons sat perched on the broken rooftops above us.

We were back in the physical plane? But then… did that mean…?

I whirled, looking about the confused faces of our party that surrounded me. "Is it over?" I questioned, hope swelling. "We're saved…?"

My azure-haired mother examined her hands with a perplexed gaze. "I… suppose? But there were still so many Golems left…"

Grandmother Crysa set a hand on her hip and hummed broodingly. "I don't know about you two, but I for one don't see a certain pair of celestial twins out here."

She was right. Where had Xavier and Alexander gone? Were they still in Aspirre, fighting those beasts?

RRRRRRRRRRRRRRRRRRRRRRRRRRRMMMMM!

A Groundquake shook the caverns, startling me. The quakes were still happening? But the four Champions had saved the Gods… hadn't they? I supposed they *had* looked terribly wounded, weakened and fractured, pieces of them chipping away bit by bit…

Like the land itself, I realized, gazing upon the devastation that had befallen Grim and its people. The living shifters had all returned, but the city of Low Rastiria was in absolute ruin. Hardly a spired building in sight had been spared. The palace was barely hanging by fragmented stones itself.

RRRRRRRRRRRRRRRRRRRRRRRRRRRRRRRRRRRRRRRRRRRMMMM!

Another enormous stalactite broke off the hidden ceiling and crashed to the ground, Necrofera and living shifters alike scattering out of its way within the city.

"Nira…" I steadied my footing, biting my knuckle. "Are you dying…?"

The twins had certainly saved us from immediate danger in Aspirre, and I had no doubts they would continue to protect the Gods from further damage…

But that meant nothing for *repairing* the wounds the Gods already fostered. If they sustained fatal injuries, it was only a matter of time before they faded entirely… along with the realms themselves. Was there a way we could help the Gods from out here? They were the realms themselves—our very cultures, the beliefs and customs practiced by its people… Rebuilding the cities may help to regain their strength, but doing so would take months. Years, even, with the level of damage the realm had already sustained.

But what of the Relics?

I squeezed my temples, straining to think. I'd seen Macarius doing something with the Orbs of Azure, just before we were thrown out to this plane. He had been displaying them to the wounded, azure fox. And then, they began to glow…

Could that have healed Iri? I wondered. *And would the Willow of Ashes do the same for Nira?*

I twirled to my mother and grandmother, growling, "Gather as many shifters as you can and lead them to the Willow of Ashes! And find the other Relicbloods—tell them to send word to their kingdoms' people!" I spun on my heels, my fox ears growing and curling tight as my teeth sharpened. "*Everyone* who is able must go to the Relics!"

62

LAST RESORT

XAVIER

*A*lex and I sped through the abyss of Aspirre alongside our gleaming ravens, keeping pace with the Ruiner and Savior who glided with us as we followed the Gods through each of their domains.

We went from section to section of the void, slashing our glimmering weapons at any Noctis Golems who threatened the realms, mowing them down mile by mile before zipping toward the next area in need of extermination.

Iri led the way in his fox form, prancing like a healthy, newborn kit. It was a far cry different than his previous state. The Orbs of Azure, it seemed, had rejuvenated him to his full strength.

The other Gods, however, were growing weaker by the second. Their luster had dulled, once radiant skin dented and cracked, flaking away piece by piece as we came upon each Aspirrian city that festered with Noctis Golems.

They were dying.

When we reached the next city—

Nira suddenly collapsed, her violet-glow dimming further, skin flaking away into ash.

We all touched down around her, Macarius and I weaving a protective barrier around us to push away the persistent Golems as Alex and Aster knelt beside the wounded Seamstress.

Then, Shel collapsed beside her as well. Rin and Ushar followed next, the four deities breaking apart.

I... AM SORRY, CHAMPIONS... *Nira whispered in my thoughts. In* ALL *our thoughts.* OUR PEOPLE HAD BEEN AWAY FROM THE LANDS FOR TOO LONG... WE CAN... GO NO FURTHER...

I flew to the Goddess's side, looking upon her deteriorating body helplessly. The others were faring no better. "There must be something we can do…!" I shivered. "We're so close…! We can't lose you all now…!"

Nira only closed her colorless eyes.

I trembled. "No… Please…"

Kris la vheh weh shae'bahl hu'leigh

My wolf ears perked, catching the lilting voice of a singing woman. A woman I loved.

Neschalist p'laven ash kemn mea la shae

"Willow…?" I could hear her so clearly… she was singing the Call of Death's Relic. She was singing the Requiem. But she wasn't alone. More voices accompanied her, strengthening as they sang louder and louder, the resolve of their voices piercing the veil between our planes.

—jaux chad'naît faquer'joul…

A second song split through the air, this time in the Marincian tongue. It was the Call of Ocean's Relic… The ballad Féurr had sung before the Pearl of Emerald, to grant us our Blessings so long ago.

…Strü aero fregĕcht necrogo…

A third song: the Call of Sky's Relic.

…Breathe ye child your life begins…

The fourth and last song to join the chorus was the Call of Land's Relic. The singing voices buzzed and tangled together in perfect harmony, morphing into one, resonating masterpiece. The Calls built upon each other in intricate layers, wavering and bold and sweet and unified toward a single purpose:

To protect each other.

The Gods began to glow anew, the synchronized voices of all the realms' shifters empowering them ten times their previous strength. Slowly, they rose. Then, with the harmonizing voices of the world filling them with love and hope…

Their weapons materialized in their grips once more.

They sprang into action, the other Champions and I hurrying to follow. The Golems ravaged the void of Aspirre with unquenchable appetites, but they were no match for our celestial unit. We slashed and we sliced, they reamed and they razed, our swirling formations mowing through each Aspirrian city in the blink of an eye.

Soon, we rounded the globe itself, returning to the parallel of Low Rastiria… where we began.

The final Golem was spotted slinking over the barrier we'd left here—and was Cleansed by Alex and my cross-slashing blades with one last streak of colorful, shimmering light.

And now, at last…

The End had ceased.

63

A LIFE WORTH LIVING

XAVIER

We *finally touched down before the trickling fountain of the Aspirrian palace grounds, dismissing our gleaming weapons in heavy, exhausted pants.*

"Is…" Alex puffed beside me, Mal settling on his shoulder tiredly. "Is it over…?"

"We've finished?" I asked anxiously, Chai flapping to the grass at my feet. "Have we eradicated the threat…?"

Nira's lips pursed into a thin smile.

IT IS ENOUGH… FOR NOW. THE GOLEMS WILL NEVER TRULY CEASE TO FORM HERE.

Aster grunted, folding his arms. "Because the Necrofera will still form in OUR plane, no matter what we do… right?"

Nira nodded solemnly. YES… IT IS A CONSTANT BATTLE WE MUST FACE. FOR THE REST OF ETERNITY, IT SEEMS.

Macarius protested, "But why? Why bother allowing them to form at all? Can you not as easily refuse to give us NecroSeams?"

AND ALLOW YOU ALL TO FACE THE INEXISTENCE YOU FOUGHT SO DESPERATELY TO PREVENT?

Macarius bit his tongue. Nira lifted her hands and weighed them thoughtfully.

DOES ONE STARVE THEMSELVES FOR FEAR OF CLEANING A DISH? SHOULD A MOTHER STRANGLE HER NEWBORN CHILD FOR FEAR OF A FUTURE TANTRUM?

We all shared grimacing looks. None of us had a rebuttal for that.

Nira shook her head. NO… YOU SHOULD NOW UNDERSTAND HOW FEARING AN ILL FUTURE CAN OFTEN CAUSE ITS CREATION… THOUGH IT MAY ONE DAY BE OUR END, WE CHOOSE NOT TO

ALLOW SUCH FEARS TO BURDEN A RICH PRESENT. AND AS SUCH, IT MAY JUST HELP EVADE THE END… AS IT HAS DONE NOW.

We were silent, hanging our heads. I flicked Macarius a sharp glare. Alex and I exchanged a glance, our emotions ringing through our Bond in perfect harmony as the next thought struck us.

"Nira," I began, my wolf ears growing and curling back. "When next will you need us…?"

Nira's radiant gaze turned to me.

THE THREAT HAS BEEN EASED FOR SOME TIME, I SHOULD THINK. WE WOULD ASK THAT YOU COME IN THE NIGHT WHEN ABLE, TO CONTINUE YOUR DUTY. BUT IF THE THREAT GROWS DIRE EVERY FEW DECADES… WHICH IT SURELY WILL, AS SUCH CANNOT BE AVOIDED… WE WILL SUMMON YOU AS NEEDED.

Alex grunted. "Then, you could say you don't need ALL of us for another few decades? You can stand to keep only some of us to Cleanse the Golems until then?"

Nira nodded. YES. THIS WOULD BE ACCEPTABLE.

"Good," Alex and I growled in unison, summoning our long, glimmering scythes. And bought our crooked blades to Macarius's throat.

Macarius's celestial face panicked. "W-wait…! What of… of forgiveness…!"

"For you, there is no forgiveness." Alex and I spoke as a single mind on this matter, our shared hatred for the cobra fueling our unified decision. "You have committed the highest sins and caused the deaths of innocent souls. Your continued life in this sickened vessel threatens the lives of countless others to come… as well as our families. For this, Macarius Lysandre, we sentence you to an accelerated rebirth." Our glares darkened. "May you choose more wisely, in your next life."

SLASH!

Our blades rang like mighty funeral bells as they tore through Macarius's crystalline flesh, his kaleidoscopic radiance bursting in a blinding flash of light as he cried out a grueling scream…

Then he puffed into stardust. In his place floated a towering, glittering crystal made of pure light.

The Savior of History had returned to his natural form: the Concept of the Past. Clunk, clunk, clunk!

The three Orbs of Azure dropped to the grass at our feet, having fallen from Macarius's hold.

Aster's geometric form faded suddenly, his glowing skin dimming to his natural skin tone. The meercat demon looked at his bronze hands with disappointment.

"Aw, man…" he grumbled, folding his arms in a pout. "Thanks a lot. Now I gotta wait another few decades to be a badass again…"

"You'll live," Alex and I snorted. Then we turned to Nira and nodded toward the sparkling Concept crystal. "We suggest you find a better vessel for him soon. One that, hopefully, isn't deranged."

Nira's hum filled our minds like static. THIS IS ALWAYS THE INTENTION… BUT ENSURING SUCH A TASK IS NEVER AS SIMPLE AS WE WOULD LIKE. EVEN SO, WE WILL TRY.

We sighed. "Better than nothing, we suppose…"

"… Xavier…" a new woman's voice suddenly flitted from beneath me, snagging my attention. I looked down, seeing that one of the Orbs of Azure was pulsating with a dim, azure light. A familiar, glittering melody was playing from the Orb, as if from a music box. Then the same woman's voice whispered from the globe's sleek surface again, "Xavier… where are you…?"

"Willow?" I separated from Alex, kneeling to pick up the blinking Orb.

In its smoky depths, images wavered and brightened. I saw my ashen-haired wife standing before the gleaming Willow of Ashes. She was surrounded by a dense crowd of shifters, all of them marveling at the Relic of Death as its wind-chime leaves twinkled beautifully in the Requiem's melody in a gentle breeze. As time grew long, the crowd thinned, returning to their broken homes to begin rebuilding. I could hear talk of a new city being planned for the Sentient Necrofera, to be located near the Crystal Caverns to the east… then, after long, the only perspective to look through next was Willow's. She was alone in the Relic's hollow cavern, kneeling before the holy tree and setting her music-watch beside her on the grass… praying.

I gripped the Orb tight, scooping up the other two before rising to my feet.

"Well, Alex," I said softly. "Aster… I think it's time we returned home."

They both nodded, relief rendering their shoulders lax as they gave long exhales.

I lifted the Orb of the Present, its surface gleaming with a steadily blooming light. The light swelled and stretched outward, creeping its way toward us hungrily.

I stole a final glance at the Gods surrounding us. And bowed. "Thank you for giving us this life…" I hushed. "We will not waste it. Of that, we promise."

They all smiled, and Nira chuckled, cupping my face in a flaming static of raw joy.

AND THAT, MY CHILD, IS ALL WE WISH FOR YOU…

The Orb burst with a blinding flash, and Aspirre vanished around us.

WILLOW

My open music-watch twinkled with the Requiem's delicate melody as I knelt before the looming Willow of Ashes.

The cavern winds licked past me, catching my long hair in its gentle flow and trilling the Relic's crystal leaves in the same melancholy tones as the music-watch, the sacred tree glowing dimly from the music.

"Xavier," I whispered in prayer, closing my eyes and hanging my head. "Please, come back…"

I'd hoped the Relic would somehow carry my voice to his ears, wherever he was in the realm of the Gods. I hadn't a clue if it would work, but… I had to try. It had been hours since we were brought back to the physical plane without him and the others. And hours still since the tremors finally came to an end.

Yet there was no sign of them.

My eyes threatened to well again, and I kept them shut to block them out. What would happen now? We'd stopped the End, yet… after what I'd seen in Aspirre—after beholding the celestial glory of my husband's new Godhood—what if he never came back?

"Xavier…" My voice thinned. "Are you bound to Their realm…? Can you not return, as a God…?"

"—Actually," a voice hummed in front of me suddenly. "I think *demi-God* is more appropriate in this case, don't you think?"

My eyes wrenched open.

Standing over me, with his grim-pale skin no longer glowing and flesh returned to mortality, was Xavier. He peered down at me with his white-pupiled, blue and clear eyes… and his lips curled into his usual, warm smile.

"What?" he asked, setting fists at his sides. "Why the surprise? You thought I'd leave you here to care for our children alone? My soul might be rotted, but I'm not heartless—*Mmf!*"

I shoved my lips against his with an overjoyed chuckle, wrapping my arms around his neck. "Oh, you beautiful, rotten bastard…!" I wiped my lids dry furiously. "Don't you dare scare me like that again or I'll Cleanse you myself!"

He returned the kiss heartily, combing a hand through my hair. Then he hesitated. "I… take it this means you don't mind having a demon as a husband…?"

"Bloods, Xavier, I don't *care*." I sighed, running my fingers over the mangled stab wound on his chest that peered through his tattered doublet. It was caked in dried blood and horrifically painful to look at. "Macarius did this, didn't he…?" I asked, morose. "Is he… Did you…"

Xavier must have guessed what I was trying to say, because he let out a hard breath. "Macarius is gone. Alex and I returned him to his original form, as a Concept. We hope his next incarnation won't be… disturbed."

I nodded, the news more relieving than I could have imagined. That was it, then. The last of the threat had been eliminated. There was nothing else to worry over, nothing else to plan, nothing else to struggle against...

Well, perhaps there was *something*.

I grumbled, "I suppose the only thing left to do is restore the realms. They've been quite thoroughly reduced to heaps of rubble." I leaned my head against Xavier's shoulder, exhaustion finally crashing over me. Then I sucked in a breath and willed myself to push away from him, turning toward the hollow's exit. "Come... We have quite the workload of repairs ahead of us."

"Oh, no you don't." He snagged my wrist and reeled me back to him, pulling us down to sit on the grass beneath the Willow's draping branches. He wrapped his arms around me defiantly. "We just saved the Gods damned world, Willow. For the past few years, we've done nothing but survive countless battles, sail across the entire globe, work ourselves damn near to death with royal duties and parenting, and watch too many of our loved ones die—myself included." He perched his cold chin over the crook of my neck stubbornly. "Now, for once, you and I are going to stay right here and do absolutely *nothing*."

I opened my mouth to protest, dumbfounded at the very idea...

Oh, Cleanse it.

"*Nothing* sounds marvelous." I took his hands and laced our fingers together, leaning my back against him and blew out a dwindling, contented sigh.

We stayed like this for what I wished could be an eternity, reveling the comfort of each other's hold that we'd been so cruelly deprived of. A soothing breeze swept past us and rattled the crystal leaves of the Willow of Ashes that hung over us like glistening chimes. Beside us on the grass, the delicate melody from my music-watch slowed to a tinkering crawl.

Until the final note rang through the empty hollow and faded into a welcome, serene silence.

A NEW ERA

XAVIER

ONE YEAR AFTER

"Are we *sure* about this?" I asked Willow skeptically, turning my wedding ring in a panic.

She and I walked alone through the gloriously sparkling walls of the newly constructed Demon Palace, made entirely from the Spiritcrystal found in the hollowed-out caverns that had once been my prison. The irony was not lost on me… but Bloods, was it discomforting. The mountain range itself had been built into the new, sixth kingdom: GrimHollow. The kingdom of demons.

The kingdom *I* was expected to rule.

"There are plenty of better candidates," I insisted, turning to Willow nervously. The beautiful glow of the arching, Crystal corridors brightened her complexion with a lovely radiance, her marriage-vines shimmering like glass in the light. It normally would have left me entranced, but the crippling anxiety that came with such an unexpected responsibility still had my wolf ears growing and my hands shaking.

I stammered. "I-I'm hardly qualified for this. Hecrûshou has been looking forward to this longer than I have, and he was a Demon King for five-hundred years—I'm still a newborn!"

"And that is exactly why the demons want *you* to represent them," Willow huffed. She pulled her long, ashen braid over her shoulder and reached for my face, adjusting the silver skull-crown hugging my head before cupping my thinly-bearded jaw. "The majority of the demons are newborns themselves. Thus far, they've spent all of their rotted afterlives as slaves to two Ancients—as were you. You shared their struggle." She smoothed out the collar of my doublet with a chuckle. "And you *freed* them. Without demanding any recompense or loyalty... They chose to follow you because you earned their trust. They feel safer with you. It's only reasonable they would want you as their king."

"But I'm already a king for one realm," I muttered, my confidence wilting further. "Granted, I'm more of an accessory for you, but... how am I expected to represent an entire *world* of Sentient Necrofera if I can only be present in the damned palace itself *half* the time?"

She shrugged. "Aren't you a Demi-God who can fly across the world in a matter of hours in the night?"

I grimaced. "In *Aspirre.* I'm still mortal out here! What am I supposed to do? Break off six pieces of my body and nail them to six summer-homes?" I wiggled my fingers. "I doubt the Necrofera will fancy an audience with a *finger.*"

She chuckled. "What of Ambassadors? You can appoint one for each realm. I'm sure Hecrûshou wouldn't object to overseeing the demon citizens in Marincia."

"—of course I wouldn't," Hecrûshou's voice interrupted sharply.

The shark demon strode into our corridor from an adjoining hallway, coming to stand before us. Strapped to his back was a newly forged, Spiritcrystal trident—one that he had acquired a special permit to wield, this time. He had promised Willow to abide by the laws of a true citizen, and he was certainly keeping to that promise indeed. His little Bindragon, Aahn, was wrapped round the fork of the glowing trident and snoozing happily.

"In fact," Hecrûshou drawled, "I would *prefer* to return home. These caverns of yours are quaint, but I tire of their rocky confines." He let out a long, smiling breath. "I should think it's long past time I went back to the open seas."

I was stunned into silence, surprised by the pang of sadness washing over me. "You... aren't staying longer...? You're leaving so soon?"

He nodded, his indigo hair wavering like translucent fins over his shoulder. "It was an honor to aid you all in your journey... but yes. It's time to return home... And I am not alone in that thought."

Hecrûshou craned his gaze over a shoulder, as if in a gesture. When I followed his eyes, I found more familiar faces stepping forward to meet us. It was our party's Ancients demons. Miranda stood hunched with her cane with a wrinkled smile at me, Khol clapped his hands in a thrill as his webbed ears flicked with excitement, Thörd stretched his dragon wings behind him while setting a hand at his side casually...

And lastly, Cilia and Kael stepped in front, side by side sharing heartwarming smiles. In Cilia's hands was a large, mirrored sphere—which I recognized as a memory holder.

I stared at the sphere with wonder, my white-gleaming eyes reflected back at me as I questioned, "Are those your memories, Cilia…?"

She nodded with pure delight. "They are. This was found in the Crystal Caverns during GrimHollow's construction. It seems Macarius had given it to La'Lunaî… and she left it in the caverns when *you* frightened her off." Cilia turned back in a chuckle. "And this young man was kind enough to bring it to me when he found it."

Behind her, Taymen peeked his head in nervously. He gave a half-hearted wave at me.

I laughed. "Well, I'm thrilled to hear it… Come to think of it, Taymen, I may have a job for you, if you'd be willing?"

Taymen swallowed and stuttered. "A-a-a… a job…?"

"There are thousands of Sentients without their memories," I observed thoughtfully. "And I'm sure there are other Somniovokers among us who could *retrieve* those memories across the realms…" I tapped my chin with a knuckle. "Do you think you could create a department of Memory Seekers? Similar to the Dreamcatchers, but strictly for the purpose of returning lost memories to new demons?"

Taymen seemed at a loss for words. Regardless, he said, "I-I… I can try…"

"Wonderful," I praised—

The giggling shouts of children burst through the halls. Then Milann, Oliver and Fuérr, barreled past us, the toddling infants of Lucas and Eryn wobbling after them in delighted screeches. The herd was shepherded by Yulia and Jimmy, who strode arm in arm as the two Dreamcatchers chatted pleasantly.

"Dad, Dad, Dad!" Milann called with excitement, the little sheep-horned princess hopping over to Willow and me. "Your new castle is *so pretty!*"

"—Pretty, pretty!" Fuérr chimed next to her.

Oliver fluttered his wings. "It's all glowy!"

Milann tugged my pant leg pleadingly. "Can we stay here all the time? Please, please, please, please *pleeeeeeeeeease?*"

I set a fist at my side. "I'm sorry, Milann, but we have to use your mother's castle also."

She crossed her arms in a pout. "I know… but why can't we stay here more than the other one? Can *I* just stay here with you?"

I sighed, rubbing my eyes. "Milann, *I'm* not staying here alone. I am not, under any circumstances, leaving my family again. Not for any reason." I flicked a daggered glare at Hecrûshou. "This was my condition for accepting this role, and I was promised it would be granted… correct?"

Hecrûshou grinned and gave a flourishing bow. "Of course, Lord of Souls… I've taken the liberty of assigning the palace's watch to your apprentice while you're away with your family."

I frowned. "My apprentice? But Hugh isn't a demon. Neither can he stray too far from Alex and me if he needs a resurrection—"

"He isn't talking about me, Master," Hugh piped from behind me. The boy was resurrected beside Vendy, their hands latched by their fingers. Standing above them and acting as a chaperones were the rabbit-eared Henry and lion-eared Syreen.

My brow furrowed at Hugh. "Then who is he talking about?" I glanced back at Hecrûshou in question. "I don't have another apprentice."

Hecrûshou's grin stretched all the way to his webbed ear. He tossed his head toward the hall as a new cluster of familiar faces came striding down the corridor: Herrin, Marian, the ghosts of Alexander and Bianca…

And Aster, who was busy scarfing down two turkey legs he held in each hand and belched rudely behind the others.

I aligned Hecrûshou's gaze with Aster, and my expression flattened. "You must be joking?" I protested. "Since when is Aster my apprentice?"

Hecrûshou looked quite amused with himself. "You and he are both Concepts of Time, are you not?" He opened a hand toward me. "You are both Ruiners of Tradition… and you are both the only two Concepts whose souls are rotted. Lord Aster may not have the strength to fully command his Necrovoking quite yet, but I should think with your guidance—and the guidance of Lord Alexander—he will prove a worthy Regent in time."

I watched as Aster tore off the last piece of one turkey leg and tossed the naked bone in the air, evoking his violet Hallows to make the bone hover with an uplifting laugh. He began to take a bite of his second turkey leg—

Kurn suddenly swooped through the air and snatched the turkey out of Aster's fingers, zooming off down the hallway to flee.

"Kurn!" Ringëd hollered after the flying ferret, trotting past Aster in an angry rush. "Did you drain my com battery again?! I swear to Bloods, when I get my hands on you, I'm making you recharge it, you alien bastard…!"

As they disappeared round the corner, I sighed and pinched my nose. This had been one Void of a journey, certainly…

"… think this could be a possible venue?" my brother's voice echoed through the corridor. Alexander's ghost floated through the palace beside the wispy soul of Bianca, their arms looped as they looked about the high arching ceiling and vibrantly glowing walls.

Bianca gave a considering hum. "It's kind of bright, isn't it? How do people sleep if all the walls are constantly glowing?"

Alex circled a translucent hand. "Xavier tells me all the walls have Sealing Runes you can press to cast illusions over them and dampen the glow."

Bianca sang an impressed breath. "Ooooooh, that could work. All right, sure. I wouldn't mind getting married here. I'll have to pay for my foster parents to sail down."

"Ah!" Alex silently snapped his spectral fingers, floating in front of her. "I nearly forgot! I queried the Reapers in the ghost-residential department to look for the records of your birth parents and… well…" He rubbed his neck shyly. "I may have sent the Herdazicols an invitation…"

Bianca squealed and crushed his incorporeal ribs, rapid-firing new questions now as he laughingly struggled to answer them all.

In front of them were Herrin and Marian. The winged Enlighteners walked backward as they scribbled in their separate ledgers and marveled at the glowing palace.

"It's absolutely beautiful!" Marian gasped as she twirled round to study the smooth, Crystal floors. She tried to touch a wall with her fingers, but her skin phased through without contact. She hummed and slid on a pair of gloves, trying again, and this time was able to find purchase. "There are certainly some brilliant architects in the demon community, aren't there?"

"You got that right," Herrin agreed as he inspected one of the engraved Sealing Runes along the wall. He tapped the rune with a gloved finger. The wall's glow dimmed all the way down the corridor into a subtle, blue gleam that wasn't nearly as harsh. He tapped the rune again to return the wall to its original brightness, writing down a new note in his ledger. "Wow… Now *that's* neat…"

I crossed my arms and called, "Herrin, Marian—the End is done and over with. What more could you possibly need to write about?"

Herrin's wings lifted as he pointed his quill at me haughtily. "Every good book needs a good conclusion. Like a wind-down, you know? Something readers feel satisfied with."

I cocked an eyebrow. "Why not a simple: *The End?*"

Marian scoffed. "After we just prevented *The End* from coming? I should think that would be inappropriate."

I pursed my lips, seeing her point, and shrugged. "Well, regardless, what are you two going to do now that your story's over? What's next for the Enlightener's Guild?"

Herrin scratched his chin in contemplation. "I'm not really sure. I guess we'll keep recording events that happen from here on. Sort of like historians, I guess? I don't know…"

Marian shut her ledger with a dwindling sigh. "Well, I for one would like a long break from note-taking after this. Perhaps I'll go out for some tea in a bit…" She peered at Herrin. "Do you want anything while I'm out, Archchancellor?"

Herrin thought for a moment, then bit his lip. "Actually… I think I'll come with you this time. I can't remember the last time I did anything that wasn't work related."

She giggled and clapped her hands. "Neither can I! I was also considering taking a holiday in Marincia—to actually enjoy the sights this time, not to keep the world from ending…" A small blush painted her cheeks as she added sheepishly, "Would you, um… like to come with me?"

Herrin went silent, his face heating red.

"Y… y-yeah. Yeah, I would." He clapped his ledger shut and shoved it in my hands, leaving me fumbling to keep hold of it—then he tossed me the quill. Herrin didn't wait to follow Marian down the hall with a thrilled smile. "You know, I bet we can ask Ringëd which islands he likes best and…"

They turned the corner, and I glanced at the ledger Herrin had left with me. Curious, I peeled it open, flipping to the last page. It held only two words:

The End.

I grinned and took up the quill, scribbling in three extra words.

"Darling?" Willow called suddenly, catching my attention. She was waiting up ahead, gesturing to a wide balcony. "Your subjects are waiting for their king."

Standing in a circle round the balcony were all the ruling Relicbloods of the realms. There was Sky King Roji, Ocean Princess Dalminia, Land Queen Anabelle, Dream Queen Myra… and now my wife, Death Queen Willow, stepping in line beside them.

They were here to welcome the sixth monarch of the world.

To welcome the Demon King.

I blew out a nervous breath, handed the ledger to Aster who took it with a puzzled scowl… and stepped out to the balcony.

I was met with a flurry of adoring cheers that poured from the droves of demons beneath me in the glistening, Crystal kingdom. *My* kingdom.

As it would be for many, *many* years to come, it seemed.

The End… But Not Quite.

NIRUSSIAN TRAVEL GUIDE

Character Reference List	
Accursius Lysandre	Lightcaster half, killed by Macarius five centuries back, cobra shifter, Seer
Aiden Rogeteller	Vassal of Xavier and Alexander, robin shifter, former Stormchaser, Aerovoker
Alexander Devouh	Half Shadowblood, twin brother of Xavier, wolf shifter, possesses seven half-Hallows with an emphasis on Necrovoking for vessel manipulation (Vassals: Vendy, Dalen, Hugh, Aiden, Nathaniel, Apson), Reaper (Messenger: Mal)
Alice Devouh	Deceased, soul destroyed. Twins' mother/ Death King's General, wolf shifter, wife of Lucas, Necrovoker, Reaper (Messenger: Ethil)
Anabelle (Ana) Goldthorn	Relicblood of Land, rightful Queen of Everland and Neverland, Land's reincarnation, Lion shifter, Terravoker/Healer/Arborvoker
Apsonald Coult	Jaq's ghostly grandfather, vassal of Xavier and Alexander, viper shifter, Hallowless
Ashya the Ravager	Ancient Demon Queen of Grim, wants revenge for her sister Charra's death, Pyrovoker
Aster Sorelles	Reincarnation of Accursius Lysandre, Lightcaster half, Sentient Necrofera, Meercat shifter, Seer
Bianca Florenne	Childhood friend of the twins, Alchemist Guild Mistress, rabbit shifter, Healer
Cayden Relekin	New Regent of Everland, Linus's lover, Rilla's eldest brother, son of the late King Galden, lion shifter, Terravoker
Cilia the Grim	Kael's wife and Everland's Ancient Demon Queen, ancestor of the Treble family, cat shifter, Pyrovoker
Claude Treble	Father of: Octavius, Cornelius, Connaline and Mikani. Descendant of Kael and Cilia. Husband of Sirra-Lynn. Cat shifter. The Party's inhouse baker and chef. Infeciovoker

Connaline Treble	Octavius's youngest sister, cat shifter, Healer
Cornelius (Neal) Treble	Octavius' brother, cat shifter, son of Claude and Sirra-Lynn, descendant of Cilia and Kael, member of Willow and Xavier's royal guard, Hallowless, Reaper (Messenger: Ace)
Crysalette Sandist	Queen of Aspirre and Dream's wife, Dreamcatcher, fox shifter, Somniovoker
Dalen Tesler	Vassal of Xavier and Alexander, hawk shifter, brother of Herrin, ex-thief, Hallowless
Dalminia Skrii'etey	Relicblood of Ocean, Wavecrasher, wife of Roji, aunt of Fuérr, Seadragon shifter, Aquavoker/Glaciavoker/Pregravoker
Daniel Tessinger	Lilli's father, Bat shifter, Necrovoker, Reaper (Messenger: Dawn)
Dream Sandist	Relicblood of Dreams, King of Aspirre, original Relic Child of Dreams, Dreamcatcher, fox shifter, Somniovoker/Decepiovoker/Seer
Edric Devouh	Twins' grandfather, owner of the Howler's Inn chain, wolf shifter, Hallowless
El Lochist	Zyl's friend, member of Xavier and Willow's royal guard, cat/blue-jay hybrid shifter, Dual-Evocator: Pyrovoker/Imbrivoker, Reaper (Messenger: Salfwy)
Fuérr Aschît'aqua	Relicblood of Ocean, the little prince of Marincia, Ocean's reincarnation, Wavecrasher, Seadragon shifter, son of Ninumel and Veyazelle, Aquavoker/Glaciavoker/Pregravoker
Genevieve Lysandre	Macarius's step-daughter, snake shifter, Hallowless
Hecrûshou the Hunter	Ancient Demon King of the Western Seas, shark shifter, Aquavoker
Henry Cauldwell	Vendy's uncle, Blacksmith, rabbit shifter, Terravoker
Herrin Tesler	Archchancellor of Enlightener's Guild, Dalen's younger brother, hawk shifter, Hallowless

Hugh Lowery	Vassal of the twins, Xavier's apprentice Reaper, younger brother of Syreen, lion shifter, Arborvoker, Reaper (messenger: Lady Lilac)
James (Jimmy) Grieves	One of the party's Dreamcatchers, elk shifter, Somniovoker
Jaqelle (Jaq) Mallory	Xavier and Alexander's friend, viper shifter, lieutenant of Xavier and Willow's royal guard, grandson of Apsonald, Hallowless, Reaper (Messenger: Bridge)
Kael Treble	Macarius's former partner, Cilia's husband, Surgeon, ancestor of Treble family, cat shifter, Infeciovoker
King Galden Relekin	Deceased, soul eaten by Necrofera. False King of Land, father of: Cayden and Rilla, Lion shifter, Terravoker
Kohl the Kindhearted	Ancient Demon King of the Northern Seas, pacifist, fish shifter, Hallowless
Kurn the ferret	Ringëd's pet ferret, secret exiled emperor from the planet *Hcah-Ah-Ah-Hcah*
Kurrick Harrow	Ana's bodyguard and lover, Lion shifter, Hallowless
La'Lunaî the Little	Ancient Demon Queen of the Southern Seas, deceased Ocean Relicblood, Seadragon, Aquavoker/Glaciavoker/Pregravoker
Lannyse Lysandre	Macarius's wife and Headmistress of the Lysander Academy, snake shifter, Somniovoker
Lëtta Russeaux	Sirra-Lynn's *Da'torr* & apprentice doctor, bear shifter, Necrovoker
Lillianna (Lilli) Mallory	Willow's Hand, Bat shifter, wife of Jaq, Necrovoker, Reaper (Messenger: Dusk)
Linolius (Linus) Rennegaurd	Everland's new general, Cayden's lover, Goat shifter, Seer: emphasis on visions of the present
Lucas Devouh	Deceased, soul destroyed. Twins' father / Death King's Eyes, wolf shifter, husband of Alice, Necrovoker, Reaper (Messenger: Barrach)

Lucas Ember	Infant son of Xavier and Willow, Relicblood of Death, wolf shifter, Hallows: Pyrovoker, Necrovoker, Infeciovoker
Macarius Lysandre	Lightcaster half, cobra shifter, husband of Lannyse, multiple Hallows: Decepiovoker/Somniovoker/Seer/Astravoker/Imbrivoker/Aerovoker
Marian	Herrin's assistant Enlightener, cardinal shifter, Seer
Matthew Inion	Father of Matthiel, First Fangs of Grim (Willow's Grand General), Necrovoker, Reaper (Messenger: Clyve)
Matthiel Inion	Willow's former fiancé, wolf shifter, member of Willow and Xavier's royal guard, Dual-Evocator: Necrovoker/Pyrovoker, Reaper (Messenger: Paschal)
Mavis & Prylan Skrii'etey	Relicbloods of Sky and Ocean, the young daughters of Roji and Dalminia, Seadragon/swallow hybrid shifters, possesses 6 Hallows: Sky & Ocean
Mikani Fleetfûrt	Octavius's eldest sister and Ringëd's wife, descendant of Cilia and Kael, cat shifter, baker and chef, Pyrovoker
Milann Ember	Xavier and Willow's adopted daughter, sheep shifter, Hallowless, Reaper (messenger: killed)
Miranda the Miserly	Neverland's Ancient demon queen, jackal shifter, Arborvoker
Myra Ember	Daughter of Dream and Crysalette, Relicblood of Dream, Dreamcatcher, widow of Serdin, mother of Willow, fox shifter, Somniovoker/Seer/Decepiovoker, Reaper (messenger: Locke)
Nathaniel Jorrechoh	Vassal of Xavier and Alexander, bear shifter, former pirate captain, Pyrovoker
Nikolai Voux	Vassal of Willow, tigerfish shifter, Glaciavoker

Ninumel Aschît'aqua	Relicblood of Ocean, King of Marincia, Wavecrasher, husband of Veyazelle, father of Fuérr, Seadragon shifter, Aquavoker/Glaciavoker/Pregnavoker
Octavius Treble	Member of Xavier and Willow's royal guard, cat shifter, son of Claude and Sirra-Lynn, descendant of Cilia and Kael, Infeciovoker, Reaper (Messenger: Shade)
Oliver Tessinger	Lilliana's adopted son, owl shifter, Seer of the Future, Reaper (Messenger: Clover)
Red Don't-Ask-Me-What-It-Stands-For	Full name unknown, Vice-president of the Alchemist Guild, hog shifter. Don't ask him what Red stands for
Revinna	Cayden's ex-wife, lion shifter, Hallowless
Rilla Relekin	Cayden's younger sister, Lion shifter, Seer
Ringëd Fleetfûrt	Seeker detective & Mika's husband, feral human, Seer: emphasis on visions of the past
Rochelle Maya	Friend of Sirra-Lynn, lizard shifter, Hallowless, Doctor
Rojired (Roji) Skrii'etey	King of Culatia, Relicblood of Sky, Sky's reincarnation, brother of Zylveia, Stormchaser, husband of Dalminia, swallow shifter, Astravoker/Aerovoker/Imbrivoker
Rossette Roroan	Vassal of Willow, macaw shifter, Astravoker
Serdin Ember	Deceased, soul eaten by Necrofera. Relicblood of Death, King of Grim, Reaper, husband of Myra, father of Willow, wolf shifter, Necrovoker/Pyrovoker/Infeciovoker (Messenger: Locke)
Shëfeaux the Gelid	Ancient Demon King of the Eastern Seas, killed by the twins, walrus shifter, Glaciavoker
Sirra-Lynn Treble	Claude's deceased wife, mother of: Octavius, Cornelius, Connaline, and Mikani. Vassal of Lëtta, cat shifter, Healer
Syreen Lowery	Sentient Necrofera, former queen of Neverland, older sister of Hugh, lion shifter, Arborvoker

Taymen Bucannan	Sentient Necrofera, Somniovoker, Fera grunt in demon troupe with Syreen
Thörd the Thunderous	Culatia's Ancient Demon King, Skydragon, Astravoker
Vendy Cauldwell	Vassal of the twins, rabbit shifter, niece of Henry, Terravoker
Veyazelle Aschît'aqua	Mother of Fuérr, wife of Ninumel, Seadragon shifter, member of the Enlighteners guild, Hallowless
Willow Ember	Relicblood of Death and Dream, Heiress to Grim's throne, Death's reincarnation, wife of Xavier, daughter of Myra (Granddaughter of Dream), fox-wolf hybrid shifter, 6 hallows: Dream and Death, Reaper (Messenger: Jewel. Vassals: Rossette and Nikolai)
Xavier Ember	Half Shadowblood, twin brother of Alexander, wolf shifter, husband of Willow, possesses seven half-Hallows with an emphasis on Necrovoking for soul manipulation (Vassals: Vendy, Dalen, Hugh, Aiden, Nathaniel, Apson), Reaper (Messenger: Chai)
Yulia Vivelle	One of the party's Dreamcatchers, fox shifter, Somniovoker
Zylveia (Zyl) Skrii'etey	Vassal of Lilliana, Relicblood of Sky, Princess of Culatia, sister of Prince Roji, daughter of King Rojired, Stormchaser, swallow shifter, Astravoker/Aerovoker/Imbrivoker

NIRUSSIAN WORLD NOTES

Dragons of Nirus: For every element of magic Hallows (with the exception of Dream Hallows), there is a dragon that embodies that element. Land realm: Stonedragon/Barkdragon/Landragon, Sky realm: Skydragon/Shockdragon/Nimdragon, Ocean realm: Seadragon/Bindragon/ Frostdragon, Death realm: Bonedragon/Flamedragon/Poisondragon.

Evocators: A shifter born with magic Hallows is called an Evocator. Most Evocators only possess one element. In rare cases, some are born with two Hallows and are known as Dual-Evocators. Only the Relicbloods have ever possessed all three of their realm's Hallows.

Land: Terravoker/Healer/Arborvoker;
Sky: Astravoker/Aerovoker/Imbrivoker;
Ocean: Aquavoker/Glaciavoker/Pregnavoker;
Dream: Somniovoker/decepiovoker/Seer;
Death: Necrovoker/pyrovoker/Infeciovoker

Hallows: These are the "Gods' Blessings", which are elemental magics to which certain shifters are born. A shifter's Hallows element is defined based on the realm they are from. There are fifteen Hallow elements in total. For each of the five realms in Nirus, there are three elements, as shown in the charts below.

LAND		SKY		OCEAN	
Rock	Terra	*Wind*	Aero	*Water*	Aqua
Plant	Arbor	*Rain*	Imbri	*Ice*	Glacia
Remedy	Healer	*Storm*	Astra	*Pressure*	Pregra

DREAM		DEATH	
Dream	Somnio	*Fire*	Pyro
Illusion	Decepio	*Death*	Necro
Prophecy	Seer	*Poison*	Infecio

NecroSeam: A ghostly thread which sews a soul to its vessel. When a shifter of Nirus dies, the soul is still bound to its body by their NecroSeam. If three days pass without a Reaper coming to cut the NecroSeam and free the soul from its deceased vessel, the trapped soul rots inside its corpse and merges into an undead creature called Necrofera that can only be killed by a weapon made of Spiritcrystal.

Nirussian Calendar: A month in Nirus is 60 days, or six weeks. One week is 10 days. There are 5 months in a year (300 days).

Realms of Nirus: There are 5 realms in this world. Land (surface realm split into two continents: Everland & Neverland), Sky (floating islands of Culatia in the sky inhabited primarily by flying shifters). Ocean (seaside isles of Marincia inhabited primarily by fish shifters), Dream (subconscious realm of Aspirre where shifters' souls visit in their dreams), Death (underground caverns of Grim where souls of the dead are protected in their afterlife).

Relicbloods: Shifters who are descendants of the Relic Children (those chosen by the Gods to be the ruler of a specific realm). The only Relic Child still alive today is Dream, who doesn't age at a regular pace due to his timeless residency in the subconscious plane of Aspirre.

The Relics: Magical artifacts of the Gods which are the sources of each realm's Hallows. (Land: Blossom of Gold, Sky: Phoenix of Scarlet, Ocean: Pearl of Emerald, Dream: Orbs of Azure, Death: Willow of Ashes)

Sentients: Necrofera who possess Hallows (Class 1), or a mongrel demon who has eaten ten thousand souls (Class 2). Sentients look like normal shifters, except their pupils are white.

Shifters: The world of Nirus is inhabited entirely by shifters, but they aren't quite the traditional shapeshifters who can transform from one human form to a full-on beast form. The shifters of Nirus are seen possessing traits of some kind (Ringëd Fleetfûrt is the only exception) but these traits usually only consist of wings, horns, claws, teeth, ears, tails, scales, fins, etc. Most shifters are born with a majority of their traits already showing (referred to as Primary Shifts), but some only appear when they are threatened or upset (teeth/talons/claws and even extra feathers/scales/fur). Mammals seem to be the main beings whose traits actually shift, with their ears, claws and teeth. Antlers and horns are always out and don't retract, nor do wings and scales. The fish shifters are the most unique due to their inherent ability to switch their Primary Shift to tails or legs when they are in or out of water, and this is the largest range of shifting that happens among the shifters.

The Void and Great unknown: A place that is considered purgatory for rotten and sinful souls in the Harmonist religion. It is believed that once the Goddess Nira has Cleansed these souls of their rot and sin, she takes them to the Great Unknown, which is thought to be the "waiting room" for souls to be reborn again.

NIRUSSIAN MINERALS/TECHNOLOGY

Olium: a lightweight, extremely durable mineral that is found in the deeper caves of Grim, where the veins are closest to the planet's magma-filled mantle and are in a constant liquefied state until extracted and left to cool. Once cooled, the metal can be crafted, but forging the material is incredibly difficult and only skilled smiths are able to handle the task.

Spiritcrystal: a mineral found in the caverns of Grim. It is a unique crystal which physical skin cannot touch. Adversely, it is one of the few things ghosts can make contact with. The Reapers use this crystal to forge their specialized scythes which allows them to cut a shifter's NecroSeam without damaging the body.

Vision-gems: minerals found in the Land realm's mines which, when broken apart, can show what the other piece is reflecting. Modern technologies led by Culatia's top inventors in 2102 A.B. have learned to harness Vision-gems to bring devices such as Vision-screens, communicators, and other numerous devices.

Levi-stones: magnetized rocks that are repelled only by the planet's core, causing them to be pushed into the air and kept suspended so long as the oppositely-charged side is facing the core. Culatia's islands are made of these stones, which is speculated by many geologists as to the reason Culatia's islands float.

Storage-gems: a gummy, gel-like mineral found in Everland's mines. When an object is pushed inside it, that object's size and weight shrinks to a small percentage of its original mass until that object is removed.

Yinklit Gel: a sap from a long-leafed plant that is native to Culatia. It is similar to the Aloe vera plant, but instead of possessing soothing properties when applied to burns, Yinklît Gel dampens all Hallows effects when an Evocator's hands are coated in the substance. If the gel is ingested, it can cause serious damage to an Evocator's Hallows for several days, and in some cases, it can wipe their magic connection permanently.

Shotri: The latest ranged weapons created by Culatia's top weapon-smiths. They require ammunition made of meta-glass pellets with entrapped elemental magics which, when fired, cause damage or temporary paralysis on a target, depending on the element the pellet housed.

Meta-glass: an alloyed material which combines Flexi-glass as the outer layer and Yinklît Gel as the inner layer. With this, Culatia's top weapon-smiths have used these to make Shockspheres, Flamespheres, Splashspheres and the like, which are then used as ammunition for Shotri.

Flexi-glass: A gummy, gel-like glass found in Culatia's mountain peaks that can be stretched and manipulated with ease while still wet. Once it has been through a kiln, it solidifies and become as fragile as normal glass.

DEAR READERS,

Thank you so much for reading *Blossom of Gold*, the fifth and final book in the NecroSeam Chronicles pentalogy. If you liked this series, I would be extremely grateful if you told others what you thought by writing an honest review. Reviews are vital to an author's career and help us not only sell books, but provide valuable feedback. Check out my review page at www.necroseam.com/reviews!

Would you like to find out more about the NecroSeam Chronicles universe, including world notes, deleted scenes, character artwork, and even recorded songs from the books? Visit my website at www.necroseam.com ! And while you're there, feel free to sign up for my newsletter to receive announcements on new releases, upcoming conventions I'll be attending, and special promotions!

I am also pleased to announce my new Patreon page: www.patreon.com/OfficialEllieRaine. If you enjoy my fantastical tales, your support would greatly help my endeavor to continue bringing magic to the world (and to you!).

Finally, don't forget to follow me on my social media accounts below:

Twitter: @AizelleRaine
Facebook Author Page: www.Facebook.com/officialEllieRaine
Official Facebook Group: *NecroSeam Official*
(www.facebook.com/groups/NecroSeam)

Thank you again!
Ellie Raine

ACKNOWLEDGEMENTS

This journey has been long and arduous at times, but I wouldn't be here if it wasn't for the fantastic team of editors, beta-readers, proof-readers, friends, and family that have supported me from the very beginning and contributed great additions to the development of the series.

First, I'd like to thank my amazing husband, Joshua, for not only being the greatest supporter and partner anyone could ask for in life, but also for giving me the single most vital piece of advice I will take with me for the rest of my career: *Just keep writing.* I know I pestered you for months about the first chapter (which I kept obsessing over with hundreds of renditions), so if it wasn't for you, I might still be stuck on the first chapter of this series.

Second, a huge thank you to my parents (and spare-parents!), brothers, and sisters who've encouraged me to keep going and offered their much-appreciated opinions. Special shout outs to Razvan, Retta Bodhaine, Jim Martin, Bryan Bushart, Y.I. Washington, and many more who wished to be left unnamed. Your constant support and helpful edits/knowledgeable insight made the books that much better.

Third, a million *thank yous* to Fiona Jayde (the absolute best cover designer there is), Tamara Cribley (the best formatter there is), and Melissa Giles (the best photographer there is). You all have put up with me and this wild experiment with such expertise and professionalism, I'm both shocked and honored you stuck with me throughout it all.

Last but certainly not least, thank you to all my friends and readers for joining me on this crazy ride! There's no such thing as a self-made woman, and you've all been such a large part of my life and journey. It wouldn't have been the same without you!

~Ellie Raine

ABOUT THE AUTHOR

Award-winning fantasy author and Amazon international best-seller, Ellie Raine, is a voracious BookWyrm when it comes to epic adventures, detailed world-building, and thrilling battles. She grew up in the suburbs of Atlanta, Georgia, where her family raised her right with a healthy upbringing surrounded by fantasy books, comics, and videogames. Her award-winning Adventure Fantasy pentalogy, *the NecroSeam Chronicles*, was inspired by her favorite fable: the Grim Reaper. It was originally intended to be a video game, but she found the book adaptation to be far more fulfilling and exciting. Her first book in the series, *Willow of Ashes*, has won multiple awards in 2019, including first place in Fantasy for the Writers' Digest Self-Published Ebook Awards. Her other works include a supernatural detective noir, *Nightingale*, published with Pro Se Productions in 2018. Ellie Raine is currently working on several other fantastical projects and only emerges from the depths of her daring tales when she is summoned by her loving king and their darling daughter: the Dragon Princess Felicity.

You can find out more about Ellie Raine and her books
at: https://www.EllieRaine.com, and learn more about the NecroSeam Chronicles and its vivid world by visiting https://www.NecroSeam.com!